Phillip Jones
"Big Dog"
12/2/10

"Today's dreams are the stories of tomorrow."

Crystal Moon, World of Grayham
View a high-def map of Southern Grayham
www.WorldsoftheCrystalMoon.com

Phillip "Big Dog" Jones' Facebook fan page:
www.facebook.com/worldsofthecrystalmoon

Principal Editor: William Zavatchin - **wjzavatchin@msn.com**

Special Thanks: To the fans, your feedback was invaluable while creating this final edition. Your input was a blessing.

I am dedicating this first book to my two sons: Christopher and Chase Jones

This printing was done by:
Worzalla Publishing Co., Stevens Point, WI • 866-523-7737

This novel is a work of fiction. Names, characters, events, incidents and places are the product of the author's imagination. Any resemblance to actual persons, people or events is purely coincidental. This story is not based on any religious beliefs.

Library of Congress Cataloging-in-Publication Data
First published in 2010 under ISBN — 978-0-9816423-2-1

Crystal Moon, World of Grayham
ISBN: 978-0-9816423-9-0

5 1 6 9 5

9 780981 642390

Fourth Edition
Appropriate for readers of advanced
seasons 13 and older.

Printed in the United States of America
10 9 8 7 6 5 4

Published by: Shapeshift Productions, LLC

From the day I was introduced to the "Worlds of the Crystal Moon" I was enthralled. When you've been in the business as long as I have, it doesn't take long to recognize real talent and a writer gifted with that rare ability to create a compelling world that not only entertains, but profoundly touches the heart, mind and soul. The Worlds of The Crystal Moon is such a story. I implore all of you to enter and explore this powerful and magical story which will stir and inspire your imagination for generations to come.

Richard Hatch (Apollo – Battlestar Galactica)
Actor, Writer, Director and Producer

Thanks to the Worlds of the Crystal Moon Artists

Todd Sheridan - Cover
sheridan.todd@gmail.com

Kathleen Stone - Black & White Illustrations
kathleen@kastone-illustrations.com

Daniel Vest - 3D Color Illustrations
dvestzeus@hotmail.com

Rick Williamson - Southern Grayham Map
rix@rixds.com

THE GODS
OF THE
FARENDRITE COLLECTIVE
In order of Power and Strength

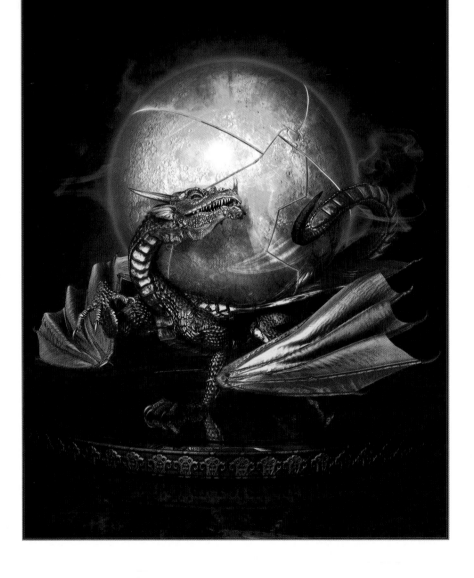

Bassorine [Bas-**sor**-in]
God of War

Lasidious [La-**sid**-e-us]
God of Mischief

Alistar [**Al**-i-star]
God of the Harvest

Hosseff [Hos-**sef**]
God of Death

Mieonus [Me-**own**-us]
Goddess of Hate

Yaloom [Ya-**loom**]
God of Greed

Celestria [Se-**les**-tree-ah]
Goddess of Beasts

Bailem [**Bay**-lem]
God of the Sun

Jervaise [Jer-**vaze**]
Goddess of Fire

Lictina [Lik-**tee**-nah]
Goddess of Earth

Owain [**O**-wane]
God of Water

Calla [**Kal**-la]
Goddess of Truth

Keylom [**Kee**-lom]
God of Peace

Helmep [**Hel**-mep]
God of Healing

Temple of the Gods
Griffin Falls

Sam Goodrich
Human

Shalee [Sha-**lee**] **Adamson**
Human

George Nailer
Human

Mosley [Mos-ley]
Night Terror Wolf

Kepler [**Kep**-ler]
Undead Demon-jaguar

Glossary

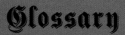

——————————— **THE DAYS** ———————————

Dawn
The moment when the sun rises just above the horizon.

Morning
Period of the day between Dawn and Early Bailem.

Early Bailem
When the sun has reached the halfway point between the horizon and its highest point in the sky, the Peak of Bailem.

Peak of Bailem
The moment when the sun has reached its highest point.

Late Bailem
The moment when the sun has passed the Peak of Bailem and taken a position halfway between the Peak of Bailem and when the sun disappears behind the horizon.

Evening
The moments between Late Bailem and when the sun is about to disappear behind the horizon.

Night
The moments after the sun has disappeared behind the horizon until it once again rises and becomes Dawn.

Midnight
An estimated series of moments that is said to be in the middle of the night.

——————————— **SEASON or SEASONS** ———————————

There are different uses for the words *season* and *seasons*.

Season
The common meaning referring to winter, spring, summer, and fall.

Seasons
People can refer to their ages by using the term *season* or *seasons*. For example: if someone was born during a winter season, he or she would become another season older once they reach the following winter. They are said to be so many winter seasons old.

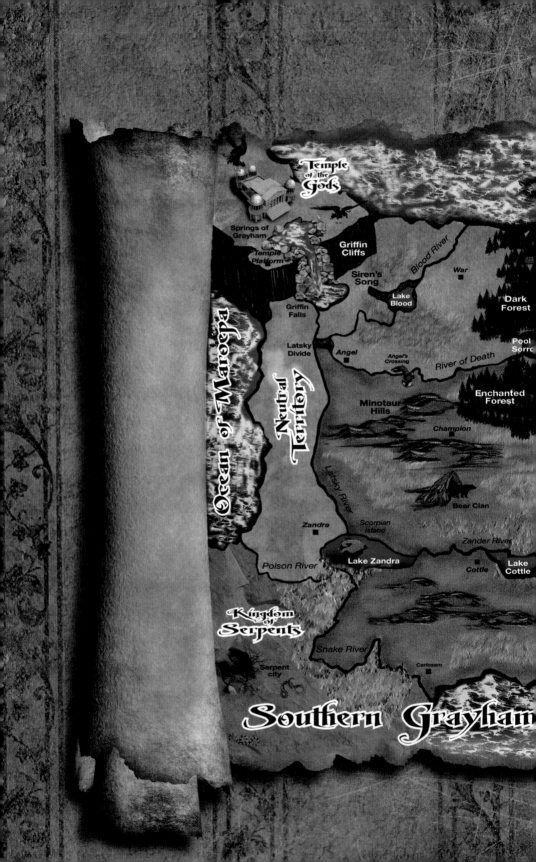

Blood Sea
Blood Sea
Barbarian Kingdom
Bloodvain River
Istumus of Change
Cat Plains
Change
Lake Latasef
Latasef
Cave of Sorrow
Gessler Village
Skeleton Pass
Mts of Latasef
Sorrow's Release
City View
Lethwitch
Lethwitch Platform
Mountain View
The Iron Chains
East Utopia
Cliffs of Latasef
Kingdom of Brandor
Ocean of Utopia
West Utopia
Brandor River
Empire
Lake Brandor
Merchant Island
Penninsula of Prosperity
Cripple River
Cottle River
Brandor Platform
Haven
BRANDOR
N
W
E
S
Ocean of Utopia

Entrance to the Pass of Tears
Leading to the Cave of Sorrow

Table of Contents

The Cripple River

Let the adventure begin…

Soul to Soul

Hello Reader...

...or perhaps I should say, Lost Soul. I truly hate to be the bearer of bad news, but unfortunately, there's no tender way to deliver the blow. I'm left with no choice but to come right out and say it. You see, you and I, well... we're dead. If it makes it easier to hear, we have perished and if a softer delivery is still necessary...your bucket has been kicked.

We can no longer call Earth, Dukas, Redbone, Langormar, or whatever world you arrived from, our home. Our souls, whether good or evil, now exist inside the Book. We're waiting for our chance to be reborn on one of many new worlds.

I know none of this makes sense and you're probably asking yourself, "Phillip, what are you talking about?" I would be forced to answer your question by saying: your homeworld is gone. You just have to deal with it.

But, know this, I'm not without compassion. I'm glad your soul was retrieved from the darkness and placed in here with me, inside the Book. I know you're confused and have many questions, not to mention a fair amount of stress which I'm sure has surfaced because of my revelation, but it will get better, I promise. Hang in there while I try to explain.

The Book, known as the Book of Immortality, has asked me to explain a great number of things for your benefit. First, there was a series of God Wars which lasted over 3,000 seasons. It was during this period of constant battling by these "so-called" deities the entire cosmos ceased to exist. I say "so-called" because I'm still not convinced they should be called gods at all.

Second, along with your beloved homeworld, the places we all knew as Heaven and Hell, everything you ever loved, everything you understood, and everything you cherished as your own, exploded into countless pieces of mass. The sadness of this devastation still wanders through space.

News of this nature can be depressing. I'm sure to many of you this neoteric truth sounds like one big pile of garesh. It's not easy to accept all was lost and your soul is now stuck inside a book, but again, hang in there, many answers will be revealed as I move forward with the telling of the Crystal Moon.

Prior to The Great Destruction of Everything Known, I was an author and lived on the planet Earth. The Book, after learning this, asked me to gather the facts necessary to tell a series of stories. I get to share the knowledge I've gained from speaking with the souls residing inside its pages, including the deities who perished, most during the God Wars. I will reveal the information acquired from questioning hundreds of fascinating creatures, as well as numerous other races. Some are immortal and living on the new worlds. I've taken great care to understand everyone's emotions, their desires, their thoughts, and the reasons for doing the things they did, and will now share these delightful, and in some cases, devilish tales with you.

Thus, I welcome you to the Worlds of the Crystal Moon. Let us begin with the first of many stories, Crystal Moon, World of Grayham. I hope you enjoy my recollections, but if you don't, garesh happens. Read anyway.

Your friend, and fellow soul inside the Book of Immortality,
Phillip **"Big Dog"** Jones.

Allow me to take you back
to a period over 14,000 seasons ago...
to a series of days just before
the destruction of a world called Earth.

The Hometown of Sam Goodrich
Los Angeles, California

Dr. Sam Goodrich put the cold stethoscope on the boy's chest and asked him to take two deep breaths. The child jumped. Once Sam determined the youngster was in good general health and his flu-like symptoms could be treated with simple over the counter medications, he wrote out his recommendations and handed them to the boy's mother.

"Mrs. Taylor, thanks for bringing Bobby in to see me. These should do the trick. He'll be fine in a few days."

Forcing a smile, Sam gave a few other words of encouragement, then shook the woman's hand before leaving the room. As he left to see his next patient, his smile faded. He grimaced and whispered under his breath, "Great, just what I want to see, another inconvenience. At least, if tonight goes well, I won't have to do this anymore."

Sam was muscular, with chiseled abs, which many women found to be their personal definition of perfection. At five-foot ten, 205 pounds, he was in amazing shape, and his cardio, not to mention his diet, was exemplary.

He was not what many would consider a normal doctor. Sam had a bit of a dark side, though he did not know its extent. For the last six and a half years, he worked tirelessly training in the world of Mixed Martial Arts Combat to develop his skills as a fighter. Today was Sam's big day, the day of his first professional fight.

For the last four years, Sam fought as an amateur. Prior to that, he spent two years learning the basics. When he started in the sport, now his passion, his good friend, John, used Sam as a life-sized punching bag. He grew accustomed to being turned into a human pretzel, learning his body could bend in ways he never imagined. Being the friend he was, John took great pleasure in delivering these lessons.

It was this friend, also a professional fighter, who had been instrumental in Sam's transformation into the machine he was inside the cage. Nine years his elder, John was one of the few people who understood Sam's motivation when the decision was made to learn the sport. Sam benefited from John's experience and knowledge, savagely absorbing it.

Today could be the beginning of Sam's rise to stardom, paving the way to leave the medical profession, one which he loathed and never desired, for a professional career in Mixed Martial Arts.

Sam was a different breed of fighter and had a reputation for potential greatness outside the cage. He was already known across the globe for his superior intelligence, graduating high school at the age of ten and finishing his Bachelor's in Science just after turning thirteen. He even earned his medical degree before turning sixteen. In short, he was a walking book of knowledge. His unparalleled ability to retain data amazed his professors and the world, but he often failed to show his brilliance.

Trying to fit in, Sam would intentionally hold back. He didn't like the idea of being the freak, the brain, the geek, or the nerd the other kids didn't want to be around. He tried hard to hide his genius, studying only what was necessary to appease his father, but his effort to blend was often ruined by his desire to take charge, creating the opposite result.

Despite his desire to please his overbearing father, Sam was unable to practice medicine. The medical community turned their backs on him, saying a sixteen-year-old kid was too immature to perform any type of patient care, let alone surgery. He was simply too young to handle real world responsibilities until turning eighteen and was unemployable.

The court supported this assessment after a number of private interviews, ruling Sam had to be of legal age before becoming a surgeon. To Sam, they were all prejudiced; an evil empire bound and determined to hold him back.

The court's ruling turned out to be the right call. Although a genius, Sam was over-confident, hot-tempered, quick to react, and lacked common sense at times. On the day of the ruling, Sam stormed out of the courtroom. "I hate you all," he screamed. "You're fools! You'll need me someday and I won't be there for any of you!" He slapped the heavy wooden doors as he left.

Sam's father fought the court's ruling, appealing the decision to a higher court. With this appeal came another rejection, which thrust an even deeper jab into Sam's pride and fueled his anger, testing the relationship with his father.

Unable to control his hostility, Sam's anger finally got the best of him. His father, again trying to help, believed Sam needed guidance from someone who could remain objective about his growing hostility. A counselor was brought in to assess Sam's inability to handle everyday life and determine a course of action.

Tammy, Sam's counselor, suggested a physical outlet, one where he could use his body to release bottled-up emotions. After many conversations, the decision was made to learn Mixed Martial Arts as a way to channel his negative energy. The plan worked. In fact, it more than worked. Sam discovered another gift. He could fight, and fight well, and because of this, a real smile finally found his face.

Not only was Sam a good fighter, but he soon learned he was an adrenaline junkie and found this brutal sport to be the best thing to ever happen to him. He no longer had to look for an emotional release. Along with healing people as the doctor his father always wanted him to be, he would silence the hatred for the medical profession by beating people up, unknowingly scarring his soul and feeding the demon hidden within the deepest shadows of his mind.

Sam's medical career developed, despite his pleas to the family to give up medicine. He hated the decision his father made to open a practice, but family money was to be obeyed. On the day of Sam's eighteenth birthday, the red ribbon was cut. The press in attendance questioned, "Sam, how does it feel to be the head doctor of a 13 story facility? Does it feel overwhelming at your age?"

"Okay, okay, lets put this in perspective. What my dad wants, is what my dad gets. Besides, I'm not the head of anything and you're misguided if you believe I am." Sam walked off and mumbled under his breath. "This is his dream, not mine."

The old man's decision to open the practice wasn't without flexibility. Sam would be able to continue training with John. He manipulated the situation and abandoned his father's plan for him to become a trauma surgeon, a position his dad revered and would have been a better career choice to appease Sam's desire to take charge.

Sam's plotting would give more time for the sport he loved and his father accepted the compromise, despite his disgust for Sam's barbaric choice to find fame in the cages of MMA. Now, Sam's life had become a balancing act between the family business, patients, training, and his love, fighting.

Thanks to Sam's worldwide reputation for brilliance, the family's practice was an immediate success. Just as his father imagined, other eager, high-achieving doctors came to work for them because of the publicity they would receive. Sam's reputation was a gold mine, but even with all the fuss, Sam kept his personal patient load to a minimum, always keeping time for his passion.

Now...fellow soul...not that it really matters, since everything would eventually cease to exist because of The Great Destruction of Everything Known, but the family's practice employed five hundred thirty-three people, including doctors, nurses, and therapists of different medical backgrounds. Sam's parents, business-minded people with administrative experience, handled the day-to-day operations. Sam offered no additional help and continued to pursue his fighting career.

❖⟨⟨⟩⟩❖

Tonight, Sam's fight would be in Las Vegas. As he left his office on the thirteenth floor, a plain looking, dark haired secretary tossed him the keys to his new convertible Mustang and winked. "Go get 'em, champ. Your dad's jet is fueled and waiting. Oh, and thanks for the new big screen. My husband and I have a bunch of our friends coming over to watch your fight. It's going to be weird seeing you on Pay-Per-View. My girlfriend, Cindy, said she can't wait for you to take your shirt off. Her husband's jealous."

Sam smiled. "Let me think. Okay, okay, tell Cindy when I look into the camera I will flex my pecs. Make sure her husband knows I did it just for her. I've got to hurry. I'll see you Monday. Wish me luck."

"Good luck," Melissa responded. As she watched him leave, she exhaled, "I so want that."

❖⟨⟨⟩⟩❖

Emotions flooded Sam as he arrived at the MGM Grand. The press and the fans of the barbaric sport swarmed his dad's stretch limo. He hadn't even fought professionally yet, but was already on the cover of ESPN The Magazine. He had to laugh at the headline: The Smartest Athlete in the World: Dumb Enough to Enter the Cage of Mixed Martial Arts Combat.

Tossing the magazine on the seat, all he could do was hope to give a good show and live up to the hype. He would hate to be the first cage fighter on the cover with a losing professional record. He smirked at the thought and stepped out of the limo.

The surging crowd pressed in as he walked toward the arena entrance. He laughed inside, thinking, *These people are fanatical. I can't believe this frenzy. They won't be so interested if I lose.*

Women were shouting marriage proposals, which startled him. One woman lifted her shirt. "Sam Goodrich, marry me, baby! I'll take care of you," she screamed.

Like any red-blooded male, Sam was not immune to a beautiful woman. He admired her brown flowing hair, long shapely legs, and curvy hips; all perfect. The coolness of the night only added to her beauty. Everything was great until his eyes focused on her teeth. Her wretched smile exposed twisted gaps you could drive a bus through. Forcing a pleasant nod, he hurried inside.

A barrage of flashing lights greeted him as he stepped through the door. Almost blinded by their intensity, he somehow managed to work his way through the mob.

"Sam, Sam Goodrich," a woman wearing a dark blue Dior business suit and a large smile shouted. She waited next to the hallway Sam had to enter to get to his dressing room. Her hair was pinned up, exposing a slender neck. Her presence was strong, but approachable. "Sam Goodrich, Martha Haige, ESPN! Please, take a moment. Allow the fans to get to know you."

"Sure thing, Ms. Haige, what do the fans want to know?"

With cameras flashing and live video streaming throughout the Pay-Per-View world, Martha changed her tone. Her smile vanished and was replaced with a more serious countenance. "You seem to be a bit of a mystery. I think the fans would like to know why you would fight in the cages of MMA. Why would a genius choose to be a part of the brutality? Can you help us understand what drives you?"

Sam searched for a response, but an answer to Martha's question left him speechless. He realized he didn't truly know the desires of his own heart.

After a long embarrassing moment of silence, surrounded by hundreds of flashing lights, Sam responded. "You'll have to excuse me, Martha, I have a fight to win." He pushed past and hurried to the locker room thinking, *Ravenous woman, you'll just have to wait until the show is over before I give you an answer.*

The locker room door closed, shutting out the noise, providing a welcome quiet as Sam changed. "Jerome, give me a minute, will you? Can you believe the audacity of that woman? Uuhhhhhhhh! I need to think before I get warmed up. Damn her! I wish John was here. I need him."

Jerome, Sam's conditioning trainer, gave an understanding nod, the light glinting off the small gold ring in his ear. "Sure thing man, but we need to start warming up. Think fast, alright? You don't need John. You know John-boy sends much love. Got to take care of the fam first. Besides, I got your back. We got this under control!" Jerome slapped him on the shoulder.

"Okay, okay, just give me a minute, will you?"

Sam watched as Jerome left the room. Martha Haige's question continued to weigh on his heart. *Why don't I know this? Why can't I answer her question? Damn it, John, I need you.*

Sam knew John's daughter needed her father after the accident. Little Fannie was in stable but serious condition after a hit-and-run as she crossed the school crosswalk with her bike. He would not have come to the fight, but John insisted. Since the accident, Sam said a number of prayers for her well-being. She was simply too young to end up paralyzed for life.

❖⟨⟨❖⟩⟩❖

His opponent was tough, a man from Brazil who held a Mixed Martial Arts record of eighteen wins, three losses, with seventeen of these wins by way of knock out. This muay-thai specialist was a literal nightmare to face as his first professional fight and everyone was betting on the Brazilian to hand Sam his first trip to the mat, knocked out cold. The press joked, the good doctor would be able to stitch himself up and save on medical bills.

After getting ready and warming up, the time came to enter the cage. Sam's stomach was queasy. He bent over in the hallway outside the locker room, grabbed the nearest trash can, and vomited. He wondered if he could make it to the cage. He felt weak and chilled, but stood up, wiped his mouth and leaned against Jerome's shoulder.

The trainer pushed back and snapped. "Man up, yo! You got this, dawg. Use that genius head of yours and get it out of the clouds. Focus, man, focus! What the hell's wrong with you?"

Sam knew Jerome was right. It was time to start thinking things through. He had to take charge of his body and control his emotions. It was time to own the situation.

As they began making their way to the cage, Sam realized the cameras to the outside world had caught him throwing up. He was sure his puddle of puke would become the cover story for the sports writers, no matter if he won or lost. Gaining further composure, he continued to walk down the corridor into the arena, enjoying the idea of the press twisting his weakness into a good laugh.

Most fighters would have been excited by now, trying to psych themselves up, but Sam's mind would no longer allow him to do anything but concentrate. He refused to let the fast-paced environment rule him. As he walked, he focused on the task at hand, taking note of everything.

As the cage door closed, Sam stared at his Brazilian opponent and nodded. He felt nothing, no fear nor excitement. He stood still, evaluating the weak points of the man's body, systematically calculating how he was going to take advantage of each area to attain victory. It was as if a switch had turned on inside him. He knew his body was prepared from his perfect 12-0 amateur fight experience. With confidence in this fact, the rest of the sport was all mental, the easiest part of the sport for him. The doctor was ready to go to war.

The referee stood at the center of the cage, pumping his fist. "Let's get it on," he shouted.

The two men met at the center of the octagon. They touched gloves and circled one another, sizing each other up. The Brazilian threw a couple jabs, which Sam brushed off with no real damage and countered with a powerful slapping kick to the Brazilian's right inner thigh. The loud smack energized the crowd.

Again the Brazilian attacked, this time lunging forward with his knee, only to pull back and strike with an accurately placed right fist. Sam arched his back in an effort to soften the impact to his face, but his reaction was too slow. He stumbled backward and fell against the chain links of the cage.

The Brazilian followed, aggressively attacking and searching for the next opening. Knees, punches and elbows rained down hard, but somehow, Sam managed to push away and create the distance necessary to regain his composure.

Sam shook out the cobwebs. *Damn, this guy is good. Think. Think. I can beat him. He's just a man.*

The two men moved in, locked up, and grabbed hold of one another's necks in a muay-thai clinch. The Brazilian tightened his grasp, pulled Sam close, and now the doctor's stomach found a new meaning for the word pain. His body screamed from the impact of a crushing right knee and before he knew it, three more rotating knees followed, one of them finding the bridge of his nose.

Dazed, everything seemed to be one big blur. Punches were now coming from all angles. He could feel the control of his muscles fading, but he had been trained to fight back. With a last effort lunge, he swung hard and somehow managed to find the chin of the Brazilian.

Now hurting, both men backed off to regroup. Nearly ten seconds went by before they re-engaged, an eternity for this type of sport. Again, the Brazilian grabbed Sam's head. He scoffed with a heavy accent, "You're not ready for dis. Go 'ome and leave da fighting to real men. I don't wish to 'urt a child."

The Brazilian's insult hit deep, opening a floodgate and awakening the dormant rage within the doctor. For Sam, everything in the arena began to melt away as the fight continued. It was as if his foe had begun to fight in slow motion. Sam's brain was trying to process each movement.

Once again, the Brazilian taunted him. "I said go 'ome, amateur. You don' 'ave what it takes, boy."

At that, Sam pulled back and surrendered to the anger rising from the center of his being, allowing his inner junkie to be fed. He struck the Brazilian with a clean, solid left hook, followed by a crushing right kick to the mid-section, causing his ribs to burn.

The Brazilian backed away. Again, they circled. Moving in, Sam landed a methodical jab, followed by another powerful left hook. The Brazilian countered with a jab of his own and followed by diving in for a takedown.

Lifting Sam high into the air, the Brazilian slammed him hard into the mat. A barrage of punches followed as the Brazilian worked to push him toward the cage. It wasn't until after a gash opened above Sam's right brow he was able to counter the Brazilian's weight. He quickly stood, backed off and wiped the blood from his squinting eye.

Sensing the advantage, the Brazilian followed. He led with a jab, then lunged in for another takedown, but this time Sam was ready. Despite the doctor's wooziness, he brought up a strong right knee, pulverizing the Brazilian's face. Blood erupted from his nose as the Brazilian fell limp to the mat.

Sam could now smell a victory of his own, a gloriously pungent aroma emanating from the adrenaline which refueled his body. "I *am* ready for this. Don't *ever* doubt me," he hissed as he threw all his weight on his opponent's back and rolled him over.

Surrounding the Brazilian's body with both legs, Sam listened to the crowd scream as he buried the heels of his feet deep into his opponent's groin. He threw his right arm under the Brazilian's chin, sinking it deep into his throat while his left elbow cupped his right hand, locking it in place. To finish the hold, Sam placed the upper part of his left arm behind the Brazilian's head. He squeezed with all his might. With a momentary loss of control, he appeased his inner demon, losing his sanity.

"Never doubt me," he shouted. With a hidden wickedness he didn't know existed, Sam tightened his grasp for the kill. "Die, bastard, die!" The demon within was now poking out its head.

It took only seconds for the Brazilian to tap and the fight was stopped. Sam had just won his first fight with a rear naked choke submission—but his arms had to be pried from the Brazilian's throat.

As Sam rolled free, he screamed, not because he was happy about his win, but more because he was angered the fight had been stopped and his enjoyment of the kill had been stolen.

A few moments passed before Sam rose in victory from the mat. As he did, he appeared relaxed, though his mind was still scrambling to quiet the rage pounding inside.

Jerome ran to him. "You did it, bro! John-boy would be proud. C'mon, man, show the fans you appreciate 'em and enjoy the moment."

It took a second to sink in, but once it did, Sam knew his fame was about to take yet another giant leap forward and his genius mind wondered what this new roller coaster would be like. He knew most men would be thinking about the moment and living it up, but Sam was not like most men. Despite the rage he had just unleashed, his mind was already months ahead of today, planning.

True, he was pleased with his victory. No man had ever taken this path. He was in full control of his destiny and the world was his for the taking.

Sam turned to face the announcer to answer his questions, but something was not quite right. He fought the awkwardness and shook the man's hand. As he did, an unexpected, evil thing happened.

The announcer's eyes turned a glowing red. Further, he exposed a mouth filled with razor-sharp, pointed teeth. Sam's heart began to pound. He tried to react, but was unable to lift his hand to strike at the threat. He was helpless and unable to respond to the orders coming from his mind. His eyelids became heavy, as if he had gone days without sleep. The overwhelming weight of his body made his knees nearly buckle. He did not know or understand what was happening.

Then, as fast as the sensation came over him, it went away. The next thing Sam knew, he was being congratulated on a nice fight and asked how it felt to accomplish such a great victory.

Realizing he was not on his knees, Sam took a second to regain his bearings. He looked again into the announcer's eyes, but this time they were crystal blue, accompanied by a large bright smile.

Confused, Sam shook off the illusion. "I am happy," he replied. "I have a huge amount of respect for my opponent. It's too bad one of us had to lose. I'm just glad it wasn't me." After speaking, he managed an unnerved smile.

The crowd cheered and, for that split second, he felt larger than life. He lifted his hands skyward and absorbed the energy.

Leaving the cage, Sam turned and looked again at the announcer. The man looked back from across the mat. Sam watched, horrified, as the red glow returned to the announcer's eyes and a mouthful of wickedly-sharp teeth began to scream their silent threats.

Sam's face showed his fear as he hurried back to the locker room with his trainer. His thoughts raced, but no rational explanation could justify what he had seen. His mind was stumped, yet his brilliant intellect knew, somehow, the red glowing eyes of the announcer and his pointed teeth seemed familiar, but how and why, he did not know.

Now...fellow soul...as Sam said in his own words on the day that I, your Spirited Storyteller, interviewed him to learn the events of this epic tale... trust me...it's epic (evil chuckle.) Moving on...Sam said, "I was scared beyond all imagination. How could I possibly recognize or feel something so sinister was familiar?"

Entering the locker room, Sam lied down on a bench. He tried to quiet his mind while allowing his wounds to be tended, but a hissing sound, seemingly from nowhere, filled the room. It pierced Sam's body, reverberating throughout the essence of his soul. A chill slithered up his spine as everyone in the room heard the words, "Your wish is granted." Sam instantly fell into a coma.

Leaving the needle to stitch Sam's wound dangling from the gash above his eye, Jerome and the cut man ran for help. They raced down the hall out of sight.

The red-eyed announcer appeared in a cloud of smoke beside Sam's motionless figure. He leaned down and whispered in the fighter's ear. "Shall we see how long it takes before your memory returns, old friend? Can you believe the idiot doesn't know I'm on to him? I'm far too clever. I have plans for us. You simply need to be reminded of who you really are. I have missed you. All will be revealed when the proper moment arrives."

Sam's body vanished.

The Hometown of Shalee Adamson
Austin, Texas

Shalee Adamson, a shapely blue-eyed blonde, pulled into the driveway of an old rundown house. She rushed up to the front door and walked in without knocking, shouting in a thick Texas accent. "Hurry up, Chanice! We're runnin' late! Our dinna' reservations are in thirty minutes and it'll take most of that ta get there."

A large woman sitting on the living room couch began to cough. "Hello, Miss K, how are ya?" Shalee asked. "Are the pain meds still makin' ya nauseous? Can I get ya anythin'? You know me, got ta save the world, might as well start with you."

Kelly gave a chuckled cough and lifted her head. She struggled to gain composure and managed to respond between coughs. "I'm sick as a dog, darlin' girl. Serves me right, I guess."

Again, Kelly coughed. "I should stop suckin' on these stupid smokes. Thank you for takin' my baby with ya. She loves you to death, ya know? I can see that'cher good for her, chile. You have the kindness of an angel. I do believe you'll save this 'ere worl' someday. Yer just ornery enough to do it."

Shalee smiled. "What kind of a Texan would I be if I didn't help out? Shoot, it's easy ta love that lil' girl. She's gotta good spirit and she's downright cute."

Kelly groaned as she shifted to find a better position, one that did not hurt as much. "That's good to hear. I can't tell ya how much my baby has grown since meetin' ya. That there Big Brothers, Big Sisters program is a genuine godsend. Chanice has said more'n once that she wished you was 'er real sister. She admires ever' thin' about ya. She 'specially loves yer style and fashion sense."

Again Shalee smiled, then turned her attention toward the hallway. "Come on, Chanice, we need ta get goin'! Do you have on the new dress I bought for ya? It isn't ladylike ta be late, ya know!"

"I'm comin', I'm comin' already! I got it on," the ten-year-old yelled from the bedroom. "Mother threw up a'gin. I'm almost done cleanin' it up."

Shalee looked around and shook her head. The house was a dump, along with the rest of the neighborhood, overrun by gangs. It was the kind of place she had worked hard to get out of.

Shalee's family, a bunch of rednecks, had become a statistic, a real-life tragedy. Only two of her seven brothers broke free from the dive they grew up in and made something of their lives. The rest followed in their drunken father's footsteps, drinking, shooting up and multiplying like rabbits. They made a bigger mess of things by adding more children to the world and these innocent little babies were growing up without proper role models.

Despite the obstacles put in front of her, Shalee had grown into a confident woman. She still lived in Austin, like the rest of her family, but put her education to work. After graduating from the University of Texas with a 3.6 GPA, she was now working on her Master's in structural engineering and held a position at a prestigious architectural firm for the last three years.

She had grown accustomed to her new life and was enjoying success. Childhood poverty had taught her to appreciate the finer things in life, right down to her exotic leather Jimmy Choo clutch. But, she never forgot where she came from, giving her mother money on a regular basis.

Shalee opened the passenger door to her new, midnight black Lexus with a tan leather interior. Chanice plopped down inside and began to cry. "Momma's killin' 'erself. I don't understand why she's smokin'. It's horrible! Can I come'n live with ya, please? I don't wanna live with my uncle when she dies. He's mean."

"C'mon now. Let's take this one step at a time, okay? You know I'll do whateva' I can ta help ya through this. Let's focus on some happier thoughts, shall we?"

Shalee wiped a tear from Chanice's face and, as always, the young girl gave a brave smile. "Chanice, I'll always be there for ya, no matter what. I love ya. Do ya understand that? Give us a smile."

"I know ya do," Chanice said, brushing away the tears. After a bit, the child's gapped smile found the conversation.

"Well, alrighty then! Since today's my birthday, what do ya say that us cleva' lil' girls go and celebrate, eat and shop. Shoppin' will make everythin' gooooooooooood," Shalee said in her best Jim Carrey impression. "High-five, lil' sis!"

"Yeah, I'm starvin'! Happy birthday, big sis!"

Shalee grabbed her iPod and chose a song, a song Chanice loved.

Lately when I look into your eyes
I realize, you're the only one I need in my life...

Swaying to the music, Shalee grabbed her hairbrush from the console and used it as a microphone while she lip-synced. Chanice burst into laughter and started dancing in the car while Shalee started singing, making up her own lyrics to the music.

My Little Sis and me...oh, oh,
We don't know how to describe
How happy we feel inside.

Chanice gave her a high-five, took the brush and made up her own lyrics.

We've got butterflies
We're going to fly higher in the sky
We can become anything we want
We're like butterflies

"Ya got it, my lil' sis! That rocks!"

Around ten p.m., Shalee walked into her home, threw the keys on the buffet table, kicked off her Marc Jacob shoes and made a cup of tea to unwind before heading to bed.

If I could only get a good night's sleep, she thought in a whiny voice. *I just need one good night's rest before facin' anotha' hectic day of presentations, clients and umpteen phone calls. Thank God motha's takin' care of my Pebbles. I'm just too tired ta deal with her lil' white behind, tonight.*

She looked at the picture of her dog, sitting on the coffee table. *What a cute lil' poodle ya are...oh yes ya are,* she thought in her best doggy voice.

Later that night, Shalee woke in a panic, sweat pouring from every pore. She wiped her forehead with her pillowcase and swung her legs over the side of the bed. Putting her feet inside the soft, pink slippers beside the nightstand, without bending over, she lifted her arms behind her head to help catch her breath. It took a minute before her pulse slowed and her breathing returned to normal. It had been 187 days since the nightmares began, and her doctor was stumped as to why her mind was taking her on these horrific trips.

Somehow, tonight's nightmare did not seem like the rest. Everything felt a bit off, but she couldn't quite pinpoint a reason. The woman in her dream seemed familiar, yet distant all at the same time and the woman's fashion sense was god-awful. It was bad enough to dream such things, but a dream with terrible Prada simply wouldn't work.

She slowly stood up from the bed, stretched her arms, and arched her back. No relief, at least not like it normally gave. She lowered her arms and looked into the dresser mirror. A frosty breath filled the air as it escaped. She touched herself, somehow feeling confused as she tried to determine if any of her parts were missing. To her relief, everything was there. She sighed as she once again watched the chilled air billow in front of her face and embraced her body with both arms. *What's wrong with me, and why is it so doggone cold in here?*

After a moment, she started to laugh and speak aloud to her reflection. "What's wrong with ya? Why're ya lettin' yourself act this way? Pull yourself togetha'. Go turn up the thermostat, and get your scrawny lil' butt back ta bed." She reached out to the mirror and slapped at the reflection of her hand. "High-five, oh yeah."

She winked in a sassy manner as she flung her head back with a rejuvenated cockiness and continued to laugh as she sauntered across the room. Passing the bedroom door, she bumped it out of the way with her hip and glided down the hallway, passing two other bedrooms and a guest bathroom. All she needed was a quick drink before going back to sleep. As she passed the thermostat, she turned it up.

The blue-eyed beauty was, despite her age, already enjoying the respect of her superiors at work. When she designed her home, Shalee created a great room where the kitchen and living room flowed into each other without separation. Her sense of taste was impeccable; granite countertops from Africa, top-of-the-line carpet from Europe, imported tile from Spain, and three different kinds of trim to match.

Tonight, as she turned on the lights, the colors on her walls seemed dull. She stopped to take note, but as she did, it began to grow colder for no apparent reason. Not only that, but the temperature began to drop so fast she became frightened. She headed for the closet near the front door to grab a coat. Before she could finish crossing the room, a rush of pain surged through her body.

Shalee collapsed, falling to the floor. As she did, she caught a glimpse of a tiny figure out of the corner of her eye. Her head slammed hard into the edge of the coffee table before the image was clear. The glass surface shattered, almost knocking her out. As she struggled to pick herself up, a steady stream of blood poured from a wound which had opened on the left side of her forehead.

Shalee's fear magnified. Her mind filled with a sense of helplessness as the red liquid pooled in front of her. Her arms began to tremble as the room started to move in circles. She slipped into unconsciousness as the image she never clearly saw, faded into darkness.

Near the fireplace, a tiny squat of a man sat on the sill of the window. No more than two feet tall, his eyes glowed red and his teeth ended in razor-sharp points. He laughed as he scampered across the room, waddling from side-to-side. He jumped up and landed in a sitting position on Shalee's stomach.

"Your wish is granted, my lady." The dwarf chuckled. "I wonder why they chose you. I bet *he* had something to do with this. You don't appear to be special. No matter, I'll discover the answer soon enough. You must be more to him than a baby maker."

Leaning forward to touch Shalee's chin, the dwarf's eyes flickered, Disappearing in a cloud of fiery smoke, laughter was all that was left behind as the home exploded, waking the entire neighborhood. Shalee was now in a coma and would be placed in storage for later use.

The Home of George Nailer
Orlando, Florida

George Nailer, an athletic, dark-haired, blue-eyed man was sitting on the bed next to his sleeping daughter as he ran his fingers lovingly through her hair. She was his everything. They spent the day going from store to store, looking everywhere before finding the cupcake maker she had been asking for over the last month.

George tried hard to be the father he had always wanted. He loved his daughter to the best of his ability. She was the only person he had never lied to, or manipulated. He may have been scum, but his little girl was his shining light to goodness.

He named her Abbie, which meant my father's joy, since that's how he felt on the day she was born. Her five-year-old heart was angelic and he loved her cute little smile. She knew how to reel him in every time she wanted something. Yes, he was wrapped around Abbie's little finger, and even though he would never admit it, all she had to do was ask and she'd get anything she wanted.

Growing up as the only child of a cruel father, George's life was filled with constant beatings and abuse. He had been forced to fight his way through childhood just to get the things he needed. Even getting food was a challenge since his parents constantly wasted most of his father's paychecks on their nasty habits during regular visits to one of the local drug lords.

George knew he was emotionally scarred. At an early age, he turned to hustling and stealing to aquire the things he needed. His perfected skills of manipulation helped his mother pay the rent, yet his mother often wasted this money on drugs. It wasn't her fault. His father was to blame for her addiction.

The past played with his head, an endless loop of loathing, degradation and shame running through his veins like a poisonous venom. Finally, on the eve of his 15th birthday, the poison spilled over. George jumped his father from behind after his dad threatened to abuse him while watching TV. He swung without mercy, beating his father over the head with his fists and anything else he could get his hands on.

His father wailed in pain and shouted for help as George's fists rained down again and again. George slipped further away from reality with each swing.

"You're a piece of garbage!" he screamed. "You're nothing but an abusive loser! I hate you! I'll make sure you never touch me, or anybody else, again! I'm not your toy! Who do you think you are? I hate you!"

The police charged in and struggled to pull George off. A moment later would have been too late. He intended to kill his father. He thrashed without concern of the consequences, punching one of the cops in the groin while trying to break free. He screamed at the top of his lungs, "Let me kill him! That scum deserves it! Let me put him six feet under! Let me kill him! Let me kill him!"

Five months later, George's stay in two separate mental hospitals had given him the time to think. With his father serving twenty-five years in prison, he finally had some peace. He had recouped some of his sanity and swore an oath—one he cherished and whispered a thousand times—writing it down to carry with him always: "If I ever have children, I'll protect them. They'll never want for anything. I'll never touch them in anger or make them suffer. I'll never touch them in an inappropriate manner. My children will *NOT* suffer like I have!"

Now, in his adult life, George struggled in his marriage to Abbie's mother, which caused him to break his oath. Instead of creating a sanctuary of safety for his daughter, he had given her a broken home. He hated his failure. Worse, he hated taking his daughter to her mother's home after their visits. The guilt tore at his heart.

His apartment was small, only two bedrooms, but elegantly decorated. He rarely spent any time in it though, because his hunger for the finer things in life was insatiable. He used others to get what he wanted, including countless women, spending most of his time living in their homes, emotionally tearing away at them until his needs were met. Once he had everything he wanted, he moved on without a goodbye or backward glance.

George took one final look at his beautiful Abbie, smiled, and pulled her door shut. Once it was secure, he turned and leaned against the wall.

"Damn, this is hard." He rubbed his hands together to try and relieve the stress. "I won't lose you, baby girl. I'll fight. I'll do whatever it takes to keep you here," he whispered while pulling the summons out of his front pant pocket.

George knew this would be the last time he would see Abbie until after the hearing. His ex-wife was suing for full custody and planned on moving out of state with her future husband. George was running low on the finances necessary to fight the fight, not having the wealth this new man possessed, but he had a plan to fix the situation.

He sighed, then began to chuckle as he made his way to his own room and fell across the bed. Tomorrow morning he would press his Gucci clothes and drop his little girl off at her mother's home before heading to work. A big-time client was coming in from out of town and George reveled at the thought of the large commission he would make as a result of implementing this new plan. As a salesman for Turkman's RV & Marine, he could sell ice to Eskimos if he needed to, and he'd lie at the drop of a hat to do it.

The next day, after hours of anticipation, George arrived at the dealership. The RV he planned to sell was fully loaded, right down to the 40-inch flat screen TV with satellite. George opened the door, hopped up the steps and headed for the window on the far side. He removed the price sticker and after a couple hours of careful manipulation, he made a few perfect adjustments. He now had a new price, one almost $30,000 dollars over list. $970,000 and he would be damned if he did not hold to every penny.

His eyes turned cold as he stared at the numbers and thought, *This is for my baby girl. You've got this one, Georgie-boy. You've got this. She's just another sucker.*

Brenda Olsen finally drove onto the lot. She had just come into a pile of money and George's mouth watered as he finally got the chance to size her up. A southern beauty with a soft accent, Brenda's pinned-up blonde hair revealed an elegant neck with an expensive pendant accenting it. She smelled of Victoria's Secret Pure Seduction lotion and her body matched her delicious personality. She was class with a capital "C" and victim with a capital "V".

Brenda was an out-of-state referral who had driven down from Georgia. He knew from prequalification it would be an easy sale and knew exactly how to go about reeling her in before she ever set foot on the lot.

During the sale, Brenda asked to see other models, but George looked her dead in the eye and replied without hesitation, "You don't deserve anything less than the best. This is a once-in-a-lifetime purchase. Settling for something beneath your class just wouldn't be right." He put an exclamation mark on his statement by smiling through a perfect set of white teeth.

George spent years developing his silver tongue, the tongue of a liar and a cheat, using it to perfection. He was a self-proclaimed King of Deception. Even his own family bought into his tangled web, hook, line, and sinker. Even worse, he was the kind of liar who remembered almost everything he said, which made him dangerous.

He took the initial paperwork to his boss and placed it on his desk. Once the manager signed off on the deal, the two shared a laugh over the buyer's ignorance. Thirty minutes passed before George took Brenda into the finance manager's office to draw up the final contracts.

As they waited, George buttered Brenda up some more. "Why don't you let me make it easy on you? I can deliver the vehicle to your home in a couple of days and then fly back."

"Oh, George, would ya? That's so generous. Thank you eva' so much. You're an adorable little peach," Brenda said as she threw her arms around him to give him a big hug.

"Well, of course, anything to keep the customer happy," George replied with a seductive smile as he thought about a woman from an old run down bar he had been in a few nights earlier. He would ask this woman along for the trip and they would have a swinging time. The RV was perfect for such an occasion.

Even as Brenda stopped hugging him, George continued making plans. He would drop the woman off at one of the local restaurants before arriving at Brenda's home. He would go in alone and make a play for Brenda's affections. He knew she was a multi-millionaire and could easily imagine spending her fortune. He wanted her money in the worst way and would even marry her to get it. He smiled inside as he rejoined the conversation and nodded at something Brenda was saying.

After finishing the deal, Brenda prepared to leave, but not without giving George another big hug before lowering herself into her car. "Drive safely, Georgie. Bring my baby home in good condition."

George smiled. "I'll do just that, Brenda. You take care now. I look forward to seeing you again. Don't you dare miss me before I get there, okay?"

Brenda giggled and pulled away.

The next day, George rounded up the lady from the bar, and after a few minutes of smooth talk, she agreed a road trip sounded fun. It was noon when they hit the road and the drive was smooth for the first few hours. George started to feel tired and wanted to rest. He had told Brenda he needed a couple of days to get the RV to her home and because of this, he could relax with no worries. He had plenty of time to spend with his new friend before arriving in Albany.

He looked at his companion. "Why don't you drive for a bit? I want to get some rest." Smiling back, she said, "No problem." He pulled over and let her have the wheel.

As he plopped down in the passenger's seat, he thought, *Now...what did she say her name was, again? Oh yeah, Tiffany. Hmpf.*

George had not made a mental note of this fact, since his attraction to Tiffany was nothing more than physical. He would never see her again once they returned to Orlando, so what did it matter if he failed to commit her name to memory? Nothing would be gained by manipulating her further.

He did, however, admire her body and longed for it from the passenger's seat. She was soft in all the right spots and although she was older, she was still young enough that gravity had not taken its effect. He knew it would be an eventful night and was looking forward to every hour of passion they would conjure up.

Tiffany had only been driving a few minutes when George heard her mumble something under her breath.

"What was that?" George asked. "I didn't hear you. Could you say it again?"

The woman pushed her soft brown hair behind her ear and smiled. Without moving her mouth, George heard her voice echo inside his head. "Your wish is granted," the voice hissed with a wickedness that frightened him.

The air in the RV's cabin turned cold to the point of being painful. The woman's eyes began to glow red and George could see the razor-sharp points of her teeth. She seemed pure evil, and as George tried to catch his breath, he realized he was in big trouble. His eyes were becoming heavy and as the sensation overwhelmed him, he slipped into unconsciousness, all the while hearing the echoes of Tiffany's laughter inside his mind.

"I have plans for you, George," Tiffany said as her eyes gleamed bright red. "Shall we leave this pathetic Earth of yours?"

Suddenly, the RV twisted into a pile of metal as it collided with an oncoming semi. The large tanker, filled with fuel, poured its liquid everywhere from a gaping hole torn into its side. As the semi exploded, it took the RV with it, throwing the surrounding vehicles everywhere. The explosion was a horrific force and tore a six-foot crater out of the concrete. In some areas, the hole was thirty feet across. Cars were thrown in all directions, some landing as far as one hundred twenty feet away.

The police investigating the scene accounted for the body of the man driving the semi, along with the other nine drivers the blast consumed. The victims were scattered in every direction, landing in small, charred, bloody pieces.

"It seems as if there was no one driving the RV," the Chief of Police told reporters. "It's almost like the driver vanished."

The short, chubby man of the law estimated that, in total, there were over fourteen dead, but there was no accounting for the missing souls in the destroyed RV.

Well...fellow soul...I don't know
if you're one who can remember old Earth,
but those were the events that happened
over 14,000 seasons, or years ago.
Allow me to take you forward
to a whole new world.

The World of Grayham

Against Our Will

It was dark, but not pitch black, yet George Nailer could not see a thing when he woke from his coma. Disoriented and with no idea where he was, he sat up. His back ached and his muscles were sore. He reached down to touch the surface he was sitting on—solid, hard, and cold. Now he understood why his body felt like hell. *I wonder how long I've been unconscious?* he thought.

George remained patient as he sat in the darkness. He rubbed his eyes and waited for them to adjust. After a while, he was able to make out what he thought were the edges of the room. The nearest wall in front of him was at least thirty feet away and extended high enough he could not tell where it ended. The edges of what appeared to be two large doors sat in the wall's center. They appeared as shadows and it was impossible to tell what they were made of.

Turning his head to the left and the right, two large pillars extended up and out of sight. Beyond, another thirty feet or so, were the edges of yet another pair of walls which stretched up and into the darkness without end. The pillars seemed to be made of the same material as the floor. *Must be some sort of marble.*

He continued to study his surroundings. To his surprise, George realized he was not alone. Two figures, mere silhouettes, not more than two feet apart, lay motionless on top of two separate altar-like platforms. Both platforms seemed sturdy, smooth and emanated a dull, shallow glow which didn't penetrate enough of the darkness to make a difference. There was not a wall beyond. Instead, the room stretched into the distance, along with the pillars, far enough his eyes could not make out an end.

This must be some kind of great hallway. I wonder who these two yahoos are. What's their story? And, why is this place so dark? Man, this place is kinda creeping me out. Ha! Who am I kidding? I've been in far worse places than this. Hey...where's my damn altar?

After a moment, George began to whisper under his breath. "What the hell's going on? Where am I? How in the hell did I get here?" As he spoke, his voice amplified to solicit a response, shouting without fear of the unknown. "Hello?"

He listened. Nothing. "Hello...would someone answer me, for hell's sake?" Still nothing. "Figures," he said, smashing his right fist into his left palm.

He turned to look at the others as one of them started to move. It was a woman, or at least what he thought was a woman, by the sound of her moans. He could only guess, since the figure was not totally in focus, though she was only lying about twenty feet away.

He knew her eyes would need time to adjust. George watched as she sat up. He said nothing, but his mind ran wild with thought. *I wonder if it's safe to say anything? Wonder who she is? Are the two of them together? If so, do I need to find the upper hand?*

It took everything to stay silent as the woman continued to stir. He wanted to speak, but his experience as a hustler knew it was best to keep the advantage in every situation. It was clear she was suffering and having a hard time adjusting to the darkness. Stretching, her hand came in contact with the other unconscious figure. She jerked it back.

"Who's there?" she said in a panic, but there was no answer.

George watched. *She's scared. Good. At least she won't be a threat. I can take her out if I need to.*

Again she asked, "Who's there?"

George smirked. *I'm definitely not the only one confused. That makes me feel better. I best stay quiet for as long as I can. There's got to be an advantage here.*

The other figure groaned and began to move. George watched the woman jump, her growing anxiety allowing him to feel even more relaxed. He enjoyed her misery. *Man, she's nearly scared to death. She's stinking terrified. I so wish I could see the expression on her face. I bet it's a riot. I can hear her breathing from here. This is classic.*

Slowly, she lowered from the altar and felt around the floor. Once confident it was safe, she sat down, scooted away from the noise and unknowingly toward George. He had to hold back his desire to engage. *I should scream, "Boo!" That would be freaking hilarious. She'd probably wet herself.*

He cupped his hand over his mouth to hold back the desire, then forced his mind to change course. *Think. That would be funny, but it would also be a disadvantage. I have to keep the advantage.*

This time, the woman used a much louder voice. "Who's there?"

The figure moved again, now groaning while grabbing at his head with one hand and pushing himself upright with the other.

George watched as the other man draped his legs off the side of his dias. *This one's definitely a guy. He groans like a man.* George tried to focus a little harder on the figure. *Just keep quiet and let the situation play itself out.*

"I said, who's there?" the woman yelled with an even more forceful tone than before. "I've got me a gun ova' here!"

George smiled as he reached down under his pant leg and patted the small firearm he always carried with him. *Well, at least I've got one, too. She sounds southern.*

"Okay, okay, relax, will you?" the man said, trying to gain his bearings. "My name is Sam, ughhhh." He rubbed his eyes and continued. "Sam, Sam Goodrich, that's who's here."

The woman said nothing. She waited for more information as George continued to secretly revel in her anxiety. *I'm loving this. She would crawl right out of her skin if I started to grumble in a freaky voice, "Red rum. Red rum." Damn, I loved that movie. Stephen King is the man.*

After a moment of silence, Sam spoke in an authoritative voice. "Who are you? Why are all the lights out? Where am I?" He began rubbing his temples. "Do you have any aspirin? My head is pounding."

George watched the woman react, searching her person for what he assumed would have been medication. As it turned out, she didn't have anything. She moved further away, frightened her inability to help would cause further tension. It was now clear she was wearing pajamas and slippers.

Wow, nice body. I can appreciate her beauty. I may not know where I am, but I know a beautiful woman when I see one. Hell...I've got to give credit where credit is due. A guy's gotta sit back at a time like this and enjoy the show.

The woman replied, speaking to Sam in a soft voice. "I don't have any. I'm truly sorry." She tried to keep her voice low, not wanting to aggravate his pain further. "If I had 'em, I'd give 'em to ya."

"Dang," Sam said, looking up, working to see his surroundings as his eyes tried to squint into clarity. Questioning the woman in waves, he said, "What is this place? Where are we? Who are you? How long have we been here?"

"I don't rightly know. I just woke up m'self, and m'eyes are still adjustin' ta the darkness. I don't know how long we've been here. I'm afraid I'm not much help." After a moment, she continued, "My name is Shalee."

"Got a last name, Shalee?" Sam responded without hesitation.

"Adamson," she answered, somewhat annoyed at his brashness. "Shalee Adamson."

"Nice to meet you, Shalee. It seems we've found ourselves in a bit of a pickle here, don't you think?" Sam said with a strong voice as he continued to try to scan the room. His brilliant mind was already looking for solutions and, as always, he was thinking ahead.

His pain began to ease as he moved his neck to look toward Shalee's silhouette. "You've got to love a good puzzle. Hopefully, I'll be able to see all the pieces, shortly," he added with a slight smile which Shalee still could not see. "Where's your accent from?"

"Why Texas, of course. Any red-blooded American knows that us Texans have the sweetness of apple pie in our voices. But, my daddy messed it up a bit. Ya know how those people from Arkansas talk, all woodsy like."

Sam chuckled. "Well I hope you brought enough pie for me."

George rolled his eyes. *You've got to be freaking kidding me. What a stupid line. Put the snake away, big boy.* Deciding the two were not a threat, it was time to pipe in. "We're in some kind of great hallway." He made sure his voice was strong, hoping to strike a nerve or two.

Shalee, with her back to this new voice, shrieked and rushed to take a seat on the altar at Sam's side. To her, Sam seemed to be less of a threat at the moment—which was ironic, since out of the two men in the room, Sam was the one who understood the mechanics of how to break someone's neck.

"Who's there?" Sam shouted. "Show yourself!"

"Hell, man, no one's hiding! I *am* showing myself. It's not my fault your stinkin' eyes can't see me yet!"

George stood and walked toward them and hopped up onto the opposite altar. "I've been sitting here in the same room. I've just been awake longer than you. My eyes have had the time to adjust. My name is George Nailer, from Orlando."

George noticed Sam had on some sort of fighting gloves and not much else, except a pair of trunks. There was also heavy tape around his ankles. *Hmmm, he must be into boxing or something,* George thought. *None of this makes any sense. Why are they dressed this way?*

The con artist continued, "When you guys started moving, I didn't want to say anything until I knew it was safe. It appears none of us have any freaking clue where we are or how we got here. The last thing I remember, I was driving an RV with some chick. Her eyes turned red, it got really damn cold and I saw her teeth turn into these crazy sharp points. Then, I passed out...and I wasn't even drinking."

Admiring George's strategy, Sam replied, "I can understand your approach. Better to be safe, than sorry, I suppose."

Sam reached up and scratched the top of his head. "This is going to sound strange, but something similar happened to me...well, at least the red eye part with the sharp teeth."

George questioned. "What do you mean?"

Sam took a deep breath and removed his gloves as he responded. "I was in a fight, my first professional fight. After my win, the announcer started to question me. When I looked into his eyes, they were also red. His teeth, like your woman's, were sharp. I felt helpless and couldn't move. The next thing I knew, his eyes were normal and so was his smile. I finished answering his questions and remember the crowd cheering. When it was time to leave the cage, I looked again and saw the announcer's eyes change back to red. I was scared. It was a fear like I've never felt before. I hurried as fast as I could to get to my locker room. I remember lying down. I felt overwhelmed and cold as my cut man stitched me up. There was a wicked laugh. That's the last thing I remember. For some reason, that laugh seemed familiar, like I've heard it before, but I don't know why."

"If your announcer's laugh was as creepy as the woman's I was with, I can't fathom something so nasty feeling familiar," George replied. "Are you sure that's how you felt?"

Sam jumped to his feet and touched his eye. "I'm pretty sure. Hmmm, the cut above my eye is gone."

"What cut?" George added.

Sam ignored the question and mumbled to himself. "I think I was cut. I had to be." After a bit, Sam shook off his confusion and turned to look at Shalee. "What's your story?" he asked, extending a hand to help her down.

"Yeah," George added, somewhat irritated Sam ignored his question.

The fact they were lost inside some dark hallway still didn't seem to bother George. This Sam guy did not seem to be much of a threat and it was easy to see Shalee was still apprehensive. Her anxiety made him feel that much better. Everything was under control.

Shalee refused to take Sam's hand. George continued to enjoy her mood and listened to her tentative response as Sam pulled back his arm. "Well... ummm...I think I caught a glimpse of somethin' or somebody out the corner of m'eye when I fell in my livin' room. Not too sure 'bout that, though. All I can really remema' is how everythin' felt so strange. Oh...and I bonked my head on the coffee table."

She reached up to touch her forehead. To her surprise, it wasn't sore. "Goodness-gracious, that's strange, I don't seem ta have a mark on me. I wonder..." Shalee's anxiety was building as she struggled to understand, but something unexpected happened to divert her anguish.

The great hall filled with an amazing light, and the group's attention turned toward it. This was good—since it was pointless to guess the purpose of the demon with the red eyes and sharp teeth—questions they would not have been able to answer, questions that could have caused panic and fear. At least for the moment, it seemed the light in the great hall was to be their saving grace.

No matter where they looked, the light's origin seemed to come from the top of the pillars. It was as if the light emanated from the marble itself, almost like powerful bulbs had been placed inside and turned on. The three moved closer and stood side by side.

"How's this possible?" Sam's mind changed course. "I don't see how they could light up like this. They're solid. I see no transparencies." He scanned the room, intently looking for an answer.

They stood huddled together, with Shalee in the middle. She grabbed each of their hands to pull them closer. Sam pulled his away and moved clear, wanting to be ready for anything that might happen next. George, however, enjoyed the touch of a woman. For whatever reason, this frightened woman's touch was strangely appealing. The manipulator took the time to look over her figure, once again, and admire it. The change in the hall's atmosphere still didn't seem to bother him.

I like the pink slippers, he thought. *Awww. They have cute little white bunnies on top of them. She's wearing designer pajamas. She clearly has great taste and a stunning...well, her everything is stunning.* After a moment, he pulled his mind out of the gutter and to the situation at hand.

They stood there for what seemed to be forever. Nothing was happening. This allowed for a good look at their surroundings. They saw the pillars were solid white with no noticeable imperfections. The large double doors nearest them were at least five times taller than Sam, and about four times his width. They looked as if they were made of a precious metal, maybe gold, and reflected off the onyx floor which had been polished to a perfect sheen.

George looked down, saw his reflection, and winked. *How ya doing, stud? Wow...I'm a looker. I kill myself.*

As a group, the three turned and looked in all directions. The hallway stretched for what Sam figured to be about the length of three football fields.

Above, they could see paintings, glorious paintings, which appeared to tell a story, but of what they did not know. Many angellic and demonic beings were fighting in an intense battle.

Sam rubbed the end of his chin as he looked up, "I bet that ceiling at its highest point has to be at least 35 to 40 meters."

George looked at Shalee, then at Sam. "What? You've got to be kidding me. You just looked up at the ceiling and wondered how high it is? What about the art? Are we not seeing the same thing? Do you always look at something so beautiful and ignore it?"

Sam shrugged. "Not always. You're right, the paintings are beautiful. I'm just a little annoyed I still have no idea where we are."

George rolled his eyes. "And, how would you know where we are by determining the height of the ceiling?"

"Some of us read. History is how. A place like this is something I should've read about. How could I not know about these paintings? A place like this is too glorious to ignore. Numbers stick with me. This place is too amazing not to be known or historically catalogued. I would remember a building with dimensions this grand. Let's look around for a bit. Maybe I'll see something that will jog my memory. I must know this place. I can't fathom not having a record of it up here." Sam poked the side of his head with his finger.

George smirked. "Sure, whatever you say, Encyclopedia Bob. Just let me know when the marbles settle. I bet I'll still be here."

After a while of marveling, the group moved to one side of the hallway, beyond the pillars. All the way down this side, about every hundred feet or so, there was another set of golden doors resembling the ones closest to them.

Sam counted eight sets and did the math. "This place must be at least a thousand feet long. Imagine the money it took to build it." As always, his mind raced ahead as he processed everything at once—the fear of the situation, two strangers dressed so differently, the cost to build such an expansive hall—and he managed to do his assessment without missing a beat.

Shalee pulled her eyes away from the ceiling. "You're right. This place must've cost a purdy penny." She pointed. "Take a look at the vertical emphasis. It's breathtakin'. The look and feel is characteristically enhanced by both the architectural features and the decoration of the structure. I just love the sweepin' flow of how the walls merge into the cathedral ceilin'. I dare say it feels a bit gothic, with a dash of Heaven and a smidge of Hell. Kinda gives me the heebie-jeebies. Never seen anythin' like it."

"Shalee, that was a nice assessment." Sam looked at George. "Hey, go check out the other side."

George sized Sam up as if he was going to object, but instead, thought, *Be a team player for now. There's a time for everything. No sense getting into an argument. This clown seems pretty smart. Maybe, I can learn something. Just play it cool. Who in the hell is he to order me around, anyway.*

George moved to the other side of the hallway and noticed there were more doors on this side. In the middle of this long stretch, there was a statue tucked behind two pillars, still not visible to either Sam or Shalee. The statue was in front of another set of even larger doors, which appeared to be different than the others. He could not see their full detail from his current position, but he could see they were, indeed, different.

George called out, "I can't be sure, but something is different about the doors a ways down. It might be worth a look. Maybe it's the way out of this joint." Sam took the lead and headed in that direction with George in tow.

"What're y'all doin'?" Shalee shouted, crossing her arms and planting her feet. "I'm not movin' from this here spot. We have no idea what's behind any of these doors. We should stay. We should stay right here."

Almost as if they shared the same brain, both men replied, "Suit yourself."

Shalee was flabbergasted. After a minute of standing alone, she ran to catch up, yelling as she did. "Well, just leave a lady standin' in the middle of nowhere in her PJ's, why don't ya? I look cute in this. Ya don't just find bunny slippers this fab everyday, you know."

Shalee was surprised at her ability to joke, considering their current situation, but her moment of bravery vanished as fast as it came. "Wait, y'all. What if some crazy person saw me and got a naughty idea?"

George thought to himself as he watched her approach. *Some guy has already had a naughty idea. No worries about that.*

Sam chided, "I was wondering how long it would take before you followed. I would hate to go on without you. I need protection, you know," he said, trying to lighten the mood further.

Shalee gave a look to kill, failing to grasp the sarcasm or realize Sam was only joking. It was obvious he could take care of himself. She was, however, subconsciously impressed with his amazing body and, if she had not been so unnerved, might have found the time to realize this fact. She may have even found the desire to touch him. His dark brown hair and soft brown eyes were exactly her type.

"Can we move together from now on?" George said in a harsh tone. "This isn't my idea of fun, so the less we have to think about, the better. Please, no more thinking for you, woman."

Sam ignored George's comment and brushed past as he continued. Shalee, on the other hand, gave him the finger and stayed on Sam's heels.

"Women...drama...emotions," George said, rolling his eyes, then followed.

They now stood in front of a bronze-like statue. It stood tall and had incredible detail. The statue was a man, no more than six feet in height, but when combined with the base, it put him another five feet off the floor. He held a staff in his right hand which had an orb resting at its top and was using it as a walking stick. On his left hip hung a long sword, which clearly was meant for one hand and was belted around the outside of his robe. A hood extended up and over the top of his head, hanging just above his eyes. Beneath the shadow cast by the hood, a scar ran across his right eye and ended near the corner of his mouth. The cut creating the scar had not penetrated deeply enough to injure the eye.

His boots extended high to the calf and looked as if they would offer solid protection. The robe beneath his chin was parted halfway down his sternum and a hint of chainmail could be seen. It was not clear how much of his upper body it covered.

Sam thought to himself, *Why does this guy seem familiar? I swear I know who this is. Dang it. Why can't I put my finger on it?*

The group continued to circle the statue. To the man's right, tucked behind the staff, was a four-legged beast that looked like a wolf. The animal seemed peaceful, as if it was with its master. They all agreed it was larger than any wolf they had ever seen.

Across the man's body was a cord which stretched from his upper-right shoulder to his lower-left hip. It extended around to his back and was attached to a sturdy-looking bow. The weapon looked worn, but battle-worthy. Sam stopped, and began to ponder.

"What is it?" George said. "You look like you've seen a ghost."

Sam murmured, "He looks familiar."

"What? Speak up, will ya? You're mumbling," George snapped.

"I said this guy's face looks familiar."

George gave Shalee a questioning glance, then turned back to Sam. "Have you been here before? How do you know this guy?"

"I don't *know* that I know him, but something about this guy's face seems familiar. I can't seem to put my finger on it."

"What about this place?" Shalee cut in. "Is it also familiar ta ya? Does it give ya the same feelin'?"

Sam took a long look around before responding. "No...this place doesn't ring any bells. I'm still at a loss. I don't think I've read anything about it. Let's just keep moving. Maybe it'll come to me."

Shalee looked at George and watched as the manipulator shrugged. As the group moved behind the statue, they noticed a quiver of arrows in easy reach over the man's right shoulder. The quiver was tucked close to the right side of his neck and angled toward his left.

On the base of the statue, near the man's feet, was a round object cradled on a golden dragon's back. The sphere had a slight blue-white glow and a rough surface which appeared to be made of a gem or some type of crystal. As they looked closer, the group saw the object looked more like a small planet of some sort. More accurately, it seemed to resemble a moon more than it resembled a habitable world. Though it was clearly made of a different material than the rest of the statue, it somehow seemed to blend. The sphere was no larger than a basketball and sat nestled in its cradle.

The platform was at least ten feet in diameter and had smooth edges. There was an inscription which started at the top and circled its way around until it ended near the floor. Shalee and George looked at the writings, then at each other and once again shrugged. Sam, on the other hand, found a starting point and began to circle the statue.

"What the hell are you doing?" George asked as he watched.

"I'm reading," Sam replied with an indignant roll of his eyes.

George shook his head in amazement. "What do you mean, you're reading? Are you telling me you can understand what's on this stupid thing?"

"There's nothing stupid about it. It's quite simple," Sam said while laying his hands across the markings. "Most every language has some sort of pattern and these symbols seem familiar, but again, I'm not sure why."

George slapped at the top of his forehead. "Ohhhh, here we go again with the familiar thing. What are you, some sort of freak?"

Sam laughed and focused. "Okay, okay, let's just take a closer look. This can't be any harder than the sixteen other languages I taught myself."

"Holy crap, man! You know sixteen different languages? Where the hell did you find the time to learn them all?"

"My father made me do it during my summer vacation when I was nine," Sam answered, acting as if it was nothing out of the ordinary, as if anyone could do it. He continued to decipher the markings.

"Ohhh, my goodness-gracious, I do believe I know who ya are," Shalee exclaimed, pointing at Sam. "If my recollection serves me right, you're the kid who was all ova' the TV and the news. I remomba' ya. You and I have the same birthday. We're both twenty-three. I was impressed when I heard about how all your languages were self-taught. I remomba' thinkin' how lucky ya were ta be goin' into your last year of high school at the age of nine. I didn't even get through the fourth grade before ya graduated. The fuss everyone made about ya learnin' all those languages. My teachers talked about ya all the time. They told us if we applied ourselves, we could be just as smart."

Shalee would have continued, except for George's rude interruption. "Oh, shut up. I get it already. He's pretty damn smart. Don't let yourself get too excited or you'll have to swim your way out of here."

At that, Sam turned, walked up to George and got in his face. "I don't know who you are, nor do I care, but if you talk to Shalee or any other woman like that ever again while I'm around, I'll have a few things to say about it...and I don't mean verbally. Women are to be respected. Get my drift? Didn't your mother teach you anything?"

George threw his hands in the air and backed up a few steps. "I feel you, man. I feel you. I'll do a check-up from the neck up. Hell, I've got the same birthday as you do, too. I know who you are. Maybe I should jump on the Sam Goodrich bandwagon as well."

George turned and walked toward the heavy doors, and thought, *I know who you are. I remember the news. You've had everything handed to you on a silver platter, Mr. Smart, Rich Ass. Life has been a breeze for you. Try living a day in my shoes, you "holier-than-thou freak."*

Shalee, annoyed with George's antics, turned to face Sam. "So don't ya think it's kinda odd we all have the same birthday? Weird, huh? I'm purdy sure I look younger than both of ya, though."

Sam studied Shalee's face a moment. "You do look young, but I think we should focus our attention on this statue. How could we possibly decifer right now if having the same date of birth is a coincidence, or not?"

"I 'spose you're right. So what does it say? Is there anythin' I can do?" she asked, watching the genius turn his attention back toward the base of the bronze figure. "I'm fairly smart m'self. I bet I can help."

Sam turned to face her, and with a low, calm voice, said, "Unless you have a pen and a piece of paper, I think I'm going to have to figure this one out myself. I need to find the patterns. I don't know why, but this language seems familiar. I feel as if I've seen most of these markings in my dreams. It's as if they are something I've already learned."

Now...fellow soul...Sam had no idea his knowledge of the symbols inscribed on the statue's base had something to do with the hooded being standing on top of it. Kinda freaky, huh?

After about an hour, Sam started to point and began to speak. "I think the symbols tell a tale of this man's great victory and how he brought home the power to control the worlds the gods lost. I'm not sure I follow it all, but it appears this power is what keeps the planets from colliding into one another."

Sam pointed to a specific symbol and began moving his finger along a path. "It says here...equal massed planets are rotating at the same distance around a single star, but on different planetary orbits. It names five planets in this story and continues to say this power is used to provide the proper separation the worlds need to keep from colliding."

George interrupted, "Yeah, yeah, yeah, blah, blah, blah, you said that already. Move ahead, will ya? My hell."

Sam took a long deep breath, his patience with George was wearing thin. Despite his irritation, he calmed himself. "Apparently, this power allows each world to support life. In short, the power acts as a governor for the worlds and monitors every function necessary to perform its job. This crystal sphere, sitting on the statue's base, is the source of this power. The crystal was lost in a large God War. It was this man who was able to find a way to retrieve the crystal and return it to the gods.

"He was rewarded with power for the crystal's retrieval. The deities who gave him this power are called, if I'm reading this right, the Farendrite Collective. I can't recall learning anything about them in what I've studied. I also don't know how many gods form this collective, but this does allude to more than one. The man's name is Bassorine, but I don't see a last name."

Sam pointed to another starting point. "This part of the inscription is talking about a prophecy. A small group, two men and a woman, will be called upon to recover the pieces of the *Crystal Moon*. This is the sphere's name. Two of the three will fight to recover the crystal's pieces, and one will fall to the wayside. It doesn't say anything more about what happens to the third person.

"To clarify, the two remaining will be asked to retrieve the pieces of the crystal before all life is destroyed and the worlds collide. If the pieces remain separated, the planets' orbits will start to shift and chaos will follow until the worlds are destroyed. If the pieces are retrieved soon enough and brought together to reform the Crystal Moon as a whole, there will be a reward. It says the races of the new worlds will be given permission to live together on any world they choose.

"Apparently, allowing the races to be joined is a big deal. I guess it will somehow prove to the gods the races can get along and live with each other on any world. I'm not sure how two people going after the pieces of the Crystal Moon would prove anything, but that's what it says."

Sam shook his head, perplexed. "The way it is now, only certain races are allowed to live on certain planets. It doesn't explain, however, what it means by races. I can only assume it's similar to the races we're familiar with."

Changing direction, Sam scratched the top of his head. "Without a way to reference a date, I won't be able to determine how old the statue is. There is something rather interesting here at the bottom. It says we are to awaken the statue and receive instruction on how to start the path of our destinies. It feels as if it is referring to us."

"What do you mean, 'our destinies?'" George questioned in a sarcastic tone. "Do you actually buy into any of this crap? This could be referring to anyone, not just us. I think it's rather vain to think we're the group it's referring to. I don't want to be the one who falls by the wayside. Doesn't that mean death or something tragic? I sell RVs and boats for a living, for hell's sake. I'm not a part of any stinking prophecy. Tell him, Shalee, you've got to feel me on this one, right?"

Shalee looked first at George, then at Sam. They waited for her answer. "I agree this all seems kinda weird. I'm just an architect and can't fathom bein' part of any kinda prophecy. But..." she paused, "but, how fun would it be, even if only for a lil' while, ta be able ta do somethin' different for a change? I mean, don't ya eva'..." She shuffled her feet. "Don't ya want to be a part of somethin' larger than yourself? What if...what if it's..."

George exploded. "You've got to be kidding me! You're nuts! I must still be sleeping." He turned to Sam. "I have officially met my first genius, who I'll bet is so far off in the head, it's pathetic. Don't get me wrong, but how could you be normal, especially with all that crap crammed so tightly in that brain of yours?" He turned to Shalee. "And, you take the cake! You're buying into this crock! I knew blondes were..."

Sam interrupted, "You finish that sentence and I'll break you in half! I never said I bought into any of this, and neither did Shalee. She simply said it would be fun to be a part of something different. I think she means she wants to be a part of something important."

George threw his hands up. "Whatever!" He walked off.

Sam shook his head in disgust, turned, and started to pace. "Okay, okay." He took a long deep breath to collect his composure. "Let's think through this for a minute. We don't know where we are. No one has come to greet us. We all share the same birthday. We woke up in the same great hallway and the three of us are standing here in front of this statue letting the unknown get the best of us. Not to mention, we're bickering. I think a better plan is in order, don't you?"

George walked back. "You're right. Let's just chill for a bit. We won't get anywhere if we don't think things through. I was wrong to get upset. I apologize to both of you. So, what do we do now?"

Shalee smiled, accepted the apology, and acknowledged they needed to keep clear heads. Turning to Sam, she said, "Well, it's sorta lookin' like you're the brains of this here operation. I, happen ta be all ears. Who betta' ta have on our side than, Puzzle Boy?" Shalee grinned flirtatiously and put her hand on Sam's shoulder.

George rolled his eyes. "Can we just get on with the brainstorming, please? You guys can get a room later."

Shalee blushed and changed pace. "Yes, let's let the brainstormin' begin, shall we?"

"Okay, okay, let's look at this, logically," Sam said, ignoring their antics. "We have in front of us a puzzle, it seems. Awakening the statue must be a metaphor. At least I hope it's a metaphor."

"What the hell do you mean, 'I hope,'" George responded. "What else could it be? Do you really believe this damn thing will come to life? Are you freaking twisted?"

Sam paused, looking over the statue once more. "I don't know, but something tells me we aren't in Kansas anymore."

"What, are you loopy? What do you mean, freak? What the hell does Kansas have to do with this? Speak up, Dorothy."

Sam frowned, glaring into George's eyes. Shalee took a step back and waited for the altercation. Not a word was said.

George held up his hands. "Look...I'm sorry. I'm listening."

Sam turned his attention back to the statue. "I know the statue won't *literally* come alive, but maybe it will produce some sort of message and give us a way out of here, or at least some answers."

Sam started to circle the object once again. The others stayed on his heels as they looked back and forth from Sam to the bronze man.

"There's only one thing that's not like the others. I'm sure you remember the jingle? 'One of these things is not like the others, can you tell which one?'"

George looked at him, floored. "Are you for real? A Sesame Street song? What the hell are you doing? A genius, singing Sesame Street. What a treat. Why would a guy with your intelligence watch such a stupid show? Better yet, why are you stupid enough to sing it?"

Sam took a deep breath to gather his calm once again. "Okay, okay, I didn't watch the show, idiot. I preferred the science channel growing up. It's the kids who come into my medical office who watch the show while they sit in the waiting room. I'm sure you know what a medical office is. Doctors work there."

"Ha!" George scoffed. "Blame it on the kids. You expect me to believe you're a doctor. I bet Big Bird will be happy to hear you're on duty. How about I tell the Cookie Monster to help make your rounds? I bet Oscar, the Grouch has a stethescope. Hey, Shalee, look at what we have here. Dr. Sam is going to save us all. My hell. Make your damn point, Doogie Howser. What were you going to say about your stupid little song?"

Shalee took a few steps back, unsure how Sam would react to George's crude assault. Sam clinched his fists. It took all he had not to punch George. After a second, he changed his mind and drilled the jerk on the upper part of his right arm. "Shut up and quit being such an ass." He smiled as he watched George fall to the floor.

"Damn it, man! That freaking hurt," George shouted, grabbing his arm after landing on the hard surface. "Sorry! Crap! Just stop, already! I'll back off!"

Sam turned toward the statue without saying another word. He calmed himself by taking three deep breaths. After a few moments, he continued to speak. "Okay, okay, so the statue of this man, his wolf, and the base they're standing on, all look to be made of bronze. The one thing that's different is this round crystal ball and the dragon cradling it."

Sam pointed to the object. "Look. If you get closer, you can see the crystal has creases, almost as if it has been put together like a puzzle." Sam counted the pieces. "I see five total and this leads me to believe, with the rest of the statue being made of the same material, we should concentrate our efforts on the sphere."

Hearing Sam's logic, George stood and walked past both of them. He pushed himself up onto the statue's base, wincing from the pain in his arm. "Damn you, man! My arm hurts. It almost gave out. This better not bruise, or I'll..."

"...You'll what?" Sam snapped.

George stared at the fighter. Soon, he thought better of the confrontation. He turned and looked down at the crystal. "Let's find out if you're right, ya big bully. Let's take it with us. I bet it's worth something." He bent over and reached for one of the crystal's pieces.

Sam shouted, "George, wait!"

It was too late. George had already grabbed the piece closest to him, separating it from the rest. Before any of them could say anything, the other four pieces of the sphere vanished, leaving George holding the remaining piece.

"Holy crap, man! Did you see that? The damn thing just disappeared. What do we do now?"

Shalee grabbed Sam's arm and moved behind his back. She felt the need to do something, but had no clue what that something was. She could not explain it, but she knew they were in for a ride.

Sam removed Shalee's hands, but allowed her to stay behind him. He turned back to George. "Get down from there!"

Before George could take a step, the statue began to shake. The floor beneath fell away, creating a large sinkhole. The base of the statue tumbled into the darkness and drug George with it. All that was left was the bronze man and the wolf, floating in mid-air.

Sam screamed, "George," as he watched him disappear. The fighter paused only a second, then moved into action. First, he turned to clear Shalee away, motioning for her to move to the other side of the hallway. She went without hesitation, her pink slippers making scuffling noises as she hurried across the floor.

Sam turned to face the floating remains. The floor had reappeared and now, both the man and his wolf were, somehow, made of flesh. "So much for metaphors," Sam muttered under his breath.

Having been caught in many stressful situations due to his fighting career, Sam kept his focus, even while Shalee screamed in the background. *Okay, okay, the man and the wolf are asleep. They could wake and become a threat. I'll dispose of the wolf first. This will leave only one opponent to fight if this guy wakes up. I'd better not hurt him. He might have the answers we need to get out of here. If I could just disable him, I could get some questions answered without a fight.*

Sam darted across the room, grabbed the wolf by its hind legs, ripped it from midair, and slammed the beast onto the floor. The animal woke and bit at Sam's arm, but missed. Sam let go to avoid its sharp teeth. The beast leapt to its feet and readied for attack.

Sam's mind took over, running the scene in slow motion to prepare for the predator's next move. The wolf ran at him, leaping at his throat. Sam moved to his right and as the beast passed, he struck a crushing right hand to the left side of the wolf's neck. His four-legged adversary landed and howled as it turned for another attack.

Sam studied his opponent, his mind searching for weak points. With all his knowledge, he did not know the creature's anatomy like he did a man's. The best way to defeat the wolf would be to get it by the throat and squeeze the life out of it. He grinned and thought, *Easier said than done.*

The wolf made three more aggressive passes. Each time, Sam managed to avoid the attack and hit the animal on some part of its body. On the fourth pass, the wolf seemed to have a change of heart. Instead of readying to attack, it turned and looked at Shalee, who started to scream. Sam tried to get the creature's attention, but to no avail. The wolf started to move in her direction, slowly at first, then broke into a run. The wolf had to pass Sam's position to get to Shalee. The fighter decided it was all or nothing. He took three running steps in the wolf's direction, calculating the angle where the wolf would be when he landed, and launched into the air.

Sam landed with all his weight on the creature's back, pinning it to the floor. The sudden impact caused the wolf's saliva to flip free from its lip and arch through the air, landing on the end of Shalee's nose. The stench was vile. She quickly wiped it off, but the damage was done. Her eyes rolled up inside her head as she fell limp to the floor. Her beautiful face changed from a look of terror to one of sweet repose as her soft image reflected off its polished surface.

Sam sat up, raised his elbow, and was about to bring it down across the back of the animal's neck when a booming voice filled the great hallway with a thunderous echo: "ENOUGH!"

Sam and the wolf were startled. Sam lowered his elbow and the animal lying beneath stopped struggling. The fighter looked over his shoulder. To his surprise, the statue-man was now awake and walking toward him. Figuring he should finish the wolf off and prepare for the next fight, Sam failed to recall the words on the statue's base. This approaching man was a "so-called" god, and by the look of things, Sam and Shalee were the two members of the group who had not fallen by the wayside.

Again, Sam raised his elbow to strike. Just before he made contact with the back of the animal's neck, he was sent flying through the air. He slammed hard against one of the pillars closest to where the floor had opened. He was pinned, suspended, and unable to move his arms, legs, and head. Even his fingers were frozen. He could not speak.

The hooded god moved to a position beneath the fighter and looked up. "Maybe you misunderstood. I said, ENOUGH!" His voice was hard and strong. The power behind it filled the air as he spoke. "My name is Bassorine. I am the God of War. I have chosen to use my statue to welcome you to Grayham. It is I who will answer your questions. You will listen when I speak. Do we have an understanding, my mortal friend?"

Bassorine waved his arm and Sam drifted to the floor. Knowing he was helpless against such great power, Sam replied, "I understand."

With the use of the word 'mortal,' Sam realized he had overlooked the godly part of the prophecy. He would have gotten his backside kicked.

Sam said nothing more as he watched the god walk toward Shalee. Bassorine stood above her and moved his hand over her body. Her body rose from the floor as if controlled by an unseen force. Floating, she stirred as she regained consciousness.

As he waited for her to regain her balance, Bassorine saw the frightened look on Shalee's face. "Be comforted. No harm shall come to you, young one." It took a series of moments before Shalee calmed down. She moved to stand beside Sam after Bassorine motioned for her to do so.

Even the wolf remained calm as it began to sniff around. The heavy-coated beast moved away from the God of War and began to explore its surroundings.

The wolf limped over to Sam and sniffed at the fighter's feet. The animal pulled back, then snorted its disapproval. Moving to Shalee, the beast seemed to find delight in this new aroma. With each sniff, its snout rose higher and higher until it took in a heavy breath of her backside. As it circled to the front, a better aroma was found. Shalee was beginning to feel violated as she stood in stunned silence. The warm air from the wolf's snout kept passing through her PJ's like nature's summer breeze.

"Mosley, stop," Bassorine commanded.

The wolf pulled back and turned to face the god. What happened next caught Sam and Shalee off guard. "What?" The beast spoke. "Her aroma is magnificent! But, his smell curled the hair in my snout. The human does not run with the rest of his pack. His odor is selfish. He does not have the smell of a leader."

Mosley walked over to stand in front of Sam. "Despite your stench, you fight well, human. I cannot remember the last series of moments in which I was hit so hard. A few well-placed blows your paws found on my flanks. I hope you are unharmed."

Sam marveled at the wolf's flawed recollection of the fight. He had already moved past the fact the animal could speak—a fact Shalee was still dwelling on—and was now working on a way to approach the situation at hand.

"Of course, I'm okay! You didn't touch me. Why wouldn't I be okay?" Sam turned his attention toward Bassorine. Respecting the god's power, he carefully chose his words. "You said you used your statue to greet us and you would answer our questions. You also said I should listen when you speak. Maybe we could begin a conversation?"

The god motioned for the wolf to stand by his side. The beast winked at Shalee, gave a wolfish grin, then did so without question. Bassorine reached down to scratch the back of the animal's head. "This is Mosley. He is the finest companion a man, or god, could have. He is a night terror wolf. On many occasions, before I became a god, this beast saved my life. He is loyal. I have given him an extended existence because of his actions. He will live many, many more seasons before he joins me in the heavens."

Sam took a few seconds to admire the animal's beauty, then raised his right hand as if in school. Bassorine motioned for Sam to speak. "Okay, okay, let me get this straight. You're a god, and you call this talking wolf, Mosley. You reside in the heavens, wherever that is, and Mosley hasn't joined you there, yet somehow, he has managed to appear by your side when you came to life or...or, whatever it was you did."

Sam paused. "I can't believe I'm saying any of this. It sounds so ridiculous and made-up." He shook his head. "Anyway, you said you used your statue as a means to greet us. We're all here in a place called Grayham? Is that about it? Do I have it straight so far?"

Bassorine sighed. "The statue was a conduit, if you will, for the purpose of our greeting. It has sat within this hall for over 10,000 seasons waiting for your arrival and serves two other purposes. The first is to celebrate the mighty victory I attained when fighting to return the Crystal Moon to the gods. The second is to hold the Crystal Moon for safekeeping.

"When placed in its resting spot, the crystal's pieces work together. They send their power throughout the five worlds. The Crystal Moon governs the planets and keeps them separated with the ability to support life. Keeping the worlds separate is just one of its many purposes."

Bassorine lifted his right hand and pointed at the paintings on the ceiling. "The Crystal Moon is kept in this place of honor for all to come and marvel, not only at its beauty, but more importantly, to recognize my glory. We felt the statue would be a fitting test to see how each of you would handle the adversity of a stressful situation."

Shalee butted into the conversation with a question of her own. "How do ya protect the Crystal Moon from bein' taken? Where I'm from, people steal things. Don't y'all worry 'bout that?"

Bassorine shook his head. "It would be a waste of someone's moments to try. The Crystal Moon is protected by my power. No one can take it unless I release my hold on it."

Sam raised his hand again and was motioned to speak. "It looks as if someone has found a way to appropriate your crystal. It's gone. It vanished just before you showed up."

The god looked at Sam, then took a moment to observe the area. Seeing the Crystal Moon was gone, he started pacing while talking to himself.

This annoyed Sam. *This is some god. Gods aren't supposed to have a weakness. They're supposed to be all-powerful and all-knowing. How could he not know the crystal's pieces are gone. How could he overlook the fact the entire base of his statue is missing? He talks just like a regular guy. An accent would be more believable. At least then he would come across as more esteemed. I would be a better god. I'd better stay calm. This guy could mop the floor with me. That pisses me off.*

Sam decided to take control of the conversation. "Okay, okay, it's clear to me there's something wrong here. Maybe we could dissect the whole situation. Could we start with a few more pertinent questions?"

Bassorine agreed and motioned for Sam to continue. Sam felt his intellect was superior to that of this "so-called" god. He would have to control the conversation in his own way. "So, how did we get here?"

Bassorine stopped looking at the area where the statue once rested and found Sam's eyes. "Your wishes brought you here. This is your chance to have everything you wanted. You succeeded at discovering the statue's meaning and how to awaken us. Otherwise, you would have been sent home. Now, you'll be able to stay and enjoy this world. Lasidious was the one who retrieved you from your Earth after you made your wishes."

Shalee listened as Bassorine motioned for Sam to speak. "Okay, okay, we have some issues here. First off, what wishes are you talking about?"

"You each made a wish. I'm sure you remember the requests you made on the last celebration you had honoring the day of your birth. You, Sam, wished to be given the chance to be the best warrior you could be, and to make an impact on the lives of others. Shalee also made a wish. It was to be able to escape her routine and have the power to make a difference in the lives of others. She also asked for an adventure. Both wishes were noble."

Now...fellow soul...Sam was floored. He thought back to his last birthday and remembered the wish he made as he blew out the candles. The problem was, he had no idea the memory of this supposed wish had been planted in his mind by Lasidious, the god known to the others within the Collective as the Mischievous One. I know, that's some pretty crazy garesh, right? Anyway, let me get back to the story.

"I remember the wish," Sam said. "But, I meant I wanted to be the best warrior I could be in the world of Mixed Martial Arts Combat. I wanted to touch the lives of others with the fame I gained. I wanted to help people *my way*—not be dragged into something I'm not familiar with, or someone else's idea of what I meant."

Bassorine nodded again. "What's done is done. It was agreed upon by the Collective to bring you here. Your gods of Earth agreed as well. Ask your next question."

Sam grit his teeth. This was heavy, a hard pill to swallow. How could he argue with a god or was this guy truly an exalted being, considering his obvious lack of knowledge of the day's events? He would argue, but it would be pointless. He could not beat Bassorine in a confrontation and he still didn't know where he was. All he could do was continue to ask questions—for now.

"Okay, okay, you said we would've been sent home if we couldn't figure out how to summon you. So, you must have released your hold on the Crystal Moon. We needed to touch it in order to complete the test, right? Maybe that's how it was taken."

Bassorine was in agreement and motioned for Sam to continue. "I'm sure you know I understand other languages. I'm also sure you know more about me than I care to guess. So, my next question is, what about George? Why was he here? Where did he go when he fell through the floor with the base of your statue? What happened to him?"

Bassorine looked puzzled. He stood in silence for a moment. "George? Who is this, George? There should only be two of you."

Sam loved the fact he knew something this "so-called" god didn't. "The writing on the statue talked about a group of three who would be called upon to recover the missing pieces of the Crystal Moon. You know, the one about two men and a woman. The prophecy where one of the group's members falls by the wayside, leaving it up to the remaining two to save the worlds and find a way to gather the pieces of the crystal before they collide?" Sam's expression mocked his next statement. "The whole, watch out for the spread of chaos part was on there as well."

Ignoring his tone, Bassorine responded. "This test was for the amusement of the gods. We grow bored and seek diversions. When I created the prophecy for your greeting, it did not read the way you described. I wrote about one man and one woman creating an empire of good, not a group of three. You were to make a difference on the worlds. The Collective agreed and thought this to be a worthy cause...a good entertainment."

Bassorine cleared his throat. "Sam, we hoped your knowledge and skills as a warrior, along with Shalee's goodness, not to mention her power, would be a strong combination while creating a glorious empire on this world. We further hoped the remaining worlds would follow in your footsteps and the races would be rejoined. They would be allowed to live together on any world they choose."

Sam started to speak, then stopped. He started again, then stopped. Bassorine looked annoyed. "Just speak."

"Okay, okay, all right. I read about the worlds and the power of the Crystal Moon. I understand the power the crystal is said to possess. If the gods agreed you wanted us to create an empire to set an example, why implement this test in the first place? Why would you risk releasing your hold on the crystal?"

Bassorine frowned. "Not all the gods were in favor of this decision. We govern by majority. It was Lasidious, Owain, Mieonus, Alistar, and Celestria who felt a test should be implemented to see if you were clever enough to undertake such a task. Lasidious was the one who suggested I allow you to touch the Crystal Moon as a way to summon me. The idea didn't seem risky. No harm should have come of it."

Bassorine's frown was replaced by a grin. "It appears part of what I have written has been changed. I believe a trick has been played and a game amongst the gods has begun. The prophecy must have been rewritten without our knowledge. This is the only feasible explanation. I fear you have been caught in a play for power. A plan is in order to stop the chaos which will spread because of this struggle.

"You will be more instrumental than ever while saving the worlds. It will rest on your shoulders to bring the balance of good and evil back into their proper place. If the pieces are not returned, the planets will begin to migrate. This could be the end of all things we have created."

"What in tarnation! What do ya mean, *we'll* need ta do this?" Shalee pointed her finger at Bassorine. "Who do ya think ya are, buddy? We didn't ask for this. Ya said I have power. I don't have any such thing. None of this makes any sense. You've brought us here against our will...against our will, I tell ya. You don't do things like this ta Texans. We don't take kindly ta folks messin' with us. I have a mind ta put my foot right up..."

Bassorine held up his hand and used his power to command silence. Tears began to flow down Shalee's face, not because of her life being forced into an unfamiliar situation, but more because the thought of Chanice popped into her head. *Oh my goodness, my lil' sis. Who'll take care of that lil' girl? How can I keep my promise ta protect her if I'm not there ta keep her in line? What if her mama dies before I get back?* All these unspoken questions and more would go unanswered as this "so-called" god bound her ability to speak.

"Let me think a moment," Bassorine said in a solid voice. He looked at Sam. "I believe this to be the handiwork of Lasidious. He is a master of deception and mischief. He must know the location of the Crystal Moon. I will check with the others in the heavens and see if they have heard anything."

Sam could not believe his ears. "You allowed a master of mischief to talk you into letting us touch your crystal? Doesn't that seem…"

Bassorine gave Sam a look and cleared his throat. Knowing he was pushing the issue, Sam quickly changed the subject. "So, what about George? He fell through the floor, along with the base of your statue."

Bassorine tapped the butt end of the staff he was holding against the front of his boot. "If Lasidious is behind this, he must have a reason for George being here. None of the others know of this mortal. I was not expecting Lasidious to place you on Grayham just yet. If I had known what he was up to, none of this would have happened. Lasidious can be quite deceptive. No one said he could not place you on this world earlier than expected. I was not anticipating a summons by the crystal until Late Bailem."

Sam rolled his eyes at Shalee, careful to only show her his disgust of the situation. "If you didn't expect us to be here until later…assuming Late Bailem does mean later…then why did you release your power over the Crystal Moon before it was time?"

Bassorine knew he had made a mistake, but was not about to admit it to Sam. The god looked him dead in the eyes. "Who are *you* to question *me* when determining the proper moment in which to do anything? I have listened to you make your judgments. I have had enough. I suggest you concentrate on fixing the problem, instead of badgering me. Do I make myself clear? I will not have a mortal speaking to me in this manner."

Sam was dying inside. He wanted to tell Bassorine he was an idiot. Instead, he held his tongue. "I'm sorry."

Shalee, now able to speak, piped up, annoyed. "Why not just kick this Lasidious guy's behind? That's what a Texan would do. You can get the Crystal Moon back yourself while y'all are at it. You should be fixin' this whole mess on your own. Ya can bring back the base of your statue and put your lil' crystal back on it. That's what ya should be doin'. Fix your own stinkin' mess and send us home. I have obligations. This problem of yours doesn't concern me. Ya said it yourself, you're the God of War. Don't ya have the power ta do that? Are ya weak or somethin'?"

Bassorine remained patient. "It is not so simple. Your misguided rant is a waste of my precious moments. Not all the gods choose a side. You should be made aware of things."

Shalee was about to speak, but the god silenced her once more. "Some of us stay neutral in events of good and evil. We believe in free will. I am the God of War, but I do not determine which alliance wins a confrontation. I love to battle, hard and fierce, but I do not care who holds the balance of power. When the Collective came to me with this idea, I agreed because of the entertainment it would provide. We are gods and if the worlds are destroyed, we have the power to create new ones. The others will view this struggle as a game. I prefer to think of it as a game of chess. You will be our pawns. The struggle for power will not manifest in the form of a war between the Collective, but more, the gods will use you while trying to keep as many of our chess pieces on the board as possible."

"I'm not someone's chess piece," Sam retorted.

"Me neitha'," Shalee said, moving to the fighter's side.

Bassorine shook his head. "You are what we say you are. There will be no further conversation regarding this matter."

"Free will. Yeah, right," Sam snapped. "What a joke."

Shalee began to object, but Bassorine silenced them both with a wave of his hand. "The only reason I care about any of this is because a trick has been played and my control over the Crystal Moon has been stolen. I would like the Crystal Moon back, but it is not essential I have it to continue existing. I will play the game better than Lasidious. He is the Mischievous One for a reason. Now that I think about it, today's events are amusing. Now, more than ever, I do not want the worlds to be destroyed. I also do not want to stop these events from unfolding. I smell war on the horizon. This new struggle for power between the races will create glorious wars."

Sam and Shalee were stunned. How could these "so-called" gods toy with worlds and each other? It took a moment for Sam to regain his composure. Bassorine allowed him to speak. "So, what about the gods who hate evil? Where are they?" Sam questioned. "Won't they want to put a stop to this insanity?"

"There are gods among us who want peace, love, and harmony, but not at the risk of a war between the members of the Collective. Also, there are gods who love chaos, hate, and fear, but not enough to fight for it. We want a simple existence and we will be amused as the drama unfolds, that is all. We allow each other to influence the beings living on the worlds, but we no longer fight one another to do it. If Lasidious is responsible for this, which I would wager he is, he did nothing more than use the greed or malice in the heart of someone to start these events. The gods would not allow Lasidious to do anything more than influence the heart of the one who wants to be influenced. This is the extent of how our power is to be used."

Bassorine paused and rubbed his neck in thought. "Lasidious will not do anything to harm your friend, unless George perished when he fell. Lasidious will tempt and manipulate, but your mortal friend will not be forced to do anything."

"We're screwed if he's alive," Sam snapped as he threw his hands in the air. "George isn't our friend. He's a jerk, the kind of guy no one likes. You should hear how he was talking. He's going to be like putty in this Lasidious character's hands."

Bassorine walked over to Sam and put his hand on his shoulder. "Listen to me, young one," he said in a soft voice. "You are in for a great adventure. I have a few gifts the Collective agreed to give each of you before this chain of events started."

Shalee, despite her anxiety, allowed a half-hearted grin to appear at the thought of what kind of gift a god might bequeath. It had to be better than the best day of shopping, and if it wasn't, what a sham to be a stupid god. She shifted from one foot to the other in guarded anticipation of the potential greatness.

Bassorine removed the staff from his hand and gave it to Shalee, but before he let go, he explained. "This is a staff of sorcery. It is the only one of its kind throughout all the worlds. Make no mistake and do not judge it by its appearance, this object can wield as much power as its master can command. Other staffs exist, but none of this caliber. Once I let go, the staff will bond with you and work for no one else. There is one complication when wielding this much power. If you use it unwisely, before you are ready, you can speed up the aging process and provoke an early death. If you handle it with intelligence, you will grow with it. If you do this at a steady pace, you will extend your life thousands of seasons."

Shalee shook all over with excitement. She was happy about the gift, excited about the idea she could live so long, but also scared to death. What if she used the power in the wrong way and, as a consequence, died faster?

"Goodness-gracious, this is like déjà vu. I wonda' if this is the same staff I have been seein' in my dreams. I..."

"Hold on a second," Sam said as he cut her off mid-sentence. "You've also dreamt of this place? Why didn't you say anything before? All this is familiar to you, too?"

"You're not the only one who dreams, ya know. This place is not familia', but this stick sure is. This is kinda excitin'. It's kinda scary, too. Goodness-gracious, how will I know if I've used too much power? I can't believe I get ta do somethin' so cool." Her mind continued, *Maybe I can bring Chanice and my family here once I know what ta do.*

Mosley laughed at her reaction and spoke with an enthusiasm of his own. "Your instincts will guide you. You will know when you have used too much power. You will get knocked to your haunches when you fail. The first moment you try something new and the effects are not what you expect, you will feel the understanding. You will learn to search for the consequence of the power you wish to summon before you command it into your service."

The wolf snorted. "You should be able to avoid bad outcomes by learning to trust your senses. This will take many moments to master and your flanks will find a new meaning for the word, 'sore.' If you spend the first while failing and use too much power, the effects can be reversed by learning to manage your growth more efficiently.

"Remember, the staff's power is only as good as your inner strength, so practice often, and start with simple commands. As you grow, the power becomes a natural part of you. You will not need to carry the staff at all moments. An impressive tool if you ask me. I have seen similar staffs before, though, as Bassorine said, this one is special."

Shalee turned to Bassorine. She lifted her free hand. "Lay it on me, big guy. Let's get started. Gimme a high-five."

With a puzzled look, Bassorine responded, "Why would I give you a lifted number, young one? How does this 'high-five' relate to your staff? No numbers need be involved."

Shalee dropped her hand, bummed. *This guy is kinda a nerd,* she thought.

Bassorine continued, "It will be up to you to name your staff." He let go of the object.

Shalee rose high into the air as the light within the great hallway faded. Her arms flew back, out of control, as her chest pushed forward. Wind filled the room as lightning struck the pillars, Shalee, and the floor around them.

Mosley followed Bassorine as the god pulled Sam back from the spectacle. "The staff is bonding with her," the god said. "She will be tired and need to sleep. She will recover soon."

After a few moments, the lightning stopped. The light returned to the hall as Shalee lowered to the floor. Her breathing was faint. The scorch marks from the lightning had ruined her pajamas. Even one of the bunny ears from the pink slipper on her right foot had fallen to the floor as nothing more than a charred remnant.

Sam reacted, fearful she might be dying. He lifted her into his arms, cradled her head, and checked for a pulse. It was faint. "What the heck did you do to her?"

Bassorine walked over and stood above them. "I told you she would be fine. Do not worry." He turned and motioned to Mosley. "Take Sam's place and give Shalee a pillow upon which to lie."

Mosley did as he was told. Sam let her weight transfer to the animal's body, then moved back.

"That should do the trick," Mosley said, nuzzling Shalee until her head rested upon his warm chest.

Sam stood, but only after he felt satisfied Shalee would be okay. "So, what am I to receive?"

Bassorine removed the bow from his back and sword from his hip. He presented the bow. "This is the Bow of Accuracy. There is none with its abilities on any other world. With this weapon, you can strike down your enemies from great distances. The enemy must be seen by your eyes. The bow will not miss if used for a just cause. It will only respond to a master with a good nature and will not allow a dark heart to pull its string. The quiver of arrows will never empty. You may pull from it forever."

The god handed Sam the sword. "This is the Sword of Truth and Might. It is also one of a kind. The sword can strike your enemies with great power and possesses the ability to search for truth when used upon them. Place the blade on your enemy's shoulder, ask for the answer you seek, and it will be given."

Sam's face lit up. "Okay, okay, so the sword helps me weed through the lies and the bow lets me hit any enemy I can see as long as it's used for good?"

"Yes and no," Bassorine responded. "Just because you like the sword, does not mean you know how to use it. The sword will only work once it feels you have earned its respect. It lives and has a mind of its own. You have much to learn, and a short period of moments in which to gain this knowledge. You do not want the blade failing you in battle. You must learn to wield your weapon. It is your responsibility to name it. Your bow, however, is not so fickle."

Bassorine moved to look at the sleeping Shalee. "Mosley will take you to the city of Brandor. I will come to you once I know more of the Crystal Moon's location. I cannot make Lasidious do anything against his will. I can only hope he sees fit to provide the clues we need to play a fair game. I will return."

With that, Bassorine disappeared and a new bronze statue appeared in place of the old, minus the Crystal Moon. Mosley looked up. "I have to admit, I look good up there."

Sam smiled and bent down to rub Shalee's back. "I have so many unanswered questions. I guess I'll just have to wait until Bassorine returns."

These questions would bother Sam. Why did Bassorine seem familiar? Why did he understand the markings on the statue? Why did the laugh of the red-eyed announcer with the razor-sharp teeth sound so terribly familiar? Why was Shalee dreaming about her staff? He needed clarification and wondered how long it would be before he would be permitted to ask the questions necessary to gain it.

"Once Shalee wakes up, do you think we should get going?"

"Yes," Mosley replied, sniffing her hair. "You may talk to me along the way to Brandor. I may know the answers to your questions."

Well...fellow soul...as you can see
there is much to learn as I move forward
with the telling of the Crystal Moon.
So, what are you waiting for?
Keep reading!

A Lost Power

George heard Sam yell for him to get down from the base of the statue, but before he could move, the shaking started and his footing slipped. He tried to put his hand on the statue's chest, but this did not help to gain his balance. He wasn't able to grab anything. The piece of the crystal was in the hand he tried to use, but he wasn't about to let go of something with potential value.

The floor, to his surprise, opened and he had been falling down the rabbit hole ever since. Everything happened so fast and the last thing he heard, as he fell into the blackness, was Sam screaming his name.

The light of the great hallway above had grown dim as he tumbled over and over. When the hole closed in on itself, he watched as the last bit of light faded away. His heart raced as his pathetic life flashed before his eyes. His little girl would be his only unselfish thought before he died. He closed his eyes tight, pictured his sweet Abbie, and waited for the impact.

The Hidden God World, Ancients Sovereign

"Do you think Bassorine has figured it out yet, my love?" the goddess, Celestria, questioned while fondling her lover.

Lasidious enjoyed her touch, then began to circle the heavy stone table at the center of the room. Their home was warm, despite being created deep within the mountain range known as the Peaks of Angels, located on the hidden god world of Ancients Sovereign. The goddess had softened the hardness of the rocky walls with many elegant touches, and just like the Temple of the Gods, the light filling their home emanated from within the rock, but only in key areas.

"I'm sure Scarface knows I've pulled a fast one," Lasidious grinned. "If I know Bassorine, he's thinking this is nothing more than a minor inconvenience. I would wager he's happy. The crystal's disappearance will start wars. You know how he loves to battle. I'm sure he'll decide to confront me while meeting with the others to ease his mind, but I should be able to crawl under his skin to amplify his anger if I strike at his ego. He won't know what hit that thick, scarred-up face of his when I'm done."

Celestria moved toward Lasidious. She was the definition of elegance. Her eyes could have stolen the blue from the clearest ocean. Her hair cascaded over her shoulders and down her back as she walked. If an imperfection was to be found anywhere on this woman, it was not on the outside. Every curve and gesture was flawless. Even her voice, an angel's voice, was sweet and soft to the ears. She was worthy of being called, goddess.

Lasidious continued to speak as he watched her move, seeking to soothe her nervousness. "Celestria, you worry too much. We have everything under control. We have only used an opportunity the others opened to find someone who wanted power and bring him to Grayham. Besides, you know the Book of Immortality wasn't yet created when we took the mortal. How could we be expected to obey a rule that didn't exist? I won't break the new ones on its pages. I'll handle the mortal as we are required. I won't do anything other than give George a reason to seek the power he wants. Clever, don't you think?"

Lasidious enjoyed the verbal pat on his own back. He smiled as his eyes changed to a bright glowing red, his teeth elongating to sharpened, fine points.

"Stop that," Celestria snapped. "I hate it when you make that face. You know I do not think you are handsome when you do that. I like my cute little devil-god when he looks striking," she oozed while stroking his face. "You are not kissable when you look so mean."

Lasidious shifted from one foot to the other. When his eyes were not glowing red and his teeth were not pointed, he was quite debonair. With short, sandy brown hair, blue eyes, and a chiseled chin, he was a tad less than six feet tall. His athletic build pleased his goddess and Celestria loved every inch of him.

He moved closer, a frown creasing his brow. "I'm sorry. You know I love you. I won't do it again, well...not in your presence anyway." Replacing the frown with another smile, he added, "I hate the despicable story we told the people of the worlds. How we ever agreed to make Bassorine so glorified is beyond me. It's ridiculous the people believe he was the one who saved the Crystal Moon and the worlds from destruction."

Celestria embraced her lover, cupped his face with her hands, and gave him a long, soft kiss. Looking him in the eyes, she placed his hand on her pregnant belly. "You know we did it because he had the power to destroy the rest of us, my pet. I, for one, have no death wish."

She adjusted a decorative setting on the table. "It is too bad exalting Bassorine was one of his conditions before agreeing to create the Book of Immortality. Lucky for us the Book balances the power he had over us. You masterfully manipulated him, my love. You are a clever little god."

Lasidious sighed. "But, he still has the sword and we both know if he figures things out, he could take it all back."

"Yes, but he is afraid to take the chance. That is why you are going to provoke his rage. You are the only one who can make him angry enough to try to take back the power he lost over us."

The goddess touched her michievous partner with a seductive playfulness as she leaned toward him. She pressed her body against his and whispered in his ear. "Have I told you today I find you amazingly handsome? We make a delicious couple." She smacked her lips and tickled his ear by flicking her tongue.

She felt her lover tremble with excitement, "I am glad you are unable to lie to me and we have found a way to trust one another, my sweet. I do not think if I were in Bassorine's boots, I would find forgiveness for the trick you played on him. I have no doubt you will be able to fuel his anger."

Lasidious looked at her belly, smiled, then frowned again. "You know I would lie to you if I could. It's just not natural for me to be so honest, even with you. Like I've said on a thousand occasions, I would never have drank your potion if your beauty wasn't so intoxicating."

After a brief period of reflection, he continued, "Who am I kidding? Being with you is the best thing for me. Drinking your potion has given me not only you, but our baby as well. I cannot wait until our baby is strong enough to allow us to tip the scale of power. It will be awe inspiring to rule the others without the voting we do now."

The goddess smiled with a dark intent hidden behind her luscious lips. "Sometimes, we have to give in order to get, my pet. You are lucky I find you irresistible, or I would never have wanted you to drink the potion in the first place. With our baby's power and the beasts of the worlds who serve me, we should be unstoppable. Baratowain's order of dragons will be a powerful force against the others when our child is ready to lead them into battle by our sides. I can only hope it will be enough to take control of everything created. We will rule without opposition."

Lasidious nodded in agreement. "The last vote we had, I was worried the others would be able to tell you were pregnant." He tapped his fingers against her expanding belly. "I sat through the entire meeting nervous to the point of becoming sick. If they ever find out about our baby, the Book will make us mortal before we have the power to rule. The consequences of being mortal are more than I care to deal with. I don't wish to be banished from Ancients Sovereign and stripped of our power. To die before our son saw the end of his first season would be disheartening. What if our alternate plan fails?"

Celestria sighed, "Maybe our initial plan will not succeed, but the alternate is secure. I also do not want the Book of Immortality to destroy us for having a child. Our baby will wield power far greater than any god has had before. After thousands of seasons of plotting, our plans are solid. Have faith, my sweet, my pet, my darling little devil-god."

Lasidious frowned at her conviction. Seeing this, Celestria put her hand over Lasidious'. "Neither the Book nor the others will be able to do anything to stop us if we succeed. With our power passing into our child, he will be able to defend us from the Book. We must stick to the plan and hide the baby from the others. Your plan to have him live amongst the mortals until he is old enough to rule is solid. The baby will protect us."

Lasidious turned and started to pace. "That's the only part of our plan I don't like. Sure, the baby will be able to defend us from the Book, but the Book and the others combined will be a losing battle until he's much older. Hiding him won't be easy."

"That is why we need to create the diversions we have been plotting," Celestria responded with renewed vigor. "And, that is why you brought this other human into the worlds. You were right; George has hate in his heart, and his desire for power will be easily channeled. All we have to do is influence him to seek out the power he needs to take control of Grayham, then wars will follow. This diversion will keep the others busy and their attention off my pregnancy. I am sure they will be watching the havoc you intend to create. We should be able to keep them from discovering our baby's birth. For now, I have news for you, my pet."

Celestria pulled her lover close and traced the edge of his lips with her tongue. "I found a family as you requested and their hearts believe a world with our rule would allow them to seek the power they are after. I will take our baby and put him with this family of elven witches. They are known by the surname Rolfe, from the Clan of Ashdown. They are located in the mountain passes of Vesper, near the village of Floren, on Luvelles. I promised them a sizeable reward. They were easily influenced and all they asked for in return was one thing."

"And, this was?"

"It was to name the baby and have him carry their name until we bring him to Ancients Sovereign."

"Did you agree?"

"I did. I agreed only because it shut them up. Besides, if I know you, they will not be watching our baby for long." Celestria ran her fingers through his hair. "Do you not agree, my pet?"

"You're right. The family of witches should do fine," he said, kissing her in return. "As always, your beautiful mind, that precious devious mind, makes me happy. I couldn't have done better myself. Luvelles, I love that world. It was by far the Collective's best creation."

Well...fellow soul...again, as your Spirited Storyteller, I should clear a few things up. After Lasidious and Celestria created their home within The Peaks of Angels, they combined their power to form a shield to keep the others from entering. This barrier of privacy became a source of contention among the gods. When the Book of Immortality was approached about the matter, it simply responded by saying, "They have a right to their privacy, as long as the *Laws of the Gods* are not broken." The Book determined the laws had been obeyed and it felt no wrongdoing. Nowhere did it say within the laws that two gods could not separate themselves from the rest of the Collective in order to enjoy each other's company.

The others told the Book they feared the couple would be up to no good and spending their moments alone without proper governing was a bad idea. The Book, somewhat angered, responded by saying, "The consequences of breaking the laws should be enough to govern their actions." The Book did, however, give caution, strongly warning Lasidious and Celestria the situation would not be allowed to continue if it felt a law was broken. The Book would send them to join the mortals and as a result, they would die a rapid death from old age.

Lasidious and Celestria knew how to cover their tracks well enough to avoid getting caught—at least they hoped they did. They brushed the threat off, the warning not stopping their plotting. Knowing their plans would take many seasons to implement and develop, they figured when the moment arrived and everything was in place, it would be too late for the Book to do or say anything. It would be forced to serve them.

After the Book made its ruling, Lasidious and Celestria watched as some of the others paired off and implemented the same practice within their homes. They knew enough of these other couples to know they would be the only pairing willing to tempt fate by having a child, which turned out to be perfect. The Book's determination had taken the others' eyes off of them and back to what all the gods felt to be more important matters.

It was in this newly created home, of Lasidious and Celestria, where they began plotting, and their plan, implemented over 11,000 seasons ago, was masterful.

Now, as I have already said, their home had a protective barrier placed around it to keep the others out. This barrier allowed for their child to be conceived without the Book sensing a *Law of the Gods* had been broken. The god-child could bring them to a higher level of glory than any other within the Collective ever achieved. Part of the plan was to keep the child from developing inside Celestria's womb until the moments were right to allow for its growth. Once born, all they would have to do is keep the child alive long enough to develop his power.

The Book was bound by one rule which superseded all others. It was to maintain a godly hierarchy. In doing so, the Book would strip Lasidious, Celestria, and the baby of their power, if the child was discovered. Lasidious and his beautiful lover would die of old age within a matter of days. As a further consequence, their child would be raised by mortals and, best case, become a powerful mystic.

Lasidious and Celestria's plans were so well plotted that, even now, some of the creatures Lasidious created to help carry out their plans were thousands upon thousands of seasons old.

Back to the story.

❖─═╬═•═╬═─❖

"Luvelles is a wonderful hiding place for the baby," Lasidious said, while giving Celestria a look of desire. "After all, this is where the others agreed to place the Source. I have no doubt we will be able to turn this decision into their demise."

Lasidious turned toward a large, cube shaped cut in the wall which served as a fireplace. Green flames burned within. He stared a moment at their wild movements, then turned his attention back to his goddess.

"The decision you made to put our son in Floren is perfect. The village is full of magic. The air smells of it. The idea the most powerful sorcerers, mages, wizards and warlocks all gather in one spot to practice the arts, is comforting. Wonderful devastations happen often and the moments of their days are riddled with magical disasters. It will be difficult for the others or even the Book to notice our son's growth. This will be the perfect place for our baby."

Lasidious thought a moment longer about the Book of Immortality. "The elven witches should be the perfect parents, but we should keep our options open." Facing his goddess, he added, "It's good you were elven as a mortal before you ascended or our son would not have the features to be allowed to live on this world."

Now...fellow soul...Luvelles is a world where only Elves, Halflings, and Spirits are allowed to live according to the *Agreement of the Gods*. Any other race listed, if not one of these three, must have special permission from the Head Master of Luvelles, Brayson Id, to come and study the arts on this world. Yes, there are beasts, giants, demons, and other beings living there, but these races do not apply. The gods only separated and applied rules as to where each of the following races could live: Elves, Humans, Barbarians, Dwarves, Gnomes, Halflings, Trolls, Spirits, and finally, the Dragons. There is another name for the Dragons, massive winged beasts which I shall describe in further detail later, but this is not the proper series of moments for this revelation.

Only a few of the five planets created are allowed to contain more than one of these specific races. Every other type of creature can quite possibly be found on them all.

"Your elven parents blessed us with the ability to make the perfect little halfling."

Celestria and Lasidious laughed together for a moment before Celestria's thoughts changed course. "Where is our friend, George? He should have been here by now."

Lasidious grinned and waved his hand near one of the walls beside the table. The rock became transparent, revealing George on the other side. It looked as if he was still falling, tumbling without an end to his suffering. His hair moved as if a great wind was passing through it. His expressions were wonderfully miserable.

"He cannot see us," Lasidious said with a laugh. "I should've told you he was here. I want him to experience the sense of falling for a bit longer. I want to give him an awful fright. As soon as you leave, I will go and act as if I've broken his fall before he hits the ground. He'll be confused. Hopefully, he'll believe I saved him. I will say I'm a traveler named Jason. I'll tell him of a map lost by the old Serpent King, Sotter, near the Pool of Sorrow. I'll inform him of a great treasure which is marked on the map. I will describe the treasure as a great gift which a man could use to control a kingdom. This should fuel his desire for power."

"Oh my," Celestria responded. "Sotter was a favorite of mine." The goddess turned and waved her hand across the room. Flowers in six different vases vanished only to be replaced with fresh flora. Satisfied everything was as it should be, she continued. "I helped Sotter realize his ability to go after the throne of the Serpent King before him. His heart was delightfully dark. When he took the throne, I knew he would make me proud. When he died, his death bothered me. That poor snake lost all of his memories before he passed. That wonderful mind just went to waste."

Lasidious approached from behind and kissed Celestria on the base of her neck. "You make our home beautiful, my love. It's always hard to lose the children who make us proud. I'm sorry for your pain."

Celestria turned to look at her heart's desire. Her sorrow for Sotter vanished as quickly as it came. "I know of this map to which you are referring. Was not the map and the reward it promised created for the dwarves on Trollcom? Was it not Lictina who created these items over 4,000 seasons ago? The map was meant to lead the dwarves into the Cave of Sorrow on Grayham, was it not? I heard they were chosen to retrieve the Staff of Petrifaction. Lictina was said to have given them safe passage from Trollcom to Grayham. She must have expected to be entertained by their venture into the cave. She must have been bored to watch such a meaningless journey."

Lasidious' excitement grew. "The staff can turn anything to stone, and yes, the dwarves were to retrieve it before returning home. The head engineer of the mines was instructed to use the staff to solidify the mud far below the planet's surface. The point was to create a safer work environment for all dwarves."

Lasidious looked forward to reveling in his own revelation. "It was Sotter who killed the dwarves and took the map, but he lost it again."

Celestria's brows furrowed, "Really? That does not make sense. I can only assume Sotter wanted the staff's power, but why? What would cause him to go after the map in the first place? It is not like he could hold the staff in a hand and speak the proper commands necessary to control its power. Can you imagine, my sweet? To watch a Serpent King mumble the commands with the staff tucked behind his poisonous fangs? How delightful."

Lasidious slapped his hands on the heavy stone table in a drumming motion. "I told Sotter about the lost map. Don't you see? Who do you think gave Sotter the idea the map's treasure would grant power? I got him thinking he needed the power of the treasure to help him rule. I never told him it was a staff he couldn't use. If I had, he would never have gone for it. It was his greed and his desire to make all of his kind fear him which made him go. All I did was suggest it might be a good idea to go alone, especially since his advisors would want to have the power for themselves. I suggested he deserved to have the power without confrontation.

"Celestria, you of all the gods should know everything about King Sotter. What was the main weakness of the Serpent Lord? I know you remember. What's the one thing his bloodline kept the rest of the Serpent Kingdom from knowing, the one thing which had to be kept secret to prevent a struggle for power? You mentioned it a moment ago."

Celestria thought a bit. "Ahhhh. His memory failed and he forgot all things short-term when he slept. I think I understand what you did, my pet." She grinned and pinched his cheeks. As she continued speaking, her hands began to wander. "You counted on that fact, did you not? You knew his short-term memory would cause him to hide the map and forget what he did with it. That was clever, my sweet. So what happened to the map, my love? Your devious little mind is so conniving."

Lasidious enjoyed the thought of his goddess' pleasure in his revelation. "Well, it certainly looks like I'm the only one who knows the map's location, and because your beauty is so intoxicating, I will tell you. Sotter had to stop after he killed the dwarves. He was exhausted. I kept him awake for over 3 Peaks before he attacked. I wanted to ensure he slept."

Lasidious spun around and flopped into a chair next to the table. "After the bloodshed, Sotter stopped by the Pool of Sorrow, removed a large boulder from the base of one of the trees, put the map into the hole, and pushed the boulder on top of it.

"From a distance, I watched him slither into the highest tree and fall asleep. When our Serpent King awoke in the morning, he couldn't remember why he was there or the fact he left the map under the boulder at the base of the tree. It's still there today and after all these seasons, the others have forgotten about the map...all, that is, except me."

Celestria leaned in and kissed Lasidious on the tip of his nose. "How great are *you*, my love, my pet, my little devil-god," she said with a sensual smile as her hand cupped his backside, her favorite part of his anatomy.

Lasidious enjoyed the moment, then turned to look at George. "Are you going to suggest to Kepler that traveling with George will be key to delivering the lifestyle the demon-cat desires?"

"Oh, yes, yes, yes, my pet. I think Kepler will make a wonderful travel companion and bodyguard for George...if he doesn't eat him first. I worry he will test George. I will work on this suggestion and see if Kepler can be influenced. Let us manipulate them to meet at the pool three days from now, by Late Bailem."

Lasidious nodded. "If the cat kills him, then so be it. We still have another mind to influence, but we should save this mind for when the moments are right. I still feel using George is a solid plan. Just make sure you stay out of sight from the others. You're starting to show."

"I knew I chose you for a reason. You are the smartest of all the gods," she said, kissing him once again. "I will leave now, my pet. You need to get the mortal going. I am sure he will be overwhelmed from such a fall. He is going to have a heart attack when he meets his first undead demon-jaguar. I would hate to see the poor guy garesh his pants before getting started on his journey to power."

Celestria leaned into Lasidious again and brushed her cheek against his. She whispered in his ear in her sexiest voice, "Goodbye, my pet, my love, my sweet, my cute little devil-god." With that, she vanished, leaving behind the echoes of her giggles reverberating about the cavernous room.

Lasidious marveled at the sensuality of his love's departure before turning his attention to George. "Let the games begin. You're about to start the adventure which will be your new life."

The God of Mischief held a picture in front of him and looked at it hard. "Well, Abbie, I hope your daddy is ready for this. Just wait until your father understands how the fiendish liquid inside the staff really works, assuming he isn't dead before he gets the chance, of course."

Welcome to the first edition of

The Grayham Inquirer

When Inquiring Minds Need to Know about their Favorite Characters

CELESTRIA is about to meet with the undead demon-jaguar, Kepler, to set up a meeting with George at the Pool of Sorrow.

LASIDIOUS is preparing for his introduction to George. The god is looking at his map of Grayham to find the best place to open up the sky and let George fall to the ground. The god has a disguise in mind and plans to teleport them both to this spot. Lasidious will play out his deception as a traveling adventurer.

SHALEE has awakened from the effects of bonding with her new staff. She is now on her feet. Sam and Mosley are walking with her, making their way through the Temple of the Gods.

BASSORINE is on Ancients Sovereign, looking for Lasidious to find out the god's intentions.

Thank you for reading the Grayham Inquirer

Mental Breakdown

Shalee had slept off the effects of bonding with her new staff, and now, Mosley is leading the Earthlings toward the exit of the great hallway. According to her watch, Shalee slept for a couple of hours, but awoke rejuvinated.

"This temple was built by the Collective as a reminder of the importance of the Crystal Moon, not only to this world, but the others as well. This is a place for all to worship and thank the gods for their bounteous gifts. It does not matter which deity a person or beast serves, everyone may worship. The strongest leaders of many packs have walked these hallowed halls."

Mosley became sidetracked. He stopped speaking and redirected his attention to the base of one of the pillars. After he sniffed its entire circumference, he shook his head, then sneezed. "Unacceptable."

Sam was curious about the wolf's reaction. "What's wrong? You look irritated."

Mosley continued to sniff, but during this series of moments he explored the base of two other pillars as Sam and Shalee watched. "It is aggravating. The pillars within this temple are unmarked. I want to claim this territory, but to do so would be disrespectful to the gods."

Shalee rolled her eyes. "Are ya sayin' ya want ta pee on the pillar? Am I understandin' ya right?"

Mosley looked annoyed. "I am saying this territory has been unclaimed. It calls to me to make it mine."

"Goodness-gracious, Mosley, who's gonna know? If it's that big of a deal, just give one of 'em a lil' squirt already and get it ova' with. We ain't gonna tell anybody." She nudged Sam with her hand, "Isn't that right?"

Sam looked at the wolf and shrugged. "If you feel the need to pee on it, then have at it. It's not my house."

It was easy to see Mosley's emotional struggle as he stood there for a long series of moments, quietly debating. He lifted his head, looked in all directions, then turned sideways against the pillar. Once he was sure no one was watching, he lifted his leg and released a quick spurt. Like a child, the wolf darted down the great hall and waited for Sam and Shalee to catch up.

It was easy to hear Mosley's excitement. "How exhilarating. I have never done anything so mischievous. My father would have been proud of me. To claim a territory as grand as this would be the talk of the pack. I cannot wait to see my brothers. Their pups' pups will forever tell this tale."

Shalee raised her free hand to her mouth and spoke just over the top of her fingers as she pressed them against her lower lip. "You'd make a good Texan, Mosley. You got a lil' rebel in ya."

After enjoying the compliment, Mosley turned his attention back to more pertinent matters. "As I was about to say, this particular temple is for the beings of Grayham. Everyone may bring their cubs, or rather, their offspring. This is the true resting place of the Crystal Moon. There are similar temples on the other worlds, though they hold only replicas of the Crystal Moon. The temples are protected by the power of the gods from every direction for a half-day's journey. This protection gives the inhabitants of each world a safe place to worship."

As the night terror wolf finished speaking, two fifty-foot long, sinister-looking serpents with large fangs and cobra hoods slithered past. Shalee grabbed Sam's arm as they rolled by and whispered, "Mosley, psst, Mosley, hey...those are some *really big* snakes. Someone should spray 'round here. Are they really allowed ta pray like otha' folks? I bet it's some sorta health risk or somethin'."

She turned to watch as the serpents undulated away, then a new thought popped out of her mouth. "Oh, my goodness-gracious, can ya imagine how many purses I could make with all that skin?" With a wave, she snapped her fingers. "It's all 'bout the accessories, ya know."

Mosley chuckled. "I can only assume you are referring to a type of bag. If so, you might want to wait until the serpent sheds. And, to answer your question, they are allowed inside the temple. There are no health risks to be concerned about. I just told you every beast is allowed to worship here." The wolf lowered his nose to the floor and sniffed around. "The serpent's trail leaves an awful smell."

Sam cut in, "What other kind of beasts come here?"

Mosley shook his head. "All kinds, of course. Have you not listened to anything I have said?"

Sam grunted. "Hmpf, your answer failed to narrow the scope. Thanks for the information, Mosley."

The wolf ignored the sarcasm. "As I was saying, Grayham's temple of worship is where the true Crystal Moon was kept prior to its disappearance, as you have seen. The gods agreed placing both of you here was a good starting point for your journey. The temple is located far to the northwest of Brandor. Your paws may be sore before we arrive."

Mosley used his snout to point to a map resting on the west wall to show how far away Brandor was. "It will take many days to get there."

Changing the subject, Shalee said, "Sam, can ya believe the beauty of this place? I still think the idea of a big snake is kinda creepy, but if you look past that, the architecture is incredible. No place on Earth can come close ta this beauty. I've neva' seen such exquisite detail. Everythin's so grand. I'd love ta study the blueprints."

Mosley interrupted. "Bassorine had the gods create many areas on Grayham to remind you of your old homeworld. The Collective wished for your transition to be smooth. If you ever see the other worlds, their look and feel will be nothing like Grayham's. My eyes had the chance to see much of Harvestom when I was a cub. Bassorine took me there after he chose me to live in service."

Sam and Shalee looked at each other and shrugged, unable to imagine the concept of another world being so accessible. Sam's mind churned with questions, but the temple doors leading to the outside world began to open. The doors were enormous and required a slow, steady pace to accomplish the task. Numerous massive hinges, almost as long as Sam's Mustang convertible and about as wide, supported the weight which was equal to thirty elephants. At more than ninety-five feet, the doors arched toward each other at the top.

Sam stared, thinking, *They must be all of two-meters thick. This can't be gold. Gold would be too heavy.* "Shalee, can you imagine the sound one of these doors would make if it slammed into the wall? This place had to cost an arm and a leg to build."

Mosley tilted his head. "Sam, I can assure you the gods accepted no arms or legs as payment for the temple's construction."

"Don't be silly, Mosley, he didn't mean it lit'rally," Shalee said, giggling. "I look forward ta seein' more of Grayham if it's anythin' like this place."

"I am sure you will enjoy yourself, Shalee," Mosley replied. "I find Sam's comment to be curious." The wolf thought a moment, then shook off the awkwardness. "The temple is unlike any other place on this world. Grayham does, however, have many wondrous destinations."

Once outside, the humans were at a loss for words. The view was breathtaking—a moment where the soul had to stop and take it all in. The temple had been built on a large plateau. The structure sat back quite a ways from the edge of a steep drop. The drop, Griffin Cliffs, was just over 7,000 feet to the bottom. All around the expansive steppe were natural springs which surfaced and pooled together before flowing over the edge. Many forms of beautiful flowers, as well as other manifestations they had never seen before, bloomed around the pools. The sight was glorious, beyond glorious, and Shalee could have stayed forever.

Sam studied his surroundings and figured there had to be at least a few hundred of these natural springs which peacefully fed into one another. The sound the water made as it worked its way into the large pooling area was soothing to the ears.

Moving closer to the edge of the cliffs, the group looked over. Sam could see and feel the energy of the falls and wondered about the volume of water released into the lands below. He could not fathom how many gallons it would take to create this kind of natural wonder. The three watched in silence as a large cloud of mist billowed up in all directions. The water from the falls hit the rocks below with such tremendous force the mist covered a massive area.

Mosley spoke. "Sam, the springs generate enough water to supply three kingdoms. The expanse of Southern Grayham's terrain slopes away from the falls."

"I've never seen anything like it," Sam responded. Taking a deep breath, he thought, *This place makes Niagara Falls seem insignificant.*

They worked their way clear of the edge and toward a large platform made of wood. The platform was large and had a railing surrounding its perimeter.

After walking up the steps, Sam turned to Mosley and started his list of questions. "Okay, okay, I can see this is clearly not Earth." Sam pointed to the east, then to the west, at a colorful planet on each horizon. The world to the east radiated many purple hues while the other permeated a spectrum of orange, spawning many more questions. "Where are we?"

Mosley looked confused. "I already told you. Your paws have found their place on Grayham. More specifically, Southern Grayham, on top of Griffin Cliffs. You saw the map inside the temple."

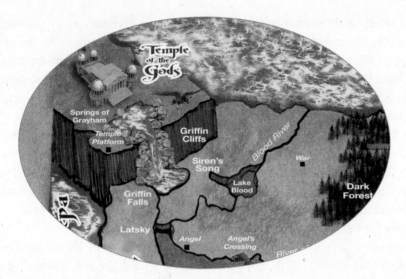

Temple of the Gods

"No, no, no! I mean...yes, I saw the map, but what I meant, where in the galaxy are we? There are no large purple and orange worlds visible from Earth with a naked eye."

Mosley tilted his head as a dog would when confused. "I am not sure what you mean. All that is, or ever was, since the end of The Great Destruction of Everything Known over 12,000 seasons ago, is where you are. You are on one of the five planets revolving around the sun. This planet, as I told you before, is Grayham. The two worlds above are Luvelles and Harvestom. Dragonia and Trollcom cannot be seen for now, since they travel on the far side of the glowing sun. Nothing else exists, other than the hidden god world of Ancients Sovereign, but the beings of the worlds do not know of its existence or how to get there. Only those of us who live in service to a specific member of the Collective know this sacred information. You would not know it now were it not for Bassorine's desire."

Again, Mosley became sidetracked. He sniffed the base of the wooden platform until he found the perfect spot. After marking it, he rejoiced, then rejoined the conversation. "What a wonderous day. To further answer your question, most of what I know consists of this world. Anything more, I cannot say. I am not sure what a galaxy is, but it is indeed an amazing name."

Sam and Shalee looked at each other for a moment. "Okay, okay, so...you don't know where Earth is, and we're on one of five planets which revolve around a single sun. The Crystal Moon's job is to keep the planets in different orbits so they don't collide. That, I can buy. Obviously, if all the worlds are able to support life and you only have the one sun, judging by the position of the other two worlds, the planets must each be on a different axis. What a logistical nightmare. Your solar system must look like a giant atom of sorts. The sun acts as the nucleus while the planets move around as equal mass electrons. Granted, this is a crude analogy, but..."

Mosley interrupted his thoughtful rant. "Sam, what are you talking about? What is an atom?"

Sam shook his head. "Oh, nothing. Forget about it. I suppose I'll just have to accept most of this, for now, since you clearly have no idea what I'm talking about. At least answer this." Sam looked toward the sun. "How many hours are in one of your days?"

Mosley gave him a blank stare. It was clear the wolf knew nothing of hours. He hesitated, "I do not know what an hour is. I can tell you we consider a day to be from when the sun reaches its highest point in the sky until the next moment it does it again. Does this help?"

"Heck, no, it doesn't help. Of course a day is easy to figure out. Don't you have clocks or watches?" he asked, pointing at Shalee's wrist. "Don't you understand the concept of time?"

Mosley looked at the object and asked Sam to explain its function. Once the beast understood how the timepiece worked, he responded. "We have no word to represent your concept of time. This is foreign to our worlds. We plan things around the different positions of our sun while it crosses the sky. For example, if you look up, you can see the sun has just risen, and is only a quarter of the way toward its highest point. We call this Early Bailem. When the sun is at its highest point, the Peak of Bailem, and when it has passed the Peak of Bailem and again midway to the horizon, this is referred to as Late Bailem. All of these terms honor the God of the Sun, Bailem.

"Just before the sun disappears behind the horizon, we call this dusk, or evening. When the sun is gone and can no longer be seen, we call the darkness, night. In the middle of the night, we have an estimated series of moments called, midnight."

Sam interrupted. "How do you possibly call 'an estimated series of moments' by one name? Shouldn't this be a single moment?"

Mosley thought a while. "I suppose if our worlds understood your concept of time, it would be easy to call a single moment, midnight. Since we don't, let us move on, shall we?"

Shalee and Sam shook their heads as Mosley continued. "When the sun is about to rise, we call this dawn, or morning. It was the Collective who named the moments of a day, dusk, evening, dawn, morning, night, and midnight."

Sam grabbed the hair on his head, looked at Shalee, back at Mosley, then spun around with his hands in the air. He laughed. "These people are primitive. I wonder where these "so-called" gods got some of those names, Earth, maybe? These people don't even have clocks. How in the heck do you live without clocks?" he said, motioning to Mosley while he spoke. "Hasn't anyone ever thought to...hmmm...I don't know, maybe create a sundial or something useful?"

Mosley tilted his head. Once Sam realized the wolf had no idea what he was talking about, he turned and adjusted his attitude. He realized his tone would get him nowhere and Shalee was giving him a look. "Okay, okay," he sighed. "I'll explain what a sundial is later. Shalee, let me have your watch. I'll take the time to get an accurate account of how long the days are here." Sam turned to Mosley. "How many days are there in a year?"

Again, Mosley looked puzzled and waited for Sam to explain. The fighter rolled his eyes. "Okay, okay, I'm twenty-three years old and where I'm from, it takes three hundred sixty-five days to make one year of my life." He pointed to Mosley and asked, "Do you understand?"

The wolf finally thought he understood. "I am old. Many seasons have come and gone since my days as a cub."

"What do you mean by 'seasons'?" Sam replied. "I've heard that expression more than once."

Mosley grinned in his wolfish way. "The season we are experiencing is called summer. We determine our age by seasons. I was born in the winter and became one season old when the next winter arrived. The next winter I became two seasons old. This continued each winter until I arrived at the age I am now, which is none of your business. Sam, you said you were twenty-three?"

"I did."

"In what season were you born?"

"I was born in the spring," Sam replied, knowing full well what the wolf was going to say next.

"Well, we also have a spring, and a fall. The seasons go in the order of winter, spring, summer, and fall, then back to winter again. This would make you twenty-three spring seasons old. Do you understand?"

Sam laughed. "I understand, but this doesn't tell me how long a year is on Grayham. It does tell me how you figure out your ages, so for that, I thank you. I'll have to figure out the rest on my own. At least the names of the seasons are the same. Sounds like your gods were too lazy to think of their own names for things they created. I swear, I feel like I'm in some sort of dream. How can any of this be real? Maybe I should pinch myself."

Shalee agreed. Mosley shrugged wolfishly (Fellow soul...I hope you can imagine how this looks.) "I did tell you the gods wanted to make your transition into this world as easy as possible. This is a good thing, considering you feel you were brought here against your will. Maybe the seasons were named the same as your Earth's for this reason. I don't know why you would want to pinch yourself, Sam, but I can assure you this is real, and you are on Grayham. You are not inside a dream, as you put it. I am sorry I am not more helpful. If I knew anything more, I would answer your questions to their fullest extent. However, I am sure Bassorine will know the answers."

"Okay, okay, you said Brandor is 'many days' from here. I'm assuming, since you don't have clocks, then you probably don't have cars either. Are we riding horses, walking, what's up? Give it to me straight. What does 'many days' from here mean?"

Sam turned and looked at the countryside far below. Everything he could see was fascinating. It was all green and the valleys and mountain ranges stretched far beyond his view. He took a deep breath as he waited for his answer. He marveled at how clean the air was. It had not been poisoned like the air on Earth. It was crisp, fresh, and pleasant.

Shalee jumped in before Mosley could answer. "Yeah, exactly what does that mean? And, by the way, I'm starvin'. I'm not gonna go anywhere else in my pajamas, nor am I gonna go anywhere on an empty stomach. After all, a woman needs ta look her best when leavin' home, and I would say this definitely qualifies as leavin' home. Do you have anythin' for us ta wear? Mine best be cute. They could've at least grabbed my wardrobe when they stole me away from Motha' Earth. Texans don't take kindly ta bein' stole away from things, ya know?"

Shalee lifted her new staff, twirled it above her head, and continued, "Hey! And, anotha' thing. How do I make this petrified wand thingy whip up somethin' really fab? Will I be able ta turn a prince into a frog and crazy stuff like that? But, I ain't kissin' him."

Mosley waited for Shalee to stop kidding around, then directed his attention to Sam. He could answer all three of their questions and was comforted.

Despite Shalee's inability to focus, this was refreshing after he had failed to answer the last few.

"I have the answers to all your questions. The gods have left suitable attire for you to wear, inside the temple. Shalee, I have no idea what you consider cute. If you do not like what has been provided, you will need to talk with Bassorine."

Shalee smiled and tapped the butt of her new staff on the ground. "Don't ya worry 'bout that, once I figure out how ta zap him good with this thingy, I'll get his fashion sense up ta speed."

The wolf laughed. "The gods will seal the temple to visitors once you have changed. They won't want the inhabitants of Grayham knowing about the Crystal Moon's disappearance."

Mosley sat on his haunches. "Your second question was how many days will it take to get to Brandor. If we travel by paw, it is a 56 Peak of Bailem journey from here to there. Your final answer is..."

Shalee interrupted, snapping, "Didn't he just say from one Peak of Bailem ta the next is a day here?" She looked at Sam for the answer.

Seeing her expression, which seemed to be a mix of anger and disbelief, the wolf's enthusiasm to answer their questions dwindled.

Sam responded, "He did...why?"

Shalee turned and gave Mosley a look to kill. "You listen ta me, ya big overgrown puppy. If ya think for one stinkin' minute I'm gonna walk 56 days ta get ta this Brandor place, you're crazy. I'm no Joan of Arc and I'm definitely not a Mormon pioneer. I don't even own a stupid wagon."

She stopped, then shouted. "Who does this shaggy mutt think I am anyway, the Crocodile Hunter's wife? For heaven's sake! There betta' be anotha' way. Where will we sleep tonight? I'm not about ta wear these pajamas two doggone days in a row, that's just wrong. They look terrible. Look at all of these burn marks."

She poked her finger through a few of the holes. "I don't have any money on me for food. This is nuts. I just got a pedicure, and my nails are lookin' absolutely delicious." Looking back at Mosley, a new thought blurted out. "I don't even have my hairbrush. How can I possibly deal with all of this without my brush? You're lucky I don't have a rolled up newspapa'."

Sam found Mosley's wide eyes. He could see the wolf was confused. He ignored Shalee and attempted to whisper into their furry guide's ear. "Just disregard her for now."

Shalee, hearing the comment, blew up. "What? Disregard me? Who do ya think ya are, buddy, some kind of king or somethin'?"

Sam held Mosley's gaze. "Like I said, just ignore her." As he continued to speak, Sam could feel Shalee's look to kill.

Mosley decided to play along and winked at Sam in his own wolfish way, then turned to Shalee. "I said it was a 56 Peak *walk*, but I said nothing about sleeping. It will take *twice* as long if we take the moments necessary to do so. Did you expect us to stop? I can make the journey straight through."

It was clear by Shalee's response, she failed to recognize the wolf's chiding. "Oh, for all the angels in heaven," she shouted. "You've gotta be kiddin' me!" She flopped down on the wooden platform and started to cry.

"I said I wanted an adventure, not blisters. I don't even have any suntan lotion for a trip like this, and I burn easy. I don't have my makeup. I don't have my deodorant. I don't have my perfume. I don't have any clean pannies. For the love of heaven, I hate this place. I swear I'll neva' wish again. Yep, oh yeah, I'll neva' wish again. Thanks, mom, for feedin' me a wonderful line of crap 'bout wishes comin' true. This isn't even close ta my idea of fun. I don't even have my new purse, and it was fab, doggone it. This has gotta be my worst nightmare." Tears filled her eyes as she put her head between her knees and continued to crumble. "I think I'm havin' a breakdown."

Sam had to smile at Shalee's reaction. He looked at Mosley and leaned in closer to the wolf before whispering again. "Just wait until she figures out she doesn't have any tampons. She's really gonna blow then."

Mosley tilted his furry head and whispered back, "What are tampons?"

Sam could only laugh. "Aahhhhh, just forget it. Let's just say where we're from, most women don't find this sort of adventure entertaining. I do hope you have another solution to get us to Brandor. I also don't want to walk 56 days. We will need to sleep."

Shalee lifted her head and whimpered, "I need a soft pilla' ta lie my head on, Mosley. I'm not cut out for this kinda thing. How can I look fab if I can't get any rest?" She buried her head again into her knees.

Sam changed the subject. "Okay, okay, so how do we get down from the top of the cliffs? They don't look scalable."

Nodding, Mosley responded, "I do have another solution to get us to Brandor. The gods made the cliffs unassailable. There are stairs, but this isn't how we will be traveling."

Mosley turned to Shalee, who was still crying, and raised his voice. "I have a way to get you to Brandor without making you walk. You can stop crying now. Let us get you dressed for the journey."

Shalee wiped her tears on the hem of her pajama top and as she did, Mosley turned and asked Sam to ring the large bell sitting at the far side of the wooden platform. "The only way to get from the top of the cliffs to the land below, without using the steps, is to ride the giant griffins who live inside Griffin Cliffs."

With that, Shalee started in again. "If you think I'm gonna ride some giant whateva' it is, you got anotha' think comin'. I'm not about ta get on some creepy, flyin' thingy. I don't know how ta ride stuff like that. Do they bite? Goodness-gracious, I bet they bite. Oh, my gosh, do they smell?"

Mosley heard enough. He leaned in and breathed on Shalee's face. She fell asleep and her body slumped over onto the platform.

"She will sleep for a while," the wolf said. "I am sure she will be far more pleasant after she has had the chance to adjust. Are all the women from your Earth like her?"

Sam smiled. "Only the ones worth keeping. I have to admit, I find her attractive. I like her sassiness. She'll grow on you, Mosley. She's just stressed right now, that's all. Ever since I got here, so many things have seemed familiar. She's from Texas and I know I've never met her before, but even she seems familiar. I would have told her, but that would have been kind of creepy. Just trust me on this, Mosley, you'll like her. I just know it."

"I hope you are right," Mosley responded.

Sam changed the subject. "Earlier, you mentioned the God of the Sun. Do all of the gods have titles?"

Mosley thought long and hard before answering. "They do, but not all the gods allow their followers to know their true nature. I would not possess this knowledge if it was not for my service to Bassorine."

"Why would they do that?"

"I'm not allowed to answer your question further, Sam. We should speak of another topic. Tell me more of your Earth."

This was a subject on which Sam could talk forever. Soon, a massive flying beast appeared from below the edge of the steep drop and prepared to land on the platform. Sam moved to the far side as the giant creature set down. The force of the wind generated by the griffin's wings made standing difficult. Sam had to grab hold of the sturdy wooden railing to maintain his balance.

The griffin—part eagle, part lion—was huge. Its feathers were dark brown with white tips. The rest of its coat was a beautiful golden tan. The beast's massive paws on its back legs touched down first while its razor-sharp talons grabbed hold of a round beam which rested just above the platform's surface. The creature lifted its head, scanned the area with its piercing eyes and shrieked.

Sam watched in amazement as Mosley walked up to the creature without fear. Though dwarfed, the wolf shouted his orders in a foreign language. To Sam's surprise, he understood pieces of the language, but again failed to comprehend why. He made a mental note and kept the discovery to himself.

"I asked the beast to wait until we return from the temple. We should hurry. Griffins are not known for their patience. Pick Shalee up and carry her."

After Sam finished dressing, he changed Shalee and cautioned Mosley, if asked, he was to tell Shalee a temple maid dressed her. Sam did not want Shalee to know he had seen her without her clothes. He wanted her dignity left intact. The wolf said he understood. Sam did admit, however, he liked the job and was glad Mosley had knocked her out.

Sam's thoughts ran wild as he secured Shalee's headpiece. *You're breathtaking. The outfit Bassorine left for you makes you look like a princess. How nice would it be if I were your prince? Ha, only in my dreams.*

Mosley showed Sam where a large pouch full of food had been prepared. The wolf explained the journey to Brandor would take six days by air. Fortunately, the moments necessary would be provided to stop and sleep, since the wolf did need to sleep.

They made sure they had everything before they left the temple and watched as the massive doors were sealed. No one would be allowed to enter until the Crystal Moon was returned.

Sam lifted Shalee onto the griffin's back, and then climbed up, securing their new weapons with straps from the saddle which rested on the creature's back. He tied Shalee in and prepared for take-off. The beast walked to the edge of the platform. Sam swallowed hard as he looked down.

"Hold on! This is going to be fun!" Mosley shouted as best he could while biting down on the straps and digging his claws into the leather of the saddle. They dropped off the edge and fell over four thousand feet before the griffin opened his wings and swooped over the undulating landscape.

Broken Back

Lasidious is still sitting at his table, watching George tumble through the transparent wall of his cave-like home. He is deciding how he wants to make his introduction as the fictitious traveler, Jason. After reviewing his map of Grayham, the god chooses the southern edge of the Enchanted Forest to stage his rescue.

Just to the south of the forest, beyond a large open field, is a place called Lethwitch. He will drop George just outside of town. This location will give the mortal the moments necessary to get the needed supplies before heading north to the Pool of Sorrow.

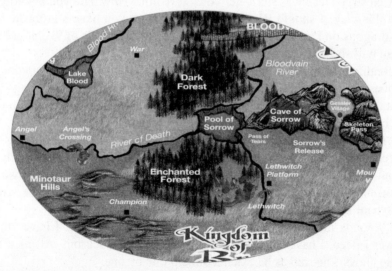

Lasidious told Celestria George would be at the pool in three days, which left no room for wasted moments for the Earthling to wander about sightseeing. The God of Mischief hopes George will bump into Kepler, as planned, and become traveling companions, if the large undead demon-jaguar doesn't eat him first.

He waved his hand and George disappeared. Lasidious stood from the table, put the picture of Abbie in his front pocket, grabbed the map of Grayham and a leather pack from his bedroom, then vanished.

The Mountains of Lataseff, Skeleton Pass

Celestria approached the demon-jaguar, Kepler. The giant cat, over thirty feet long from the tip of his nose to the end of his tail, had a smooth, shiny, black coat which revealed his powerful muscular structure. His claws were sharp as knives, terrifying to most, but not Celestria, Goddess of Evil-Natured Beasts.

The cat yawned as she approached. His large mouth had tasted the death of many men. Kepler's teeth were white, except for the yellowish stains at their base from the blood of man-flesh. As he closed his mouth, he stood and stretched his legs, neck, and back.

"How dare you walk within this pass and come into *my* home as if you belong," he snarled. "Can you not see the dead which lie with their bones scattered? Are you not afraid of my skeleton army? I should summon them to gut the likes of you where you stand! This is my territory!"

Celestria's face was stern, her voice forceful. "How dare you talk to your god this way! I should take you and everything you have and throw it to the dragons on Dragonia." Her voice echoed off the walls of Skeleton Pass. "You will show me respect, demon!"

Realizing who he had insulted, Kepler lowered his head. "My apologies, goddess. If I had known you were coming, I would have made things presentable." The giant cat pushed a half-eaten barbarian torso behind him with his back paw as if embarrassed about its presence.

"Never mind your chaotic untidiness, Kepler," Celestria replied as she watched him squirm. "I am here to inform you of great things which are about to happen. The moments have come for those who want power to stand up and take it. This will forever change the powers-that-be within Grayham's kingdoms."

"Sounds intriguing," Kepler responded. "Why tell me? I have all the power I need. I have ruled my pass for hundreds of seasons. All men fear these claws," he said as he extended them one by one.

The goddess walked by, brushing her hand along his fur as she passed and sat where he had been lying. "Kepler, you have been bored for many seasons. I know the secret of how you rule this pass. I watch you from the heavens and see how you lie about and wish for something to happen. I only tell you because I know of a man who is strong and possesses the wit to rule this world. I have foreseen this man to be the master of Grayham. He will send this world into darkness. Would I be correct in saying this would make you a happy little demon, my pet?"

Kepler hated how the goddess called him a "little demon," and her "pet" but said nothing to correct her. "Sounds interesting," he said with a hint of disdain. "All I'll need to do is lie here and wait for this to happen. I'll have my own private den of misery. I can't complain about something so grand. These eyes function best when I prey upon the weak in the darkness."

The goddess knew Kepler was more interested than he let on. "This man will be at the Pool of Sorrow three days from now. He should be camped near the outlet where the pool releases its water into the Cripple River. For all I know, he may not find you worthy of his company."

"Not worthy of his company?" the demon snarled, then let out a ferocious roar. "I'm *more* than worthy to be in his presence! He should be honored to have me at his side. I would be the best choice as an advisor to the one who rules the territories of Grayham. I alone can handle this power. I am the master of the hunt."

Celestria was pleased with his response, but did not show it. She knew of Kepler's immense pride and hoped it was large enough to take the bait. She moved to stand beside the demon and began to stroke his flanks.

"I know a beast of your abilities could be quite useful on this human's journey, if you are worthy, my pet," she said as she reached up to touch the point of one of his teeth. Again, she leaned into him. She felt Kepler cringe and smiled inside. "Perhaps, you should meet this human and sell your abilities. See if he accepts your companionship. I warn you, Kepler, this is a strong-willed, hot-tempered human. I would not make him angry if I was you. I would hate to see you end up on a skewer, cooked for supper."

The beast let out another angry roar. "I'm no one's supper! I will track this man. He will see I'm the perfect travel companion. I'll allow him to rule with me at his side. If he doesn't accept my offer, I may find it necessary to pick his bones from between my teeth before I return."

"Careful, Kepler," the goddess cautioned, moving to stand in front of his massive mouth. She tugged each of his whiskers as she continued in a soft tone. "I know you are strong, but I warn you, I would not toy with this human. He is powerful."

The goddess scratched the underside of his powerful jawline. "You will need to make your way to the Pool of Sorrow before the end of the third day if you are to find him."

Celestria turned and pointed at what appeared to be the right leg of a barbarian he killed earlier in the day. "I will put a blessing on your dinner. This will give you the stamina you need to make it to the pool before the human arrives. It is your decision. After you eat, you would need to hurry."

"I am powerful, but a journey of this magnitude would take thirty Peaks. I cannot cross such terrain without peril. Are you saying this meal will allow me to make the trip around the mountains in only 3 days? Why are you doing this, goddess?"

Celestria rubbed her hands through the fur on each side of his snout. Though her size paled in comparison, she was firm and loved the way the demon-cat loathed every moment of her touch.

"Yes," she finally said as she backed off. "That is exactly what I am saying. As I have said, it is up to you. I am doing nothing, other than blessing your food, and giving you information. Of all the great cats who serve me, you are my favorite. It must be your decision to fulfill your destiny. I cannot do it for you. However, I need to warn you. I will be gone for quite a while. I will not come to you again. This is your only chance to grab the power you have always wanted. It will be up to you to make friends with this human and keep him from killing you." The goddess gave a sinister smile, kissed the tip of Kepler's gigantic nose, and enjoyed the cat's disdain before vanishing.

The undead demon-jaguar let out a mighty roar which caused the birds sitting on the top of the pass' steep walls to take flight. He shook to rid himself of the goddess' unwanted advances. After a moment of staring at the blessed leg, he started ripping the bloody flesh from the bone.

North of Lethwitch

George was sick to his stomach. The blackness opened and spit him out like rotten food. He appeared high above the ground and now, he could only focus on his death. He had been falling for so long, he welcomed an end to his suffering.

Just before impact, he closed his eyes and waited. To his surprise, the next thing George knew, he landed on something soft. A loud scream erupted beneath him as his descent came to an end.

George waited before opening his eyes. He was not sure if he was dreaming, but he felt alive. He could hear the cries from under him. Whatever he landed on was badly hurt. He opened his eyes and lifted himself off a massively heavyset man. He checked to see if he broke anything before attending to the fool. Everything seemed intact, except his clothes, which had taken a beating. The man cried out once again, in pain.

"Damn, man, you all right? You saved my life, thank you!" George said.

"I think I've broken my back," the man wailed.

"Is there anything I can do to help?" George grabbed the man's bag and rifled through it to see if there was anything he could use to assist.

"There's a powder," the man groaned. "It's in a copper tin. Add it to the water in my leather hide." He groaned again. "It will act as a painkiller. You could help me get up against a tree. I have friends who should be coming this way. They should be able to lay me on their wagon and take me to the healers' vestry."

George did as instructed, thinking, *Yeah sure...they'll take you to a healer if your big ass doesn't break their wagon, first.*

As George watched the powder fall through the hide's opening, he further thought about what just happened. After a moment of absent pondering, he administered the tonic. The mixture seemed to have an instantaneous effect as the wounded became intoxicated.

"Ahhhhhhhh, that's better," he said with a slurred voice.

George took this opportunity to move him against the nearest tree, grunting as he struggled to move the man's weight. In a winded voice he said, "Why did you catch me?"

"I didn't catch you. I had no choice. You fell on top of me." The man was feeling no pain as he spoke. "I was walking and the next thing I knew, you landed on top of me. It's not like men fall from the sky everyday. Did you fall from one of the hippogriffs?"

"Damn, that sucks. I guess I'm kind of sorry and grateful at the same time. I hope you can forgive me," George said, contradicting the real truth within his mind. "I don't know what a hippogriff is. I'm not even sure what happened. One minute, I'm on a statue looking at a rock, and the next, I'm falling to my death. If you hadn't come along, I think I'd be eating dirt right now."

"Lucky me. I cannot say I fully understand what these 'minutes' are you're referring to, but my name is Jason, nonetheless. I'm from Lethwitch. I'm an adventurer and traveler. Who, may I ask, are you?"

George stood, taking note of Jason's odd response. *How could he not know what a minute is and why is he dressed like Robin Hood? Must be some kind of freak.*

George shrugged, his eyes spotting a town in the distance. The town sat on the far side of a large, gently sloping field covered with brightly colored flowers, none of which George had ever seen. He turned his head to continue his survey. Just north of their position, not far from the tree Jason was resting against, sat a dense treeline of a forest. "Everything is so bright and green. This place is beautiful."

"You're right, it is beautiful. The gods bless us. What's your name, boy?"

"Where are my manners? I wasn't thinking. I apologize. My name is George, from Orlando, Florida."

"Well, George, from Orlando, Florida, well met."

"You'll have to cut me some slack here, man, I'm at a loss for words."

"You speak in a strange manner," Jason slurred. "Your fall must've been traumatic." Lasidious groaned for effect. "I cannot say the place you hail from is familiar to me, but I can extend my hand in friendship."

"Yeah, yeah, yeah, sure thing. Friends it is. Is the town over there the one you were talking about?"

"The town you see is indeed my home," the man responded with a goofy smile.

"Where are we? What were you doing out here in the first place?" George asked, turning his attention back to Jason. "Do you always hang out in the middle of freaking nowhere? What's wrong with you?"

"I can't say there's anything wrong with me, other than my back. You're between the town of Lethwitch and the southern border of the Enchanted Forest. I like to travel. Recently, I found out a secret. I..."

George picked up on what was about to be said and focused. "I have secrets, too, Jason." He wanted to capitalize on the situation. "It looks as if your secret will have to wait until that back of yours heals. Maybe you could tell me what it is. I could help you accomplish it as a way of thanking you for saving my life."

The RV salesman knew he had no intention of helping, but wanted to know the secret just the same. He hoped the information would help him figure out the mess he was in, or at least the mess he thought he was in. "I owe you one. It's not everyday I break a guy's back while he's saving my life. Let me help you finish your task." He gave the man another drink and waited for its effect to cloud his judgment.

"What could it hurt?" Jason responded after thinking it through. "You look like a trustworthy fellow, strong, too. I would appreciate the help. What do you say we split the gains once you've completed the task? There's enough value and power to go around. I see no reason why we can't share the rewards."

George liked what he heard. The words "power" and "value" suggested the task was something he might want to undertake after all.

Jason continued. "Do you get tired of being pushed around? I do. I heard of a map which was lost just northeast of the Enchanted Forest, near the Pool of Sorrow. It's actually a lake, but they call it a pool anyhow. Rumor has it, the map has been lost for many seasons."

Struggling to focus, Jason looked at his hands as if something commanded his attention. Once he determined nothing would come of his pondering, he continued. "The map is under a large boulder beneath the tree closest to the pool's outlet which flows into the Cripple River. The map shows where a treasure is hidden. It is said to be inside the Cave of Sorrow. I was going to retrieve it and sell it for a substantial profit. The map is worth an amount of coin I've never had or been able to imagine. The only thing worth more than the map is the treasure it leads to. I would go after the treasure myself, except I cannot find a way to get past The Beast inside the Cave of Sorrow. In order to get to the treasure, you must get past him. I'm scared, to say the least."

"Wait a second," George interrupted. "This map is worth a large amount of money. So the treasure has to be worth far more than that. Exactly what is this treasure, anyway?"

Lasidious knew he had George's full attention. He also knew from watching George back on Earth, the mortal was greedy. He would want the treasure and power it would bring. He smiled within as he continued to play the role of the wounded adventurer. "The map is said to lead to a Staff of Petrifaction. The staff is able to turn anything into solid stone, but for one problem."

George rolled his eyes. "Are you for real? A staff that turns things to stone? Do you really expect me to believe that? I think the medicine is messing with your head."

Jason looked George in the eyes. He squinted hard as if trying to focus. "Why would you doubt what I'm saying? The medicine is strong, but it hasn't effected my mind."

George thought, *Oh my freaking hell, this guy is totally serious. I'll just play along for now.* "Anyway, so what's the problem with the staff?"

"Are you sure you want to know?"

"Definitely. By all means, continue."

A look appeared on Jason's face, unsure if he should go on. After seeing George's conviction, he continued. "The staff can only be used by the dwarves of Trollcom. I'm sure you know of Trollcom. The good thing is, it's worth a large amount of coin...or it could be..."

"It could be what?" George asked without hesitating. "It could be what?"

Jason acted as if he was thinking. He motioned for George to come closer, then whispered, "The staff isn't solid. Its center holds a liquid. If a man was to drink it, he would receive the ability to turn things to stone."

"Really?" George asked as he backed away. "Sounds like B.S."

"I assure you this is all very real and not this 'B.S.' you speak of."

George rolled his eyes and decided he would continue to play along. "If what you're saying is true, that would kick ass. Sounds like some really serious power if you ask me. Can you imagine the money a guy could make with this kind of ability? How could this be real?"

Jason motioned for him to keep quiet and come even closer. He winced, pretending to feel pain. "I don't understand what you mean when you say something 'kicks ass,' or what 'money' is, but I do understand you see the value of this artifact. I swear what I speak of is the truth. I, for one, believe it's not the coin we should be thinking about. If one of us had this power, we could go into the world and take control of Grayham. Imagine the wealth which would come from controlling kingdoms. It would be far greater than using the power to make coin." Jason smiled. He knew this kind of power would appeal to the Earthling's desires.

"Oh, hell yes. If I can get my hands on that staff and drink its liquid, I could gain some serious power. I could get rid of that wicked ex-wife of mine. Abbie would be able to live with me." He looked at Jason, then added, "Of course, I would need to take my new best friend with me once he's back on his feet."

"But, of course," Jason responded. "I can tell you're a man of your word. I would do anything for a loved one of my own. I just have one question. Do you have the courage to face The Beast inside the Cave of Sorrow?"

"Hell if I know." George scratched the top of his head as he imagined The Beast's appearance. "Courage isn't the problem. The problem is, I'm not the best fighter. What should I expect and what does it look like?"

"I'll tell you everything I know. The Cave of Sorrow is home to Maldwin, a hideous monster which uses visions of sadness to drive those who enter his cave insane. The visions encourage his victims to commit suicide. They walk down the Pass of Tears and throw themselves into the Pool of Sorrow. It is said you can hear them weeping as they descend the pass. Once they are in the pool, they swim deep below the lake's surface. When the moment comes they realize what has happened, they don't have the air necessary to resurface before drowning."

Jason pretended to need another drink. After three large swigs, he wiped the dribble from his chin. "Any man who enters the cave's opening accepts the risk of losing himself to The Beast's visions. Few have lived to make their way through the cave, but there are those who have done it. The only way out, if you manage not to lose your mind, is to exit through Sorrow's Release. This exit cannot be seen from the outside. It is said to take 8 Peaks of Bailem to find a way through the cave."

What the hell is a Peak of Bailem? George thought. "Sounds like a pain in the ass. It also sounds fake." He put both hands on top of his head. "Even if this is true, how am I supposed to do all this? How am I going to stop this Maldwin from screwing with my mind if I go in? How am I going to live long enough to last these '8 Peaks of Bailem?' Even if I do find my way to this 'Pool of Sorrow,' how will I lift the 'boulder' to get to a map which has been buried for so many seasons?" George was becoming anxious.

"I have asked the same things myself," Jason replied. "I understand your troubled mind. In the town is an old mage who has mastered some beneficial uses of magic. They may come in handy. This man could help you on your journey. I'm sure he would have a spell which could assist you through the cave. The Beast is not aggressive. It only uses visions to drive men insane. If you could find a spell which would allow you to block his visions, you could get close enough to kill him."

"Kill? I've never freaking killed anything. I'm not sure I can do it." George looked up and saw the worlds of Luvelles and Harvestom in the afternoon sky. He shook his head, closed his eyes, then reopened them to see if what he saw was truly there. Once he determined they were real, he pointed upward and looked at Jason for a response.

Lasidious enjoyed George's confusion. Instead of addressing the matter within the human's head, the God of Mischief continued with the conversation as if he failed to notice. "I understand the thought of killing is troublesome, but don't you think The Beast deserves to die? His visions have killed many who've harbored him no ill will and simply made the mistake of entering the cave."

George shook his head again. *Where the hell am I? I can't tell this jackass I'm lost. He won't trust me if I do. I'll give him another drink and figure it out later. This place is trippin' me out.*

George ensured Jason was comfortable before continuing. "I suppose The Beast is bad since it's hurting people. I guess killing him would be the best thing to do in order to save others from dying. I like the idea of the reward. Maybe I can handle this after all."

"Good," Jason replied. "You should go into town and buy the supplies you'll need. I'll give you my map. It'll help you get to the Pool of Sorrow. You can also have my pack. This should give you a head start."

George hesitated. "Exactly how am I to do that? I don't have any money to buy anything. Hell, I don't have a pot to piss in right now. All I've got is what's on me."

Jason eyed George. "I get the sense when you say 'money', you mean what those of us from Lethwitch refer to as coin. Seeing what's on your person, you'll need no pots in which to piss. It appears my eyes have spotted something of value on your wrist. It looks as if it might be worth something."

Well...fellow soul...true to form, and George being a jerk, the object Jason was referring to was a Rolex watch an old widow lady in Orlando gave George on Earth. She came into the dealership to buy a new forty-five foot Meridian Yacht, which gave him an excellent opportunity to work his way into her life. He spent six months giving her the attention she was missing and collected numerous expensive gifts along the way. The widow paid a small fortune for the watch. It was almost a piece of George's anatomy.

"Hell no," George snapped. "This watch is worth a ton of money. I won't part with it. I can't replace it."

"I understand," Jason nodded. "It has sentimental value. Too bad, though, I would hate to miss an opportunity to gain this kind of power. The way I see it, you could always buy it back once you have the means to do so."

George thought for a moment while giving Jason another drink. "I imagine I would have a little cash...or coin I mean, left over. I'll need a larger pack to carry food, and I'll also need to get this guy to sell me the spell you mentioned. What did you call him again?"

"A mage," Jason responded.

"I might also want to get a couple of those leather water pouches you have."

"What about a weapon to kill The Beast, some torches for light, a hunting knife, and supplies for healing?"

George reached under his pant leg and pulled out his small pistol. "I almost forgot I had this. It's one of the smallest .22 caliber pistols made. Some of the gangs back home use them. They can be hidden in the palm of your hand. It's only able to fire one round. I usually carry one more in my pocket." He reached inside his front pant pocket as he spoke, fumbled around a bit, and produced the bullet. "The two of these should do the trick, don't you think?"

"I'm not sure what a pistol does, but if you're saying it can only work twice, then I would consider purchasing another weapon. Maybe a sword or a dagger would be good to have as a back-up. I would also do a few other things. First, I would change the way I talk. If you respond to the people in town the way you've spoken with me, they may not understand.

"The second thing I would do, is hurry. I heard someone else is on their way to retrieve the map. It seems I'm not the only one who knows. I would hate to see you lose this opportunity to another adventurer. It was for this reason I was trying to work up the courage to go myself. You might want to procure some additional spells to catch this individual to keep him from getting what you deserve."

"Then, I better get moving. When will your friends arrive so I can leave? I want to make sure you get on the wagon." George laughed within, *Best place for a drunk, anyway. Ha...a wagon. I kill myself.*

"Don't worry about me. They'll be here soon. I'll have them take me to Lethwitch to wait for your return. The pool is almost a day and a half from here if you walk, so you'd better hurry to town. I would wait for this other adventurer if I was you and figure out a way to stop him. Maybe you can get some useful information before entering the cave. Now hurry and go."

With that, George started to run through the field toward the town. His mind raced with thought. *How could any of this magic crap be true? Let's check into this a bit further and see what I can learn. If it's all a bunch of B.S., I'll go my own way. Hell, I would have never thought a floor would open up and swallow me whole, either. Maybe there's something to all of this. Poor Jason, that drunken fool actually thinks I'm going to share the reward if there is one. Screw him and his wagon. And, what's up with these extra worlds in the sky? That purple one seems kind of cool.*

Lasidious watched until George was out of sight. As soon as the coast was clear, he changed back into his normal appearance and removed the picture of George's daughter from his pocket. "Well, well, Abbie, your daddy is working hard. Do you think he can handle this?"

Laughing, Lasidious vanished.

First Flight

It has been six hours, according to the digital watch Sam took from Shalee, since the griffin dropped from the platform at the Temple of the Gods. Sam is a bit nauseated from the movement of the giant beast. The entire period of moments during flight, Shalee remained asleep.

Sam watched the countryside pass beneath as they swooped, following the elevations of the terrain. He was awed by the beauty. Gentle sloping hillsides, farmer's fields filled with crops of plenty, children fishing in scattered ponds of all sizes, sporadic forests with treelines reaching for the sun, and he appreciated all of this amidst his desire to barf.

Taking a closer look at the griffin's shadow as the beast passed above the ground, Sam studied the position of the front talons and back paws of the creature. They were tucked close to its body to reduce drag. The beast's beautiful eagle head was pushed far out in front of the rest of its body to guide the way. The rest of its massive form, other than the gigantic wings extended far on each side, was stretched out.

Sam took note of the long padded saddle they were sitting on. The large leather surface had sufficient cushion to pad their backsides, and many lengthy leather straps allowed them to tie in. The ride had been safe and unless the creature decided to roll or make a drastic movement, they would finish the flight without problems.

He looked at Shalee as she leaned against him. She had a peaceful look on her face and he admired her beauty. Just before take-off, he tied her in to keep her safe. Every now and again, he pushed her blonde hair clear to get a look at how exceptionally breathtaking she was.

He was impressed by Mosley's balance and watched as the wolf bit down on two of the leather straps, one from each side of the saddle. The wolf placed the straps under his right front paw and turned to speak. "How are you two cubs doing back there? The first flight is usually the hardest."

Sam hesitated, amused about being called a cub. "I'm doing fine, for the most part. How long are we going to be on this thing before it lands?"

An unexpected voice shouted from the direction of the eagle's head. "I'm not a thing, human!" The griffin's head snapped around as it shrieked. "My name is Soresym! You will refer to me in a respectful manner if you need to speak of me in the future. I have the mind to roll over, snatch you up, rip you apart, then drop you to your death for your ignorance. You should watch your tongue, or I shall pluck it from you."

Sam realized his mistake and apologized, asking forgiveness. The beast grudgingly accepted and, after a moment of silence, turned his head back into the direction of flight.

"We should be landing on Angel's Platform by dusk," Soresym continued. "Beyond, you won't be traveling with me any longer. My kind only travels between Angel's Platform and the Temple of the Gods. After this, you'll be traveling with my cousins, the hippogriffs."

"We don't like transporting your kind. I can't stand to be near any of you humans, or any of the other wretched beasts on this world. The gods require us to do so in order to live within the cliffs beneath the temple. I would not be doing this now, but Bassorine requested this ride. You should've walked down the steps inside the cliffs. You're not of noble blood. My kind would rather feast upon your flesh than be servants to the people of this world. I suppose it's a sacrifice worth making to live in such a glorious home."

Sam looked at Mosley after apologizing again. On this occasion, he chose his words far more carefully. "Is it my imagination, or does every *glorious creature* on this world understand how to speak English? How can any of this be possible?"

Mosley laughed and replied, "Not all of us 'glorious creatures' have the ability to speak your language. Most speak a language of their own. Only those in service to the gods can speak all languages of the worlds."

Sam nodded his understanding. "I didn't see the steps Soresym mentioned leading into the cliffs. Where are they?"

"The steps are hidden. The gods built them for the common people. They must use them to worship while visiting the temple. The griffins are for those who have noble blood or the coin necessary to travel aboard them. If it wasn't for Bassorine, your journey to Brandor would have been a much longer one."

Sam nodded again. His mind took a turn as he looked at Shalee's watch. *It's a good thing this works off kinetic energy.* Sam determined by the position of the sun, combined with the griffin's explanation of when they would land, the days seemed to be similar to the ones on Earth. He would reset the stopwatch as the sun disappeared behind the horizon, then stop it the next day at the same general time. He hoped to get a good spot on the horizon so his calculation would be close to accurate. Sam knew a large change in terrain would throw off his estimation, and wanted as little error as possible. He hoped they would be on the ground when this took place.

Mosley told Sam, Shalee would continue to sleep through the night and most of the next day. He also explained there were many landing platforms scattered across the lands of Southern Grayham, all with a small village, town, or city where they could spend the night.

From the way it sounded, the hippogriffs only flew during the day, unless ordered by the kings of Grayham. It was only possible to fly to one landing platform each day, due to the distance between them. When they arrived at the village, Mosley would make the arrangements necessary for the night.

Sam looked at Shalee and wondered how he was going to explain everything. He still had a hard time believing what he had learned, let alone trying to make sense of it all to someone else. Animals talked, griffins, along with their cousins, the hippogriffs, acted as airborne transportation, and that was just the start of it. Magic, gods, swords, kingdoms, and everything he thought to be myth were said to be true. He had no idea about money and how it worked. He knew nothing of the culture, or even how to speak with the people to make a smooth transition. *I am truly out of my element,* he thought.

He wondered if his home on Earth was going to be repossessed. He was not there to pay the bills. He had so many questions for Bassorine, and yet, this "so-called" god was not around. He could only look forward to their next meeting to get his answers. There was still one question which bothered him most. Why did Bassorine seem familiar?

Sam moved his hand through Shalee's hair as they flew. He realized his heart was growing warm toward her. She was beautiful and she had been leaning against him during the entire flight. He imagined he felt this way because she was the one thing left in his life which resembled anything normal. He held her close as he tried to stop staring at her lovely face.

After flying over the Blood River, a name Sam remembered from his mental snapshot of the map back at the temple, he knew it would not be long before they landed. When he saw the platform standing high in the air, he knew they were about to set down. He looked forward to a belly full of hot food and hoped he would be able to settle his mind in order to get a good night's rest. Sam smiled as they made their approach. The little village below looked like one out of the hills of old Scotland.

Now...fellow soul...if you're not one of the souls who lived on the planet Earth, you might not know what I'm talking about or have any clue as to where old Scotland was. I would have to say, it sucks to be you. Garesh happens and keep reading. Anyway, back to the story.

It seemed as if people who made their homes outside of the king's cities always lived this way. Their homes looked to be made of stones stacked on top of each other. The roofs were made of large bundles of straw tied together and angled to allow the rain to run off. The entire village was bunched together. Sam could not wait to see how big the towns and cities were, especially if the people of this world called this a village.

Not far from the landing platform, Sam saw a stadium, or rather an arena of some sort. It seemed to be out of place. *If Shalee were awake, she'd probably criticize the arena's architecture. It's nothing like the rest of the village.* In fact, the arena reminded Sam of Rome. Mosley was right, Grayham did remind him of Earth in some ways, but the setting sun splitting two colored worlds was a little far fetched.

The arena was not large, but big enough for hundreds of people to gather. He wondered what kind of sport or theatre was performed there. He would check it out if he had the time.

As they landed, Sam took note of the watch and stopped its timer. The flight had lasted eight hours and ten minutes. He grabbed all their gear, along with bags holding their old clothes, and jumped from the griffin. Sam tied the bags together, hung them across Mosley's back, then pulled Shalee off of Soresym, and draped her over his left shoulder. He was careful not to strike her head against the bow as he adjusted the sword on his hip. Preparing to walk down to the village, Sam saw the sun was about to fall below the horizon.

"Thanks for the ride, Soresym. It was an honor," Sam said while walking toward the front of the griffin. He looked into the beast's eyes. "Again, I'm sorry for my ignorance. It's easy to see how your kind is far superior to us humans. I'll make sure to speak your name with respect whenever I say it from now on."

The flying beast looked down. "Maybe you're not so bad after all, human. I may decide to honor you by calling you Sam. It's clear your remorse is genuine. I accept your apology. On occasion, I run into one of you two-legged beasts I take a liking to. I sense you might be one of those men. Someday, our paths will cross again. May the god you serve be with you as you travel."

Sam laid his free hand on the beast's feather-covered neck. "I hope we meet again. Fly safe, and may the god you serve be with you as well."

Sam turned and looked at the horizon. He reset the timer as the sun disappeared. He found what was left of the purple colored world which Mosley called Luvelles. He watched as it disappeared behind the opposite horizon. The night sky was odd. No stars, no moons, nothing on which to focus for navigation. It was an eerie feeling. As the pitch black of a new kind of night surrounded them, they would need to wait until the landing platform's torches were lit before making their descent.

Using Shalee's staff for balance, Sam motioned for Mosley to lead the way. They headed down the long flight of stairs resting high above the ground. The quaint village below was beginning to fill with the flickering torch lights of a new reality.

The Grayham Inquirer

When Inquiring Minds Need to Know about their Favorite Characters

BASSORINE is looking for Lasidious. The God of War's anger is increasing. Bassorine has spoken with nearly everyone within the Collective on Ancients Sovereign. No one has any idea where Lasidious is. The God of War can be heard throughout the hidden god world as he keeps calling for the God of Mischief to show himself.

SAM has followed Mosley to an inn where he laid the sleeping Shalee on a bed. He left with the wolf to find dinner and have a mug of ale or two to calm his nerves.

LASIDIOUS is inside his home beneath the Peaks of Angels. Although he can hear the screams of Bassorine echoing throughout the world, he is ignoring them. The protection his beautiful goddess and he put on their home has kept the God of War from popping in. He is laughing with disdain.

Thank you for reading the Grayham Inquirer

Breaking and Entering

As Sam was finishing his flight, George hurried through the field toward the town of Lethwitch. Dusk was approaching as George looked back at the place where he landed on Jason and wondered if the poor schmuck's friends had picked him up.

Turning to enter the village, it was only a short period of time—or rather, a short period of moments—before he realized he stood out like a sore thumb. Anyone he tried to speak to would have nothing to do with him because of his appearance. He was still dressed for the road trip to deliver the RV. The people just stared when he approached and walked away.

The men of the town were rugged and wore leather clothing for the most part. Some wore softer-looking clothes, made of a material George had never seen. The women had a better style and wore long dresses, yet still with an old world feel.

He smiled. *At least the women feel it's important to accent their curves. This place is like some kind of renaissance Beverly Hillbillies' town. How funny is that? I can just imagine how great this place would be for a TV pilot.*

George looked himself over, lifted his arm and sniffed. *I probably smell. Look at me. I'm a wreck. I must look like some kind of bum to these people. Holy hell, I really stick out. These clothes could use some attention. Damn... my new slacks are torn. Crap, and my shirt, too. This must've happened when I landed on Jason. Poor bastard.*

The pocket of his shirt hung by a stitch or two. His shirt, pants, belt, wallet and cufflinks (all Gucci) were out of step with the town's fashion. His shoes, not meant for sprinting through fields, looked like garesh and were scuffed from his rugged run.

George pulled the rip on his pant leg apart, only to see his thigh had suffered a good-sized bruise. He figured adrenaline was the reason he had not noticed the pain until now. He knew if he did not figure out a way to blend soon, no one would speak with him and he would not get to the Pool of Sorrow before the other adventurer—well, if anything Jason said was true, of course.

George studied his surroundings as he walked around the town. A few hours passed before he found a solution. He watched as one of the town's merchants locked the front doors of his store for the night. The older man shook the lock to double-check it, then disappeared into the next alleyway.

George looked at the sign above the door. *Hmmm, I can read the writing. Maybe I'm not so far from home after all. The Old Mercantile, eh? Let's let things get a little darker and I'll pay this joint a visit.*

George knew dusk was not the best series of moments in which to perform a robbery. Waiting until it was good and dark before circling to the back of the store was the smart thing to do.

He noticed earlier there were some stables down the road. While passing, he had seen a piece of iron laying on the ground with a sharp point on one end. He hurried to retrieve it. He wanted to make it back to this spot and keep scouting for the right moment to make his move.

This would not be the first robbery in George's life. His high school had been his mark on four occasions, his foster dad's home twice, and the city's recreational center near his mother's home had been a target on a dozen different series of moments when he was seventeen. He loved to go swimming at midnight. With a record for all his breaking and entering, he was only seventeen when he was caught for robbing the local bar to steal beer for his friends.

This place is ripe for the picking. There's no security in any of these buildings and with my experience, I can rip this joint off without breaking a sweat. Maybe I won't need to sell my watch after all.

The buildings of the town were built with a combination of shaped stones and wood. The windows were not made of glass and if the store had been open, he could have jumped right through. Large, heavy wooden doors had been lowered over the top of the openings to cover the holes, with iron hasps holding them closed. The roofs were covered with a unique style of wooden shingle which appeared to lock together, but without climbing up, he would not be able to tell how. There were no streetlights or electricity, and many of the town's children were lighting torches placed in various locations since the sun and the freaky-looking purple and orange worlds were about to set. The roads were made of cobblestones and had been well-maintained to keep vegetation from growing between them.

This standard of living was far beneath George's personal requirements. *How could these people live their lives this way? I would never want to live like this. It doesn't look like there's electricity, and I doubt there's hot water without fetching it from a well and warming it up. Smoke stacks, too. I bet there's not a heater inside any of these stupid places.* George chuckled. *This place is barbaric. Maybe I'll even run into a few genuine barbarians one of these days.*

When the right moment arrived, George circled to the back of the mercantile, within the shadows of torchlight, and prepared to enter. As it turned out, he did not have to use the iron bar in his hand. The door was not fully secured. When he tugged at the lock, it popped open. He slipped inside with a smirk and shut the door. *You've got to be kidding me. These people are idiots. Holy hell, it's freaking dark in here.*

George activated the light source on his watch to get an idea of his surroundings. He crept through the darkness and was now standing in front of what he thought to be the man's cash drawer. The thief opened it, triggered the light on his Rolex again and looked inside, but saw nothing. Nothing, that is, except a small piece of twine that most anyone else would have ignored. George took a closer look, then reached in and tugged, lifting the base of the drawer into the air. He removed the thin slab of wood and beneath it were coins. *Bingo. Must be my lucky day.*

It was dark, but from what he could see, the coins looked as if they were made out of the same metal. On further inspection, he noticed a distinct difference. There were three different names engraved on each type of coin: Jervaise, Owain, and Helmep, each with a distinct size difference. The largest was Jervaise; the second, Owain; and the smallest, Helmep.

The size must have something to do with their value. Oh, well, looks like I'm gonna have to take them all. What a bunch of suckers. Who would just leave something like this unsecured? They're too trusting around here. Good for me, I think. You're the man, George, you're the man.

Cleaning the storeowner out, he took one Jervaise, seven Owain, over fifty Helmep, and put them into a small leather pouch he took from one of the shelves. He removed his old clothes and put on some tan leathers. After fumbling around, he found a pair of wool socks. Boots were next. He found a pair which looked to be his size and tried them on. They were a perfect fit. *How can people wear this stuff? I hate this leather crap. I've got to find something better when I can.*

Seeing the large leather backpacks near the rear door, he headed for them and dumped the contents of Jason's pack inside. Next, he balled up his old clothes and shoved them in. Before lifting it, he stuffed one of his old socks inside the smaller pouch full of coins, then placed it within the wadded-up clothes inside the new pack. *That should keep them from rattling as I move through town.*

George reached for a belt hanging from a series of nails on the back wall and was about to put it on when he heard two voices. His heart raced. He was only a few feet from the door. He tiptoed across the room and put his back against the wall. He could smell smoke. The men were close. Their tobacco carried a powerful aroma and an even stronger high as it made its way through the cracks of the door and to his nose.

His thoughts ran wild. *Get your pistol. Just shoot them if they come in. Come on, George, think, damn it! That would cause too much noise and give your position away. Think man, think! What about this belt?*

He took the belt and stretched it between his hands. George's thoughts continued to scramble as he looked at it. *Damn! This thing is useless. I can only use it on one of them, but what can I do with the other guy? Why didn't I take karate when I had the chance? Because I was too lazy, that's why. Damn, this sucks. I don't have the training for stuff like this. They're gonna kick the crap out of me if they find me. What if they find the money? Holy crap, they're gonna be really pissed. Oh, my hell! My heart's going a hundred miles an hour. Just be quiet, man. Just keep quiet, maybe they'll...*

"Jonathan Walker Smith!" a lady's voice yelled.

"What?" the man shouted back. "That woman will never leave me alone," he muttered.

"I understand," the other voice responded. "My old heel is always yelling for me to do something. I wish I could shut her up."

"Jonathan Smith, you get in here and beat these kids. They won't listen," the lady yelled again.

"Be right there, honey," he said in a charming manner. He added so his friend could hear, "You old bat. Can you blame them?"

The men laughed and headed their separate ways. George stood still against the wall and waited for his heartbeat to slow before putting on the belt and heading out into the night. When leaving the store, he made sure everything inside was in order. He smiled as he secured the lock. *A good thief always covers his tracks. I still need to take karate.*

George made his way through town to an inn which he had seen earlier in the day. He took the backpack and rubbed it in the dirt so it didn't look so new. Further, he added a little character to his leather shirt and pants before heading in. He stood inside, watching the people move about and now, no one turned a head to take notice. He sighed with relief.

The ale people were ordering cost one Helmep coin. He listened as a man ordered a room and handed the lady behind the desk one Owain. It was not long before he figured out that one Owain was worth four Helmep. Once he felt comfortable he understood the financial transactions, he walked to the desk and stood in front of a pretty lady.

"What do you want?" the lady snapped, not looking up from her logbook. "I'm not going to take anymore lip from you Cottle boys. I've had enough of your comments about how wonderful my new dress fits my bosom. That whole city is full of undesirable men, or perhaps I should say, children. Don't any of you know how to treat a lady?"

George took a step back from the verbal assault and thought a moment before re-approaching. "Miss, I'm not from Cottle and, although you're very beautiful, I would never presume to have the nerve to say something that wasn't welcome. I'm sorry you've been mistreated. Some men don't realize, if it wasn't for good women, there wouldn't be any good men. But, I do."

The lady stopped dead in her tracks and turned to look. She took note of George's deep-blue eyes, dark-brown hair, and olive skin. They captured her fancy. Her blue eyes beamed with satisfaction as she pushed her long blonde hair behind her ears and looked him over from head to toe. She noticed his thin athletic build and was pleased with everything she saw.

"Well now, we have a man who understands how to talk to a lady. How can I help you, honey?" she said, adjusting her bosom to a more ample position, the same bosom she had just finished bitching about being complimented.

George smiled inside. "Well, Miss, I just came in from out of town and was jumped by two thieves on my way here."

"Thieves? What are thieves?" she said, her eyes cocked.

Her response caught George off guard. "Uhhh, ummm, you know, people that want to take your stuff and run off with it?"

A look of understanding appeared on the woman's face. "You mean, you were ransacked by mishandlers? That's terrible. What did you do?"

"Yeah, mishandlers," George responded without missing a beat. "How silly of me. I misspoke. Anyway, I started to shout. It was all I could do. All they took was my sword and water before running off. I thought they would've wanted more when they knocked me to the ground, but I think my shouting scared them. They must have gotten nervous. I'm a little shaken, my back hurts, and I would like a room for the night. If you have any water and some food I could take with me, I'd be much obliged." George gave a wince for effect, reaching for his lower back.

"Oh, honey, that's terrible. We can't have a visitor being treated like that, now can we?" The woman was eager to please. "Let me see what we have available. I do have a room, but I'm afraid it isn't the best one we offer. The bed isn't worth sleeping on, if you ask me, but the owner of this inn...that would be my mother...is too cheap to do anything about it."

"That'll work fine. I really need the rest and some food. It'll have to do." George grabbed his back and winced, yet again. "This back of mine is telling me to just call it a day." Reaching for his backpack, he gave his best smile. "How much do I owe you?"

"Oh, honey, don't you worry about a thing. That room isn't even worth the coin. Like I said, the bed is dreadful. How about this? I'll have some food brought up and some hot water to soak that back of yours. You can just pay me for the food, and we'll call it even."

"That's very kind of you. You don't have to do that," George said, smiling inside as he put the final touches on his deception. "I can pay."

"Nonsense, honey, I'll bring the water up once my replacement arrives. We have boar on the menu today, hunted locally, and if you have more expensive taste, sea turtles from the Ocean of Utopia. What would you like?"

The liar's stomach did not necessarily like the idea of either one, but figured he would try the boar since it sounded like the lesser of two culinary evils. "I'll take the boar, I guess. Do you have some bread you could add to it?"

"Of course, honey," she smiled. "You go and head on up. I'll bring it up as soon as it's prepared."

"Thank you, you're a lifesaver." With that, George took the key to his new room, paid her three Helmep for the food, and turned to head for the stairs.

"Oh, and one more thing, honey," the lady said with a big smile. "My name is Athena. Perhaps, you can tell me what a 'lifesaver' is when I bring your food up. It sounds like a good thing."

"I will do just that. Thank you again, Athena."

George returned the smile and started up the stairs, congratulating himself on the deception while evaluating both the woman's personality and her appealing figure. He liked her soft blonde hair and natural beauty. He did not see any benefit Athena could give beyond what he already received, so he decided to be nice when she brought his meal and not take advantage. He would try to thank her with a kiss and send her away smiling. He did not know why he would stop there, but he did know this was unusual for him. Something about this woman was intriguing. He wished he had the moments necessary to figure it out.

It was only a short while before Athena knocked at the door. She brought the plate of food in and instructed some of the hired help to dump the hot water into the bathing tub. Once done, she motioned for them to leave and turned to face George. "Is there anything else I can do for you?" she asked with a big smile. "Perhaps, keep you company while you eat?"

"As a matter of fact, there is," George responded. "Come on in and make yourself at home."

While asking questions about the town, he found out where the mage lived. He also learned, despite Athena's ignorance on the subject, magic was real, although she had never seen it used.

Through subtle questioning about the pricing of things he would need for his journey, it sounded as if he would have enough coin to purchase what he needed without selling his Rolex.

As the moments passed, George explored an unexpected attraction for Athena. He asked her to turn around while he undressed and kept himself covered with a towel until he was in the tub. Something about this woman commanded his respect and it was obvious she liked him. The kiss he planned on giving her when she left would need to wait.

George wanted to ask about the two colorful planets in the sky, but determined this level of ignorance would not serve a purpose. "Thank you for the wonderful evening, Athena. I hope you won't be upset if I excuse myself to get some sleep. I'm exhausted."

Athena assured him with a soft voice, "Everything is well, honey. All I wanted was to make sure someone took care of you after your run-in with bad luck. Mishandlers are terrible people. All criminals belong on Dragonia."

George was dying to ask more questions, but he did not want his ignorance to ruin their conversation. He leaned forward, placed his cheek against hers and whispered, "I wish the women where I'm from were as sweet and as beautiful as you."

He was surprised at how this sounded. He actually believed the compliment. "I'm sorry, Athena, but I'm so tired. If I don't get some sleep, I'll fall apart. Will you eat with me before I leave in the morning?"

"I would like that. See you in the morning?"

"In the morning. I look forward to it." George had to admit, he really liked this woman. The way she treated him and the soothing sound of her voice when she called him "honey" piqued his interest. He was not the type of guy to get involved, but this woman was so much better than anyone he had ever dated back home. She had a class about her he could not explain. If he had known more of what the future would bring, he would stay a while to explore this possibility.

George went to sleep that night wondering what had happened to Sam and Shalee. Not that he cared one way or the other about their safety, but more because he was curious. He looked up at the night sky through the window and focused on the idea the sky was completely dark. There was not a star to be seen, and the funky colored planets were also gone. He could not be certain where they went. As he went to sleep, the last thing he remembered thinking was how his daughter, Abbie, would enjoy this adventure. That is, if she did not freak out about how dark the room was when the torch was extinguished.

In the morning, Athena was there to eat with George. She kept her word and the liar kept his. Her sweet smile was intoxicating. He enjoyed watching her over breakfast and longed to be near her. Her hair, body, soft-blue eyes, and the way she blushed when complimented, softened him inside. He wished this moment would last forever.

Once they finished eating, he held her hand and walked her outside. George gave her a long kiss goodbye and, for the first series of moments, he enjoyed a woman's kiss without attaching it to a game or con. This kiss, to his surprise, was real and full of passion—yet it was also sweet and tender. When he pulled away to leave, he saw the longing to know him in her eyes. He wanted to know her just as much. He smiled and took her back up to the room without saying a single word. Spending valuable moments he did not have, he finally experienced his first act of true unselfishness as he lost sight of himself while holding a real conversation with Athena.

Before he left, George assured Athena he would be back. The funny thing was, he meant what he said. He had no desire to lie to this woman. He would be back to see her and found he was truly smitten. The same woman he had manipulated the night before to get a room had found a crack in his cold-hearted armor. She had stolen a tiny piece of his manipulative heart and, for the moment, turned him into a decent human being. He smiled both on the inside and out as he held her hand for as long as he could before letting go. He was saddened when she left to start working for the day.

After a few moments, George decided standing in the doorway would get him nowhere. He turned back to the business at hand. He had shopping to do and would need to take the moments necessary to buy a new sword, dagger, knife, rope, water pouches, torches, and food for his journey.

After reaching the home of the mage, George realized he was nervous. He had no clue what to expect. He knew nothing of magic or how he would attempt to manipulate the topic. *Just play this one safe, Georgie boy. That's what's best for this situation.*

Prior to knocking, he took a quick calculation of what was left. He now had one Jervaise, which was worth four Owain and three Owain worth twelve Helmep. He also had thirty-three Helmep, which was this world's smallest currency. By his calculation, the total worth of his coins was sixty-one Helmep, if he broke it down to its simplest form. All he could do was hope he had enough.

George knocked on the door. A tall thin man answered, wearing a long, bluish-gray robe. He was older, sporting a matted beard and a mustache stained from many seasons of pipe smoking. He was not the most pleasant-looking and his hygiene was atrocious.

"What can I do for you?" the man asked, his breath stinging the inside of George's nose even from where he stood.

George choked down his desire to say something rude, and explained. "I'm going into the Cave of Sorrow. I was told to seek your help. I could use a spell to block the visions of The Beast. Oh, and if you have one, I could use a spell to help trap food."

"Cave of Sorrow, eh?" the mage replied. "Come in, boy. You can call me, Morre. My brother just left or you could have met him."

As George walked past, the desire to vomit rushed through him as the stench of Morre's body odor clubbed him upside the head. *What the hell! This guy is a disgusting old man. Take a damn bath for goodness' sake.*

George struggled to think beyond the stench, swallowing hard before forcing a smile and responding, "My name's George. It's nice to meet you, Morre. I'm sorry to barge in on you like this. Maybe I can meet your brother on some other occasion." *I bet he's just as disgusting as you are*, he continued to think as he waited for a response.

"Perhaps...however, if you're going into the Cave of Sorrow you may never get the chance. I'm probably the only one in these parts, besides my brother, who can help you, but only to a point."

"What do you mean, 'to a point?'"

"From stories I've read, it takes almost eight days to find your way through the cave. The spell I can give will last about two days and I only have two of them prepared and not enough supplies to make more."

George thought a moment. "That should be fine. I only need two. I don't plan on using the spell until I sense the first sign of The Beast. While the spell takes effect, I'll trap him and bind him so I can get a large headstart through the rest of the cave. If he catches up to me, I'll use the other one to finish the journey to the cave's end."

Morre nodded. "I never thought of that approach. It sounds like you may be clever enough to pull this off. What will you use to bind The Beast?"

"A rope," George replied, without hesitation. George thought, *The real trap will be a gunshot to the head.* But, as usual, he lied. He had no intention of trying to spare The Beast's life. He continued, "All I've got to do is figure out how to trap him once I'm inside the cave."

"That's simple," the mage replied. He turned and led George to the far side of his library. "I think I have three snare scrolls. All you'll need to do is read from the scroll after planning where you will lead The Beast. The spell sets an invisible trap which will hold him in place for a significant series of moments. It won't limit your ability to walk across the affected area. What I'm trying to say is, you'll be able to walk through the affected area without being trapped yourself. This should allow you to make your actions look natural while moving within the cave. You wouldn't want The Beast to be following you and see you jump over the area and give away its location, now would you?"

"Definitely not. I want to make sure he's captured."

Even though he had not originally planned this approach, George decided the three scrolls would come in handy. He told the mage he would buy them all.

Morre did some calculations and after a moment, he came to a number that was intentionally overpriced. "That will be four Jervaise."

George did the math and realized he didn't have enough to buy everything. "Damn," he said. "I'm three Helmep short. Is there any negotiating room here, Morre? What can I do to make up the difference? Perhaps, I could do some sort of a favor to work it off."

The mage thought a moment and, after a bit of pondering, turned to

George with an idea. "I'll sell you the scrolls for the coin you have, if you'll deliver a message to a friend of mine who lives in the Siren's Song. I use the word friend loosely. He's a large ball of energy called a wisp—a Wisp of Song. If you can find him, and I assure you he's difficult to find, please give him this magically-sealed envelope. I have found the artifact's location he asked me to seek. I'm sure he'll reward you with an answer to any specific question you may have. Make sure your question is solid. The wisp is all-knowing when it comes to treasure or matters of power."

"Wow," George said, stunned. "I'll deliver this envelope once I have completed my task, if that's okay. I swear I'll get it done. But first, I would like to know more about this Wisp of Song."

The mage took a few more moments to give additional details. "The wisp makes its home within the mist of Griffin Falls. The pool hidden within the mist is called Siren's Song. The vapor spreads across a large area due to the sheer power of the water hitting the bottom of the falls. This ball of energy hides within the fog. Since the gods have protected the area around the temple, the wisp isn't an aggressive creature.

"The sphere uses a song to communicate with those who find it. For those who are willing to perform a deed of service, the wisp will give a gift for the completion of the task. The journey to fulfill the deed's requirements always involves danger. In almost every case, the explorer doesn't return from the attempt.

"This gift is in the form of a song the creature creates within a person's mind and discloses the location of an artifact of great power or answers any question asked of it. I'm sure the sphere will give you the information you require after delivering this envelope, but I encourage you to ask a simple question. You'll be one of the lucky ones who doesn't have to perform a deed of service."

George was already thinking of a question for the wisp. He turned and rubbed his hands together before speaking to the mage once more. "I'll get the envelope to this Wisp of Song, you can count on it. I must be going now. I need to arrive at my destination before someone else does. I have a journey ahead of me. I'd better hurry. Will you please show me on this map where Siren's Song is?"

Morre pointed to the destination, then showed George the quickest path to the Pool of Sorrow. He waved goodbye and shut the door. He watched out the window as George hurried down the streets of Lethwitch, then turned and walked into the library where the goddess, Celestria, appeared.

"Hello," Morre said, as he changed his appearance. Morre, now Lasidious, kissed his lover's voluptuous lips. "My portion of the task is handled, how about yours?"

"Oh, my love, my pet, my sweet, my cute little devil-god." Celestria cupped his head in her hands and kissed him again, "You are a wickedly sweet man. I have truly missed you. Everything is as planned."

"I love you. You're everything to me," he replied. They moved to the entryway where Lasidious set something on the floor. With that, they vanished, returning to their home on Ancients Sovereign.

Soon, after the gods took their leave, the door of the home opened and the real Morre walked inside, his natural, nasty-smelling odor followed him. The mage looked at the floor of the entryway. As he bent down to retrieve the note laying beneath a small leather pouch full of coins, he let out a huge, juicy-sounding fart that crept through the home like a poisonous cloud. He had to wave his hand to clear the air, grunting his own disapproval of its foul stench. The smell reminded him of the large helping of sea turtle he had eaten the night before. After a moment, he redirected his attention back to the note. It read:

Dear Morre,

Thank you for the scrolls. I've given you far more than their value since I have inconvenienced you and took them without your knowledge. Please forgive the intrusion on your home, but I assure you, it was necessary. I wish I didn't have to leave before meeting you. I have heard so many good things. Again, I'm sorry, and I hope to one day apologize to you and your brother in person.

Sincerely,
George Nailer

Morre scratched his ass and farted again. He grinned, the forced explosion warming his hand. He turned, picked a piece of the previous night's sea turtle out of his teeth with the same hand, then headed into town toward the local vault. With each bounding step down the front steps, an additional moist note of flatulence was released.

***Fellow soul...don't you wonder if the
vegetation wilted as Morre walked past?
How rank was this guy?
Ohhh, to be a fly on the wall.***

The Truth be Told

Sam woke from a great night's sleep after having a delicious supper, compliments of Mosley. They stayed at Angel Village's best inn and Sam was grateful for the wolf's company. He admired the beast while looking across the room, watching as he slept in front of the cold fireplace. Since their hippogriff was not scheduled to take them to their next destination until the Peak of Bailem, there was no rush to get the day going.

He directed his attention to Shalee, who slept on the bed with him. He had been careful not to touch her during the night, putting her staff between them. The bed looked to be almost as large, if not larger, than his king-sized bed back home. They had plenty of room.

Her rest seemed so peaceful. Every now and then she moved from one side to the other. Sam was glad for her movement. As a doctor, he knew it was not good to stay in one position for too long.

She's beautiful. What is it about her I like so much? I can't put my finger on it. Do I really like this kind of drama? She's a bit of a diva, but what a diva she makes. I bet those pretty hands have never seen a day of real manual labor. This woman is going to be my Achilles' heel. I wish I could lie beside her and hold her.

He moved from the bed to the window. The room felt as if they were staying in some sort of cottage instead of an inn. As his bare feet made contact with the cold flat stones of the floor, he stopped, closed his eyes, and imagined he was in a castle. He took a deep breath and stretched. It was a breath which managed to add to his fantasy. He admired how clean the country air smelled. The world of Luvelles was in clear view as he looked up into the morning sky, its purple hues added to his enjoyment.

Sam had always been the type of man who had to fight with his mind to fantasize. This struggle was something which bothered him throughout his life. Being a genius had its disadvantages. He could never escape his own need to stay in reality. Once again, just like most other moments in his life, his mind brought him back from the fantasy of walking on castle floors and dropped him in the cold reality of a simple village, full of everyday simple people.

Adjusting his gaze, he looked down at the people below and laughed inside. *This reality is something I used to believe was fantasy. At least my mind can't remove me from this. It's a refreshing break to get away.*

From the smells penetrating the air, breakfast was being prepared somewhere. Taking another deep breath, Sam thought of George. *I wonder where he is? Is he dead? If not, what's he up to?*

If Sam had known, at that very moment, the same guy he watched fall through the hole back at the Temple of the Gods was having breakfast with Athena, he would have felt a sense of relief. But, dwelling on questions he could not answer would get him nowhere. He turned from the window and moved across the room to wash his face. The water he poured from the pitcher had turned room temperature and he knew the slight chill would help get the day going.

Mosley shifted near the fireplace, but did not wake. As Sam looked over at Shalee, the God of War, Bassorine, appeared next to the bed. Startled by the appearance, Sam watched as the god looked down at the sleeping woman. Sam whispered. "I was wondering when you'd be back."

Bassorine turned from Shalee and walked toward him. "There's no need to whisper. The others cannot hear us. This conversation is between the two of us. I am here to understand your mind and inform you of the current situation regarding the Crystal Moon. This would be a good series of moments in which to ask questions you may have."

"Finally," Sam sighed, taking note of the god's interesting use of the words, "series of moments." "My thoughts have gone in many different directions."

Bassorine nodded and motioned for Sam to proceed. "I would like to know why you seem familiar? Is it possible we know each other? When I read the symbols on your statue, how did I understand their meaning? I even understood a portion of the language the griffin, Soresym, uttered. Why?"

Bassorine walked back toward the bed. He leaned over and pushed a straggling piece of hair clear of Shalee's face. "Your questions will require lengthy explanations. I am not sure you're ready to hear what I have to say. We should focus on easier questions for the moment and come back to these particular matters once you have had the proper series of moments to adjust. I trust this would be acceptable, yes?"

Sam thought a moment. "I don't need any time, or 'the proper series of moments' to adjust. I would like to have this conversation before you leave. For now, let's do it your way. I trust *this* would be acceptable, yes?"

Bassorine grinned and motioned for Sam to continue. Sam shrugged, then changed course. "I have plenty of other questions. First, what exactly is the current situation regarding the Crystal Moon?"

The god nodded, pulled a chair across the room, placed it by the window, and looked through the opening. "The Village of Angels has the potential to be a good starting point for your rise to glory, but we will talk of this later. Many things on Grayham will remind you of old Earth, as I am sure you have already discovered. The situation regarding the Crystal Moon is unique. None of the others within the Collective have been able to find Lasidious. It is as if he has vanished. I intended to speak with Lasidious to find out the Crystal Moon's location, but have been unable to do so. It was my hope, with this information, the gods would come together and vote on how these new events are to be handled. Alas, without Lasidious, we are no farther along than when we last spoke. I am disturbed, to say the least."

Sam splashed another handful of water on his face. "I'm not sure what to say. This creates some additional concerns. May I ask these questions?"

"Sam, do not ask permission any longer. I am here to speak without formalities."

"Sounds good to me." Sam dried his hands. "My biggest concern is, the Crystal Moon is what keeps the worlds from colliding. Your statue said the crystal provides for the balance of life. You said if it wasn't retrieved and put back in the temple, everything would be destroyed. How long do we have before this happens?"

Bassorine looked away from the window. "There is no way to determine this quantity of moments. The Crystal Moon has governed the worlds for over 10,000 seasons and has placed each planet in its optimal path of travel. Each world has been given a precise speed within its orbit and has the ability to maintain consistent days and nights. The only immediate effect is the Crystal Moon will no longer be able to change the position of the planets in order to create new seasons. Grayham is in the middle of a warm and rainy season. This should allow for life as normal to continue within this extended season. The people will talk, not understanding why the rain continues, but I do not see this being a cause for alarm. The Crystal Moon has governed all five planets in a similar fashion. The seasons on the other worlds are the same."

Sam jumped in, "That's great, but how long will it be before the worlds start to drift? What will happen when they begin to migrate?"

"As I have already stated, I do not have an answer. It is impossible to tell. Once the planets begin to drift, the changes will be unnoticeable, at first, but they will magnify. For all I know, the worlds could take more than a season before they begin their migration. The Crystal Moon has been governing the worlds for so long, it is how you would say on Earth, 'a crap shoot.'"

Sam was anxious, but more than anxious, he was annoyed a god would not know the exact answers to his questions. Maybe these "so-called" gods were simple enough to screw with things on a cosmic level and nothing more. To Sam's way of thinking, a deity should be all-knowing as well as all-powerful.

Sam calmed himself. "Is there anything else I can do while I wait for you to tell me where the Crystal Moon is? Maybe I should be preparing to retrieve it."

"I cannot say you are the best man for this journey. In light of these new events, you lack certain requirements. You do not have noble blood coursing through your veins. You do not have the fame necessary to gain an audience with kings. Only kings are powerful enough to do something about this situation. Only kings can control wars which will be created as a result of the Crystal Moon's theft. This is most unfortunate. I was looking forward to your rise to glory."

Sam decided he had enough. He was not about to cower to Bassorine's position, simply because he did not have the power to stand up to him. He was not about to let his life be taken over without a fight.

"Okay, okay, hold on for a moment. It was the gods' bright idea to bring me here in the first place," Sam barked. "Now that I'm here, you're telling me I'm not good enough for the job? I understand what's involved. I'm not an idiot. I understand you might want to keep the theft of the Crystal Moon confidential. Your 'so-called' Collective will have a mess on their hands once the people of the worlds find out the Crystal Moon is gone. Their belief in you will fade once they know you won't stop the planets from colliding. You said I could speak freely. Tell me why you're not powerful enough to keep the worlds from migrating without the Crystal Moon's governance."

Bassorine laughed. "You are bold when given permission. Maybe I should have chosen my words more carefully. To answer your question, it took fourteen of us to create the worlds, and the power it would take to keep them from migrating is more than the Collective can handle on a continual basis. This is why we created the Crystal Moon. Each of us poured some of our power into this masterpiece. Each piece of the crystal was made so they could not be drained of their power. I would like to tell you the gods are all-powerful, but this is not the case. We have weaknesses and limitations in this pathetic existence."

Bassorine removed a long sword hanging from his hip, placed the tip of the blade on the floor and spun it as he continued. "If I convince the gods to use their power to keep the worlds from migrating, we would soon use what is left of our power. The worlds would eventually be destroyed, anyway."

"Okay, okay, so create another Crystal Moon to replace the one Lasidious took," Sam reasoned.

Bassorine shook his head. "As I have said, it took fourteen of us to create the Crystal Moon. Lasidious will not help us make another. There must be a method to his madness."

Sam had to think. He had never thought of a god as having a weakness, but the concept made sense. It explained how Bassorine failed to know everything. If there were limitations to his power and his knowledge, then the term "god" now meant something completely different than what it meant before.

"Okay, okay...well, then what you've told me confirms what I wanted to say. I think you would want the people, not to mention the beasts of the worlds, to continue to worship and maintain a normal life while the Crystal Moon is missing. What happens when they know you cannot do anything to save them? What happens when they find out they're expendable, simply because you can create another world with a sizeable population to worship you?

"I would laugh at the god I served if he could do nothing because the others allowed one of their own to destroy everything. You've all taken this 'free will' crap to a whole new level. At least, if you have me handling the situation, the politics on Grayham would be handled the right way, and you wouldn't lose your worshippers. If anyone is smart enough to figure this mess out, it's me. So, go tell your godly friends, I won't just sit here and do nothing or you might as well send me back to Earth."

Well...fellow soul...Bassorine hoped Sam would summon the desire to undertake the task, but wanted Sam to make the decision to fight for the right to do so. Bassorine knew he made a mistake by allowing the Book of Immortality to be created. If he had not done so, he would destroy Lasidious and take back the Crystal Moon—or would he?

The god knew if Sam chose to go after the crystal, Shalee would follow in his footsteps and Shalee was the key to accomplishing his own masterful plans. Helping Sam would allow Shalee's power to grow and of all the men on the new worlds, Sam was the best choice for the job. It had been far too many seasons since he had captured Sam's soul and placed it on Earth. He missed their old relationship, but revealing this relationship was not beneficial at the moment. Anyway...back to the story.

"You have made your point, Sam, but there is much you do not know." Bassorine turned to look out the window, his face growing serious. "I am the God of War. I love a good battle with everything in me. What you are about to do by volunteering is going to be far beyond war. This journey encompasses the survival of everything in existence, and I do mean everything. It is true the gods can create another group of worlds, but there is nothing wrong with what exists."

Sam interrupted. "There's something you're not telling me. I can feel it. I've been in this situation with you before. Don't ask me how I know this, but I know. This is not the first series of moments in which we've had a conversation that feels this vague. You need to level with me. I'm not interested in being left in the dark. What are you holding back? How could you say these worlds affect the survival of everything? How could what happens on five worlds cause destruction throughout an entire cosmos?"

Once again, Bassorine sighed, but during this series of moments, it carried the weight of the world. The god stared at the heart of the fighter and watched it beat. "Sam, what I am about to tell you will be upsetting, but I swear it is the truth. There have been many stories created for the people to believe. Most are not true. I would send you back to your homeworld, except for one problem. Your planet, the one you call Earth, is gone. It no longer exists."

"What do you mean, 'it no longer exists?'"

Compassion filled Bassorine's expression. "A man with your intellect understands what 'no longer exists' means. I am saying Earth has perished. Allow me to finish what I have to say, then ask your questions."

The god waited for Sam to nod. "When the God Wars started over 14,000 seasons ago, the battle for power extended to every galaxy and solar system. The story the Collective created to tell the people of these worlds...the story

I was the one who brought home the Crystal Moon to the others...is not true. I have always been a god, since the beginning of what you earthlings called 'time'. The story claiming I was given god-like power was conjured to give the beings of the new worlds something to believe. It allows them to have something to be thankful for and gives them faith. This is similar to the way your gods of Earth gave their creations their own sense of faith, a way to worship, rewarding the faithful to Heaven, the unfaithful to Hell."

Sheathing his long sword, Bassorine continued. "The fact is...all gods back then, no matter what world they governed, used Heaven and Hell as a place to send the souls of their dead. Even the gods who ruled worlds and didn't believe in free will, simply sent their followers' souls straight to Hell. They were kept in this place of torture until the moment came to be reborn, thus beginning the same vicious cycle.

"All gods allowed the souls of the dead to be reborn. This is where the idea of reincarnation came from. The gods who did not believe in free will toyed with the souls they governed, allowing many of them to be reborn as mere maggots. They would live for a matter of days before returning to Hell, again allowing the cycle to repeat."

Sam opened his mouth to speak, a thousand questions resting behind his eyes, but Bassorine held up his hand and commanded silence.

"Make no mistake, the gods are strong. We are the beginning and the end, but we can be destroyed and have weaknesses. During The Great Destruction of Everything Known, thousands perished, and those of us who survived elected to be governed by rules we did not have before. We have done this voluntarily. The laws implemented have things which were overlooked. We can vote to fix these things, but not until the events which have been set in motion stop.

Bassorine walked to the pitcher of water and took a drink. "The Book of Immortality was created to govern our laws. I regret its creation. I have the power to stop Lasidious, but our laws bind my resolve. I cannot stop him without risking the Book's power, and my own destruction."

Moving back to the window, he continued. "Allow me to explain the Book further. As I have said, those of us who survived the God Wars decided to create the Book of Immortality. Each of us poured some of our power into the Book and made it strong enough to dictate our actions. Its purpose would be to keep the Collective from warring against one another for all eternity and hold our new laws within its pages. If a problem arises, it is for the Book of Immortality to govern the punishment and determine a solution. We are no longer allowed to destroy one another to manipulate specific outcomes.

"We would no longer control the will of gods, men, or beasts. Instead, we would give them the freedom to make choices on their own. The Book allows free will, as long as we do not break the laws within its pages."

Bassorine turned from the window and found Sam's eyes. "It is the concept of free will which started the God Wars. Your gods of Earth, along with myself, and others, were among those who supported the idea of giving all creatures the freedom of choice and ran our worlds accordingly. Every deity had a hand in the creation of Heaven and Hell and as I have stated, they were created to hold the souls of those who perished. Where their spirits ended up was determined by how each soul chose to live their life and how well they followed the rules their god or gods, in some cases, established. Heaven was a glorious place of happiness, while Hell was not so desirable. No matter what, it was the free will of men which sent them to either place.

"The gods who fought against free will started the wars. Gods you are familiar with: Ra, Sekhmet, and Harrah all chose to fight. Even the Fallen Angel, Lucifer, who you personally knew as Satan, rose up and struck down countless numbers, god and angel alike, as they drew more to their cause."

Sam interupted. "What do you mean, I 'personally knew' Lucifer? How could I have possibly known Satan? I am not personally familiar with any of the gods you've mentioned, beyond what I've read."

Bassorine cleared his throat. "I apologize, Sam, I simply misspoke. I did not mean you actually knew Lucifer. Please, allow me to continue."

"Okay, okay, by all means. Who's going to stop you? I don't have the power. You might as well get it all out in the open."

Bassorine smirked at Sam's candor. "As I was about to say, once the wars started, everything exploded out of control. Everything was destroyed. Even the most ancient of beings, including the one I loved most, my brother, fell in battle. In the end, it was those of us who came together to create the collective of the Farendrites and fought side-by-side who survived to see the conclusion of the wars.

"The battles lasted over 3,000 seasons, or what you would call Earth years. It took those of us who were left another 800 seasons to create this new, smaller solar system, which is over 10,000 seasons old. We had to search long and hard for materials to do so, since matter was sparsely scattered and almost nothing remained. These five worlds are all we have been able to create thus far. We continue to bring materials from the far reaches of what used to be other galaxies and store them to expand this new solar system into a galaxy of its own.

"The Collective wanted you, Sam, to create an empire here on Grayham. We wanted your example to be what the other races would emulate. If the others followed your lead, we intended to allow all races to be joined. We expected there would be problems, problems similar to the ones you had on Earth. We hoped with your intelligence, a job of this magnitude could be accomplished. You and Shalee have good hearts, full of kindness. Your intelligence and experiences from Earth could be used to avoid mistakes when bringing the races together."

Bassorine pushed the chair back to the table. He then returned to the window and leaned against the sill. "The Collective's first goal is to separate four of the five worlds after the races unite and move them each to a solar system of their own within an expanded galaxy. The fifth planet, known as Dragonia, will be given a new name and become the new Hell. This place will punish the souls of evil beings until they are reborn to try again to live a better life. The dragons of Dragonia are to be given a new home and separated to live peacefully apart from all others.

"We plan to create a new Heaven and once again allow the souls filled with goodness to live in glory until their opportunity to be reborn arrives. For now, we hold all souls, whether good or evil, within the pages of the Book of Immortality. The Book keeps them safe until the moment arrives for them to live again. As it is now, evil is not punished."

Again, Bassorine found Sam's eyes. "As for me, I am millions of seasons old. This is the first real threat, since the new worlds were created, that an end to all things could come again. With the Crystal Moon's disappearance, we may be forced to rebuild once the dust settles. I hope the people are strong enough to make it through this."

Bassorine moved to the table, grabbed the chair, spun it around and sat in it backwards. "What I am about to tell you is of utmost importance. Before your gods of Earth perished in the God Wars, they told me and three others about you, Sam. They spoke of the blessings given before sending your spirit to Earth. The gods with me that day were Lasidious, Keylom, and Alistar. The gods of Earth told us about your superior intellect and how you were the best choice to preserve and bring forward through the seasons. I chose Shalee because she would be a good mate, having been given the perfect anatomy for childbearing. There were other reasons I chose her, reasons I have hidden from the others within the Collective. All I will say is this... Shalee will be powerful."

Bassorine changed his direction of thought. "Lasidious must have brought George forward for reasons I do not know. He did this without the knowledge of the Collective. I cannot think of any reason why Lasidious would do this. If he would have brought a magical being forward, the gods would have felt the disturbance. His actions do not make sense. I suspect the answer will be evident, soon.

"As you know, it was the Collective who voted to have Lasidious retrieve you from Earth. We agreed to keep you preserved until we saw the perfect opportunity to place you on Grayham. As I have said, the gods felt your knowledge would be essential while building an empire.

"I fear Lasidious has taken an opportunity meant for the good of all beings within the worlds and manipulated it for his own agenda. I am still bound by the Book of Immortality's rules and cannot start another war over this. It appears Lasidious is exercising his right to make a mess. This is the only logical explanation. He wants a stronger following of man and beast. Maybe that is what this is about. Even Lasidious falls under the Book of Immortality's governing. All he can do is influence those willing to do his bidding. Unfortunately, the hearts of those who inhabit the worlds can be persuaded to do evil. If you look at your own planet before the wars happened, your different governments on Earth were about to destroy life with their own Weapons of Mass Destruction."

Bassorine watched as Sam poured a glass of water and chugged it. Once he felt Sam had been given a moment to digest, he continued. "Sam, I was listening from above when you asked Mosley about the days here on Grayham. Allow me to put your mind at ease on these issues. The days are identical to your old Earth's. The number of hours in a day is the same. The people on the new worlds have no concept of time. You should be able to use this to your advantage when planning your next move. A season, or rather a year, is also the same number of days as old Earth's. There is much which will remind you of your planet and your watch will work fine until its kinetic source fails. I am surprised it has maintained this ability while you were held in stasis over the seasons."

The god stopped talking. He watched as Sam took a seat on the edge of the bed near Shalee. Sam couldn't think of one single question. His mind and heart were overcome by everything Bassorine divulged.

He couldn't fathom the fact his own personal god of Earth was supposedly destroyed, along with Heaven and Hell. How could any of this be true? Earth was gone. His family, his house, his car and everything familiar—

destroyed. The idea he was one of only three mortals to be spared the Great Destruction in all of creation was overwhelming. The fact the only beings to survive the God Wars, other than himself, Shalee, and George, was the Collective, required a complete reboot of his mind. How could he possibly deal with all of this?

Bassorine saw the effect on Sam. Knowing the mortal needed relief from his thoughts, the God of War walked over, touched him on the head and said, "Rest, my child, rest. Let blessed memories be forgotten." With this, Sam fell into a deep sleep.

"When you awake, *oira toror'*, you will find peace within you. You will understand all I have divulged. If you still desire, I will allow you to create the glory you need in order to gain audiences with kings. You are going to need help to save all that is."

Bassorine walked over to Mosley and woke him. He told the night terror wolf to extend their stay at the inn and keep watch. Before leaving, he gave Mosley instructions on how Sam could gain the notoriety necessary to earn an audience with Southern Grayham's largest royal family, The House of Brandor.

The Unicorn Prince's Horn

George left Lethwitch. On his way out of town, he passed a group of men who were talking about the robbery of the Old Mercantile the night before. He smirked, returning to his old self. *Now that was a nice piece of handiwork. Those poor chumps never saw me coming. What a bunch of morons.*

For the rest of that day and through the night, George moved at a slow jog or a fast walk, rekindling his torch with many strips of tattered cloth. He knew he had to hurry and only stopped to eat or pee on a tree. He thought about his lovely Athena, wondering if his little Abbie would approve. He had never brought a woman around his daughter, but his heart said Athena could be the first. He wondered how long it would take to get back to his beautiful little girl. *My precious Abbie, I can't wait for you to meet Athena. I just know you'll like her. Athena is special,* he thought, his heart beaming. *Daddy will be home soon.*

Along the route, there was no shortage of trees. He was told to leave town and make his way north along the Cripple River until he reached the outlet where the Pool of Sorrow released into it. The Enchanted Forest followed the west side of the riverbank and was so dense light struggled to find its way in. George had no desire to go near it. The whole scene was just plain creepy.

He was beginning to feel exhausted from his jog. The weight of his pack had not made his task to get to the Pool of Sorrow any easier. If it had not been for his training while competing in triathlons, he would have stopped long ago. He heard many strange noises coming from the forest during the night, some of which sounded like screams of frightened animals. With each scream, a response from something more aggressive filled the night air. He was horrified and the adrenaline produced by his fear was the only thing keeping him moving.

When morning arrived, the noises stopped. This was his chance to get some rest. He looked at his watch. He had been moving at a steady pace for almost sixteen hours. His body was about to shut down. He lowered to the ground, rubbed his cramping muscles, grabbed something to eat, and laid his head on the stolen backpack for a nap.

He set the alarm on his Rolex for eight hours and looked over the map Jason gave him. Some of the townfolk said the journey was a solid two-day walk if he stopped to rest at night. He smiled. He had been pressing hard almost the entire time. He was now within a few hours of the pool and would arrive at his destination before dark. He could only hope it would be easier to sleep and the noises around the Pool of Sorrow would be far less frightening.

George adjusted the backpack under his head and used his old Gucci shirt to cover himself. As he fell asleep, he listened to the sounds of the river's cascade and plotted his adventures. His dreams were of Athena, his baby girl, and him spending their moments together. It was a lovely dream of Abbie flying back and forth between the two of them as they pushed her on her favorite swing.

Angel's Village, Sam and Shalee's Room

When Sam woke, Shalee was sitting next to him on the bed, rubbing his back. He rolled over, stretched his entire body, then sat up with a big smile. Shalee's beauty was stunning and, for the moment, all he thought about was her. The fighter, teacher, doctor, genius, and wannabe lover, brushed his hand across her face.

Mosley had been sitting at the base of the bed, waiting for Sam to wake. When the wolf saw him moving, he jumped up and plopped down across his legs. Both humans smiled and the mood in the room felt lighthearted and peaceful.

"Thanks for watching over me, you two. You look beautiful, Shalee. Do you like your outfit?"

Shalee grinned, then pulled the cloth away from her waist. "It's kinda cute. I need ta take it in a notch or two and add a dash of *me* to it, but I should be able ta salvage this world's attempt at acceptable fashion. I do like the... hey Mosley, what did ya call this headpiece again?"

"It's called a Gashal."

"Yes, the Gashal. I like the way it lays on my head. The little gems are fab."

Sam chuckled. "You were given a beautiful dress and all I received was a rugged leather outfit. Now, how fair was that?"

"But, ya pull it off, nicely," Shalee responded.

"I suppose."

Mosley broke into the conversation. "I was wondering when you would wake. I was starting to think Bassorine had knocked you out for good. We haven't left this den except to get something to eat. You slept like a bear through all of yesterday and last night."

At that, Sam rose from the bed. The sound of Bassorine's name brought back everything the god had told him. He stood at the window and looked out at the world of Luvelles while the other two sat confused, watching.

"Are ya okay, Sam?" Shalee asked.

Sam motioned for them to leave him be for a moment. He reviewed everything he heard the morning before. Accessing his photographic memory, he listed everything:

*1. Shalee was brought forward for the purpose of having my children and to be my mate. **Note to self:** Be careful how this news is broken, she may get angry. I don't fully know what the other reason is, except Bassorine said Shalee will be powerful.*

2. The gods of Earth were destroyed in the God Wars, along with thousands of others. Only fourteen deities make up the Farendrite Collective.

3. Bassorine has always been a god. The story he was given power for bringing the Crystal Moon to the others is untrue. Bassorine is millions of years, or seasons, old.

4. Earth was destroyed. My family, Shalee's family, George's family... all dead. My home, jet, boat, and brand new Mustang convertible, all destroyed, along with my father's medical center.

5. The Crystal Moon is used for the purpose of separating the planets, all equal to Earth's mass, and monitors their movements. It controls their distance from the sun, speed, orbit alignment, rotation, axis tilt and other functions for each world to support life.

*6. The gods do not have the power to govern the worlds indefinitely. They would run out of power if they tried. It is because of this each of them poured a portion of their power into the creation of the Crystal Moon. **Note to self:** Ask Bassorine how the gods can pour part of themselves into something.*

7. The Collective cannot make another Crystal Moon without Lasidious' help. He caused this mess, so making another is unlikely.

8. The people of the worlds were told the story of Bassorine's retrieval of the Crystal Moon to give them something to believe. The story is also untrue, but it does give them something, a sense of faith and peace.

9. It was true the faithful on Earth, depending on which god they served, went to Heaven.

10. Hell was a real place before it was destroyed.

11. The Book of Immortality is more than just a book. It has its own soul. It is a being the gods created to govern and hold the laws of the Collective within its pages. The Book currently keeps the dead souls—good or evil—within its pages until the moment arrives for them to be reborn.

12. The idea of reincarnation is true. **Note to self:** *Who would've ever thought such a foolish notion was an actuality.*

13. The gods allow all beings, no matter what race, to have free will. Even the Collective functions under the concept of free will and are not allowed to impose their will on the beings of the worlds. The Book of Immortality enforces this. **Note to self:** *I wonder what it would be like to meet a book that has a soul. The idea of a book having a soul has to be fabricated. I would bet this story is also untrue.*

14. The gods planned for us to come forward through time. They kept us someplace safe until the moment was right to place us on Grayham. They want us to create an empire and set an example for the races on every world to emulate. **Note to self:** *I don't like the idea I was put into stasis. It pisses me off.*

15. The Collective did not intend for George to be brought forward, but Lasidious manipulated this for reasons the others do not understand. The gods cannot do anything about this. Like them, Lasidious has free will. Bassorine has the power to destroy Lasidious, but if he does, he will be punished by this "so-called" Book.

16. It is the intention of the Collective to separate four of the five planets and give each their own solar system.

17. The fifth planet—Dragonia—is to become the new Hell. The dragons will be given their own world to live on, away from all others. **Note to self:** *I don't believe dragons are real.*

18. The gods plan to make a new Heaven for the souls of those who are good. **Note to self:** *If this is true, I had better receive a guaranteed ticket to get in once all of this crap is over.*

19. The years, days, and hours of this world are the same as those of the now-destroyed Earth. Shalee's watch will work fine, despite the people's ignorance of time. **Note to self:** *I'm not about to wear a girly watch, no matter how 'fab' it is. I'll figure something else out.*

20. I don't have noble blood, nor do I have the fame to do anything useful. How do I gain it? I need to meet with the people in power to get anything done around here. **Note to self:** *This also pisses me off.*

21. I know I'm forgetting something. I don't know what it is, but there's something about this place. **Note to self:** *Until it's resolved, this is going to drive me nuts.*

Sam had been standing motionless for a while, before Shalee walked up behind him and touched his shoulder. "Sam, are ya okay?"

He realized he was being rude. "I'm sorry. Something is bothering me. I feel as if I've forgotten something important. I can't put my finger on it, but I know something is missing."

Shalee rubbed her hand across his back. "I'm sure you'll think of it. It'll come ta ya. Just relax. You can always ask Bassorine 'bout it later."

Sam turned to face her. "I'm sure you're right." He pulled her close and, for the first moment since their arrival, he made an advance. If she was to be his mate, why not get started? "I think you're stunning."

Shalee was shocked by the compliment, but could not keep from smiling. The only thing she could think to do was give him a hug and a gentle pat on the back. "Why, thank ya, Sam."

"You pat?" Sam joked. "My friends pat when they hug. I pat when I hug my buddies. I pat my grandma. Let me show you how to hug someone you're interested in."

With that, he caressed her arms, then wrapped his around her and pulled her close. He held her for a series of moments which seemed short lived and enjoyed the fact she did not pull away. "Now, that's how you hug someone you find attractive," Sam said, releasing her.

"Well now...who said I find ya attractive?" she responded in her thickest Texas accent. Shalee turned, grabbed her staff, and left the room, smiling as she exited.

"Ouch! That had to sting," Mosley said as he looked at Sam. "You might want to see if you have any fur left on your haunches. She took a bite right out of you. Nice try, though. I must admit, if I were a human, I would have tried myself. I saw a different side of her while you slept. She cried a lot, understandably, considering what you have lost. She misses her family and a special litte girl cub named Chanice. She spoke of a den which she built on your homeworld and how it suited her taste more than this establishment.

"She understands humor, something I am thankful for, considering the fit she threw on the griffin's platform. We laughed about many things. I think she finds the idea of marking my territory and our swine having three nostrils to be delightful."

Sam was still mulling over his rejection and failed to hear the wolf's attempt at humor. "That backfired," the rejected Doctor of Love muttered. "I could've sworn that would've worked. I guess I'm not her type."

"Don't be so quick to judge, Sam. My wife rejected me on nine separate occasions before she kept this old night terror wolf. She kept gnawing at my fur, telling me I was not clean enough. I never did understand why she liked to bathe. It's just not wolf-like."

"Okay, okay, hold on just a moment. Did you just say you have a wife? Since when do wolves get married? Do all animals get hitched on this world?"

"Not normally. Perhaps, I should clarify. My wife died many seasons ago...100 seasons, to be exact. When she did, I was lost. It took many seasons to stop feeling the pain her death caused my soul. I met her on the bridge at Angel's Crossing. She was traveling with a group, guiding them to the city of Champions. I happened to be heading in their direction with a cure for a disease spreading throughout the caves of the Bear Clan on that day.

"Her name was Luvera, and she was, by my kind's standards, a perfect creature. Her coat, eyes, teeth, body, and tail...oh, that tail was exceptional in any wolf's eyes. I would give anything to have her back. I miss the warmth we created in our secret den.

"Luvera lived in service to Keylom and was blessed because of it. Many things we had in common back then. We spoke every language of both man and beast. We talked for four days before we had to go our separate ways. I was destined to be with her. I wanted her to have my pups. Bassorine was the one who made it possible for us to meet."

Mosley held his head high as he spoke. "We found ways to be with each other. We traveled together doing the work of the deities we served. After three seasons we asked if we could adopt the tradition of marriage, common to the humans of this world and make it our own. As I have said, I had to ask her on nine separate occasions before she said yes. Our request was approved and we were united. I had to agree to bathe on every third day before she would say her vows. It was awful, but a price worth paying to be near her. I was with Luvera for over 300 seasons before she died. I cherished her with everything I am and can still remember our last hunt together."

Sam stood in amazement. "Wow! 300...that's a long time, I mean, that's alot of seasons. The men where I'm from would've considered that their personal hell. Being attached to someone for so long must require patience. I imagine it would be nice to find someone you love so completely you could have spent an eternity together. I hope I can find such a love someday. So, this Keylom is the god your wife served. How did she die?"

Mosley hung his head. His green eyes started to swell as his ears fell back and he started to cry. "I have never spoken of this to anyone other than Bassorine." A tear fell to the floor. "I will tell you now, but I do not want to dwell on it once spoken. She did serve Keylom. He is the God of Peace. Luvera served him with undying loyalty. He is a giving god, worthy of her service, but it was her service which ended her life."

"How?"

The tears blurred Mosley's vision as he continued. "A demon-jaguar named Kepler killed her. He is the Lord of all Giant Cats on Grayham. It does not matter if they are alive or undead, good or evil. Kepler uses fear to rule his feline subjects, no matter what god they serve. He has the ability to control the spirits of dead men, making them serve his will. He has the ability to move invisibly within the shadows, even the smallest of shadows. It is for these reasons, along with his size, he dominates the world of cats and rules their territories. He preys on the weak."

Sam swallowed hard. "He sounds like the perfect nightmare. Even sitting here I worry about crossing his path."

The wolf began to scratch at his neck. "Kepler is an undead creature. He lives in a place called Skeleton Pass, which he has ruled for as long as I can remember. He has a small army of skeleton warriors which patrol this area, killing every man who tries to pass."

"Okay, okay, hold on just a moment. You're telling me he's undead and there are other undead under his control? So, how did Kepler kill your wife, and why?"

"I do not believe Kepler had any reason to kill her. She was in his path and suffered because of it. My wife was delivering a message from Keylom to the Unicorn Prince, Ultonen, who lived within the Dark Forest. The message was sealed for his eyes only. I cannot speak about the purpose it served. I would have gone with her, but on this trip, I was detained. Bassorine had a job which required my attention.

"Before I tell you how she died, let me tell you this. The horn of a unicorn has marvelous abilities, even if separated from the rest of the creature. The horn can be used to aid anyone who possesses it. Aside from the healing power to cure most ailments, all poisonous plants or animals will burst and die in the presence of the horn. When held near, or in the presence of anything poisonous, the horn will start to sweat, giving a warning of danger to the holder."

"Really?" Sam interrupted, again. "Sounds like fiction and, for argument's sake, if it's not, why would Kepler want the horn in the first place? Can poison harm an undead creature?"

"I assure you this is real, and no, Kepler cannot be harmed by poison. He was hired by the Barbarian King in the city of Bloodvain to hunt down the Unicorn Prince. Kepler was told if he retrieved the horn, the king would stop sending his armies through Skeleton Pass when invading the Kingdom of Brandor."

The wolf began pacing, becoming more agitated as he continued his story. "Luvera was standing in front of the prince, delivering Keylom's message, when the attack occurred. The prince was bowing in appreciation when Kepler made his move from the shadows. He rushed from the darkness and knocked my wife onto Ultonen's horn, impaling her through the heart. I was told she died instantly and was gone before she fell to the ground. She was unable to manage even the smallest of howls."

"Oh, my gosh!" Sam exclaimed. "I'm so sorry! Is there anything I can do?" He realized how ridiculous his question was.

Mosley looked at Sam and forced a smile. "It has been 100 seasons, as I have said. There is indeed nothing that can be done. Her soul is in a good place. I am sure Keylom saw to this."

Sam knew exactly where Luvera's soul was said to be—it was within the pages of the Book of Immortality, supposedly waiting for her chance to be reborn—but he said nothing to Mosley. It was clear the wolf did not know what happened to the souls of the dead and where they were kept after perishing.

Sam's mind began churning. "Something had to give the Barbarian King a reason to go after the prince's horn, something more than detecting poison. Any of his subjects could have tested his food."

"The murder of the prince served three purposes," Mosley replied. "Two of the purposes were far more important than testing the king's food. He wanted the horn for its healing properties and to show the unicorns they were vulnerable to attack. They would learn, even with their magic, they could not stop one simple beast, employed by the Barbarian King, from killing their prince. The king intended for all unicorns to serve him. The murder of the prince sent a clear message he was to be feared. To this day, the unicorns remain loyal to the king's house. The Barbarian King's thirst for control was insatiable and he dominated everything through fear."

Mosley stopped what he was doing and stared at his tail. After a moment, he balled up and began to gnaw at its tip. He continued speaking between snips. "I suppose I can understand a king's desire to rule. His actions must have been instinctive. Even I was the leader of my own pack for many seasons and commanded three separate territories."

"Okay, okay, I agree with you. That makes sense. I understand the desire to use the healing properties of the horn and sending the message of fear to gain power."

Mosley inserted, "I have not spoken of the effect the horn had on the king, an unexpected effect. The barbarian used the horn to heal himself. One day he realized he was receiving the benefit of an extended life."

"That's medically impossible," Sam scoffed.

Mosley lifted his hind leg and scratched at his neck, again. "Your dull eyes are still focusing on what your packs from your homeworld knew to be familiar. You must remember, many of the beasts within the worlds governed by the Crystal Moon are magical. The barbarian's extended life was a magical benefit, not a medical one."

Sam struggled to wrap his mind around the thought. "Let's just say, for argument's sake, this is true. I bet if the Barbarian King had known, he would've gone after the horn for that reason alone. How long will he live?"

Mosley paused long enough to sneeze. "The barbarians are an aggressive race. They fight among themselves for fun. When the king was injured while fighting, he used the horn to heal himself. Once the Barbarian King understood the healings were making him stronger and younger, he did things to intentionally hurt himself. He retired to his chambers and cut himself in order to use the horn's power. It is not known how often he used the horn. Only the gods and a few others knew."

"Okay, okay, how on Earth...I mean, how on Grayham, could a secret this big be kept from the world? The man is outliving his subjects. Doesn't anyone question this?"

"Of course they questioned, but the Barbarian King did not want anyone to know. A secret of this magnitude would cause a massive power struggle and start a war amongst the people of Bloodvain. The king told his subjects he had found a spring and its waters granted longer life. He told them the spring dried up when he visited again to gather water for his cubs or rather, his grandchildren. I would not know any of this if it were not for Bassorine. Bassorine watched from Heaven as the king used the horn over and over again. I was told the gods were not pleased, but they do not take away the free will of man or beast."

Sam felt pity for Mosley, thinking, *He doesn't know there's not a Heaven.* He sighed. "This free will crap can give everyone a lot of room to cause problems. What's this Barbarian King's name?"

Mosley growled. "Sam are you not listening? I have been speaking about the past during this entire series of moments. You need to pay attention. His name *was* Bloodvain, Bude Bloodvain. He recently passed. It seems the horn's benefit does not stop the aging process completely. His great-great-great-grandcub, Senchae Bloodvain, has taken the throne.

"Bude told Senchae about the horn's benefits before he died. The only thing worse than the new king's use of the horn, is Senchae has been the

Barbarian Champion for the last 15 seasons. He is the strongest and best warrior the Barbarian Kingdom has ever seen. The barbarians fight to the death when entering their arena. The fact Senchae Bloodvain is still alive should give you an idea of what kind of warrior he is to survive in such a hostile den."

Sam walked across the room and looked out the window. A group of small children were taking turns at tossing a small wooden hoop, attached to a string, in an arching motion. It was their goal to catch the hoop on a metal spike which protruded from a wooden post. It was a simple game. The joy on their faces warmed his heart. Sam turned back, found Mosley sniffing the hearth of the fireplace, and refocused. "This Senchae guy sounds intense. This guy is someone I can relate to. I love to fight. I just won my first professional fight before I..."

Mosley did not let Sam finish. "I would not get excited about this man's abilities. I also would not get any bright ideas about challenging him and living. Allow me to explain how the barbarians fight in their arena. They are a vain race, vain to the point of stupidity. All Barbarian Kings throughout history have kept an open invitation with the humans of Grayham to fight in hand-to-hand combat for the crown. Any human who can beat the barbarian's best warrior, without weapons, and wearing a cloth to cover his loins, will be rewarded with the crown. This means all barbarians will bow to that human and serve him. Many humans have tried for this power and failed. The current barbarian champion, since Senchae Bloodvain's retirement, rules the arena. He is called Churnach Furgus. In order to fight the kingdom's best, you would first have to kill their second best.

"Bloodvain is a nightmare. His sheer size intimidates any man. He towers over you and is easily as well-defined as you are, Sam. He is well-known within the kingdom for his ability to fight for long periods without getting tired. The king trains with angered bulls to keep in shape. He strikes the bull, causing the beast to charge, then meets the creature as it slams into him head-on, wrestling the bull to the ground. He does this over and over while striking the bull with heavy blows. The beast hits the ground exhausted and can no longer continue.

"Before Senchae became king, he would serve the bull to the leaders of his grandfather's army as a gesture of respect. Now that he is the leader of this bloodthirsty pack, Senchae is loved by his army and does not need to rule by fear. He rules through respect and respect alone. He is loved, though his control over his kingdom is just as strong as his grandfather's ever was."

Sam was impressed, but still looked for a solution. "My experience is...a big man is also a slow man. I'd bet that's his weakness. I admit, he's powerful if he's fighting bulls, but if a man were fast enough, he could cause Senchae serious damage."

Mosley laughed. "I did not finish telling you about his training. After he fights this single bull and clears its body, Senchae brings in three fresh bulls and, as before, he makes each of the bulls angry. He uses this as his training for speed, working to avoid the attacks of the other two while entangled with the third. Not only does the king have to move to avoid collisions with the others, he also must move the weight of the third bull he is holding. This exercise is intense and far beyond any champion before him. The new champion, Furgus, has tried to emulate the king's training, but despite being powerful, he cannot fight three bulls at once. Furgus fights one for both power and speed."

Sam lowered to the bed. "Okay, okay, I'm sold. This guy is a true champion. How am I going to achieve the fame I need to gain an audience with the people holding power? How can I fight men like the one you've just described and live to tell about it? I'm pretty tough, but also a hundred percent sure both these guys, Furgus and this King Senchae, would kick my butt."

Mosley stood from the bed and jumped to the floor. "I have some ideas, but it will take everything in you to gain the glory you need. You must work hard if you are to become the leader of the packs within Brandor."

Sam's eyes widened as the reality hit him. "So, then it's true? I'm to become a leader?" His question was filled with hesitation.

Mosley shook his head in disbelief. "Sam, for someone so intelligent, you have a short memory. Did Bassorine not explain it is the desire of the gods for you to build an empire on Grayham? Do you not want to be the leader of such a pack? Are you frightened of such glory? Does your fur not stand on end when faced with the challenge of saving the worlds? Perhaps, you should tell Bassorine you fall short of the gods' expectations. I cannot help someone who is not strong of heart."

"Whoa, whoa, whoa, whoa, whoa...hold on there a second, Mighty Dog. I never said I was afraid of anything. It's not like I have anything to go home to anymore. If I don't do something, who will? I misspoke. I guess it's all just hitting me now. I am the man for the job. Where do we start and what needs to be done?"

"You will be a fine leader, Sam. Your eyes show pride. We should eat before beginning your training."

Mosley led Sam downstairs for a large breakfast. They were going to slow their journey to Brandor to work on gaining the glory Sam needed.

The wolf sniffed at Sam's greggled eggs, then sat on his haunches on the wooden chair. A plate of rare corgan strips was set in front of him. "First, you will need to learn how to use your sword, while increasing your strength and stamina. I have already sent Shalee to begin her enlightenment with her new staff. Her growth should be captivating.

"Angel's Village is the perfect place to start. When you are ready, we will introduce you to arena fighting. This should allow us to make the coin necessary to keep ourselves fed and warm at night." Mosley smiled and winked. "I know how important it is for Shalee to have a comfortable den in which to lie."

Sam's voice was filled with anxiety. "Arena fighting? I thought you said that was to the death."

Well...fellow soul...it appears there is more to
Sam than meets the eye. I am dying to tell you everything,
but all things intriguing are best left for later.
Even though you can't see it,
I just stuck my soulful tongue out at you.
Ha, ha!

The Grayham Inquirer

When Inquiring Minds Need to Know about their Favorite Characters

GEORGE is sleeping just east of the Enchanted Forest on the banks of the Cripple River. Not much else to report here.

LASIDIOUS & CELESTRIA are together in their home on Ancients Sovereign. They are working out the final details of a few plans before Celestria leaves for the world of Luvelles where she will spend the remainder of her pregnancy.

BASSORINE is still trying to find Lasidious. The others on Ancients Sovereign are becoming tired of listening to the God of War yell.

SHALEE is on her way to the local School of Magical Studies. She is scheduled to start training with her new staff.

SAM & MOSLEY are having a hearty breakfast, waiting for the man who teaches at the local School of Weaponry to show up. This man will train Sam.

Thank you for reading the Grayham Inquirer

The Training Blues
-or-
Should I Say, Bruises

Shalee left the inn smiling about Sam's advance and sought out the local School of Magical Studies. Angel's Village, according to Mosley, was a good place to begin her training with her new staff. She admired the simple touches of the village. Though the architecture was not anything to write home about, it felt peaceful. Simple things were her passion anyway and, although the buildings could use some attention to their design, she saw many areas of intricate detail.

Everywhere she turned, the pride of the village folk was evident: a sign perfectly painted, carefully placed stones creating a well's mouth, cobblestone walkways running from the street to each store front and steep, tightly bound straw-bundled roofs which allowed the rain to run off.

As she walked through the streets, she came across a young boy who appeared to be no more than eleven seasons old. He had in his hand a sharpened pencil of some sort, but it wasn't anything like she had ever seen. Also, on top of an old, smoothed-over piece of wood, a good-sized piece of parchment had been centered. He was sitting, facing a group of trees which grew a fruit which resembled peaches. Her curiosity got the best of her and as she leaned over the young man's shoulder, she found herself being taken by the arm. The boy guided her to a position where she was left standing in front of the trees.

"Just stay still for a moment, my lady," the boy said, holding up his hands as if to ensure she would stay in the desired position. "You'll be my focus. This will be far better than drawing some stupid old trees."

"But, I don't have the time, I mean...the moments. What's your name, lil' man?"

"Trace. My name is Trace Chaslend. Please don't go. Please. I promise to capture your beauty."

Shalee had to smile. He was an adorable child. His cute, chubby, freckled face and his red hair made her melt. How could she possibly say no to such an innocent request?

"Well, how darlin' are *you*. As long as ya promise ta get my good side, I'll stay."

"That's going to be easy. You don't have a bad side," the boy said, with a gap-toothed smile.

"Now, now, now...you already know how ta make a lady blush. You're far too young ta know how ta schmooze a woman, Trace."

"What does 'schmooze' mean? You talk funny. What makes you sound like that?"

"Don't you worry yourself 'bout stuff like that. You just go on ahead and draw up your lil' picture, but hurry, I need ta move along."

"Yes, my lady."

A while later the boy turned the picture around.

"What do you think?"

Shalee gasped and thought, *Maybe Bassorine's fashion sense ain't so bad after all.* "Trace, it's downright beautiful. I don't think I've eva' met a young man with so much talent. I'll rememba' your name 'til the day I die. You've filled my heart with such happiness today, Mr. Chaslend.

"I'm glad you like it, funny lady, but I better go before mother gets upset. I'm causing her to be late. Bye!"

"Bye, Trace," Shalee watched him rush off.

When Shalee found the School of Magical Studies, she stood outside for many moments before walking in. She was nervous, almost to the point of making herself sick. It took everything she had to keep from turning around. *C'mon Shalee, stop bein' such a chicken,* she thought. *Ya don't even know what ta expect.*

The front part of the school was a store. The walls to either side had shelves lined with many things, both creature and plant-oriented. The jars were labeled: Baby Bat Wings, Spider Legs, Mandrake Root, Dragon Scales, Snake Skin, and many other items she had never heard of. She guessed she had an idea what they were used for, her favorite show on Earth being her only frame of reference. The show was about three witches who fought demons in an effort to rid their city of evil. One of these witches had an incredible sense of fashion, but all of them used ingredients such as the ones here to make their magical potions. She was not in the store long before an elderly woman, with beautiful gray hair and soft features, walked into the room holding a staff.

The outfit did not accentuate her body's curves at all. Shalee thought, *Oh, my goodness-gracious. I need ta call the Fashion Police and report this crime. If I'm gonna train with this woman for any length of time, she'll need fixin'. It'd be a shame ta allow her beauty ta continue ta be squandered by*

such horrid fabrics. Now, how do I tell her? How do the women on Grayham handle tragedy?

The woman's smile grew larger than life when she saw Shalee. She hurried over, bouncing with excitement. "You're my new student, child!" She clapped her hands together, then reached out to take hold of Shalee's arm. "Oh, thank the gods the day has come. I've been expecting you for many, many seasons and have been looking forward to your arrival. My name is Helga Kolinsky."

"Hello...I think. Ummm...my name is Shalee," she responded. "Ya say you've been expectin' me? How so? I don't recall anyone announcin' I was comin'."

"No, no, no, child. It is not like that. I have dreampt you would be coming to study with me for most of my life. I have prepared for this day and longed for it to arrive since the celebration of my eighth winter season. I have much to teach you."

Needless to say, Shalee was unnerved by the woman's confession and started to hurry out of the store. In her haste, she noticed the door was not getting any closer. Looking down, she was shocked to see her feet were not touching the smooth stone floor. She frantically moved her legs, but was going nowhere.

Helga Kolinsky laughed as she circled Shalee. "Oh, child, I have known you were going to try to run out of my store since I was a young girl. Do you not think I have prepared for this special day?"

Shalee went from surprised to angry. "Ya best put me down or I'll..."

"You will what, child?" the woman responded with a soft voice. "You are suspended and cannot move. You will do nothing until I let you down and I am not going to until you calm yourself and open your mind. If you will just think a moment, you will realize I am familiar to you. We have had conversations in our dreams. You know who I am. Concentrate, child. Think your way through this. Our spiritual visits have prepared you for this day."

Shalee struggled to the point of exhaustion before giving up and relaxing. She took a deep breath and thought back to her dreams. To her surprise, she remembered Helga's face. In fact, this lady was one of the few things she had a peaceful feeling about. Sure enough, her Prada still sucked, but it was a bit more fashionable in her visions, nowhere close to the tragic mess Helga had on now. The rest of her dreams had been of terrible creatures and wars.

Shalee sighed as she spoke. "I do rememba' ya. I don't understand how, but I know ya. Lemme down. I'm ready ta listen."

Helga waved her hand and Shalee slowly touched the floor. "Oh, child, child, child, now that we have that bit of awkwardness out of the way, you and I can work on something a bit more constructive."

"I brought coin for the lessons," Shalee said, watching as the woman moved beyond a large bear rug that hung in front of an opening, leading to a spacious room in the back.

"Your coin is no good here, child." Helga shouted loud enough to ensure her voice could be heard through the rug. "You have much to learn and will need to pay attention, not coin. Bring your staff and we will get started."

Shalee was cautious as she moved past the rug into the next room, which was large and wide open. Thick pillows, made of leather and stuffed with straw, lined the walls. Even the beams in the middle of the room and on the ceiling were covered with this padding. The floors had some sort of mattresses placed side-by-side, covering the entire surface. The only things missing, at least in Shalee's mind, were a few pieces of gymnastic equipment.

"This is where we will start your training, child," Helga said with a large smile. "Never mind all the padding, it tends to come in handy every now and again with a new sorceress."

Shalee looked puzzled. "Handy? Am I ta become a sorceress?"

"You will see what I mean about the pads and yes, you are to become a sorceress if you choose to be one. You, like any other person in this world, have the right to do anything you want. I would guess you are a little curious, yes?"

Shalee nodded, then presented her staff to Helga. "So what do I do with this thingy? I have no clue where ta start."

Helga took the staff from Shalee's hand and lowered it to one of the mattresses in the center of the room. "First, you must name the staff, then quiet your mind. You must learn to speak with it through your soul. You will not actually talk to it, but rather, learn to feel its power flowing through you. This is usually the hardest part. I am going to leave and give you the quiet moments necessary to work on this feeling. Some women find this experience to be quite a pleasure once they understand what to do. There is only one piece of advice I must give. Make sure to name your staff using a short word, one with no more than two syllables. Trust me. This is very important. One or two syllables only, child, nothing more. Don't forget."

Shalee watched Helga leave the room. She turned her attention toward the staff. "This is downright weird."

Shalee studied the room, taking note of every detail. *This place does seem familiar,* she thought, *I wonda' why?* She felt comfortable, like it was some sort of second home. *I think I know this place. Did I bonk my head and I don't rememba' comin' here? This is strange.*

Shalee turned her attention back to the staff and nudged it with her toe. She sighed. "So, shall we get ta talkin'?" she asked as she bent over to pick up the staff and held it in front of her. "I can't believe I'm talkin' ta a petrified piece of wood. Anyway, first things first. I need ta name ya. What's a fabulous one-or-two syllable name that tickles me pink?"

Shalee thought a bit, then smiled as she remembered a name which made her feel good inside. She would use the name of a magical item from a movie she had seen on Earth. The name rolled off her tongue every time she said it. It was the name she had given her favorite coffee cup. The cup held the one drink capable of getting her day going. It was the perfect name, fit for her new, petrified wooden friend. No one was here from Earth to object, so why not steal this perfect name for her own use?

"I think I'll call ya Precious. Oh yeah, I like that. How does Precious sound ta ya?" She slapped the top of the staff with the palm of her hand and sassily said, "High-five."

Once the staff's name had been uttered, Shalee found a new admiration for the staff. "So, how do I feel your power, Precious?" she said, giggling at the thought of talking to the stick.

Shalee spent the next hour or so in the back room of Helga's store, staring at the staff, waiting for something to happen. She concentrated with everything in her to feel something. When this did not work, she lied down and held it in hopes her touch would help her feel something. She wanted to feel anything, even the smallest sign or hint. At one point, she became frustrated enough to play peek-a-boo.

Now...fellow soul...can you imagine seeing this, a grown woman, sitting in a room, all alone, covering her face, and yelling 'peek-a-boo' at a large petrified wooden stick? I find this amusing. Enough of my senseless babbling, back to the story.

Shalee was sure anyone seeing this display of idiocy would have put her in a padded room and thrown away the key. She laughed. She was already in a padded room. The irony of the situation was amusing.

Shalee lied down, again, beside the staff. Giving up, she quieted her mind. This was enough. The staff was now able to communicate. Though gently at first, the sensation grew, sending waves of energy through her body. The feeling caused her to tingle with a sensation she had never felt. Sitting up, Shalee stared at the staff. She felt awesome. Her body tingled.

"Lordy, Precious, that was good stuff. I gotta get me some more of that. High-five, lil' darlin'." She slapped the butt end of the staff.

She lowered to the mattress and concentrated, but nothing happened. Now, she became frustrated, knowing what she was missing. *What am I doin' wrong? I'm missin' somethin' here. Allrighty, let's think this through. What was I doin' when I felt the tingle?*

Shalee thought for many moments before it came to her. *I was doin' absolutely nothin'. I was just lyin' here, doin' nothin'. That's it, just sittin' here, feelin' relaxed. My mind wasn't boggled.*

Again, she lied down and, after a bit, cleared her mind. The staff sent another wave of its power through her, but this time a much stronger one. Her whole body filled with warmth, causing her to tingle in places she didn't know was possible. There was nothing she could remember that ever made her feel this good. Shalee sat up and looked at the staff once more and, after a few long moments of admiration, she spoke.

"That's better than...oh, my," she giggled. "You can do that ta me anytime. Let's try that again, okay, Precious? And, I do mean...you're Precious. My goodness-gracious, I couldn't have named ya better if I'd thought foreva'. Ya just keep on makin' me feel like that and I'll neva' wanna leave this room. Would ya like ta be the first petrified piece of wood ta have a wife?"

Shalee rolled back onto the mattress. She realized how ridiculous the marriage proposal was, yet she could not stop smiling and talking to her wooden friend as she rolled about. Now, she wanted the staff to make her feel as good as it possibly could, for as long as she could keep her mind quiet. "Go with it, Shalee. Don't worry about anything." When she managed to do so, the staff sent more of its power through her.

Shalee absorbed the warmth. Every hair stood on end as the intensity grew. She started to cry large tears of joy. Her hands grabbed hold of the mattress as she allowed the feeling to consume her. She was about to have the most incredible experience of her life. And, before she had the moments to think, an intense rush, far beyond anything she had ever felt, consumed her. Every muscle in her body tightened as she giggled with a deep sense of satisfaction. The sensation seemed to last forever. After a long series of moments, her muscles relaxed. Exhausted, Shalee drifted off to sleep.

Sam's Training Begins

Sam finished eating breakfast with the wolf and they were now on their way to a field just outside the village. Mosley had recruited a local instructor named Barthom Jonas from the School of Weaponry, BJ for short.

As they headed to the field, Sam looked over his sword. He remembered Bassorine's exact words when he was handed the sword at the temple. *"This is the Sword of Truth and Might. It is one of a kind. The sword can strike down your enemies with great power and possesses the ability to search for truth when used upon them. Place the blade on your enemy's shoulder, ask for the answer you seek, and it will be given."*

Sam also remembered Bassorine saying, *"The sword will only work once it feels you have earned its respect. It lives and has a mind of its own. You have much to learn, and a short period of moments in which to gain this knowledge. You do not want the blade failing you in battle. You must learn to wield your weapon and it is your responsibility to name it."*

Now...fellow soul...do you remember me telling you about how Sam failed to show his intelligence every now and then? Well, you're about to get a perfect example of how overconfident and stupid the genius can be. I love this part.

Sam didn't know what the god meant about earning the blade's respect, nor did he believe the sword lived. *Maybe it's just an expression of some sort,* he mused, as he moved the blade around in front of him. He was surprised at how light the weapon felt. He had never spent any of his moments around swords, but the blade was appealing and the markings on the hilt were mysterious.

"Hey, Mosley, do you know what these markings mean?"

"I do not, but a weapon of this nature will reveal the meaning of its markings to its owner, once the proper relationship has been established."

"That's hard to believe. It sounds fake."

BJ replied, "Maybe you're not worthy of knowing such things, son."

"Yeah...sure," Sam scoffed. "All King Arthur had to do was pull his blade from the stone and his sword worked from day one. Why is this blade so fickle?"

The wolf looked up from the rock he was sniffing next to the path leading out of town. As he lifted his leg and began to pee, he asked, "Who is King Arthur? What pack does he lead?"

Sam smiled, realizing his point had fallen on uninformed ears. "Oh, never mind. Just finish marking your rock."

When they reached the field, BJ faced Sam, and motioned for Mosley to step aside. "Sam, show me your blade and reveal its name. A man cannot fight with a sword he hasn't named. That would be a dishonor, not only to the sword, but its maker. Let's hear it."

Sam looked at BJ, then at his sword. "I haven't named it yet. I haven't put any thought into it yet. What should I name it?"

"Only you can answer that question, son," BJ said. He was an elderly man, strong from many years of instructing at the school. His dark hair was graying and his brown eyes were full of wisdom. He wore light leather armor pants and similar boots. His shirt was made of a white fabric which buttoned up the front.

BJ continued. "The naming of a sword must come from within. It wouldn't be noble for another man to name your blade."

Sam looked at the weapon and thought a moment. "Okay, okay...when Bassorine gave it to me, he said it was the Sword of Truth and Might. So, I guess..."

BJ dropped to one knee and bowed. Sam lowered the blade and redirected his attention. "What're you doing?"

"Son, you don't realize what you have in your possession," BJ responded, keeping his head lowered in the sword's presence. "This is a sword given by a god. I didn't realize it was a blessed gift. This is indeed a great honor. This weapon could command the Ultimate Power. One does not simply *use* a sword like this. A man must ask permission from the blade to command it. I, as your teacher, must ask permission before I can instruct you with it in your hand. Please, son, I beg you. Bow and ask for forgiveness. Permission is required to continue your training."

"What?" Sam said, exploding with laughter. "You've got to be kidding me! It's a piece of metal. How on Grayham can I ask it for permission to do anything? It's unable to speak. This thing isn't alive, because if it is, it sure hasn't said one thing to me since I got it. Whatever power it's said to have, I'm sure it'll have to come from within me." Sam looked at BJ and Mosley, and watched as a deeper level of concern appeared on their faces.

Both the instructor and the wolf took a few steps back. Sam watched, his worry growing with each step. "What are you guys doing?"

Sam no sooner finished his question before the sword grew red hot in his hand, forcing him to release it. The sword rose from his palm and into the air, then turned and brought its point beneath Sam's chin as if some unseen force was controlling it. The sword made three thumping taps to Sam's jaw with the flat of its blade and started to speak.

"Sam," the sword said in a commanding voice. As it continued to speak, its blade pulsated, emanating a shallow light with each syllable. "I had such high hopes for you. It appears you are nothing more than an ignorant boy who has learned little since his arrival on Grayham."

As the sword continued, Sam watched the pulsating light intensify as the sword emphasized its points. "I have waited for more than *10,000 seasons* to be wielded by you. I was created, along with your bow, when the gods molded the new worlds. I am disappointed someone with your intelligence has not been able to come into this world and figure out, what you used to consider normal, is long gone. If the Book of Immortality can be given, not only a soul, but also the power to govern, then maybe a sword of my caliber can communicate. It appears the gods have made a mistake. Return me to Bassorine. I have waited for nothing. You're useless!"

Sam was floored. A sword had just floated in midair, scolded him, called him 'an ignorant boy' and 'useless.' This world was throwing his mind some serious curve balls and he was failing to knock them out of the park.

Sam watched as the sword started to move away as if leaving. He regrouped and chased after it. "Hold on a moment! Okay, okay...I'm sorry. I had no idea I was doing something wrong. I also had no idea you could speak. I would still like to train with you. I'm sorry for my ignorance. I apologize."

The sword continued to scold. "It seems to me, for such a brilliant man, you spend many of your moments apologizing for your ignorance. If I remember right, you had to apologize to the griffin, Soresym, for calling him a 'thing.' I hate to admit it, but I find you to be rather pathetic."

The sword turned and placed its blade beneath Sam's chin once again. "I might allow you to train with me, but you *will* ask properly."

Sam dropped to one knee. As he spoke, he realized he still did not know the sword's name. He improvised the best he could. "I am sorry for my ignorance. If you will allow it, I would appreciate the honor of training with you."

The sword held its position for a long while, observing Sam's mannerisms. Noticing Sam had kept his head bowed and was sweating, the sword said, "Apology accepted. BJ, be sure to beat the ignorance from him. Teach him true humility."

BJ dropped to his knees, along with Mosley, and bowed his head. "I will do my best. Thank you for blessing me with this opportunity."

The weapon floated toward Mosley, stopped, and hovered in front of the wolf. "If it is your responsibility to watch this human, I suggest you teach him to be respectful of things he does not understand. You are failing in your duty."

The wolf nodded, "Message received. Consider it done." With that, the sword returned to Sam and descended back into his hand.

"Thanks a lot!" Mosley growled. "Maybe you could stop and think from now on when you speak. You are making me look bad. Do not apologize for your ignorance. I do not care and I am not in the mood. I am going to check on Shalee. BJ, train this fool. Oh, and one more thing, I have never met a stupid genius. Sam, you are the first. You are stubborn and hardheaded. You remind me of a new cub. I dare say you would be considered the weakest of the pack." Mosley turned and began to run toward the village.

BJ shook his head, stood and motioned for Sam to put the sword back on his hip. "Until you name the blade, *boy*, you cannot train with it."

Tossing the virgin swordsman a wooden stave, BJ laughed, "We'll start with these. This will hurt *you* far more than it'll hurt *me*. I'm going to enjoy beating you senseless."

Helga's School of Magical Studies

Helga walked into the training room in the back of her store. She smiled as she saw Shalee lying there asleep. *Aahhhhhhhhh, I remember what that feeling was like,* she thought. The sorceress leaned over and shook Shalee to wake her up. Shalee struggled to open her eyes. When she realized what was going on and Helga was in the room, she started to explain what had happened.

Helga listened, smiling as she saw the excitement on Shalee's face. After a brief series of moments, Helga motioned for Shalee to stop talking. "There is a reason you have been given these feelings. It is the staff's way of keeping you motivated to learn how to master it, child. When you begin learning how to command your new power, you will make mistakes. We all have. You will try to use more power than you are strong enough to handle. The effects of this can be harmful to a sorceress while training. I should know, I have broken more than one bone. The good thing about this process is the staff will reward you for success. This is the one thing which keeps most young sorceresses from quitting when they fail."

Shalee pushed her hair clear of her face. "So...are ya tellin' me every time...ugggh, I mean, every moment I succeed and do somethin' good, the staff'll reward me with anotha' incredible series of moments?"

Helga looked to the ceiling for a response. "Hmmmm, how to answer. I'm saying, for a while, you will have some wonderful experiences when you succeed, child. Eventually, the sensation from your successes will fade, and you will be left with only the result of what you are trying to accomplish. Most young sorceresses keep trying to learn beyond this initial period of training because, as they learn to control stronger power, they also gain the benefit of a longer life from the success of this control. But, beware the failures, as they can shorten your life. If done properly, and with careful training, the benefits of your staff could extend your life more than 1000 seasons.

"I am 247 seasons old and don't look a day over 60, child. I would have aged better, but I took a road that was not smart when I was younger, commanding power I was not ready for. It took me quite a while to reverse the effects to live this long. I wanted to be the best teacher I could be when you arrived. I tried to grow faster than I should have."

Shalee hung on every word until Helga was finished. Her response was energized. "Holy mackerel, Mary Kay would love ya. Your skin looks absolutely delightful for a woman your age. If ya ask me, 247 seasons seems like an eternity. I bet you're the best teacha' eva'. I'm pretty doggone tough. I should be able ta handle this magical wonderland. Let's get started."

Shalee grinned with a playful wickedness as she made her next statement and winked. "So, what-da-ya say? Let's get ta workin' on my first success. I don't wanna keep Precious waitin'."

Just then, Mosley entered the room from his run back to town. "Yes, let us see her try something."

Mosley began to sniff at the mattresses covering the floor as Helga started to leave the room. The sorceress stopped and stared the wolf down, "Don't you even think about it, mutt." She tapped the butt end of the staff against the wooden frame outlining the opening to the storefront. "You can pee outside like the rest of the dogs. You may be Bassorine's messenger, but you will mind yourself while you're in my presence."

Mosley gave a low growl, but submitted by sitting on his haunches. Helga left the room. When she came back, she carried a softball-sized steel ball and bent down to whisper in Mosley's ear. "Let's see how she handles a little failure before I allow her a first success. Let's give the child a challenge."

Mosley huffed, "Do whatever you like. This is your territory. Clearly, you have already marked it."

"Clearly," Helga said with a condescending tone. "You just stay right here. I'll scratch the back of your ears later, if you're good." The sorceress moved to the center of the room and placed the ball on one of the mattresses. Seeing all was as it should be, she moved away and told Shalee to take hold of Precious.

"Let's start with something to challenge you, child." She pointed to a target painted on one of the pads on the far side of the room. "I want you to point your staff at the target, then command the ball to fly through the room and hit it."

"Goodness-gracious, how do I do somethin' like that?"

"You will need to learn the Elvish language to command your staff. You must say the name of your staff and follow it with the Elvish name of the object you are trying to command. You must say this with authority for anything to happen. You must speak with words strong enough to get the desired result from the object you are commanding. The staff will retrieve what you want to happen from your mind's eye and deliver the desired result. It will happen providing you possess the power to obtain the result. Your thoughts need to be clear and focused. If you do not have the strength, child, the result will be failure. How this failure manifests will vary in many ways, but we shall talk of this later."

Shalee thought long and hard. Once she was sure she comprehended everything, she replied. "I named my staff, Precious, so I got that part. What's the Elvish name for ball?"

"The name for ball is *koron*," Mosley replied, as he looked up from sniffing Helga's feet and snorted his displeasure.

Shalee and Helga looked at Mosley. "What?" the wolf said, in a bragging manner. "I speak every language. I work in the service of Bassorine. At least he values the service of this lowly, mutt."

Shalee watched as Mosley and Helga stared each other down. "Um-mmm...maybe we could focus here, guys?" She waved her hand between them to capture their attention. "Focus, y'all. Don't make me throw a lil' bit of Texas into this argument."

Shalee raised her staff toward the target. Once sure she had everyone's attention, she continued. "Anyway, let's give the name of this ball a shout, shall we? Let's make this ball whiz right on through the room and blast that target. Y'all ready for this?"

Helga motioned for Mosley to move back. Commanding the staff, Shalee hollered, "Precious, *koron!*" The ball launched from the floor and flew across the room. It hit the target with a tremendous force. The padding was destroyed, but that was not all. The ball knocked a hole through the wall and blew up a large wooden barrel of water across the alleyway. The women and children surrounding the barrel, on the far side of the alley, screamed and ran for cover.

Shalee bent over, put her hands on her knees, and trembled as she received the benefit of the successful command. Her body quaked as she started to laugh and cry during the same series of moments. It took a while before the sensation subsided. She turned to look at her astounded audience with a large smile on her face and wiped the tears from her cheeks.

"Woo, hoo, hoo, hoo, hoo! That was incredible. I gotta assume that's what shoulda happened," she said with total satisfaction as she continued to giggle. "Oh my goodness-gracious. I'm lovin' this staff." Looking at the petrified piece of wood, Shalee continued, "How precious are ya, Precious?"

Mosley walked over and began to sniff Shalee. Before he could get too carried away, Shalee reached down and grabbed under his snout and lifted his head until their eyes met. "What do ya think your doin', buddy?"

The wolf allowed his jaw to rest in the palm of her hand as he responded. "The smell of your success is intoxicating. Is my nose too cold? Does my curiosity bother you?"

Shalee straightened up and with pointed finger, pretended to draw an X across her mid-section and across her behind. "Wolfs not allowed," she exclaimed in a stern voice. "Keep your dirty nose outta these areas. Otherwise, you can sniff whateva' ya want."

Still stunned, Helga broke her silence, "Shalee, you are going to be powerful, child. I have never, in all my seasons of training, seen anyone complete this exercise. I have picked up many a new sorceress from the floor after they slammed into the wall. Child, let's try something else."

Tough Lessons Learned

Shalee was excited by Helga's revelation that no other young sorceress had ever commanded the steel ball to hit the target. It was satisfying, and with Helga in a hurry to start the next lesson, she was in a hurry to continue.

Helga moved one of the mattresses from the floor and lifted a hidden door beneath. A dark staircase was revealed and disappeared under the school. Helga turned to Shalee. "Use your staff, child, I wish to see what I am doing. The Elven word for light is *me'a*."

Once Shalee understood how to pronounce the word, she lowered the tip of her staff in the direction of the darkness and shouted, "Precious, *me'a*!"

The stairway and room beneath lit up. With eyes closed, Shalee stood motionless, once again receiving the benefit of the successful command. "I think I'm gettin' the hang of this magic stuff," she giggled. "Was that the next thing ya wanted me ta do?"

The elderly sorceress smiled and started to walk down the stairs. "That is not your lesson. That was far too easy a command. I thought I would allow you another good experience before we make things harder. I will be back in a moment with your next lesson."

Shalee waited while Mosley began to sniff the fresh hole in the wall. Suspicious of the wolf's intent, she said, "Mosely, don't ya do it. Helga's gonna get mad."

Mosley lifted his head and found her eyes. "I would never. I intend to respect that cantankerous woman's wishes."

From below the floor, Helga responded, "I heard that, mutt!"

Shalee could only smile as she watched Mosley return to sniffing. Soon, Helga returned with five pieces of dried wood. She motioned for Shalee to close the door behind her and replace the mattress.

Helga headed toward a corner opposite the hole and began to prepare the area. Using her own staff, she commanded the padding from the floor, walls, and ceiling to peel away and reveal an area perfectly covered with large sheets of iron.

Shalee was amazed as she watched the padding float about the room and settle in a neatly stacked pile against the opposing wall. On more than one occasion, Mosley had to duck as a few of the mattresses flew over him. When Helga was finished, all that was left was a secure resting spot for the wood.

Annoyed, Mosley redirected his attention after getting an idea of what the sorceress was thinking. He motioned for Helga to speak with him in the next room. "Are you sure this is a good lesson to teach on her first day?" Mosley asked, concerned. "If the task is what I am thinking, it should be done by someone with keener senses. She is nothing more than a cub, magically speaking."

"Who is the teacher here, you or me, mutt? Isn't there something you desire to go and smell? I want to see what her limits are."

Mosley lifted his leg and released a spurt onto the rug beneath Helga's feet. "Perhaps, I feel I have already found the smell I was seeking. Shall we continue this confrontation or shall we return to more important matters?"

Helga scowled, shook the moisture off her shoe, then stormed into the training room to set everything in place. She summoned two pails of water and continued to eye the wolf as she commanded her magic to place the buckets at a distance safe enough they would remain unaffected in case something went awry.

Once the older sorceress calmed her nerves, she called Shalee to her side. "Child, there are many forms of fire we can command. There are simple forms, like striking a piece of flint to start a campfire. Then, there are much stronger forms which burn hot enough to turn things to ash before you can snap your fingers." Helga turned to look at the wolf and made sure she had his attention. She snapped her fingers to emphasize her point.

Seeing Mosley cringe, Helga enjoyed his discomfort, then returned her attention to Shalee. "What I would like you to do is start with something simple, then work your way up. The good thing about this exercise, you'll be able to use the same command for each. The only difference will be what your mind tells the staff to do. As I have said, child, your staff will look into your thoughts for the desired effect. It will draw from this and use your inner strength to produce the outcome. The Elven word for fire is *naur.*"

"So...your wantin' me to set the wood on fire?" Shalee asked. "Seems simple enough."

"No, child, I want you to think of how you can use fire to create different outcomes. Fire can be molded and shaped to serve you in many different ways. It can be used for more than just destruction and warmth. This exercise will test your mind and also your limits. Let me give you an example of a way fire can be used that is not destructive."

Helga pointed her staff and spoke her words of power. A thick wall of flame formed. Feeling the heat, Mosley backed to the far side of the room. Shalee felt nothing and watched in amazement as Helga walked into the flame and turned around. She waved at her student and after a long series of moments, exited the fiery wall before it dissipated.

"Now, that's what I mean by non-destructive, child." Helga smiled as she gave the wolf a vengeful wink. Finding Shalee's eyes, she continued. "In my mind, I told the staff to allow the mutt to feel the heat. The two of us, along with the room, didn't feel a thing. My mind called for the fire to be smokeless so it did not permeate the room. As you can see, I am unharmed. Fire can be used as a tool to create perceptions of power, like you just witnessed." The older sorceress turned her head. "Do you see what I mean, wolf?"

Without saying a word, Mosley lifted his leg and released a continuous stream onto the stack of mattresses. His deep green eyes commanded Helga's attention as he responded while cocking his head in a condescending manner. "A good stream of moisture has the ability to put out a fire. Do you see what I mean, cantakerous woman?"

Helga began to raise her staff. Shalee intervened. "My lord in heav'n, you two need ta stop. Can we focus here, please? This is supposed ta be my series of moments to train, not y'all's to argue. Anyhoo...can we just get on with it? Gimme some space and I'll whip ya up one of them fabulous walls of fire."

Helga pulled her attention off the wolf and placed it where it belonged. "No, child, that was advanced magic. You are not ready to try something of this magnitude. You will need to start simple. It is going to be up to you to figure out what your limits are since you are a much stronger student than I've ever had. I want you to think of many ways to manipulate the wood with simple uses of fire. Be careful not to hurt yourself. Your power will develop and, through the seasons, you will progress to stronger uses. You'll advance to combining Elven words to make objects work together, but this concept is far beyond your abilities."

"What do ya mean? How can I combine words ta make objects work togetha'?"

"Oh, child, I will not answer your question. I should not have said anything. Focus on what we're doing."

"Shucks, us Texans can handle anythin'."

Seeing Helga was not going to cave and reveal any further information, Shalee looked at the pile and raised her staff. She pointed her new petrified friend, and shouted, "Precious, *naur!*" A ring of fire appeared around the wood. The heat could be felt, but was not uncomfortable. There was no smoke and slowly, the flames faded.

Shalee enjoyed the benefit of her successful command, but the strength of her command was causing her body to tremble so much, she had to lean against her teacher until the intensity subsided.

"Well done," Mosley cheered. "I am impressed. You are the kind of cub who would make any wolf proud. Once you have collected yourself, see what else you can conjure."

"Oh, my goodness-gracious," Shalee said, once she was able to stand. "Whew! I'm sweatin' like a hog on a hot summa's day. I bet I look a fright. I'm just lovin' this magic stuff. I can't express ta ya how much. This is definitely not like anythin' I've eva' learned before. Just lemme catch my breath," she said as an aftershock hit.

"Take the moments necessary to recover, child. This is indeed a wonderful day for you. I must say, I'm jealous. I haven't felt that way for more than 200 seasons."

Shalee took her hands from Helga's shoulders and smiled. "Sucks ta be you. Shall we try somethin' else?"

Shalee raised her staff, prepared her next thought, and spoke her words of power, "Precious, *naur!*" The top piece of wood on the pile started to burn, but the ones below remained unaffected by the flame. The fire burned hot and strong and took a considerable amount of power.

The benefit of the success began to control Shalee's body as the spell dissipated, bringing her to her knees. She reached down with one hand for balance as the tears of joy ran down her face. The sensation lasted a much longer series of moments. Shalee collapsed to her back and inhaled to catch her breath.

"Ohhhh, child, child, child, I've never seen anyone command fire on their first day. Not only did you command it, you segregated it to a specific piece of wood and did not allow it to touch the others. This is the most exciting day of my life. It's best you stop. It is getting late and I think, after a day like this, I would be exhausted if I were you. I've never met a woman lucky enough to shed so many wonderful tears and experience the joy of life as much as you."

Shalee agreed. She was getting tired, but she wanted to try just one more thing before she left. "What're the Elven words for wood and life?"

"Oh no, child! It is not wise to be toying with combining words. This is not something I would teach you for quite a while. I should have never said anything. I'm sorry."

"Sweet molasses, Helga, I understand what your sayin', but I'd like ta know the words. I feel as if I'm onto somethin' here and I really think I can handle it. Just trust me, would ya?"

Shalee lifted herself from the floor. Helga and Mosley looked at each other, shrugged, then moved a few steps away. Mosley whispered to Helga as he reached up with his back paw and began to scratch his neck. "This is either going to be really good, or really bad. I am not sure how you are supposed to judge her growth. She is able to lead a pack of her own and is unlike any of your other students. I say we watch and allow her to keep going until she marks the boundaries of her magical territories."

"Agreed," Helga whispered back. "That's the smartest thing you've said all day, mutt. I will protect us just in case." She waved her hand and an invisible wall of force encircled them.

Shalee asked, "So...what're the words?"

"*Taurina* is for wood and *coia* is for life, child. I ask you, again. Think. This is not the best idea."

"Gotcha! I know how ya feel. But, how am I ta determine my limitations if you, as my teacha', don't know how ta judge my progress? You said you've neva' met anyone who was able ta do what I've done. Let's just see where that lil' ol' line is drawn in the sand."

"Okay, child. But, I think we can look for this line some other day. You should rest."

"I'll be okay, don't y'all worry. I'm tough. I can handle a lil' failure."

Helga looked at Mosley. "It's clear she's not going to listen until she finds a rock wall to run into." Mosley nodded.

Shalee thought for a moment, then a smile spread across her face. Remembering something Sam said when they were in the Temple of the Gods, she uttered, "This should be purdy cool. I know no one has eva' seen somethin' like this 'round these parts." She lifted her staff and spoke in a forceful tone, "Precious, *taurina naur coia!*"

The remaining pieces of wood jumped from the floor and formed a small being shaped like her favorite childhood character, Elmo, from Sesame

Street. The wooden creature had a coat made of an intense fiery fur and moved as if it was alive. As it started to dance, Shalee waited, anticipating the reward for her success, but it never came. Something was wrong. Fiery Elmo stopped, turned toward Shalee, and with a sad look on his face, exploded, sending a shockwave through the room. The wave hit Shalee so hard her body lifted from the floor and flew through the air like a rag doll thrown by an angry child. She hit one of the columns holding up the roof at its center and knocked her shoulder out of joint. Landing on the floor, Shalee's arm twisted under her, snapping with a loud cracking sound which could be heard in the alley outside. She screamed as the pain shot through her body. Having landed in a nasty position, it wasn't possible to move her without creating another wave of pain.

Helga darted out of the room and went for a healer while Mosley walked over to the injured student and breathed his soothing breath over her, sending Shalee into a peaceful sleep.

Sam's Training Continues

BJ beat on Sam after Mosley left. The wolf had called Sam a "fool" and because of this, Sam was bothered. BJ was delivering hard lessons to many areas of Sam's body. He had been hit in the head on three occasions, lower back four, upper back twice, chest eight, both arms a combined seventeen, and his feet swept from under him another seven.

BJ extended his hand to pick Sam off the ground. The novice swordsman had just had his feet swept out from under him yet again and had fallen hard. Not only that, but his wooden stave was taken before landing, adding further insult to injury.

The teacher shouted, "I've told you on many occasions to watch your weight when you're moving in to strike. Leaving yourself wide open will get you killed. A weapon won't be the only thing your opponent will use against you. Their hands, feet, legs, elbows, and heads are also dangerous. Now, get up, watch your balance, and be ready for anything, not just my weapon. I swear, I feel like I'm teaching a child of only five seasons."

Sam was frustrated, but he was not a quitter. The two men kept at it for a while longer and after a few more trips to the ground, Sam held up his right hand and motioned for BJ to stop. He limped over to where the sword rested in its sheath and picked it up. Sam bent to one knee and whispered to the blade. "I've thought of a name for you."

Before anything else could be said, the ground started to tremble. The shaking lasted for nearly ten breaths before it stopped. Sam turned and found BJ's eyes which were looking around, confused. It was clear BJ had no idea what was going on.

"I take it you've never been in an earthquake?" Sam said as he stood to buckle the belt holding his sword around his waist.

Sam's weapon was the first to respond. The blade removed itself from its sheath and hovered in front of Sam. Again, the blade pulsated with a shallow light as each syllable was uttered. "BJ has no idea what you are refering to, Sam. Walk with me. We need to talk."

Sam did as instructed and waited for the blade to continue. "The people of Grayham have no idea what an earthquake is. This is a term used only on your old Earth and is beyond their level of comprehension. The gods have not used natural disasters as a way of controlling the population. This world does not have enough beings, as your Earth did, to justify such means. This quake is a result of the Crystal Moon's inability to govern the worlds. You must focus, Sam. You must rise up and be a better man if you are to save the worlds. I sense it in you. You could be the best, but not without my help. I cannot help you until you are ready. You said you had a name for me. What is it to be?"

Sam's mind raced as he struggled to accept the sword's revelation. It was not until after the blade thumped him under his chin he was able to refocus. "Okay, okay. I was thinking of using the name, Kael. Would this be acceptable? It means, Mighty Warrior."

The sword sighed, "Kael is a fine name, but a man should be confident in his decisions. I have given you permission to train with me. Act like a leader. Do not seek my approval. Demonstrate your ability to command. I will not allow you to fight with me in combat until I feel you have gained the skills necessary to keep from embarrassing me. I would rather this world come to an end than be held by weakness."

Sick of being chastised, Sam turned to face BJ. He knew he could not divulge the Crystal Moon's lack of governance over the worlds. He shouted, "I've given my sword a name. It's Kael. It means, Mighty Warrior." He lifted the sword and took a stance. "Come on, let's see how you handle this," he said, directing the point of the blade toward the teacher.

BJ was still focusing on the ground around him. Sam thought, *This isn't good. I need to get his mind off the tremor. The people are not ready for this. I need to work harder.*

Sam shouted again to get BJ's attention. "Come on, everything's allright. I've been in places where the ground shook on many occasions. It's not a big deal. Hey! I've named my sword. Let's see how you handle the power of the gods, *old man*!"

Hearing the words, "old man", BJ smiled and walked to his bag. He lowered his wooden stave and picked up his weapon. "This blade has seen many seasons of battle, *boy*. You need to be taught humility."

BJ wiped the sword's hilt with a towel, then threw it to the ground. Securing his grip, he turned to face Sam. Without a word, he lunged, knocking Kael from Sam's hand. A quick swipe with the tip of his blade was all it took to cut across Sam's left thigh, deep enough to draw blood.

"Damn it," Sam yelled as he looked down at the fresh cut. "What the heck did you do that for? Train me! Don't kill me!"

BJ's voice was firm, "Just because you hold a sword of the gods doesn't mean you understand how to wield the power the sword possesses! You'll come to know this if I can make you understand this isn't some sort of game. You'll be killed if you enter the arena without the necessary skills. Your stance is terrible, your balance is off, your movements are slow, and your ears aren't listening."

BJ moved to gather his things. "I cannot believe where you're from they call you a fighter. I don't think in all my seasons I've ever had a worse student. Stop your whining and let's get moving before it's too dark. I'm hungry and need ale.

"Pick up your sword and put this bandage on your leg. I'll help you stitch it up when we get back to the inn. Dusk is approaching, and we have a lengthy walk to the village. You might want to keep a supply of bandages in your pack. I have a special mud the Merchant Angels delivered from the healers on Harvestom. You can put it on your stitches. You'll heal enough by morning we'll be able to train. It won't, however, get rid of the scar. I hope you learn fast. If you don't, you'll be an ugly man before I'm done teaching the likes of you."

It took a while to reach the village. The walk was quiet. When they arrived, the two headed for the inn and went up to the room. Opening the door, they saw Helga standing over Shalee with Mosley lying on the bed next to her. Sam forgot about the pain in his leg and rushed to Shalee's side. He looked her over, scanning the splints the healers had placed on her arm. Satisfied all was as it should be, he looked at Mosley. "What happened?"

"I should be asking you the same thing," Mosley responded as he sniffed at Sam's blood-soaked wrap. "It appears you have learned a few lessons to-day. I cannot remember the last moment I saw a man with so many bruises. You look as if you have been dominated. You stink."

Sam looked at his upper body, which he had not bothered covering with a shirt. Smiling, he walked toward BJ and patted him on the back. "I suppose that's the sign of a good teacher. BJ is not political about his verbal criticisms, but he'll break through this hard head of mine...hopefully not literally. This is all new, but I swear, I'll learn."

BJ grunted, "Shut up. There are no politics in battle, only men who live and die. Take a seat before I knock you down. Sit on the edge of the bed. I don't have all day to teach you how to stitch. Let's get going." The teacher pulled a needle made of bone and some thread from his bag.

Sam removed the items from BJ's hands. "This is something I already know how to do, but I could use the mud you told me about. I'll be ready in the morning, I assure you."

BJ tossed the mud, threw his bag over his shoulder and walked from the room. "See you bright and early then. I'm going to beat you, tomorrow. Sleep on that."

Sam frowned, cleaned his wound, stitched himself and grunted with each pass of the bone needle as it pierced his skin. Once finished, he applied the mud, and wrapped it with bandages before turning his attention to the wolf. "Mosley, what happened to Shalee? How long will it be before she's back on her feet?"

"I imagine it will take her a few Peaks to recover." Mosley stood. "I will return soon," he said as he left the room, uninterested in anything else Sam had to say.

After staring at the door, stunned at the wolf's demeanor, Sam moved across the room. He sat down in the chair, still in the same spot where Bassorine had left it. He lowered his head into his hands and began to cry, the emotions of his new life overwhelming him. He missed Earth. He missed his family. It crossed his mind to pray, but his god was said to be dead. He felt small and in control of nothing. A tear fell to the floor. How could he possibly put on a strong face for Shalee?

The Grayham Inquirer

When Inquiring Minds Need to Know about their Favorite Characters

BASSORINE is still upset. He has been unable to find Lasidious. His anger is building.

The God of Mischief is watching part of his overall plan fall into place. Celestria and Lasidious have finished some last-moment plotting within their home. Both gods will head out to put these plans in motion.

HELGA, leaving the inn, stopped at the healers' vestry. She instructed them to check on Shalee in the morning. She needed to clean up the mess the young sorceress had made while training. The explosion has left many of the mattresses and padded walls charred.

THE OTHER GODS are in the Hall of Judgment, home of the Book of Immortality, located on the hidden god world of Ancients Sovereign. They are speaking with the Book about any options they might have to force Lasidious to come to a meeting which would put an end to Bassorine's annoying ranting. Bassorine's anger has become taxing and their patience with Lasidious is running thin. However, the Book cannot do anything but remind them Lasidious has done nothing wrong and it is his free will to show up whenever he decides.

Thank you for reading the Grayham Inquirer

Here Kitty Kitty

Hours earlier, George awoke on the bank of the Cripple River. He jumped up when the alarm went off and once again, hurried toward his destination. His muscles were tight and every joint ached, but in spite of the pain, he pressed on, wanting to arrive before nightfall or at least shortly thereafter.

To the northeast, a mountain range extended as far as he could see. George looked at his map. The mountains started near the Pool of Sorrow. He was certain he was getting close; his excitement was building. One more look showed the Pass of Tears to be east of the pool and it was this pass that would lead to the Cave of Sorrow.

Working his way north, George sensed something was wrong. He felt he was being watched or worse, followed. With each casual glance toward the edge of the forest line, he saw nothing, yet something inside knew there was a presence in the shadows.

He increased his pace. *Just focus on getting to the pool*, he thought, reminding himself of the goal. *Just focus.*

Jason said the pool would be where he would find the tree with the boulder under it. Beneath the boulder would be the map, if there really was one, and on it, the location of the staff inside the Cave of Sorrow.

Try as he might to focus on the journey and prize that awaited, he could still feel the presence of something lingering in the shadows of the forest. He hurried on.

I'd better not look in the direction of the trees anymore. He wanted to give whatever was watching the impression he wasn't aware of its constant stalking.

George reached his destination only to discover what everyone called a pool was actually a huge lake—one so wide he could not see its other side. He thought back to his conversation with Jason. He remembered hearing the adventurer say the Pool of Sorrow was a lake, but the size had been reduced to something far smaller in his mind because of its name.

Under normal circumstances, he would have taken the moments necessary to enjoy the view, but instead, he had to figure out how to deal with his Peeping Tom. He could sense whoever—or whatever it was—watching. It was unnerving. He knew, or at least felt he knew, it would not be long before something happened. He did not know why, but the alarm in his head was screaming he was in danger and he fought to keep his wits.

Studying the area where the lake and river joined, he noticed a line of massive rocks which created a path crossing the waterway's outlet. The stones spanning the distance could not have been positioned more perfectly, even if they had been placed by a set of giant hands.

Calculating the distance to be over sixty yards or more from start to finish, he made his way to the crossing. As he did, he reached around and pulled his leather pack from his back.

Climbing to the top of the first boulder, George studied the large flattened surface of the stone. It was easily over eighteen feet long and half as wide. After observing the water passing between his current position and the stone beyond, he knelt.

From the shadows of the forest, two yellowish-brown eyes watched. The sun was sinking below the horizon, and the moment for the beast to make its move was approaching. Beneath its fur, powerful muscles rippled, anticipating the satisfaction of closing the distance between the human and its place of hiding.

Water rushed through the gap between the first and second boulder. Rising from his crouched position, George struggled to gain his balance, distracted by the view. Beyond the outlet, the terrain's drastic change in elevation caused a temporary lapse in concentration. The movement of the water created a powerful sound below. He shook his head and turned his attention to the rocks beyond. Jumping seemed possible, yet intimidating. The gushing of the torrent would kill him if he fell, but if he didn't jump, he would be left vulnerable to whatever was stalking him.

George removed a torch from his pack and lit it with an old cigarette lighter from Earth. He tossed the torch to the rock beyond to offer additional light to the landing area.

He counted to three, then jumped. When he landed, he collapsed, grabbed his right ankle and screamed in pain. Rolling to a seated position, he removed his boot, keeping the corner of his eye on the forest and his head lowered. His face could not hide his anguish. He was sure whatever stalked him could see his concern and this weakness had to be penetrating the dusk like a beacon.

He rubbed his ankle, put his boot back on, wincing as he did, and tied it tight for support. He stood, careful not to put too much weight on his foot, and tried to take a step. Again, he fell to the stone's surface and grabbed his ankle. Feeling like a wounded animal, he fought the urge to scream.

As the sun split the horizon, shadows lengthened. Then, as if a switch had been turned on, a loud horrifying roar filled the air. George turned to look. Out of the forest, a large, dark figure made its way toward him. Slowly at first, then faster as the beast began to run. George could only sit and watch in terror.

George hobbled to a standing position, put his weight on his good leg, and clenched both fists. His heart pounded out of control as the thumping footsteps grew louder. Once the beast was close enough, it launched into the air. Before the monstrosity could land, George corrected his posture, balanced his weight on both perfectly good ankles and smiled. His injury, a ruse to flush out his attacker, was no longer needed. Raising his right hand, George screamed, **"Stop!"**

Now, he could only watch. The beast landed on the first stone and prepared for the final spring with its powerful haunches that would send it crashing into him. Its legs started to uncoil, but three of four paws stayed firmly planted, trapped on the stone. The weight of the beast's upper body continued forward, as its free paw bridged the gap between the stones and swiped at George's legs.

This unbreakable snaring of the remaining feet caused the beast to slingshot into the stone's solid surface. The creature's face smashed into the boulder before the rest of its body. One of its legs, its neck, and the lower portion of its jaw crunched on impact, filling the air with horrid cracking sounds.

Despite the beast's advance being nullified, the damage had been done. George's legs had been swiped from under him and he was now dangling above the unforgiving rapids as they crashed into the rocks below. His descent stopped only after he grabbed hold of one of the jagged protrusions of the rock's exposed face. He struggled to pull himself up, the rough edges cutting into his forearms. It took every last ounce of strength to save himself and as he rolled to safety, he listened as the massive creature let out a cry of pain so deafening he had to cover his ears.

George retrieved the torch. Looking down, he noticed the lower portion of his right pant leg had been shredded. The material was saturated. Blood flowed from three gashes which had opened on the outside of his right calf. The wounds were wide, but not too deep. The beast's claws had hit their mark and his leg burned like hell.

George reached for his pack, rifled through it and searched for anything to stem the flow of blood. There was nothing, not a single aid, other than his Gucci shirt. He ripped the left sleeve free from the garment and used it as a tourniquet, but the flow was too much. He tore off the right sleeve, and still the cloth was not enough. He needed another plan. Rifling through his pack, he looked for a different solution.

Damn it, he thought, as he turned to look at the torch. *I can't believe this. This is gonna suck.*

After removing the saturated sleeves from his leg, he reached under his opposite pant leg and pulled a dagger free of its sheath. He held the blade in the flame. Once sure the steel was hot enough, he took a deep breath and placed the glowing flat surface on top of each gash to cauterize the wounds. His skin sizzled and his hair burned. The smell of cooked flesh filled the night air and caused him to vomit onto the rock where he was sitting.

He managed to wipe the tears from his eyes and turn his attention back to the injuries. He held the torch close. He had not got it all. A portion of the middle gash was still bleeding. He lifted his head toward the sky and shouted his disgust, "Aahhhhhhhhhhh, damn it!"

After taking many deep breaths between continued curses, he again placed the blade against his skin and suffered the torture until he was sure the cauterization was finished. "Aahhhhhhhhh!"

It took many long moments to calm his nerves, but once he had done so, he turned his attention toward his attacker. After staring at the beast for what seemed to be forever, George saw it was a large cat of some sort. The lack of light made it hard to tell, but despite the struggle, he was sure it was feline.

The beast's moans continued to fill the blackness of night and with each cry, shivers ran down George's spine. Many moments passed before the human's nerves allowed clear thought. He crawled to the edge of his rock to get a closer look at his enemy. Biting down hard, he suffered the shooting pain of his movements.

The giant cat's free paw lifted to strike, but the pain caused the beast to retract its primal weapon. A single claw grazed the rock's surface. This was all it took. George's magic trapped the limb.

George realized the beast was no longer able to move. After a few erratic swings with his torch to entice another strike, he felt confident the creature was bound. This newfound confidence gave him the courage to get an even closer look, but the wound on his leg made the jump between boulders seem impossible.

After thinking things through, he tossed his pack across the gap and beyond the cat's massive form. He felt the lack of the additional weight would make the jump possible.

George held the torch high to study the area. Once sure he had his spot, he rocked back and lunged forward. As he landed, the wound caused his leg to give way. He stumbled forward and came to a tumbling end onto the broken body of the beast. The cat thrashed as the torch sizzled against its fur. The saber's wicked cries filled the night once more as the pain sent it into a temporary state of shock.

George scrambled to a small, secluded spot on the massive stone. The pain in his leg was excruciating. He needed to collect himself. His skin burned. He took what was left of his Gucci shirt and after holding the torch high again, he dangled it into the fresh water of the pool below. Once the cool material had been applied to the wound, he was comforted.

He stood and stared at the giant cat. He moved the flame around to get a better look. *Amazing. The Snare Scroll worked,* he thought as he hobbled closer.

He could not believe it was only a few short moments ago when he read the words of power from the scroll as he knelt. The only thing left to chance was whatever followed would need to cross the path where the trap had been set. As luck would have it, faking an injury worked to draw the beast exactly where George wanted.

The sight of the creature was impressive. The power the magic must have had to stop such a creature was tremendous. *I can't believe this magic crap actually works. This place is freaking nuts. Abbie would be scared to death of this thing. I have got to tell her this story. This is so nuts. This is nuts...it's nuts...it's nuts...it's nuts.*

As he held the flame closer, he could see the beast had different shades of brown fur. Its broken leg was bent underneath in a horrific position. *This thing must weigh over a ton. I doubt it would fit in the bed of my truck.*

The cat continued to moan as George limped around the helpless creature and winced with every placement of his right foot. The beast's lower jaw was so mutilated it looked fake and lay awkwardly to one side. Both of its fanged teeth had broken off and were resting on the stone not far from its head.

George's mind was beginning to fight the reality of what had happened. He thought he was ready for anything this world had to offer, but this was the first series of moments in which anyone or anything had made an attack on his life. His sanity wasn't solid and was continuing to deteriorate.

He remembered seeing this sort of beast in a children's movie he had watched with Abbie not long ago. He remembered the cat having similar-looking teeth. George's anger grew as he realized he could've been killed.

"I thought sabertooth tigers were extinct," he shouted as he hovered over the animal. "What else does this world have in it? I don't think anything in this damn place is normal! Mages! Magic staffs! Treasure maps...and now, extinct beasts! It doesn't matter! It doesn't freaking matter! Bring it on! Let's see how far from normal we can get!"

He kicked the saber in the gut as payback for his wound. The pain of the impact not only caused the cat to cry out, but also sent George back to the edge of the rock to dip his shirt into the water to help soothe the pulsating throb.

The human had never felt more out of touch with reality in his life than he did now. He was losing control of his emotions. As he shouted a new set of fresh curses into the night, his loud exploits were being observed by yet another set of hidden eyes nearby.

Again, George moved close to the cat. During this series of moments, he would take a new approach. He began to torture the beast with the flame. The cat tried to defend itself, but could not. George watched as the beast's fur sizzled and its flesh fried. The saber went from an angry roar to excruciating cries. George's heart grew colder with every moan the beast made. He resented the attack on his life. He lowered the torch onto its body again, feeling no remorse.

Soon, the torture of the flame was no longer enough to soothe his need for vengeance. Reaching toward his hip, George drew his sword. Three separate occasions, he tapped the flat of the blade against the bone protruding from the cat's broken leg. Laughing, he reached down and twisted the lower portion of the saber's broken jaw. Not only did he twist, but he tugged at it as well. He enjoyed the beast's suffering. George had never experienced this type of pleasure.

"Here, kitty, kitty!" he taunted, poking the point of the blade into different areas of the giant cat's body and savoring its cries. He was careful to make sure the point entered deep enough to draw blood, but not so deep it would hit an organ. He did not want to kill his enemy. The torture he was administering was far too enjoyable to stop now.

"Payback's a bitch," he shouted. "You tried to kill the wrong guy!"

He limped over to pick up the bloody teeth from the rock, then mounted the beast in a straddled position and lowered them in front of the cat's pain-filled eyes. He jeered, "I'm going to make a necklace with these. I will tell my children how good you tasted tonight." After pushing the points of the cat's own teeth into its neck, George leaned back and shouted into the night air. "Here kitty, kitty," and laughed wickedly. A pain filled groan followed.

He slid off of his furry chair and circled the beast again, poking it some more with the point of the blade. With each step, he continued to scream while kicking at its jaw, "Here, kitty, kitty! Oh, here, kitty, kitty! My pain is your pain!"

Becoming bored, he raised his sword above his head, pointed it down toward the cat's neck and plunged it clean through, taking the sabertooth's life.

George leaned against the cat's lifeless body, opened his pack, and removed his old pair of pants to wipe the sweat from his forehead. He took a moment to breathe, allowing his heartbeat to slow and the rush of adrenaline to stop before he stood.

Methodically, he severed all four legs of the beast to release the creature from the unseen trap. Amazed at the beast's weight, despite the missing legs, George had to cut the saber into twelve smaller pieces before tossing them from the rock to the ground.

Gathering some wood from the forest, he built a fire near an old, dead tree trunk which lay on the ground. The piece of deadwood, close to the Pool of Sorrow, provided the perfect place to sit near the shoreline. It was evident the trunk had been pulled from the forest some seasons ago. A fire pit sat close to the log, the ash mostly blown away by the wind, but at some point, others had used this spot to build a fire of their own.

As he removed the shirt from his wound and dipped it again into the Pool of Sorrow, his senses were triggered. Something wasn't right. His gut feeling was telling him to beware. He was not alone and needed a plan.

George returned to the saber and cut the dismembered cat into smaller pieces of bloody flesh. He put them into a pile and saved a few choice cuts to cook for dinner, and sat on the log. The now-experienced *Slayer of Giant Cats* figured the bloody flesh would serve as a distraction for any aggressive beast which might come along.

The night carried a slight chill. The fire provided a much needed warmth and kept the area dimly lit. He had collected enough wood to keep it burning hot, tall, and strong until morning. His brief period of Boy Scout experience told him the flames would act as a deterrent for most animals, and with this knowledge, he smiled with satisfaction.

It took a bit of tugging, but George was able to remove the meat from the end of the skewer. He had chosen a cut from the beast's haunch and was eager to enjoy the experience. He marveled at the tenderness, despite the fact it had been held so close to the flame. All-in-all, his first helping of sabertooth was a pleasure. He knew a real chef would have done a better job, but George did not care. His stomach was full and he was satisfied with his success.

From the darkness, the demon-cat, Kepler, watched as George pulled the meat from the stick and started to eat. He was nervous, not wanting to startle the man when he approached. This human was strong, just as the goddess foretold. He did not want to end up like the Sabertooth Lord. Being eaten did not make for good conversation. Being cut up like his subject was not his idea of a good first encounter. He would approach with caution and avoid giving the impression he might be a threat.

The demon-jaguar moved forward, making just enough noise to make his presence known. He had watched from within the forest shadows as everything transpired and caution was the proper course of action. The brutal slaying of one of his best subjects, even to Kepler's conniving mind, was pointless.

Kepler had been appalled as he watched the human strike his blade against the tiger's broken leg, only to cause it pain. He saw the look of pleasure on the man's face as he twisted the saber's broken jaw. The countless number of pokes with his blade was humiliating to all cats. He could smell his subject's flesh as the heat of the flame scorched it. In his entire existence, Kepler had never made one of his victims suffer the way this human had. The demon-cat had always killed his victims in an instant—which made the sight of today's events troubling, even to his undead heart.

He had a newfound fear of this man. He thought back to his conversation with the goddess as he approached. *"I warn you, Kepler,"* Celestria said, *"this is a strong-willed, hot-tempered human. I would not make him angry if I were you. I would hate to see you end up on a skewer, cooked for supper."*

The demon had now seen firsthand what Celestria meant. George seemed to have no problem cooking anything he killed. Kepler was not about to end up as a flavor of the day.

Kepler feared no man prior to this night. The goddess foresaw this man to be a powerful ruler. He would send this world and others into darkness. The cat now believed this to be true. He hated admitting it, but he was afraid to approach after seeing how easy it was for the human to kill his best subject.

The jaguar crept toward the fire, but to his surprise, George did not stop eating. Did the human not notice him? Or worse, maybe he simply did not care about his presence. Whatever the truth of the matter, the demon was cautious, assuming the man was not worried about his company. *This human could raise his hand to summon the power to stop any confrontation.*

Kepler turned up his nose as he walked by the pile of bloody pieces and continued to study the man. His mind was calculating as he circled the flames. *How could this human ignore me? He fails to acknowledge my presence. This is my territory. My lands. Has he not heard of me? Has my reputation not reached his lair?*

George knew the jaguar was approaching. The fire cast enough light to see the beast out of the corner of his eye. *Holy crap! He's huge! He could bite me in half. The top of his back has got to be higher than I am. He's gonna kill me. What to do? What to do? Think George, think, damn it!*

George decided not to lift his head for fear of making any movement other than what he was already doing and continued to eat instead. Terrified, every hair on his body stood at attention. The black cat was much larger than the saber, maybe another fifteen hundred pounds or so, which made his heart beat violently against his ribs, creating a wicked surge of blood through his neck. The pulsing pounded in his ears, strong enough to drown out the creature's heavy footsteps as it drew closer.

George watched as the powerful movements of the cat dwarfed the pile of bloody parts. He wanted to jump up from the driftwood log and run, but knew the wound on his leg would get him nowhere.

The jaguar stopped. It was all George could do to keep the fear from his face. The sight of the solid black cat, with burgundy-red glowing eyes, amplified his desire to run, but he held firm. He continued to eat, not wanting to change anything he was doing in hopes the cat would move on. The saber's remains had to smell appetizing. He could only hope he had a chance of escaping a certain death.

George thought, *If I live, I'll never camp in this world again. I'm helpless. I knew I should've used another Snare Scroll. I don't have the skill to fight this big of a cat. This damn sword won't kill it. I'm sure of that. I'm so dead. I'm so definitely dead. Damn, how could I have been so stupid? I should've used another scroll. Damn those Boy Scout books. This thing isn't scared of fire. He's just ignoring the pile. I'm so dead. Think, George. Just sit here and play it cool. Keep eating. Keep calm and show no fear. Ignore it. Maybe it'll just go away. Oh, my freaking hell, please go away!*

Kepler stood near the fire, motionless. Now, not more than fifteen feet separated the two of them, and his mind was also racing.

This human doesn't care about my dominance of this territory. He must be truly powerful. He doesn't appear to be nervous. I've never been ignored. I cannot let him live to tell about it. This is humiliating. Every cat on Grayham would laugh if they knew. If I try to kill him, he'll use his power. I'd be no better than the Saber Lord. What should I do? I should lie down and see how he reacts. I should move carefully. Perhaps maintain a regal posture.

George was relieved to see the jaguar lower to the ground. The stare of the burgundy-red eyes continued to burrow a hole into his soul. He kept reminding himself he did not want to do anything the massive animal would see as an aggressive movement. From everything he read about wild animals, he knew no movement was the best movement. He did not change a thing, and kept eating.

Kepler and George continued their mental stand-off for a long, long series of moments, each believing the other, at any moment, could take the other's life. Finally, Kepler's anxiety broke the silence. "Are you not scared, human?" the demon-cat questioned, careful not to sound too intimidating.

After hearing the beast speak, George started to laugh, not because he wanted the beast to think he wasn't scared, but more because he had run into yet another crazy thing this world had to offer. He couldn't fathom a giant cat could talk. It sent him over the edge, laughing so hard it hurt. Tears flowed from his eyes as he lost sight of the fact his life could be in danger.

Kepler was now more convinced than ever of the human's power. The man's hysteria added to the feeling this human cared nothing about his presence. He watched the man roll around and act the fool.

The jaguar continued to speak. "You don't have to be rude. It was only a question. I don't see what's funny."

George, through all his laughter, heard the beast. Taking a few moments to gain his composure, he noticed the cat shift, almost as if nervous.

Kepler was worried the man might be toying with him. He figured it was a good idea to say as much as he could before the man calmed down. He might not have the chance later. "I had no idea you humans could be so rude and show so little respect. I don't cross the boundaries of your territories to insult you."

Now...fellow soul...I must take a moment to interject something here. I find it somewhat humorous George had no idea he was hurting the giant undead demon-jaguar's feelings. It boggles me to this very day, as I hang out inside the Book to tell you this story, how a soulless demon could feel this kind of emotion. Anyway, enough rambling from me...back to the story. As I was about to say...

...the cat's feelings were hurt as he continued, "I would like to converse. You look as if you could use company. Traveling without the rest of your pride can be a lonely journey."

Kepler glanced at the pile of food and swallowed hard at the idea of eating one of his own. "Care to share?" He nodded in the direction of the saber's leftovers, then waited for the human's response.

George fought to relax, took a few deep breaths, then reached over to grab one of the pieces of meat next to him. He threw it at the giant cat's front paws and started to laugh. "Eat up, I don't freaking care," he said as the insanity swept over him again.

Kepler's ego never felt smaller than it did right now. How to react? This human was not afraid. His power had to be great—great enough to allow him to act without concern. Now, more than ever, his existence might be in danger.

Kepler decided to say something to command the human's attention. "I'm here to assist with your rise to power. I was told to create an alliance and this alliance would bring the territories of this world under our control. We could hunt freely, without opposition, and dominate."

This caught George off guard, but his laughter covered his surprise. He took a short series of moments to quiet himself. He sat up to look at the beast, but his temporary state of insanity was still not allowing him to think straight.

"Oh, you were, eh? Unbelievable. Why would I want to have a large pussycat travel with me? What are you going to do to help me? Are you going to lick people to death?"

He cackled. His mind was so far gone he was making fun of the beast which only moments earlier terrified him.

The demon-cat, taken aback by George's ridicule, had never been made fun of or allowed anyone to speak down to him. "I have skills," Kepler retorted, unsure of his own conviction in the statement. "I can do far more than lick someone to death."

George stopped laughing and sat up, continuing to hold his belly. "I can't remember laughing this hard. Oh my gosh, my stomach hurts." He reached up to wipe his tears, feeling as if he were in a dream.

"I'm sure your big furry ass has many skills. Quick, show me how flexible you are. Lick yourself. I'm sure this will be the ability that gets us into power. Why don't we run around and introduce ourselves throughout the land? How do you want to say it to everyone? How about this? My name is George, and this is my sidekick, Captain Ball-Licker." Again he started to laugh.

Kepler's self-esteem was sinking to an all-moments-low and he was becoming angry. He didn't know what to say that would make any difference, so he decided to walk away. He stood up. "I'm sorry to have bothered you. My name is Kepler, not Captain Ball-Licker. I will not allow you to attack my character. No one speaks to the *Master of the Hunt* in this manner." He held his head high and started walking.

George, seeing the cat was about to leave, stopped laughing and fought to bring himself back to reality. There might be something he was missing. Why was this beast under the impression that he, of all the people on this world, was the one it should form an alliance with? None of this made any sense, but he never passed up an opportunity to manipulate a situation.

"Hey, Kepler," George called in a relaxed tone. "Come on back, and I'll stop being such a jerk."

Kepler stopped and turned to look. After a moment, he continued to walk away.

George had one shot at this. He needed to get the upper hand before there was no hand to play. "Suit yourself, Kep, but I'm disappointed you're not witty enough to pass my test."

Kepler stopped again. *What is this human talking about? This was a test? Did the human know I was coming? Could he have known and simply killed the saber as a message? If it was a message, it was received. Garesh! I have to know. I would love to rip his throat out.*

The jaguar turned and headed back to the campfire. "I don't like tests, human," the demon growled while lying down.

George did not miss a beat. "Let me ask you something, Kep. Why would I want your company? What do you bring to the table that would help us dominate?"

Kepler didn't know what to say. He stayed quiet.

"Come on, Kep, talk to me," the manipulator continued. "You clearly want to travel with me. What makes you think I need a travel buddy? Why would I want someone like you assisting me on my quest to rule this world? Give me a good reason and I'll promise never to call you Captain Ball-Licker again."

Until now, George's only concern had been to get the staff inside the Cave of Sorrow. He would have figured something else out from there, but he did like the sound of dominating a world. He wanted to know more.

"As I have said, I have skills. I am undead. I am *demon*. I am the *Lord of all Cats*. They obey my commands. I have other talents which may prove useful as we travel. They can be easily demonstrated." Kepler roared to restore his self-esteem, then sniffed his disdain.

What Kepler did not realize, his statement gave George a big clue about why the sabertooth had attacked. It also gave the human the idea Kepler may have seen the events of the night and watched the saber die. The demon all but said, at least to George's way of thinking, he was behind the attack on his life. In light of this, George felt the giant beast was scared. Kepler had given George an ace up his sleeve.

George decided to ask a few questions. He hoped his thinking was accurate and, if it was, he could use Kepler's fear to his advantage. He led the beast down an unsuspecting road of admission. "So you're undead? Impressive. You're also the Lord of all Cats?"

"I am."

"So...you're their ruler. They are under your command, doing whatever you tell them, right? I wish I had that kind of a following. Very impressive," George encouraged, sure to sound positive.

"Yes," the demon responded, his self-esteem growing as he sat up tall. "I do have quite the following, as you put it. They do as I order. I can see you're impressed. All prides in every territory fear me."

"So...your orders are the ones they always listen to and they would never do anything against your wishes. Is that right?" George said with an admirable tone.

Again, the jaguar confirmed the statement and pushed his chest out even farther. He was now feeling strong once again. "I told you I had skills of my own. I can do far more than lick myself. Are you impressed? Do you see the value of my talents?"

George smiled inside as he now figured the moment was right to bring the jaguar down a notch. "I'm impressed, but it seems I'm missing something."

He changed his expression as he continued, making his statements sound factual to let the beast know he was on to him. "I'm sure you would agree with me, Kepler, it isn't a coincidence you're here after I had a run-in with one of your subjects."

The jaguar's delayed reaction confirmed George was right. The demon had ordered the attack. He was now sure the demon had seen his subject butchered. "I'm sure you can see I'm a little annoyed, Kepler."

The demon's face showed the guilty verdict, but he tried to cover it up with a lie. "I swear to you, George, I didn't order the saber's attack."

Despite his denial, Kepler knew what was coming next. His pride had led to his downfall, moving down a forked road and taking the wrong path when it mattered most. He dreaded what his ears were going to hear next.

"You'll never be able to lie to me, Kepler, so why don't you just level with me? You had me attacked and your friend over there died while you watched. Why the deception? You're not here to travel with me, are you? You hoped I would be an easy meal. Be honest. I'm in no mood for more of your lies."

Switching to a harsher tone, George added, "I won't travel with you if I can't believe in you, Kepler." He watched for the cat's reaction.

The demon hesitated before speaking. He was unsure what George would do if he lied again. No matter what, he was between a rock and a hard place. Best own up to the attack, then try to explain his reasoning.

"I did give the order. I watched the saber die. I wanted to see if you were strong enough to handle the attack. It's not worth giving my allegiance to someone who cannot defend himself. The deception, when I first approached, was intended to start a conversation, but the things I have said about coming here to travel with you are true. We could rule the territories within the three kingdoms."

After he listened to the demon's response, George thought a moment. He knew he had a huge advantage over the jaguar, as the beast thought he had killed his friend. He was unsure what the beast's perception was of the event. He asked Kepler to explain what he saw.

The demon felt this to be an odd request, wondering why the human would want to relive the slaughter, but he did not argue. "I ordered the attack and watched..." Kepler finished his account by saying, "I'm not sure what else to say, other than I decided to offer my services to you after bearing witness. It was, after all, what the goddess thought I would enjoy doing."

The deceiver had no clue what Kepler meant by "the goddess," but he did not want to lose the upper hand. "What other skills do you offer, Kep, other than being the Lord of all Cats?"

"I can capture the souls of men with dark natures. I steal them before their hearts stop. I trap them inside the bones of their lifeless skeletons. Once this has been done, they must do my bidding until I decide to release them. I can hide in the smallest of shadows. This ability gives me a chance to stalk in situations where stealth is required. Simple things...things which affect normal creatures, don't harm me. I walk the world as undead. Poison and extreme cold are harmless annoyances. I am *King of the Hunt*."

George smirked. "King of the Hunt, eh? Take it easy, stud."

The demon pondered the word "stud," then dismissed his confusion. "I'm skilled at gathering information and these claws are unmatched when the moments show no solution other than to kill. If these traits are not what you consider employable, we have nothing further to discuss. I will hunt on my own."

George liked a lot of what the jaguar said. What could it hurt to have the beast travel with him, as long as he could maintain the illusion of power. He would travel with the beast for protection and use this illusion to maintain command. He wanted this fantasy to remain strong until he was able to re-trieve the power of the Staff of Petrifaction. Once he was able to turn things to stone, he would re-evaluate his need for the demon.

Turning to Kepler, George thought of two questions. He hoped the an-swers would make the next couple of steps in his journey much easier. "How do you feel about lifting heavy boulders and are you immune to the effects of The Beast inside the Cave of Sorrow?"

Kepler's response was everything George wanted to hear. They decid-ed to call it a partnership—for now—and since the night was late, George turned to sleep. It was a few hours until sunrise and there was a big boulder to find. As George went to sleep, he contemplated how he was going to maintain this perception of power. He would dream of Abbie, along with Athena. They would take his little daughter to an amusement park and eat cotton candy. It would be a pleasant dream.

Kepler, on the other hand, was relieved he was able to accomplish the task Celestria recommended. The demon was happy to be in George's ser-vice. He yawned and decided to go sit on a nearby boulder to ponder the day's events as the fog began to move in across the lake. Closing his eyes, the breeze was soothing.

From a branch, high above in a nearby tree, Lasidious watched the uniting of the two travel companions. He lowered his eyes to the rock at the base of the tree. It was this large stone the map rested beneath and it would soon be discovered. He realized he was right about George's ability to seize power and hoped the earthling could distract the gods. He needed this diversion to hide Celestria, allowing her to give birth without fear of discovery. He enjoyed the luck involved this evening, but he knew this kind of luck simply followed those who were clever enough to find it. Smiling, the God of Mischief vanished.

The Grayham Inquirer

When Inquiring Minds Need to Know about their Favorite Characters

IT IS A NEW DAY and everyone is up and moving in their own little part of Grayham. Celestria and Lasidious are inside their home, once again, on Ancients Sovereign, plotting.

GEORGE is with Kepler at the Pool of Sorrow. After waking, Kepler sent for help to move the boulder which supposedly sits atop the map.

SAM is training with BJ in the field just outside of Angel's Village. The fighter is being humbled by yet another series of beatings, despite showing a significant improvement. Kael, Sam's sword, has already commented on Sam's growth, saying he is doing much better than the day before.

THE HEALERS have attended to Shalee, replacing her bandages and applying more healing mud to her arm. She is tired from the experience, but not in too much pain. Despite her injury, she smiles as she looks across the room toward the fireplace. She is holding Precious and is commanding the fire to do many different little things—making sure to only use simple commands so she can enjoy the benefits of her successes. What a naughty little sorceress.

HELGA is working on a few new lessons for her protégé. The older sorceress has every intention of making Shalee practice with her broken arm. She plans to retrieve her student from the inn, not long from now.

MOSLEY is talking to the manager of Angel's Arena, setting up Sam's first fight to give the Earthling a taste of the intense competition in Grayham's arenas. This particular battle will not be to the death, but neither will it be without injury if Sam does not fight well. The competition, using wooden staves as the weapon of choice, will continue until a cry for submission is uttered. In this fight, Sam will be required to inflict enough pain on his opponent to make him yield. Compensation for a victory will be ten Owain coins, or two, if he loses.

BASSORINE is in a meeting with the Book of Immortality, trying to convince the Book that Lasidious is up to something. He tells the Book Lasidious and Celestria cannot be found, but it does not give the answers he wants to hear. The Book reminds Bassorine its pages contain no law requiring the gods to check in with the others. It also reminds Bassorine if a meeting of the gods is called, attendance is not mandatory. Lasidious does not have to show. Lasidious has not broken any rules and everything he has done up 'til now is acceptable. Bassorine tries to object, but the Book reminds him if free will was to be taken away from any soul it would feel an emotional wave of sorrow flowing through its pages. Since no rules were broken, the Book has felt nothing. Therefore, no steps need to be taken. The God of War storms out of the Hall of Judgment, screaming for Lasidious once again, feigning his regret of the creation of the Book as he passes by Keylom on his way out.

Thank you for reading the Grayham Inquirer

Kroger the Ogre

The Home of Lasidious and Celestria
Ancients Sovereign

From within their home on the world of Ancients Sovereign, Lasidious and Celestria laugh as they listen to Bassorine's screams. They are thrilled with the successful pairing of George and Kepler, created at the Pool of Sorrow.

"You should've seen Kepler's face when George tortured the Saber Lord," Lasidious sniggered. "It was all I could do to keep quiet. When Kepler introduced himself, he was so careful about it. You should have seen how George kept his cool when he saw the giant cat. How the mortal thought to use the snare scroll to trap the saber is beyond me. I just knew he was going to get his head taken off when Kepler sent the cat after him. It appears George is smarter than our initial assessment suggested and has solid instincts."

"Truly, my love, my adorable devil-god?" Celestria purred, rubbing Lasidious's forehead with her thumbs. "Do tell..."

The Mischievous One enjoyed her touch. "It was perfect. He set his trap, then acted as if he was injured...a beautiful deception. I was proud of my puppet. He had the nerve to laugh at Kepler and jest at his expense. He told Kepler his only skill was licking his privates and assigned the beast a title, Captain Ball-Licker. I nearly died when I heard the insult. Kepler did nothing. He appeared scared. I think he believes George wields magic. I still can't comprehend where George got the nerve. I thought for sure he would garesh his pants when Kepler appeared from the shadows."

Celestria cupped her lover's face in her hands. "You are so cute when your vicious mind overflows with pride, my love." She kissed him and touched her belly. "Your baby grows, my sweet, and I will be leaving for the village of Floren soon. As we discussed, I will need to stay until the baby is born, and no longer use my power. We cannot allow the others to track me.

Using my power will only increase the risk. I want you to be patient, my pet. I may not be able to be with you, but I will be thinking of you. You are my heart's desire."

Passion filled their kiss. They agreed it was Lasidious' responsibility to carry out their plans until the baby was born. Celestria kissed her devious lover once more, then left to spend the remainder of her pregnancy with the elven witch family, Rolfe.

The Pool of Sorrow

George and Kepler are waiting. It will take the rest of this day, and most of the next, before Kepler's summons for help to remove the boulder from beneath the tree will be answered. One of the dead Saber Lord's relatives has been sent north into the Dark Forest to fetch help from a giant ogre named Kroger.

Angel's Village

Helga walked through the door of Shalee's room, unannounced, to get her student moving for the day. The elderly woman caught the young sorceress-in-training using her staff to command smaller successes, then enjoying the satisfaction. Shalee was in the middle of one of her pleasurable tear-filled moments when Helga barged in. The older woman laughed. As a young sorceress-in-training herself, she did something similar—only she had been smart enough to lock the door.

Shalee was embarrassed by the intrusion and jumped out of bed, her face damp from the tears of joy. She tried to hide her embarrassment behind a pillow.

"Don't ya knock?" Shalee snapped. "It's just not ladylike bargin' in on anotha' woman like that."

Helga fell to the empty bed. Holding her stomach with laughter, she tried to answer, but could not.

"Very funny," the younger woman said, turning away to hide a smile. "I bet ya did the same thing and know exactly what I was up ta. You can't blame me, ya know. Precious has given me plenty of happy thoughts. This here staff is my new definition of goodness-gracious."

"Oh, child, child, child, you don't have to tell me. I didn't leave my room for days when I first began my training. My teacher was displeased, to say the least."

The women laughed and the moment of embarrassment vanished and was replaced with a perfect period of bonding as Shalee taught Helga how to give a high-five.

"My friends and lil' old me, gave each otha' high-fives back on Earth when somethin' felt special-like or funny. I think you and I could be good togetha'. Besides, I could really use a friend. I have cried so much since learnin' all my loved ones have passed. I wish the pain would go away."

Helga was sympathetic. "Oh, child, I love the idea of being your friend. Anything I can do to help ease your pain, I will. I know what it's like to lose a loved one. Pain like this should not be suffered alone." Helga lifted her hand and gave her new best friend another high-five to seal the bond. "Shall we speak of other things to get your mind off such torture?"

Shalee nodded. "So...now that I've had my first failure, the rest should be smooth-sailin', right?"

"Let's hope this is the case, child. We best get going. I have a few things planned we need to get to. I hope you don't fail again. I would hate for you to break your other arm and not be able to practice."

"Ya know it, girl," Shalee said with sass as she threw up her good hand for another high-five. Both women enjoyed the moment, then Shalee changed her clothes before heading out.

Once they arrived at Helga's school, Shalee was anxious to get started. She was amazed at the healing properties of the mud which had been used under her bandages. Even though she had broken her arm the night before, she could tell the moments necessary to move past the injury would be minimal.

Once in the padded room, Helga removed a few of the mattresses from its center and replaced them with four large buckets of water. Turning to Shalee, she said, "This exercise is similar to last night's, but during this series of moments, I want you to manipulate the water in different ways. Don't even bother asking to combine words, child."

Shalee smiled and did not argue. She looked at the four buckets, and, after a bit, she asked Helga for the elven word for water. The sorceress gave it to her, figuring it was a simple request, but Shalee had other ideas, her Texas pride shining through. She raised her staff into the air and shouted, "Precious, *nen coia*!"

Helga looked at her student and threw up a wall of force to protect them. Shalee had fooled her teacher by combining the elven word for "life," *coia*, with the word for "water," *nen*. All Helga could do was wait for the outcome and hope for the best.

They watched, apprehensively, as the water began to lift into the air and form into a shimmering image of a falcon. The detail the command retrieved from Shalee's mind when creating the flying beast was spectacular. Her memories had come from the nature channel while on Earth and the falcon had been her favorite ever since she had first seen it. The bird looked like a piece of crystal, except for its graceful movements in flight. After a while, it began to make sweeping passes above their heads as the staff responded to her changing thoughts.

Eventually, Shalee could feel her power beginning to fade. She decided to end the command by flying the bird above Helga's barrier of protection. The command further instructed the falcon to stop above the older woman's exposed head. Shalee allowed the watery image to fall on top of Helga, drenching her. She would have laughed at the sight, but the success of the command was demanding her attention.

Shalee lied down and allowed the rush to consume her. She fell asleep and could not be awakened for the rest of the day, due to the intensity of the experience. Sam had to make his way to the school and carry Shalee back to their room.

Helga followed and tucked the covers around her student, in awe of Shalee's power. It had taken the older sorceress almost ten seasons of her life to accomplish what Shalee had done in two days. She smiled inside and wished she could give her new friend a high-five.

The Pool of Sorrow

The next day, the giant beast-man hurried, responding to Kepler's summons. From his home in the Dark Forest, Kroger, an oversized ogre, emerged and crossed the boulders of the outlet's crossing.

George heard thunderous footsteps as the giant approached and watched in amazement as the massive beast of a man crossed the outlet and dwarfed the rock where the 2,500 pound Saber Lord was killed.

As the ogre drew closer, Kepler explained Kroger was cursed at birth with gigantism. His mother died while giving birth. Though it was not Kroger's fault, his father resented him and had abandoned the newborn in the Dark Forest. Kroger was raised by the most unlikely of families—a group of Dread Gorillas. They had taken him in as their own and no one could explain why. The Dread Gorillas were so fierce they ate their own if a weakness was found. Perhaps, they saw the ogre as unique and respected his differences enough to let him live.

The ogre was easily thirty feet tall and wore furs to cover his mid-section. His feet were bare, toughened from many seasons of exposure. He carried a massive club with spikes. A large wrap ran up across his chest and over his shoulders to support a huge pack which George figured could hold a small car. The pack had something inside, but George could only see the bump the object made. Kroger was not a handsome creature. Scars covered his body from many seasons of wrestling with his gorilla family in play.

Lucky for George and Kepler, the giant could cover great distances in a short amount of moments or they would have still been waiting for him to arrive. Kroger had run the same distance the saber messenger had traveled, but in a quarter of the moments.

In spite of his difficulties, the giant was a happy person, singing as he walked over the crossing. George could tell from the sound of his voice, this big guy was not one you would expect to score high on an IQ test.

Dusk was approaching and George took charge of the situation. He introduced himself to Kroger, treating him with respect. After a few moments of necessary befriending, he excused himself for two purposes: to empty his bladder on yet another unsuspecting tree, and to allow Kepler to instill the proper amount of fear in the giant's mind about George's perceived power.

Once George rejoined the group, he asked Kroger to remove the stone and the giant lifted the rock with ease. As he watched Kroger playfully toss it up and down, he figured it probably weighed close to two tons, this estimation based on similar boulders which were delivered to his apartment complex for landscaping. George watched in awe as the ogre threw the rock into the torrent waters below the outlet's crossing. *Wow! This freak would make a good bodyguard. This place is trippin' me out.*

George jumped into the hole and moved the dirt around. It took a few moments, but he finally uncovered the map. He did not understand how the paper could look so new, but said nothing. The weight of the stone sitting on it should have destroyed it, yet the paper had not absorbed any moisture from under the rock. It was as if the map had been drawn that morning. George did not dwell on this fact. Like everything else in this world, it was just one more messed up thing.

Kepler and Kroger were curious, but George pulled the map back to keep nosey eyes from seeing it. "Easy, my powerful friends," he said. "There's going to be something in this for all of us, but for now, I ask you to let me figure out a plan. This map is going to help us gain a tremendous amount of power if we do things right. Just be patient and we'll have everything we want."

Kepler desperately wanted to look at the map, but was learning that George was not stupid. If he said the map was going to help them gain power, then he could only assume the human knew what he was talking about.

Night was coming and George wanted to study the parchment. He ordered the duo to gather wood for a fire and soon they were all sitting by the flame. Kroger and Kepler stared at George while he memorized the details. The human was shocked at how easy it was to read. The location of the staff was clearly marked, resting behind a hidden door, which guarded it, just inside the cave's entrance. Once inside, there were only two ways out. The first was to make it through the cave's eight-day walk and find the exit called Sorrow's Release. The second was to find The Beast within the cave and kill him to release his control over the entrance, risking a deadly confrontation.

George remembered what Jason told him about The Beast. He said it was a hideous creature who used visions of sadness to drive anyone who entered the cave insane. The visions make his victims commit suicide—walking through the Pass of Tears, weeping, and throwing themselves into the Pool of Sorrow. They swim deep enough that when the moment comes, the moment when they realize what has happened, they do not have the air necessary to surface before drowning.

The idea of dealing with The Beast was of little concern to George. He remembered Kepler said he was immune to its visions since sadness was an emotion his demon's heart could not feel—or so the demon thought.

With George's mind working overtime, it wasn't long before he had developed a plan. "Listen up, guys. I have a job for us to do, but first, I'm hungry." George rubbed his belly. "What do you guys say we get something to eat?"

"Food!" Kroger shouted in a booming voice. He reached into his gigantic pack and pulled out a dead corgan. He ripped the cow-like animal apart and offered it to the group.

George laughed, realizing what the bump in the giant's pack had been. He thanked him for the meal, watching as Kepler and Kroger ate their supper raw. George, on the other hand, found a stick to hold his meat above the flame.

After everyone was finished eating, they sat by the fire while George explained his plan. Once the look of understanding appeared on their faces, he put the scroll in his bag and lied down, suggesting they all get some rest. He placed the bag under his head to keep curious minds out and drifted off to sleep.

The Grayham Inquirer

When Inquiring Minds Need to Know about their Favorite Characters

THE NEXT MORNING, George, Kepler and Kroger are up and on their way through the Pass of Tears, traveling toward the Cave of Sorrow. They plan to camp a safe distance from the cave's entrance once they arrive. George wants to avoid any unexpected encounters with The Beast, Maldwin. They will review George's plan before entering.

SAM, MOSLEY and BJ are on their way to Angel's Arena. BJ wants to give Sam a sense of what to expect before his first fight. The fight is scheduled as the last one of the evening. Sam, however, is not sure the idea to put him in the arena this early in his training is a good one. The trainer wants Sam to practice and familiarize himself with the sandy surface of the arena floor.

SHALEE is once again with Helga after sleeping through the night. She still feels weak and they have decided to stick with simple commands as they continue her training. The past few days have been wonderful, despite her broken arm, but using the staff has taken a lot out of her. The rewards Precious has given have been exhausting. She has never shed so many tears of joy in her life.

As training continues, the rewards she expected from these simple commands are beginning to fade. Helga explains Shalee has moved to an advanced skill level and from now on, the benefit of easier commands will only add small extensions to her life.

CELESTRIA is now with the elven witch family on the world of Luvelles. She is posing as a distant relative. The story, if asked, is she has traveled to be with them until her baby is born.

LASIDIOUS plans to make his appearance to the Collective. He has sent word for the Book of Immortality to call a meeting inside the Hall of Judgment. The Book has invited the gods to attend and as expected, with the exception of Celestria, every god informs the Book they will be present.

Thank you for reading the Grayham Inquirer

A God Falls

Inside the Hall of Judgment
Ancients Sovereign

The meeting was held in the Hall of Judgment, the home of the Book of Immortality. The vanity of the gods ensured everything on Ancients Sovereign was breathtakingly beautiful and this room was no exception. It was difficult to enjoy the beauty of this place as many harsh words were being thrown around by those in attendance.

"I am outraged at your deception and the theft of my Crystal Moon," Bassorine yelled, while glaring at Lasidious.

The Collective was sitting around the heavy stone table within the Hall of Judgment. One of them, Keylom, due to his individual body composition, was unable to sit. He stood and listened to Bassorine scream across the table's surface as his centaur hooves clapped against the polished floor.

"I would never have released my hold on the Crystal Moon if I had known it was your intention to peculate its pieces."

Lasidious laughed in a taunting manner. "You're outraged. Who cares? I have broken no laws within the Book's pages. This Collective doesn't call me the Mischievous One for nothing. Did you really expect the release of your governance over the Crystal Moon to be without recourse? Have you become dense? Deception is what I do, imbecile. I couldn't care less how you appear in the mortals' eyes. It was your vanity which drew you into my plan. You're pathetic, Bassorine, a sorry excuse for a god."

"What," the God of War screamed, "my vanity? How was I so vain?"

"You have the biggest ego in this room. It didn't take much to convince this panel you should appear to the mortals after they touched the crystal. You enjoy looking *almighty!* Your vanity liked the idea or you would've never agreed to allow this to happen."

Bassorine tried to speak above Lasidious, but he stumbled over his words. It was easy for the God of Mischief to take control of the conversation.

"You stumble when you speak. This weakness helps make my next point. Face it, Bassorine. You're not the brightest of the gods. When it comes to planning a war you're adept, but when it comes to thinking long-term, you should leave it to the others. There would be nothing created if you were the only one to survive the wars. You have no imagination. We needed your *power* to help us create the things within the worlds, nothing more. You're useless and everyone around this table knows I'm right."

Lasidious could see Bassorine moving toward the edge of his seat as he continued. "Let's face it. If you had any brains at all you never would've allowed the Book to be created. The funny thing is, not only did you allow it, but you allowed me, of all the gods, to manipulate its creation. I did it right under your nose. Thank you, Bassorine. Some of the loopholes within its laws are wonderful."

The others exchanged quizzical glances from their seats as Bassorine responded with a few well thought-out statements. Keylom cringed, the sounds the beautiful centaur's hooves made managed to heighten the tension in the room as his weight caused them to clap hard against the floor.

Bassorine stood, drew his sword and jumped up on the table. He pointed his blade at Lasidious as he threatened, "Allow me to show you stupid! Let us see how stupid looks when I am standing above your lifeless corpse!"

Bassorine began to walk across the table toward Lasidious, but before anything more could be said, he flew across the room and slammed hard into a nearby wall with a thunderous thud. The entire hall shook from the collision, leaving the thick marble damaged.

The Book of Immortality rose from its golden stand. The Book realized the meeting was out of control and the moment had come to take action, which it did by knocking Bassorine into the wall with its power. In all its seasons, since the Collective agreed on its creation, the Book had never used the power resting within its many pages. Until now, the Book had always settled things with logical communication. Everyone in the room was stunned, even Lasidious, though he had hoped this would happen. It was the God of Mischief's goal to put the Book in a defensive position, forcing it to protect him.

The Book spoke. "Bassorine, this meeting will not become a battlefield. You *will not* harm Lasidious. He has the free will to say anything he wishes, just as you do. I suggest you calm yourself before you do something which requires further discipline."

All watched as Bassorine picked himself up from the floor and dusted off his long, tan leather coat. The others stood and waited for his reaction. The God of War finished shaking off the debris and scoffed as the white marble chunks fell. He lifted his head high. Everyone knew he was the strongest—able to destroy each of them, but it was the Book's job to keep the gods from fighting. Its power was not to be taken lightly, no matter how dominant Bassorine was.

He was the only god within the Collective with a weapon capable of destroying the Book. Angry, he debated in his mind what his next move would be. He watched as the Book hovered above the table and moved to a position above its golden stand.

Now...fellow soul...I need to take a short series of moments to tell you a few things. When the Collective created the Book of Immortality, they left two weaknesses. One weakness was Bassorine's sword. The gods agreed, on the day of the Book's creation, they needed a way to take back the control given to the Book if it ever became necessary, but they did not leave room for error when doing so, which brings me to the Book's second flaw.

This flaw is a slowed reaction. The problem is...this moment of weakness is minimal, a split moment if you will, extremely narrow. Only Bassorine has the skill necessary to react fast enough to capitalize on this advantage. Anyway...enough babbling from this soulful tongue, back to the story.

Bassorine calculated these facts, knowing he would have only one shot to destroy the Book—realizing another governor of the gods could be created, if needed. With the Book out of the way, he could destroy Lasidious. If he did, it would set an example to the others within the Collective. They would learn they should never deceive him again. Even better, he would once again be all-powerful. Lasidious' actions could be his excuse to take back this ultimate level of glory—or, was this level of glory truly ultimate?

Lasidious, sensing Bassorine's hesitation, took a few more calculated shots at his ego. "See what I mean, you overgrown corgan? You're no better than a side of beef after a killing. Only you would attack me in front of the Book. You're not as almighty as you would have us believe. Accept the fact I've taken the Crystal Moon. Bury your head in the sand. Accept defeat. I have won this battle." Lasidious laughed at Bassorine's expense while the others remained on edge.

The God of War's pride swelled. His hatred for Lasidious grew stronger with every breath he took. His desire to destroy the Book and take his vengeance was cosmic. The deception of the god, along with his verbal lashing and the attack from the Book clouded his judgment. He could not think of a series of moments in which he wanted to fight more in his entire existence. Bassorine watched Lasidious smile and laugh, daring him, taunting him, luring him to attack. With every breath he took, Bassorine sized up the Book, and calculated the best way to destroy it.

The God of War quieted his mind and took a few deep breaths. After a moment, his decision was made. He would fight. He was ready to go to war. Methodically, he began walking toward the group, acting as if he was going to put his blade away. Reaching the heavy table and seeing the gods were beginning to sit, he quickly lifted his sword into the air. The blade began its deadly descent toward the Book's heavy cover. None of the others expected this, except Lasidious.

The God of Mischief hoped this day would come. This moment had been a part of his plan all along. He knew one of the laws within the Book's pages allowed for the gods to protect its existence. The Book could be defended with any use of power necessary, without punishment. Lasidious knew he didn't have the power to defeat Bassorine, but he didn't need it. Then again, if this part of his plan failed, he would be dead. He was aware Bassorine's blade was the only thing in existence which could destroy the Book of Immortality. If Bassorine caught it off guard, the Book's ability to protect itself would not be fast enough. All Lasidious needed was to buy the Book a single moment in which to defend itself and he was ready to do this.

As Bassorine's blade arched through the air, Lasidious reached forward with his hands and sent a wave of force strong enough to push the Book out from under the thunderous slam the blade made as it hit the Book's golden stand. The weapon continued through the heavy stone table before cracking the floor and coming to rest.

The Book flew across the room and landed on the floor, unharmed. Lasidious sent another wave of force into Bassorine, knocking him backward, buying the Book the moments necessary to respond.

Lasidious was not strong enough to knock Bassorine into a wall like the Book had, but he only needed to take away the god's balance long enough for the Book to react.

Regaining his stance, Bassorine leapt across the room toward the Book, trying to make up for the lost moment. His blade arched through the air and met its target with a thunderous collision, but it was too late. A powerful field of protection surrounded the Book's heavy ancient binding.

The repercussion of the two powerful forces colliding sent everything in the room flying hard against the opposing walls. The collision of bodies surrounding the table was so strong they broke through the walls and landed in the countryside, scattered beyond the structure. Except for Bassorine and the Book of Immortality, the others within the Collective were now lying dazed in the grass with pieces of the hall surrounding them within a billowing cloud of dust. The rest of the structure had fallen on the two in battle.

It took a while for the rumbling to stop. The sound of the event had been heard as thunder throughout all the worlds. The gods lying on the grass stood to look at the spectacle. With the dust settling, all that was left was an enormous pile of marble, gold, and the now shredded tapestries which had been scattered throughout.

The deities looked at each other and waited. They were about to declare the Book and Bassorine destroyed when they heard a noise from under the pile's center. Lasidious swallowed hard at the possibility it could be Bassorine. If it was, he knew he would be dead in a matter of moments. Bassorine would not find forgiveness. The God of War's blade would split him in two.

The pile of marble started to shift and lift into the air. The pieces floated away and settled toward the edges of the rocky debris. Lasidious took a deep breath and held it as he waited for the answer which would determine the remainder of his existence. From the center of the pile rose the Book of Immortality. Lasidious exhaled as the Book float over to the group. "Bassorine is gone and will no longer be with us. I have destroyed him."

Some of the gods fell to their knees while others stood in disbelief. They had all known Bassorine and, despite their differences, admired him. But, true to their vanity, they shook off their loss, realizing there was one less being more powerful than them at the top. Lasidious allowed his dark heart to relish the fact this part of his plan had fallen in line. He was now the strongest of the gods. The only hurdle which remained was to find a way to take control of the Book. Thousands of seasons of plotting were coming together.

The Book spoke. "I'll need a new hall. I want it built right away. If anyone breaks another law, they will meet the same fate as Bassorine. It is a rule within my pages, for every fallen, a new deity must take the place of the one left behind. This replacement is to be chosen per the wishes of the fallen. I will announce the name of the ascended when we convene to honor the Mighty Bassorine's passing."

The Book floated toward Lasidious. "Is it your intent to allow everything created to be destroyed? If it is, then this is your right to do so. No one will do anything to stop you. There is no rule stating you cannot destroy the Crystal Moon."

The Book turned to the others and shouted. "I cannot fathom how any of you could have forgotten to create such an important rule!"

Lasidious responded. "I don't want the crystal or the worlds destroyed. I'm simply bored, and wish to play a game. I have scattered the crystal's pieces and have given each individual hiding spots. There's one piece on Grayham at the moment, but this could change."

The God of Mischief smiled. A malicious intent rested behind his grin. "I intend for all of us to play a game, that is, if you choose, of course. I have protected each piece of the crystal. No one can touch them, except for me, now that Bassorine is gone. You'll be given a choice to join a team. Those of you who join me will create a team of evil and try to collect three of the five pieces of the Crystal. The other team will be one of good and will need to do the same. For every piece collected and placed together, it should allow enough power to be sent throughout the worlds to keep them in their proper orbits and allow us the moments necessary to finish the game.

Mieonus' dark hair cascaded over her shoulders. Her red and black gown exposed the flesh of her thigh as it complemented her gentle curves. She responded as she tapped her lifted heel against a piece of the hall on which she stood. "As a consequence, the theft of the Crystal Moon has already caused tremors on many of the worlds. We do not have the moments necessary to play your silly game. Everything created is in jeopardy because of your foolishness. I have no intent to appease your twisted desire."

Lasidious watched the hate in the goddess' eyes as he chuckled at her expense. "Tremors are not our true concern. The planets shifting from their orbits would be more of a concern. They should not start to shift for nearly a season. The Crystal Moon's governance will only effect the land masses of the worlds during this period. This will create chaos, fear, tragedy, and tension on the worlds. We can enjoy the mortals' misery as the theft of the Crystal Moon leaves them with little choice other than to battle for the pieces of the crystal. When a team adds a piece of crystal to the first, it will give us the moments necessary to toy with the worlds."

Lasidious moved past Mieonus. As he passed, he reached out and flipped her hair with his hand. He enjoyed Mieonus' irritation as he watched her stomp her heel against the marble. "If we do this right, Mieonus, we will be amused and the mortals will suffer because of my game. You worry too much. The pieces of the crystal will work to govern the planets as long as two of them are bonded. I see no reason why we cannot enjoy the mortals' suffering until the first two pieces find their way to one another."

Mieonus' expression changed. Her delight in what Lasidious proposed brought forth a change of heart. Her disgust vanished. "Your demented mind is delicious, Lasidious. I will enjoy their heartache."

Seeing the goddess' pleasure, Lasidious continued, "If our team wins and collects the majority of the crystal's pieces, the worlds will fall under our control. Evil will rule and govern the Crystal Moon. If the other team is victorious, the worlds will be dominated by good, and they will likewise be given control."

"What will keep you from cheating?" Alistar adjusted the hood of his robe. "You'll have a distinct advantage. There is no way to monitor fair play. I will not play a game in which there is not an equal chance of winning. How do you propose to solve this problem?"

Lasidious pretended to ponder. "I give the Book my word I will not cheat while on my team. If I do, the Book will sense this deception and I'll be destroyed. This will be enough to keep me in line. If I find it difficult to play, I'll resign and watch. I've never been much for teams anyway, so this may very well happen."

"Sounds fair," Mieonus responded, "when do we start?"

Lasidious clapped his hands and rubbed them together. "The influence we have over our followers will be our weapons, or tools, you might say, to manipulate. You could even call them our chess pieces. If I remember right, Bassorine loved chess."

The God of Mischief smiled at the thought of Bassorine's destruction. "We will play a game fit for the gods. The only rules: we cannot force our pawns to do anything they don't want to. As the laws of the Book of Immortality state; 'Free Will is to be cherished above all else.' The second rule: all the worlds will continue to trade merchandise without interruption, since it is necessary for their survival. None of us will do anything to influence trading or the game will end and the crystal's pieces will be destroyed. The goal is to get the beings of the worlds to strategize for the pieces of the Crystal Moon and fight to capture them. As I have said, the team that captures three pieces first...wins."

Lasidious moved to a piece of stone debris and hopped on top of it before making his next statement. "If the game is not played, I will destroy the Crystal Moon. The worlds will follow, destroying themselves, and our followers. However, without Bassorine, we will be unable to create another Crystal Moon. We will have to rebuild and start over. I think we all remember how tedious *that* was. You can now choose to play or not." Lasidious smiled and said, "Who would like to be on my team?"

The gods looked at each other. As expected, they all enjoyed the thought of this new diversion. Of the thirteen remaining, Lasidious now had a team of eight, including himself and Celestria. He watched as Bailem stepped forward and took the other team leader position over the remaining four.

Before Lasidious left, he shook the hands of his team and called for a meeting in his home. He would allow for their entrance and gave them a period of the day to be there to start their planning.

Bailem did the same as the Book of Immortality made one final statement before they left. "It appears this follows the rules of free will. I don't see any laws within my pages being broken. Let the game begin."

The Grayham Inquirer

When Inquiring Minds Need to Know about their Favorite Characters

LASIDIOUS, the God of Mischief, and his team are in his home, deep within the Peaks of Angels. The gods present at this meeting are Yaloom, God of Greed; Mieonus, Goddess of Hate; Hosseff, the Shade, God of Death; Jervaise, the Spirit, Goddess of Fire; Lictina, the female Lizardian, Goddess of Earth; and Owain, the Dwarf, God of Water. The one god missing from the meeting was Celestria, the Beast Goddess.

Planning has begun. Lasidious informed his team of what has transpired so far. He told them of George, Kepler, and Kroger's alliance. He gave them up-to-date information, telling them George's group is on their way to the Cave of Sorrow. Lasidious is unable to give his team the exact location of the first piece of the Crystal Moon on Grayham because of his promise to the Book of Immortality, but he did say he might change his mind and put two pieces of the crystal on Grayham instead of one. They all agreed the things Lasidious has done up 'til now are good and congratulated him on his destruction of Bassorine.

BAILEM—an angel, now the God of the Sun, is holding his own team meeting. The gods present at his home are Alistar, God of the Harvest; Keylom, the Centaur, God of Peace; Calla, Goddess of Truth; and Helmep, God of Healing. None of them know where to start. All they know is the first piece of crystal is somewhere on Grayham. The meeting seems somewhat pointless, but they hope to recruit the newly ascended to their team once the Book introduces this individual.

SAM has finished his early morning training and is now familiar with the arena. Back with Shalee, he has a few moments before his fight to think. He is worried and is using Shalee as a sounding board. Sam's fight will be the last fight of the evening, and by all estimates, the fight will end before dusk.

HELGA is working hard to plan stronger lessons for Shalee. The older sorceress has given her pupil a few days off in order to accomplish this task. Bassorine visited Helga the night before his destruction, during the estimated series of moments called midnight. He told Helga Shalee could handle an aggressive growth in her skills. He would not say why or how her student could handle this, but he did say Helga was not to speak of their conversation with Shalee or anyone else. The God of War left the older sorceress with many unanswered questions.

CELESTRIA is helping the witches clean their home and prepare her baby's room. She hasn't been this excited about anything since she became a goddess. It has been well over 100,000 seasons since she set up anything without using her power. She is finding this to be quite the challenge.

MOSLEY stayed with BJ after Sam's training. When the fights started at the Peak of Bailem, the trainer excused himself and headed for the nobleman's box to watch the fights. Mosley was looking for Sam when the Book of Immortality appeared in front of him.

Thank you for reading the Grayham Inquirer

A God's Gifts and a Revelation

"Mosley, we must speak," the Book of Immortality said before teleporting them to a secluded place on the god world of Ancients Sovereign. They reappeared in a valley, nestled into the mountain range known as Sylvan Spirits, not far from Hosseff's home.

This garden-valley was tormented and was like no other garden Mosley had ever seen. The vegetation seemed angry. The groups of trees, scattered throughout, appeared ghost-like. Their long limbs reached toward their neighbors and plucked their leaves, then tossed them to the ground, as if disgusted. The various forms of bushes were at war. They rustled, taunting one another in a territorial confrontation. They moved back and forth, removing their roots from the ground while invading another's domain. After establishing this new place of dominance, they would plant their roots to maintain their superiority until a bigger, stronger bush pushed them aside. Even the grass lamented. The transparent white blades moaned as the wind whipped across their tops. There was nothing peaceful about this place. The God of Death had clearly enjoyed creating his garden.

The Book, wanting a quiet place to speak, opened its heavy binding. A thick powder began to fill the air. It settled on the vegetation. It wasn't long before the trees' branches fell limp. The bushes stopped rustling and the cries of the grass silenced.

The Book did not give the wolf the chance to adjust to their surroundings or say anything, but rather, continued talking. The night terror wolf could only stare at the Book's black binding as the thin slit, functioning as its lips, opened and the words poured out.

"Mosley, I have much to say and only a few moments in which to say it. Listen carefully. Some of what I'm going to tell you will be upsetting, but emotions will need to wait. I realize none of this makes any sense. I assure you it will very soon. I ask you to be strong. When the moment is right, you can grieve.

"Bassorine has been destroyed. You are to become the new God of War. You are Bassorine's choice."

Mosley knew of the Book, but had never seen it before, nor did he understand its function. He struggled to set his surprise aside and instead, worked to focus on what had just been said.

"Destroyed? How could this be? There is no stronger pack leader than Bassorine. This is not possible, is it? What do you mean, I am to become a god? I am but a pup compared to Bassorine. Why would I be exalted? This does not make sense."

"There aren't the moments to explain. I can't afford for the others to know of our conversation. I must hurry. You're to be given godly power. It will be your job to fulfill Bassorine's role as the God of War. That's all I can say for now."

The Book of Immortality did not wait for a response. Instead, it began to impart the power of the gods to Mosley, enlightening him to their ways. The knowledge of everything the Book knew to be true (or rather, portrayed to be the truth) was forced into the wolf's mind like the destructive nature of an avalanche mowing down a tree-covered mountainside. Even the fact his wife was not waiting for him in Heaven and her soul only rested within the Book's many pages was now known. This hit Mosley hard. All he could do, for what seemed to be forever, was stare at the Book and wonder on which page her soul rested. Mosley tried to organize his thoughts, but found the information overwhelming.

"Mosley, I'm sorry for the abruptness of my actions. It may take a while for you to adjust. According to the laws within my pages, you're allowed to bestow two gifts on anyone you choose. You must say goodbye to those you love and return here, to live on Ancients Sovereign.

"The gifts cannot be wealth, knowledge, or love. They must be something to aid a person, or beast, through life. The gifts cannot give any one being or person the power to control the free will of others. Again, Mosley, I'm sorry for any inconvenience this may cause, but there are things which must be done, my friend, and done quickly to ensure the safety of Bassorine's secrets. They must be done to ensure the future. Search your memories. I've given you everything you were meant to know. The day grows short. Now go."

The Book disappeared, leaving Mosley to teleport himself to wherever he wanted. Mosley thought about it for a moment, then spoke out loud, but no one was there to listen, other than a few blades of grass which were beginning to wake and moan.

"What if I do not want to be a god? Do not get me wrong, I like the idea, but you could have at least asked first. Maybe I would have wanted to spend more of my moments on Grayham. I did not want to know there is not a Heaven or my wife's soul was put into a Book, even if the Book has a soul of its own. How can I get rid of this deep pain? I do not wish to mourn again. Can someone talk to me, please? What a way to give a god his power. This is anti-climactic."

Mosley always wanted to be like Bassorine and figured the Book of Immortality had this knowledge, but what an unremarkable way to make it happen. Thinking things through, he came to realize the power he held. He commanded the feelings for the loss of his wife to be hidden. He would deal with his emotions later. Once the pain subsided, he smiled.

Hmmmm, this god thing could come in handy. I bet I can mark all my territories at once from the highest of heights. I wonder how accurate I would be. This would drive all wolves mad.

Coming back to reality, the wolf knew he did not have the moments to ponder his territorial dominance. He had to be back on Ancients Sovereign by nightfall, and he couldn't say long goodbyes. He had to get going, but wanted to try on his new name for size.

"Hello, I am Mosley, God of War," he said aloud as he trotted around. "Hey, look at me. I am Mosley, the furry God of War." He liked how it sounded. There was a ring to it. As he bounced around the grass, the wolf felt a poke from behind. One of the bushes was awake and had decided it wanted to plant its roots where the wolf stood. The bush rustled as it tried to push itself into this new spot.

Mosley whipped around, and growled. The bush backed off. Delighted in his small victory, the wolf started to boast, "I am Mosley, the new, dynamic, vigorous, vehement, forceful God of War. Do not make me angry. Do not make me mark your territories with my godly smell." He lifted his back leg and peed in the bush's direction. The plant uprooted and hurried to another spot. Mosley flicked out a sharp nail. "Bow before me. This nail shall strike fear into the roots buried within this garden. I am to be feared. Do not mess with me or I shall breathe my mighty breath and make you slumber."

Another random thought popped into Mosley's head. His smile widened as he shouted, "To all the giant cats of the worlds, I will shed and you will choke on my deadly fur balls." The wolf laughed and said it again in many different ways. He could only hope his fighting skills were better than his ability to talk garesh, but he would have to find this out later.

For now, he concentrated on the fighter and, before he knew it, he was standing in front of Sam. Sam and Shalee were caught off guard by the sudden appearance. Shalee jumped back, raised her staff, and began to yell a command. Sam reacted by throwing himself into a defensive posture and raised his hands, ready to strike.

Mosley overreacted, closed his eyes, and used the same method of defense he had always used throughout his many seasons. He breathed on the humans in an effort to protect himself, a reaction not necessary for a god, but an old habit that would need to be changed.

Hearing two thuds, the wolf opened his eyes. Seeing the awkward position Sam had landed in, he shook his head and thought, *Ouch! That is not good. That had to hurt. Good thing I am a god or his leg would never mend before the fight.*

With a nod, Sam's leg slowly began to twist from beneath his weight, the crunching sounds of the bones stinging the wolf's ears as the appendage came to rest in its proper alignment. After a few more minor pops, the leg finished mending.

Another nod was given. The humans woke and stood from the floor. Mosley looked at their confused faces and gave a cute, wolfish grin as if nothing had ever happened. "Hey, guys, miss me?"

Shalee sighed. "Mosley, ya scared the bejesus out of me. Since when do ya know how ta pop in and about like that? How did I end up on the floor?"

"Yeah, what the heck?" Sam added.

Mosley was not sure where to begin. He decided he would answer questions later. "I have a lot to say, but most of it will have to wait. I will not answer questions, Sam. You have a fight to win. For now, I will say Bassorine has been destroyed. He is no longer the leader of his own pack."

"Destroyed? What are you talking about?" Sam snapped.

"That would qualify as a question, Sam. I said no questions until later. I need you to listen. I am here for a reason and need you to let me do what I came for. Bassorine was destroyed and it was his choice I take his place."

Mosley stuck out his furry chest. "I am the new God of War, but not as powerful as Bassorine...yet. More power will come, but for now, I must bestow two gifts on someone before returning to the god world. I am giving them both to you, Sam, if you will allow it."

"Okay, okay...hold on a moment. What do you mean by, 'bestow two gifts?' What do you mean, you took Bassorine's place and you're the new God of War?"

Mosley smiled. "Sam, you are unable to refrain from questions no matter what the situation. I expected as much. Allow me to put it this way. All you need to know is, I am one of the gods. I am here to give you two gifts. Do you want them or not?"

Sam looked at the wolf. He didn't believe a word Mosley was saying, but figured it would be best to play along. He was dying to ask another question, but thought better of it. "Well, of course I want them. Anyone would want a gift. Lay it on me, buddy."

Sam spoke with a touch of innocent sarcasm and a big smile on his face. Despite his lack of belief in the things the wolf said, the last series of moments he doubted something on this world, a sword scolded him for his ignorance and tapped him on his chin. He didn't want to look foolish again.

Mosley sniffed the corners of the room as he continued. "We both know your rise to glory is going to be a savage journey. What I want to do is help speed your quest. The gifts I can bestow will assist you through life."

Mosley stopped in one of the corners and curled his nose at the foul stench. A spot of blood had been spilled by one of the arena's combatants while being attended by healers. "Nasty. This man smelled as bad as you, Sam. The men of your species carry a horrid odor."

"Okay, okay, already. I get it. I stink. Can you just get on with what the gifts are, rather than bash on me about how bad I smell? Gees, Mosley, what kind of friend are you?"

Shalee covered her grin with her hand and waited for the wolf to respond. "As I was about to say, I have thought about what to give you, Sam, and my decision is this; you will receive two gifts to assist in the arenas of Grayham. I want these gifts to increase your ability to fight and be a natural part of your body."

Sam's excitement was evident. Maybe he wouldn't be so hasty and give his four-legged friend some credit. He was practically crawling out of his skin as the new god continued.

"I will bless you with greater natural strength for the first gift. You will be able to lift your body weight, amplified by six, above your head. For the second, I will endow you with greater natural reflexes. This will allow you to move quicker and respond as fast as your mind can think. We both know this is fairly fast. You would like both of these gifts, yes? With this blessing, you might even be classified as a real fighter."

Sam was like a child in a candy store. He could not stand still, waiting for Mosley to tell him what to do. His doubt in his furry friend vanished. "Okay, okay, yes, yes, and yes! What do I have to do? Did I tell you, Mosley, you're now my favorite god?"

Mosley laughed and looked at Shalee who was just as excited about Sam's gifts as he was. "I think he is going to get an aneurism from all the excitement," Mosley chided.

Shalee nodded. "I agree. So what does he have ta do?"

"Nothing. There are benefits to being a god," Mosley replied. "Sam has to do nothing other than allow me to let the gifts flow into him."

Without hesitation, Sam readied himself. "Okay, okay, start flowing."

Mosley walked over and touched one of his paws to Sam's left foot. The transfer of power was instantaneous. The fighter felt an electrifying surge move through his body. Not painful, but rather a soothing current which massaged his insides as his body accepted the gifts. He could feel his strength increasing. His feet felt light as he watched his body change. He looked at Shalee to confirm what he thought he was seeing was actually happening. He saw her nod. His body was growing bigger and stronger.

Shalee stood aside and could see the effects the gifts were having. Sam's height was increasing as she watched his mass grow. His legs, arms, chest, back, and neck all became thicker and, to her wondrous delight, that was not all. She loved this new Sam, but his new look was just as wonderful as before. She had always desired him.

Sam's new six-inch-taller frame balanced the additional weight. He had just enough body fat to look healthy. His shoes burst open, allowing for the growth. His pants were not only too short, but shredded. Shalee grabbed Sam's old pair of fighting trunks and made him put them on. Sam dropped his pants and, for the first series of moments since their arrival, Shalee saw the fighter in all his glory. His shoulders were broad, arms were like cannons, his neck thick and his jaw line had tightened enough to accent the perfection. His abdomen called to her—and the rest, well—Sam was perfection.

Shalee lost herself in this new look, admiring what she longed for since they met. The staff was a grand thing, but now Sam would get all her attention. The moment had arrived for her to become Sam's.

Shalee ran off at the mouth, saying things which were out of character and downright unladylike—things best left to the imagination as she stared at his body. Sam and Mosley could only look at her in shock.

Embarrassed, realizing what she had said and blushing bright red, Shalee apologized. "I'm so sorry. I don't normally act a fool. I don't know what came ova' me. Goodness-gracious, it's just so hot in here. Can we forget I said any of that?"

Sam looked at the new god and winked. "Looks like you've given me more than two gifts, Mosley. The ladies won't be able to resist me now."

He turned to Shalee and smiled. "I'm glad you like the look. I've always liked yours as well." He addressed Mosley once again. "You really know how to hook a guy up, my friend."

Sam looked over his new six-foot-four inch, 275 pound frame and marveled at its splendor. Excited, he blurted out without thinking, "Well, I'm sure I can inseminate some strong babies with Shalee now. What do you think, Mosley?"

Mosley rolled his eyes at the humans. Neither of them had much self-control.

Shalee looked at Sam. Her mood went from anxious embarrassment to utter surprise and soft-heartedness. She moved to him, looked into his eyes, and spoke with a softness as she held his gaze. "You look at me special like? You see me as the woman you would want ta have your children? If I had known, I would have neva' walked out of the room the otha' day and made you believe I didn't feel the same for ya. I've always found ya attractive, Sam. I promise, I'll neva' play ya, again. If ya still want me, I'm yours."

Mosley rolled his eyes, feeling awkward as Sam pulled Shalee close and kissed her. "Oh, I want you. You can believe that," he breathed. "You're forgiven for the other day and just so you know, I spoke with Mosley about how to pursue you. I was willing to enjoy your desire to play hard to get. This new look just made my job a little easier, it seems. If it's all right with you, I would like to skip the part of chasing after you."

Shalee smiled and stroked Sam's face, saying everything without speaking a word. They allowed each other to feel the passion they had both avoided. He kissed her again in farewell and headed outside to the village. He wanted to find a new pair of leather pants before entering the arena. There were only four more fights before they would call his name.

Shalee stood in complete silence. Her heart was at peace. No woman on Grayham could be happier than she was. After a few moments of watching,

Mosley broke the silence. "Hmmmm, hmmmm, I hate to ruin your desire to mate, but I need you to listen. Did Sam tell you everything Bassorine told him? Do you know your pack on Earth was destroyed?"

Shalee frowned at the way Mosley phrased his question, but answered despite her irritation. "He told me some of it, but I was so tired. I know Earth was destroyed and I'm not sure how I feel or how ta deal with it. I miss so many people and it's hard ta believe they're gone. I have been tryin' not ta think 'bout it. It hurts a' plenty. When I've got the moments ta think, all I do is cry." Tears began to run down her face.

"Shalee, Bassorine brought you here for the purpose of mating with Sam. He hoped the two of you would form a union and have pups of your own, but it appears Sam failed to tell you this part."

Shalee wiped away the tears and responded with a sniffling chuckle. "That lil' devil, he was gonna pursue me no matta' what I said. I could've played much harder ta get if I'd known. I think that's so cute. It's downright adorable."

"I am glad you feel that way," Mosley sighed, "but there is a much bigger reason you are here...much, much bigger than having Sam's cubs."

"As if havin' his kids isn't enough of a responsibility, already. What else can ya throw at me? Motherhood can be a real challenge, ya know."

"I am sure you are right. What I did not know, until after being enlightened and receiving my power from the Book, was Bassorine told the Book of Immortality many secrets after its creation. Did Sam tell you about the Book of Immortality?"

Shalee thought a moment. "He said its pages are where the souls of everyone go since Heaven and Hell were destroyed. It all sounds entirely made up and fake ta me."

Mosley sat on his haunches and scratched the fur on his neck with his left rear paw. "That is part of what the Book does. It also holds the laws of the gods. The gods have to live by this charter no matter what." The wolf thought a moment. "The information I am about to share with you was given by Bassorine and protected by the Book of Immortality. Bassorine did not share this information with anyone else. I would not know this now, but it was Bassorine's wish I be told. Bassorine instructed the Book to divulge this information, only if something happened. The Book and Bassorine created many plans of their own, though I do not know to what extent or how this planning may affect the future."

The wolf took a deep breath. "One thing I do know, you will grow quickly and have abilities far greater than any sorceress before you. Your gods of Earth spoke with Bassorine before you were born. It was a secret meeting which only Bassorine and these earthly manifestations knew about. It was during this meeting he asked these gods not to divulge the information they shared between them...and they didn't, making sure they kept this pact sacred.

"Your gods were asked to give you the ability to absorb the energies which live all around you. Bassorine asked them to allow you to channel these energies at a much higher level than those who are normally able to do so. He requested you be given a gentle heart and a strong will. This is why you learn so quickly and are so kind. This is also why you are so stubborn and display a bit of drama. You have the ability to become a goddess without having to ascend. You could be the most powerful woman, even more powerful than the gods on Ancients Sovereign, without having to leave for the God World."

"My Lord in Heaven! If my motha' was here, she would soil her pajamas ta know her lil' girl was so blessed. Wow! A goddess! I don't know 'bout that. I would need a much betta' wardrobe than this old thing. And, what do ya mean by 'energies,' anyway?"

"I do not think it is possible for me to describe these energies, literally. Allow me to improvise. I will call them miniature beings which cannot be seen, living all around everyone. They are beings only certain souls can absorb. They flow into your body when you command magic and become a permanent part of you."

"So, you're tellin' me these lil' life forces enter my body and stay there? What happens once they're inside me?"

Mosley smiled at her concern and began gnawing between his legs searching for a source of irritation. He managed to continue their conversation during his exploration. "Let us say they are the building blocks of the magical foundation within your soul. The bigger you can make your foundation, the stronger you will become. The power you will come to command will be tremendous. You..."

Shalee interrupted. "Why would Bassorine ask the gods of Earth ta do this? Why would he choose me?"

"It was not that Bassorine specifically chose you, but it was more a matter of your birth order. After they spoke of Sam's abilities and what skills he would carry throughout life, they sent him to Earth. The gods then found an imperfect soul. Your soul, Shalee, was also incomplete. Joining both imperfections provided the perfect union. I do not know further details or how to explain what this means. You were simply incomplete. This was the only way for the gods to fix your deformity."

"So, you're sayin' I'm special only because I was screwed up? Well if that doesn't just put a damper on things. How's a girl supposed ta live life knowin' she was no betta' than a mutt? I..."

Mosley stopped her short. "I know many mutts who have lived valued lives, Shalee. Be careful who you insult. Mutts have feelings, too. It would appear you are flawed. According to the knowledge the Book of Immortality passed to me, Bassorine has plans for you, but I do not know all of what they are. He was the God of War for a reason, and he never failed to create a strategy."

"I thought ya said Bassorine was dead. How could he have plans for me? Don't ya mean, he *had* plans for me?"

"I said what I meant to say, Shalee. Bassorine has plans for you.   This plan involves the Book. When the Book of Immortality was created, Bassorine liked the idea of its creation, but he did not trust the others. If any of the gods found a way to take control of the Book, someone would need to be strong enough to take it back. You are the only one who will be able to summon the power necessary to take back this control. I know nothing more of Bassorine's plans for you."

Shalee stood in silence. After contemplating everything said, she responded. "Goodness-gracious, Mosley, I'm not powerful enough ta fight the gods. I can't even fathom the concept."

"You will be able to, someday, Shalee, I assure you. The only reason I am able to tell you this now is because the others do not know I have been given my power. This is my only chance to say anything without the worry of being watched. The Book of Immortality knows you could be the only thing to protect its existence. Make no mistake...there are those living on the hidden god world who are deceitful and hungry for power."

"I believe ya. I can only imagine. With that kinda power there must be a ton of temptation ta go with it. So what do I do?"

"You will become powerful as I have said, but this power will make you the prey of others. I want you to be careful, and even though you are going to learn how to command magic like no one has done before, unexpected danger will find you because of it. Do not use your power unless you must. Try to avoid attention."

Shalee laughed in frustration. "Sam Hill, how can I become powerful if I don't use my power? It doesn't work that way. I have ta use it in orda' ta grow. It sounds like I'm screwed. This is a sure-fire damned if I do and damned if I don't situation."

"I understand how your power works, Shalee, and I know you must command it to grow. I agree you find yourself sitting on the blade of a double-edged sword. It is up to you to find a balance and try to grow without attracting attention. You can do what you want, but consider yourself warned. You will know when you have become strong enough to worry, then you can make the needed adjustments. I must go before I run short of moments. I have many goodbyes to say before I leave. I suspect, someday, you will join me on the god world. Speak of this conversation to no one, not even Sam."

"Doggone it, Mosley, why can't I tell Sam?"

Mosley sighed. "You will be putting Sam in danger if he knows. I will protect your thoughts so this information cannot be stolen. Guard it well."

The wolf touched his paw to her foot to protect her thoughts. Shalee asked him what he meant. He simply said, "Trust me. Just remember, I am the only one of the gods who has the knowledge of what Bassorine has done. Do not speak of this, and protect those you love. Will you please tell Sam I forgive him for not saying goodbye, and I understand his excitement? I wish the best for him during his fight. I also wish you well. I'm sure this will not be the last series of moments in which we speak. You can help Sam with your abilities if you put your mind to it, but I cannot tell you how to do so."

With that, the new Wolf-God of War vanished.

The Fight

Sam was angry when he came back from his unsuccessful search for a new pair of pants and Shalee was dying inside because she could not tell him anything Mosley had told her. Sam returned with an issue. This issue gave Shalee a chance to focus on something else. She had never been good at keeping secrets, but then again, she had never known a secret of this importance.

Sam had worked himself into a panic and was storming around the room. "I can't go out there looking like this! I will be the laughing stock of the village. These trunks are too tight. I look like a giant Richard Simmons. Paint me green and I would look like a queer hulk. I'll be damned before I go out there looking like a freak. You should see how the people of the village were staring at me in these stupid shorts."

Shalee smiled and threw Sam his old pair of torn leather pants. "Goodness-gracious, we can't have ya lookin' silly like, now can we? Why don't ya put these on as best ya can. I got me an idea."

"Why would I do that? They don't fit!"

"Sam Goodrich, don't ya make me stomp this purdy lil' Texas foot on the ground," she said, not liking his tone. "I said put 'em on as best ya can. Now git. I wanna try somethin'. I have an idea. I just might be able ta fix your pants and your boots."

Sam did as he was told and pulled on the shredded mess. He watched as Shalee raised her staff and pointed it at him. "Wait! What the heck are you doing? I don't want you using your magic on me. What if you screw up? Save all the hocus pocus for someone else. My gosh."

"You shush up and stop bein' such a baby," Shalee poked. "I know what I'm doin'. Just stand there and be quiet. I need ta concentrate."

Once again, she lifted her staff and pointed it at the leather pants. "Precious, *lanne*," she shouted with an authority that surprised Sam.

To the fighter's amazement, the leather started to grow and add to itself as if it were alive. It did not take long before he was standing in a perfectly formed piece of clothing.

"Holy cow! That's incredible! I can't believe this!" Sam stopped and took the moments necessary to adjust his mind. "I'm going to thank you for this later," he promised, lifting her in the air and planting a big kiss on her cheek.

Shalee enjoyed the affection, but in the back of her mind, she realized the staff had not rewarded her for the success. There would be no more tears of joy and she knew the intimate relationship with her petrified, wooden friend would soon be over. However, she grinned, she had a replacement—her relationship with Sam. The transition could not have been more perfect. She wanted to make Sam happy.

Sam lowered her to the floor. Shalee commanded Precious to repair his boots. Like the pants, the leather mended itself and formed perfectly to his feet. Sam bent over to kiss her again as BJ walked into the room. All the trainer could see was the large back of a much bigger man. Not recognizing his student, the trainer turned to excuse himself, thinking he was in the wrong place.

Sam called to him, "BJ, wait. Don't go!"

The trainer reentered the room, and stood there, stunned. BJ could see it was Sam's face, but nothing else resembled the person he knew. He rubbed his eyes as if he was in some sort of dream and looked again.

"Sam...is it really you?"

"Yes, yes, it's me. You won't believe me when I tell you. I've been given two gifts by our new God of War, Mosley."

The trainer pondered a moment before speaking. "If you mean your size, I can see that. But, aren't you referring to the wolf? Isn't Mosley the wolf? Bassorine is the God of War."

Before Sam could respond, the bell of the arena sounded. It was his turn to fight. On the way out of the room, he told BJ he would explain everything later and made sure the trainer would study his fight. He wanted to get as much feedback as possible.

Sam was the first to enter the arena. He still did not know who his opponent was. As he entered, the crowd cheered. The atmosphere reminded him of the professional fight he had in Vegas, except for being outside and the mat being made of sand. The arena and style of fighting were far different than anything he had ever known, but the screams of the crowd were the same. He raised his hands into the air and allowed himself to enjoy the moment.

He walked across the sandy surface to his position and grabbed his wooden stave. He moved it around and was surprised his actions were much quicker than they were while training with BJ. *With Mosley's gifts, I can open up a can of godly whoop-ass. BJ's going to flip when he watches this fight.*

Then—Sam's opponent entered the arena. As if a light switch was toggled, Sam's demeanor changed. He was all business as he sized up the man who moved across the arena floor to take his place. His adversary was a few inches shorter and much thinner. He did not look to be much of a threat until he started to move the wooden stave around with great precision. Sam had never seen anything like it. The man's movements were so fast. He muttered under his breath, "This is going to hurt. So much for godly whoop-ass."

As Sam crossed the arena to engage the opposition, he reminded himself there were no rules. In this world, a fight was a fight. No matter what happened, there was no referee. It did not matter if he took a shot to the groin, head-butt to the face, had sand thrown in his eyes, or any other cheap shot—he still had to fight his way through it all. It was the truest form of fighting in which a man could compete.

The wooden staves collided hard, echoing across the arena as the people began to cheer. A quick crushing elbow smashed into the side of Sam's head, followed by another stinging strike by his opponent's stave flat against his upper back. Sam had watched the man spin effortlessly as he moved from one strike to the next. The force of the blow to his back made his nerves scream and was strong enough to knock him into a stumbling fall, but Sam managed to control it by rolling to his feet. Though a severe blow, he once again stood ready to defend. The pain sent a thunderous message—pay attention.

His adversary attacked with the tip of his stave. The thrust, part of a combination of moves, was meant for Sam's belly, but he blocked it. A spinning leg followed, however, knocking Sam to the ground on his back.

As he fell, Sam saw the man continue the sweep to his feet, and followed this graceful movement with another powerful, potentially life-ending downward strike. Again, Sam managed to block the advance just before it made contact. The strike was forceful. If it had crushed into the side of Sam's head, the fight would have been over, as well as his life.

Sam brought up his left leg, twisting for the right angle as he did, and slammed his foot hard into the backside of the man's knees. This brought his foe to the ground, but he managed to land on his knees, ready to swing. Sam rolled and managed to avoid the wicked slice. He felt the rush of air as the weapon passed.

He stood and backed up, taking the moments necessary to regain his composure. He moved far enough away to think and began to replay the downward strike meant for his head in his photographic memory. His opponent was trying to do far worse than make him quit. Even the swing which missed his face was powerful enough to cause permanent damage. His rival was not trying to make him submit—he was trying to mutilate him.

Again, Sam reviewed each attempted strike in his mind. He felt like a dog backed into a corner. He was out of his element, and now, his fear needed to be channeled. He had no choice but to turn his fear into an angry storm. If he failed to do this, he would die.

Sam closed his eyes, looked deep within, then opened them. This round, he would deliver the pain. He no longer had an opponent. He had an enemy. Sam began to circle as his anger grew with each breath.

The man rose from his knees. Noting the change in Sam's eyes, he approached with caution. Some moments passed as they sized each other up. Suddenly, the man threw himself into a roll as Sam's raging mind took control and slowed every movement. Sam watched his enemy come out of his roll and attempt to deliver a strike, but Sam was ready and blocked it. His mind continued to slow the advances, blocking three other strikes meant for his head, stomach, and groin. Sam countered with a punch which pounded his enemy's temple. The hilt of his wooden stave assisted the blow's impact, his knuckles sinking deeper than normal.

Stunned, his rival tried to reach out, but Sam spun away, escaping the man's grasp, keeping him off balance. As he exited his spin, Sam sent his stave cutting through the air toward his enemy's reaching forearms. Using his new god-given strength, Sam brought the wooden weapon down as hard as he could. His foe's left arm was pulverized, snapping like a twig. A loud cracking filled the air, sending the crowd into a frenzy.

Sam watched his enemy's wooden stave fall to the ground, but despite the pain in his arm, the man moved to retrieve the weapon. Sam's inner demon no longer allowed him to feel compassion. His rage had grown far too great and he was now out of control. The sound of the man's arm breaking, along with the crowd's cheers, fueled the fire inside of his hardened heart. He wanted vengeance for the attempt on his life, and once again, he replayed both strikes in his mind.

Sam kicked his foe in the head, stopping him from retrieving his stave. He waited for the man to regain his composure and allowed for his arm to reach out to grab his weapon. As he did, Sam's blade cut through the air again and broke the man's right arm as it made contact. Another loud snapping crackle could be heard, but now it was not only his opponent's arm which broke. The contact was so severe the wood of Sam's weapon splintered into many pieces.

Realizing his stave was useless as an offensive tool, Sam adjusted. He snatched his adversary's limp arms and twisted. He enjoyed the man's cries as his broken bones ground against each other. Sam yanked unmercifully, feeling the limpness as if they were wet noodles. His enemy fell forward. Unable to catch himself, the man's face broke his fall, slamming into the sandy surface of the arena as his scream of pain pushed the sand from beneath his mouth.

With no opposition, Sam's next strike was wide open. His enemy was unable to lift from the ground to defend himself in any manner. Sam's rage-filled insanity took no note of this helplessness and, without hesitation, he jumped into the air and landed with a crushing knee to the base of the man's neck. Another loud crunching sound covered the man's cry of surrender. The screaming fans were fueled by the noise, the force of the strike leaving his opponent out cold. Sam was fighting like a merciless, rabid dog, unable to think of anything but the all-out victory.

He reached for the broken right arm and twisted it into a triangulated position behind his foe's back. The man woke from his unconscious state, but would not have the chance to call out his surrender. Sam's boiling adrenaline ignored his enemy's defenseless position as he raised his right leg high into the air and brought all of his two hundred seventy-five pound frame down as hard as he could. The blow landed on top of the enemy's shoulder blade between the scapula and the man's spine. The force of the knee was enough to break not only the scapula, but also the ribs beneath. The ribs tore violently away from the spine and, once again, bone-crushing sounds filled the arena.

The spectators did not cheer. They had become quiet, understanding the severity of what was happening to the fallen warrior. They all knew this fight was not one meant to be to the death, but Sam's mind was cold and still in full survival mode. He was unable to consider the man's future, nor was he able to feel compassion as he was *sure* the man would kill him. His fury forced him to keep going. Sam was now an insane torturer, not a fighter.

He rolled off the dead body and toward his foe's stave. His mind was clouded, unable to realize his enemy was already dead. He delivered another series of thunderous blows, striking over and over again to the back, arms, and head, tearing away at them like an enraged beast. Sam was lost to his own gentle soul, which for the moment could not claim him and turned away in rebuke. It was not until after a voice cried out from the crowd to stop, that he stopped.

It was Shalee—the only voice strong enough to bring him back from his insanity. Hearing her voice, Sam became aware of the man's lifeless body and his feelings returned as what was left of the gentleness of his spirit embraced him.

The compassion of the doctor brought forth a sorrowful remorse over what he had done. He stopped, backed away from the body, and grabbed his head with his free hand. Rage turned to disbelief, then horror and finally, a tragic grief-filled sorrow.

He moved in and knelt on one knee. Slowly, he lowered the weapon to the ground and frantically reached to feel for a pulse. Nothing, not a single beat could be found. A wave of emotion swept through him as he realized the consequences of what he had done. He fell back to a sitting position, brought his knees up, buried his head in his forearms, and wept.

The crowd was silent—not a whisper or comment, only shocked looks as they stared down at the arena floor watching Sam wail. The only sound heard was his sobbing. This was the first life he had ever taken. He had not only taken the life, but lost himself while doing it. He knew he was now a murderer, the antithesis of a healing physician. Mr. Hyde had temporarily controlled the good Dr. Jekyll, and as a result, left him with a heavy heart, making it nearly impossible to move. He knew his father would not have approved.

BJ calmed the nobles and instructed them it would be a good series of moments in which to leave. Once everyone cleared the box, the trainer ran to the arena where Sam continued to sit. BJ had been in many fights in his life and knew full well the emotions his distraught pupil was feeling. He once lost control in the arena himself and paralyzed a young boy of only 18 seasons.

BJ arrived to find Shalee sitting with Sam in her arms, doing her best to comfort him. BJ reached down and lifted her up, motioning for her to come a few steps away.

"Young lady, I admire your efforts to comfort, but Sam's pain is something you cannot fix. Until you have felt the destruction of the arenas, you can't understand his torture. Go back to the inn and wait. I will bring Sam to you once we have spoken. He has broken no laws and will face no consequences."

BJ cupped Shalee's chin, forcing her eyes to find his. "The result of this fight is a good thing. The gossip which will spread will work in Sam's favor. As he fights in the arenas of Grayham, his opponents will know of this outcome. This will instill fear in the hearts of weaker men. This is a glorious day."

Shalee failed to understand BJ's candor. The barbarism of this world made her sick to her stomach. She whispered, "My Lord in Heaven, how can killin' a man be okay, BJ? It's just not right, I tell ya. I should stay with him. He needs me. Killin' isn't okay where we're from. You don't understand us, BJ. You can't understand us. It's just not possible."

BJ walked Shalee to the arena gate and removed a torch from the wall. He handed the light source to her. "Do as I say and go. Men are the same, no matter where we are from. You will listen, young lady and trust a man with my seasons understands the struggles of battle. This is not up for debate. Now go."

Frustrated, Shalee did as BJ commanded. She motioned to Helga she was ready and was grateful she had a friend to talk with. However, before she left, Shalee turned to BJ and gave a command of her own.

"Ya betta' tell Sam I'm here for him. When you're done with all yer conversin', he'll need me. Don't ya eva' doubt that." Having said what she needed to, Shalee left.

BJ shook his head, grabbed a torch of his own and walked over to stand above Sam. The trainer watched as the arena morticians carried the dead away on a stretcher with three slave boys holding light sources to guide their way. The sun had fallen behind the horizon and now the pitch black of night was upon them.

He turned his attention to the weeping fighter and lowered the torch. As the light flickered off Sam's crouched posture, BJ's voice turned fatherly. "Get up, son. Be the man you need to be. I'm not about to let any student of mine sit there and feel sorry for himself. Stand up, dust yourself off, and act like a true warrior."

Sam lifted his head and let out a penetrating cry of remorse. "Aahhhhh-hhhhh!" His cry served to finish corralling the demon roaming through the depths of his mind and forced it back to its hiding spot.

BJ was patient and watched as his student stood, brushed himself off, and began to walk toward the arena's gate. BJ followed and again used a fatherly voice while moving into a better position to walk alongside. "I know how you feel, Sam. I once paralyzed a boy after becoming enraged. The arenas of this world carry with them much emotion and just as much death. You aren't the first to kill someone. You will come to terms with this tragedy, I promise. In a short while, your name will be known throughout the world. You are going to be considered great."

BJ put his arm around his fighter, encouraging him all the way to the inn. When they arrived, they stopped outside. The trainer spoke sternly, but softly. "Sam, I want you to look into my eyes. Let me know you've heard everything I've said."

"I heard you," Sam replied. "I just don't know how to move on from here. I've never killed a man before. How do you move on from something like this? This goes against everything I believe. I was trained to be a doctor. I never wished to be a murderer. This is contra to being a healer."

"You *don't* get over this. A man must learn from his experiences and use them to grow into a better warrior. You've done something awful. I understand your pain. I also have beliefs and values, but sometimes we must adapt in order to survive. You'll be okay, son, and you will find peace. You're a fighter. We all understand the risk involved when entering the arena.

"The opponent you faced tonight has killed twelve men. I didn't know this until one of the nobles mentioned it. I would have stopped the fight, but it's against the laws of Grayham to do so. Only you and the man you faced could stop it. If you hadn't killed him, he might have killed you."

Sam thought a moment and realized BJ was right. "Okay, okay, I see your point. I agree. He would have killed me. This is a tough pill to swallow. I need the moments necessary to think."

BJ sighed. "I can tell you how I got over my anxieties if you want to know, but you must take me seriously. You should do exactly as I suggest. Are you going to listen?"

"I promise. Please tell me what to do," Sam said, expecting to hear some kind of great wisdom from the older man.

The trainer nodded. "You have something going for you. Upstairs you have a beautiful woman, and there is no better counsel than a woman's touch. I want you to do what I did when I needed the chance to heal. Go up there and allow her to fix this. Women have a way of making things better. Shalee can make your pain seem less invasive and you'll heal faster. If you don't feel better in the morning, I want you to come and find me."

BJ pulled Sam close and gave him a hug. "You'll be okay, son, I promise. You and I are going to be close. You're growing on me."

Sam smiled and returned the embrace. "I could use a friend right now. Thanks, BJ...you're not so bad after all."

After a moment, Sam entered the inn. As he did, almost every face in the place stopped and turned to watch him pass on his way up the stairs. The news of his victory had already reached this far and no one uttered a word. Sam took a deep breath as he stood in front of the door to his room. He turned the knob and entered.

To Sam's surprise, Shalee greeted him with open arms. She did not speak, nor did she try to make anything better. As he walked across the room to greet her, another tremor shook the village for nearly five breaths.

Sam's demeanor changed as he pulled Kael from his sheath. Sam looked at the blade and commanded it to speak. "Kael, tell me all you know of the Crystal Moon's inability to govern Grayham."

Shalee watched in awe as the blade lifted from Sam's hand and began to float in front of the fighter. The pulsating light of the weapon created an eerie feeling throughout the dimly lit room as the blade responded. "I know nothing more, other than the Crystal Moon has lost its ability to govern the land masses of this world. There needs to be urgency in all you wish to accomplish. Sam, you and BJ need to begin your travels to the arenas of Grayham and fight your way to a visit with kings. You need power to solve a problem of this magnitude. The only way to accomplish this is to stand before the King of Brandor and challenge him for this power."

"And, how does one man challenge a king?" Sam snapped.

As Kael lowered back to Sam's hand, he simply responded, "We have discussed this already. You need to be a leader. A leader does not ask, he shows."

Sam stared at Kael, speechless as the blade came to rest in his hand. After a long series of moments, he looked up to find Shalee's eyes as the lantern resting on the table flickered.

Shalee could see his despair as she pulled Sam close. After sitting with him on the edge of the bed, she held him. She lifted his chin from her bosom and wiped the tears from his eyes. Leaning forward, she kissed him ever so softly. "What are ya gonna do, Sam? Whateva' it is, I'll stand beside ya."

Sam reached up and wiped the tears from his cheeks. After breathing in and filling his chest with a much needed wind, he responded. "I'm going to be the best. I will suffer the brutality of this world and see to it the people have a home. I will not allow their lives to be taken from them the way ours have."

As Sam continued, his eyes held Shalee's with conviction. "They want an empire...we'll give them one. The two of us will show this world something they have never seen before. We have no choice. We must be the leaders the people need. We just need to figure out how."

Shalee's smile widened. "Goodness-gracious, Mr. Sam Goodrich, that was downright sexy. You just turned this lil' Texas beauty on. Come here. You can talk like that ta me wheneva' ya want."

She brushed her lips across the areas of his face. Her cheeks met his, their warmth causing him to become excited. When she closed her mouth across the top of his ear and began to nibble, Sam was lost. He took control and pulled her toward him with an enjoyable intensity Shalee had never experienced. Their longing for one another fueled their passion as they loved away the night.

The Grayham Inquirer

When Inquiring Minds Need to Know about their Favorite Characters

IT'S A NEW DAY on Grayham, and the moments to rise and shine have arrived. Sam is lying with Shalee's head on his chest. The night had been explosive and ohhhh so passionate. Shalee feels satisfied and her heart is filled with love. BJ was right. Sam feels much better. The lovers decide to snuggle before getting up.

THE BOOK OF IMMORTALITY is preparing the ceremony to honor Bassorine's passing. The event will be held on top of the Falls of Faith where Bassorine used to sit when he wanted to think. Once the ceremony ends, the Collective will turn their attention to other things, just as if the late God of War never existed.

GEORGE, KEPLER, and KROGER kept their campfire going throughout the night. In an effort to help, the demon-jaguar offered to use his saliva on George's leg. The cat's spit has healing qualities and better yet, an instantaneous soothing effect. The wounds on George's leg have started to mend. They will go over the plan George made once more before entering the cave.

BJ and HELGA are meeting for breakfast to discuss Sam's fight. As they talk, they find they have much in common. Although neither speaks of it, there is a romantic interest growing between them.

CELESTRIA is making the best of her stay with the witch family, teaching new potion recipes. She can't believe the family calls themselves witches. They are idiots, but she knows they will not draw attention to her baby after he is born.

MOSLEY woke up inside his new home. Bassorine left behind a perfect place and the wolf is admiring his new view. He is standing outside, looking across the valley below and taking deep breaths from high atop Catalyst Mountain.

LASIDIOUS is thinking through his plans for the near future. He misses Celestria and knows the moment is approaching for him to step down as his team's leader. He's okay with the change as it is just one more part of his master plan.

Thank you for reading the Grayham Inquirer

Daddy, Help Me

The Cave of Sorrow

George took a deep breath. "Let's go over the plan once more before you go inside, Kep. Kroger and I will stay out here to give you the moments necessary to find a spot to hide within the cave's shadows. We'll wait until you're set, then I'll climb to the top of the cave's entrance and hide while Kroger bangs his club into the ground to capture The Beast's attention. Hopefully, he'll be curious and come see what all the commotion is about. If he does, it should lead him past you. I want you to push him out. Remember, you'll need to stop short of the entrance. We don't know how the spell The Beast uses to control it works. Once Maldwin is out, I will kill him with my gun. If I'm unsuccessful, Kroger can bash him."

George looked at his companions. "Do you understand it may take a while for The Beast to hear the commotion and come looking? It is, after all, one hell of a big cave. I'm counting on the walls inside to echo the sound of Kroger's club."

Kepler and Kroger nodded. The demon headed inside as George set the timer on his Rolex. After a couple of hours, he climbed to the top of the cave and signaled for Kroger to start pounding on the spot he previously circled on the ground.

Ancients Sovereign

Mosley awoke and stepped outside onto the porch of Bassorine's old home high atop Catalyst Mountain. The view was breathtaking and the air smelled of pine. The cabin overlooked two valleys, one to the east, one to the west, and both were filled with grazing animals. Bassorine gave the mountain its name. This had been the late God of War's way to remember the many wars he had been the influence behind, or better yet, catalyst of.

The home itself was not unique, but none of the others within the Collective lived in anything like it. Bassorine was rugged and the dwelling left behind was nothing more than what those of us from old Earth would have called a log cabin. And now, with Bassorine's destruction, the home fit Mosley's tastes as well as he sniffed around to mark his new territory.

Today was a special day for the night terror wolf. He would have his chance to meet the others. The Book of Immortality said his introduction would be short and to expect a rush of interest after Bassorine's Passing Ceremony.

He spent a good portion of the night howling his delight at the many different abilities he now possessed. All of them were useful, but he especially liked the fact he could conjure a rare corgan steak and it would appear before him. He enjoyed three or four before he went to sleep, ignoring the fact he would never need to eat again if he chose not to.

It was important to look good for the ceremony, knowing the others were snobs. A bath, no matter how much he hated the thought, was in order, not wanting to turn up noses. He knew Luvera, if she were here to see this day, would be proud as the tub of hot water appeared before him with nothing more than a simple nod of his snout. He grumbled as he put the first of his paws in and pretended to speak to his lost love. "This is not wolf-like, Luvera. This is unnecessary torture and unbecoming for a beast of my stature."

Now...fellow soul...for Mosley being such a smart wolf, he sure didn't use his head on this one. Sure, he thought far enough to create his own bath water and make it appear in front of him, but I find it funny he failed to think beyond the idea of a simple bath. A smarter use of his godly power was all it took to clean himself without water being involved. I'm sure he's going to be upset once he finally realizes he bathed unnecessarily. Poor wolf. Anyway, back to the story.

The Cave of Sorrow

Hours passed while George sat above the cave's entrance. Kroger continued to slam his club into the ground. The noise was taxing to George's nerves. A hole formed at the center of the clearing as a result of the devastating slamming—a good five feet across and equally as deep, with the trees resting atop the pass shaking with every hit. George told himself it might take a while, but he had not calculated the boredom he would feel sitting in one spot for so long.

Suddenly, to his surprise, something scurried out which could not have been The Beast. The creature was not hideous at all. George opened and closed his eyes in disbelief, straining to get a better look. It was a large dark brown rat, yet small enough to fit in his pack. He watched as the rat rose up in front of Kroger and looked toward the giant.

The ogre grabbed his head, lowered to the ground, and once he was sitting on his large butt, started to cry. George knew for sure, by the way Kroger was reacting, the rat was Maldwin. The visions had an instantaneous effect on the giant. George realized he needed to protect himself before anything else happened. Reading from the scroll purchased from Morre, the giant's booming cry covered his voice as he spoke the words necessary to release the spell, shielding his mind. As before, when he used the snare scroll, the paper vanished into thin air when finished.

A new plan was in order. The original plan wasn't going to work. Kroger was no longer useful. George knew his pistol would do the job since The Beast was small, but his intentions had changed and shooting the rodent was now a last resort.

Watching from above, George observed the way the rat's visions affected Kroger. A new idea was beginning to form. He would make his presence known and act in a similar fashion as the ogre. Instead of sitting on his butt and crying, he would feign his sadness to get close enough to the creature to trap it. Adding the rat's abilities to his new group would be a benefit. If Maldwin's ability was salvageable, killing him would be a waste.

He climbed down from the top of the cave, careful to make as little noise as possible. For the moment, Maldwin had his back to him. In his mind, George ran over the plan once more. He still felt it was worth a shot, especially with the scroll protecting his mind. What harm could it do to try? He questioned his judgment once more, but the answer was the same. The rat's talent could come in handy. The plan could backfire and if it did, he was prepared to shoot.

He reached the ground and noticed Kepler was close to the entrance yet far enough away not to disturb the magic The Beast cast upon it. He turned and pulled the blood stained sleeves of his old shirt from his pack and wrapped his hands for protection.

George was now within ten feet of Maldwin. The rat still had no idea he was there. The opportunity was wide open for the taking. George lunged and landed on top of him.

Maldwin let out a squeal of terror as George closed his hands around his body. The successful hunter of large rats shouted as he lifted the animal into the air. "I got you, you little snot! Your visions don't work on me. I bet you never saw this coming, did you?"

George set the terrified creature on the ground, pinning him, waiting for him to tire. Maldwin squealed as he fought, but struggle as he might, he could not break free or bite his captor to release the grip. George mocked the rat's struggle as he watched. Maldwin tired and his body relaxed. George adjusted his hold to one hand, then reached under his pant leg and drew his pistol. He pointed it at Maldwin's head.

"Can you talk, rat?" He shouted, then waited for a response as he tightened his grip. "I asked if you can talk! Every other damn thing in this world can talk, so you'd better be able to!" When nothing came from The Beast, he continued, his voice amplified. "This is your last chance! If you can't talk, I'm gonna kill you!"

Again nothing, George lifted his pistol and was about to pull the trigger when the rat spoke. *"As sel a ip te yalema quay!"*

The words were clearly a language, but nothing George could understand. "English, you little freak, speak English! Do I look like I speak Ratanese?"

From inside the entrance of the cave, Kepler growled. "He wants you to spare his life. He'll do anything you want."

George found the jaguar's red eyes. "You understand this...this...this..."

"He's a rat," Kepler snapped. "What's wrong with you? Of course, I understand him. You have made your point. You have displayed your ability to pounce. Your prey is scared. Idle threats no longer serve a purpose. Stop letting the excitement affect your judgment. I consider your display to be most unbecoming of a leader."

George thought, *Damn it. I have to think faster than this. Come on, George, you need to be smart you freaking idiot. You're going to lose your advantage if you don't think.*

George adjusted his attitude, then responded. "Well, don't you have many talents, Kepler? Having you around is going to be just what I need. I have a linguist and a politician all wrapped up in one big, undead demon-jaguar. This is going to be the start of a long, beautiful friendship, my friend. Remind me to treat you well as we travel. I shouldn't have doubted your abilities. You make me proud."

George made sure Kepler saw his smile, knowing this simple reassurance would go a long way. The jaguar seemed nervous over the last few days and being complimentary, however untrue his intentions, would help the cat relax. His manipulative mind was working better now.

Kepler did feel a sense of relief. The jaguar shouted from the cave something only the rat could understand. *"Uh uyat gote say!"*

George watched as the rat twisted his head and responded, *"Le fuat yoor tekle!"*

Kepler walked from the cave and back into the open. He moved close to George and sat down. "I told him to release his magic on the cave's entrance. I can help him talk with you. Would you like me to translate?"

The manipulator thought a moment. George had no idea how stupid he was about to sound. "Tell him it's clear neither you nor I are affected by his visions. Tell him I don't intend to kill him. Tell him I would like him to join us on our travels as we seek control of this world. Tell him I offer a chance to do something other than live in the cave. Tell him I would like to employ his abilities and put them to better use. Tell him killing everyone who enters his cave is pointless and solves nothing. Tell him there will be rewards for traveling with us. Tell him a life of luxury will follow. Tell him we will rule this land and he would be wise to stay with us. Tell him if he says no, I won't harm him. Tell him I want something from inside the cave, and after I retrieve it, I'll let him go. I think if you tell him that, it should be good enough for now."

Kepler smiled as a jaguar would. He looked at George and for the first series of moments since their introduction, he decided to make a joke. "Really, that's it, nothing else? Are you sure? Are you absolutely positive that's all? You want me to tell him, tell him, tell him, tell him, tell him, tell him, and finish it off by telling him some more. Are you sure you don't want me to tell him something else? I would hate for you to miss an opportunity for me to tell him something. It's not like you haven't given me enough to tell him already. Will that be all I should tell him, or would you like me to tell him anything else? After all, telling him is what you want, right? How about I tell him now? Should I tell him right now? Tell me what to do. Please, tell me. If you don't tell me, I might not know when you want me to tell him."

George rolled his eyes. "Just tell him, damn it!"

The demon-cat laughed and after a few moments of speaking with Maldwin, began to translate. "George, he said to tell you..."

George cut him off. "I get it already. I sounded like a bloody idiot. You've made your point. Get on with it."

Kepler chuckled. "He'll travel with us only because he hates the cave. He's lived in this place because his family is trying to avoid being hurt by the humans of this world. Much of his family was killed by your kind. He only uses his visions in defense. He's the sixth generation to live in the cave. He has many relatives inside, but he's the only one who has this ability to use the visions to make the humans go away. He can manipulate the visions for many different kinds of emotions, not just sadness. He said there is only one within his family who can command the gift at any given moment. The skill has been passed to each generation and his family decides who will be given the gift when the one who possesses it dies.

"Apparently, his family was originally given the gift as a way to help with some sort of test. He doesn't remember every detail, but he does know this is why they received the power. A group of dwarves was to be kept out of the cave. The family was to use the gift for this purpose, but the dwarves never showed up. I guess they had something to do with the test. His family decided the gift was something they would use to keep the humans away once they had the power. It's a comfort to them, but it is not used in a malicious manner. His family simply wants to live unharmed within their own territory."

Kepler's conniving mind remembered the reason why the dwarves never showed. He was friends with the Serpent King, Sotter, long ago. He knew it was the snake who murdered them, but he never knew why Sotter did it. The Serpent King had a runner deliver a message, asking Kepler to keep his cats from attacking while slithering through the Enchanted Forest. The message was, he had dwarves to kill near the Pool of Sorrow and they had a map of his kingdom. He was going to get it back and did not want interference from Kepler's subjects. The message never said what the dwarves were doing at the pool or anything about the cave, but as Kepler thought through it all, he realized George had the map. Kepler could only guess, but figured George intended to make the serpents serve him or at least use the map in some way to gain power over them.

The map must have secrets, the demon thought. He now wished he had cared more about what the Serpent King had been up to. He didn't know why the map would take George inside the cave, especially if it was about the Serpent's Kingdom.

The demon further thought, *Why would the dwarves need to enter the cave? This must be the reason George needs to go inside. What is he after? Is it what Sotter wanted? Why would two different beings have the same desire to prowl this territory?*

Kepler would wait to find out until the human exited with the answer. He thought it best not to say anything since he couldn't do anything about it anyway. George was too powerful and would destroy him if he tried to force the answers out of him. Besides—his friendship with George was growing and he could see George's mind looked for an opportunity in every situation. Maybe this was not a bad alliance after all.

Kepler moved to the mouth of the cave and used the rocks as a way to scratch his back as he continued to talk with George. "Maldwin said...if you give him and his family a place to stay, a place safe from harm, he will travel with us and be loyal. He asked for your word you'll provide this place once you have gained the power to do so. He also asked us to seal the cave once you have whatever it is you seek inside. His family can use other smaller escapes, created throughout the seasons, to search for food. He wants to say goodbye to his family before we leave. This is important to him. He promised his loyalty during many other moments throughout the conversation, as well."

George thought a moment as he stared into Maldwin's frightened eyes, then looked at Kepler. "Do you believe what he says? Do you think we can trust him?"

"I do. I also think he could come in handy. I must admit, I like the way your mind works. He doesn't have a devious bone in his body, but he'll do whatever it takes to protect his family. I would allow him to travel with us if I were you. I can teach him to speak with you as we quest for territorial dominance."

George smiled at the cat's use of the word 'quest.' "Tell Maldwin..." He stopped and realized he was about to do it again. He took a deep breath and continued. "Oh, my freaking hell, don't *tell* him anything. *Inform* Maldwin I'm agreeable to everything he wants. I would like him to stay with you while I retrieve what I've come for.

"When I come out, Kroger can seal the cave after the rat has said goodbye to his family. Oh, and please ask him to give Kroger some better visions. I'm sick of listening to the big ox cry. I'm about to go nuts. All this sobbing is killing my ears. I would hate for the big guy to smash our little friend once he releases him from the sad crap he is seeing. Maybe some happier thoughts would be a good idea to stop this from happening."

Kepler pondered George's use of the word 'crap.' Unsure of its meaning, he shook it off and communicated everything to the rat. It didn't take long before Kroger's crying turned to smiles. The big guy warmly hugged himself and started to sing in gorilla tongue.

George rolled his eyes at the sight. *You've got to be kidding me. He's snuggling himself now. How did I ever sign up for this? I don't remember the application for this job asking if I had experience with gentle, giant morons.* "Give me a break," he said while throwing his hands up. He entered the cave, shouting, "I'll be back. Keep an eye on them, Kep, will ya? I think you'll love what I'm going in for."

The demon watched as George disappeared into the darkness. He couldn't wait to get the answers to his questions. What did the dwarves want in the cave and was it the same thing George was after? He allowed himself to get lost in thought.

Kepler looked at Maldwin and spoke in the rat's language. "Does the cave have other secrets?"

Maldwin nodded. "My visions are not all that protect this cave. Fear also surrounds what is hidden. Your friend may not scurry out of the darkness. His days of scavaging may be over."

Kepler lifted his head and as his red glowing eyes found the cave's entrance, he began to laugh. "We shall see if George is truly a master of the hunt, after all. Fear, how delightful."

After a few more moments of pondering, Kepler turned to face Kroger. The demon-cat also understood gorilla. This reason alone allowed him to befriend the giant long ago. The knowledge of this language saved his life when being threatened by Kroger's club. He shook off the thought and watched as the simple-minded big fella sang. The song was a lullaby his gorilla mother sang to him as a baby. Even Kepler's vicious heart had to smile at the sight of this pathetic-looking sweetness.

George made his way into the cave. Realizing more light was needed, he pulled out another torch from his pack, fumbled around in the darkness, and produced the antique cigarette lighter. The lighter had been passed down from his great-great-grandfather, a lie he told everyone. The truth—he stole it from a Vietnam veteran while doing charity work for the VA Hospital in Orlando. He refilled the lighter not long ago and considering how dark the nights were on this world, he would need it, and could use it for quite a while before running out of fluid. It was one of a kind and he carried it everywhere, despite the fact he did not smoke.

He lit the torch and studied the map. Once he had his bearings, he headed for the secret door. The cave was moist and wet inside, the floor slick and smooth, like massive amounts of water had raged through it for years. The air was stale and he would need to be careful of his footing. He tried to grab hold of the walls for better balance, but they were just as slippery as the floor. It was clear why it took eight days to go from one end of the cave to the other. Hurrying would only cause him to fall, but there was one good thing about the smooth wet surfaces. When the light was cast, they reflected the torch's glow.

It took over an hour to get where the secret door was marked on the map. Setting the torch down to free his hands, ensuring the moisture on the floor didn't extinguish the flame, he moved toward the walls and reached out to feel around. He just knew there had to be some kind of hidden latch or switch to toggle. He checked the area, but found nothing.

Frustrated, George went for the torch and picked it up. He held the burning stick high above his head and let the light fill the room. From the way things looked, he might need to exit the cave and ask the rat for assistance. Letting out a sigh, he noticed a spot about twenty feet deeper where the light failed to reflect. George moved toward the area and stood in front of it.

Again, he held the flame high. It was as if the light went through the wall, outlining an entrance, yet it still looked to be solid.

It was worth a shot. He reached for the slick surface. He intended to feel around, but instead, the solid-looking barrier faded away in front of him. His hand destroyed the magic as it passed through the illusion to reveal the path ahead. *No freaking way. You've got to be kidding me,* he thought. Without wasting any more of his moments, he stepped inside.

A long narrow corridor stretched in front of him with no visible end. He was about to take another step when he heard something familiar. His daughter's voice filled the darkness. "Daddy, help! Stop it! You're hurting me!"

Fear seized George's mind. Again, Abbie's voice echoed, "Don't touch me! Aahhhhhh! Daaaaaddy!"

George called out, "I'm coming, baby! Daddy's here! Whoever you are, get your damn hands off her! I'll be right there, Abbie!"

George's hand trembled as he lifted the torch high. He moved further down the corridor, toward his daughter's cries. The walls and floor of the cave were different now. They were not smooth like before. Instead, they were jagged and rough. Footing was easier to find, but the end of the corridor was not visible beyond the torch's glow.

With each step, his daughter's helpless screams echoed. His heart raced as he quickened his pace. "Daddy, make it stop! It hurts!"

"I'm coming, baby! I'm coming! Leave her alone you son of a bitch! I'll kill you when I find you!"

Over two thousand panic-filled footsteps pounded against the cave's surface before the light of his torch cast a glow on a single door at the corridor's end. The door was solid, made of a thick wood, maybe some sort of oak, and was painted red. A small half-arched window rested eye-level at the door's center. Beyond the door, no light was visible through the window.

George slowed his pace and approached with caution. He lifted the torch toward the window. Suddenly, his daughter's face appeard on the other side and screamed, "Daddy, save me!" Then, the face vanished and the window went black.

George freaked. He snatched the doorknob and twisted. It was locked. Again, he twisted and pulled with all his might, shouting, "I'm here, baby! I'm here! Get your damn hands off of her! I'll kill you, I tell you! I'll kill you!

George reared back, ensured his footing, and kicked the door with all his might, but nothing happened. The barrier held firm and remained unpenetrable. Constantly calling to Abbie to let her know he was coming, George kicked at it over and over, pounding away until he was exhausted and unable to lift his leg.

George fell to the floor, his chest heaving to catch his breath. As he did, his daughter's voice continued to scream, "Daaaaaaaddy! Make it stop!"

His face was covered with tears as he lifted himself up from the floor and prepared for another assault. He was about to lunge forward when a light appeared on the other side, illuminating the window. Again, he held his torch high, but during this series of moments there was something different. A heavy iron door knocker now rested at the door's center just below the window.

George lifted the hoop with a balled-end and bashed it against the door three times. He waited, removing his pistol from beneath his pant leg. He pointed the gun and whispered, "Answer it you son of a bitch, answer." He lifted his voice higher and shouted, "I'm coming, baby! Daddy's right here!"

The lock on the other side of the door was released. As it opened, a set of familiar faces appeared. They were George's worst nightmares. His ex-wife, her mother, and the bastard responsible for trying to take his daughter away all standing in a row, with his ex motioning for him to come in.

The room beyond was a kitchen, elegant and with many expensive appliances. He touched the wall. It felt real. He was no longer in the cave. Nothing made sense. He scanned the rest of the room. Abbie was sitting at a large table all by herself, crying. Her face was red, eyes blood-shot and her fear was evident.

George dropped his torch, holstered his gun, and darted across the room. He lifted Abbie from her seat and tried to hold her tight, but her form faded into nothingness. *What the hell is going on here?* "Abbie! Where are you, baby?"

He turned to face his ex-wife and watched as her fiance handed her the court summons, taunting George as he did. Once a kiss had been exchanged between the couple, the man vanished in a blue cloud of smoke.

"What the hell?" George demanded.

His ex-wife lifted her hand and pointed at her mother. She chuckled hauntingly as she responded, "Ask her!" She slowly began to dematerialize. Her body became transparent and faded away.

George took a defensive position and faced his ex-mother-in-law. She now had a large wooden spoon in her hand and was stirring a sizable bowl of macaroni and cheese. As she glared at George, a calamitous grin appeared. Regurgitating, she burped up small chunks of meat and spit them into the bowl.

She lifted the delicacy and tilted it toward George. Taking a few steps forward to peek in, he saw the partially digested pieces turn into miniature pigs. He became sick to his stomach as they began to devour the macaroni.

He was now more unnerved than ever. "I said what the hell is going on? Don't make me ask you again. Start talking!"

The woman dropped the container to the floor. As it hit, the bowl shattered. What was left of the macaroni took form and added to the creatures' numbers. George tried to avoid the tiny swine as they swarmed between his legs. They began attacking the soles of his boots. Many small chunks were torn away and an equal number of swine were crushed beneath George's weight before the rest darted across the room and through a hole in the wall.

Finding his ex-mother-in-law's eyes, he watched her laugh as she lifted her hand and pointed toward the table where Abbie originally sat. She hissed, "Your daughter is in danger, George! She's in danger!"

George's heart sank. A chill ran through his body as every hair on his arms stood on end. Before he could utter a word, the image of the woman faded as the others had. The kitchen melted away and the darkness of the cave once again appeared, lit only by the torch laying on the floor.

He moved to pick it up. He shoved the flame forward in order to light the way ahead. "Hello!" he shouted. He took a few steps, moving the torch from side-to-side and circling to see if he was alone. "Abbie, where are you?"

He felt lost, helpless, and terrified. "Abbie! Daddy's here, baby. I need you to call out to me. I'll find you."

He took a few more steps, continuing to move the flame from side to side. The light found the edges of what appeared to be an altar, similar to the ones Sam and Shalee were on back at the temple. The altar began to glow, shedding light throughout the cavernous room. He could see everything and laying on top of it was the staff he was after. As he approached, his mind went wild. He stopped and took note, realizing the only way into the room was through the same red door which now sat more than thirty feet away. As if triggered by his attention, the door dissolved and revealed the way back to the rest of the cave.

He hurried to the opening. Beyond, there was nothing but the long corridor. He shouted again, "Abbie! Abbie! Answer me, baby!"

He stood still for many long moments and waited for a response. Nothing. It was as if he was living a dream. As he turned around to face the altar, the room went dark. The only thing which remained lit was the staff resting at the altar's center and the torch laying on the floor.

George fought to clear his mind as he grabbed the torch and held it high. His love for his daughter made it hard to focus. The sight of the staff and the way it was lit toyed with his mind. His thoughts raced.

Am I sane? Am I still sane? He lowered the torch to check out the soles of his boots. As the flame lit their surface nothing was out of the ordinary. It was as if he had never been attacked. *What the hell?*

He moved to where his weight crushed the pigs. There were no remains. *You've got to be kidding me. I'm losing it.*

After many long moments of turmoil, George convinced himself everything had to be a hallucination. He turned his attention to the staff and thought, *I hope you're real.*

He boldly walked over and reached out. As his hand made contact with the object, he quickly pulled it away. *Freaking crap, it is real!* He took a few steps back from the altar. Now his mind was racing in a whole new direction. *If the staff is so powerful, it's got to be trapped. I could die if I take it. That's it, it's rigged. The staff is the trigger.*

Sweat built up on his forehead. He scanned the altar and moved to check out the walls, ceiling, and floor for anything out of the ordinary. He saw nothing other than a few small cracks. Nothing seemed alarming. Returning to the altar, he froze. All he had to do was reach out and take the staff, but he could not make himself do it. He just knew it was trapped and his life was in danger. He scanned the room again, his heart pounding. If he did not take it, he would live, for now. He knew he would not be able to defend himself once Kepler learned he was powerless. Either way, he would die.

I'm damned if I do and damned if I don't. He was in a bad spot and now, more than ever, he wanted to go home.

After what seemed like hours of standing there staring at the staff, he gathered the courage. Reaching out to take it, he took a deep breath, let it out, then breathed again. Counting in his mind, *ONE...TWO...THREE,* he lifted the staff from the dias and ducked.

From his balled position, he opened his left eye. *Ha! I'm still here.*He opened his other eye and without out moving, scanned the room. "I guess there aren't any poison arrows on this trip, eh, guys?" Looking around for someone to answer, George realized his insanity and started to laugh.

George stood and backed his way out of the room. Despite having the staff, he called for Abbie one last time. He waited to hear her voice, a voice which never came.

A Big Stone Statue

George decided he would stop long enough to drill a hole in the butt end of the staff. He wanted to drink the liquid inside its hollowed center and ingest the power Jasòn spoke about. The wood was hard. Even with the sharp point of his knife, it was taking forever to make a hole. He looked at his watch and realized he had been at it for over five hours. Finally, the staff gave way and revealed the liquid inside. He held the hole tight to his mouth and lifted the staff. He directed the flow, pouring it into the back of his throat beyond his tongue, wanting to avoid the taste as much as possible, in case it was vile.

He thought the draining would never stop. It was difficult to take in this much fluid without tasting it, no matter how hard he tried. As luck would have it, the drink went down without triggering a gag reflex. He swallowed all of it, careful not to miss a single drop. Lowering the staff to the ground, he waited for something wonderful to happen. He thought of the movies and pictured how the receiving of a power should look. Nothing—not a single tingle or quiver was felt. No white light, lightning, or loud noises. George only experienced an upset stomach from drinking so much, so fast.

Maybe Jason was wrong. Maybe the liquid in the staff doesn't give the power to turn things to stone, he thought. *Shouldn't I feel different?*

He looked at the staff laying on the cave floor. After a moment, his thoughts focused and he grabbed it. Try as he might, the staff would not change. He had to be doing something wrong, or Jason was misinformed. He hoped with everything in him it was just a matter of time, or rather, a matter of moments, before he would figure it out.

When he exited the darkness of the cave, the sun had already gone down. Everyone was sitting back from a Kroger-sized fire, the light flickering off the walls of the pass as it penetrated the blackness of night.

It was Kepler who noticed him first. "I thought you were never going to come out. Slick in there, isn't it? I thought you might've fallen and hit your head. It's hard to prowl when your paws are not formed for the task, wouldn't you agree?" Kepler further thought to himself, *He survived the cave. Fear must not control his instincts. Perhaps territorial dominance can be accomplished with this human.*

George threw the staff toward Kepler's feet. "It's definitely slick. It took forever to find what I was after. Here it is."

Kroger became excited when he saw the staff. "Oh, George, you got pretty stick us play with. Kroger like play stick. Let him have." The giant reached down to pick it up. The staff bent and broke under the weight of his finger before he could lift it, leaving a sharp point on one of the pieces that wedged beneath one of his huge fingernails. The beast man cried out in pain as big tears began to flow from his eyes. He fell to the ground. Kepler tried to console the gentle giant, but nothing worked. The demon could not get him to stay still long enough to remove the splinter.

"It hurted Kroger," the giant screamed as he sobbed. "Stick mean to Kroger. Make stick stop pain to Kroger. I no like stick no more, George." He threw himself on the ground and clutched his finger with his other hand.

Kepler was lost as to how to handle the situation. Kroger's foot slammed down in his fit, nearly smashing Maldwin.

"George, make stick no hurt Kroger, George. You give Kroger mean stick. I no like stick no more, George."

This carried on for far too many moments. The giant baby rolled around without regard to the safety of the others. At one point, his toe caught a few pieces of wood from the fire and sent them flying. Everyone was running around to avoid being squashed. George had seen enough and his breaking point had been reached.

George exploded with all his energy. "Shut up! You stupid idiot! If you don't shut up, I'll leave you here by yourself!"

Everyone became quiet, even Kroger. Babysitting the giant was going to be a pain in the butt, and George knew it.

"Kroger, listen to me," George screamed. "Sit up right now!" The giant did as he was told. "Don't make another noise. I want you to stop whining. I'm going to fix your finger and you're going to stay still. If you don't, George will be very mad at Kroger. Do you understand me?"

The giant nodded as another tear fell to the ground and splashed next to George's foot. He sighed and stuck out his hand. As George walked toward it, the giant turned his head, shut his eyes, took a deep breath and held it as he prepared for the pain.

George snapped out a few more comments before removing the big splinter. "I've never seen a bigger baby in my life. You would think someone was going to kill you, Kroger. I'm sick of listening to your whining. I just want you to be still."

George reached out and grabbed the sliver. He sized up the situation and leaned in to lay his free hand on the end of the giant's finger. To his surprise, the skin started to turn gray and began spreading. The grayness moved past his finger and into the giant's hand. George jumped back and moved away, watching in horror. Nothing could be done to stop it. He knew this was going to look bad to the others and looked at Kepler.

"What's happening?" Kepler growled, his eyes burning a bright garnet-red, while taking a defensive posture. "What are you doing? This isn't necessary! Stop this! Now!"

Kroger watched as the change moved up his arm. "What happen me? I no feel my arm. It sleeps, yes?" The beast-man was confused and could not understand. He continued to speak. "I make sleep stop. Arm wake. I wake now. You see, George."

The ogre's arm was heavy. Kroger struggled to lift it into the air. The collision it made when it slammed into the ground shook the area around them, adjusting the fire which rekindled itself. The entire forearm crumbled into rubble. Kroger now understood it was George's fault this was happening. "My arm rock, George. Why you do me this? You hurt arm more. Why? George not friend to Kroger? You no like Kroger no more? Kroger like George. Kroger be good. George to fix Kroger. Please, George, no make Kroger die!"

Kepler backed away from his human travel companion, but his voice remained harsh and cold. "You're turning him to stone! His whining wasn't bad! Stop this, before he meets his end!"

George had no idea what to do. He looked at the ogre. "I didn't mean to do this, Kroger. George likes you. I'm so sorry, big guy. You're my friend. I'm sorry. Please forgive me."

The grayness was growing faster now, passing through the giant's shoulder. Soon it would reach his heart and there was nothing he could do to stop it. All he could do was stand there and watch. Before the last beat could be finished, his heart became solid and the giant knew it was over. Kroger's eyes filled with confusion as he looked into the human's. George could feel his own heart breaking.

Kroger's speech grew softer as the last of his air left his body. "It okay, George. I like George. Me still friend." This was the last thing the thirty foot tall, gentle giant would ever say.

Kepler circled the backside of the statue. He didn't know what to think. He felt George had done it intentionally, but his demeanor, standing with his head lowered, said something different. The demon-cat thought, *He did apologize. It seemed sincere. Was it an act, or is he truly remorseful? Could he not stop the change? How did he do it?*

The rat asked the jaguar what to do. Kepler responded by telling Maldwin to stay put. The demon needed the moments necessary to sniff out the situation. *Why would George want to turn him to stone? He would've simply left if he had been told. This doesn't make sense. The ogre could have been a tremendous ally.*

"George, I don't want to upset you, but this doesn't seem to be something a human with your intelligence would do," the demon said. "Despite his whining, Kroger could've been a valued member of our pride. Please, explain your logic? I would hate to think you're this irrational, temper or no temper. This seems stupid and not becoming of a man seeking power."

"I know, I know, I can't explain it," George replied. "I didn't mean for this to happen. I didn't want to harm him. I have no idea how to control the power I received from the staff. I didn't think it worked. I need to figure out how to control it, or I'll be turning everything I touch to stone."

"What are you talking about?" Kepler snarled. "Are you saying you can turn things to stone and you have no understanding of how? This is the power you went into the cave for? How could this be? The staff is broken. Do you not need the staff to control the power the staff commands?"

With Maldwin shouting, the demon was finding it hard to concentrate. The furry critter was confused and scared. He wanted some answers. The cat turned to the small beast and asked him again to relax while he figured things out.

George looked up, motioned with his hand for Maldwin to calm down, and moved to take a seat. He reached down to balance himself on a tree which Kroger had fetched the night before. He had asked the big guy to bring him a small stump to sit on, but instead, Kroger returned with an entire tree. He laughed when he saw it and figured, to Kroger, it probably was small. George called him his "adorable dumbass" that night.

Before he could finish lowering to the tree, George noticed a bug resting where he intended to sit. He reached down and flipped the centipede-looking creature from the spot. The anthropod flew through the air and before it hit the ground, it was rock solid. George backed away and so did the others.

"See what I mean? Now what? The staff had a liquid in it. I was supposed to be able to turn things into stone when I wanted to, not whenever I touched something. The power should work in such a way I can walk up to anything and change whatever part I choose. Kep, I should be able to walk over, touch you and turn your leg to stone and leave the rest of you unharmed. It looks like, no matter what I do, it's all going to turn to stone. I'm all ears if you have ideas. I swear to you I didn't want to hurt Kroger. Sure, he was a moron, but he was likable. I would never hurt anyone I had an alliance with, no matter how much they annoyed me. I would send them home first. It doesn't make any sense to kill my friends. I might have needed him, someday."

Kepler explained the situation to Maldwin. The rat was asking a million questions. He was not going to stop, so it was best to talk with him. As Kepler spoke, the rat's demeanor changed. When the rodent replied, he related a story of a similar situation he was involved in. The rat had come close to killing his own mother when he received the gift of his visions. He could not control them at first. It took the family watching throughout the moments of many days to keep his mother from jumping into one of the deep shafts scattered throughout the cave. The point Maldwin was trying to make was he could understand how this whole situation could be a tragic accident. Despite his understanding, the rat said, *"Ah ilyel sey, George,"* which when translated, meant, "Don't touch me, George."

George waited for Kepler to translate. When Kepler finished, he felt much better. The alliance with his new companions was strained, but still intact.

George looked at Kepler. "So, what the hell do you think I should do to get control of this? I don't want to turn you or the rat into statues. Do you have any ideas?" He moved back to sit on the tree.

Kepler thought a moment. This was new to him. His own abilities had always been under control. After a bit, he came up with a solution.

"You need to practice to command the power. Since you emerged from the cave, I have seen two things turn to stone you've touched. The first was Kroger, and the second was the bug. I have also seen two things which have not turned to stone. The first was the staff and the second was the tree when you lowered yourself onto it. If I'm right in my observations, you have only turned things to stone made of flesh and blood. Again, you just need to practice. Seems simple enough, and..."

George interrupted. "I can't go around touching everything I see. I will kill it all and leave a trail of stone leading right to us."

Kepler laughed. "No, no, no, I have things you can practice on. Things already dead, made of bone. Bone is a part of us. You should be able to find the governance of your power by using them. You won't need to kill anything."

George sighed, "That sounds a hell-of-a-lot better. Where will we do this and what things are you referring to?"

The demon looked at Maldwin, then back at George. "We promised Maldwin you would seal the cave. Without Kroger, this will be impossible. I'll summon my skeletal warriors. You can practice on them until you learn how to command the power to make it work. I can summon more if need be, but once we get to five hundred forty-one, I'll be fresh out of ideas and you'll have to practice on living creatures. This should solve your problem with Maldwin. We both know, at least for a while anyway, you won't be able to control the power. We'll have a few intimidating statues surrounding us. I suggest we start at the mouth of the cave. You can leave stone skeletons along the entire length of the pass. This will leave quite the impression for anyone who comes this way. I think Maldwin will agree his family should be safe. The skeletal warriors, combined with the ogre, should frighten most anyone. Even I would hesitate if I saw this."

George's excitement returned. "That's an awesome idea. Are you sure you don't mind? What about your home and the protection the skeletons provide?"

Kepler smiled and jumped up into Kroger's stone lap to lie down. After shifting to a comfortable position, he responded. "I can only assume 'awesome' means good. I said you had to stop at five hundred forty-one. I never said this is all the warriors I command. I'll still have hundreds guarding my pass and I can always create more as we travel. I do like to ravage man flesh, especially those I can make serve me. There is something I want, but the revelation of this desire I'll save for later." Kepler lowered his eyes. They flashed bright red. "Do we have an agreement?"

"It's a deal." George moved to shake Kepler's paw, but thought better of it. "We'll have to shake on it later, I think. When will the warriors arrive?"

Kepler let out a low roar. Behind him sat two rocks at the base of the cliffs. Two black jaguars made themselves known to the group and appeared before George's eyes. He had a clear view from where he sat and watched the beasts jump down into the brighter light the fire cast in their direction.

They were equally as large and intimidating as Kepler—seeming to appear out of thin air.

George's heart rate skyrocketed, but maintained his position on the tree. Kepler had his posse with him and he had not known it. It was not a good feeling, but he'd be damned before he'd show any weakness. He had been through this once before, but this time, or rather, this series of moments, he had a true advantage and not just his bluff. He calmed himself and waited for more information.

Maldwin, despite the human's inability to control his new power, jumped up and sat next to George for protection. The rat was having one heck of a day. His world had been turned upside down. He had been jumped on, threatened, pinned, yelled at, negotiated with, joined George's group and if that was not enough, he was sitting here with three very large cats, two of them moving in his direction. He felt like dinner. Cat and the rat was not a game he wanted to play.

Kepler cleared his throat. "Speaking of territorial dominance, allow me to introduce my brothers, Keller and Koffler. The three of us are identical. I'm the oldest, by only moments. This is how I create the perception I'm everywhere within my pass. We hunt to keep everything under our control. My brothers will collect my undead army. It will be 12 Peaks of Bailem before they return."

George took a deep breath. "So, you're the oldest and the leader?"

"I am. The power to control the skeleton warriors is mine to command. I've given my warriors orders to obey my brothers. They will use this governance to order my army to come. My brothers will be assets as we dominate the territories of this world."

"I can see why you're not concerned with keeping your home protected. You have plenty of back-up," George rubbed his hands together and pondered. "Twelve days is a long time...uggh...I mean, 12 Peaks is a lot of moments to be sitting here."

George shook his head in disgust. "Damn this place. It would be so much easier if there was a word for time. I swear, it feels odd to say moments and mean time. Not only that, but you guys use the word moment or moments as if you understand exactly when the moment is. This is stupid. It's ridiculous. It's unfathomable, well...almost unfathomable. Good hell. What dumb son of a bitch thought of this system of communication? Even Athena looked at me like I was a moron when I used the word, time. Thank goodness she explained."

Kepler shook his big furry head in disbelief. "I do believe you're ranting. Who is Athena? Why speak of something you cannot change? I assume you have a point to this nonsense."

George rolled his eyes, then adjusted his thoughts. "Just forget about Athena. She isn't our focus at this *moment*. Anyway, since twelve days is a large period of *our moments*, maybe a new plan is in order. Why don't we leave Maldwin here? We can run to Lethwitch and stock up on supplies. This will kill a good 6 or 7 Peaks. If we take our time, uggh...I mean our *moments*, and stay a couple nights, it will give me an opportunity to experiment with this new power and maybe I can find something to put over my hands. When I touch my clothes they don't turn to stone. Maybe a pair of gloves would act the same way. I sure as hell hope so."

The demon turned and sent his brothers to Skeleton Pass. He looked at Maldwin and told the rat it would be a while before they left the area. The rat said he understood and would wait until they returned.

"George, maybe you could explain the meaning of this word, 'time,' as we travel. Many of the things you say are strange. I believe if I am to hunt with you, we should have an understanding of each other's ways."

"I'll think about it." With that, George and Kepler headed for Lethwitch.

The Grayham Inquirer

When Inquiring Minds Need to Know about their Favorite Characters

IT'S A NEW MORNING on Grayham and Sam is getting ready to catch one of the hippogriffs to travel to his next fight. Shalee is also making the trip, along with their trainers. The next arena is located just outside of Lethwitch. They intend to stay seven days before moving on to the next town.

The tremors have Sam worried and upon further communication with BJ, Sam decides if he is going to gain the fame needed to meet the King of Brandor, he must fight twice every seven days over the next seventy-seven days—twenty-two fights in all—and win every one. His ambitions are adding up to one city, town or village every seven days. He must fight in the city of Champions for the Golden Chalice of Brandor.

MOSLEY attended the ceremony honoring Bassorine's passing. He has decided to join Bailem's team. He is with them now, telling them everything he knows, or at least, everything Bassorine wanted him to share.

MALDWIN called his entire family out of the cave. They have gathered around the stone statue of Kroger as the rat explains he will leave with his new travel companions and soon they will have a better, safer place to live. He hopes George will be okay with the size of his family. There are easily over two hundred fifty of them. Imagine the noise and the rat droppings on Kroger's stone lap.

GEORGE and KEPLER are on their way to Lethwitch. They have walked through the night and have agreed to stop for a rest just after the Peak of Bailem. George has set the alarm on his watch to ring five hours later and is showing his jaguar friend how the Rolex works. Kepler is asking questions about the device—questions George wishes to avoid answering, but cannot.

CELESTRIA is going nuts. The elven witch family has been nagging her to answer the questions their small minds can conjure up. If it were not for her baby's safety, she would have left already.

ATHENA is sitting behind the counter at her work, going through the logbook and singing. She has been happy since her breakfast with George, and looks forward to seeing him once again.

LASIDIOUS is more than ready to step down as his team's leader. The gods have been called to a meeting, scheduled for Late Bailem. He plans to announce where he is going to hide one of the pieces of the Crystal Moon.

Thank you for reading the Grayham Inquirer

What Irony

George and Kepler's Napping Spot

"So, you have your Rolex watch," Kepler said after hearing much of what George explained. "I understand it keeps what you call 'the time' according to your Earth's day, which has twenty-four hours, and it takes twenty-four hours for your sun to rise, travel across the sky, then rise again. I also understand what you call a 'minute.' I think this concept would make things easier if we had something like your Rolex to plan our days on Grayham. You should keep track of this 'time' and see if our days are similar to the ones from your Earth. What I don't understand is, how did you get here?"

"That's the fuzzy part for me, too. One minute, I'm driving with this beautiful woman in an RV—I'll have to explain what an RV is later—and the next thing I know, her eyes changed color, her teeth grew sharp, and the cold, ohhhhh, the cold was like needles to the skin. After that, I woke up in a great hall with huge pillars and golden doors. I was one of three in that hallway. The others were from my world and had no idea what was going on. The man said his name was Sam, a pompous bastard if you ask me, but he was pretty damn smart. The woman was annoying and not worth talking about. We found a statue, and this guy, Sam, was able to read what was on it. It had a prophecy about the three of us and also talked about a crystal. I think he called it the Crystal Moon."

The demon-jaguar interrupted. "You mean the Crystal Moon in the Temple of the Gods?"

George shrugged, "I don't know for sure. I can't remember. Everything was so crazy that day. The inscription on the statue talked of a man's great victories and how he brought home the power some gods lost to control worlds. Apparently this power, which Sam said the Crystal Moon generates, is what keeps the five planets from colliding. It said something about the planets all rotating at the same distance around a single sun. I know there's more, but I'm not recalling it right now. Wait, I do remember Sam saying there were five planets and some guy named Bassorine was given power and made god-like."

The demon jumped in. "I know what you're referring to. The place you're talking about is the Temple of the Gods above Griffin Cliffs. The man you speak of is the God of War, Bassorine. He is the mightiest of hunters. He's all powerful, but we can speak of this in one of your Earth's 'minutes.' You're right. The Crystal Moon, which rests on the statue of Bassorine, sends out the power necessary to keep the five worlds separated. Bassorine's power protects the crystal's pieces, keeping them safe so no man or beast can send the worlds into chaos."

Kepler stopped talking when he saw the expression on George's face change. "What is it? You seem bothered."

The manipulator's anxiety was evident. "Maybe we can keep walking while we talk. I have a gut feeling I'm not going to be able to sleep once you hear everything I have to say."

"Sure, we can walk. I sense you are troubled."

George sighed, throwing his backpack across his shoulder. He made a mental note it didn't change to stone. "You said the Crystal Moon was protected and this "so-called" god, Bassorine..."

Kepler cut him off. "There is nothing *'so-called'* about the gods. They are to be feared and respected. If you know what's good for you, you should talk respectfully."

George turned to Kepler. "If this *'so-called'* god was so *'all powerful,'* then I wouldn't have been able to take a piece of his crystal before I fell through the floor, now would I? Didn't you say his almighty power protected it? I shouldn't have been able to take a piece of it, right?"

Kepler snorted his irritation. "You took a piece? Do you not know what you've done? You've doomed us all."

The demon began to pace. Kepler took a few deep breaths, realizing his outburst was getting them nowhere. "Where is this piece of the crystal and what do you mean when you say, you fell through the floor?"

George hesitated, eyeing the giant cat for a moment. "Now keep calm when I tell you this." He took a deep breath, and thought, *Crap, he's going to kill me.* "I don't know where the piece is."

The demon let out a deafening roar. George prepared for the worst, holding his hands up in case Kepler attacked. The demon's explosion stopped. Turning to find George's eyes, and while walking toward the dwarfed, vulnerable human, the beast's muscles rippled beneath his fur as he gave George a stare which cut through the man's soul. With a cold tone, he growled, "You're telling me you have enough power to remove one of the Crystal Moon's pieces. You took it and have *no* clue where you put it. What else haven't you told me?"

George was scared and desperate, despite the fact he had readied his hands to turn the cat to stone. He knew the jaguar could sense his fear and spoke with caution. "I said I have no idea where the crystal is, because I fell through the floor when I touched it. I lifted one of its pieces. It wasn't just me who thought we should touch the crystal in the first place. Sam thought it was an answer to a riddle written on the statue."

"You lie!" Kepler snarled. "I've read the statue on a hundred different occasions. It says nothing of a riddle."

George snapped back, grabbing hold of what was left of his backbone. "HEY! I didn't ask to be brought to this ridiculous world! There was a riddle! You call me a liar again and I'm gonna get pissed off!"

Kepler snorted his disgust, exasperated with his inability to kill his irritation. "Hmph...finish your ridiculous story."

George clinched his fists. It took a while before he was able to take a breath. Still angry, he continued. "The statue said something about three people fighting to recover the pieces of the Crystal Moon. One will fall to the wayside, but it didn't say anything further about what would happen to this third person. The only reason we touched the crystal was because it was the only part which didn't look like the rest. When Sam said it looked like the Crystal Moon had five different pieces, I jumped on top of the statue's base and grabbed one. The next thing I knew, the rest of the pieces disappeared into thin air, except for the piece I had in my hand..."

"You had a *piece* in your hand?" Kepler said in disbelief.

"Yeah, yeah, yeah, blah, blah, blah...I'm not making this crap up. The damn floor started to shake and the base of the statue fell out from under my feet. Then, I fell through the hole with it. I remember the man and his wolf didn't fall with me. They stayed suspended as I fell away from them. I can only assume the one prophesied to fall by the wayside was me. I don't know what happened to Sam or the woman. It felt like I fell forever before the darkness opened up and I landed on a guy named Jason. I had no clue touching the Crystal Moon would start a cosmic problem."

Kepler returned to pacing. "George, put your hands down. There's no struggle between us...we're allies. Have you not learned anything from your experience with Kroger? We may get angry, but we don't fight amongst ourselves."

The giant cat shook his head, snorted, then continued, "I don't believe you could make up such a ridiculous story. I'll accept this foolishness as fact."

George's fists clinched even tighter as he lowered his hands. Rather than speak, he waited for the demon to continue.

"All right...so, you fell through the floor and the Crystal Moon disappeared. You have no idea where the people are...the ones with you in the temple...or any idea of where the piece in your hand went? Hmmm...you clearly have enough power to get past Bassorine's hold on it. All this appears to make sense, except for a few things."

"What *things* are you talking about?" George snapped. "Tell me, and I'll clear them up."

Kepler grinned within at George's expense. He enjoyed the human's irritation. "You said you fell on a man named Jason. How long ago was this, and where?"

George thought back. "About 10 Peaks, just south of the Enchanted Forest, north of Lethwitch."

The demon sneered his disbelief. "Since your arrival ten days ago, you've learned about the map, killed my subject, found out about the cave, learned the staff was inside, and went in to retrieve the power to turn things into stone? I would like to know how you learned so many things in such a short period of what you call, 'time.'"

"That's easy to explain," George said with a wild grin. "I also failed to tell you I robbed the mercantile in Lethwitch to get the coin necessary to pay for the scroll I used on your Saber Lord."

Kepler laughed for a moment, then realized what George had said. "What do you mean, you used a scroll?"

George knew he had said too much. He sat on a mound and started flicking tiny ants, sending the newly made stone statues flying everywhere. He was going to level with the jaguar and tell him the truth. "Like I said before, I landed on a guy named Jason. He was a big guy and I broke his back. He was in a lot of pain, so I reached in his pack and gave him a liquid which numbed it. The medication made him talk way too much. Jason told me about the map and its secret. The map would lead me to where the staff was located inside the cave. He told me I wouldn't be able to command the power by using the staff, but there was a way I could get the power out of it. He said I would need to drink the liquid that filled its hollow center. If I drank it, it would give me the same power the staff would have given to its intended owners. Apparently, the staff was meant for some dwarves."

"Dwarves, what dwarves?" Kepler responded, as if he didn't know.

"Jason told me the dwarves were from a place called Trollcom. I have no clue where that is. When your Saber Lord attacked, I got lucky. I felt something in the forest watching me, so I knelt on the first rock of the crossing and used something called a snare scroll to set a trap. It was dumb luck he ended up where I wanted. I was overcome with anger when I tortured him. It wasn't until I drank the fluid that I gained the power to keep you from killing me. I was bluffing you during this entire series of moments. I have no power other than the ability to turn you to stone."

As George finished telling his story, he flicked another tiny ant statue toward the feet of the demon. "So...how do you like me now?"

Kepler had to laugh. "You stalked your prey skillfully, George. You surprise me. To think after I saw you kill the saber, I feared you. When I approached, you just sat on the log, eating. I thought you were powerful and simply held up your hand to stop the attack. Using the scroll was brilliant. Of course, I was angered to watch the torture of my subject. To know, during those moments, you did it only because you lost your temper...interesting. It pains me to know you have only just now found a real power to command. Granted, it's a good power, but you couldn't have kept me from killing you before this. What irony. Well, George, my friend, I'll enjoy our hunts together until the day I cease to be on this world."

Kepler rolled on the ground, laughing. "When I think back, the look on your face when Kroger was turning to stone, it's funny, knowing what I do now. You didn't have a true understanding about what was going on. I bet you were frightened. I bet you thought your alliance with me was ruined.

Kepler laughed a while longer before he sat up and faced the human. "As funny as this all is, we have a problem. The Crystal Moon is missing and the worlds will come to an end. I wonder how long we have until this happens."

"I don't know, but if Bassorine had his power on the Crystal Moon to keep any man or beast from touching it, then why was I able to? I had no power to do this. I'm just a guy with a quick wit, one who wants to gain some respect. Something else must be going on here if he's as all-powerful as you say."

"Perhaps," the demon responded. "I agree you shouldn't have been able to remove the crystal. I'm sure everything will be revealed in this 'time' of yours. For now, let's rest a bit and continue to Lethwitch when we wake."

Lying down, George reset the alarm for a few hours. Before he went to sleep, he reached for his wallet. He wanted to look at his baby girl's picture and dwell on her for a few moments. When he opened the wallet, the photo was missing. He rifled through the compartments of the leather billfold. It was nowhere to be found. His eyes were heavy, the exhaustion of the last few days overwhelming him as he cried himself to sleep. His dreams made up for the missing photo, dreaming of Abbie and Athena.

Angel's Village

Sam and Shalee walked up the stairs to the top of the landing platform with their trainers. To Sam's surprise, the griffin, Soresym, just brought the last of the servants from the Temple of the Gods, all of whom were grumbling about the temple's closing and being out of work. The fighter walked over to the giant flying beast.

"Soresym, how are you?"

The large eagle head turned to look, his keen eyes surprised to see Sam's face sitting on top of a much larger body. "You look familiar, human. The person I know with this face was much smaller. There must be a relation. It's bad enough one human should suffer with such ugliness, let alone two. Who are you?"

Sam rolled his eyes. "Soresym, you know who it is. It's a long story. If we were riding with you, I'd tell you about it. One of the gods has given me a couple of gifts. I've thought of you on many occasions since our last meeting. I didn't know you thought I was so ugly. It's hard to compete against your majestic appearance."

Soresym chuckled, "You jest. Well done, Sam. It is unexpected to see you. Your looks are not as tragic as I portray. I may have thought of you as well. I would like to hear the story of your gifts. Perhaps, you could share with me how you've grown. I would have ignored you, but I recognized the woman. I see your female companion is awake. The last series of moments I saw you, young woman, you were unconscious. Who might you be?"

Shalee looked at Sam, a little unsure how to react. Sam responded, seeing her hesitation. "Soresym, I would like you to meet my beautiful girlfriend, Shalee."

"I see," the griffin responded. "So, you're the one who has the stomach to mate with this male of your species. I am truly sorry. Shalee, you would not remember, but I'm the one who gave you a ride to this village. I'm glad you're rested and feeling better. It will be an honor to have your beauty aboard my back."

"Why goodness-gracious, aren't *you* just flatterin'. Thank ya, Soresym. I don't rememba' the ride. Please forgive me."

"Nonsense, your male companion made enough ignorant comments when we first met to make you look like a Tralapataise."

"Oh my, that sounds beautiful. What would a Tralapataise be?"

Soresym lowered his head and made sure his eagle eyes found hers. "A Tralapataise is the rarest, most elegant and delightful smelling flower on Grayham. I only compare such beauty to true grace."

"Why, Soresym, if *you* were a man, I'd eatcha up. You may flirt with me anytime. I like men who can talk somethin' special." Shalee turned and gave Helga a high-five.

BJ grumbled and spit off the landing platform, watching it fall to the ground far below. "Stop with these ridiculous gestures."

Helga looked at Shalee, then Soresym and whispered, "He's so cute when he's grouchy."

The griffin chuckled, then looked at Sam. "Don't worry about your woman, Sam. You have nothing to fear. It is not possible, with my anatomy, to mate with a female of your species. I will allow her to stay yours."

"Gee, thanks."

Shalee and Helga giggled as they watched Soresym look toward the horizon. "Sam, where are you off to today? I will give you a ride. Since the gods shut the temple, the rides I give are few and far between. I told the others this would be my last trip. I will travel with you and you will explain how this extra size was added to your frame."

Sam responded to the order, "Sounds like a plan."

The griffin turned to look at Shalee. "The weather is perfect for flying. Climb up and don't worry. I can easily carry the four of you, but it will be a tight fit. You will need to sit close together."

Everyone climbed aboard and sure enough, they had to tuck together. BJ sat at the rear just behind Helga. He had been watching the older sorceress and thought she was beautiful. He put away his grouchiness and replaced it with something more tender. Taking the opportunity to reach around her waist, he pulled her close and whispered in her ear, "I'm doing this for your safety. It's only right. A man should see to it the women around him are safe."

Helga managed to twist around to find a sly smile and an adorable wink. She accepted BJ's advance and nestled in tight against his chest. She put her hands on top of his and enjoyed their ruggedness. Neither Sam nor Shalee were aware of the exchange as the griffin launched from the platform.

Shalee was disappointed she had not experienced this during the first series of moments she had the chance. She made a mental note to no longer throw fits regarding things she knew nothing about. Sam and the giant griffin talked the entire trip. Many laughs were exchanged.

The World of Ancients Sovereign

It was Early Bailem when Mosley arrived and began sniffing around the God of the Sun's home on Ancients Sovereign. Bailem's abode felt capacious as the wolf trotted around looking through the many grand openings leading to the outside world. Giant stone columns, all white as snow and 144 strong, sat perfectly placed, supporting a dark stone roof with an enormous circumference.

At the top of the structure, a dodecagon gem with a canary hue had been set, without fault, at the roof's center. A beam of light materialized as it passed through the gem and slowly moved across the floor. Mosley teleported onto the roof to get a better look. At just over twelve paws wide, he admired the gem's size.

Mosley watched as the sun's rays penetrated the jewel's facets. His godly eyes were now able to see far more than they used to. The million crystallizations within the jewel were mesmerizing. Curious as to their effect, Mosley teleported back inside and watched as the beam approached one of twelve angelic statues, all standing atop a large circular base. A diameter of 48 feet separated the twelve. Each statue had a gem implanted into a smaller circular base on which it stood.

Eventually, the beam struck the gem beneath the statue resembling Bailem and gave it momentary life. The statue adjusted its robe, assumed a new position, then looked to the ceiling before solidifying.

Mosley was astonished. He had never seen anything like it before. The wolf waited for the beam to pass across the floor to hit the jewel of the next statue. It was during this series of moments that one of Bailem's fallen brothers animated and assumed a new stance. The statue lifted both arms high, turned his hands level to the floor and spread his resplendent wings.

He looked directly at the wolf and smiled, solidifying again as the beam moved beyond his jewel. The plaque on his base carried the name, Metatron. He would remain this way until his gem was lit again the following day.

Mosley searched his godly memories. The weight of all he knew to be true was overwhelming as he studied the names on the other eleven plaques. To the right of Metatron, moving clockwise, the names read: Michael, Gabriel, Uriel, Raguel, Ramiel, Chamuel, Iophiel, Cassiel, Sandalphon, Azael, and finally Bailem, formerly known as Zerachiel.

Mosley knew Metatron, also known as Lucifer, was one of three archangels to be scorned. The trio rebelled and joined with Harrah, Ra, and Sekhmet to induce the God Wars after receiving their diminished status within the heavens. Mosley struggled to shake off the thoughts of the devastation. The death toll of The Great Destruction of Everything Known was too much to suffer. He had to use the fur on his legs to wipe the tears from his eyes.

A long series of moments passed as the wolf took note of the careful positioning of every statue. Bailem had taken great care while creating the only form of a sundial in existence. Over 3,713,875 separate animations of each statue had occurred since the creation of the God of the Sun's glorious structure. The home rested on top of the highest mountain called Bailem's Aubade on Ancients Sovereign.

Now, with the Peak of Bailem past, the others have convened and Mosley has already explained everything he knew of Lasidious' plan to play a game. The wolf is telling the gods what he has learned of the third person retrieved from Earth, a person they know nothing about.

"His name is George and leads no pack other than the one he is trying to form on Grayham. He was brought forward by Lasidious. He must feel this human can be easily manipulated to accomplish things on his agenda. Sam said George is a mean-spirited man. Shalee does not care for him either. As we all know, there were clear plans for Sam and Shalee. When I became enlightened, I gave my gifts to Sam to help his rise to glory. This should help our cause while assisting the mortals to gain an audience with the King of Brandor. We will need the Kingdom of Brandor to fight for the Crystal Moon's pieces when the moments arrive. Sam and Shalee will need to be a key part of this."

Bailem stepped forward. The god was short, heavyset, and balding. What hair he had was a grayish-brown. He was pleasant to look at, wearing golden robes with dark trim. His long tail hung to the floor and his angelic wings were folded against his robe. He was said to be the only angel to survive the God Wars and was known as the God of the Sun.

Bailem held his hand within the beam generated by the gem as he spoke. "Thank you, Mosley, for shedding light on current events. If I might ask, what were the two gifts you bestowed? Sam won't be able to gain an audience with the King of Brandor unless he defeats each arena's best fighter. Even if he survives the city of Champions, we all know who he'll face in Brandor's arena."

"Justin Graywind shows no mercy," Calla added. Her dress was modest, accented with lace and though not stunningly gorgeous, she was far from ugly. "The General Absolute has never been defeated."

Helmep further added to the conversation. "Every opponent who has entered the arena with Justin has died before they could be carried out by the king's healers."

Helmep was tall and thin, well-built with blond hair, hazel eyes, and he wore a tan robe with gold trim and a brown cape. He was handsome and his smile carried a wonderful charisma. "The healers in Grayham's arena are exceptional. They are the best who serve me on Southern Grayham. The general doesn't leave room for them to work. When he's done, they are done."

The gods were becoming sidetracked as they conversed about the many swift deaths Justin delivered. Mosley called for order. "We must ensure Sam is invited to Brandor. A few simple suggestions is all it should take. The gifts I gave Sam have increased his strength and his agility. This should help him gain an audience. Shalee can assist with her sorcery."

Mosley lifted his snout into the air, "As much as I would like to keep talking about these things, the moment has come for us to leave for the meeting Lasidious has called. I suggest we disband."

Everyone agreed and vanished. When they reappeared, each found Lasidious and his team sitting on the grass outside the newly constructed Hall of Judgment with the Book of Immortality floating nearby. The new hall was identical to the old, just as the Book insisted. It was normal for the gods to snap their fingers and create anything they wanted. The new hall had been constructed in less than forty breaths.

"I'm glad everyone is here," Lasidious announced. "I have made a decision. Rather than putting a piece of the Crystal Moon on each world, there will need to be at least two pieces of the Crystal Moon on Grayham. I want to ensure they are rejoined. I'll announce where the first piece has been hidden in the near future. Until then, I would work on strengthening your team's position on this world. Be ready for anything. Thank you all for coming. I will now excuse Celestria and myself from our team. We will create an unfair advantage if we play. When the moment is right, I will reveal information on the crystal's pieces. Your teams will have equal numbers. I'll see all of you in 60 Peaks."

With that, Lasidious vanished, and left the others looking at each other. The God of Mischief's next destination was the town of Lethwitch.

Warning to the Barbarian King of Bloodvain

Lasidious appeared in front of the mage, Amar, the brother of Morre, whom Lasidious had impersonated the last series of moments he was in Lethwitch. Amar worked in his brother's store—the same store where George purchased the magic scrolls—whenever he was on Grayham. He was an older man with gray hair, but unlike Morre, he did not wear a beard, nor did he smell. The mage was startled when the god appeared, but throughout his many seasons, he had come to expect the unexpected and was able to dismiss the shock. Realizing who was standing in front of him, Amar bowed before his god.

"Hello, Amar," Lasidious said. "It has been a while, my friend. How's your brother?"

Amar kept his head lowered. "Hello, My Lord. We are well. To what do I owe this visit?"

"Please stand. I'm here to talk as friends, not as your god. It pleases me you're doing well. I'm here to inform you of things to come."

The mage rose. "I don't understand."

"I know, my friend. The other day I was here in your store. I took a few of your scrolls and sold them to a man. His name is George. There was also a note, thanking your brother."

"I know of the note. My brother spoke of it. He said he was overcompensated for the scrolls. I was fine with the transaction and have since heard my brother say he has made replacements. I would have paid better attention to what scrolls were taken, but I had no idea I would receive this visit, My Lord. Why would the insignificance of scrolls cause your visit?"

"I'm glad you were pleased with the finances of the transaction, but this isn't why I've come. The scrolls are of no consequence. The man I spoke of will be seeking power while on this world. He'll be arriving in Lethwitch within 3 Peaks. George is the type of man you've been waiting for. I know you wish to seek your path of glory and this man could help. If you choose, it would be wise to ally with him until it benefits you to leave his company. His heart is as dark as your own. I have determined you would be good counsel on his journey. He travels with the undead demon-cat, Kepler."

"Kepler? My Lord, Kepler is a vicious killer without honor. Can the cat be trusted? I have heard stories about men who have tried to go through his pass. He kills without mercy, as if for fun."

Lasidious laughed. "Kepler can be trusted, Amar. Likewise, you have killed without mercy. The jaguar has honor, but this isn't something you would know. Like you said, you have heard stories. The man I speak of is ruthless. He's not from this world. He has traveled here from the past. It's in his character to seek as much power as he can obtain. He has aligned himself with The Beast, Maldwin, from within the Cave of Sorrow, as well. He also had an alliance with Kroger before he killed him."

"Kroger, you mean the ogre from the Dark Forest, My Lord?"

"Yes."

"Kroger is a gentle giant. Why would he want to kill him? Why would I wish to travel with a man who doesn't respect his allies?"

"Tisk, tisk, Amar. You have also stolen breath from your allies. You forget with whom you speak."

Amar hung his head. "My deepest apologies, My Lord. It's not everyday I speak with someone who knows my secrets. Please forgive. How was George able to align himself with The Beast? The creature's visions are deadly to all men."

"There is no forgiveness necessary, Amar. I find your mind pleasant. To answer your question, George is immune to Maldwin's visions. He needed the scrolls purchased from your brother to protect Kroger's mind, not his own. The giant was with him when he went to the cave. It was at the cave George killed Kroger by turning him to stone."

Amar's eyes widened. "Stone? That's a treasured power. There's no one on Grayham, other than myself, who can command it. Did he use a staff or spell?"

Lasidious reveled inside. He knew the mage was impressed. "He commands the power, but is having difficulty controlling it. His ability is natural and because of this, greatness follows him. He uses neither staff nor spell to control his magic."

Amar could not believe his ears. "How is this possible, My Lord?"

"How is unimportant. It would be wise for you to align yourself with George. You could be his counselor and teach him to direct his power. You have been to Luvelles and have trained under your good friend, Head Master, Brayson. You understand the dark arts better than anyone on Grayham. You're the most powerful mage on this world. I have seen to this because I knew this day would come. I would keep our relationship a secret and would not speak of it with George."

Amar bowed. "I'll do whatever you ask, My Lord."

"No, Amar, I'm not here to ask anything of you. I'm here to inform you of things which are happening. It is my desire to see you become powerful. Consider my visit a suggestion...an idea you may want to think about. You must want this for yourself. I don't wish you to do anything that's not your heart's desire. I'll give you a vision of George. If you choose to befriend this man, your wisdom will come in handy and your rise to glory will soon follow. I wouldn't speak of this with your brother. His service to his god is a fool's service. He wouldn't understand the desires of your heart. You should make this decision on your own. If you choose to pass, I shall look fondly upon you...just as I always have. After all, we are friends, are we not?"

"Yes, My Lord, I would like to be your friend. I've never seen myself as your friend. I am your humble servant and have always lived to serve you."

Lasidious put his hand on Amar's shoulder. "You are, indeed, my friend and I extend my hand to you this way. You're a free man, with free will, and I respect you as the man you have become. I couldn't be prouder of the way you have served. The moment has come for you to seek your glory. I'll watch from above as your biggest fan."

Amar was happy with the way his lord had spoken. "Maybe it would be best if I took my staff and went to find this George."

Lasidious agreed, but reminded the mage George was not yet in town. The god suggested it would be wise to gather the materials he would need to travel with his new allies. He watched Amar run from the store and into the night with his staff held high to light the way. The Mischievous One uttered three simple words before he left for his next destination: "What a cretin."

With that, Lasidious vanished.

The Next Morning
City of Bloodvain

Lasidious' patience was wearing thin as he waited in his pen for the Barbarian King of Bloodvain to arrive. He had taken the form of a thick-horned black bull and was due to enter combat with Senchae Bloodvain for his daily training. He thrashed around inside the corral, playing the part of an enraged animal, and tore some of the fencing apart. When the handlers approached, he sent them flying through the air, landing in awkward positions and breaking bones.

"Today, you face a spirited one, My King," the general of the barbarian army commented. "I've never seen this bull before. His eyes have spirit. His stare calls for battle. He's much bigger than the others. This will be a glorious kill."

King Senchae Bloodvain nodded at the general and other high-ranking members of his army. Removing his clothes, he looked across the arena while tying up his long hair. He was an enormous man—slightly over eight feet four inches. It was customary for the barbarians to fight to the death. Today would be no exception. King or no king, he would fight in nothing but the furs covering his loins. If today was his day to die, then so be it. He weighed nearly five hundred fifty pounds, with muscles bulging. He was well known throughout his kingdom for his ability to fight for long periods without tiring. Today, as he did everyday, Senchae would train with angered bulls. He would beat the first to death with nothing more than his hands and feed it to the leaders of his army.

The king looked at the bull. "He is a fine beast and worthy of dying by these hands. I hear your son, Churnach, conquered yesterday. He makes the kingdom proud."

General Fergus responded. "It was his eighth victory since you surrendered your belt as champion. He fights to glorify all barbarians."

"Tell your son I see weakness in his training. He must shed blood often to maintain his dominance."

"Yes, My King. He speaks of training as hard as you. His efforts fall short of your glory. He tries, yet I believe many, many moments must pass before he matches your skill."

"Let us hope this isn't the case. I believe your son could be as good a champion as I. For now, let's kill the beast so we may feast this evening, then bring in the others. Agreed?"

"As always, I look forward to watching its blood stain the arena sand. We will feast tonight before we sleep with all our women, Sire."

"You bed your women. I shall stay loyal to the Queen. I would suffer her wrath if these eyes wandered. She can be forceful, for a woman. A man who respects his love, lives a good life."

The men enjoyed the fantasy of the queen's power over the king. The general knew his king's loyalty to his queen was given out of respect and not fear. Senchae would never look at another woman. He held true to his vows.

Now...fellow soul...Senchae Bloodvain is the type of man who governs his army and High Council through respect. Unlike his grandfather, Bude Bloodvain, and most other kings before him, he achieved this respect throughout the Barbarian Kingdom's arenas over 15 seasons prior to taking the throne. Every fight is to the death. The vanity of this race has kept the challengers coming for thousands of seasons. Senchae is still considered, even though he does not compete in the arenas any longer, the most feared barbarian champion to ever live.

Senchae is the strongest and fastest barbarian the kingdom has ever seen. Since he was crowned, Senchae has sat on the throne, ruling with a strong hand, yet still trains harder than any other. Unlike his grandfather, he maintains a belief the respect of his army should be earned, not commanded. The king's reputation is so beloved, the rest of his kingdom remains loyal. He is proud, a great husband, good father, and just like all other barbarians, believes killing is just a game.

The leaders of his army and the High Council are allowed strong opinions, unlike his grandfather's monarchy. Bude Bloodvain was a much weaker king, controlling his armies through fear of his crown. Senchae chooses to listen to his men before making a decision, but the men know it is the king's right to have the final word.

"General, let dinner out of its pen. I shall sport with our food before I beat the life from it."

"Yes, Sire." The general looked across the arena and shouted, "Release the beast!"

Lasidious exited the holding area where he had waited patiently, or at least as patiently as an angered bull would wait.

"The beast seeks to command your respect, Sire," the general shouted as he moved to sit in the king's box. "Best watch your backside, his horns look to be a good fit."

"Ha! Shall I trade you places, Furgus? I'm sure such intercourse would pleasure you far more than I. The way you look upon this fine animal feels amorous. Do I dare say you must be in love?"

The other members of the king's army laughed. The general accepted the slam and forced the dark skin surrounding his eyes to remain relaxed, hiding his displeasure. "Witty, My King, I must remember with whom I jest."

"Indeed, Furgus, my respect for you as the leader of my army stops at beastly pleasure. Perhaps, you should focus on other things." Senchae's smile widened as the bull charged.

Lasidious lowered his head and rushed in. Bloodvain grabbed a horn in each hand, then used Lasidious' momentum to throw him to the ground. The bull-god landed hard, followed by the king's crushing punch to the side of his neck. Keeping in character, the bullish deceiver bellowed. Digging his hooves into the sand, he rose for another attack. Lasidious snorted, shook his head for effect and charged again, allowing the king to throw him once more before taking the offensive. Much to the bull-god's amusement, the general and his men cheered for their king.

Lasidious knew what he had planned was going to be accepted by the men and interference would not be an issue. Again, Lasidious charged and allowed Bloodvain to grab his horns, but during this series of moments, he held firm as the big man tried to twist for the throw. When the king could not complete his maneuver, he was caught off balance from the attack. The bull-god drove him hard into the ground, then rose to drive his head into the king's groin. He was careful not to do any long-term damage, but forceful enough to stun Senchae and pin him.

The general ordered his men to stay put, reminding them it would be an insult to help their king. They obeyed the order.

The god threw his bullish figure onto Senchae, putting much of his 3,100 pounds on top of the barbarian to keep him pinned. He watched the giant man struggle, punching, trying to break free. Senchae's blows were ineffective. He could not find the leverage to injure his opponent.

Lasidious sat there, careful not to put too much weight on Senchae, and waited for him to tire, but the king did not. Senchae realized the bull was not fighting. He relaxed and hoped the bull would get up. As he waited, he found himself caught off guard. The bull spoke.

"King of Bloodvain," Lasidious whispered.

The king shook his head, closed his eyes, then reopened them. He was not sure what he heard and was further stunned as the bull continued. "Senchae, I bring news of your demise. There is weakness beneath your crown. You are unworthy of ruling a nation of barbarians. In the Kingdom of Brandor a man is seeking power. This man will kill your champion."

"How do you speak, beast?"

Lasidious snapped, "Bind your tongue, barbarian!"

Senchae's eyes were wide with disbelief as the bull continued. "Killing you is not my intent. You will listen or this encounter will end with your last breath. Do you understand?"

Senchae's pride took over. "Who are you to speak to a king? Get off of me!"

Lasidious lowered his horn and brought its point to rest against Senchae's throat. He pressed and allowed the barbarian to fight. Struggle as he may, Senchae could not better his position. Defeated, the king stopped contesting.

Lasidious enjoyed Senchae's despair. "In the Kingdom of Brandor, a man is seeking power. He will visit your kingdom. This human is to be feared.

You will not need to seek him. He'll be coming for you. Your kingdom's reputation will be damaged if your champion loses to this human. I know you have your laws, but if I were you, I would handle this myself."

Again, Senchae's pride swelled. "How do I know you speak the truth?"

Lasidious pressed his horn deeper against the king's throat and waited for a response, one which came without hesitation. "Stop this! I'm listening," Senchae uttered, gasping for air.

Lasidious released the pressure against his throat. "You'll know this man when you see him. He travels with the undead, Kepler. You're familiar with this demon-cat, the one hired into your great-grandfather's service to re- trieve the Unicorn Prince's horn. The cat now serves this human. This swine of a man can fight like no other. The looks of this human are deceiving. He'll destroy your champion. I've come a long way to give you this message. I'm sure your horn can dull the pain I've left in your groin."

Senchae watched as the bull rose and walked toward the holding area. After disappearing into the stables below the training grounds, he stood and followed. By the moment Senchae arrived, the bull was nowhere to be found. He was left standing alone and confused.

Two and a Half Days Later
The Town of Lethwitch

When George and Kepler arrived just before the Peak of Bailem, Leth- witch was in a big stir. Kepler stayed outside of town due to the reaction his presence would cause. It was hard for the demon to move unnoticed. There were not enough shadows during the height of the day.

The excitement in the air was evident. George followed the crowd to the outskirts of the east side of town near the Cripple River. Cheering erupted from inside a massive arena. He wanted to go inside, but lacked the coin. He was forced to live vicariously through the others going in and out. After speaking with some of the people, he realized the fights were like the gladi- atorial combats held in ancient Rome.

Now...fellow soul...for those of you who are not familiar with Rome, this was a civilization which lived on one of the destroyed worlds called Earth. Unlike that civilization, the gladiators of Grayham are all free men, not criminals or slaves forced to fight. These combatants are glory seekers and for as long as anyone can remember, the games have always been a part of Grayham's culture. Let me get back to the story.

George needed to find more of this world's coin to gain entrance to watch the fights. This was an opportunity to pass the moments of his days while waiting to go back to the Cave of Sorrow. The competition was going to last for the next two days. This was perfect and far from boring.

With malice in his heart, George headed back into town to a familiar spot. It did not take long before he was standing outside The Old Mercantile. It was the middle of the day. He would need a different approach. He walked in to look around. To his delight, the store was almost empty. *Most of the town's people must be at the fights,* he thought.

There were only two people in the store: an elderly gentleman behind the same counter he had robbed before and an older woman, maybe the man's wife or an assistant. By the way she stocked the shelves, she had worked there a while. Given her attention to detail, he would have bet they were the proprietors.

The old man came out from behind the counter. "Hello, friend, how may I assist you, today?"

The woman heard the greeting and also stopped what she was doing and came over to stand next to the man. "Hello, young one, it's a beautiful day outside. I hope you're enjoying yourself."

Well aren't these two clowns sticky sweet. Poor bastards, George thought. "It is a lovely day. How are you?"

The old man reached in his pocket and removed a coin. He began to fumble with it through his fingers. "So how can we assist you today? Why are you not at the fights?"

"Oh, just been busy, I suppose. I'm looking for a pair of gloves and thought a nice place like this would have some. Do you think you could help me out?"

"Sure we can," the gentleman replied. "This is my wife, Jannica. My name is Carldon. We carry a wide variety of items. Let me help you find what you're looking for." As he finished his statement, he dropped the coin.

Jannica shook her head as she watched it roll, then excused herself. Once Carldon retrieved the coin, he showed George where the gloves were. They were on display, near the boots, on a shelf close to the middle of the room. As George followed, he surveyed the rest of the store to ensure there was no one else around. They were alone. While Jannica was busy adjusting the boots, George took a deep breath and reached out to touch Carldon on the back of his neck. His transformation was instantaneous. George could tell his new stone figure was going to topple. Carldon had been in mid-stride. Hurrying, before Jannica could hear her husband's body hit the floor, George reached around to touch her forearm. Jannica's transformation was just as quick as Carldon's, but she didn't fall.

The killer watched as Carldon broke in two pieces as he hit the floor. The sound encouraged George to rush to the door and look to see if anyone heard the commotion. The street was quiet. No one had noticed a thing. He didn't hesitate. George headed for the money drawer and sure enough, the old couple was just as trusting as before. George found an amount equal to 14 Owain, then bolted the back door shut and created a sign to hang in the front window. The sign read: Closed for the fights. See you in four days.

He grabbed a pair of gloves, exited the store, locked the door, and moved to the alleyway. Once there, he took a deep breath. *Murder is easy.* As he put on his gloves, the smile on his face disappeared as he further thought, *This is not good. Abbie would not approve. I can't make this a habit.*

Shaking off the thought of his daughter's disapproval, a new thought entered his mind. *I wonder what Athena's up to. Perhaps, I should buy her a gift.*

He found some flowers and went to the inn where Athena worked. His moment of arrival was terrible. She wasn't there. The lady behind the counter recognized him. "Hello, George. If you're looking for Athena, she won't be back until tomorrow night. Those are beautiful. Are they for my sister?"

George smiled as he thought, *Wow...something on this world is the same as Earth's. At least flowers mean something to the women.* "Yes, they're for your sister. I should attach a note since she's not here." The note said:

Dear Athena,

I want to give you these flowers to let you know you're on my mind. I miss your beautiful face. Your smile warms my heart. I'm sorry I missed you, but I will be back tomorrow night. I hope you have longed for me as I have longed for you.

With fondness,
George

Saying goodbye to Athena's sister, George left for the arena, feeling bummed. Tomorrow night would be a long time to wait. He wanted to see Athena now, but after thinking it through, he remembered he could not control his new power. Her absence was for the best.

After making his way back to the arena, George was about to buy his way in when a familiar voice shouted. "Oh, my goodness-gracious, George, is that you? I thought ya were dead!"

He watched as Shalee approached. She continued her rant. "The way your skinny little behind fell through that hole, I could've swore I'd neva' see ya again. Are ya allright? Did you bonk anythin'?"

Great, here comes the blonde ditz. How could Texas even claim a woman like this? I hate annoying women.

George did, however, like what she was wearing. A white dress, black lacy sweater, but nothing like you would find on Grayham. The outfit clung to her bosom and waist. Her blonde hair was pulled back in a ponytail, exposing a graceful jawline. George forced a smile as she stopped in front of him.

He pretended to care. "I was wondering what happened to you. Looks like you figured out how to add a little kick to the boring clothes they wear around here."

Shalee looked down. "Oh, this ol' thing," she said, pulling at the fabric. "It was a gift. Sam gave it ta me after he won his first fight. It tickles my fancy how he spoils me. I had ta adjust the waist and bodice, plus take the sleeves off. I even made this matchin' sweater from an interestin' black material I found at an adorable lil' fabric shop near The Old Mercantile. The place just looked so tiny, but they sure had some cute things for sale. I think the women 'round here like my fashion. Ya wouldn't believe how many come up and ask 'bout it. Maybe I can start a new trend. How's this sound to ya. Can ya imagine the sign: Shalee's Purdy Prada? Can't ya just feel the ring to it, George?"

George ignored most of what she said. Instead, he focused on the part about Sam winning his first fight. "Sam, he's fighting? So, he's here with you? Tell me what's going on with him."

"George, ya need ta learn how ta entertain a lady's ambitions. I'll tell ya 'bout Sam, but first, tell me what happened when ya fell through the floor. I was horrified. You had to bonk somethin'. Perhaps, you shoulda bonked it harder. Maybe you woulda learned how ta listen when a woman talks. I didn't think we'd ever see ya again. I thought ya were dead."

Blah, blah, blah, George thought, then made up a lie. "I fell to a room below and was knocked out. The next thing I knew I was in this town. Nothing too exciting has happened since. It's been kind of boring, if you ask me. Not much to talk about. So, tell me about Sam."

Shalee rolled her eyes. "Ya just don't get it, do ya? Anyway, I'm not here to educate the hopeless. Let me see...where ta start? The place we woke up was the temple controlled by the gods. Sam and I have been workin' ta gain the fame he needs ta win an audience with the King of Brandor. I've been workin' on my power with my new staff." She held up the staff. "Precious, I'd like ya ta meet, George."

The liar was intrigued to hear more. "Well, hello, Precious. Shalee, when did you start naming large, petrified shafts. I can only imagine what you do with it. And, what do you mean by your 'power'?"

Shalee took a deep breath. *He's the same ol' pig.* "Where ta begin? Hm-mmm...goodness-gracious, that's a tough one. Since we met, I've become a sorceress-in-trainin'. I'm really excited 'bout it. I'm kinda good at it. I'll have ta show ya, sometime. Ya just might be impressed."

"That's crazy." George said, then thought, *Yeah, right. I don't believe any of this.* "What about Sam? What's his story?"

"Sam's doin' fine. He's been fightin' in the arenas. He fought yesterday and won his second fight. He has anotha' one tomorrow. He really loses his mind when he gets in there, but fightin' is necessary to gain an audience with the King of Brandor. I swear, it takes me foreva' ta calm him down. He's killed two men. He gets so enraged, it's scary ta watch."

George smirked. "Sounds like he needs anger management."

"I agree. Well, I kinda agree, anyway. Even though he has killed his last two opponents, he's becomin' well-known. Last night, everywhere we went, people treated him like a celebrity. The people of this loopy world love barbarism. I don't understand it. It just makes me sick."

"Are we talking about the same guy I know? I realized he was a tough guy and all, but I didn't think Sam was that much of a stud."

Shalee nodded. "Oh, he's the same guy, all right. There's one big difference, though. The new God of War, Mosley, gave Sam a couple of gifts. One enhanced his body, makin' him a much bigga' guy than the last time ya saw him."

"I thought the God of War was Bassorine?"

"He was, or at least he used ta be. Bassorine was destroyed and Mosley took his place. You'd like Mosley, George. Sam and I traveled with him before he ascended ta become a god."

"What the hell are you talking about? Are you telling me you've actually traveled with a god since we arrived?"

"That's exactly what I'm sayin'. I know what ya mean, though. Sometimes I sit in my room and think this all has ta be some sorta dream. It's so hard ta believe that everythin' I thought ta be fantasy is real. I can't believe we've been on Grayham for two weeks. So much has happened. Sometimes, I just can't stop myself from cryin'."

"No kidding, I'll second that emotion. I wish I could say my life has been as exciting as yours."

Shalee looked at his hands. "Why are ya wearin' gloves? It's kinda warm for that, don't ya think? It's not fashionable."

"You and your stupid fashion. It's a long story, don't ask."

"I would take ya ta see Sam, but he's trainin' with BJ. I'm just waitin' for Helga ta watch the fights. I've been trainin' so much I need a break."

"Is Helga your trainer?"

"She is. Even Helga likes my fashion. So there. I've got her wearin' it now. Hey, you're welcome ta sit with us. I'll buy ya an ale."

"I'd like that," George replied, thinking, *I couldn't care less about your fashion sense.* "Maybe we could all have dinner tonight and catch up."

Later that Evening

Sam was with BJ, in a farmer's field just south of town, when Shalee showed up to tell Sam about running into George. The fighter was interested in meeting for dinner. Tossing his wooden stave to the ground, Sam proceeded to get dressed, then tended to his trainer's wounds.

"It looks like the old man has gone soft on me," Sam said as he applied the healing mud to BJ's leg.

BJ grumbled, "Give me a couple gifts from the gods and watch what I do to you. You're lucky you've been blessed or I would beat you senseless."

Sam and Shalee laughed. After a few moments passed, BJ lightened up and began to laugh as well. They headed out to meet George for dinner.

The Grayham Inquirer

When Inquiring Minds Need to Know about their Favorite Characters

SAM and Shalee are making their way to the tavern across town to have dinner with George. Amar is sitting at the bar observing. Lasidious is also sitting in the tavern—invisible to all—watching events unfold.

CELESTRIA has retired to the room which has been provided by the elven witch family. She is having a pleasant conversation with two squirrels sitting on her window sill and watching them eat the nuts she set out for them. Their conversation is a wonderful stress reliever after her interactions with the witches. They are driving her mad. She is counting the days until her son's birth—and her departure.

MOSLEY has just left another meeting with his team of gods. They were all in agreement he should visit Keldwin, the King of Brandor.

ATHENA is singing as she washes the dishes at her mother's home. She is excited about her flowers. They have been brought to her from work. She cannot wait to see George again. She has read the note over and over, anxious for her shift to start tomorrow night when George will be back.

SENCHAE BLOODVAIN is holding the Unicorn Prince's horn close to his groin. The healing power the horn possesses is starting to soothe the pain. He cannot believe how black and blue his inner thighs are and is contemplating the talking bull's words while struggling with his pride. Never before has he been in a near-fatal position. Although his men do not regard him any differently—their respect still intact—something still gnaws at him. He would have preferred an honorable death to the bull's mere departure, but taking his own life now would be cowardly, so his only option is to swallow this bitter pill.

Thank you for reading the Grayham Inquirer

A Soul Rescued

George waited for his dinner companions to arrive as he finished his second mug of ale. A gray-haired man approached, wearing a light green, hooded robe and holding a staff. He sat at George's table.

You've got to be kidding me, George thought. *Who's this S.O.B.? This schmuck looks like Merlin.* "Look pal, I have people coming. You might want to take a hike."

The man grinned. "I'll make this quick, George." Amar watched the surprise on George's face. "Yes, I know your name. I've been sent to assist you on your journey. I know you need help with your...let's just call it, your gift, since we are in mixed company. I can teach you to control it. With my counsel, you can master it."

The liar leaned across the table. "Who the hell are you to tell me I need your guidance? Whoever sent you is mistaken. I don't need your damn help."

The mage leaned in. "Lasidious sent me. I am Amar."

George feigned his interest. "Oh, so *you're* Amar. Why didn't you just say so? I feel so much better." He changed his expression to something more sinister. "I don't give a crap what your name is. I didn't ask you to sit at my table. I don't need your guidance. Tell Lasidious to mind his damn business. You're wasting my moments. It's best you go, before I make you wish you had." *I hate presumptuous people. This guy is freaking me out.*

Amar's expression was filled with concern. "You speak of Lasidious as if you do not respect his power. The gods are to be feared." The mage stood from the table. "I'll be outside the arena at the closing of the games. If you want my help, get back to me. Think about this. How could I possibly know about your gift? I'm here for a reason." With that, he closed his eyes and vanished.

Now, more than ever, George was confused. *Holy crap. The son of a bitch just disappeared. How did he know my name. How did he know about my new power?* He leaned back in his chair and grinned. Shaking his head, he further thought, *There's never a dull moment around this place. I have so got to write a book about this for my Abbie.*

George decided he would find Kepler after dinner and ask about this Lasidious character. He lifted his drink from the table, slammed down the rest of his ale and waited for his guests.

When Sam and Shalee arrived, George could not stop staring at the fighter's body. "Holy cow, man, look at you. You're a horse. Put an axe in your hand, throw on a red-checkered shirt, and call you Paul Bunyan. I thought you had muscles before, but this is sick, hella sick. Shalee told me where you got the size."

Sam interrupted. "This is a conversation best left for places a little quieter, don't you agree? I have a lot to tell you about this world. There are many things we've learned. I'm hoping to compare notes and see if we know something you don't, or vice-versa."

George looked around and figured it was a good idea to wait. They changed the subject and had a nice dinner. After the meal, they left the tavern and headed for the inn.

⊷✦⊶

Lasidious watched the three of them leave. He remained invisible and followed. He wanted to hear their conversation.

⊷✦⊶

George was glad to learn the inn was not the same place Athena worked. He did not want to mix business with pleasure. This meeting, in his mind, was all about gathering information. It had nothing to do with friendship. He couldn't care less if either of them existed. He just wanted the scoop.

Everyone filed into Sam and Shalee's room. Sam was the first to speak. "It's good to see you, George. I thought you had become a tragedy, but after speaking with Bassorine, I began to think you might've survived, since Lasidious has plans for you."

⊷✦⊶

Lasidious smirked. The god moved to sit in a chair across the room, maintaining his invisible cover. *This should prove interesting.*

"What the hell are you talking about? That's the second time..." George stopped and, after giving a smirk, continued, "...I mean that's the second *moment* I've heard that name, today. Can you believe how stupid this place is? These people are so primitive. They don't even understand the concept of time."

Sam responded, "It's not they don't understand the concept, they just don't have a word for it, but I do agree, it's odd. It feels foreign to speak this way. Anyway, it appears Lasidious has plans for your *moments*."

Shalee chuckled at Sam's use of the word and watched as George responded. "I don't even know who Lasidious is. I woke up outside of town and have been here ever since. Who is this guy, anyway?"

Shalee responded, "He's the 'so-called' god who retrieved us from Earth."

"She's right," Sam added, "he was directed to bring only the two of us, but brought you as well. But, the gods don't understand why. Even Mosley is clueless."

George gave an inquisitive look. "Shalee said that name earlier. Who in the hell is Mosley?"

"Goodness-gracious, George, I already told ya, he's the new God of War. Weren't ya listenin'?"

George looked at Shalee. "Blah, blah, blah...whatever." He turned to Sam. "I'm listening."

"Same old George. Okay, okay, Shalee and I were supposed to create an empire as an example for the worlds to follow, but it looks like this has been put on the backburner, now that the Crystal Moon is missing. Shalee was brought forward to be my mate."

Shalee slapped Sam's arm, taking the opportunity to act as if she didn't know what Mosley told her. "Hey, you neva' told me that part." She desperately wanted to tell Sam the rest of what she knew, but she remembered the wolf told her it was dangerous to say anything.

"Maybe we could talk about it later," Sam said, rubbing the sting out of Shalee's slap.

George covered the grin on his face. "You, poor girl, you have to sleep with this big guy. Yuck." He moved to the window and looked down at the torches lighting the cobblestone streets. "I don't know anything about this god, Lasidious, but maybe I'll meet him, someday. If he has plans for me, he'd better say something. I've got to get back to my daughter."

Sam looked at Shalee, both of them knowing George's daughter was dead. "Shalee and I have been so overwhelmed we lost sight of your disappearance. I'm grateful you're okay."

"I agree, man, it was stressful when we arrived," George replied. "I didn't handle things very well. I hope you both will forgive me for the way I acted. I'd like to catch up. Nobody around here has any clue of the things we share in common. It'd be nice to keep this bond, assuming you guys don't mind. Maybe we can figure out a way to get home."

"We forgive ya, George. I'm sure we all need our own lil' slice of forgiveness for things said that day. I seem ta rememba' flippin' ya the bird."

Sam glanced out the window and chided, seeing an opportunity to lighten the mood before giving George the bad news. "I'm sure we would all agree I'm the only one innocent of any wrongdoing. It's not like I punched you in the arm."

For the moment, they all laughed, then Sam's face grew somber. "Okay, okay, so you already know about the five worlds and the Crystal Moon. What you don't know is the gods created a Book after the God Wars destroyed the cosmos. They call it the Book of Immortality and it holds the souls of the dead. There's no longer a Heaven or a Hell. It doesn't matter if a person is good or bad, everyone ends up in this Book, until it's their moment to be reborn."

George responded. "That's pretty deep. Sounds fake."

Sam nodded and continued telling the story about Bassorine being given god-like powers, explaining the story was a monumental lie told to those living on the worlds.

Sam reached up to scratch the top of his head. "Bassorine said the gods of Earth sent our souls to Heaven or Hell, depending on how we lived."

"So, all that crap is true," George responded. "You're telling me what the Bible says is true. I'm going to Hell for the things I've done? Damn! This sounds so unreal, but if you think about it, with the way this world is, I'm almost inclined to believe anything."

"Okay, okay. I suppose if you're worried about your soul, it's good Hell is gone. As I've already said, it doesn't exist any longer. There's something else you need to know."

"I'm listening."

"As you know, everything was destroyed in the God Wars. The only things which exist are these five worlds and one sun."

George laughed in disbelief. He repeated all he knew so far. "You're trying to tell me this guy, Lasidious, is a god. He was told by the others to bring you two to Grayham, but somehow, he managed to trick them and brought me here for reasons no one knows. You are destined to be an example on this world and these 'so-called' gods presumed Shalee would want to be your mate and have your babies while you run around ruling an empire. I would say this gives new meaning to the word *presumptuous*. Is this story for real? It seems like a gigantic pile of crap to me."

Sam nodded, affirming, "I swear it's true."

George looked at the floor. "It sounds farfetched...like some sort of fantasy. You're saying everything was destroyed in the God Wars? Nothing remains of the gods of Earth? If the only things which remain are these five worlds, then..."

Sam watched as he saw the light come on behind George's eyes. Shalee grabbed Sam's arm and held it tight, remembering how she felt when she learned everything was gone, including Chanice and her family.

George reached for his wallet. Remembering the picture of his daughter was missing, he crumbled to the floor. Under normal circustances he would never show a weakness, but the loss of his daughter was not a normal circumstance. George started to cry as he came to the realization of what Earth's destruction meant to his life. It was more than he could bear and the disturbance of this revelation overpowered his emotions.

Shalee rushed to his side, but George held up his hands and motioned for her to stay away. "Don't come near me," he screamed as he pushed himself back against the wall. "I'm dangerous! Stay back!" His grief was hellish, the memories of his daughter filling his mind. The pain of her death, tormenting.

"She was so young," he sobbed. "I loved my daughter more than anything. She was perfection. She loved me no matter what anyone said. She didn't judge me or look for my faults. She loved me because I was her dad. Oh, God, help me. My baby girl...my baby girl...this hurts. Your daddy loves you, baby," he screamed again as he looked up to the sky. "I know my baby is in Heaven." He wailed as he remembered. "There's no Heaven. How can she find a safe place for her tender soul to rest if there's no Heaven? I don't know how to stop the pain. My little girl won't know Athena."

The dreams of his baby girl going to the park with them would never come true. The thought amplified his pain and ripped his soul. "My heart. Oh, it hurts. I have to go. I have to go. I have to go, now!"

George picked himself up, then ran across the room toward the door. Before he left, he turned. "This is where we part. I need to find a place for me now. I'm lost. Please don't follow." He slammed the door behind him.

Lasidious stood from his chair, maintaining his invisible cover. He walked through the solid door to see where George was going. He did not want to lose sight of his work-in-progress.

Shalee started to follow, but Sam grabbed her arm. "You can't stop his pain. He needs to figure this one out on his own."

"What if he kills himself? I can't imagine a child of mine dyin'." Shalee fell to the bed. Her sympathy for George's pain was pulling at the core of her heart. "I couldn't deal with that kinda guilt."

"He won't kill himself. He's a better man than that. Something tells me he'll fight back and land on his feet. He mentioned a woman's name. Maybe he has a shoulder to cry on."

George was devastated as he walked down the hallway with the invisible god giving chase. The manipulator became more enraged with every step. His hate was enough to fuel the whole of Grayham twice over.

His mind questioned. *How could the one good thing in my life be stolen from me? How could these "so-called" gods destroy everything I consider precious and dear? Why did my baby have to die?*

His mind screamed this agonizing cry over and over again until he was lost in tormenting sorrow. *Why did my Abbie have to die? Why did my Abbie have to die? Why did my Abbie have to die?*

He stopped at the top of the stairs and looked out across the dining area of the inn. People were sitting and drinking, unaware of the danger lingering at the top of the stairs. He removed his gloves.

"The gods have taken my baby girl, now it's my turn. I'll kill your followers. I'll have my vengeance. I'll kill 'em all," he hissed under his breath with a reinforced evil. "An eye for an eye…just like the Good Book said."

His eyes grew dark, his hate so intense it literally changed their color as he scanned the room. The baby blue faded and was lost to his resentment. They were now the black of the darkest night. Never again would their color return, as the last piece of goodness in George's heart vanished.

Lasidious watched with concern. In all his seasons of existence, he had never seen a revulsion so intense. Even he could not believe George's emotion could cause the color of his eyes to abandon itself. The god knew this was not good for his plans. He would follow George until he could fix the problem.

George clapped his hands and scanned the room. He decided to kill everyone below, starting with the men and working his way to the women. He flew down the flight of stairs, touching them all as they ate, shouting over and over within his mind, *Everyone must die!* The taste of vengeance was sweet. He would kill every follower of the gods. *Kill them all!*

The town would have had more deaths, but it was late when George exited the inn. He stole a torch from a nearby wooden pole and headed toward the southern edge of the Enchanted Forest. Along the way, another twenty-nine people were transformed into statues. Once he arrived, he lifted his head to the sky and screamed, "Kepler!"

After a bit, the giant cat appeared from the shadows. He could sense the shift in George. Something inside the demon warned to keep his distance. The blackness of George's eyes burned its way through the jaguar's undead heart. The torch and the way it lit the murderer's face amplified the intensity of his depraved stare. The demon waited for orders.

"Go into town and find a man named Amar! I want you to do this before morning and tell him to come find me! I'll be waiting in the forest for your return! Go!"

Kepler wanted to object, but he did not want to argue with the hate flowing from the human. For the moment, he would do as he was told. He turned and charged into the darkness for the shadows of town.

George headed into the forest, found a clearing and started a fire. He lifted his head toward the starless sky and shouted. "Lasidious! Lasidious! I know you can hear me, if you're a god. I know you're watching. I'll kill everything I see if you don't show yourself."

"You called?" Lasidious answered, appearing as Jason. The Mischievous One morphed into his true form. "I'm here. What do you wish to say?"

George darted toward him and grabbed hold of the god's right hand. To the murderer's surprise, nothing happened. Lasidious laughed. It echoed in George's brain as the god's eyes turned bright red and his teeth to sharpened, fine points. Lasidious lifted only a finger. George was forced backward and hung suspended in air. Once the mortal's body floated a good distance away, the god lowered his finger and forced George into a seated position near the fire.

Now...fellow soul...according to the laws scribed onto the Book of Immortality's pages, the gods are allowed to defend an attack to make a point. On the other hand, they are not allowed to kill the soul responsible for the attack. No law has been broken.

Lasidious surrounded the area with an invisible field, allowing them to talk without fear of being heard by the others. "How bold of you, George. Did you truly think your power was strong enough to transform me? Are you not familiar with what the term, 'god,' means? Did you not think I would have the power to stop something so trivial? I would have never told you how to get this power if I couldn't defend myself against it? Think! This is unbecoming. I would have expected more, much more. Now...how about we start again? You can speak to me as if I'm someone you respect."

George screamed. "Why would I respect you or any of the gods? It's your fault the God Wars happened! My daughter is dead because of them! Kill me now and get it over with! You've taken everything from me...everything that means anything! I have *no* desire to listen to what you have to say!"

Lasidious leaned forward and allowed his eyes to burn a hotter red. "George, you're wrong. The gods are not responsible for starting the wars. The wars began as a result of the handiwork of an angel. Perhaps, you remember his name...Lucifer. *He* was the one responsible for your daughter's end. The Morning Star, *himself*, failed to value your daughter's life. *His* lack of compassion caused her end, *not mine*. George, I know your heart. What you have lost, doesn't have to be lost forever."

The blackness of George's eyes held the gaze of the god's, without waiver. "My daughter is dead. I don't care about what you and your heavenly counterparts have destroyed. All I care about is Abbie. She was everything: my light, my soul, my smile, my comfort, my desire to keep going, and the only person I ever loved. I would never lie to her. I would never hurt her. I'm lost without my baby. You took her from me. I have nothing to live for since you destroyed Abbie, along with everything else in your damn war. What could be so important you had to destroy my little girl? Why don't you take a hike and screw yourself? I want nothing to do with you."

Lasidious laughed as he reached in the pocket of his dark blue robe. "I will pretend you didn't speak to me this way, George. Look at this." He pulled out a picture of George's daughter and gave it to him. He watched the Earthling tremble as he held the picture near his heart. "Sometimes, what we think is lost, isn't lost at all. Your daughter's soul is resting inside the Book of Immortality. The Book holds the spirits of the dead until the moment arrives for them to be reborn. I personally retrieved your daughter's soul when Earth was destroyed and placed your precious little Abbie inside."

"You what?"

"I knew this day would come and we would have this conversation. I can get your daughter back, but it will require effort to be put into our moments. I have a plan; one put in place long ago. I thought you would be the right person to help carry out this plan. I saved you by bringing you here before Earth was destroyed. Once I learned of your daughter, I went back for her soul. She was lost in the darkness of space surrounding your destroyed world and I plucked her from it. There were billions of souls there that day, but I only retrieved hers from the darkness. I asked the Book of Immortality to give her soul good dreams. The Book agreed, but questioned why I would do something so against my nature."

"Yeah, and why *was* that?" George scoffed. "I'm sure you're just a peach."

"Touché." Lasidious' eyes changed to crystal blue. "I told the Book...a soul as tender as your Abbie's touched my heart. That was the end of our discussion. I poured happy thoughts onto the page where her soul rests. She is living an existence where she is at peace. In her reality, you're the best father a girl could ever have. You take her to the park. You play together and get ice cream cones."

George shook his head. "Are you saying she's all right?"

"Completely. I even gave her a little dog called Tidbit. This vision and other pleasant implanted memories play over and over. She's reminded of how great her loving dad is, every single day. She laughs as you get ready to go home and the dog pisses on your foot. She even thinks her mother is happy and you have a great marriage. George, I've given her a pleasurable existence."

George wiped tears from his cheeks. "I would say, other than the ex-wife part, it seems to be a good thing you've done for my Abbie. So, are you telling me I can get her back? When can this happen?"

The god smiled. "I'm saying, your life was spared from the destruction of Earth. I should be able to, *one day*, rejoin you with your daughter. Holding the power to bring your daughter back is the key. I have a plan to gain this power. For now, I'm bound by the laws written within the Book of Immortality. I have plans to rectify this problem. For this to happen, I need someone on Grayham to take over and create monumental distractions. These distractions will be necessary for me to move without recourse while the gods watch the events unfold."

Lasidious walked over and put his hand on George's shoulder. "In other words, I need a smoke screen. I believe, if we work together, you could see your daughter again. We could have this done in one of your Earth years if we work hard. However, my plan is contingent upon one thing...you being strong enough to create the distractions I'm asking for. I cannot make you do this. You must want this. It must be your free will which chooses to undertake such a task. What do you say, George? Are you with me?"

The mortal thought long and hard before responding. "I suppose I'm with you on two conditions. When you get the power to retrieve Abbie's soul, you do it, immediately. I'll need to be updated on our progress as we go. I also want to have plenty of coin. I don't want to worry about finances while doing your dirty deeds. If you agree, I'll bring a hell to this world like no one has ever seen. This should keep the others off your ass."

"Agreed," Lasidious responded. "It's dangerous for us to have these meetings. We would not want the others to listen in and diminish our advantage. If you will open your mind, I can keep our conversations between us. No one will be able to look into your thoughts and retrieve anything we say. This will allow me to give you the updates you require. I'll talk with you in your dreams. I'll do this as part of our agreement, but as I have said, this must be your choice."

"Then, this is what I choose. Let's get the show on the damn road," George said as he clapped his hands and rubbed them together.

Lasidious touched him on the head and, after a moment, he moved away. "It's done."

"What, that's it? What a downer. I didn't feel a thing. You need to work on your special effects when you do something godly. Hell, when I received the power from the staff, all I ended up with was a bellyache. You need to step it up a notch. You suck at this."

"You and those movies locked in your head. They make me laugh, George. I know about your special effects from Earth. I will work on something better for the next series of moments in which you receive a power."

"Hell, yeah, that sounds much better...maybe some lightning, thunder, or how about something catching on fire. Blow some crap up. But, don't forget the rain to put it all out."

"I get it, George. You want drama. I'll show you some. By the way, I cleaned up your mess in town. The people you killed live again. I'm glad I had my eye on you. You could have stirred the pot beyond well-done. You need to be cautious of the trail you leave. People would've been scared and started talking. If someone identified you, an angry mob could have given chase. You're not immortal. You don't need this kind of excitement, just yet. The moments for this will come."

Lasidious touched George's head and smiled as the murderer's eyes turned back to the soft blue they had once been. "I don't think your lady-friend would have liked your eyes looking so sinister. From now on, we will only visit in your dreams or when I'm sure it's okay to appear face-to-face. Your Abbie is waiting. Make me proud."

The god vanished as Kepler showed up. The demon's speech was reserved. "Has your mood changed, or should I go? Your eyes look better."

George had not known his eyes were a problem until Lasidious said something. Now, Kepler had also made a comment. "Relax, Kep, I have nothing to be mad about any longer. I'm sorry for yelling. What do you say we get some information out of this mage when he gets here?"

The demon turned and looked into the trees. Amar stepped forward. The mage moved to the fire and sat near George.

"It took some convincing to get him to come," Kepler growled. "I don't think he likes me."

George focused. "Amar, I'm glad you decided to join us. Let's finish our conversation. How do you think you can help, and why would I want this help?"

**The King's Castle
The City of Brandor**

Mosley appeared in the sleeping king's bedroom. As he sniffed about the chamber, his green eyes spotted a shallow glow at the room's center. The glow emanated from the embers within a circular fireplace. The chamber was spacious and sculptures of previous kings stood in every corner. The stone walls, between these six figures, were covered with colorful tapestries. A large, heavy wooden shutter had been left open to allow the cool night air of the outside world to infiltrate the room.

The wolf moved to look out the window. From this position, located at the top of the highest tower, he could see the stone slabs of the streets leading away from the castle. The longest of these streets had thousands of torches spanning its distance on either side, one on every storefront, and stretched for miles. The street ended at Brandor's arena which acted as a beacon. The glow from hundreds of torches sitting at its top softened the darkness of the night and appealed to the wolf's senses.

Mosley moved to stand at the foot of the king's bed. He scratched at the footboard and waited for Keldwin to awaken. When he did, the king leapt from his bed, grabbed his sword, and readied for battle.

"Easy, Keldwin, I am not here to hurt you. I trust I have found you well. How is your son, Aaron?"

Hearing his name, Keldwin looked hard through the fading light and waited for his eyes to adjust. "Mosley, is that you?"

"It is. I have come to speak of important matters. I request you get dressed and gather the leaders of your army. Please...meet me in your throne room."

"Since when do you give orders to a king? No one has given you permission to call me by my name. What on Grayham possessed you to think entering my chamber is permitted?"

Mosley continued to push the man's patience. "Keldwin, you would be wise to join me in your throne room. I am not just anyone, any longer. I now command a vast pack. I would look at my request as a suggestion. You can come or not, but I will be there. I intend to speak with your army."

"I'll have you flogged, wolf! How dare you talk to me this way! Guards, remove this pest from my room!"

"The guards cannot hear you, King of Brandor. This 'pest' is no longer just any wolf. I have been given immortality. I am one of the gods. I would appreciate it if you would gather your men and meet me in the throne room. Please."

"Mosley, you bore me with these lies. You...a god. Ha! Since when would the gods want the likes of you to join them? Leave me to my rest and I may forget you had the arrogance to enter my chamber."

"I'll leave as you request, but..." Mosley smiled within as he finished his statement. "...I guess I will have to seek out better men than you to listen to what I have to say." Mosley sniffed the air in the room. "I smell weakness."

Keldwin, upon hearing the insult, became furious and attacked. He lifted his blade high and brought it down across the wolf-god's back. The blade passed through Mosley's body as if thin air had been struck and crashed against the stones of the castle floor. The king watched in horror as Mosley turned and faced him. The wolf growled and showed his teeth. His dark fur stood up on the back of his neck as he maneuvered Keldwin into the open arms of one of the past monarchs. Once the king's royal bum was pressed tightly against the sculpture's cold surface, Mosley snarled.

"Keldwin, you can do as you choose, but I would think twice before you turn your blade on me again, Old King. I am, indeed, the new God of War and demand respect. Please, gather your men and bring them to the throne room. I, and some of the others, wish to speak with you."

"Others? What others?"

Mosley moved toward the door and sniffed at the stones on either side. Once satisfied he had his mark, he lifted his leg and began to urinate. As the stream flowed, he looked at Keldwin, "The other gods, of course." Mosely vanished.

Keldwin swallowed. It took him a while to recover, but he managed to get dressed. When everyone made their way to the throne room, the group consisted of the king, his son, Aaron, the General Absolute, Justin Graywind, and the gods: Mosley, Helmep, Alistar, Keylom, Calla, and Bailem.

Bailem stepped forward and prepared to introduce everyone. He kept his beautiful white wings close to his back and adjusted his robe to a better position around his portly belly. His tail moved back and forth as he spoke. "This conversation is private to those of us in this room. We cannot be heard by anyone on the outside. All of us can speak without fear. Mosley, you may tell the king why we've come."

"Keldwin, your god, Bassorine, is no longer. I have taken his place. We have not come to make demands. We are here to inform you of events soon to occur. You will need to strengthen your army to its full potential and make ready for war if you are to survive. There is an enemy building its forces, the likes of which this world has never seen. For now, the threat is minimal, but it will soon be powerful. The Crystal Moon has been stolen from the Temple of the Gods. Its pieces have been scattered."

"Who took it?" the king demanded, forgetting the company he was keeping.

Alistar answered. "Lasidious has decided to play a game with the fate of the worlds. Two pieces of the crystal will be placed on Grayham. The gods have been divided. Three of the five pieces of the Crystal Moon must be secured, or all will be lost. Grayham, as you know it, will fall into darkness."

"And, if we capture these pieces?" Keldwin responded, seeking a glimmer of hope.

Mosley answered, "If we succeed, the world will be without suffering, and your bloodline shall rule the greatest of all packs forever. You should prepare to go to war for the pieces on Grayham. The pieces need to be rejoined to keep the worlds from a sure annihilation. I'm sure you have felt the tremors of the ground beneath your feet."

The General Absolute spoke out. "There have been no tremors in Brandor, Lord Mosley. The ground beneath my feet has remained firm and strong, but reports of this shaking have made it to my ears from Angel's Village. If these tremors relate to matters of war, then this will require my attention." Justin Graywind addressed the king. "Sire, I would like the chance to question."

"By all means, General."

The general walked forward and approached the gods as if they were mortal. "I have received word from the village of Angels, their ground shook on two occasions. It was said to be a mere series of moments. No damage was done. You said an evil builds, yet I have no reports of this from my runners. Our only foes are the barbarians to the north. We haven't been at war for many seasons. I've heard nothing of a plan to attack."

Bailem stepped forward. "I understand your concern, General, but I can assure you this force does strengthen itself and will make itself known without warning. Like we said, the gods are divided. The others strengthen their position with the people of this world. The threat is real."

The leader of the king's army rubbed his head as he moved around the room, his bicep bulging as his arm moved back and forth through his long hair. "Your point has been made. I'll get every man called into service to prepare for battle. How long do we have before we see the first signs of this movement?"

Keylom stepped forward, his hooves clapped against the stones of the throne room floor. "General, this answer is unknown."

The king moved to take a seat on his throne. He grabbed a wooden goblet filled with ale and took a drink. "You would ask me to call every man in my kingdom into service and wait for an undetermined amount of moments? The finances for such a calling would be tremendous and ruin my kingdom's economy."

The God of the Harvest, responded. "Keldwin, your crops are due to be harvested in 45 Peaks. I'll bless the soils of your land. Your crops will be bountiful. You'll be able to use the finances from such an abundant harvest to fund your army's preparedness."

The king thought a moment and took another swig. "It would take three full harvests to make this kind of coin. I would like to know your intentions to address this issue. Without your help, Brandor will have to take its chances and wait to call our men into service."

Alistar response was swift. "Send word to every farm, village, town, and city. When they harvest their crops, they are to plant again before morning. If they do this, I'll bless the soil. The following morning their crops will be grown again. This will continue until three full harvests have been gathered. I assure you...they will be abundant."

The general interjected. "This is good news, but how will the people get this abundance to Merchant Island? They do not have the means."

Once again, Alistar answered. "General, I'll bless an area of soil outside of each populace. You can use this area to plant Garanto Trees. They will grow through the night and become tall and strong as if they have grown for many seasons. Use this wood to build harvest wagons. Use them to carry the harvest to the coastal cities of West Utopia, Haven, South Utopia, and Carlosam. Once there, use the king's fleet to transport the harvest to Merchant Island. You will need to build barns to store what you are unable to get to the coast until your next trip.

"Make sure you have the people in your kingdom stock their homes. This will assure your men their families are fed. The harvests will give your economy enough coin to sustain this calling. You can also harvest enough trees to rebuild the run-down areas of your kingdom."

Alistar hesitated, pulled a map of Grayham from beneath his robe, then continued. "Your first harvest is not for 45 Peaks. This gives you the moments necessary to build your wagons."

Alistar circled a number of key areas on the map with the tip of his finger. A mark was left as if some sort of lead protruded from it. "I'll take my leave to bless these areas. You should plant the trees before this day's end." The god waved his hand near the wall. Bags of every kind of seed appeared, each bag marked. "I've placed similar bags throughout your kingdom. You can find them in your royal storehouses." With that, Alistar vanished.

The king stood from his throne and walked to Mosley. "It appears there's work to be done. I apologize for my arrogance. I'm sure the general will agree, we will need to use our army."

"Wise King," Mosley said as he reached up with one of his back paws and scratched his neck. "I am sure the arrogance would have been similar on my part if someone claiming to be a god appeared as I slept." He smiled, wolfishly. With that, all the gods left for Ancients Sovereign.

𝕸𝖎𝖓𝖔𝖙𝖆𝖚𝖗

Just Outside the Town of Lethwitch

As they sat around the fire within the Enchanted Forest, George informed Amar of the trouble he was having controlling his new power. George tried to focus on Amar's life, not his own. The manipulator did not want to lose whatever advantage he might have. He felt confident Kepler understood what he was trying to accomplish. At one point, the cat winked as he cleaned himself by the fire.

George was relieved when he learned Amar would be helpful while learning to control his new power. Kepler's skeleton warriors were no longer necessary.

Amar had grabbed ten rats from the cellar of his brother's store before coming to the forest and threw them in a small cage. One by one, he pulled them out and gave instructions. It took only four deaths before George had his first success. He was able to limit the transformation to a single leg. The rest of the rat had been spared a solid death and George watched as the rodent hobbled in front of them.

Kepler lifted his head from between his legs and stopped licking himself long enough to comment. "It appears you're getting the hang of it. You might be able to keep from killing us all."

George shook his head, then pulled another rat from the cage. During this series of moments, nothing happened. He smiled as he tossed the rat into the air and watched as Kepler snatched it in his mouth. A crunching sound could be heard as the rat's bones snapped beneath the heavy chomp. Amar had to dodge as a squirt of blood shot passed his face.

Amar frowned. "This is a new robe. I don't want it soiled. I have no desire to smell as foul as my brother."

Kepler stood, walked over to Amar and sniffed. "You are human. You will always smell foul."

George snickered. "Knock it off, Kep. We're here to learn, remember?"

Kepler growled and lowered to the ground as George reached into the cage and pulled out another rat by its tail. He lifted it into the air without changing any part of it.

"That's very good," Amar said, "but can you change its heart without turning the rest of it?"

"I can try," George responded with a questioning look, "but how will I know if it worked?"

"Because it'll fall over dead, simpleton," Kepler sneered. "It is, after all, the heart you're turning to stone. It's a major part of the body. How could you possibly dominate territories while asking such ridiculous questions? Perhaps, I should assign *you* a title. How shall we say it? How does this sound? George, The Ludicrous."

Irritated at the cat's remark, George smirked, shook his head in disgust and directed his attention toward the rat. The critter began to shake. Moments later, George tossed the dead rodent on the ground and stared directly into Kepler's eyes.

Kepler gave a half-hearted grin and once again began to lick himself. He mumbled between licks. "Give humans a taste of power and they feel invincible. Remember, we are allies, George. Your power does you no good if I swipe your head from your shoulders."

George searched for a cutting response. "Well, aren't you a brave kitty?"

Kepler lifted his head from between his legs. His eyes flashed as he responded, "It would be prudent to change the subject."

Satisfied with Kepler's irritation, George watched as Amar cut the rat open to witness his handiwork. Sure enough, the heart was the only thing turned to stone. Everyone around the fire—including the invisible god—praised George's success, though Kepler's cheer was forced.

Reaching in the cage again, George threw another rat to Amar for inspection. During this moment, he changed just the lungs, as he intended. Again, everyone praised his work. When he arrived at the tenth rat, his skill level was strong enough to change a specific toenail, then let the creature loose in the woods. George was pleased with himself, to say the least.

After a bit, he sat next to Kepler. Amar was talking to the jaguar when Kepler felt George's hand. The giant cat sprang over the fire to the far side of the clearing and snarled, "Not funny, George!"

The jokester rolled on the ground in amused satisfaction. "Oh, my hell, you should've seen your face, Kep. Amar, did you see him freak out? He crapped himself."

Amar's brow furrowed. "I don't know what 'freak out' or what 'crapped' means, but it certainly sounds funny."

George rolled his eyes. Kepler calmed down and was able to laugh at his own expense. Once the atmosphere settled, George's mind began to plot.

He poked the fire with a stick. "Kepler, please go back to the cave and fetch Maldwin. Your brothers need to know your skeleton warriors aren't needed. Amar and I will go into Lethwitch and prepare for the journey to Siren's Song. Let's meet up on the north side of Angel's Village in 20 Peaks. After we reunite, we'll head west to the Latsky Divide and follow the river north to Siren's Song. I..."

Kepler interrupted, "Why are we going to Siren's Song?"

"For more power, of course. I need to speak with the wisp inside the mist."

This seemed to satisfy the demon. The journey to fetch Maldwin would give him a break from the humans. He turned and headed for the cave. Amar walked with George into town. On the way, the mage informed George his family had once served in King Brandor's court. They would be able to take the hippogriffs to Angel's Village. When he realized George had no clue about the flying creatures, he explained. George liked the idea. The journey to Angel's Village would only take 2 Peaks by air. They would be able to stay in Lethwitch for quite a while.

* * *

Lasidious decided it was the proper moment to leave. He had learned enough and his presence was no longer necessary.

* * *

Leaving much later than expected would allow George to watch Sam's last fight. He could also spend the moments necessary to get to know his beautiful Athena. He would get a room at the inn where she worked and make sure he was there when she showed up.

When they arrived, the two men shook hands and parted ways after agreeing to meet at Early Bailem on the 17th day. George continued inside the inn. The lady behind the counter smiled as he entered.

"Back already, I see," she said. "I don't believe we've met properly. I'm Susanne, Athena's favorite and only sister. I had the flowers taken to my mother's home. I'm sure Athena loved them. She's just south of here, visiting our mother's farm. My sister has never gone home to talk about anyone, except you. I hope you're worth it," she said, giving a half-serious-half-questioning grin.

"Oh, I wouldn't count on it," he responded with a smile. "I'm a big pain and I don't think I would pay even one Helmep for me."

Susanne smiled. "What're you going to do to keep yourself busy until she arrives?"

"I was thinking about going to the fights. Do you know when they start?"

Susanne turned and grabbed a local event calendar, which was scribed once every 25 Peaks. "It looks as if they start at the Peak of Bailem, tomorrow. Is there a particular fighter you're interested in?"

"I have an old friend fighting and I want to watch. This will be his third fight. He won his first two."

"Could you tell him Athena has a single sister? I have room for a strong man in my life."

"I will, but I'm not sure how his girlfriend would like that. She's training to be a sorceress."

"Well then, I want no part of him. I would hate to be turned into a vestlechick."

Unsure of what a vestlechick was, George responded as if he understood. "You're right, that would be terrible. Thank you for your kindness, Susanne. Will you tell Athena my room number when she arrives? I look forward to getting to know you better. Hopefully, I'll meet the rest of your family someday."

The Next Day
Lethwitch Arena

George was amazed by the brutality of the fights. Many of the men had been carried off on stretchers, followed by a trail of healers. *I hope Sam is good*, he thought as he looked down to study the arena's archaic form of a program. *Your opponent's bio reads like a mysterious nightmare. There's nothing here.*

The champion of Lethwitch was undefeated, with eleven wins—some of which ended in death. Other than the number of wins and deaths, the schedule said nothing else about Sam's opponent. Unlike the other fighters, his profile only had a name. It said: The Beast from the West, Terrogon.

The fight was to be with a sword and shield, no body armor—to the death, unless the roll said otherwise. George got the attention of a man sitting to his left. "What does it mean, unless the roll says otherwise?"

The man's breath smelled of ale and a woman to his right grumbled at his ignorance. The man responded with a slur. "A favorable roll can give the champion a choice to change the style of battle. The champion of every arena is allowed this roll. I feel sorry for the man who faces the beast."

George looked across the arena's sandy surface. *I wonder what's going through Sam's mind. If only I could find a way inside his preparation room.* He had tried to get below the arena. *Damn those two guards.*

Shalee stood over Sam, rubbing his shoulders. After a moment, she moved away and picked up her staff. She looked at BJ and Helga and asked the trainers to leave them alone. Once she was sure the coast was clear, she turned to Sam. "Are ya ready, darlin'?"

"As ready as I can be. You know it scares me when you use Precious on me. Sure, you mended my pants, but are you sure you can make this work? I don't want to end up like some kind of magical hamburger."

Shalee laughed. "Don't be silly. I wouldn't want my baby ta be hamburger eitha'. Well, I do like hamburger, though...so maybe..."

"You're not funny. Can you get this over with? I trust you know what you're doing. Hurry up."

The sorceress gave him a quick kiss. "Just in case," she said, giggling as she lifted her staff. "Make me proud, Sammy-kins. Precious, *tiuka helma*!" Her voice was strong and forceful.

Sam could feel a difference in his skin. Even though his appearance had not changed, he knew the command worked. He grabbed Kael and used the blade to test the effect. He watched as the razor-sharp edge of the god-sword crossed his skin, leaving no mark behind. "Not even Kael is cutting me!"

Kael had a few things to say. The weapon pulled away and rose from Sam's hand, its blade pulsating as it spoke. "The use of Shalee's magic doesn't mean your opponent's blade won't kill you. It only means your skin has toughened and smaller wounds will not open as easily. Strikes made by hand, foot, or even the blunt force of a shield, should feel less painful. If your opponent is able to stab you with the point of his blade or make a deep slice, you will die. Do not make the mistake of thinking you're impenetrable."

"Great. Thanks a lot, Kael. Leave it up to you to bring a guy's high down," Sam joked.

The sword had come to understand the fighter's humor. "You need to prepare your mind." The blade floated over to Shalee. "Please, excuse us. I have matters of importance to discuss with Sam before he enters the arena."

Shalee did as the sword requested. When she left, the blade lowered to the bench beside the fighter. "Sam, you must fight with me today."

Sam could not believe his ears. Until now, Kael had said he could not wield him in any form of combat other than training. "Are you sure? You're not worried I'll embarrass you?"

"I have something to tell you before you can take me into the arena. I need to tell you what the markings on my hilt mean."

"Of course. I'm all ears."

"The message reads:

> *Bound by honor and righteousness,*
> *a true warrior who has lost everything*
> *will command this Sword of Truth and Might.*
> *His wisdom and valor*
> *will be his true power to lead the masses.*
> *The power of the Elvish word*
> *will strike down his enemies before him.*"

"Kael, I'm grateful you told me their meaning, but I don't know the Elvish language."

"*Val arrna,*" Kael responded. "It means Storm of Power. All you must do is remember these two words. When you engage your enemy, speak them both. If you need help, the power of the words will allow me to guide your movements. Be careful. You don't want the people knowing you wield a sword of my calibur. Place my markings near your mouth and speak the words aloud. I must feel their power. Once I do, I'll assist when needed. Today, your enemy will suffer a quick death."

"Okay, okay, do I really need to kill my opponent? I don't want to kill anyone else. I've done enough already."

In a soft voice, the sword responded, the pulsating of the blade humming as it did. "Sam, this fight is between two beings who wield sharp weapons. Do you think there's another way? This fight will be to the death. This was made clear on the event schedule."

"You know I don't read the event schedule. It gives me anxiety. I..." Sam hesitated. This was the first series of moments in which he realized he was expected to go into the arena to take a life. His first two fights ended in death only because his foes were trying to do more than subdue him. In this fight, he was going to kill or be killed. He would have to release his rage from the beginning.

The bell of the arena sounded, jarring Sam from his thoughts. He only had a couple of moments to find his position. He headed out with Kael in hand.

The crowd erupted as Sam entered. From the stands, George marveled at how well-known Sam was. They chanted his name while stomping their feet. The fighter moved into position and held his hands high to absorb the energy of the screaming masses.

When Sam saw his enemy walk through the arena doors, he was shocked to see the beast. It had a bull's head, a massive human torso, and powerful, cow-like legs ending with sharp hooves. He knew this type of beast from books he read as a kid. It was called a minotaur. Long horns, at least two feet in length, extended on each side of its head.

Sam watched the beast bellow like an angered bull. The creature's muscles tightened as it threw its thick arms outward, level with the floor of the arena.

From the intense feeling of the crowd and his opponent's dark stare, Sam knew he would die if he was not ferocious. He called upon his inner demon. It was screaming to be freed. Sam opened its cage and let it rush to the forefront of his mind. His demeanor changed as the hate poured out of him. His heart turned to ice as he walked in to engage.

The arena headmaster shouted while lifting his hands, motioning for Sam to stop. "As champion, Terrogon is allowed his roll!"

The crowd chanted for the bowl. The minotaur bellowed in Sam's direction and snorted as he moved to stand over a podium. The circular dias had been placed on the arena floor below the headmaster's box. The beast reached inside a large wooden bowl and grabbed seven dice made of the bones of past champions. After shaking them in his massive hand, the dice rattled around the bowl before coming to rest. Four of the seven dice was all it took to indicate Terrogon had his choice of battle.

The minotaur lifted his shield and blade into the air. Once sure the headmaster understood his intent, he tossed them to the ground to signify combat without weaponry. It was now illegal, under the laws of Grayham, to use any object crafted by hand to win the fight.

Lifting Kael in front of his mouth, Sam whispered, "I'm screwed."

Sam was not surprised Kael did not respond. The pulsating of the blade would have enlightened the crowd as to the power the weapon possessed. Sam held his head high as he walked to the area of the arena where Shalee, Helga, and BJ sat. He tossed Kael to BJ, then discarded his shield, tossing it to the sand.

Shalee called to him, "Sam, ya cannot fight! Ya need ta concede! Dyin' in the arena won't accomplish anythin'!"

BJ would have spoken, but Sam motioned for him to stop. After a moment of deep thought while staring at the stone wall surrounding the arena's yellow sand, Sam found Shalee's eyes. "We have nothing to go home to. This world is all we've got. If I don't fight for these people, who will? You know the task we're facing. To quit because of fear only prolongs the death we'll suffer. I couldn't live with myself if I didn't fight. I have to be the best I can be. Would you have me do less?"

George studied Shalee's face from the other side of the arena. Though he could not hear their conversation, he could see her look of despair. He was surprised at his level of concern. Though against his character, he wanted to help, but he had no idea what he could do. He lifted his hands in front of his face and crossed his fingers. "Fight like a mad man, Sam. Kick this thing's ass," he whispered.

Sam nodded at BJ, then at Helga. After one last reassuring look to give Shalee a sense of confidence, he turned to face his opponent. He pushed his neck side to side, cracking the bones, then began his approach.

Terrogon gnashed his teeth and flexed to intimidate, but Sam was no longer in control. His inner demon, centuries older than Sam's own consciousness, now ruled him. Sam charged.

The minotaur met Sam's advance with a rush of his own. The two collided. The force nearly knocked both combatants unconscious. The beast-man was the first to recover. He lifted Sam above his head and threw him across the arena and watched as the human landed with a thud. Terrogon turned to the crowd and lifted his arms skyward to bask in the glory of the moment.

Sam struggled to push himself up. He appreciated Shalee's magic. Without it, he would have been knocked unconscious. Trying to match the beast's power, despite his godly gift of strength, was a flawed plan. He needed to be swift.

Sam shook out the cobwebs as the bull-man turned from the crowd. Again, the beast charged. Sam crouched and waited until the last possible moment. Just before Terrogon made contact, Sam rolled backward, secured a horn in each hand and used his legs to send the minotaur flying. The bull-man collided with a single pillar at the center of the arena, loosening its foundation.

Sam hurried to his feet and followed. As the beast's massive muzzle lifted from the sand, Sam grabbed the hoop which dangled from its nostrils and ripped. The bull-man's flesh clung to the pin which secured the hoop as it tore free. The minotaur reacted to the pain and kicked. Its right hoof collided against Sam's ribs and, despite Shalee's magic, a gash opened. Though no bones were broken, the collision was so severe the flesh dangling from the hoop's pin fell to the arena floor as Sam flew backward and landed in a balled position.

The minotaur rose, reclaimed his bloody flesh and ate it to demonstrate his superiority. The crowd groaned its disgust. Angered by the people's response, Terrogon placed his heavy hands against the pillar and pushed. At over 30 feet tall and three feet wide, the pillar toppled in Sam's direction.

Sam lunged from beneath the object of death. The pillar missed by a narrow margin as he rolled to his feet. The arena floor gave way, the weight of the stone being too much to bear. Each section of the pillar fell into the darkness lit by torchlight and killed four men waiting for their moments to fight.

The crowd's energy amplified the mood as the hole opened and delivered its sentence. George sat in his seat, stunned. He could not believe how sadistic these people were. Their thirst for blood was insatiable. He thought to himself, *Damn...at least when I killed the owners of The Old Mercantile they didn't feel anything. How could these people be so cruel? Getting crushed has to hurt.* As soon as George finished his thought, he lifted his voice and shouted, "Kick his ass, Sam!"

The woman sitting to George's right turned and grumbled. She was heavyset, probably around her fiftieth season and wore a yellow dress. The dress had no sleeves and the hairs under her arms were so long George could see their ends. The woman had a grouchy grandmother's voice as she spoke. "You aren't from around here, are you? You should watch your mouth. Those who sit around me root for our champion. You understand, boy?"

Out of the corner of his eye, George watched as the minotaur threw Sam across the arena. As Sam landed, everyone surrounding the old lady stood and threw their arms up, cheering, but not the woman. She just sat there, staring at George as if he had some sort of disease.

George put a smile on his face. "You're right. I'm sorry. Who am I to be sitting here insulting you like this? I will cheer as expected."

The woman turned forward and growled, "That's more like it."

George listened to the crowd moan as Sam kicked the minotaur in his loincloth covered nuts. As Terrogon cried out, George took the opportunity to remove his glove, then touched the old woman on her hand. Every bone, muscle, and organ from the top of her neck down turned to stone, but her skin remained unchanged. Despite most of her bodily functions being shut down, simultaneously, George knew her mind was not dead yet. He watched as her eyeballs rolled in his direction. He stood, smiled, and nodded, then said, "It was nice to have met you. Please, don't get up, I'll find my way out." As he moved passed, he watched the woman's eyes gloss over.

Meanwhile, on the other side of the arena, Helga had to take Precious from Shalee. The hot-headed Texan was finding it hard to watch. She desperately wanted to help Sam, but it was against the laws of Grayham. The young sorceress-in-training had threatened to kill the minotaur with her magic twice already and Helga felt it best to secure her only weapon.

Since she couldn't use her power, Shalee resorted to the next best thing and started screaming. BJ and Helga could not believe someone so beautiful could sound so ugly. "Sam Goodrich, ya best grab him by his junk, drag his sorry ass 'round this arena, and use that god given strength of yours ta shove your foot right up his backside! No one treats my baby this way! Ya tell him I said that when ya knock the sense out of him!"

Shalee turned to look at Helga. "Can ya believe the nerve of that thing? I ought ta..."

Helga put a finger against Shalee's lips. "You'll do nothing, child." The older sorceress took Shalee by the arm and sat her down. "I suggest we pray to the gods we serve. Sam needs all the help he can get, child."

Shalee rolled her eyes. "You go on ahead and do that. I'd rather watch this fight. Who in their right mind prays at a fight? That's downright weird." Shalee stood up, looked across the arena, then shouted, "Kick his butt, Sam!"

Sam fought to pick himself up after being thrown into the wall below the headmaster's box. He tensed as Terrogon charged again. With head lowered, the beast rammed him into the wall. Blood rolled down Sam's chin, his internal organs taking much of the damage. The beast backed up, saw Sam was unable to move, and began to scuff his right hoof through the sand.

From his cave-like home beneath the Peaks of Angels, on Ancients Sovereign, Lasidious watched the green flames within his cube shaped fireplace. He could see the images of Sam and understood the situation was critical. He moved to the stone table at the center of the room, grabbed the four remaining pieces of the Crystal Moon, then returned. "Use this to your advantage, old friend. The moment has not come for you to die, my brother." Lasidious began to shake the pieces of the Crystal Moon.

Once again, the beast-man slammed into Sam, pinning him against the wall. The blood flowed from Sam's mouth as the ground beneath the arena began to shake. The quaking was severe. The seismic activity was enough to get the beast's attention. The minotaur turned his back to Sam. Terrogon looked confused as he watched the sand sift into the hole at the center of the arena.

Seizing the opportunity and understanding this was his only chance for survival, Sam reached deep within and reacted. The fighter lunged forward, grabbed the end of the minotaur's left horn with his left hand, and used what was left of his strength to pulverize the horn's base with his right fist. The horn snapped, becoming a weapon. Before the minotaur could react, Sam spun around and plunged the horn deep into Terrogon's back, piercing his heart.

The crowd screamed as the bull-man fell to his knees, but Sam wasn't finished. He pulled the horn free with his right hand, reached over top of the minotaur's shoulder with his left, and grabbed the beast's chin. Pulling his enemy backward, Sam used the horn and plunged it over and over again into Terrogon's massive chest. After letting the minotaur fall to the sand, Sam spit a mouthful of blood onto its muzzle, then collapsed.

The arena was in a frenzy. The box holding the Minotaur King and his guards was the loudest of them all. Their cries called for justice. They were already claiming Grayham's laws of combat had been broken and were demanding a meeting with the arena's headmaster to discuss punishment.

It didn't take long for the arena's healers to surround Sam's motionless figure. There wasn't a moment to spare, yet putting Sam on the hide of their stretcher was impossible. It was easy to see Sam's condition was critical. His internal wounds were responsible for his faint breathing. The eldest of the three healers, dressed in an earth-colored robe, reached into a large leather case and removed a pouch filled with a reddish-yellow liquid. Pulling the cork from its mouth, Jaress knelt next to Sam, then lifted the fighter's head onto his right knee. Forcing Sam's mouth open, he poured the liquid to the back of the fighter's throat and pushed his jaw shut.

BJ arrived and knocked the bowl from its pedestal. The trainer shook his head in disgust as he watched the dice tumble, then lowered next to Sam.

Jaress placed Sam's head on the arena sand. After pushing his graying braid behind his back, Jaress looked at BJ through weathered eyes. His voice was strong. "His condition is severe. I have given him the essence of the griffin. It is too bad our reunion is overshadowed by these grave circumstances."

BJ's eyes widened as he held his brother's. "Jaress, how did you acquire the griffin's essence? I know of no other healer on Grayham with access to such a treasure."

Shalee and Helga arrived to stand behind BJ as Jaress responded. "You can thank Soresym for saving your friend's life. His Majesty sent word for me to come to the landing platform the night of your arrival. The Griffin Lord gave me his essence and instructed it to be used only if your friend was to fall in battle. I know of no other man fortunate enough to have this bond."

Shalee was a mess and her eyes were filled with tears. Helga held her arm as the young sorceress spoke. "Will Sam live? Is he gonna die?"

Jaress found Shalee's gaze. "A griffin's essence is a powerful thing. I will watch your friend throughout the night. We should know by morning."

"His name is Sam," Shalee said in a soft tone. "He's got a name. Please use it."

"Yes, my lady."

Shalee knelt and lifted Sam's head onto her lap. "When can he be moved? We can't leave him lyin' here all night."

Before an answer could be given, the loud voice of the arena's headmaster filled the air. "Barthom Jonas, leave your fighter with the healers! There are matters to discuss!"

"Now what?" Helga questioned. "You're needed here. What could they possibly say that's so important?" She turned to look at Shalee, "I'm sure everything will be allright, child."

BJ's face showed his concern. He stood and put his hand on Helga's shoulder. "I suspect this has something to do with the Minotaur King. This may not be news we care to hear. I will return when I know more." BJ rushed off.

Seeing the griffin's essence was beginning to work, the healers accompanying Jaress rolled Sam to his side and lowered him onto the stretcher. Jaress led the women into the healer's vestry below the arena.

Athena's Work

It was just after Late Bailem when Athena started her shift. She placed the flowers from George on the end of the bar in her mother's inn. It was just a matter of moments before she would see him again and get the kiss she so badly wanted. She moved about the inn, singing as she did her odd jobs. She was dusting the bar when George arrived. Flying across the room, she jumped into his arms.

"Hey, honey," she glowed. "I'm glad you're here. I would love to finish the conversation we started."

George pulled her close and gave her a warm kiss. "I missed that smile of yours. I'm going to be in town for a while. I was hoping we could get to know one another. Maybe one of these evenings we could find a secluded spot to have dinner."

Athena kissed the end of his nose, winked, then excused herself. She ran into the back room and rummaged through the kitchen. After a while, she returned with a basketful of food. "Let's go. I'm free for the evening. My mother will be okay without me. We have extra help during the fights. There are torches out back. We'll need to take a few with us for when it gets dark."

Leaving the inn, George admired the purple hues of Luvelles. He also admired the orange hues of Harvestom as both worlds approached their horizons. He liked the collection of moments called evening. The colors of the worlds, as they set in opposite directions, though much smaller in size than when he first saw them, felt vibrant as the sun closed in on the end of the day.

He had learned while traveling with Kepler, both worlds would continue to move farther away from Grayham's orbit and eventually be unable to be seen. The demon said the red world of Dragonia would be the next sphere to become visible, followed by the dark world of Trollcom.

George felt romantic as they held hands and walked south out of town. Soon, they came to a natural spring which boiled to the surface. It was tucked behind a wall of foliaged trees. The area, some sixty feet across, was closed-in and hid a gazebo-like structure made of hardened clay. The gazebo was covered with blooming flowers of all colors and sat at the water's center. A quaint bridge led to the structure. Its natural enchantment was intoxicating.

Dusk was approaching. George reached for a torch. "Not yet, honey," Athena whispered as she placed a single finger across his lips. She led him to the gazebo and continued to whisper. "Just watch. The torches are for later. We don't need them now. Shhh."

Soon, the pitch black of night fell across the land. George could not see a thing. He reached over, found Athena's ear and leaned in. "What are we waiting for?"

Athena covered his mouth, "Shhh."

The flowers growing on the gazebo and the trees surrounding the pool began to glow, but it wasn't just any glow. They gave off a light directly opposing their natural color during the day. The pool's depth mirrored their warmth. George felt as if he was in the middle of a galaxy, floating amongst stars of many colors.

The flower petals began to move back and forth in a massaging manner. Small puffs of pollen were released from the flowers' centers. A plethora of fragrances filled the night air as each puff drifted against the breeze. One by one, the puffs worked their way to their destinations. It was as if the flowers were in the middle of some sort of mating ritual.

George watched as a blue puff found an opposing yellow flower. The flower opened, allowed the puff inside, then closed its petals. The color of the puff merged with the color of the flower. Soon, the flower opened and a melody began to fill the night as if the flower had a voice of its own. As the song progressed, the flower took on its new color and radiated a vibrant green.

"I can't believe this," George blurted.

As soon as he spoke, everything went black. Athena nudged his arm. "I told you to shush. Now, we have to use a torch. You ruined the mood."

"Aahhhh, man, I'm sorry. That was freaking cool. We've got to do this again."

Athena wasn't sure how to respond. She was confused by the way he phrased things. Seeing her confusion, George changed the subject. "I'll get us some light."

George fumbled in his pocket and pulled out his lighter. As soon as the flame appeared, Athena's eyes widened. George smiled, placed the torch in one of the brackets attached to the gazebo's side, then waited for the questions he knew were coming.

Their conversation would be without pause as he explained how the lighter worked. Athena was intrigued by the many subtle differences of how the two of them spoke. Their conversation bounced from one subject to another as they held each other while sitting at the gazebo's center.

As the second torch died, they made their way to a place only Athena knew. A little cottage, still twice the size of George's old apartment, was lit with many oil-filled sconces. He held their last torch high as he examined the stonework. It was meticulous and great care had been put into every detail.

Athena walked to the door and opened it. "Mother," she shouted, "I brought home that adorable man I was telling you about! Can he stay in the spare room?"

George was taken aback by Athena's forwardness, but after a moment of thinking it through, he stepped inside and shouted, "Mom, we're home!"

After sitting on the bed and talking with Athena throughout the night, they decided to get some sleep. George leaned in and gave her a soft kiss. One kiss led to another and before the two of them knew it, they were tickling each other on the bed.

For the first series of moments in George's pathetic life, other than his daughter's birth, he felt happy. He knew his goose was cooked—this woman had captured his heart. All he had to do was figure out a way to ensure she ended up in his life. He knew this would be a challenge, a challenge he looked forward to facing. He rolled Athena over, pulled her close, and while remaining clothed, he cuddled her as they drifted off to sleep.

Lethwitch Arena

When the sun rose, Shalee and Helga were sitting next to Sam who remained unconscious in the healer's vestry beneath the arena. Jaress returned, carrying breakfast, corgan milk and muffins. "Any movement while I was out?"

"I'm afraid not," Helga replied.

The heavy wooden door to the vestry opened. BJ walked in, followed by the arena's headmaster, Lorund. Upon seeing them enter, Shalee stood from her seat, set her muffin on the table next to Sam and braced herself for the news. Realizing the looks on the men's faces appeared grim, she retrieved Precious from the corner of the room.

Lorund, a strong, gray haired man with brown eyes, was the first to speak. He was still dressed in his black leather armor which bore the symbol of the Kingdom of Brandor. "The Minotaur King has requested Sam's life in exchange for the death of his champion, Terrogon."

Shalee gasped, "Why? Sam beat him fair and square. He's practically dead already. I won't let 'em have him."

"Child, it's not that simple," Helga responded. "There are laws combatants must live by in the arena. Hear the man out."

"Law or no law, I'm not gonna let 'em have him. I'm not givin' Sam ta some bull-faced losers." Shalee began to tap the butt end of Precious on the floor. "I'll give 'em what for. You just tell 'em ta come on down here and I'll show 'em anotha' way ta die. I dare them ta try ta take Sam off this table. I can't stand a sorry loser."

BJ began to laugh. "I admire your spirit, Shalee, but you will not need to use your magic on anyone. After a long debate, we have determined Sam's actions were acceptable. The fight was to be without weapons. Terrogon was the first to use a weapon during the battle. When he tried to use the pillar to crush Sam, he broke the law by which he chose to fight. Sam's use of Terrogon's horn as the instrument of death has been justified. Sam no longer had to abide by the rules set by the roll of the dice."

"That's great!" Shalee exclaimed. "So, Sam's free ta go when he wakes up? For goodness' sake, that's a relief."

Lorund shook his head in disagreement. "I would not consider this a joyous outcome. The race of minotaur will know of this. Sam will be despised. If I were you, I would see to it Sam never runs across another one. The Minotaur King will not allow him to live if he ever sees him again."

"Goodness-gracious! That's not very nice. Sore losers. They wouldn't make good Texans. We would've been downright embarrassed ta have folks like that livin' in our state."

Lorund looked at BJ, then at Helga, then Jaress. "What is she talking about? Is she foreign?" He turned to look at Shalee. "Is Texas on one of the other worlds? I have read nothing of it in all my studies. I have never heard anyone speak as you."

Helga cut in, "You know how young ones can be. I will handle her. You go on ahead. I'm sure your family is expecting you. Thank you for clearing matters up."

Lorund nodded. "There are other matters to which I must attend. I have been informed there is a woman sitting in the arena who has passed. Her weight is abnormal, even for her size, and will require a significant number of men to carry her away. It's as if she is made of stone."

It wasn't long after Lorund's departure that Sam began to stir. Jaress quickly moved to keep the fighter still. Once Sam's eyes opened and the fighter realized where he was, the healer explained everything. After Sam acknowledged he understood, Jaress uncorked the essence of the griffin and lifted Sam's head.

"I need you to drink. This is a powerful elixir. Your wounds will heal, quickly."

Sam took three large swigs. With as much as he ingested, his body began to tingle. Despite the blood loss, the paleness of his skin faded.

Sam managed a weak voice, "That doesn't taste like any medicine I've ever had. It was sweet. What was it?"

"The essence of His Majesty, the griffin, Lord Soresym," Jaress responded with admiration. "I know of no man on Grayham who has ever been given this honor."

Sam began to chuckle, but the pain caused him to stop. Once he collected himself, he responded. "I knew we bonded, but I had no idea Soresym considered me to be worthy of his essence. Exactly, what part of a griffin does its essence come from? Is it a special gland of some sort?"

BJ looked across the table at this brother. "I would love nothing more than to explain. Please, allow me this honor, Jaress. You owe me."

Jaress shook his head and rolled his eyes. "I thought mother settled our dispute. Besides, I cannot. I've given my word. The Griffin Lord said this question would be asked. I have been given special instruction to deliver this answer." Jaress looked at Sam. "The essence is collected when a griffin allows a healer to harvest its urine."

Sam grimaced, his face showing his disgust. BJ and Helga began to laugh. Shalee was the first to respond. "That's downright nasty! Are ya standin' there tellin' me Sam just drank a truckload of piss? What on this world would eva' make y'all decide to drink somethin' so foul in the first place? Who was the first fruit loop ta look at a stream of urine comin' out of a big old griffin and think, 'I wonder if that'll fix me?' Goodness-gracious, y'all are drinkin' griffin piss. I neva'."

It took a while, but Sam managed to put a clear thought together. "If drinking Soresym's essence is what it took to save my life, then I'm honored. If no man has ever been given this honor, why me?"

Jaress could only smile. "Lord Soresym said you would ask this question. His response: it is to get even with you for calling him a thing. He further said, he hopes you hate the taste. His Majesty laughed as he launched from the landing platform and flew into the night. I did not expect the delivery of this message to be so enjoyable, but I cannot help myself."

Sam looked at Shalee. "It wasn't as bad as it sounds." He began to smile. "Griffin's must be made of raspberries and lemons. His urine tasted like lemonade. If the idea wasn't so disgusting, I would bottle it and sell it. At least it would be a healthy drink." He poured what was left of Soresym's essence into his mouth and swallowed. "I'm feeling much better."

Shalee rolled her eyes. "You're nasty."

That evening, over dinner, BJ and Helga sought each other's attention. Both trainers flirted and were careful not to allow their students to see their momentary exchanges of quick smiles and playful winks. It was clear to BJ something was there and he wanted to explore the possibility of Helga's companionship.

After dinner, BJ excused himself and asked Helga if she would join him for an evening walk. When Shalee offered to tag along, BJ declined, and said it would be nice to converse without students present. Sam and Shalee thought nothing of it and retired to their room.

The two trainers put some distance between them and the inn. BJ reached down and took Helga's hand. They walked east out of the city. Helga used her staff to light the way as they stopped at the center of a bridge which spanned the distance over the Cripple River flowing from the Pool of Sorrow.

They knew their attraction for one another was mutual. It was on this beautiful night, beneath a pitch black gentle sky and hundreds of glow bugs surrounding them, that Helga commanded her staff to go dark.

The gentle rippling of the river passing beneath the bridge amplified the mood. BJ put his hand under Helga's chin and lifted. A passionate kiss followed.

Helga giggled as they separated. "Well now...Mr. Barthom Jonas, you're quite the kisser and delightfully delicious."

The Grayham Inquirer

When Inquiring Minds Need to Know about their Favorite Characters

2 PEAKS of Bailem have passed. Kepler is with Maldwin at the entrance to the Cave of Sorrow. The jaguar realized he was going to run into a problem on his way to the cave. He commanded one of his giant feline subjects from the Enchanted Forest to travel with him. As expected, the rat refused to leave. His family would not be protected while he was gone. Without the stone Skeleton Warriors promised, Kepler knew it was pointless to argue.

To fix the problem, Kepler told the rodent he would have one hundred of his finest monitor the cave and the Pass of Tears. They would not leave and would be ordered to protect the rat's family. Maldwin agreed and Kepler sent word to his brothers by way of his feline subject. Maldwin instructed his family to stay hidden until the skeletons arrive, then the pair left for Angel's Village.

SAM, Shalee, BJ, and Helga have arrived in the town of Mountain View. Soresym enjoyed giving them their ride and relished the idea that Sam had to use his essence. A rare bond has formed between the griffin and his human companions.

Sam and Shalee have been impressed with the town's scenery. Many of the views surrounding the landing platform are breathtaking.

YALOOM, the God of Greed, has taken over the leadership of Lasidious' old team. They are plotting. Based on what Lasidious said at the gods' meeting, they have determined a course of action. They will put the Barbarian Kingdom in the strongest position for the war they know is coming. When the moment arrives that their meeting is over, a plot to assassinate the King of Brandor's son, Aaron Brandor, and the General Absolute, Justin Graywind, has been finalized and put in motion.

MOSLEY spent the previous day mourning his wife's soul. He hates the idea she is in the Book of Immortality. The wolf is now with his team. They watched from the god world as the King of Brandor sent his runners throughout the kingdom to deliver his orders. Alistar revealed the locations of the blessed soil and Keldwin has ordered the first harvest of the massive trees which will be used to build the harvest wagons.

Building these oversized wagons is going to be quite the task. The runners have called for a meeting with the nobles of each city, town, and village to explain what must take place. They have also informed the nobles two of the king's engineers will arrive at each location to help with the proper design and construction of the wagons. The final approved drawings show each wagon will have nine axles and fifteen horses will be needed to pull them.

GEORGE and Athena spent the last three days on her mother's farm. After that, they agreed they wanted to stay in her mother's guest house. Their longing for each other is growing and they anticipate making noise.

CELESTRIA is still months away from delivering her baby boy. The elven witch family is testing her patience. She wants to destroy them, but continues to remind herself of the goals she had set with her lover. She has retired to her room to speak with the squirrels.

LASIDIOUS is with the Wisp of Song, deep inside the mist of Siren's Song, below Griffin Falls. The Mischievous One tells the creature about the envelope he gave to George. He also says the human will be traveling to meet with him and in return for the envelope, the god asks the wisp to tell George how to win the crown of the Barbarian King.

SENCHAE BLOODVAIN is still on edge from his run-in with the talking bull. He is sitting in his bedroom chamber holding his unicorn horn and has skipped his training for the first series of moments in over 16 seasons.

Thank you for reading the Grayham Inquirer

Duke Barthom Brandor

BJ has taken Sam to a quiet place outside of Mountain View to train with Kael. The clearing they are in is surrounded by trees at the base of the Mountains of Latasef. BJ trained here as a younger fighter many seasons ago, but today, Kael, will be the instructor.

"Pay attention, Sam," Kael snapped, his blade pulsating with a brighter intensity. "I have taught you the command, *val arrna*, which allows me to guide your movements. It is the basis for every other command to be built upon. The next word you will learn is *naur*. What I want you to do is hold me up and speak all the words at once. You will need to speak with a strong voice. This is necessary to release the power of the words."

Sam thought he understood and lifted Kael into the air. "*Val arrna, naur,*" he shouted. The blade burst into flames. Sam dropped it to the ground.

"What are you doing?" Kael screamed as the ground caught fire. The blade went cold and BJ stomped out the flames. "Why did you drop me?"

Sam was speechless for a moment. "I didn't want to get burned. I'm sorry."

The blade grumbled. "You would not have been burned. It's your command which releases the power. This means you're protected from anything you tell me to do."

"Okay, okay, so I'm protected," Sam barked. "You act like I should just know this."

Kael snapped back. "Of course you should know this. You've done it on a million different occasions."

Sam looked at BJ, confused, then reached down to pick up the blade. "What the heck do you mean? How could I possibly have done it on a million different occasions?"

Kael was silent for a long series of moments. "I meant nothing. Continue your training. Don't drop me again, or I won't let you train with me further."

Sam desperately wanted to ask another question, but figured it best not to push. "I said I was sorry. I won't drop you again. Besides, I'm the master here. You'll do what I tell you. I'm sick of being pushed around."

The sword went silent, again. Sam refused to speak first. Eventually, the blade spoke. "Perhaps, you are becoming a leader. I will mind my place. Please, let's try this again. Speak the words of power."

Sam stared at the blade, conflicted. It didn't take long before BJ snapped. "Enough of my moments have been wasted. I'm tired of waiting. Just say the words, boy."

Sam lowered the weapon. "Can't a guy think around here?"

"Shut up and say the words."

Sam shook his head, lifted Kael high and shouted. *"Val arrna, naur!"* The blade ignited. He began to move it around. He touched it to his skin. Despite the sword's explanation, he was surprised the blade felt cold. He held it out toward BJ. "Can you feel anything?"

"Of course I can. Kael already told you how it worked. Have you become dense?"

Kael laughed at Sam's expense, then pushed forward with the lesson. "Now that you have commanded the power and it is active, you can build on it, like you would the stones of a home's foundation. Let's imagine you are in battle and have commanded my flame, but the enemy is lining up in front of you. You need to bring them down quicker. You can extend my area of coverage without changing my weight or balance. You can swing at will and not worry about your allies. This power will cut through your enemies while passing through your friends, without harm. I want you to lift me up and say the word, *ngw*."

"Wait a moment," Sam responded. "So, after I say this word, let's say there is an enemy on the far side of BJ. Are you telling me I can pass the blade through his body and only kill the enemy beyond?"

"That's exactly what I'm saying and it doesn't matter if an enemy is beyond BJ or not. If you consider BJ to be a friend or ally, then I *will* pass through him, leaving him intact. We are connected spirit to spirit."

"No way! This has to be the coolest thing I've ever heard. Okay, okay, so how do you pronounce that word again?"

It took a couple of attempts for Sam to learn how to pronounce a word with no vowels. Once he understood, he lifted the sword and released its power. Sam was floored to see Kael's blade extend nearly another eight feet. He moved the sword around. It felt as if nothing changed. Even when he brought the sword to his side, the blade adjusted to pass through without hitting the ground, then re-extended itself. Sam spun around and, after a bit, caught BJ off guard and passed the blade through him.

"Watch it, boy," BJ screamed. "Just because you know it won't hurt, doesn't mean I want the power tested! I should troblet your sorry back-side!"

Sam smiled, then lowered Kael to his side. "If you could, old man." The fighter moved to stand beside the trainer. "Don't be mad. You know I care about you."

BJ grumbled and moved away.

"So what's next?" Sam inquired, as he looked at Kael.

Kael's magic subsided. "I can see you like this form of training. Let's try a new command. The word for ice is *khelek*. I want you to do the same as before, but instead of commanding fire, I want you to command the word for this new element."

Sam lifted the blade. "*Val arrna, khelek ngw!*" Kael once again extended and an ice-cold flame appeared around his blade. "Ohhhh, wow, this is cool! But, why would I need to have both fire and ice? Why not just stick with one?"

Again, Kael grumbled. "Sam, for such a smart man, you can ask the dumbest questions. Do you think you would fight a fire-breathing dragon with its own element?"

Sam nodded. "Okay, okay, I see your point. Are you telling me there are dragons on this world?"

"The dragons live on Dragonia. I don't imagine you would need to worry about them, but some enemies will still have an ability to withstand certain powers. You may find yourself in a battle where you will need to use a different power to strike."

"If I'm fighting beasts of this nature, will they have magic of their own? How will I defend myself?"

Kael's blade pulsated. "At any point you feel you need protection, you can use the word *var* and the name of what you need to be protected from. For example, you could say *Var alu*. This will protect you from an enemy using water as a weapon. If you need to protect those around you from this same foe, you can use the words *Vara alu*, which will extend the area of protection to fifteen feet around you."

Sam thought a moment. "So let me give you an example. Let's say I'm fighting one of these fire-breathing dragons. I would say *Val arrna, ngw khelek* to bring forth the icy flame on your blade, then I would follow this up with *Var naur* to protect me from its breath of fire. Is this what you're saying?"

Kael confirmed. The training continued.

Shalee and Helga are Shopping

Shalee purchased a new belt designed with many pockets sewn into it. Helga explained how useful substances could be kept in the pouches and Shalee would be able to command her staff to retrieve them, if necessary. Before Helga could explain anything else, and per Shalee's character, she pointed her staff at the belt and commanded Precious to change its appearance into something far more fashionable.

"I think I just might be able ta wear this, now," Shalee said while waving her arm and snapping her fingers. "I wasn't about ta wear that hideous thing. It didn't even have lace. Can ya believe it?"

"Everything is fashion with you," Helga said, shaking her head. "Will you pay attention, child? We need to put some key ingredients in these pockets so you can command Precious to combine them for the effect you want. It's like cooking. When you bake bread, you need different ingredients. Your staff is able to summon fire, lighting, ice, and wind, naturally. You won't have to worry about those since they can't be kept in a pouch. We have twenty-five pouches to fill, so we should choose wisely and prepare an arsenal of commands which will use the ingredients available to you."

"I agree, we'll need ta choose our ingredients wisely, but we won't need ta prepare an arsenal of commands."

"How so, child? I've been doing this for many seasons and I know what I'm doing."

"Don't ya remamba'? Ya taught me that Precious can read my mind," Shalee replied. "All I need ta do is command the staff ta *create* and let it look into my mind for the desired outcome."

Helga moved to the far side of the room. She flopped down on a bench and thought a moment. "You may have a point, but it would require a significant use of power. I have spent my whole life saying each word for every ingredient. What you're describing seems too simple, but it sounds possible. We'll try it once we fill the pouches. I can't imagine you have this kind of power, but we shall see.

"You will need to make sure you buy more ingredients as they diminish. The staff will only need to draw from a very small amount, no matter how large the effect, but you will run out."

Once again, Shalee smiled and looked at the older sorceress. "For goodness' sake, why would I do that when all I need ta do is tell Precious ta multiply what's already there? Once we have the supplies, I'll never need ta go ta anotha' store ta buy 'em, again."

Helga was floored. "I can't believe I've lived this many seasons and never tried to do that. I have always waited till I ran out and found a place to buy more. Poison can be expensive, child."

Shalee laughed. "You just watch me whip up somethin' here. I'm sure it'll work." She went over to the store owner and asked the lady to bring her a vial of poison. The lady did as requested and produced a tiny glass cylinder filled with a green gel. Shalee asked for a bowl. The lady returned with one and sat it in front of her. Shalee spooned some of the gel into the bowl, lifted Precious and spoke her command. The poison began to bubble as it multiplied upon itself. A fume filled the room which caused all three women to cover their noses. The smell subsided and before they knew it, the entire bowl was full.

The lady behind the counter watched as Helga took a bit of the poison from the bowl and put it inside a cup. She lifted her staff and, with a forceful voice, spoke her command. The sorceress flew back and landed on her butt.

"Goodness-gracious." Shalee panicked. "Are ya okay?"

"Help me up! I'm fine!"

Shalee did as she was told, then turned to hide her smile. After she collected herself, she turned back and began to brush off Helga's backside. "I suppose there is a bright side ta your failure."

"And what would that be?" Helga snapped.

"At least ya didn't waste all the coin you've spent on ingredients all those seasons. Isn't that just a purdy lil' thought?"

Shalee picked up Helga's staff as the older sorceress grumbled. After handing it to her, Shalee looked at the lady behind the counter. "Why don't *you* give it a try?" she said, smiling.

"My staff is best left under the counter."

The women enjoyed choosing the twenty-five ingredients. Shalee had everything she needed: a vial of water, poison, sand, cloth, steel, which had been ground to a fine powder, straw, sulfur, dragon scales (four different types) and various other creatures' parts. She had a vial of explosive powder and three types of oil—one of them for nothing more than cooking. With the power Shalee used to multiply the woman's inventory, she did not have to pay for any of it. It was a successful day of shopping, and they left to go out of town to try a few new commands.

Later that Night
South of the City of City View

Mieonus arrived behind a tavern south of City View. The cliffs nearby had been the point of entry for Brandor's Army 75 seasons ago when they attacked the Barbarian's Kingdom. On that day, neither the city nor the tavern existed.

Now...fellow soul...allow me to give you a bit of Southern Grayham's history. 75 seasons ago, the King of Brandor, Jahronus Brandor, sailed his fleet up to the base of the cliffs to unload two hundred of his finest soldiers. They scaled the rocky walls and carried with them long thick ropes. Once at the top, they signaled for the fleet to return. It was the king's objective to secure heavy iron chains to the top of the cliffs so the rest of his 10,000 men could ascend.

The army made a special catapult which was attached between two of the king's largest ships and used it to throw a massive iron ball to the top of the cliffs. The two hundred men at the top wove their ropes together to keep them from snapping. Once this had been done, they wrapped this larger rope around the backside of a number of thick trees which served as a series of pulleys. The men secured one end to the ball, then dropped the other end to the ships below. Large iron link chains were secured to the opposing rope's end, then the ball was pushed over the side of the cliff to lift the chains upward.

Due to the ocean's depth, the army had to devise a way to sever the rope before the iron ball pulled the chains up and around the trees and back into the ocean forever. They created a series of bladed harpoons to ensure they didn't miss. The men fired over forty shots in the direction of this reinforced rope. It was the job of the two hundred men at the top of the cliffs to see to it the chains did not fall in the opposite direction.

These men threw their weight on the chains and drove special iron bars between the links. The operation would have failed except for the cuts the chains made in the massive trees. The cuts stopped the progression of the chain long enough for the men to secure it. The army attached large ladders to the chains and began their invasion on the Kingdom of Bloodvain. And now, because of this military activity, a tavern sits on this very spot and was given the name...The Iron Chains. So, enough of my little history lesson... back to the story.

Mieonus had been assigned the task of initiating the assassination of the King of Brandor's son, Aaron Brandor, and the General Absolute, Justin Graywind. The goddess knew there was a relentless killer named Dawson Drake, inside the tavern. He was known for skillfully killing his victims and was considered the deadliest assassin in all of Grayham.

Dawson Drake, known by the name, Double D, had not used his real name since the age of fourteen seasons. His father, a drunken piece of garesh, beat his mother on a regular basis. She loved Double D with all her heart, but could not defend herself against the advances of her husband.

After another long night of merciless beating, Double D leaned over and picked his mother off the floor. She made a mistake, saying in a blood-filled raspy voice, she would give her last Helmep if someone killed her husband.

Being a good son, Double D attended to her wounds and after ensuring she was asleep, he took her last two coins from her secret stash as payment and entered the darkness. He left with murder on his mind, stalking his father from the shadows cast by the city's torches as he returned from another night of heavy drinking.

The situation was perfect for a killing. The torches leading away from the city gates of West Utopia were becoming few and far between. As luck would have it, he and his father were the only ones around. He crept up on the much bigger man and buried a dagger deep into each kidney. As Double D stood over his father, he watched as the brute took his last breath. He enjoyed the kill, savoring the idea his father knew it was his own son who ended his life. This was just the beginning of Double D's merciless career.

The assassin was always a hard person to find, and the only way to get in touch with him was through a man called Assistant Kane. Once contact had been made with Kane, it was difficult to get Double D to accept the job for anything less than 25 Yaloom, the highest denomination in the land. The goddess knew when she entered the tavern Double D would not be open to her request. It would be a tough sale to get him to accept the job.

Mieonus decided not to approach as a goddess, but rather, would show up as Assistant Kane. She needed a way to deal with the irritation of the assassin if he became angry. She moved her arms in front of her and as she did, a new appearance emerged. She was now a tall, thin, handsome man with long black hair, wearing brown leather pants and a black shirt.

The goddess walked into the tavern and headed for a spot at the bar next to Double D. As she sat, she spoke in a whisper. "We need to talk. I see you're still accepted by the barbarians. How do you avoid being killed?"

The assassin was a shorter man with an athletic build. His hair was long and he dressed in black from head to toe. He was not ugly, but he was not considered handsome. His eyes were brown and his long brown hair fell across his eyes as he looked down at his ale.

"I thought I told you to never meet me in person."

"I know. There are extenuating circumstances," the goddess replied.

"I don't care about the circumstances. You know how I work. This isn't the day I'll make an exception."

Kane stood from the bar. "Too bad. The job would have paid 100 Yaloom. We would have been rich. I'll see if Tiara wants the job."

The goddess left the bar and started to walk down the trail leading into town. The next thing she knew, she was lying flat on her back with a dagger to her throat.

Double D hissed. "Move and I'll cut you through. What could be such an important job it would pay 100 Yaloom, Kane?"

"Someone wants the Prince of Brandor, and the General Absolute dead. Let me up. This is not how I intended to do business. Maybe we could walk and discuss this."

"The job is suicide!"

Kane shrugged. "I'll leave and tell them you said it can't be done. I'm sure they'll find someone to go for that kind of coin."

"I never said it couldn't be done. I said it was suicide...suicide for anyone, but me. I wouldn't do the job for the price. It'll take twice that much."

The goddess laughed and started to walk away. "I'll tell them you said that, but don't expect me to return with an answer."

"Kane," Double D shouted, "One hundred fifty!" The assassin watched as the man kept walking. "One hundred twenty-five! That's my final offer! Don't push me, Kane!"

"Deal! You know where to find me for your coin when the job is done."

"I need supplies for the job. I'll need an advance."

Kane turned and threw a bag filled with coins and watched the assassin catch it.

"I see you came sure of yourself."

"I'm a businessman. Did you expect less?" With that, the goddess walked down the path and out of sight.

17 Peaks of Bailem have Passed

George walked up the stairs of the landing tower with Athena. Amar was waiting for him at the top. The moments George had spent with Athena were wonderful, and he was more than confident he wanted this woman to be in his life, forever.

The previous evening, George explained he had to travel to the Siren's Song to meet with the wisp. The idea he was being this forthcoming surprised him. He was unable to lie about where he was going. His love was deep. Athena deserved the truth and when she got it, she did not question him. Instead, she smiled and instructed him to be careful. She asked when she would see him again. He told her the truth, saying he did not know, but he would try to get back to her as soon as he could. George wanted her to believe in him so much, he gave her his Rolex that evening over dinner and asked if she would consider moving to wherever he settled down. Her response was everything he wanted to hear, saying it would be okay as long as she could visit her family every now and then. Their last night together had been passionate after retiring to Athena's mother's guest house.

George greeted Amar, then turned to kiss his beautiful Athena. "Tell mother I said goodbye."

Athena liked how he had taken her family in as his own. "I'm sure she will ask five hundred questions when I get to work. I've never taken this many Peaks off in my entire life. My sister is expecting all the naughty details. I'm so excited. I don't have to embellish and make anything up." She moved in close and put her head to his chest as she giggled. "I love you, George."

This was the first occasion in which he had heard those words uttered from Athena's mouth. He looked into her eyes and said, "I love you, too." For once in his life he had told a woman he loved her without it being some sort of game.

Amar said goodbye to Athena and as they climbed onto the back of the hippogriff. George displayed a bright smile which would not go away as the hippogriff took flight. The two gazed at each other until they were nothing more than tiny specks.

The City of West Utopia

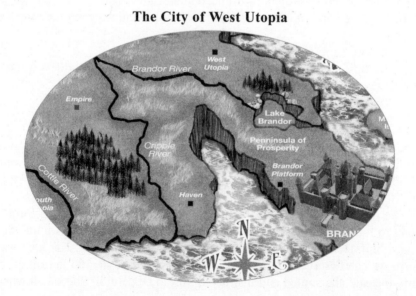

Sam won both fights in the town of Mountain View and had moved on to West Utopia. His opponents in this arena suffered the same fate as all the others. His record was now seven wins with zero losses, all by way of permanent knock out.

Now, Sam and Shalee planned on taking the day off from training. They wanted to spend quality moments together without the crowds following them. Sam's rise to glory was starting to show real promise and this small getaway was necessary to stay sane.

BJ and Helga bid their students good day and took the opportunity to run off and find some quality moments of their own. Their secret relationship has blossomed since their first kiss just outside of Lethwitch. BJ is smitten with Helga. Creating excuses to be alone with her is becoming tiresome and he plans to stop hiding his feelings from Sam and Shalee.

⊷⊱╪•╪⊰⊶

Now...fellow soul...Grayham is similar to Earth in yet another way. It has its own version of the Paparazzi. Instead of the constant snapping of photos, they want Sam to sit still to be drawn for their stories. The drawings are hung on the information boards found at the center of most populated areas. With as many moments as it takes to sit for an artist, Sam and Shalee would much rather have photographers in their faces.

⊷⊱╪•╪⊰⊶

After all the artists of West Utopia had been satisfied, Sam and Shalee were able to pack a lunch. It was just past the Peak of Bailem when they headed out. As they were leaving town, a young child dressed in fine clothing, ran up and bowed. The boy held a piece of parchment in his hand.

"Can I help you, young man?" Sam asked.

"Your presence is commanded at Duke Barthom Brandor's home."

Sam looked at Shalee and laughed. "Well, who are we to turn down a request to meet our first Duke?"

"This is not a request, sir. It's an order."

Sam's mood changed. "And, if I don't want to come, young man?"

"Sir, I beg you. If you don't, I'll be beaten for incompetence."

Shalee slid in close. "He's just a boy, darlin'. Ya said ya wanted glory. I suppose, with glory, we'll have ta put up with a few pompous jerks now and then."

Shalee's accent softened Sam's mood. The fighter turned to the boy. "Lead the way."

The child led them through the city and up a hill to some large estates. The area reminded Shalee of the Roman architecture she studied during her travels on Earth. The scene was fascinating. It was fun to see this sort of architecture in a form other than ruins. It was pristine and functional.

Sam, on the other hand, was not so impressed. "You'd think the gods would have at least given the people of this world some other ideas for their city's structures. I know it was supposed to make our transition easier, but give me a break. It's not unique. Everything since our arrival, though beautiful, appears to be from some period of our history on Earth."

Shalee rolled her eyes. "For heaven's sake, Sam, this place is delightful. Who says these ideas were ours in the first place? Maybe they were used before Earth was eva' created, in some otha' culture, by some otha' world. What if the gods simply recycle their ideas ova' and ova' again?"

Sam nodded. "Point made. I suppose that wouldn't surprise me after all we've learned. I wonder what the other worlds look like. Bassorine did say they are different from Grayham. I just wonder how different."

As they continued to walk, more massive columns lined the road leading to the duke's home. The detail of the sculptures which had been chiseled into the columns were remarkably life-like. Beautiful grapevines stretched between them and were held by the stone hands of the sculptures' outstretched arms. The fruit was being harvested by slaves. The cobblestones of the road were perfectly placed on top of tamped rubble beneath to allow for the drainage of water.

The duke's home was enormous, making both visitors feel anxious as they entered. They were taken to a large room and as the doors opened, a group of well-dressed people in a flowing assortment of colored cloths greeted them. Shalee was relieved she had made them dress up for their special day together.

A fat, jovial man walked up and introduced himself. "Welcome! Welcome! I am Duke Barthom Brandor. I trust you are enjoying your stay in West Utopia. I have heard much about you prior to your arrival in our fair city, Sam." Barthom looked at Shalee. "I don't believe I know who you are, young lady." The duke reached out, took Shalee's hand, then kissed the top of it.

"Well, aren't ya just all proper-like? It's nice ta meet ya, Duke Brandor. My name is Shalee."

"Your speech is intoxicating." The duke looked at Sam. "I do believe a woman as beautiful as the one you have on your arm should be given the right to call me by name."

Sam nodded. "I'm sure this would make things far more pleasant for the lady."

"Then it is settled. Shalee, you may call me Barthom. Sam, since I have extended the courtesy to your lovely companion, I will allow you the same privilege."

"Thank you, Barthom. To what do we owe the pleasure of being called to your home?"

"I watched your fights. I must say your reputation is understated. I don't believe I've seen such a presence in the arena since my King's General Absolute. I dare say you could find yourself in the arena with Graywind. This would be a fight I dare not miss. He, like you, has killed every man who has entered the arena against him. I do hope you're able to make it that far. I would love to watch you shove his vanity down his throat."

The room erupted with laughter.

"Seems you have earned a room full of fans, Sam. I'm sure they'll be following your career, however long it is you live." Barthom motioned for Sam to grab a drink.

A maidservant approached. She was carrying a tray of cups filled with wine. Sam grabbed two of them, handed one to Shalee, then responded. "Let's hope I live longer than your average fighter."

A pessimistic smile appeared on Barthom's face as he lifted his cup and tapped it against Sam's. "Indeed, let us hope."

<hr />

Sam and Shalee found their day with the noble and his friends to be a pleasant one. As they left, their host sent them away with a few gifts.

Sam received some of the duke's finest handcrafted black leather armor. The seal of the duke's home, a red dragon, had been placed on most every piece: the chest, arm bracers, greaves and on the back of the boots.

Shalee was given six bolts of expensive fabric of assorted colors. As they left, she realized she did not have a place to put them. She had been so busy running around with Sam, staying at one inn and then another, she hadn't thought of getting a place of their own. She spoke with Sam about the problem as they headed back to the inn. They decided they would discuss the issue with Helga.

Helga and BJ were sitting at the bar drinking ale when the two arrived. They saw the older couple flirting with one another but didn't say anything. BJ was about 61 seasons and, even though Helga was over 247, she did not look a day over 60. They stood in the background and watched as Helga reached over and touched BJ's arm. It was clear there was more to this relationship, but neither Sam nor Shalee had noticed until now.

Sam crept up on their trainers. As BJ touched Helga's hand, Sam cleared his throat and watched the couple jump. "Look what we have here," Sam said in a fatherly voice. "I guess I'm going to have to start keeping a better eye on you two kids. We leave you for the shortest amount of moments and come back to find you flirting. I'm shocked."

"Oh, get lost," BJ grumbled. "We have lives, too. I never would have thought I could look at another woman after my wife died, but traveling with Helga has given me a new perspective. We have something here that's good for the both of us."

Helga was embarrassed. "Sam, please know we still intend to make your training the best we can offer."

Shalee jumped into the conversation. "Don't be silly. I don't think that eva' crossed our minds. The idea is ratha' charmin', really. Sam and I were talkin' the other day about the two of ya and agreed *you* are like parents ta us. You're not just our trainers, you're our friends. We've grown ta love ya and see ya as family."

Shalee's sentiment was everything Helga wanted to hear. Her eyes grew misty. Grabbing a towelette, she dabbed the moisture from them. BJ looked at Sam, shrugged, then rolled his eyes as guys do when this kind of thing happens. After a moment, BJ placed his arms around Helga. "I suppose the cotlum has been let out of the bag. We can be more open with our love."

"Love! Have you two been doing this long enough to use such a strong word?" Sam said, ignoring the fact he had no idea what a cotlum was. "Where was I when the courting was taking place?"

BJ turned to Sam. "Ha! Since you consider me like a father, the place you have been when Helga and I were courting is on top of my daughter. This incestuous relationship between the two of you must stop." The trainer smiled as he sat back on his stool.

Helga stopped crying and slapped BJ on the arm. "He's always talking that way, child. He can be so naughty. Why, last night he said..."

Shalee grabbed her ears and spoke over Helga's voice. "T.M.I. T.M.I."

Sam agreed, chuckling, "Yeah, way too much information."

Helga and BJ enjoyed the phrase and tuned into what Sam had to say. "We just received some gifts from Duke Barthom Brandor." He pointed to the pile sitting across the room. As soon as BJ saw the armor, he jumped from his stool and ran over to take a look. Lifting the chest piece from the floor, he held it up in front of him. The excitement could be seen on his face as he threw it over his head to try it on. The armor was too large for his smaller frame, but it didn't curb his enthusiasm.

"Sam, do you realize what this means?"

The fighter followed and picked up the bracers. "It means we have met our first noble, why?"

"It means far more than that," BJ responded. "It means the house of Brandor will be talking about you as your career develops. It means the king knows who you are. When something like this happens, a fighter usually receives an invitation to come and fight before he completes the fight requirements. You've only completed three cities. If you can win your next few fights, you could get an invitation to go to the city of Champions before you finish fighting in Empire. Sam, all you have to do is see to it your victories have large statements attached to them. If they do, we'll be on a fast pace to the King of Brandor's personal Tournament of Champions.

"There is far more than fighting at this tournament. It's a citywide event which lasts for ten Peaks. Sixty-four fighters are invited and none of the fights are meant to be to the death until the last two. If a fighter survives, he's given a chance to fight the General Absolute. Many want the glory attached to this victory, but all have died from this choice. The general is merciless and, although he's an honorable man, he believes the arena is a glorious place to die. The leader of the king's army steps into the arena prepared to die...and equally prepared to kill."

BJ took off the chest piece and placed it on Sam. He admired the fit and tightened it. "The first day of the tournament is to celebrate the sixty-four fighters and the General Absolute. The next seven are filled with glorious battles. The field is narrowed until only one fighter remains. On the ninth day, this man is given his chance to face the general. The tenth day is the highest form of exaltation a warrior can achieve. The winner is celebrated and invited to the king's personal dining table. For as long as I can remember, the general has been the one celebrated. I don't think he cares about dining with the king, since I imagine he probably does this often as the leader of the army."

BJ reached up, grabbed hold of his student's head and placed his forehead to Sam's. "Glory could be yours. If you were to beat the general...you would be one of the most powerful men in the kingdom. Only the king and his son would be above you."

An enormous smile crossed Sam's face. "I can make the impression needed to win our invitation to Brandor. Mark my words. I will win...convincingly."

Sam pulled away and headed for the bar. He was about to order an ale when Shalee tapped him on the shoulder. He turned and saw the look of fright in her eyes. "What's wrong?"

Shalee put her hand on his chest. "Didn't ya hear the part where BJ said every one of the general's opponents has died when fightin' him?"

"I heard it. What's the big deal?"

"Doggone it, Sam, I know you're not dumb. He's killed everyone. For heaven's sake, don't ya think that's a big deal? Geesh! I don't want anythin' ta happen ta ya. I love ya, ya big ox."

"Okay, okay, hold on a second. You know I love you, too. BJ also said, I don't have to fight the general if I don't want to. So, let's not worry about it."

Sam said this to help Shalee relax. He knew he would fight the general, if given the chance. He had no choice. How else could he get into a position of power? Shalee would need to understand when the moment arrived to make the decision to fight.

Shalee seemed to be okay with his answer. She turned to Helga and asked if the sorceress would make a quick detour to the city of Brandor to find a place for them to live.

BJ thought it was a great idea. Being this close to Brandor, it would take Helga only 4 Peaks to fly down and find something suitable. All she had to do was take a separate hippogriff. She could find a home, then catch another flight a few days later to meet in Haven. BJ further suggested she take the bolts of cloth and leave them in Brandor. BJ wanted to go, but he would not have the moments necessary to get back before Sam's next fight. Helga agreed to leave the next day.

Retiring for the evening, Shalee watched to see if Helga slipped into BJ's room. She smiled as she went to bed, crawling in next to Sam. "Can ya just see the love they have for one anotha' in their eyes. I think it's cute. It's downright adorable. Don't ya agree?"

"Yeah, sure, whatever floats your boat. Now, get over here and float mine."

The next morning, the group headed for the landing platform. While walking through town, they noticed a higher level of military activity. The king's soldiers were carrying trees to the mill. Sam stopped one of the men dressed in chain armor. The man wore a black tunic, with red trim and the king's symbol at its center. "What's going on?"

"The king has given orders to build harvest wagons. His Lordship has received word from the gods the harvests will be bountiful. The wagons will be needed to transport the bounty to the coastal cities."

"Why are the harvests transported to the coast?" Sam inquired.

The soldier gave Sam an odd look. BJ waved the soldier on and answered the question. "The harvests are shipped to Merchant Island to determine their value. Once a value is assigned, they're distributed throughout Grayham. Each world has certain benefits they provide the others. Goods are exchanged between worlds and delivered by the Merchant Angels."

Sam furrowed his brow. It was easy to see another question was coming. BJ took the liberty to answer without waiting for the question to be formulated.

"The gods have created a group of beings whose sole purpose is to move merchandise between the worlds. The merchandise is delivered to their own Merchant Island. After a value is established, the goods are distributed, just as they are here. No one has ever seen a Merchant Angel. There are special areas where the angels assemble, gather the goods, then take them away. But, this only happens when everyone is gone."

BJ put his hand on Sam's shoulder. Leading the group, he continued. "Sometimes, when government officials from two worlds agree to allow a member of another race to visit, it is the Merchant Angels who transport them. The ride is said to be dark and miserable. The gods have created special containers to transport live beings, but the ride is said to be spent in the dark. When criminals are caught on Grayham, they are transported in this manner to Dragonia as punishment. I believe, if the dragons don't kill them first, the other criminals living there do, or maybe the demons get them, or even the vampires for that matter."

"Okay, okay, now I've heard it all," Sam responded. "Vampires! Really? Yeah right. You know...it wasn't long ago I would have said you were full of it for saying something so outlandish, but not anymore. I'm sure Stephenie would have loved this place, if she was here."

BJ's brow wrinkled, "And, who's this Stephenie?"

"Oh, not that it matters, anymore. She was an author on my homeworld before its destruction." Sam further thought to himself. *I wonder what page of the Book of Immortality her soul is resting on?*

It wasn't long before the group arrived at the base of the landing platform and began their ascent. Sam's mind was still dwelling on the Merchant Angels. "BJ, can you at least eat on the journey when the angels take you to the other worlds?"

"I don't know anything more, Sam. You'll have to study on it later, when your moments allow."

Once at the top, they waited for BJ to lift Helga onto her hippogriff. The trainer blew her a kiss as the giant beast lifted into the sky.

Soresym showed up not long after. Shalee was standing on the platform when his majestic form settled. The wind created from the massive beast's wings made her thankful for the railing lining the perimeter.

The force of the wind had ruined Shalee's hair style. She pulled the tangled mess into a ponytail. "So much for lookin' cute for ya today, Soresym," she joked. "How can I show ya fab if ya keep floppin' my hair all ova' the place?"

The griffin enjoyed her candor. "I'm sorry, Shalee, but I do not have an essence capable of fixing your hair."

BJ covered his smile as Sam poked back. "Ha, ha, very funny. He has a chance to pee in a guy's mouth and the King of the Griffins considers himself a comedian. Soresym, you're just a bowl of laughter. Tell me again, why do we like each other so much?"

After a brief period of friendly banter, they lifted off to wing their way to the city of Haven.

A Father of Seven

Lasidious has decided to visit the world of Luvelles. He is chatting with the Source, the most ancient of dragons. The Source is the only one of his kind not living on Dragonia. It is his job to test all those who seek magic's greater power to determine if they are capable of looking into the Eye of Magic. If deemed capable, the Source grants them access. It is not enough to just be capable. The seeker must be worthy. If they are—the seeker lives. If they are not—the seeker's soul is swallowed and their body is lost within the Eye forever. Since Lasidious does not want to make another appearance before the gods at the moment, planning the future is in order and the Source is a good place to start. Who better to speak with than a dragon, with a six hundred foot wing span, inside his cavernous home?

The City of Haven

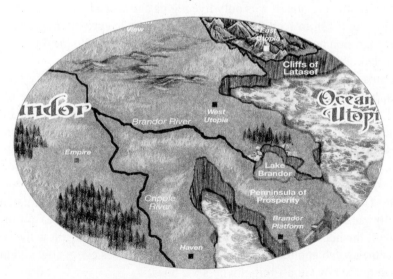

Brandon Smith, a strong-willed, handsome, family man, comes from a long line of farmers and makes his home near the city of Haven. His family is known throughout the valley for their kindness. They are also known for their ability to make well-crafted iron shoes for the area's horses. He is a good father to seven beautiful children and his wife, Josephine, is an average-looking woman with beautiful green eyes and a heart of gold. After bringing six boys into the world, they were blessed with a beautiful girl.

Family comes first in Brandon's life and, even though he is busy with them, he maintains a strict training schedule which he follows after the children go to bed. His wife puts the children down every night after dusk, then Brandon trains in their barn with three of his friends. He goes on to participate in the fights each season when they come to Haven.

Brandon named his sons: Brandon Jr., Jonathan, Mathew, Jasper, Mark, and Chase. His little girl, Adriana, is now three seasons old and her brothers, starting from oldest to youngest, are twelve, ten, nine, eight (twins) and five seasons. His oldest, Brandon Jr., is a strong boy who has worked with his father in the fields of their farm since turning eleven, the same age Brandon's father and his father before him put their boys to work—a family tradition.

Jonathan is an athletic child and spends countless hours playing with his father's wooden training swords. He was almost eight before he could carry a stave properly, but once he could, his mother couldn't keep the thing out of his hands.

Mathew is quite the fisherman. If he cannot be found, he is on the river going after the big one. It was only five nights ago when he came home carrying enough fish to feed the family. Brandon made sure the boy received the recognition he deserved and helped the child prepare the meal for a special celebration of his catch.

Twins, Jasper and Mark, are mama's boys. They are the family scoundrels, but know when their father speaks, they better listen. On the other hand, they run rough-shod all over their mother. It took a while, but Josephine finally figured out their weakness. When the two boys get out of hand, she sends them outside to pick a sturdy switch off some nearby wishershyle trees. When they return, she places the switches on the table and informs the boys the switches are for their father to beat them with when he comes home. The kids know it will hurt, and it is this style of mental warfare which usually puts them back in line. Most often, Josephine finds a reason to let them off the hook before Brandon returns. It is rare for her to allow the boys to get the switch applied to their rear ends, but she does every now and then to ensure the boys don't forget who's the boss.

Chase, is the charismatic one of the bunch. He not only has his grand-mother and grandfather wrapped around his little finger, but all the neigh-bors as well. He is the kind of kid who can talk to anyone, despite being five seasons old. His mother's friends love pinching his chubby cheeks.

Brandon took Chase into the city last spring and stopped at a local place to eat, melted goat cheese on potatoes—Chase's favorite food. On that par-ticular day, three beautiful women who were leaving the eatery, stopped, pinched Chase's cheeks and called him 'cutie.' Chase turned his head and even at the early age of five seasons, watched their beautiful backsides all the way out the door before turning around and saying, "Father, every girl in this town loves me." Brandon laughed that day and rubbed his hand through the boy's hair before heading home.

Adriana, the baby of the family, has thick blonde hair and facial features like her father. She is spoiled—a real daddy's girl. She thinks her father walks on water and Josephine has taught Adriana how to butter Brandon up when she wants something. If Brandon has an Achilles' heel, Adriana is it.

Brandon met his wife when he was a boy in school. They are the same age and now, at 30 seasons, they have been together as a couple since he asked his wife to be his at the early age of ten seasons. When Brandon was 16 and of legal age to leave his father's home, he went to his wife's father and asked for her hand in marriage. Their fathers were good friends, and because of this, permission was granted and a beautiful wedding was cel-ebrated.

Josephine did not waste any of her moments starting their family. She became pregnant on her 17th seasonal celebration. Children had been an experience which forced both of them to change, but they managed to hold their vows sacred and grow together.

It was on Brandon's 18th seasonal celebration he became old enough to fight in the arena and has been fighting each summer season ever since. It was just before his wife gave birth to their first child that he won his first fight. The money from the victory helped to make payments on a piece of land he purchased from his father. His father is a good man and loved by everyone.

On Brandon's 20th celebration, after he had struggled to make his way for the previous four seasons, his father decided Brandon had learned how to be a man and let him have the land without having to pay further. That day had been a wonderful celebration. The entire Smith and Rosslyn fami-lies had attended. Both families were from the area and numbered over one hundred ninety-seven strong.

Today, was another great day. Brandon's family was getting ready to head into the city to watch him fight. They would drop Chase and Adriana off at the grandparents' house before heading to their favorite inn. The only thing that changed throughout the seasons was how many kids accompanied them to the fights.

After checking into the inn, Brandon went down to the arena at dusk and, as he always did, read the fight schedule for the next day's events. Just like every season, he knew nothing about who he was fighting. He noticed his opponent was his height, but thirty measures heavier.

Brandon was the only fighter who never entered the lottery because of his connections, and was also the only fighter who did not travel from city to city. His dad's brother was the arena headmaster and, as his uncle had done every season, he saved the one fight without weapons for Brandon. His wife had been firm. No weapons were to be involved. She insisted he could not fight with anything that would split him open. His only option had been to fight hand to hand. It was his good fortune and the fact his uncle was employed by the arena which allowed him to fight in the same event each season.

The next day, Josephine woke them all and, as per tradition, they made their way to the inn's dining area. This was a series of moments in which the kids could order whatever they wanted. They laughed and told stories over a diverse selection of food.

After breakfast, Brandon prepared to leave for the arena. "I love you all," he said, smiling, as he reached down and rubbed the top of each boy's head. "Maybe, after the fight, we can all go to papa's house and swim in the pond. Would you like that?"

The children's answer was everything he wanted to hear. He loved throwing them into the air and watching them land with a splash in awkward positions. After a few more moments of playful chiding, he embraced each one and turned to face his loving wife.

He caressed Josephine's face as he looked into her eyes. "I consider myself a blessed man." He reached down and touched her belly, covered by a yellow sundress. His seventh son was growing inside, though they did not know the baby was a boy. "Did you know...each day I have you as my wife, it feels as if I have a new reason to rejoice? You are the backbone of this family. I love you so much."

Josephine's smile widened. She reached up and rubbed her hand across the stubble on his cheek. Her green eyes found the soft blue of his. "Be safe, my love. Find the honor you seek in battle. Make our families proud."

No further words needed to be said. The look on his wife's face said it all. They embraced, another soft kiss followed, then he was off.

The bell sounded. The moment had come for Brandon to take his place on the sand of the arena floor. As he entered, the locals knew who he was and cheered. He looked to the seats where his family sat and waved at his kids before blowing his wife a kiss. He crossed his arms over his chest to express his love. Once this had been done, he turned to prepare his mind for the fight.

The crowd quieted as his opponent entered. Their reaction was far from normal. Their moans seemed to express concern, but Brandon did not know why. He had never seen this man. This was nothing new since most fighters' careers lasted less than a season. They were usually dead or stopped participating due to the wounds they suffered.

Despite the crowd's reaction, Brandon readied himself and the signal for the fight to start was given. He moved toward his foe and after they touched fists in the center of the arena, he threw himself into a roll and grabbed a handful of sand. He tossed the sand into the man's eyes and followed with a continuous assault, striking at his foe's face, ribs and kidneys. As Brandon circled, he dodged his foe's blind strikes, and delivered a powerful knee to his hardened stomach. Brandon moved around and around, pummeling every opening he could find. Seeing an opportunity, he jumped onto his opponent's back and locked in a choke.

Brandon was surprised at the man's power. His arms were peeled away as if he had no strength of his own, then he was thrown. He picked himself up off the sand and watched as the man wiped at his eyes. He had to hurry, the sand would not give him an advantage much longer and this man was far too powerful not to capitalize on this vulnerability.

Again, Brandon darted in. He planted a crushing fist to the side of the man's face, then moved back. To his bewilderment, his opponent was still standing. He needed to try something stronger. Landing a crushing kick to his foe's chest, Brandon sent him rolling backward—a roll which didn't stop his opponent as he returned to his feet.

Brandon's bewilderment turned to shock. He had never seen anyone take this much abuse and still be standing. His strikes were solid. Any other man would have fallen unconscious. He would need to try something stronger, maybe an elbow to the side of the head.

He jumped high into the air, intending to come down across the blind side of the man's face, but instead, his opponent twisted and sent a blind punch in his direction, one which pulverized his throat. The crushing shot sent Brandon stumbling to the ground. As a true warrior would, he pushed himself to his feet, but beyond that, he found he was hesitant to move. Not because his opponent was a threat, in fact, his foe was still fighting to clear the sand from his eyes. No, this was different. He couldn't breathe and further movement would shorten the air supply he had left. The strike to his throat had crushed his windpipe. This would be the last series of moments in which he could look upon his family.

The lack of air was already having an effect. He stumbled over to where his family sat and gave his wife a look. He saw the pain on her face as she cried and he longed to take it from her. He watched her pull the twins close and bury their faces in her dress to keep them from watching. Brandon Jr., Jonathan, and Mathew stared at their father with horror-filled eyes. There was nothing they could do and they knew it. Their little hands grasped the stone wall of the arena in front of them with enough force their knuckles turned white. Feeling their despair, Brandon fought the pain and crossed his heart with both arms as a last gesture. He pointed to each of them and winked to show them their father's love.

The last bit of his air ran out. Gasping for more would only serve to frighten his children further. He knew it was pointless to fight for the oxygen he needed as he lowered to his knees. Selflessly, he fought back the convulsions with everything in him, not wanting his children to see his suffering. He won this final battle. He was able to keep his body steady as he felt for his own pulse. The beats continued to fade, just as his family did, from his sight.

Sam stood at the center of the arena and studied the crowd after he cleared the sand from his eyes. He wasn't getting the normal reaction he was accustomed to since his first fight in Angel's Village. He walked over to the fallen warrior and looked down. Feeling the need for compassion, he placed his arms under Brandon's lifeless corpse and lifted him from the ground. The crowd's reaction told the story. This man was well-loved and he would be missed. Sam looked up toward the seats with Brandon in his arms. A woman in the first row stood with her children tucked against her. They wept, but held their heads high. His heart broke. Tears filled Sam's eyes as he held the woman's gaze.

An Unheard Prayer

Sam carried Brandon from the arena and into the healer's vestry, where his body would be prepared and given to his family for a proper Passing Ceremony. This had been the type of fight Sam felt he could make his opponent submit. His training the previous day had been dedicated to this style of fight. He had hoped to secure his victory without causing another death, but it was not meant to be. For this man to be lying here was devastating.

He looked down at Brandon's figure and watched as the healers gave way to the mortician. The people adored this man, a local farmer and ironworker. He overheard the crowd surrounding the woman in the first row say she was his wife. He thought back to how she wept when he looked at her. The dead man's sons were strong boys. They held their ground and didn't look away. The oldest nodded and showed Sam respect as he held the boy's father in his arms.

"What's his name?" Sam asked the mortician. "It's clear he was important."

A large lady, dressed in black, with her hair tied in a bun, responded, "His name is Brandon Smith, or *was* Brandon Smith. He was the father of seven children—six boys and a girl. Another child is expected. Everyone who lives here knows him. His whole family is loved. He fought in this arena for 12 seasons."

"May I wait until the family comes? I would like to express my regret for their loss."

The look on the woman's face suggested his request was an odd one. "Suit yourself," she shrugged, "but I don't know how well you'll be received."

After a while, Brandon's wife walked into the room. When she entered, Sam was standing over her husband's body with his back to the door. She paused, caught off guard by his presence. She swallowed and moved to the opposite side of her husband's body. Sam watched as she leaned over to hug Brandon's corpse and kiss him on the forehead. She did this for what felt like an eternity. To Sam's surprise, she maintained her strength.

She rose to face him. She started to speak, but stopped to catch the tears that wanted to escape. After three agonizing breaths, she said, "What's your name, fighter?"

Sam wanted to make up a name and run from the room. He had to search for the nerve to speak. "My name is Sam."

"Well...Sam," she sighed, "my name is Josephine Smith. This is..." she paused to collect herself. "This *was*...my husband, Brandon. He would have been proud to know you. The way you handled yourself, the way you have shown my family respect by carrying him from the arena, he would have found you to be a man of honor. He would have believed his death to be honorable. My husband felt to die in battle was glorious. As much as I would like to be angry with you, I cannot dishonor Brandon's death with such emotions. I would like to invite you to his Passing Ceremony. It will be held tomorrow. I'm sure he would have felt honored if you were to attend."

A young boy walked into the room. Sam watched as he moved close to his mother. Just as she had done, he bent over to kiss his father's forehead. As the child stood up, he handled himself with a presence Sam felt to be far above his seasons. He walked around the table and stuck out his arm. Sam felt small as they grabbed hold of each other's forearms.

Brandon Jr. looked into Sam's eyes and nodded, "You are a mighty warrior, sir. My father's death was glorious. I can only hope to be so honored that I might die in this manner. I will follow your career. Do not let my father's memory die with you." The boy, accepting his role as the new family patriarch, released his grip and left the room.

Josephine spoke after her son left. "He will be strong, for now, but he will seek solitude. My husband taught our sons that fighting in the arena is glorious. He told them if anything were to happen, they were to hold their heads high and be men. Brandon Jr. will cry when he gets home. For now, he will honor how his father wanted him to act."

Sam fell to his knees and apologized for her loss. His emotions were so intense Josephine had to comfort *him* and encouraged him back to his feet.

"Don't cry, Sam. My husband would've found this to be a praiseworthy death. His wish would be you not mourn him, but rather, celebrate him. After his Passing Ceremony, I'd like you and your family to come to the farm and celebrate with us. It would be an honor...if it wouldn't make you feel uncomfortable."

Sam confirmed he would be there for the passing and the celebration, asking where he was to go and apologized again. As expected, Josephine was gracious and told him everything he needed to know. Saying she would see him later, she placed her hand on his face to reassure him.

Sam left the room, joining BJ and Shalee, who were waiting. Without saying a word, they left for the inn. Once they were settled in their room, BJ explained the other fights had been canceled in Brandon's honor. The arena's banker told BJ they were going to pay every fighter as if they had won both fights. He also said most of the city's merchants would shut their doors for the ceremony.

"Can you imagine how many people will be in attendance, Sam?" BJ asked. "A populated area isn't considered a city until it has reached 16,000 souls. If most of these people knew Brandon and his family, this will be a monumental event."

Sam moved to stand over a wooden table, sitting not far from the cold hearth of their room's fireplace, and poured a drink of water from a sturdy pitcher. The drink did not quench his thirst the way it normally did. After three more, and a long period of silence, Sam spoke. "I can only imagine what it would be like to be so well-loved by a community that everyone mourns your death. I don't know how I can step back into the arena. How am I going to face all these people? You should have seen his wife. She was so gracious and kind. Even her son was strong. Going to Brandon's Passing Ceremony and the celebration afterward will be far worse than battle. There is no way I can step inside the arena again."

As soon as Sam stopped speaking, the ground beneath the city began to quake. The shaking lasted for 17 breaths.

From inside the Source's cavernous home on Luvelles, Lasidious shook the remaining four pieces of the Crystal Moon as he held them together in the palms of his hands. After he finished, he held the crystal's pieces just above a shallow river of lava which flowed through the dragon's cave and watched as Sam's image materialized.

The God of Mischief laughed as he watched the misery on Sam's face. Lasidious looked up and found the Source's massive set of eyes and shouted, "Oh, he'll fight again!" He lifted the crystal's pieces skyward. "He'll definitely fight, again! You'll see!"

The Source's voice was booming. "You find too much pleasure in toying with the mortals. I have seen many gods fall because of the games they have played with those they have created."

Lasidious frowned, "You worry too much. I am the Mischievous One for a reason."

The dragon leaned back and spread his mighty wings. A torrential wind filled the cavern. Lasidious' hood flew back from the top of his head as the dragon responded. "Perhaps, you're right. Or, perhaps, your fate will be the same as those who perished before you."

"Baaahh!" Lasidous vanished.

The dragon's laughter shook the mountain. Many of the stones, laying on the top of the cliffs, toppled.

After feeling the quake, Shalee pulled BJ aside and told the trainer this was her series of moments to handle Sam's despair. The trainer did not argue and left the room.

Shalee turned to Sam, "Sweetie, ya have no choice. Ya gotta fight. Ya said it earlier when ya fought the minotaur, you're fightin' for everyone. This man knew what he was doin' when he entered the arena. He knew there was a chance of not leavin' alive. It's obvious Brandon was a good father and taught his children the arena is a place of honor. Goodness-gracious, ya can't let this slip ya up."

"Okay, okay, hold onto that thought. You're not making sense. Brandon didn't have his wife use magic to help him absorb punches like you did for me. This guy should have kicked my ass. The punches he hit me with, and that damn kick to my chest, should have knocked me out. He died because *we* cheated *him* out of his victory. There's no honor in this kind of battle. I'm tired of killing. I'm tired of justifying my actions because I need to save this world. How can I face Brandon's family knowing what I've done? How can you expect me to fight?"

Shalee moved close and placed her hand on his heart. Her voice was soft, but firm. "I want ya ta listen ta me, Sam, and I mean *you* listen well. *You* trained ta make that man submit, not ta kill him. I saw ya swing. Ya couldn't even see when ya made contact. It was nothin' more than dumb luck that ya won. We both know there's much more at stake 'round here than one man's life. If we don't find a way ta gain an audience with the King of Brandor and find the pieces of this stupid Crystal Moon, everythin' will be destroyed. Now answer me this; with what ya know about Brandon, don't ya think he would have wanted ta die so you could go on ta save the rest of his family?"

Sam thought long and hard before responding. "I don't agree with your logic. I believe Brandon would have wanted to spend every last moment he could with his family before this world came to an end."

Sam moved to sit on the edge of the bed. He grabbed one of the pillows and threw it across the room. After watching it hit the door, he continued, "This place really pisses me off. The gods are a bunch of morons. I will keep fighting to save the people of this world, but I will not dishonor Brandon's death further by allowing you to use your magic on me ever again. I will fight like every other man. If I am supposed to die, then so be it. I will not look Brandon's family in the eye and know that I plan to cheat others out of their victories."

Kael began to pulsate as the blade hung from Sam's hip. "I think you have finally become a leader, Sam. I could not be more proud."

Sam reached down, unsheathed the sword and lifted it in front of his face. "Oh, shut up! Who asked you?"

Brandon's memorial was like no other Sam had ever seen. It was held at the Peak of Bailem—Brandon's favorite moment of the day. Brandon had always said a hard working man's day was about over by then, since he woke so early.

There were thousands of people who surrounded the family as they stood on top of a hill. They lifted Brandon into the air and laid him on a stacked pile of wood. Josephine and all the children surrounded the pile with torches. For the first series of moments since his arrival on Grayham, Sam listened to a prayer being shouted from the top of the hill. The prayer was addressed to Bassorine.

A tear fell from Sam's eye. He knew their words were falling on ears that did not exist any longer. He did not have the heart to tell them their god was dead. Maybe it didn't matter, since every soul ended up in the pages of the Book of Immortality anyway. Why destroy the beliefs of a family in mourning. It didn't seem right.

To Sam's surprise, Brandon's father called him over to stand next to Josephine and handed him a torch. As the man squeezed his arm, he looked at the fighter, "My son would have wanted you to light the fire with his family. It's a privilege to have the man who defeats you in battle honor you in this way. It will help start the healing process for this family."

Sam took the torch, then looked at BJ. The trainer nodded. Sam turned to light the fire.

Late Bailem has come and gone and the party is just getting warmed up. Sam is sitting on one of the many chairs the family has set up around the farmhouse, watching a scene like nothing he has ever experienced. As far as he can see, people are eating and laughing across the farmer's land. No one appears to be sad, not even the family. They all celebrate to honor Brandon as their fallen hero.

The moment came to give the toast. Each of Brandon's nine brothers took a turn. Delbert, Brandon's father, also spoke, followed by Brandon's wife. Once she had finished, Josephine turned to Sam and asked him to make a toast of his own.

It was agonizing. It wasn't the idea of speaking in front of thousands of people, but more the pressure of speaking about a man he knew so little about. The fact so many people loved Brandon made him feel Brandon was worthy of something grand. He thought for as long as he could, then addressed the crowd.

"In all my seasons as a fighter, I've never met a man who was so beloved by everyone who knew him. I consider myself humbled to have met such a man. I only wish I could've known his qualities outside the arena. From what I know of Brandon's life, I believe he would have been the kind of person I would've cherished. I will, forever, remember this day. The love which has been displayed here is worthy of the gods' recognition. I know Bassorine will reward Brandon for a life well-lived. Let's raise our glasses and celebrate this fallen warrior."

The crowd erupted as Sam finished his speech. Many of them moved to place their hands on his shoulders. After things calmed down, Sam turned to Josephine and whispered in her ear. He led her to a less crowded spot and handed her a bag full of coin. "I've decided to give the winnings I received from your arena to help ease your family's burden. Take it, and know that I care. I will forever be there for you, if you need me."

Overcome with emotion, Josephine held the bag close and began to cry. "Sam, you are a good man. I...I'll..." Some of the women noticed Josephine's demeanor and sought to console her. They realized what Sam had done. It was not long before the gathering knew of Sam's generosity. He would leave Haven with a reputation as not only a fighter known for his barbaric victories, but also for his compassion and kindness. His actions on this day would catapult him to a new level of glory.

5 Peaks of Bailem have Passed

George, Amar, Kepler and Maldwin had gathered at Angel's Village before continuing on to the Siren's Song, a journey which took over 4 Peaks of Bailem. Dusk was approaching when they entered the mist, which reminded George of a cool, foggy evening in Florida.

They followed the river which flowed away from Griffin Falls. The moisture in the air thickened the farther north they walked. The mist created a climate which gave life to vegetation unlike anything George had ever seen. Soon, darkness fell and Amar's staff was necessary to light the way. After many long moments, they stopped to lie down. With the moisture in the air, they could only hope to get a good night's rest.

Kepler growled, "The mist from the falls has saturated my coat. I feel heavy. How can I prowl in these conditions?"

Amar lifted his staff, waved it in a circle and whispered a command. The moisture covering the demon-cat evaporated.

Maldwin's nose twitched with excitement. *"A yay alesoot tenguan yo maiyne."*

The jaguar nodded. *"Tele pomayn og foway."*

Maldwin cleaned one of his front claws as he responded. *"Nep, nep, osay poryolamay."*

George cut in, "What the hell are you two jabbering about?"

Kepler chuckled, "He wants Amar to keep his magic to himself. He said if it is used on him, he will give Amar nightmares. I, for one, appreciate the burden of my soggy coat being lifted.

"You're welcome," Amar said as he set the staff on the ground and motioned for the rat to relax. Once he saw the rodent lie down, the mage reached into his robe and retrieved a pipe.

George gave him a look of disgust, "Are you for real? Don't light that nasty thing around me. You're going to end up smelling like your brother. Do you really want to smell like that nasty old man?"

Amar looked at his pipe, then at George. He was torn between defending his brother or agreeing with George's assessment. After a while, he simply put the pipe away.

As they slept, George dreamed of Abbie. In his fantasy, Lasidious had returned his baby girl to him. They were with Athena, fishing. On Abbie's first cast, she caught a good-sized trout which almost pulled her into the water. The day was good, until the darkness fell across the pond. The next thing George knew, he was standing alone and both of his favorite women were nowhere to be found. He called to them, but there was no answer. He knew the darkness had swallowed them. He started to panic. He screamed over and over again, desperately hoping for an answer, when a speck of light appeared. It was small at first, but grew as it came closer. The light turned into a large sphere. He was scared, but could not run. He looked for an escape, but all he could see, beyond the light, was blackness. The ball was floating through the air and as it was about to crash into him, an electrifying scream filled his head.

George woke with a start and sat up. Confused, he scanned the area, but his eyes could not see anything beyond the campfire's light. All of his companions were asleep. His clothes were saturated from the moisture of the mist. He turned to grab his bag from behind a massive root which protruded from the ground. Inside, he found a torch and pulled it free. Something told him he needed to leave the group. He could not explain the feeling, but knew it had to be done.

He stood up, careful not to make a noise, grabbed his pack and walked toward the sound of the river. Once sure the light would not wake the others, he lit the torch and headed out.

The elevation changed at a rapid pace. It was not long before he was hiking, not walking through the darkness. The hillside grew even steeper, elevating his heart rate as the river's rapids made its descent over the rough terrain.

He kept moving, pressing ahead with sheer determination. Eventually, he reached the top of the hill where the area flattened in front of him. He stopped to take a few deep breaths before continuing. He wasn't sure how long it had taken to get to this point, but it had been quite the hike.

A large pond stretched out in front of him as far as he could see. He should not have been able to see anything, but a strange greenish glow filled the air. To the far side of the body of water, Griffin Falls could be heard crashing against the rocks. It was the force of the falls which caused the mist to fill the sky.

From the depths of the water, a light appeared and made its way to the surface. George recognized the light as it approached. It was the same light from the sphere in his dream. He knew it was this creature who had called him to this spot. The water fell from its smooth surface and soon, the large ball of energy floated in front of him.

There was a long silence as he stood watching. Then, as he was about to speak, the air filled with a song. The sound was beautiful, heavenly in fact. Though the lyrics were in another language, somehow, he could understand their meaning. Through its song, the creature called itself a wisp. Further, it requested to be called by the name, Cadromel. The sphere told George he knew why he was there and asked for the envelope. George removed it from his pocket and held it in front of him. This seemed to satisfy Cadromel. He asked if George was prepared to give the envelope in exchange for information.

George nodded, "I am ready to listen, please continue."

Once again, the lyrics filled the night air. The harmonics of the wisp's heavenly sound reverberated against the water of the pond. George watched as tiny waves beneath the sphere rolled away just as if a pebble had been dropped below it. As the wisp's song came to an end, the gentle roll of the waves dissipated.

George looked at the center of the wisp's mass. "I understand. I already know the question I would like to ask. I would like to know how I can use my ability to gain the power necessary to rule this world?"

The wisp began to pulse, its melody releasing short bursts of baritonal tones. It was as if the creature was laughing.

"What's so stinking funny? Don't you know the answer?" George snapped.

The wisp went silent. The light within dimmed. Then, suddenly, the creature emanated a blinding light combined with a thunderous bass toned eruption. Within this much darker melody, a powerful message was delivered. George heard it loud and clear, despite having to cover his ears. "Who are you, mortal, to speak with the wisdom of the ages in a manner most unbecoming of the god whom you represent? Kneel before me on the banks of this pool or the information you seek will remain locked within my eternal mind. Bow now...or leave my home, none the wiser."

Frightened, George did as he was told. He rushed to take a knee and lowered his head. He kept his eyes shut to protect them from the blinding light penetrating the night. His mind ran wild with thought. He had no idea the wisp thought he was here to represent a god. He now knew it was Lasidious who was responsible for sending him on this quest. "I'm sorry, Cadromel. Please forgive me for the way I spoke."

The wisp's light faded. The song went silent. An extremely long series of moments passed before the sphere decided what he wanted to do.

Now...fellow soul...do you remember me telling you at the beginning of this story how I interviewed everybody involved? Do you remember I said I knew everyone's desires, their thoughts, and their reasons for doing the things they did? Well, allow me to take you inside the wisp's mind...

As Cadromel sat with his light diminished, he thought, *This mortal possesses the knowledge I desire on his person. If I send this human away without revealing the answer he seeks, I will never know Lasidious' mind. Ohhhh, how I miss the days of slaughter. If only I could devour this mortal and take the envelope from him. Curse the gods and their laws of governance over the temple. Why do they protect the weak on this world?*

George was nervous to move. He might as well have been a statue. Never in his life did he feel more insignificant than he did at this very moment. It felt like sweat was pouring from every gland and the moisture of the mist made his clothes heavy. His mind screamed, *Stay still, George. Stay still. Just be still. Don't piss this thing off anymore than you already have. Who knows what this freaking thing will do? Holy hell. I miss Earth.*

The glow within Cadromel's sphere returned. *I shall give this insolent human what he is after. I want him out of my sight.*

The wisp's melody was soft and carried a sense of peace as it delivered the information necessary to rid itself of George's presence. Soon, George knew all about the Barbarian Kingdom. The barbarians would not know of his ability and he could enter the arena without suspicion.

Once again, the light of the sphere became blinding. When George lowered his hands from his face, the wisp was gone and so was the envelope. He had to wait for his eyes to adjust before heading back to camp. Though shaken from the experience, he knew how to put his power to its best use, but had he created an enemy while gaining this knowledge? His face carried a chaotic expression all the way back to camp.

After making his way down the mountainside, the others were awake and the night was fading. They expressed concern about his absence, though Maldwin's worry was the only genuine expression in the group. George informed them of his meeting with the wisp and said he had a plan in place. He would fight for the Crown of Bloodvain.

"What? Are you an imbecile?" Kepler growled. "The barbarians are the most ruthless two-legged fighters throughout all the territories of Grayham. They don't allow magic in their king's arena. You won't be allowed to challenge their champion."

Amar jumped into the conversation, "I agree. How do you expect to do this when you're commanding the arts? Without them, you will be pummeled into a pile of garesh."

"What the hell is garesh?" George responded.

Annoyed, Amar replied, "You know, garesh. When a horse lifts its tail and drops it to the ground."

"A pile of garesh, he says." George laughed. "I think I like that term. I'm gonna start using it."

"I like cheese, George!" Maldwin shouted, looking for a way to chime in. The group turned to look at the rat. The rodent desperately wanted to get in on the conversation and this was the only phrase Kepler had taught him that everyone could understand.

George stopped laughing. "I really like this damn rat." He leaned down and scratched the top of Maldwin's head. "You guys are right. The Barbarian King won't allow anyone to enter his arena who uses words of power or magical items. The king will only allow a fighter to wear a fur loincloth to cover his family jewels..."

"Family jewels?" Amar quizzed.

George rolled his eyes. "For real? You really don't know what that means? This place drives me freaking nuts. Family jewels is another name for your privates, Amar. You know, the part that hurts when I kick you between the legs for interrupting me, you rotten bastard. Where I'm from, we also call it 'your junk.' Don't make me kick you in your junk."

Amar had to grin. "I apologize. By all means, please continue. My junk is fine without your foot being in it."

Kepler snarled, "Stupid humans!"

Maldwin shouted at Kepler in his own language, wanting to know what the humans were discussing. After Kepler explained, the rat rolled over onto his back and began laughing as he reached down with his front claw and grabbed between his back legs to express his understanding of the word, junk.

Again, George laughed. "Now, that's the funniest damn thing I've seen on this world."

The group enjoyed the series of moments before George continued the conversation. "Anyway, as I was going to say earlier, the king won't let me in the arena in anything but a cloth. There are no weapons allowed. Think about this for a moment. I don't need to speak words of power or use magical items. My ability works naturally and all I have to do is touch someone. Not only that, but I can turn a specific part of his best fighter to stone and they'll never know it."

"Yes they will," Kepler responded. "They harvest the heart, lungs, kidneys, liver, and the brain before placing them in jars for their passing celebrations. They'll know if you have done something when they open their champion and see his insides are made of stone."

George thought a bit. "So, what do they do with the rest of the body?"

"Well..." the jaguar collected his thoughts. "For those barbarians who are held in high regard, they burn them on the Blood Sea. It is the sea which swallows them, then everyone goes home to celebrate."

"There you have it," George blurted. "I'll turn the parts to stone which won't be cut from the body. The sea can cover up the truth. I'll turn the inside of their champion's Adam's apple to stone, or maybe the inside of a small part of his brain so he can't get signals to the rest of his body. This would give me the moments I need to move in, smack him around a bit, then run. I'll figure it out before we get there, I'm sure."

Amar looked at Kepler, then he began to pace. "When Lasidious told me I should travel with you, George, I didn't imagine you had this kind of nerve. If you pull this off, you'll be ruler of the Barbarian Kingdom. We'll be enemies of Brandor."

Amar massaged the end of his chin. "My family lives in Lethwitch. If we become enemies of Brandor, you must promise we won't attack Lethwitch."

George agreed, "You're right. This does present a problem. Athena's family is also from Lethwitch." He agreed not to attack the area only because he cared for Athena's family.

George pulled out his map. The moment had come to formulate a new plan. "Kepler, it'll take you at least 20 Peaks to reach the Blood Sea platform since you can't ride the hippogriffs. Why don't you go to the platform and wait for the rest of us to arrive?"

Amar stopped him. "Without kicking me in my junk, I need you to listen. We already have a problem. We cannot fly to the Blood Sea platform. The hippogriffs do fly there, but they won't take someone out of Brandor and fly them into barbarian territory. The rule of the kingdoms states: no man can fly into a kingdom he's not from. The only exception to this rule is Angel's Village, because it's protected by the gods. The closest landing tower anywhere near Bloodvain's is in Gessler. This is a place where the roughest crowds from both kingdoms have a tendency to migrate. This village is considered neutral territory and not owned by either kingdom."

Kepler jumped in. "That's because I dominate the passes surrounding the village. Gessler has been a good supply for my brothers and me to build our skeleton army. We stay out of the village for the most part. Since most men will not walk through my pass, the only way to get to the village is by hippogriff. But, on occasion, we find a fool. We catch nine or ten victims a season walking through our pass. I can't use them all for my army. Never could quite figure out why. Maybe it's because..."

"Kepler, will you get to the point?" George snapped.

"Sorry! I think what Amar is trying to say is, you'll need protection while in Gessler. Since the crowd isn't pleasant, I have an idea. Instead of meeting at the Blood Sea platform, I'll make my way to Gessler, but it will take 23 Peaks to get there. I want you to arrive the next day. My brothers and I will be hiding in the shadows in case you need us. Get off the hippogriff and make your way to an inn called The Bloody Trough. You won't see us unless you're attacked. When night makes it easier for us to move undetected, leave your window open for us to enter."

George responded, "Kepler, it scares the crap...wait, I mean it scares the *garesh* out of me that you can hide like that. I can't tell you how happy I am you're on my side. That's a good plan. We should do it. Will you ask Maldwin if he can project his visions to a group of people?"

The demon, although unsure where George was going with this new question, spoke with the rat. "He said yes, but if it is too big of a group, they'll all see the same vision."

"Exactly how big is 'too big of a group' before they start seeing the same thing? How many people can he project his visions to before he has to stop?"

Again, Kepler asked and responded, "He said more than three and they'll need to see the same image. He projected his visions to his entire family before a portion of the Cave of Sorrow collapsed. Back then, his family totaled over five hundred."

The manipulator smiled and started to plot. "Holy garesh, five hundred. I bet he has no clue if he can do more than that. So, what we know is, three or less, he can project separate visions and more than three, they all need to see the same thing. Is that what he is saying? Oh, and express to Maldwin I'm sorry about his family."

Again, the undead cat asked the rat to confirm. "He said you're right and he imagines he can project his visions to much more."

George put his hands behind the back of his head and started to ramble off another plan. "Let's figure out what the three of us will do until Kepler gets to Gessler. I think we should go back to Lethwitch. We can spend quality moments with our loved ones and work on the problem regarding rival kingdoms.

"We can introduce Maldwin to everyone who'll need to move out of Brandor. Once we take over the throne, we'll need to bring them to Bloodvain. I don't know how else we'll be able to guarantee their protection unless they're with us. I'll introduce Maldwin to Athena's family. He can use his visions to manipulate their minds and gain their affections. He can make them think they'll need to move. Kepler can keep his skeleton army under control and force them to provide safe passage through his pass."

George took a moment to think. "Oh, holy garesh, I almost forgot. Kep, this next part is really important. Maldwin might want to brainwash everyone to like your skeletons. Do you think you can explain everything?"

Kepler began to grin as a jaguar would. "At least you didn't tell me, to tell him, you said to tell me, to tell him, that I should tell him something, during that series of moments. I would hate to listen to that again. Should I tell him now?" The demon finished poking fun with a wink.

"Just shut up and tell him," George said with a laugh. He was starting to feel a strong bond with the giant cat. His feelings for Amar were still up in the air. Beyond learning to control his power, he didn't see much use for him. He figured he would take a wait-and-see attitude.

Kepler laughed and reviewed the plan with George. He wanted to make sure he did not mess it up since he would not be there to fix any problems. The jaguar suggested they walk as he informed the rat of their plans. They walked until the Peak of Bailem before Kepler stopped and said his conversations with Maldwin were complete.

"The rat will do everything you want, George. The signal for him to know who to use his visions on will be given by squeezing his tail. Maldwin will take care of the rest. He has asked for one favor in return."

"So, what's the favor?" George responded, sure it would be something large.

"He wants you to leave a pile of food behind when you go to Gessler."

George turned to look at the rat and before he could say anything, the rodent said, "I like cheese, George!" The critter grinned as he showed his two large front teeth and twitched his nose.

Everyone laughed. Maldwin's statement fit the conversation. Kepler informed the rodent he would have his pile of cheese when George left for Gessler. Not long after, they split up, parting ways for their own destinations.

Three Nights Later

Fellow soul...before we go on to the next part of the story, allow me to interject another small history lesson about another inn on Grayham. This particular lesson is about The Bloody Trough located in Gessler Village.

The inn acquired its name before it was built. Six seasons prior, when people first began to travel to Gessler, the center of the village was used for watering horses. The people built a six-foot-high, thirty-foot-long, sloping rock wall on this spot. Twelve different troughs, six on each side, also formed out of rock, had been laid into its base. A natural spring provided water for the entire area. The people of the village figured out a way to direct some of the water to the top of the wall. Once there, gravity directed the flow to each of the troughs.

One night, while the village slept, about one season prior to the inn's construction, a double murder was committed. The bodies of the beheaded men were thrown across the top of the wall. The corpses plugged the flow of water. When morning rolled around, one of the troughs at the end of the wall was marked by the aftermath. The blood covered the trough's rock edges and marred the water red. Though the stains faded over the next season, this one trough had been labeled. The family who built the inn decided to name it, The Bloody Trough, after the incident. To this very day, a man can take his horse into the tunnel and leave it to drink. Anyway, enough of my soulful babbling, back to the story.

Double D had made his way through the first part of Skeleton Pass and was now sitting on a stool at The Bloody Trough. He was drinking his ale and contemplating his trip through the second part of the pass when an unexpected event happened. He had been paid over a season ago by one of the nobles of the Barbarian Kingdom to kill an arrogant sergeant for sleeping with his wife. This type of job was not one he would normally accept, but the pay was up-front and substantial.

When he accepted the contract, someone talked. When his future victim heard he had been hired to kill him, he ran before Double D could set things in motion. As always in life, things have a way of coming full circle. This particular barbarian, dressed in furs and heavy leather pants, just walked in to sit at the bar. The assassin knew the man would have no idea what he looked like and, because of this fact, he decided to toy with him.

"How's it going, friend? Is it still raining? Slight chill out there, eh?"

"Hmpff," the man grunted.

The assassin smiled at the shortness of the exchange and asked another question. "Where you from, friend?"

The man did not respond and kept drinking. He tried again. "Say, friend, where you from?"

The barbarian turned. "I've no desire to speak with garesh. You're pathetic, a sad excuse of a man from Brandor. You're less than a man. I'd rather spit on you." He slammed his empty cup on the bar and demanded another ale.

The man from the north was large, over seven feet tall, and like most barbarians, he was strong. His long, dark hair hung to the right side of his rock-jawed face. The coldness of his eyes would have scared most men, but Double D was not most men.

The killer excused himself and walked to the far side of the bar to take a seat. He would wait for the big man to go out to the waste shed to relieve himself. Watching him pound one drink after another, the assassin knew it would not take long before the need would arise.

When the barbarian did go, he stumbled out and into the night. Double D followed, watching from the shadows as the barbarian opened the door to the shed. He gave his unsuspecting victim a few moments, then pulled a cloak from his pack. He took the hood and lifted it over his head and as he did, he vanished beneath the veil of magic.

Without a sound, Double D opened the shed. He stepped inside and let the door shut. The barbarian looked in his direction. He watched as the barbarian grumbled and turned to continue peeing into the large hole provided for The Bloody Trough's patrons.

Double D shook his head from within his invisible veil. Many of the men from the north were crude. When drinking, the less educated liked to drop their pants around their ankles to show their manhood. They didn't care for privacy or meekness. This didn't bother the assassin, in fact, their animalistic mannerisms made his job easier.

Double D moved toward his prey. With the big barbarian's back to him, he removed the hood of his cloak. He rematerialized with a big smile crossing his face. He looked down at the leather pants bunched around the barbarian's legs. A large knife rested in a sheath on the big man's belt. It was army issue. The pride of the barbarian kingdom was carved into its handle. The assassin moved closer and crouched to a position where he could reach the blade.

The man was so intoxicated, his stream of urine was moving all about as he swayed back and forth. At one point, the stream caught the edge of the barbarian's pants. The splash from the spray landed on Double D's hand. Disgusted, the assassin pulled the blade free of its cover. He lifted the tip of the weapon to a position just a matter of inches from the barbarian's buttocks.

The blade—thirteen inches long, two inches high and 3/8 of an inch thick at its widest point—had hooks along the top which rolled back toward his hand. The barbarians took pride in the fact that a sharper blade could not be found on all of Grayham.

The assassin shoved the blade hard into the man's rectum. He lifted upward in the direction of the hooks and ripped the knife free, pulling chunks of flesh from the barbarian's body. He ducked to avoid the large man's elbow as he spun around. Blood flowed freely in all directions as his intoxication caused him to lose control of his spin. His pants tightened around his feet causing him to fall face first into the large hole.

The assassin made sure his victim saw his face. Once satisfied the barbarian knew his imminent death had been dealt by the hand of the man he earlier degraded, Double D nodded. He lifted the cape's hood back over his head and darted out of the shed, leaving the barbarian bleeding profusely and lying in a pile of piss and garesh. The village people would find him the next morning, but not before the big man released some of the most horrific screams the assassin had ever heard, screams which would go unanswered. These tormenting sounds, which filled the blackness of the night, would leave an everlasting impression in Double D's ruthless mind. The moment had come to keep moving. He made his way to the other side of the village and entered the second part of Skeleton Pass.

Sick of this Royal Crap

The Town of Empire

Sam, Shalee, BJ, and Helga arrived in the town of Empire five nights ago. Empire is a small town with little military presence, despite being part of Brandor's kingdom.

Sam has already won his first fight in front of the populace who worship fire. His fight was to the death and his ribs took an awful beating. They are bruised, and he does not have the necessary Peaks to heal before his next fight.

Meanwhile, Shalee has worked with Helga to increase her power. She continues to astonish the older woman with her successes. Shalee has still suffered just the one failure since her first day of training in Angel's Village. For privacy, the girls have been practicing outside of Empire in a heavily wooded area. Not one soul has bothered them and this spot has proven to be a great place to go back to each night.

The night is beautiful and if Shalee could see, the sky would be clear. Shalee is still not comfortable with the idea there are no stars twinkling in the blackness. Helga's staff is planted in the ground and acting as their light source.

Helga moved back and watched as Shalee commanded Precious to rip a massive tree from the ground and send it flying high into the air. Foreseeing a bad outcome, Helga grabbed her staff, pulled it free, then put up an invisible wall to protect them. The trunk, almost eight feet in diameter, crashed into the ground. The area around them shook. The noise was deafening. The limbs splintered in all directions. Wooden missles thumped against Helga's magic and fell to the ground as nothing more than harmless pieces of kindling. The ladies rolled with laughter.

After a few exchanged glances of amazement, the foolhardy women began to wonder if the people in town had heard the collision. They decided it was best to stop training for the night and started a fire after collecting many fresh pieces of the kindling which laid scattered about. They would sit for a bit and talk.

"Oh, my goodness-gracious, that was loud," Shalee giggled as she held her stomach.

"I know, child, I know. I hope no one comes out here to yell at us. I had no idea you were going to send it that high. I felt like I bounced when it hit."

"Ya should've seen your face. Your big ol' eyeballs were just a poppin' when it was comin' down. I knew ya were gonna put up a protective wall. I'm glad ya did. We could've been punctured all ova'. I'd bet those fire worshippers would just love us for makin' all this kindlin'."

Helga knew the younger sorceress was commanding power most students would never command in their entire lives. It did not make sense how such a thing was possible, despite Bassorine's visit. Shalee had long since passed Helga's abilities and the only reason the student needed her around was for emotional support, if even for that. She felt like a mother to the young woman. This was the main reason she stayed. She thought back to what Shalee had said in West Utopia. The moment had come to let her student know she had surpassed her abilities, hoping Shalee would continue to need her friendship.

"Shalee, I have something to say, child. I must admit, I'm nervous about telling you."

Shalee could see the worry-filled eyes of her friend. "What is it? Why the long face?"

"Well, child, I've been trying to figure out how to tell you that I cannot teach you anymore."

"Why?! Do ya have someplace ta go? Did I mess up? I can fix it if you're upset with me. This Texan doesn't have so much pride I can't apologize."

"No, no, no, child. It's not like that. I'm not mad, nor do I want to stop being around you. Your power has grown beyond mine. I cannot teach you because you are better than I am."

Helga scooted next to Shalee, pulled her close, then hugged her. "I'm sad to say this, but I fear I'm not much use to you any longer."

Shalee returned the embrace and, after a moment, pulled away, tears filling her eyes as she spoke. "I already knew my abilities were beyond yours. Rememba', you bonked your butt. Shoot, I just didn't want ta say anythin'. Just because ya can't teach me any longer doesn't mean I don't need ya. You, BJ, and Sam are all I've got. I need ya now more than eva'. Who else would I talk with and who will shop with me when Sam needs ta buy me stuff?" Shalee smiled as she wiped her eyes.

"Do you want me to stay with you then, child?" Helga asked, looking for confirmation.

"Goodness-gracious, Helga, ain't ya listenin'? Yes, of course. I need ya. You're like a motha' ta me. The motha' I had on Earth is dead. She would have been happy ta know you're taking care of me."

"Well, then, it's settled. Now, you're stuck with me for good." They embraced again.

Thinking about how to advance her skills, Shalee said, "If you're not able ta train me, who is, and where do we find this person?"

After a moment of thoughtful consideration, Helga responded, "We've already been to a place where there is such a person. His name is Amar and he lives in the town of Lethwitch. He's much stronger than I am. He could teach you further. He's the only person on Grayham who can help you grow beyond what I've taught you. He is the only man on Grayham who has traveled to Luvelles and studied the arts. If you'd like, we can seek him out once we've gotten Sam to the city of Champions."

"I don't want ta leave Sam until afta' he has met with the King of Brandor. I hope he can keep his winnin' streak alive. Goodness-gracious, what am I sayin'? He has ta keep his winnin' streak alive or he'll be dead. He doesn't have anotha' fight scheduled for submission." Shalee groaned. "This just makes me sick. I hate the fact he won't let me use my magic ta help him. I can't handle watchin' him get stitches. His ribs look terrible." She grimmaced. "Let's pass on findin' Amar for now. I'm sure I can think of somethin' ta challenge myself 'til the moment is right. All we have ta do is think of somethin' absolutely absurd, then try it." She slapped her hands together, "*BAM,* we have another purdy lil' lesson."

"I suppose, child."

"Besides, I have been dyin' ta use some of the new elvin words ya taught me. I'm just waitin' for the propa' moment."

"Until then, maybe you can try raining down fire or manipulating some other outlandish control over the elements. Who knows what you're capable of?"

Shalee agreed, then changed the subject. "We need ta find a way ta get the king ta listen ta Sam. Maybe you and I can figure somethin' cleva' ta speed this whole process up." Shalee smiled, "Give us a high-five, girl."

⚜ ⚜

Unbeknownst to the women, they were being watched from the shadows. The stare of the being within this hiding spot was filled with disturbed thoughts.

⚜ ⚜

The sorceresses stayed up through the night and spent most of it talking about girl stuff. When morning arrived, the moment had come to go back to town and eat breakfast with the boys. The swine meat and greggled eggs were delicious and, as always, the conversation quite pleasant. Afterward, everyone prepared to go to the arena for Sam's fight.

⚜ ⚜

Now...fellow soul...I need to tell you something about Empire. This town is considered to be the jailhouse for the whole of Grayham. This arena's headmaster lives in forced service to the King of Brandor, and he acts as a sheriff, of sorts. He is not human and lives in humiliation. Farogwain is a serpent noble, a relative of the Serpent King, Seth. His nobility is what spared him from being transported to Dragonia, but this immunity did not exonerate him from being punished for the crime he committed against an officer in Brandor's army.

Thirteen seasons ago, Farogwain devoured this man's son while traveling to the Temple of the Gods. Because the serpent's murderous actions happened during a time of peace, Farogwain has been forced to live in shame. He has been ordered by Brandor's senate to spend the rest of his life disposing of Grayham's unwanted. Seth was left with no choice. He did not want to go to war with Brandor. He had to surrender his slithering cousin to the king, and he did it himself.

Farogwain's mind is sadistic and, as a result, Empire's large, oval arena is the most barbaric setting throughout all the worlds. This stage, on which the fights are hosted, is like no other. The faces chiseled into the stone walls surrounding the sandy surface look tortured.

The faith of the people living here makes Empire's arena unique. Their faith is different from the rest of Grayham. The people pray to a god no other populated area worships, and they cherish the eternal fire. This town is one of the few areas where Jervaise makes a seasonal appearance. While in her ghostly form, she seduces the people into worshipping her. The town sculpted a statue to honor the goddess some 6,000 seasons ago and placed her likeness at the center of the battleground.

The Goddess of Fire's statue is surrounded by a circular pool of flame, 30 feet in diameter. Seven other, smaller pools, all square, and nearly twelve feet across are also burning. They have been scattered across the arena's floor. The pools have been positioned to serve as obstacles to keep combatants separated when they enter the arena at opposing ends of this high temperature battleground.

As if this isn't bad enough, whenever the fights come to Empire, there is one fight filled with convicted felons. These criminals are awaiting transport to Dragonia. They are positioned by each pool. Some are in pairs, while others are in groups of four, but each felon is harnessed and holds a key. Generally, the most ruthless of these criminals are placed around the circumference of Jervaise's pool.

All of these convicted beings are used to heighten the hostility of the fighting environment during the Man vs. Beast Battle. They are all chained by a single wrist, leg, or tail and the weakest felons, capable of holding a weapon, are given one. Their metal leashes require a key to be set free. However, the key is held, or secured, somewhere on the body of another criminal within reach.

It has been decreed: a criminal who slaughters another, will be spared transport to Dragonia for 10 Peaks. Further, for a criminal who extinguishes the life of a primary combatant—a combatant who enters the arena by choice—transport to Dragonia will be delayed by another 30 Peaks. If a prisoner manages to kill both free combatants, man and beast, transport will be delayed for a full season. This prisoner will be given the option to remain on Grayham and allowed to fight while trying to secure enough victories to earn freedom.

Since banishment to the dragon world is considered a death sentence, the Man vs. Beast Battles in this town are the most ruthless and fierce on Grayham. This is a criminal's only chance to lengthen what is left of their life and those who enter want to win any reprieve.

Now...fellow soul...the reason I have told you this—Sam is about to enter Empire's arena and the lottery has handed him the Man vs. Beast Battle.

"Sam, this is not good," BJ said, after being informed of the lottery's results. "I've always hated the way this town's arena has been governed. I still hate it. Brandor claims the serpent's punishment is degrading. They say Farogwain despises his service to the senate. I think he enjoys the slaughter which happens during the battle the lottery has handed you. Sam, this fight is a fool's fight. There's no honor in this battle. I recommend you withdraw your entry."

Sam stood from the wooden bench in his preparation room beneath the arena's floor. He passed his hand across the rough stone walls as he moved to grab another sconce and lit it before the other ran out of oil. "Okay, okay, why would I withdraw? If I do, we will have to start the 22 fight requirement from the beginning. I don't want to kill more men than I need to, just to escape a single fight."

BJ put his hand on Sam's shoulder. "You need to listen to me, son. This is the only battle I would recommend that any man walk away from. You are entering without a weapon. You are fighting a bear who equals your weight, amplified by five and..."

Sam rolled his eyes and interrupted. "Hold on, BJ, it's just a bear. I've learned a lot since we began our training. I can handle this."

"No, son! This is more than a single battle. In this arena, the Man vs. Beast confrontation is a series of battles within a much larger battle. You won't be fighting just a bear. According to the lottery's registry, you will be fighting another 28 souls. They are criminals, fighting in desperation. There is a prize on your head. If they manage to get free of their bonds, they will come for you."

"Okay, okay, hold on just a moment! So, you're saying I'm fighting 29 total and all of them want to kick my ass? What kind of messed up lottery is this?"

Before BJ could respond, Farogwain slithered in. The headmaster's serpent body coiled up and filled much of the preparation room, forcing BJ and Sam toward a wall opposite the door. His cobra hood expanded and the rattle on the end of his tail shook. Once the reptile was sure he had their attention, his rattle silenced. "I sense fear in you, human. Today is a glorious day to watch your blood stain the sand of my arena."

From behind the serpent, just outside the door, Shalee's staff tapped the stone floor. She moved the finger of her free hand back and forth. "Hmm, hmm, hmmm! Excuse me, Mr. Slitha' Pants! Today is also a good day for lil' old me ta be castin' some hocus-pocus on your cold whateva' ya call 'em. I should create me some brand new snake skin boots. Don't ya be comin' down here and makin' your threats. You just ran across a genuine Texan. I was a child when I learned how ta cut snakes' heads off. Ya best take yourself on out of here before I get mad."

Farogwain's coils tightened, his rattle shaking wildly as his head lowered to a height level with Shalee's. His annoying hiss was barely above a whisper. "You're brave for a female of your species. You speak like no other on Grayham. I wonder if you taste as good as you sound. Perhaps, your bones will break in a melody within my coils."

Before another word could be said, Shalee slammed her staff against the stone floor and shouted, *"Precious, fea en' naur, lom!"* Her body erupted in flames and the look of her flesh turned spirit-like. The heat caused the serpent to pull back and press against the far wall.

From within her personal inferno, Shalee began to laugh. The power of her magic echoed the sound throughout not only the room, but the catacombed hallways beneath the arena floor. Once she saw the serpent's eyes were filled with fear, she stopped laughing and whispered in a hiss of her own, free of her accent. "Do you always talk back to gods, Farogwain? Mind your place. Today, I will spare your life, but you will leave this room before I change my mind. Now, be gone."

The fire surrounding Shalee's body dissipated as she took a few steps back and gave the serpent room to exit. As the serpent undulated past, without saying a word, Shalee looked over her shoulder at Helga. The older sorceress was standing down the hallway with her hand cupped over her mouth to silence her laughter.

As Shalee walked back into the room, Sam and BJ were still looking at each other, shocked. Shalee said, "Well, that was just downright nifty, don't ya think? Me, a god, who would've eva' thunk it? What a delightful deception. So, Sam, what's this about ya fightin' 29 souls, anyway? Were y'all plannin' on tellin' me?"

Again, Sam and BJ looked at each other. They turned and responded at the exact same moment, saying the exact same thing. "Of course, we were. We were just about to come and get you."

Helga bounded into the room. "Oh, child, child, child, that was exhilarating. I believe a high-five is necessary." The women sassily threw up their hands, clapped them together and bumped one another's hips. Shalee added, "You go, girl! I told ya I was gonna find the right series of moments ta use those new words."

BJ cleared his throat. "I hate to interrupt your celebration, but we have a problem. Sam refuses to withdraw his ticket. He cannot win a battle of this magnitude. If it was just the bear and not another 28 souls, he would have a chance."

Shalee looked at Sam. Before she could say anything, he held up his hands. "Don't even suggest it. I'm not backing down and I'm not going to fight with your magic protecting me. If I'm meant to die, I'm going to do it without dishonoring Brandon's death. You know I must fight to save the people of this world."

Kael took it upon himself to lift from Sam's sheath and hovered to a position in front of the fighter's face. The sword's blade pulsated as it spoke. "BJ is right, Sam. You need to withdraw your ticket. This is a fool's fight."

"Kael, ya took the words right out of my mouth. There's no glory in dyin' in a fight ya cannot win. It's downright stupid."

"Okay, okay, hold up. First of all, Kael, I didn't ask for your opinion. Second of all, there's not much choice here. Even if I do quit and start the 22 fight requirement again, who says I won't land the Beast vs. Man fight the next series of moments we return? What are we going to do, quit again, and again, until we draw the fight we want? I have no desire to keep killing."

Shalee tapped the butt end of her staff on the floor as she pondered. Eventually, she came up with a plan. "Ya know what...why don't ya just go on up and take your position on the arena floor when the bell sounds? I got every-thin' unda' control. Don't ya worry 'bout a thing." Shalee and Helga left the room.

Sam looked at BJ. "I wonder what she's up to."

"I don't know, but it is Shalee we're talking about. Who knows what goes through that woman's mind?"

It was night when Sam entered through the gate on his side of the arena. All the pools, scattered about the arena floor, had been lit and illuminated the battlefield. To his surprise, the sandy surface was empty and there were no opponents visible. Curious, he walked further out to get a better look at his surroundings.

When Sam spotted Shalee, she was sitting in Farogwain's personal booth. The serpent was coiled against the far corner, clear of the sorceress. It was evident the reptile wanted to avoid further confrontation.

Sam shook his head in amazement. As he looked down, he saw two rows of criminals. The rows consisted of two giant cats, a minotaur, one wolf, and the rest were human. They were all standing beneath the headmaster's box, bound to the wall in chains. Sam thought to himself, *Damn, she really cleaned house. There's nobody to fight. So, where's the bear?*

Helga entered the serpent's booth. She had a dagger in her hand and handed it to Shalee. Shalee spun it around in her palm, then tossed the blade down to the arena's surface. The knife stuck in the sand, not far from Sam's feet, then she shouted, "You go on and fight your lil' fight now! I got ev-erythin' unda' control!" She pointed down at the criminals. "They won't be botherin' ya none!"

As Sam grabbed the knife, the bear's growl filled the air. Its gate, on the opposing side of the arena, opened. The kodiak-looking beast adjusted to the emptiness of the battlefield. Above the bear's gate, in another observa-tion box, sat a larger group of bears which were growling at their champion. It didn't take long before the beast realized he only had one enemy. He turned and charged.

Sam secured his footing, gripped the knife in his right hand, and waited for the bear to close the distance. The beast's heavy paws thumped against the sandy surface as the people of Empire filled the stadium with their cheers.

As the bear drew near, it stopped running and rose up. His mouth opened wide and a powerful roar covered the screams of the fans. Sam did not wait for the beast to lower onto all fours. Instead, he dove into a roll. As he exited, he stabbed the bear's right rear paw, then ripped the knife free and began running to the far side of the arena.

Limping, the bear gave chase. As Sam passed one of the pools, he spotted a heavy chain meant to harness one of the criminals. He grabbed it and with all his god-given strength, ripped the chain free from the block it was secured to. He started to spin the linked weapon around in his hand. Again, the bear stopped and lifted up as the chain whipped around in front of him.

Sam gathered the chain into a ball and tossed it skyward. As the bear watched the weapon arch over its head, he removed the dagger from his mouth and dove into another roll. He stabbed the bear's left rear paw, yanked the knife free and began to run again.

Passing a second pool, Sam ripped another chain free. He tossed the majority of the links into the fiery oil. He waited for the bear to limp his way back into battle. Once the animal was close enough, Sam pulled the chain free in a slinging motion and ensured the weapon landed across the beast's back.

The bear rose up to free himself of the irritation. Again, Sam pulled the chain, and moved to the far side of the pool. Passing the pool's far corner, he made sure the chain's heavy links passed through the oil, reigniting the fire. As he waited for the bear to follow, he laid the chain onto the arena's surface, parallel with the pool's edge. He used the fire on the tether to create a natural barrier he knew the bear would want to avoid. Using himself as bait, Sam drew the beast in.

As the powerful animal passed between the chain and the pool, Sam jumped to the opposite side of the flaming barrier and threatened to stab the bear on its flank. The beast rose up to defend itself. Seizing the opportunity, Sam jumped toward the bear, planted both feet on the center of the beast's exposed chest, then kicked. The heavy-coated animal flew backward into the pool and was engulfed in flames.

Sam came down hard as he landed across the hot links on the same side where he had injured his ribs only days earlier. Despite the cracking sound beneath his sizzling skin, he forced himself to roll off the chain, suffering additional burns as he did.

The crowd of the arena erupted as Sam stood. Holding his side, he stumbled over to BJ who waited on the other side of the gate he had entered. BJ handed the fighter a pouch filled with Soresym's essence. Sam did not drink right away. Instead, he poured some in the palm of his hand and splashed it against his burns. He watched as the skin began to heal. After taking two large swigs, he handed the pouch back to BJ.

When Sam tried to leave the arena the next day, after collecting his winnings, BJ ran up to him. "There's a rumor going around. Someone of great importance is here. No one is allowed to leave until this person speaks. They have posted guards at every exit."

"Who is it? I have a headache and my ribs still hurt. The pain in my head has been getting worse all day. I want to go back to the inn and drink the rest of what Soresym gave me."

"You'll have to wait. They're not telling anyone who is here, but when someone is given this kind of privilege, it's usually a member of the Royal Family."

Sam rolled his eyes. "Whoever it is puts his pants on just like you and I do. I'm not in the mood for dealing with a pompous jerk who wants to throw his royal weight around."

A male voice, from behind Sam, spoke. "Pompous jerk, he says. I heard you were a strong man, but I wouldn't have imagined you viewed royalty with such disregard."

Sam turned to take a look. The figure was well-dressed and he had clearly heard everything Sam said as he walked up.

BJ knew who was speaking, backed up against a wall, and dropped to one knee. Sam didn't care in the least and turned to defend his position.

"It's not that I view royalty with disregard, I'm just not in the mood to kiss someone's ass today. I have a headache, I feel sick, and all I want right now is to get some sleep. Who are you anyway?"

BJ shouted to get Sam's attention. "Sam, shut up! The man you're talking to is Prince Aaron. He's the King of Brandor's son."

Sam whirled around. "So what! Like I said before, he puts his pants on just like you and I do, unless you know of some kind of royal secret I don't."

The Prince laughed, "Sam, Sam, my good man, you're clearly out of sorts today. I'm glad I came, and not my father. He would've had you beaten for your words. I, on the other hand, would like to think I can understand people's frustrations. Maybe we could walk a bit and have a nice conversation, just the two of us. I have come a long way to see you, and I would appreciate the company."

Sam studied the royal figure. Prince Aaron had sandy blond hair, blue eyes, and although his frame was not a fighter's frame, he was fit. His black robe was trimmed in gold. Embroidered at the robe's center was a red shield with a gold outline. At the center of this shield sat a golden scale, the crest of Brandor.

Aaron ordered the healer to fetch something for Sam's headache. "Perhaps, when the healer gets back, we could walk together."

Sam took a deep breath. "Sure, no problem, I'll talk with you, but I need to piss first. I'll be right back."

While Sam was gone, BJ made an attempt at damage control. "I'm sorry, Your Grace. He is hurting. His last few fights have been brutal."

The prince assured the trainer it was unnecessary to apologize, but this didn't make BJ feel any better. "Everyone is allowed a bad day every once in a while. Duke Barthom Brandor has assured me Sam is a true gentleman. I am sure our conversation will be pleasant."

When Sam returned, he followed the prince into the cobblestone streets of the town. The prince's personal guard cleared the way as they went, barring people from stepping outside their heavy wooden business doors. Aaron smiled as he watched the children poke their heads above the watering troughs as they passed.

"Duke Barthom Brandor has spoken highly of your character, Sam. I heard about what you did for the Smith family in Haven. I can think of no other fighter who has given his winnings to the family of his fallen opponent. After hearing of this generosity, I spoke with my father. He was impressed. He will be holding his tournament early this season since we may be going to war. With the way your reputation has spread, my father has decided to extend an invitation. It seems you have turned the heads of the right people, Sam. The rumors about your skills have proven to be true. Since I've received my father's permission, you now have two more victories to your name. The King's tournament will start in 7 Peaks and I would like you to return with me to Brandor. I don't normally deliver this sort of invitation, but I wanted to see what the commotion was all about."

Sam was grateful for the invitation, but he was thinking about the upcoming war. "You said we may be going to war. Is this what all the wagon building is about? Are they not for harvesting? What can I do to help?"

"I can see why people like you, Sam. You have just been extended the highest honor a fighter can be given, yet you're more interested in what I've said about the war. It's refreshing to meet someone with such an unselfish nature. To answer your question about the wagons, I first need your word. You must swear to secrecy on this subject. Can I trust you, Sam?"

"Of course, you can trust me. I swear pretty good when I need to. Heck, I can keep my mouth shut for a good bit of dirt."

"I don't think I've ever heard someone speak as you do. I find it entertaining." The Prince smiled, then his demeanor changed. "The wagons are for harvesting. The gods have promised there will be three bountiful harvests within a short period of Peaks. We need the wagons to get them to the coastal cities. From there, the king's fleet will take the harvests to Merchant Island."

Sam cut in, "Was Mosley a part of this conversation?"

Aaron gave Sam a look, unsure how to respond. "Why would you speak of Mosley?"

"You said the gods have promised a bountiful harvest. Since Mosley is a god, I assumed he would have been part of this conversation."

"He was. How do you know of Mosley?"

"Shalee and I were the first to talk with him after he became the new God of War. He told me about Bassorine's destruction. How's the wolf doing, anyway? Has he been back to see you since the gods gave you this information? I was hoping to say a few things to him when I bumped into him next."

The prince took Sam by the arm and led him into a pottery shop. He ordered his guards to clear the area. Once this was done, he spoke. "Whom have you told Bassorine is dead?"

"No one. Only Shalee, BJ, and Helga know. I understand the importance of keeping information like this quiet."

"You've done well, Sam. We'll speak more about this in Brandor."

The prince reached into his robe, produced a pouch and tossed it to Sam. As the fighter caught it, he heard a heavy clinking sound.

"There are 25 Jervaise in that pouch. If my accounting is right, this will equal what you would have won over ten victories in the arena. This is your reward for being so gracious to the Smith family. It's also meant to give you the means to come to Brandor and live. I think it would be wise for you to leave with me in the morning. You can bring your friends and we'll finish this conversation with my father."

Sam was unsure how to react, so he tossed the bag in the air and caught it. "I guess I'll see you in the morning." He watched as the prince extended his hand for him to kiss it. Sam thought to himself, *There is no way I'm going to do that.*

The fighter took the prince's wrist, turned it over to expose his palm, then shook it. He followed this up by saying, "I am not from your world. Where I'm from, we show respect in different ways. I have much to tell you, but for now, I'll ask you to be patient with my ignorance of your customs."

The prince was shocked, but after a moment, he looked down and secured Sam's hand. He allowed his arm to be moved up and down.

Sam said, "I do hope this will be the start of a great friendship."

"I hope so too, Sam. I look forward to tomorrow's conversation and the explanation of your customs. I didn't realize the gestures on the other worlds were so different."

"I'm not from any of your worlds. As I said, I have much to tell you. See you in the morning."

"Agreed," Aaron replied. With that, the prince walked out of the store, escorted by his guards.

❖❖•❖❖

When Sam arrived back at the inn, BJ, Helga, and Shalee were waiting for him at the bar downstairs. BJ was a wreck, worrying that Sam would say something to upset the prince. The women were trying to calm BJ, since his ranting was getting a little loud. Sam walked in behind them just before BJ said, "...then, the todlum said, with the prince standing right there, he puts his pants on just like he does! And, if that wasn't bad enough, he said maybe there was a royal secret to putting pants on. I was so embarrassed! I wanted to sink into the ground. So much for getting an early invitation to the city of Champions. I'm sure everything has been blown to garesh."

Sam smiled. He tossed the bag of coins over BJ's shoulder and watched it thump onto the bar. "You're right! We didn't get an invitation to the city of Champions."

BJ shouted, "I knew it! You messed it up! What'd I tell you ladies? He's a todlum!"

"Goodness-gracious, BJ, what is a todlum? You're not makin' any sense."

Helga responded, "A todlum is someone who is thick in the head, child."

"Oh shoot, in Texas, we called todlums, numskulls."

Sam rolled his eyes. "Well, I may be a todlum, but we still did much better than being invited to the city of Champions. Look in the bag, you old grouch!"

Once BJ saw what was inside, he clinched the bag and whispered. "This is a substantial amount of coin. Where did you get this?"

"The prince, of course. I sold him a new secret about how to put on his pants. You should have seen his face. He was so impressed. His eyes got really wide and his mouth started to water. He was so thankful, he pulled out a bunch of coins, threw them in a bag, then tossed it to me. He even invited us to his father's tournament in Brandor, which, of course, I had to turn down because the secret wasn't worth that much. Apparently, his father's tournament is being held early this season since there is an upcoming war."

BJ growled. "That's absurd! Why would a member of the royal house give you this much coin? Why would he pay you to come and fight in his father's tournament?"

Sam looked at BJ and whispered, "Have you ever heard of keeping quiet so the whole world doesn't know we've got this kind of coin on our person? Let's go up to the room and talk."

Once they were in the room, Sam explained how the coin was a reward for his generosity to Brandon's widow. He told the trainer they were to meet the prince in the morning to go to Brandor.

BJ responded, "So we're leaving for Brandor and we'll be meeting with the king? What should we wear? I don't have my best clothes with me, or my armor."

Sam looked at Shalee. "Looks like someone's star-struck."

Shalee laughed. "Maybe they have room on this world ta start a celebrity magazine. I betcha BJ would be tickled pink."

"What're you two talking about, child?"

"Oh, nothin' worth explaining. Pay us no neva' mind."

"I'm not going to see the king looking like a beggar," BJ announced. "I'm going to buy some nice clothes. You all might want to do the same."

Shalee walked over to Sam and nestled up to him, speaking in her cutest voice. "Baby, don't ya just want ta take your lovin', sweet, wonderful, sexy, kind, generous, perfect, sublime lil' magic-user shoppin'? Don't ya just want ta spoil me? I'll make it worth your while."

Sam rolled his eyes at BJ and sighed. "See what you've started, old man? Let me have the coin and I'll go buy us something."

The City of Brandor

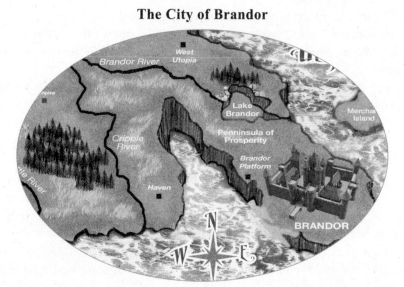

"I'm sick of all this royal crap," Sam said. "Ever since we met the prince, I've bowed more than I care to. I'm telling you right now, I'm not going to kiss this king's butt tomorrow. If he can't have a normal conversation, then screw him."

He turned to face Shalee. "I had the world in the palm of my hand on Earth and I didn't need to kiss anyone's royal ass. I don't have anything on this world. I just know I'm going to have to suck it up tomorrow and kiss his butt to get anywhere. Crap, this really pisses me off."

Sam pulled Kael from his sheath and started poking the tip of the blade into the wood of the bed's footboard. "I know I should be more patient, but I've killed so many people since we've arrived, and for what? It was all just to get *here*, and now that we are, I'm about to lose my mind. We don't know if this guy will even listen to us. How am I going to make a king believe I'm here to create an empire to set an example for the worlds to follow? How am I going to get him to let me go after the Crystal Moon's pieces? He'll see me as a threat. Aahhh, I need a break. I need a vacation."

Shalee could only smile at Sam's outburst. "Would ya just relax? Maybe ya don't have ta kiss his royal behind, after all. Just be bold."

The sorceress took Kael out of Sam's hand. Seeing the damage the blade caused, she commanded Precious to fix the marks the sword cut into the wood, then returned the blade to its sheath. "Ya know I've got your back, Sam. I realize the way the king and his son treat people isn't the way *you* would."

"So, what would you have me do?"

"For heaven's sake, show 'em your strength. Just shake the guy's hand like ya did Aaron's and see how it goes. I know ya don't like the politics of this place. Use the fact we're not from here ta cut through all the red tape. If it doesn't work, just piss him off." She tapped the butt end of Precious on the floor. "I'll take care of everythin'. I'll do it all nice and tidy-like. When I'm done, we'll have his attention. His lil' ol' ears will open up. After all, we have been sent here by the gods. Let's act like it. Let's take charge of the situation."

Sam turned and walked to the window. They had been given a room in the castle by the prince. The king's city stretched as far as he could see. The architecture was different from the Roman style of West Utopia. Brandor reminded him of something King Arthur would have lived in. Although this city was built with great attention to detail, he liked the city of West Utopia better. It simply had more class. He was surprised the king would allow his realm to have so many different looks. If he were king, there would be some sort of consistency to the grand design. He thought, *Isn't this hodgepodge something that should bother Shalee, and not me? After all, she's the architect.*

After a moment, he turned to face Shalee. "Exactly how would you have my back? I can only assume you're referring to using your magic. I don't know everything you can do. Give me an idea of what you're talking about here. Give me some news that'll make me feel better. I really need it right now."

"I can do far more than that," she said, scanning the room. In one of the corners of their castle suite, she saw a potted plant with loose gravel. She grabbed it, ripped out the plant, and handed the pot to Sam. With that, she moved to the other side of the room.

"I want ya ta take a handful of that gravel and throw it at me as hard as ya can."

"What? I can't do that. I'd hurt you."

"Don't be so sure, darlin'," she responded with a laugh. "I wouldn't tell ya ta do somethin' unless I knew I was goin' ta be okay. So just throw it, ya big sissy."

"Are you sure?" Sam said with a look of uncertainty.

"Just throw it and I'll make it worth your while." She licked her lips to emphasize her point. "Do I need ta say more?"

Sam grinned as he grabbed a handful. He reached back and threw it as hard as he could.

The sorceress had already lifted Precious and was speaking her command. The pebbles stopped in front of her and stayed suspended in mid-air. She moved around them, methodically circling the floating stones while she plucked them one by one from the air and turned towards her lover. She handed them to Sam as she spoke, allowing her hand to massage his chest as she moved away.

"Be a darlin', would ya? Put the rest of them back for me. I'll be in bed waitin' for ya." She leaned in and whispered seductively in his ear, "Please hurry, Sammy-kins." She smiled, patted him on the behind, then removed her clothes as she walked across the room.

Sam turned back to face the floating rocks and, with haste, gathered them into the pot. He thought, *Sammy-kins, hmmm, I like that. That woman is a tiger.*

The next morning, after Early Bailem, Prince Aaron guided Sam and the rest of the group into the king's throne room. As the prince entered, everyone was told to bow. Aaron signaled to come forward and approach the throne. They did as they were told, lowered to one knee and waited for the king to enter. It was a long wait, which angered Sam. He was sick of all the royal protocols wasting his precious moments. Bow here, bow there, bow, bow, bow, and bow again was the only thing they seemed to do in this stupid city.

Aaron sent one of the slaves to inform the king they were waiting, but somehow this news did not seem to create urgency on his father's part. After being on their knees for what felt like forever, the king entered. They lowered their heads and waited for the signal to lift them.

The king was a handsome man with long dark hair that complemented his brown eyes. He also had the body of a fighter and looked nothing like his son. His wife had been a beautiful handmaiden whom he married after taking the crown of Brandor many seasons ago. His decision to marry a woman without royal blood was not well accepted, but through the seasons, she became loved by all. It was her fair complexion which colored their son's appearance. She died not long after giving birth and the king never remarried because his heart would not mend.

"Stand, fighter. Let's have a look at what all the commotion is about," the king said to Sam and watched as his order was carried out. "I must admit, you appear to have a presence about you." The king motioned for the rest of the group to stand, "I welcome you all to Brandor."

They did as instructed without saying a word. Sam, however, was not one for all the formal gesturing and stopped the king's party in full stride. He was not about to spend all day on these meaningless formalities.

"Look," he said in a matter-of-fact tone. "I'm sure we can spend all day greeting one another. I would even bet that, under different circumstances, it's fun and has its place, but can we skip to the part where we get something accomplished? I have knowledge of things you may want to know. The quicker we get going, the sooner we can win this upcoming war."

As Sam was speaking, BJ was squirming inside. He knew this was not the way things should be done and he expected the king to explode.

Although she didn't show it, Shalee was more than ready to back Sam up. As agreed the night before, they wanted to get something accomplished and they were not about to be brushed off. She was holding onto Precious, ready to make an impression.

The fighter walked up the steps to the king's throne and stuck out his hand. This caught Keldwin off guard. He was unsure how to respond, so he looked to his son for guidance as the guards took a readied stance.

"I told you his mannerisms were strange, father. He says he's not from this world and has been brought here by the gods to create an empire. He claims they are to be an example to the worlds. It was Sam and his friends who were involved in the Crystal Moon's disappearance. Sam said three of them came to this world from a place called Earth."

The King stood and moved behind his throne. He didn't care much for what he heard, especially the part about Sam creating his own empire. "So, you're the one responsible for taking the Crystal Moon. Do you know what this has done to the fate of all the worlds?"

Sam ruined his momentum and interrupted with a voice loud enough to cover the king's. "Keep your royal britches on, Keldwin. Put your listening ears on and pay attention. No one said we're responsible. Aaron said we were involved. I knew this was going to be a waste of my moments. If this is all you managed to get from your son's words, then I'm disgusted and would never serve a king with such weakness."

BJ was about to die as he listened. He knew what was coming next. Sam would be hung before sunrise. For that matter, they would all be hung. Even the prince was fidgeting.

The king was astounded at how Sam spoke. His lack of respect was inexcusable. "Guards! Seize them! Take them to the dungeon!"

This was Shalee's cue to take action. She jumped to her feet and yelled, "Precious, *iluve sal!*" Almost everything in the room froze. The only ones who could still move were the king, Sam, and herself.

Keldwin looked around before turning his head to Shalee, and unsheathed his sword. In turn, Sam brought Kael from his resting spot on his hip and pointed it at the King as he yelled, "*Val arrna, naur!*" The blade burst into flames. "Not so fast!"

Shalee watched Brandor's leader take a few steps back to avoid the intense heat of the god-sword. As he did, he lowered his own, defeated. Shalee, seeing things were under control, began to move through the frozen figures scattered about the room, touching them sensually as she went.

"My King," she sighed, "You're bein' far too hasty. It seems you've let that lil' ol' crown of yours get ta your head. You're just not listenin'. If you'll pay attention...right now...I'm calling ya, My King."

Shalee passed her right hand across the blades of Keldwin's frozen soldiers as she continued to speak. "Your men keep their weapons sharp. Ya must be proud of your army. I would ask that ya open your mind and realize your ways aren't the only ways. We're not from your world. We won't be bullied, nor will we spend all day wastin' our moments on your senseless traditions."

The sorceress continued up the stairs which lead to the throne and walked behind Keldwin. She rubbed her hand across the nape of his neck and could feel him tremble. "Where we're from, we treat otha' folk the way they treat us. You're not givin' us the respect we deserve, My King."

Shalee floated back down the stairs and removed the weapons from his guards' hands. "We have no intention of bowin' ta ya until ya speak with us as equals. You'll treat us with respect and as friends. Once you've done this, you'll have our loyalty and we'll adopt your customs. We'll conform ta your silly lil' illusions of respect. People don't respect ya because they bow ta ya, Keldwin. They respect ya because you've earned it. I would imagine your people bow only because they fear your crown."

The sorceress placed the swords at the king's feet, then backed up. "I watched as ya hid behind your throne to command your guards ta seize us. It's a sign of weakness and I don't respect a weak man. I would only respect a king who has the nerve ta get somethin' done with his own two hands. I respect a man like Sam. Ya need a man like Sam helping ya, Keldwin. I won't stand here and allow ya ta make a mockery of him. Ya haven't earned our respect ta command us ta do anythin' yet, My King. If ya want me ta bow, I suggest ya stop all this childish nonsense before I become angry. Ya wouldn't like me when I'm angry."

Shalee moved back up the stairs and removed the king's sword from his hand. She turned it around and tapped it on his chest. "Ya don't wish ta see me angry, do ya?"

Keldwin shook his head, unable to speak as the sorceress continued. "We have been brought here by the gods and we have no intention of leavin' until we find a way ta save the worlds. I think we should be workin' togetha', don't you? You'll find a spot within your army for Sam. And, it betta' be an important position. Consida' this a non-negotiable request. I'm sure ya understand what non-negotiable means. We have come here ta help ya find the Crystal Moon. I'm sure ya can understand my position on this matta'."

The sorceress lowered Keldwin's sword to the floor with the others. She stood and brushed her hand across his face before moving to stand behind Sam. "Do we have an understandin', Keldwin? If we don't, speak now. I suppose, if it's necessary, I can use a much stronga' magic than ya have just witnessed ta make my point."

Keldwin felt disheartened as he lowered himself to his throne. He took the moments necessary to think. After a short while, he responded. "Is anyone hungry...or is it just me?"

Sam laughed and grabbed the man's hand, pulling him up from the throne. He put his arm around the king's shoulders. "Now, that's the best thing I've heard all day. Do you have any pancakes?"

Sam and the king were about to leave the room when Shalee commented. "My King, no one will rememba' this day's events and we will now adopt your customs. Thank ya for listenin', Sire."

The king forced a slight smile. "It appears I was being hasty. We have much to talk about over breakfast."

Sam and the king turned and walked through the doors. After they were gone, Shalee stood by the doors before releasing her magic. The men were confused by the absence of Sam and the king. They exchanged glances between their empty hands and the pile of swords. Shalee giggled as Helga winked. She pretended to give her friend a high-five as she left the room to catch up with the men.

Helga turned to BJ and grinned with a hint of mischievousness. "I may not be able to teach her how to command her powers any longer, but I can still teach her how to be a vixen with them. I guess it all went as planned."

BJ looked at her. A hundred questions filled his eyes. "What are you talking about? What's a vixen? Did Shalee teach you that word?"

Helga smiled and licked her lips as she responded, "She did, but it's nothing for you to worry about. Just wait 'til I teach you how to use the phrase… who's your daddy?"

Taking him by the hand, she led BJ and the confused Prince Aaron to find the king.

The Grayham Inquirer

When Inquiring Minds Need to Know about their Favorite Characters

SAM, Shalee, BJ, Helga, and the prince spent the rest of the day with Keldwin. All parties enjoyed getting to know one another. They shared information which needed to be exchanged. And now, with Late Bailem approaching, the king is about to give an address, announcing the details of his upcoming tournament.

DOUBLE D is still traveling to the city of Brandor. He is now only 3 Peaks of Bailem from the city's gates.

GEORGE, Maldwin, and Amar are due to arrive in Lethwitch tomorrow and have decided to stop for a night's rest. They will sleep at an inn located inside the city of Champions' gates not far from the landing platform.

KEPLER is on his way to Gessler Village. His trip has been uneventful. When he reached the northern part of the Dark Forest, he asked Hestin, a grave raven, to deliver a message to his brothers. He wants the cats to be at Gessler landing platform when he arrives.

THE GENERAL ABSOLUTE, Justin Graywind, is with the army's high-ranking officers. He is being briefed on the field reports needed to create new orders. As expected, the wagons are being built in an orderly fashion. Each populated area of Grayham will have more than seventy new harvest wagons ready within the next 17 Peaks of Bailem. The carpenters and engineers are working with the king's army through the nights.

The general knows they only have another 20 Peaks of Bailem before the harvest. He orders his men to scatter throughout Grayham to ensure that all men, no matter what their normal occupation, are helping in the process. He also follows up on the progress of the harvest barns in certain areas and has given his officers enough coin to hire four hundred men to build these barns. After a few more orders are given, he closes the meeting and makes haste to join the king at his dining table.

CELESTRIA is still living with the elven witch family. She has now taken up walking to avoid them as much as possible.

LASIDIOUS has been on the world of Luvelles. Five nights ago, he felt Shalee's power from afar. He excused himself from another long conversation with the Source and went to see what was going on.

Lasidious put a warning spell on Shalee the day he brought her to the Temple of the Gods. He secretly listened in on a conversation between Bassorine and the Book of Immortality in the Hall of Judgment. The late God of War told the Book that Shalee was special and would command great power. This news prompted Lasidious to put the warning on her. At that point, Bassorine became suspicious and put up a barrier through which Lasidious could not hear further.

Lasidious would never have dreamed Shalee could become so powerful so soon. Something more had to be behind her growth, but he did not know what it was. Whatever the reason, he needed to find a solution or George would be in trouble.

Lasidious had watched Shalee and Helga from the shadows near the town of Empire. The tree Shalee launched into the air was massive and the power necessary to do this was substantial. He was glad he had introduced George to Amar sooner than planned. He knew their relationship would need to be short-lived. George would not want Amar around if he felt threatened by his power, and Shalee's power would command Amar's attention.

Once George had an idea of how strong Amar was, he would turn him to stone. Lasidious knew he would need to implement another part of his plan sooner than expected. He needed to appear to George in his dreams and offer him some helpful information. He just hoped the Earthling's hunger for power was strong enough to stomach the next step.

MOSLEY had been watching from the hidden god world, Ancients Sovereign, and enjoyed every moment of what happened in the king's throne room in Brandor. He was impressed with Shalee's speech and decided the moments were ripe for an appearance during the king's upcoming dinner. He has grave news to deliver to King Keldwin.

Thank you for reading the Grayham Inquirer

A Taste of Death

When General Justin Graywind arrived, he apologized for his tardiness and introduced himself to the group. He took his normal position to the left of the king with BJ and Helga to his left. To the king's right was Prince Aaron, followed by Sam and Shalee. Keldwin ordered the servants to bring their meal as he informed the general of everything he knew. For obvious reasons, he did not mention the events which transpired in the throne room.

Keldwin explained how the general was the champion of Brandor's arena and, like Sam, had killed every man or beast who entered the arena with him.

Upon hearing about Sam's successes, the general lifted his glass. "This is most impressive. You have come to our world and adapted well. I'm sure you'll be a worthy opponent when we battle."

Sam looked at Shalee who, after hearing Justin's comment, seemed angry. He remembered telling her he wouldn't fight the general, and now that he knew the full extent of her power, he wasn't about to break this promise. The fighter was unsure how to respond, but as it turned out, the king pushed the conversation forward.

"General, I'm not going to allow you to fight each other. I have plans for you to work together to strengthen our kingdom. With this man's knowledge and his abilities in battle, I am placing him under your command."

"I understand," the general responded. "It'll be nice to have a sergeant who's well-trained in battle."

The king looked at Shalee and took a deep breath. The sorceress was now looking directly at him, waiting for his response. He knew the general was going to be displeased with his next statement. "No, my friend, Sam will not be a sergeant. He'll be your second in command."

"What?!" The general exploded as he stood from the table. "You can't be serious! What does this man know of commanding an army?"

Sam was about to interject and inform Justin of what he felt to be extensive knowledge of the wars he studied back on Earth, but Mosley appeared on top of the massive table. Startled, Sam and the general drew their swords. Once they realized who it was, they lowered their weapons.

Justin bowed and was the first to speak. "I'm sorry, Lord Mosley. I didn't know you'd be coming. I meant no offense by my actions. Please, forgive me."

"General, your actions were acceptable. You are a man of war. I would have expected nothing less."

Sam and Shalee took an entirely different approach to the god's appearance. They reached up and hugged him.

"Mosley, how are you?" Sam said, squeezing the wolf tighter as he continued. "It hasn't been the same without you around. One moment you're traveling with us, and the next, you're off with the rest of the Collective. I miss you, buddy."

Shalee could not contain her excitement as she spoke in her cutest doggy voice. She rubbed her hands through his fur, "I missed my Mosley. Yes, he's so cute. He's just so cute." She laughed as she kissed his snout.

Mosley couldn't stop himself from laughing. Shalee was a favorite of his and her advances, despite the obvious looks of confusion from the king, were welcome in his heart. "I missed you also, Shalee, but I am not so sure about you, Sam," he said, grinning wolfishly. "You still stink."

"Dang," Sam responded with a big smile. "Smack a guy in the chops when he's down why don't you?" Sam gave the wolf another big hug. "Get another whiff while you can."

After a moment of continued looks of disbelief between Justin and the king, the wolf began to speak. "I am sorry for my absence, but I have been attending to important matters. Being a god is not all it is presented to be. The others are lazy and are not much help. Sam, I am glad to see you have gained an audience with the king. Shalee, I watched the entire event unfold from the god world when you met in the throne room."

Keldwin felt uncomfortable that Mosley had seen what happened, and hoped the wolf wouldn't say anything in front of his general. Mosley could feel the reluctance of the king and turned to relieve his worries, projecting his thoughts into the king's mind. They were heard only because Keldwin wanted to hear them. *Don't worry, Keldwin. Your secret is safe. I will not tell the general of your fear of Sam and Shalee. You will remain the dominant leader of your pack.*

Upon seeing the king's relief, the wolf-god addressed the room. "I agree with His Majesty's choice to place Sam as second in command. It is the best thing for this kingdom."

The king sighed with relief. "Lord Mosley, is there anything else we should know?"

"As you know, Sam was chosen by the gods to create an empire for the other worlds to view as an example. I tell you this, Keldwin...the knowledge this man has will benefit your son and his armies. It is hard for anyone to set an example for others to emulate during moments of war, but this is the reason he is here. It is not necessary for Sam to be the leader of this kingdom to help your son create this empire, but he will be the most important part of it. I hope you and your general have enough strength to let him make your son's kingdom the example the gods want it to be. If you can do this, other worlds will adopt your customs and the gods will allow the races from each world to be united. It is your choice, Keldwin."

The king was a bit unnerved. Like his general, he was concerned about how Mosley had phrased a few things. The wolf had referred to *his* kingdom as his son's more than once.

"Lord Mosley, you spoke as if I won't be here to see these things happen. You have spoken of my kingdom as if it wasn't mine, and made it my son's. Is there something to become of me?"

Mosley jumped down from the table and moved to the king's side. "Keldwin, I hate to deliver negative enlightenment, but your body is fighting a disease and has been for over a season. Your body's ability to fight this is beginning to weaken. By morning, you will start to feel the effects of this disease and your healers will not be able to stop it from killing you. Your days as the leader of Brandor's pack are numbered."

"Am I to die right away, Lord Mosley?"

"No, Keldwin. I am here to bless you so you can see the end of your tournament. This will be my gift to you. As per your custom, your son will become king, and the general, his advisor. This will leave the position of General Absolute open. The second in charge of your army assumes this position. By default, Sam will be the new General Absolute. I believe this to be a wise move. Your confidence in this man is not misplaced. This change will be hard for the officers in your army to accept, but I will be present when you tell them. I am sure the loyalty of your people will remain strong."

Prince Aaron waited for the god to finish speaking. Once done, he jumped from his seat and argued his father should not be allowed to die. The king held up his hand, silencing Aaron. "Be strong, Aaron. Hold your head high and be proud. Everything is as it should be."

Keldwin stood and started to pace. He moved along Sam's side of the table as he spoke, "My son is brave and will make a fine king. When I die and the general becomes Aaron's advisor, Sam will become the General Absolute. I agree, Lord Mosley, this is per our custom."

Keldwin thumped the back of his son's chair. "Aaron, you don't have an heir. I suggest you get busy and find a wife. You'll need children to survive you once I'm gone. I know this isn't how you envisioned finding your wife, but you've enjoyed sowing your royal oats long enough. The moment has come for you to do your duty."

The prince stood and embraced his father. "I promise. I won't let you down. I'll lead the people with the wisdom you've taught me."

The king smiled and, for a moment, allowed himself to be proud. "It is my wish that, from now until the moment I pass, when we aren't in the company of others, everyone in this room calls me by name. Let us talk as equals. I would like to enjoy this pleasantry before I die. I find myself wanting friends right now, not loyal subjects. This isn't something I wish to command. I want it to be from your hearts. It's acceptable to say no."

Everyone in the room spoke at the same moment, calling him "Keldwin," confirming their acceptance of the idea.

After a moment of silence, the king kissed his son on the forehead and said, "But, *you* still have to call me, father." Shalee and Helga started to cry.

The king turned to the general. "Ready Sam for his new position.He'll need to know everything about our army."

The general stood from the table. "My King, I mean, Keldwin, it will take at least 10 Peaks to impart this much knowledge. The moments necessary to accomplish such a task are not available."

Mosley responded, "Justin, you must remember Sam was chosen by the gods."

"I do, Lord Mosley, but this doesn't mean he can learn such a tremendous amount of information in such a short period of moments."

Sam slapped the table. "Justin, prepare to be impressed. I think you'll find I'm more than capable. You only need to speak the information once for me to have it committed to memory. The faster you talk, the quicker we'll be finished."

Justin looked at Sam. "I can speak for days about our policies and our army."

Sam turned to the king. "Keldwin, if what Justin says is true, then I'll be ready to be sworn into command in a couple of days. Trust me."

Mosley looked up from sniffing the base of Keldwin's chair. "Sam is able to see anything someone says as if it is written in his head. He can quote conversations from when he was only two seasons old without missing a word."

The general turned to look at his soon-to-be second in command. "This is impressive. Second in command might be a waste of your skills. A messenger boy might be a better position for such a memory. With a mind like yours, I could send many unwritten messages throughout Grayham and not worry about my letters being opened by the enemy. It sounds like you might be able to handle that." Justin made sure he smiled so everyone would know he was trying to be clever.

The king laughed along with the others and spoke to the group. "I'll announce Sam's position to the officers at Early Bailem. I'll have the cooks prepare a hearty breakfast and instruct the hippogriffs to fly through the night to get the officers to their assigned destinations. They will swear to silence until we have announced the changes to the kingdom. Justin, spend the next 3 Peaks briefing Sam. We'll have his ceremony before the Royal Court and the kingdom on the fourth Peak when the tournament begins. This announcement will be made inside the arena and word will spread. The arena's mob will already know of Sam's victories, and with Mosley present…" The king paused, then turned to the wolf.

"Lord Mosley, we have a problem. No one in our kingdom knows you're the God of War. How will your presence create an authoritative impact on my officers, let alone the fans of the arena, or even Grayham for that matter?"

"Keldwin, do not worry. Call your meeting in the morning with your officers and I will make a grand entrance. Have your runners spread word through the city that Bassorine has been destroyed and a new god has ascended. Make sure the news spreads like fire. On the day the tournament begins I will make an entrance like no one has ever seen. I am sure we will turn the heads of the people and give them confirmation I am their new deity. After this, the people will recognize Sam's new position."

The king confirmed his service. "I believe this will work, My Lord. If you were to speak in support of everything which is being done, it would help ease the people's minds."

"Agreed." Mosley bowed, said his good-byes, then vanished.

The general clapped his hands and three slaves ran into the room. He told them to find his officers and make sure they did not leave the city without first attending breakfast at Early Bailem. The slaves darted out to fulfill the command.

The general looked at the group. "Since we're all on a first name basis, we should toast to these new events on such a fine night." He smiled big as he lifted his glass high. "Here's to my new friends and a four-legged wolf-god."

Everyone lifted their glass in a mutual cheer: "Hear, hear!"

Later that Night, the City of Champion

George, Maldwin and Amar stopped for the night. George figured they would arrive in Lethwitch tomorrow, before Late Bailem. George was anxious to see Athena and wanted Maldwin to put their plan in motion right away. The plan was for Maldwin to brainwash Athena's family into believing that living with George in the barbarian city of Bloodvain was a delightful idea. He would introduce the rat to Athena's relatives and let the rodent do the rest of the work.

They had checked into the inn closest to Champions' landing platform, located just inside the city gates. The flight on the hippogriff from Angel's Village had been uneventful, but George had enjoyed the ride. He told Amar he would see him in the morning as they walked by the mage's room. He was exhausted from the trip and was more than ready to lie down.

George had been carrying the rat in his pack since the beast was too small to keep up. This closeness gave him the necessary moments to teach Maldwin a new phrase. Once Maldwin understood the phrase, George realized they were starting to bond and he was becoming quite fond of the rodent.

After a quick bath, George ate a couple of biscuits, then lied down for a night's rest. It was not long before he was dreaming of his little Abbie and his beautiful Athena. The dream was pleasant, but Lasidious interrupted. The God of Mischief was requesting a conversation and wanted to enter George's dream. As agreed that night in the Enchanted Forest, George opened his mind. "George, my friend, how are your travels?"

"I'm sure you already know. Why don't you skip to the point? What can I do for you?"

The Mischievous One snickered. "I suppose I do make small talk at moments, but I've come to tell you something important. I fear there's an obstacle which could stop us from achieving your goal to get your daughter back."

"Then let's figure it out and move on. What do I need to do?"

"As always, George, you don't disappoint. The woman you arrived with on Grayham has discovered she has incredible power. This will present a problem for us. I need to know how you feel about Amar."

"What? Why? What does Amar have to do with Shalee?"

"Nothing yet, but once Amar finds out about her power, he will seek her out to destroy her."

"What the hell are you talking about, man?" George replied. "Are we talking about the same Amar I know? Why would he seek out Shalee? This guy isn't even worth having around. He's a spineless wimp. You should've seen the look of concern he had on his face when I said I wanted to fight for the crown of Bloodvain."

"I agree, Amar doesn't have the backbone to fight for great things, but he is the most powerful mage on Grayham. I told him he should keep his power hidden from you until the moments were right. If he goes after Shalee, he'll become impossible for you to control. This will destroy your chances to get your daughter back. I don't want this, George, do you?"

"Hell no! So, what can I do about it, other than turn his ass to stone, or is that what you want me to do? Is that even possible, considering his power?"

Lasidious gave a sly grin. "I don't want you to do anything you don't want to. The choices you make need to be your own. I'm going to tell you a way you can become just as powerful as Amar, but this needs to be your decision to go after this new level of glory."

With his eyes still closed, George rubbed the scruff on his chin. "Level of glory. I like the sound of that. I'm all ears. Lay it on me. He's a dead man."

From within his home on Ancients Sovereign, Lasidious stood next to the green flames of his cube shaped fireplace. The god looked into the fire and stared at the vision of George as the blaze delivered the human's message. Satisfied with George's answer, he gave his response, just as if George was in the room.

"A person's soul doesn't immediately leave their body when they die. This is a lie the gods have told the beings on all the worlds to stop those who would attempt to do exactly what I'm about to tell you to do. Only the most ancient of elves on the world of Luvelles have this knowledge. Under the right circumstances, a soul's power can be drained before it leaves for its new home within the Book of Immortality."

"What do you mean, 'under the right circumstances?'"

"I mean you would have to kill Amar to take his power for yourself. The problem is, you must do it right in order for Amar's soul to stick around."

"That's it? I don't even like this guy. Are you saying if I kill him in this certain way, I can steal his power? If that's what you're saying, I'm all ears."

"I'm saying that killing Amar is just a part of it. Unfortunately, it is more complex than simply ending his life. It requires you to be an artist." Lasidious waited for a response.

George rolled his sleeping eyes. "Drop the drama, man. Get to the details and I'll go drop his ass. I'm cool with Kepler and Maldwin, but Amar is a chump. I couldn't care less about Amar or his family. I vote we bust him up."

Lasidious was surprised at how cold George had become since his arrival on Grayham. Now that the human had taken life, he loved the rush. The god knew George was loyal to those he cared for, and this made the human a perfect machine to do his dirty work. Without these loyalties, George would be unable to accomplish their overall goals. He was happy at how his choice to bring this Earthling forward was turning out.

"I will tell you everything you need to know, George, but it might be more than you can handle."

"Blah, blah, blah, spare me the drama and tell me what I need to know. If this is what it takes to get my Abbie back, then I'm game."

Lasidious smirked. "This is the only way to ensure you won't be stopped by Amar's power. He's powerful, at least by this world's standards. The addition of Shalee's power would make him unstoppable on Grayham. The Head Master of Luvelles doesn't make friends with just anyone. This should tell you the extent of Amar's ability."

"How in the hell did Shalee get so freaking powerful anyway?"

"I don't know, George, but does it really matter? Don't you think we should figure that out later?"

George was glad he had let Lasidious into his dream. "Alright. Tell me what I've got to do. I'll make it happen while he sleeps."

"Your love for your daughter is strong. I hope it's strong enough to do what I'm going to tell you next."

"Come on, man, get to it already!"

As George listened, it didn't take long before his facial expressions began to show his disgust. "Are you freaking kidding me?" George shuddered in his sleep. "Uhhh, my hell, man, that's so uncool. I like your sick mind, Lasidious, but that grosses me out. You can't really expect me to do that. So what if his power goes with him when his soul goes to the Book? It just means he won't be a threat any longer."

Lasidious sighed. "George, you're smarter than this. I told you Shalee is a dominant force and Amar will want her power. If you're not able to command magic of your own, you'll lose the battle with the Kingdom of Brandor. She's one of many people who could destroy you without Amar's magic. His power can make you untouchable to most everyone on Grayham. Once he understands he can control everything without you, you're going to be a waste of his precious moments. He'll get rid of you."

"I see your point, but what you're asking me to do is not my idea of a delicacy. Hell, I don't even have a bottle of wine to chase it down. This is some kind of *Silence of the Lambs* garesh."

"George, as always, you and your references to your movies of Earth are intriguing, but to get serious, you'll need to keep Amar from speaking his words of power. If you do this right, you can perform this task while he's still alive."

"What do I look like, Lasidious, some kind of Dr. Frankenstein? Even if I could do it right, how will I keep him from dying from shock? I don't have any anesthesia."

The god nodded. "At least you're thinking in the right direction. You won't need medication, George."

"I would love to know how that's possible."

Lasidious took the moments necessary to explain a process which George could use to accomplish the task. A wry smile appeared on George's sleeping face. "Damn, Lasidious, you're one morbid S.O.B. I love the way you think. So how do I...?"

It took a while longer for Lasidious to answer all George's questions and explain the rest of the details necessary to accomplish the job. "...as I have said, you cannot stop his soul from finding its place in the Book of Immortality, but you can strip the power from it before it leaves his body. You only have one shot at this. You'd better do it right."

"Damn, just the thought of it makes me want to barf, but I can do anything for my Abbie." George hesitated. "But, I swear, if it tastes like garesh, I'm going to haunt you forever, Lasidious."

The god laughed. "I'm sure it won't taste pleasant, but it'll be worth it, I assure you."

With that, the dream and the connection between the two faded. George was left dreaming of his Abbie. Slowly, his little girl turned, found his eyes, and yelled, "Dad, get up! Save me!"

George woke with a start. He pulled on his boots, buttoned up his shirt, and left the sleeping Maldwin behind as he shut the door to their room. He went to Amar's door and knocked. When the mage answered, George told him he could not sleep and asked Amar to walk with him. Shaking his head, the mage decided to get dressed and go, if for nothing else other than his curiosity. It was not long before they left the inn.

George made small talk as they walked out of the city. He spoke of how he missed his Abbie and the desperation he felt to get her back. He further explained the pact he made with Lasidious and that the god had promised he would return Abbie if he took control of the Kingdom of Bloodvain. Every response the mage gave George about how he would do anything for a daughter of his own, if he had one, served to strengthen the killer's resolve.

Not far outside the city's gates was a smith's barn. The lock was secured. George gave it a tug. "I need a hammer from inside. Amar, use some of your hocus pocus to manipulate the lock."

The mage held up his staff. He spoke the simple command and the lock released. The men entered and pulled the door shut. George took a seat on a wooden bench near the forge and tossed his torch inside. George studied his surroundings as light filled the room. "Sometimes, I feel like I'm going crazy. I miss my family, Amar."

The liar was now in full manipulation mode. "I want to tell you something. When I first met you, I didn't like you much, but I've grown fond of you over the last few days. You remind me of my uncle back home. I really need someone I can trust in my life. I was wondering if you needed a friend? How would you feel about that? If you don't want to, I'll understand. I'm sorry I've bothered you if this is the case." The manipulator finished off his deception with some tears to add effect.

Amar sat next to George. "I don't have any problems being your friend. I would prefer to travel this way. I also want this, but I've had my doubts, just as you have. I didn't think you cared for my companionship. I must say I'm surprised at your request. What made you decide this?"

George played the part by hugging the mage. "I've been so alone since my arrival. I can't tell you how grateful I am we'll be friends. It warms my heart to know that I've found companionship worth keeping on this world."

George placed his hand on Amar's right shoulder. "I have news which will make you happy, my new friend."

Amar's brows lifted. "What kind of news?"

"Well...it's like this. I know where you can gain a significant amount of power above what you already command." George enjoyed the surprise on Amar's face. "That's right, I know of your power, Amar. I also know of a woman who has substantial power. Her abilities would increase your own if you seek her out and take them from her before her soul leaves her body."

Amar questioned, "How do you know of my power? I have said nothing of it. And, how do you know the secret of the ancient elves?"

"I'm a smart man, Amar. Your knowledge of this secret comes from the same source as my own. Now that we're friends, I'll tell you her name if you want to know it. This is my way of showing you it is my true desire to be your buddy."

"George, this is valuable information. I would like to know her name." Amar further thought, *If this is true, I'll be unstoppable. I can take the Barbarian Kingdom as my own. I'll dispose of you and keep the barbarians' throne for myself.*

"Friends for life, right?" George said with a big smile. "Let's take this friendship to new heights until we rule this world."

"I agree. We will dominate," Amar said with a calm voice as he waited for George to reveal the woman's name. Once he had it and her location, he would teleport to where she was. He would come back and kill George later. He would also need to kill the rat and Kepler. He would not want to leave anyone alive who would have a desire for revenge. This would mean Kepler's brothers as well.

George spit in his hand and stuck it out. "Where I'm from, this is how we become friends. You spit in your hand and I spit in mine. Once we shake, we become brothers. We'll become true buddies. You do still want to be my friend, right?"

Amar smiled. If all it took was one mouthful of spit in his hand to get the information he needed to dominate this world, then it was worth it. He lifted his palm, spit in it, then extended it.

George grabbed his hand and smiled as he shook it up and down. "Amar, I'm so glad you fell for this line of garesh."

Amar's eyes widened and he started to speak, but it was too late. His tongue and lips were now stone. He ripped his hand away and tried to move, but his feet were heavy. They were also stone and both of his hands were beginning to change. The pain was severe as he watched the grayness cover them. He tried to move again but became unbalanced from the weight in his shoes. He fell backward to his butt. George walked up and touched his nose, putting a stone blockage on his spinal cord. The pain stopped as George pushed him to his back.

Amar wanted to call forth the power to stop his attacker, but he could not. His tongue was too heavy. He could not pronounce the words necessary to command the devastation he wanted to inflict.

"Ha! Cat got your tongue?" George sneered. "Just relax a little bit. Don't be so bitchy. Your eyes are cussing at me. That's not very nice. And, you seem so tense. You must be eating wrong."

George peeled back the sleeves of Amar's robe. "You know what, I didn't do a very good job. What was I thinking? How could I be so rude. Turning your hands to stone isn't very giving. After all, we are friends. You deserve more. Allow me to fix it for you." The killer smiled as he touched the mage's flesh over and over. Small areas of Amar's arms turned to stone, spot by spot, with each touch.

George leaned over and looked into Amar's eyes. "Hey, I wish I had a marker. I'm curious. I wonder if all these dots have a pattern. Oh man! How am I going to know which dot is first? Wait. I know. Check this out." Again, he placed his finger on Amar's flesh. Tiny stone numbers appeared by each dot. "That's better. Hey, Amar, I'll tell you a secret. If anybody figures this out, it's going to spell your name...Gullible.

"I wonder if you would have had the ability to lift your arms if I didn't place the block on your spine. I wonder if you'd be able to pummel me with your new look. Hmmmmm, I guess we'll never know. What a shame."

Standing up, George moved to a corner of the barn. On his way, he passed several shields bearing the symbol of Brandor which were crafted earlier in the day. He spoke from the shadows, "Give me a moment, will ya, I gotta piss. I'm sure you don't mind. After all, you can't feel anything. Man, I hope you can't feel anything. Speak up if you can feel something. You're so quiet over there." He chuckled.

After tying the fly of his pants, George reached in his right front pocket and pulled out the old cigarette lighter. He tapped the lighter's butt end on each shield as he moved passed to take a knee next to Amar.

George ripped the mage's robe apart. "Yuck! I hate a hairy chest. You're not a swimmer are you? Allow me to get rid of all of this for you." He took his knife and started to cut away the flesh to expose the sternum beneath. "You know, Amar, I hate to say this, but I'm not a doctor. I'm not even qualified to be doing this. Heck, I don't even play one on TV." He leaned over and looked into Amar's eyes again. "You know, it sucks when you don't know what my jokes mean. You probably wouldn't laugh anyway. Grouch."

Peeling the last bit of flesh away to expose the sternum, George grimaced. "This may leave you a little out of it when you wake up. Oh wait, what am I saying? You're not ever going to wake up. I know, I know, I know, I should probably say I'm sorry, but I think you already know I would be full of garesh."

Again, George leaned over and looked into Amar's eyes. "You wouldn't have any idea how I should bust your chest open, would ya? Maybe that hammer and the chisel near the forge will work."

The helpless expression in Amar's eyes spoke volumes. George responded, "Ahhhhh...you don't like that idea. I can see you're a little upset. Come on, buddy, stop giving me the silent treatment. Geez... you act like you've got a tongue made of stone or something." Again, George laughed.

Amar wanted to respond to his attacker's malevolent chuckles, but all he could do was watch as the smithing hammer pounded hard against the chisel, creating an eerie wickedness which echoed off the barn's walls. A tear rolled from his left eye and came to a rest in his ear. The mage watched his pumping heart get ripped from its cavity. The last thing Amar saw was George taking the first bite as the last bit of light faded from his eyes.

Outside the smith's shed, Lasidious stood beneath one of the torches lighting the road to the city and watched as George found the special effects he had asked for. The light show was spectacular. He knew Amar's powers were now George's to command. He wondered how the heart tasted.

Lasidious would appear to George in another dream later that night and teach the new mage how to use a portion of his power. The great thing about George's new ability was he could command it naturally. He would never need to speak words of power or use magical items. This was the Mischievous One's most fascinating creation yet and it was all done within the laws of the Book of Immortality. He had not taken anyone's free will, but George had. He loved loopholes.

Later that night, George lied down on the bed in his blood-soaked shirt. It was not long before he went to sleep, but it was short-lived. Lasidious wanted access to his dreams. The god took just enough of the new mage's moments to teach George how to teleport from place to place. He would need to appear to George some other day to teach him further.

The God of Mischief didn't want George anywhere near the city of Champions when the rumors started to spread about Amar's death. He informed George the innkeeper was suspicious. The blood on his clothes prompted her to call the guards. They were on their way up to check things out.

The dream ended. George rolled out of bed and moved to the far side of the room. After picking Maldwin up from the hearth of the fireplace filled with glowing embers, he closed his eyes, and concentrated as Lasidious instructed.

The door to the room burst open and the guards entered, screaming for his surrender. They had their swords held high, but the room was empty.

The next thing George knew, he was standing outside Athena's mother's farmhouse. He was about to knock on the door, but instead, he decided to address the blood on his clothes first. Taking up his knife, he set Maldwin down on the ground, and turned away so the rat could not see what he was doing. He cut the top of his head, allowing the blood to drip down his face.

He knocked. He would feign an assault and say he had been jumped by the same guys who tried to rob him during the first series of moments on the night he met Athena. He would concoct a story of how he had obtained the upper hand and would allow Athena's mother to tell her daughter the story so he would not have to tell Athena a lie, as if this made it right somehow.

The door opened and, to his surprise, Athena was standing there. She freaked out when she saw the blood and pulled him inside, shutting the door behind them. Maldwin looked up from the ground, unsure about what he should do. He just sat there, twitching his nose, staring at the door until it opened and George scooped him up to bring him inside.

"Sorry, little guy," George whispered. "Babe, this is Maldwin. I know he's a rat, but I really like him and he's my pet, so don't freak out, okay?"

Athena responded in a scolding voice, "George, put the rat down and sit! You're a mess! What happened?"

**Well...fellow soul...I don't know about you, but I
think if it were up to me, I would have asked
Lasidious to give me a vintage wine of some sort
before I ever agreed to eat a bloody heart...Yuck!
I suppose the love we have for our children
can make us do stupid things!**

The Visions Begin

Athena cleaned the blood from George's face and stopped the bleeding. She asked many questions, but George wouldn't answer. All he would say was, "Don't worry about it, babe, I'm okay." Each moment he said this, he gave her a kiss and changed the subject. After a while, Athena gave up and stopped questioning.

George was glad he was able to avoid telling her a lie. He felt bad enough that Maldwin was going to manipulate the minds of the rest of her family, but he would not deceive her. He had to draw the line somewhere and, in his twisted mind, this was the line.

The next morning, George could see the rat was anxious. He figured it was because they had teleported without Amar in the middle of the night and the fact he had blood all over his clothes didn't help. When he had a moment away from Athena and her mother, he took Maldwin outside to console him. He used the phrase he had taught him on their journey from the Siren's Song, making sure his smile was big when he made the statement. Wanting his furry friend to feel settled, he said, "Everything is A-okay, man!"

Maldwin looked into his eyes, then relaxed and twitched his nose. It was clear the rodent wanted to say something, but did not know how, so George waited. After a moment, the little guy said the only thing he could think of. "I like cheese, George!"

The liar smiled and took him inside. "Hey mom! Do you have any cheese?" Once Mary produced it, Maldwin scurried into a corner and started to eat. George turned to Mary and smiled. "He's cute, don't you think?"

"If you like big rats, I guess he would qualify as cute. That's not my idea of a fine pet." Mary pulled out a chair and sat down. "So, what have you been up to, George? You seem to find yourself getting trobletted a lot lately. Athena told me the night you met, you had been attacked outside of town. Now, you show up at our door, bloody and refusing to offer an explanation.

Do I need to worry about you, mister? I don't know what to think. Do you always find trouble so easily."

George moved across the room and stood in front of her. Putting his hands on her shoulders, he looked her dead in the eye. "I assure you I'm not trouble. I've had a little bad luck for sure, but I think everything is going to be okay. How could things not be when I've got so many beautiful women in my life?"

His charismatic line of garesh seemed to pacify Mary. "Don't worry about me, mom. I'll take care of your little girl."

She leaned back far enough to catch his eyes and slapped her hand on his chest. "You better. The two of you have much to discuss." As she finished her statement, Athena entered the room. "There are preparations which need to be made. You need to talk with your girlfriend."

"Mother," Athena shouted. "I was going to tell him later today, but you just had to stick your nose in it, didn't you?"

Mary walked up to her daughter and kissed Athena's cheek. "That's what I do. I'm entitled, young lady, because of what I went through to bring you into this world. Love you, sweetheart!" She smiled and left the two of them standing in the room.

George looked at Athena. "So, you were going to tell me something. What is it?"

Athena took a deep breath and moved close. She nestled into him for quite a while. It was obvious to the master manipulator he was being buttered up for something big. He played along. What she had to say was creating distress, but George knew whatever it was, they would be okay. He loved her enough that whatever help she needed, he would figure something out.

"Honey?" she whispered.

"Yes, sweetheart, what is it?"

"You know I love you," she responded with a questioning glance.

George knew it must be big, or she would not be leading up to the knockout punch so slowly. He was too good at this game not to recognize a set-up when he heard one. He continued to play along.

"Yes, baby, I know you love me with all your heart."

"You know I would do anything for you, right?"

"Yes, I know you would do anything for me."

"You know my family loves you, right?"

George put his chin on top of her head. "Yes, babe, I know your family loves me."

"You know I would go anywhere with you, right?"

"Yes, I know you would go anywhere with me."

"I really, *really* love you, George."

"Babe, you're stalling. I love you, too. Why don't you tell me what it is, so we can talk about it? I promise I'll be there for you no matter what."

Athena started to cry. "I won't get mad if you leave me." She had never been in a real relationship and the only men she had dated treated her without respect. She loved George with all her heart, but she was afraid he wouldn't want her after what she had to say.

George sensed what was going on and he smiled, knowing there wasn't a problem at all. He pushed her back so he could see her eyes, then held her gaze with a passion he had saved for only one other in his life. The memory of his Abbie filled his heart.

"I will take care of both you and our baby, Athena. I'll never leave you. I have a few things to do before the baby's born, but I promise, your family will see how strong our love is."

"How did you know?" she gasped. "I haven't told anyone but my mother. I can't be sure, but my body speaks to me. It's telling me I am going to be a mother. I was waiting for you to come back before I said anything to anyone else."

George pushed her hair clear of her shoulders, exposing her neck. He admired her beauty. "I will say this; you're terrible at delivering bad news. Besides, what made you think I'd feel this was bad news?"

"I don't know. You're the only man I've ever lied with. I was worried you wouldn't want me after you found out. I've always been mistreated by the men who've courted me. I've given you so much more than I have anyone else. I was frightened this news would chase you away."

George pulled her close, then asked her to get ready. He assured her his love was genuine and wanted to take her to get something to eat. The fact he was the one to take her innocence only made him feel that much stronger about their future.

When Athena left the room, he took Maldwin in his arms and scratched his neck, something he had learned to do on their way back from the Siren's Song. He called to Athena's mother and, as she entered the room, squeezed Maldwin's tail. The rat looked at him for confirmation. George nodded.

He set the rodent down to ask Mary a question. "Mary, I want to marry your daughter. I would like your permission. Will you give it to me?"

The woman's smile stretched from ear to ear. "I knew you would be good for her. So, when's the wedding?"

George explained it would be best to do it within the next few Peaks since he would be traveling. He wanted to make sure Athena was not showing when they formed their union. He assured Mary he would be settled before the baby's birth and they would all be taken care of.

The woman accepted his answer and they set a wedding date. Once agreed upon, she darted out of her home for Athena's sister's place to start planning. The wedding would be held the day after tomorrow.

Athena came back into the room. She was now out of her pajamas and in a beautiful full-length dress. "Is this pleasing to your eyes?"

He put his left arm around her and placed his right hand on her tummy. "I will love you until the day I die. I have something to ask you over breakfast. Are you hungry?"

The City of Brandor

Shalee, BJ, and Helga were not allowed to attend the king's breakfast meeting, since it was for military ears only. Though they knew what was going to happen, BJ still felt left out and decided to go for a walk. His pride was hurt and the girls let him go. They had shopping to do.

The night before, the group had taken the general to see their new home, walking together as they drank their ale. Afterwards, the general took them to a large estate. By Sam's estimation, the home sat about a mile from the arena. Justin announced this was the home of the army's second in command.

"Sam, once you have been sworn in, this palatial home will be yours. I will see to it you are reimbursed by the king's treasurer for the expense of the other home."

Neither Sam nor BJ, as well as the girls, could believe their good fortune, but waited until they were back in their quarters before discussing it.

Shalee spoke with Helga in an excited voice. "Goodness-gracious, did ya see the size of that place? Me-oh-my, it wasn't what I imagined livin' in back on Earth, but I think I can work with it, girl." She threw her right hand in the air to give a sassy high-five.

The older sorceress returned with a proper amount of attitude. "You go, girl!"

BJ looked at the two women. "What on Grayham is all that nonsense about? You women have been doing some silly things lately. Shalee, you've taught her too much of this Earth talk of yours. I don't even recognize her."

"Oh, lighten up, you old fart," the 247 season old woman said with a chuckle. "Shalee has only taught me a few of her mannerisms from her old home. There are plenty more I need to learn. Besides, I think they're fun. You're just gonna have to love them with me." She leaned over and purred in BJ's ear, "You just wait until I explain the phrase, 'baby's got back.'"

Shalee and Helga laughed and again did another sassy high-five.

Sam looked at BJ and rolled his eyes. "The women from Earth often acted a little off-in-the-head. Don't even try to figure them out. It's impossible. They come from a planet called Venus."

When Shalee heard Sam's snide remark, she gave her lover an evil grin and lifted Precious into the air. "Let the games begin," she announced as she began to stalk Sam.

Sam had played this game before and knew what was coming as he turned to run away. Shalee began chasing Sam around the room. She sent tiny electric shocks from the tip of her staff into Sam's buttocks. Moment after moment, the macho fighter jumped into the air screaming like a little girl. "I love you, baby...ouch! I love you, baby...ouch! I love you, baby... ouch!" Even BJ had to laugh.

The next day, Sam woke up early, kissed his beautiful sorceress, and told everyone goodbye. He assured BJ that, once he could do something about the situation, BJ would have a place of importance by his side.

Sam went to the king's dining hall to wait for Keldwin with everyone else. When the king entered and greeted his officers, he thanked them for coming and shook everyone's hand before changing the tone of the meeting.

Sam could see the slight hint of pain on Keldwin's face. The effects of the disease were beginning to bother him.

"I have called everyone here, not only to sit at my table and eat a fine breakfast, but to discuss issues of great importance."

The king moved around the long table as he spoke. The legion leaders totaled eleven men, not including the general and the army's second in command, Michael, the man who was about to be demoted. Michael was sitting next to Sam near the head of the table. The other eleven occupied seats of importance along the length of the table, with the prince sitting at the far end.

The king's army was just over 50,700 strong and the Kingdom of Brandor always had the advantage over the Barbarian Kingdom's numbers.

Keldwin continued. "I have a few things to say, some of which will not sit well, but I've received word these decisions are best for this kingdom. This confirmation comes directly from the gods."

The room filled with whispered commotion as the officers looked at each other, the seriousness of the meeting increasing. The general stood and called everyone to order.

As the king continued, Keldwin walked behind each officer, circling the entire table before stopping behind his chair. "Bassorine has been destroyed."

Before Keldwin could speak another word, the table again became agitated and questions filled the air. The general stood and commanded their silence. "Didn't I just say this meeting will come to order? There will be no more speaking until the king has finished!"

The officers knew not to question Justin's authority. His reputation as a mighty warrior was respected. Everyone quieted and once again, the king took the floor.

"As I was saying, Bassorine is gone. A new god has taken his place." The royal man's eyes scanned the room as he watched his officers throw each other glances. Never, since he had been king, had a god made his presence known to the leaders of his army. He knew this would come as a shock. Keldwin had never met Bassorine, but knew Mosley from the work Bassorine had him doing before the wolf ascended.

He waited for them to digest the information before continuing. "The god who has replaced Bassorine, is Lord Mosley. The wolf will be joining us for breakfast."

He knew this statement would get a reaction, since most of his officers had met Mosley in the past. The table once again buzzed with commotion, but the king stopped the general from shouting, allowing them to talk amongst themselves.

After a moment, Keldwin raised his hand and the room quieted. "As I was saying, gentlemen, Mosley is our new god, and..."

The king was able to speak no further. A powerful wind filled the room, intense enough each man had to steady his glass. As the wind settled, a brilliant light appeared a few yards behind the king's chair. The men shielded their eyes and when the light dissipated, Mosley stood in its place. Despite the king's warning the wolf was coming, the frightened men backed away from the table.

The general covered his mouth with both hands and turned his back to the men to keep them from seeing his smile. Keldwin, on the other hand, did not show any emotion. For the next few moments, the room was in chaos.

Sam, knowing what was coming, moved to a clear area of the room away from the table and knelt on one knee, along with the king, the prince, and the general, adding to the importance of the god's appearance. The men stayed in this position with their heads lowered until the rest gathered their nerve and knelt.

Mosley had added additional size to his appearance for the occasion and looked to be twice his normal girth. He sat on his haunches and pushed his furry chest out in a majestic posture. He looked stunning. His white teeth, tail, and coat had been brushed to a regal shine. He looked better than perfection.

With everyone kneeling, the canine spoke. "Great King, I request to be a part of this meeting. I am here to voice my opinions. I have things to say which will be useful. Please stand, Keldwin, so we may talk."

The king rose and followed Mosley to the far side of the room where they could speak in private. Mosley leaned in toward Keldwin. "Do you think they bought it? They did seem a bit nervous. I feel an impression has been made. What do you think?"

"The men will listen to everything you say. It was a fine entrance."

"But, do you think the entrance was dramatic enough? Was it worthy of a pack leader of my stature?"

"Ohhhhh, more than dramatic, My Lord. The men have never seen anything like it, I assure you."

Mosley sniffed Keldwin's fingers. "The disease is spreading. How are you feeling?"

Keldwin hesitated before answering. "I feel as good as a man can, considering the fact I'm dying."

"I understand." Mosley snorted to clear the disease's smell from his nostrils. "Please kneel, Keldwin. I will give you the blessing you will need to see the end of your tournament."

The men watched their king take a knee. Mosley touched him on top of the head with his paw and a glow surrounded Keldwin's body as he hovered above the stones of the floor. Only a short period of moments passed before the king returned to the floor and rose to his feet.

"May I give your men an order, Keldwin?" Mosley asked.

"Please, by all means, My Lord!"

Mosley turned to face the group. With an authoratitive voice, he commanded them to sit. The wolf enjoyed the anxiety on their faces as they rushed to take their seats.

"Great King, I will sit for the moments necessary to listen as you speak."

Keldwin loved being called a "Great King" in front of his men. It gave him renewed vigor to carry on with the meeting. "Thank you, Lord Mosley. I was about to tell the men there are changes coming to our kingdom." The king forced a smile as he studied the faces of his men. "I'm dying. I will be dead not long after my tournament."

The room buzzed with commotion. The king allowed the General Absolute to explode. "I said to keep quiet! The next man I have to tell will be put on the arena's lottery! I feel bad for the soul who has to face me!" Justin's strong facial features added to the intensity of his statements.

All the officers knew this was their last warning. No one would dare speak again unless they were asked. Sam, on the other hand, sat across from the general and thought, *I bet I could defeat you if given the chance.*

Keldwin cleared his throat. "Michael, I will be temporarily removing you from second in command and placing Sam in your stead. When I die, Sam will become the new General Absolute and General Graywind will become the advisor to my son. Michael, you will return to your responsibilities and assist Sam in our upcoming war." The king turned to look at Mosley for confirmation that what he said was correct.

"This is correct, Great King," the wolf replied in a strong voice.

Keldwin continued. "Are there any questions?"

The first one to raise his hand was Michael. "My King, with all due respect and I mean no offense, who is Sam? Why should he be able to show up out of nowhere and move into a position I have earned?"

The general was about to jump out of his seat and rip Michael apart for his ignorant nerve, but the king was wise and recognized the situation. He motioned for Justin to relax.

"The last series of moments in which I looked into my chamber's mirror, Michael, the vision within still showed me as king. Any position given throughout this kingdom is because I allow it. If I remember our laws...laws *my* family created with the help of the Royal Court and the Senate, they allow me to have final authority during moments of war. The gods have told us war is upon us. I have ordered the general to activate our armies, as you know. This means this decision is mine alone to make."

Keldwin leaned over the table, his expression stern, "Michael, I would ask you to explain why you feel you have the right to question your king? Do you question the knowledge the gods have about Sam? It was by their referral that Sam will be given this position. It's true, he's not from this world, but he is a warrior with a great tactical mind. A referral such as this would be foolish to ignore. Who here at this table will agree by raising your glasses?"

Everyone in the room lifted their drinks, saying, "Hear, hear!"

With the issue settled, the king continued. "I'll announce Sam's new position at the start of my tournament. I expect you to leave after breakfast and carry out the duties General Graywind has assigned. I have sent word for the hippogriffs to fly through the night. Each of you has an important job to complete for your kingdom. Do it well and with honor."

The king turned from the table and looked at Mosley. "Do you have anything you wish to say, My Lord?"

The oversized wolf-god moved close to the table, lifted his front paws onto the edge, and looked down at the men. "The gods have brought Sam to this world, along with his soon-to-be-wife, Shalee. They are powerful beings and worthy of your respect. I would hope this relationship does not need to be tested before you accept they are worth following. I leave you now, but will be watching from the heavens." With that, the wolf began to dissolve into a million pieces . They floated up and through the roof.

Once the room settled and the king saw everyone was calm once again, he turned the meeting over to Sam before making his exit with his son and the general.

Sam stood and moved to the head of the table. "Does anyone have questions?" Sam was still thinking about Mosley's comment that Shalee would become his wife. Until now, he hadn't even thought about it, but he had to admit he liked the idea. He would address the idea again after he finished with the men sitting in front of him.

Every officer had a hand in the air. Sam sighed as he pointed at one of them to begin.

Town of Lethwitch

It was over breakfast when George asked Athena to marry him. She was delighted, *of course*, and dragged him to a jeweler friend of hers. George smiled as he paid for the ring, ignoring the fact the money had come out of the pockets of Amar's pants. He realized this was the first moment he had given someone other than his daughter a piece of jewelry. His first wife had bought her own. He enjoyed giving instead of receiving. He was elated as he watched his beautiful Athena's smile grow.

Before they left, the jeweler told them she would have the ring ready the next day, early enough to retrieve it before the wedding. The next stop was to buy the new bride a gown, and George something to wear that would make him look dashing. Both items of clothing would be ready to pick up during the same series of moments as the ring. After they were finished shopping, George suggested that Athena head back to her mother's farm. He had seen a store earlier in the day which caught his eye. He had a great idea.

After Athena was out of sight, George turned and headed back up the road. He was looking for the store filled with boxes and bags of all sizes.

As he entered, he studied his surroundings. Despite his general distaste for ruggedness, he admired the craftsmanship sitting on every shelf. Each container was the result of a laborious art and had been made of one kind of hide or another. In every case, the leather had been treated and the smell was inviting.

From a backroom, an older gentleman appeared. He was dressed in a white shirt and a brown leather vest which had been tied up in front. His long gray braid hung to the middle of his back and swung from side to side as he moved to stand behind a counter opposite the shelves holding his masterpieces. Behind the counter hung three different pelts and two tails, possibly cut from some sort of racoon.

"Hello, son," the older man said with a smile. "People around these parts call me RJ, the leather guy. I'm sure you saw it on my sign outside. How can I help you?"

George reached out and grabbed RJ's forearm, which was the town's customary way of greeting and thought, *Who is this hillbilly-flowerchild? Thank goodness his art looks better than he does.*

"It's nice to meet you, RJ. I'm George. I saw your boxes through the window. I'm especially interested in that one over there."

RJ moved to grab the box and brought it back to the counter. He handed it to George. "I just finished crafting this one 3 Peaks ago. I think I like how it turned out. I was just getting ready to start another one. Perhaps I should put a different design on it so it stands apart."

"That's a great idea," George replied. "I'm getting hitched, tomorrow..."

"Hitched?"

"Yeah, you know, I'm going to have a wife."

An understanding appeared on RJ's face. "And, are you here to buy her a gift?"

George held up the box and studied it. "I am. She's totally worth it. She hits my hot button, if you know what I mean."

"I'm fairly sure I understand your meaning. You speak different than the rest of the town."

As George studied the box, he responded, "I'm just visiting from another world. Let's get down to business, shall we?"

"Do you think you can make the next box with the words 'Athena's Treasures' on the upper left hand corner of the lid? I'm sure she would love it if it was personalized. Maybe you can add some kind of design to surround the words across the bottom and the right hand side. Oh...and, do you think you could have it done by morning?"

"For the right kind of coin, I can have anything done by morning."

George gave a sly grin. "Coin is not an issue, RJ. I'll see you in the morning. Just remember, this woman is special. The box needs to equal her beauty."

"In the morning, then. I'm sure your lady will be pleased."

It was now past the Peak of Bailem. George needed to put his plans in motion. He stood up from the empty plate, shoved the last bite of biscuit in his mouth and looked at Athena. "Hey, if you were to ever move, which of your family members would you want to be near you?"

Athena answered his question. George asked if she would take him to meet them all. She agreed and as they left Mary's home, George grabbed Maldwin. He threw the beast in his pack and headed out, holding Athena's hand.

It would take most of the afternoon to find each of these family members. When the moment arrived that they were finished, Maldwin had learned the faces of everyone to whom he would be sending his visions.

They stopped by a dairy outside of town and purchased a block of cheese, then headed home. On their way, George noticed military personnel moving about and asked Athena what she knew of it.

"Giant wagons are being built for the harvests. Word has spread the harvests will be bountiful. The king has declared they were blessed by Alistar. Some of the town's men have been hired to build barns on the far side of mother's farm to hold it all."

"How do you know all this?"

"It is posted on the message boards at the center of town. The king has paid these men to carry out his orders. This is an unusual way of doing things."

"If a god is blessing the crops, there must be something big about to happen."

"What do you mean?"

"I have no idea. I'll let you know when I know." George thought, *Where's Kepler when I need him?* He knew the demon would be able to get answers he was after as he stalked around unseen in the shadows. He would need to find out what was going on after his wedding.

As Maldwin shifted in his pack, George remembered what Kepler said before they separated: *"...the rat would need to be provided a quiet place to send his visions."* George took the little guy to Mary's barn and left him with his block of cheese. It would take the rat quite a while to reach everyone in Athena's family to get them to one of their midnight meetings. The manipulator hoped the first meeting would be held the next night.

The next morning George woke, kissed his fiancée's soft lips, and excused himself to check on Maldwin. When he arrived, the rat was sleeping on a bale of hay, the block of cheese untouched. The new mage tiptoed over and whispered, careful not startle his new pet.

"Maldwin, Maldwin, wake up, little guy."

The rat stirred. When he looked up at George, the mage could see his exhaustion. The rodent pulled his way over and lowered his head on George's lap. George rubbed his head and assured him everything was okay. The visions the rodent sent had been hard to deliver.

He didn't want to push his little ally any further. George supported the rat's head as he moved out from under it and lowered it to the hay. He was about to make his exit when a faint voice called out. "George, everything is A-okay, man."

George smiled, walked back into the barn, tore off a chunk of cheese, and laid it next to the little guy's paws before leaving. The meeting Maldwin had set for Athena's family would be held on this night, after the wedding. They would learn of the wondrous idea of living with George in the Barbarian Kingdom and how peaceful this existence would be.

George grabbed Athena from inside the house and walked down the road, holding her hand. His plan was coming together. They needed to hurry to town, grab the rings, their clothes, and return to the farm to get dressed before Late Bailem. He would also need to teleport back into town to pick up the treasure box. He wanted it to be a surprise. He needed to hurry. He barely had enough moments to get everything done before saying, "I do."

Two Weddings and a Funeral

While Athena was introducing George to her family, excitement was building in Brandor. Sam left the breakfast meeting with the officers of the king's army and hurried out into the city to find Shalee. He was shocked at how hard it was to find a woman who stuck out like a sore thumb.

When he found her, Shalee was with Helga. The ladies were in one of the local jeweler's stores. When Sam walked in, a heavyset man, working behind a polished wooden counter, was placing an emerald-looking gem into an elegant, tiara-like headpiece.

The comment Mosley made was still circling in his mind. He felt it ironic he should find his future mate in a store filled with jewels. The setting only served to heighten his anxiety. "Hey," Sam said, giving Shalee a kiss on the neck.

"Howdy, sweetheart. I'm just lookin' for a good reason ta spend your hard earned coin on me. How was your lil' meetin'? Did Mosley make a good showin'?"

"He did. He was impressive. He scared the king's officers to death and he looked twice his normal size."

Shalee looked over her shoulder and grinned at Helga. "So, did everyone freak out? I bet they just freaked."

"Yeah, did everyone freak?" The older sorceress chimed in.

Sam could only grin at how Earthly Helga sounded. "Oh, they freaked out all right. But, Mosley said something which has stuck with me all morning."

It was easy to see Sam's hesitation to talk about whatever it was, but that didn't stop Shalee from asking. "What did Mosley say ta get ya so worked up? Do I need ta take ya back ta the castle ta help ya relax? I could always chase ya around with Precious."

This did not bring the normal smile to Sam's face. Shalee knew something serious was on his mind. "I'm sorry, sweetheart, what's botherin' ya?"

Sam looked at her with an intensity she had never seen. "Mosley said you and I are going to be married."

Shalee didn't know what to say. Helga chimed in, "Just leave it to the mutt to meddle in the affairs of others. If that mongrel wasn't a god, I'd peel the fur off of him."

Sam held up his hand. "No, no, no, it's not like that. Mosley wasn't meddling. Shalee, did you say anything to him about getting married," Sam queried, "maybe when I wasn't around?"

"For heaven's sake, I wouldn't do somethin' like that," Shalee responded as she pulled him close. "But, I've got ta say, I like the idea. He's truly a smart wolf."

"Hmpf. Smart for a mutt," Helga grumbled.

After hearing Shalee's response, the concern Sam had about talking with her vanished. He was able to be his usual bold self and approach the conversation with confidence. "I also like the idea. Come on. Let's find Keldwin and ask him to marry us."

"Oh Sam, I can't think of anythin' betta'. Ta be married by a king, it sounds so romantic."

"Let's go then." Sam clapped his hands to show his enthusiasm. "We don't have the moments to waste. Keldwin will be leaving us soon. I think we should ask him this very second."

Helga screamed at the top of her lungs and started to run around the shop. "My babies are getting married! My babies are getting married!" She stopped dead in her tracks, then turned to look at Shalee. "Hey...what's a 'second?' That does mean you want to do it now, right?"

Shalee laughed at the woman's antics. "I'll explain what a second is later, and yes...it means now."

"Then, go get married!"

Shalee kissed Sam on the cheek. "I guess we're gettin' married. Mom has spoken."

The brilliant-minded doctor, fighter, lover, soon-to-be second in command, and friend was suddenly engaged. He grabbed Shalee, lifted her up, gave her a big kiss, then rushed her off to find the king.

As they hurried to the castle, Helga was sent to find BJ. Sam wanted the trainer to be his best man. Shalee would choose Helga as her maid of honor. Everything else would take care of itself. All they had to do was find Keldwin.

When they entered the throne room, they found one of the servants and sent him to fetch the king, making sure he relayed the message as urgent. They knelt and waited for Keldwin. It seemed like forever, but it was only a few moments. Though the king had been sleeping, he hurried, thinking it may have something to do with Lord Mosley.

"Sam, what is it you so badly need? Why did you wake me?"

"Keldwin, do you remember saying you wanted us to treat you as a friend when others were not around?"

"I do."

"Okay, okay, that's good. So, here's the deal. We're here to do just that. I have decided to marry Shalee and there's no one we want to perform our ceremony more than you. We can't think of a better friend in which to give this honor. We would like this to be our gift to you."

Keldwin was speechless. Never had he been so touched. For the first series of moments, other than Justin Graywind, he felt like he had real friends. Sam and Shalee would remember this day for the rest of their lives. Being a part of it was, indeed, a gift. He felt honored and blessed as he wept.

Keldwin walked toward the group and motioned for them to stand. He embraced each of them and, when he came to Sam, he kissed his forehead and smiled. "You've honored me. I would be pleased to perform your ceremony and honor you in return."

The king clapped his hands and a slave ran into the room. "We have much to do. I want my seamstress, cook, jeweler, and driver brought to my throne room!"

The slave ran from the room. The king turned to face the group. "This wedding will be one to remember. You shall be married at the start of my tournament. You will be married in front of thousands of my people from all over my kingdom. A union has never been performed in the arena. Everyone will know you throughout the land."

Shalee shouted, "Howdy-doody! Big group hug, y'all! High-fives all around!"

Sam looked at BJ and, as usual, the trainer rolled his eyes. Shalee did not let BJ's lack of enthusiasm ruin her mood. She turned to Helga and slapped hands with the older woman. Keldwin, seeing the joy in their eyes, reached out with both of his hands and exchanged his first set of high-fives.

BJ rolled his eyes again, "Ohhh, brother."

Keldwin told the slave who appeared to make sure everything was done as Sam and Shalee commanded. He excused himself and went back to bed.

Sam and BJ left the palace. Just like most bone-headed men do when the moment comes to plan a special occasion, they figured they would leave the planning of the wedding to the women. They mindlessly headed into the city to grab a few ales.

Shalee would have been upset, but Precious would make quick work of the tasks at hand. The young sorceress had a special wedding dress in mind—as most women do when they plan their weddings as young girls—and ordered the seamstress to bring an assortment of fabrics to the throne room.

When the woman returned, she was carrying ten bolts of assorted colors. Shalee and Helga lined them against the wall to get a good look. The ladies huddled and agreed on the perfect combination—a predominantly white dress with a dash of pink. Shalee raised Precious into the air and spoke her words of power. The seamstress stood in disbelief as the fabrics lifted from the floor and disappeared into a big ball of light. When the light faded, a flowing masterpiece was left floating in mid-air.

The women exchanged a bouncing embrace, pulling the seamstress into the celebration. Shalee retrieved the dress and tried it on. She was stunning—a mortal beauty without equal. The lines of the dress accented every curve and the pink brought out the glow on her face. She took off the dress and gave it to the seamstress, asking her to make sure it was put in a safe place.

When they walked through the kitchen doors, the head cook seemed to be displeased they were in his domain. Shalee laughed and told Helga that chefs on Earth had also been protective of their kitchens. Seeing everything was in order, Shalee scanned the entrance to the kitchen to determine how big a cake she could make. Each requested ingredient—with the exception of the cinnamon, since no one had a clue what it was—was present and accounted for. Even the pile of wood she requested was stacked next to the counter.

Once again, she lifted Precious and spoke the words of power. The magic created a blinding light. Many moments passed before the light faded. A cake like no other was left behind on a large table with wheels. The creation was nine layers, each supported by shaped wooden columns. Shades of icing worked in unison to tell a story of love. Angels, made of sculpted sugar and dressed in yellow robes, were sitting around the edges of the cake, their legs draped over the side, wings spread, and hands folded in front as if praying. Nine of these heavenly figures sat on the first level, their numbers reduced by one with each level as the cake ascended until a sole angel rested on top. This angel was dressed in a red robe, also made of sugar. His white feathered wings were spread and circled forward to protect two figures within them: the figures of Sam and Shalee.

The king's head cook was astonished by the beauty of the pastry. Over seven feet tall, the bottom layer alone had a diameter nearly six feet wide. Shalee had even created a small cupcake for the chef to taste. He was delighted and left her with a standing invitation to come into his kitchen at any moment she pleased.

The women left and made their way to meet with the jeweler. Shalee used her magic again to create the rings, but the lady who brought the gems screamed when she saw the magic work. The woman darted out of the room and, despite Helga running after her, would not come back.

All in all, the day was productive. When Shalee retired for the night, she laid her head on Sam's chest before realizing everything was not finished. She forgot to make Sam's tux. Once again, she sent a servant for the seamstress with a message to bring materials fit for a groom. When the lady arrived, Shalee hurried, thanking the seamstress with a hefty tip.

Wedding Day

Sam and Shalee planned to marry just after the Peak of Bailem. They dressed together, agreeing the old Earth tradition of the groom not seeing the bride prior to the ceremony was ridiculous.

Helga and BJ had left for the arena. The moment had come for Sam and Shalee to join Keldwin, Justin, and Aaron in the king's carriage. The men were dressed in their best military regalia.

The king was the first to speak. "Shalee, I must say I've never seen a gown like the one you have on. I'm impressed. I wish my kingdom shared more of your taste."

"Why, thank ya kindly, Keldwin. If you'd like, I could whip ya up somethin' special-like for the final day of your tournament. I'll command Precious ta enhance your good looks. The ladies will think you're debonair."

"I'd like that, but it's our tradition to wear our best armor. Maybe you could do something special to make it look better."

"I'd be honored, Keldwin."

"What a bride you'll be on this wondrous day. Your beauty makes the gods jealous."

"Hear, hear," the general responded. "Sam, you're a lucky man. If ever you have a day you need a break from such grace, you can send her my way."

Sam laughed and looked at the prince. "And, how are you today, Aaron?"

"I'm fine, thank you. I would like to know the name of your attire. I would like Shalee to make me one someday."

Shalee did not give Sam the chance to answer. "Oh, Aaron! Ya know somethin'...you'd look mighty handsome in a tuxedo. Sexy even."

"Tuxedo." The king laughed. "A funny name, but if you say it will enhance his looks, I would like you to create him one as soon as possible."

"Agreed," the general responded. "The boy needs help."

The pleasantries of the conversation continued until the group arrived at the arena. As they entered the arena's massive gates, the people cheered for their king. The women who lined the walkways marveled at the beauty of Shalee's dress. Even the men admired the couple's outfits.

"Shalee," Keldwin said, pulling her close. "Are most of my people admiring your attire to the point they do not notice their king's arrival, or is this just my misplaced perception?"

Shalee kissed him on the cheek and whispered in his ear, "What can I say, Keldwin? When ya look this fab, they just love ya."

"I can only assume 'fab' means beautiful. You are stunning."

"Ya can say that on a thousand separate moments, ya sexy beast," Shalee responded while sliding her hand sideways through the air and snapping her fingers with a sassy sexiness.

The king chuckled, "Your mannerisms are growing on me, Shalee." Keldwin placed his hand on hers, then continued walking with her arm resting atop his.

When the Peak of Bailem arrived, trumpets sounded to signal the start of the tournament. The king, along with Aaron, Justin, Sam, and Shalee, walked to the center of the arena and waved to the crowd as they waited for Mosley to make his appearance.

The daylight turned to darkness as the clouds lowered to a position just over the arena. They looked angry and lightning struck the arena floor. The clouds finished their descent and settled onto the sandy surface. Now, nothing could be seen and the screams from the frightened crowd filled the air. Sam was unable to see Shalee, even though he was holding her hand. When the clouds dissipated, all that was left was a larger than normal wolf-god. The crowd's fears vanished with the haze and the screams were replaced with their cheers. Once again, Mosley had made quite the impression. The king held up his hand to silence the crowd.

Keldwin signaled for the announcement to be made. A large man standing at the top of the arena shouted to let everyone know Sam was to take the place of Michael as second in command. As expected, there was a lot of commotion as the crowd buzzed about the decision. This was Mosley's cue to speak. Deciding to make his point on a larger scale, the wolf expanded to a height of forty feet. The horror could be seen on the people's faces.

"People of the Kingdom of Brandor, hear me!" Mosley's voice matched his giant size. "The gods are aware of your king's decision. Know this, Sam will strengthen the leadership of your army. Your kingdom will benefit by his presence."

Keldwin admired the god's ability to make a point. He turned toward Sam and motioned for him to bow. The king used his sword to swear him in. When Sam stood, he was the new commander. Now, only three people in the kingdom possessed more power. As he rose, the crowd welcomed him. Seeing the success of Mosley's message, the moment had come to move on.

The wedding was next. Keldwin signaled for everyone to take their places. BJ and Helga made their way to the center of the arena where thirty well-dressed men, carrying long trumpets, formed two long lines facing each other in front of the king. The trumpets were made of silver and were thin, while the men were dressed in black with silver ruffs extending from their chins to the bottoms of their coats. Their shoes gleamed with perfection in the sunlight, contrasting against the white sand of the arena floor.

Sam and Shalee were given room to stand in front of the king to say their vows. The prince and the General Absolute took places behind Keldwin. The armor of the three men had been polished by Shalee's magic for this occasion. They lowered their arms as they stood at attention.

After BJ and Helga took their places next to Sam and Shalee, Mosley decided to give them a gift. He returned to his normal size and moved to stand beside the king. He lowered to his haunches and kept his head held high. In a thunderous voice, the wolf announced, "This wedding is blessed by the gods."

The people shouted their approval as the wolf used his power to enhance Keldwin's ability to be heard by everyone. Once the vows were complete, the king sealed the union. He motioned for the couple to kneel and join hands. He took his sword and blessed their union by lowering the blade to touch each of their shoulders. Once this had been done, Keldwin commanded the couple to stand. He announced to the Kingdom of Brandor that Sam and Shalee were bound for life.

The trumpeters lifted their instruments. A tunnel formed as the music filled the air, indicating the moment had come for Sam and Shalee to leave the arena. The king kissed them on their foreheads and waited for the couple to begin their first walk as husband and wife.

Keldwin, Aaron, Justin, BJ, and Helga, followed, single file, as everyone exited. Once the musicians cleared the sand, Mosley was the only one left. He made a grand exit, expanding once again into a giant. He lifted his head and howled. As the mob grabbed their ears, the wolf vanished.

After the crowd settled, the first fight was announced. The stadium erupted as the tournament began. Sam and Shalee went back to the castle to celebrate their new life together.

Later that evening, the party began with royalty filling the king's ballroom. Sam stood on a table, resting at the center of the polished floor, to call for a toast. As he tapped his mug of ale to command the group's attention, he thought, *Welcome to Wiltshire, England, everyone. Too bad they wouldn't know what I'm talking about, if I said that. I bet Shalee would laugh.*

Once he had everyone's attention, Sam looked at Shalee and began his toast. "To my beautiful wife, you know my most intimate mind and my weaknesses. I cannot hide my gratitude for allowing me to love you. I embrace the sharing of our secrets. The change in me is due to your love. I will be forever blessed. Here's to my wife, my companion, my heart, my soul...I will be forever grateful. I love you."

Shalee rushed to stand beside him on the table and a long passionate kiss followed as the room filled with applause. Sam lifted his mug. "It has come to my attention, the people of Brandor have never seen a wedding cake. My wife has prepared this special gift for you. With your permission, My Great King, let's have the cook bring it out for these fine people to partake."

The king agreed and clapped his hands. From between a large set of double doors, the massive cake appeared on a polished wooden cart. The room gasped at the grandeur of the pastry. The delicacy was a hit.

BJ and Helga, after saying a few words of encouragement to the newlyweds, managed to sneak away. Helga's staff lit the way as they moved to the center of the royal garden behind the king's castle. They lied on the grass, giggling as lovers do when falling in love. They enjoyed the idea of the garden being considered off limits to commoners. Being naughty only heightened their experience.

Helga commanded her staff to go dark. They sat up and pulled each other close. They remained quiet and waited. They looked about the garden and watched as the flowers began to illuminate. Thousands of puffs radiated as they floated from one flower to another. They kissed as each bloom's melody filled the night air. The mood was set as passion followed.

No words or sounds were uttered as the couple's personal interlude sang a song of its own. The lovers' bodies discovered their own special brand of happiness.

After a long while, BJ looked into Helga's eyes and whispered so the flowers would not go dark. "I love you more than I have loved any other. You've taken this broken heart and given it back, whole and renewed. You've helped me to feel again. For so long, my heart was hard after the passing of my wife, but you've managed to soften it. I will always cherish you for this."

Helga's heart melted. "I love you too, you big grouch..." She smiled as she nestled into him, "...with all my heart. I will love you as you deserve to be loved."

Helga used her staff to cast a romantic light throughout the garden. The rest of that night would be filled with childlike giggling as they chased each other around the statues scattered throughout the garden.

The Town of Lethwitch

George and Athena were also due to be married this evening. When Late Bailem had arrived, George was finishing the running around he had to do. Although it was later than expected, he now stood in front of an assistant to one of Brandor's senators in the torchlight to speak his vows. Athena's mother had tried to get the senator himself to perform the ceremony, but most every member of the kingdom's government was at the king's tournament.

Mary and this particular senator had been friends since childhood. Even though he was from a royal bloodline, they had found each other irresistible, often running off together despite the laws which forbade it. They continued in secret until his parents found out and put a stop to their relationship. Royals did not like to mix bloodlines with commoners, despite what the king had done many seasons ago. Mary often wondered what her life would have been like with Ralton Brandor. But, as she looked at Athena on her wedding day, she realized this was the life she was meant to have.

The ceremony was going to be simple, yet Athena's entire family was in attendance. George's heart was filled with happiness, and for the first series of moments in his pathetic life, he was committing to something lifelong other than his daughter. He would no longer use women for the things he needed or wanted. He would have to rely on his charisma to get what he wanted without the added bonuses. He would be loyal to Athena and give her, at least in his mind, the respect she deserved. There was a new child on the way and he was not about to let this one have a broken home.

The assistant kept the vows short, but sweet. The family applauded as the party was moved to Mary's barn to celebrate, creating an atmosphere which reminded George of some kind of hillbilly square dance. Everyone was enjoying the festivities. There was even a potluck dinner laid out on many of the tables. The only thing missing was a wedding cake—and a whole lot of class. They settled for fresh fruit dipped in a sweet cream. George told himself he would marry Athena again once he had the moments necessary to do it right.

George took Athena by the hand and knelt on one knee. He handed Athena her new treasure box. "This box is to hold the memories of our life together." He opened the lid. Inside was one of the flowers which he had picked near the gazebo. The flower's petals were still glowing, despite being plucked from its tree.

"Oh, George, how did you manage to do this? It's beautiful."

"I'll tell you later. Do you like it?"

"I do. It's perfect."

George smiled as he listened to the ladies' comments surrounding them. They complimented Athena on how romantic her new mate was. George thought, *It was easy to pick the flower. Hell, all I did was teleport next to it and pluck it before it realized I was there. I can't believe the damn thing stayed lit up like that. What luck!*

George took Athena for a walk just before midnight. Since the entire family was there, Maldwin sent a vision to them. They saw how great it would be to live with George in the Barbarian Kingdom.

The newlyweds went to the bridge, spanning the river, just outside of town. They dangled their legs off the side. Under the torchlight, they tossed pebbles into the water.

George loved Athena's voice. He kept the conversation going as he pulled his wife close. Everything she said was important. His love for her was self-less. They stayed for the majority of the night. When he decided Maldwin should be finished, they prepared to leave. After kissing Athena, he said, "I have a surprise for you."

"You do? What is it, honey?"

"I'm able to do things which will allow me to come and see you more often as I travel. I need to show you what it is. I want you to understand how I can find my way home to you every night. I want you to keep this surprise a secret. Will you do this for me?"

Athena looked puzzled. "I thought you said your travels were going to take you far to the north?"

"I did."

"So, how do you expect to be with me if you are there and I'm here?"

George pulled her close. "I'll show you, but you have to promise to keep it a secret. Will you do this?"

She was hesitant to agree, but she embraced him and put her head on his chest, which was her favorite place to be. "If it lets us be together, then I promise."

George smiled. "Close your eyes."

"Why?"

"Trust me. Just close them."

Once she had done so, he closed his own. When they reopened them, they were standing in his mother-in-law's guest home. Athena shrieked, backed away from George, and started ranting. "What kind of sorcery is this? How can I be in my mother's place? Where's the bridge? Where's the water?"

George expected her reaction. "Babe, sit down." He took her arm and guided her to the table, where he pulled out a chair. He watched her face as the seat's legs screeched across the floor.

"Are we really here? How is this possible?"

The mage pulled another chair close and took a seat. "I thought you would be happy that I can come see you each night. Once I get where I'm going, I'll be able to come back and forth until the moment arrives for you to come and be with me. Doesn't this make you happy?"

Athena started to cry. "Why didn't you tell me about this before we said our vows, George?"

George was taken aback. "Let me ask you this. If I had told you, or shown you, before we got married, would it change the fact I've always loved you and have been good to you since the first moment we met? Would it have stopped you from marrying me?"

Athena looked into his eyes. "No, George, I love you and I would die if I couldn't be with you."

"Well, if you love me...and this love is unconditional," he said, brushing his hand against her cheek, "then why are you so upset about something that will allow us to be together? I have the ability to do so much more than what I've just shown you, but it has nothing to do with how much I love you. I love you because my heart wants to be yours. I'm sorry I've upset you. Will you please forgive me?"

Athena melted at his plea and stood. She motioned for him to stand and embraced him. With her head on her favorite place, she cried, "I'm happy I'll be able to see you so often, but this scares me. Whatever it is you can do, whatever these things are, I think it would be best for you to show me. I don't want to be scared of the unknown."

"Baby, you have nothing to be scared of. I will always protect you and your family. I'm much more powerful than you realize, that's all. Just know when I leave here, I'll be going to set up a wonderful home for us. I won't let you or our baby down."

Athena whimpered, then whispered, "I'm glad I have you. I've never been this happy. I want to be with you. I want you to do whatever it takes to make sure we have a happy home. Just give our baby a good life. I will follow you anywhere."

George lifted his bride into his arms and carried her into the bedroom. He would enjoy the night and leave in the morning for Gessler. He no longer had Amar and the cost to fly on the hippogriffs was steep. There were 13 Peaks left before Kepler would be in Gessler, but it would only take him seven days to get there. He wanted to become familiar with the village so he could teleport as he pleased. The more places he became familiar with, as Lasidious had instructed in his dreams, the easier it would be to get around this world.

As they went to sleep, George dreamed of Abbie. The dream was sad and his little girl kept screaming, "Daddy, save me!" He tried to run toward her, but was unable to do so for reasons he could not figure out. The dream was hellish, but thanks to Lasidious, it was cut short as the Mischievous One asked to be allowed into his mind. George gave him access.

"George, we need to talk."

"You could've shown up a little earlier. The dream I was having was awful. Are you sure Abbie's okay, Lasidious?"

"Yes, she is, George. Like I told you before, her soul is in the Book of Immortality. I've given her many good thoughts of you and her mother. You don't need to worry about your little girl. She's safe."

"Then, what do you want?"

"First, I think congratulations are in order. I see you have a fine woman lying next to you."

"How do you know I'm lying next to Athena? Are you here?" George was starting to feel uncomfortable the god knew so much. "I am dreaming, right?"

"Yes, George, you're dreaming. I know many things, and I keep track of my favorite subjects."

"Favorite, my ass. What do you want?"

Lasidious chuckled. "You'll always be the same old George. Anyway, this visit is not about what you can do for me. It is more about what I can do for you. I have come to enlighten you on the extent of your power. You are about to be a force on Grayham."

"Force, huh? Do I need to do anything?"

"No. All you need to do is lie there. I will enlighten you with everything you need to know. When you awake, you'll be hungry and thirsty. I know your journey to Gessler begins in the morning, but it may take a while for you to recover and feel strong enough to get going."

George agreed to let him do his thing. Lasidious filled his mind with the details of how to use his power and after this lengthy explanation, the God of Mischief left. George woke with an awful thirst. He asked Athena to prepare him a meal and he drank the water in not only the guesthouse, but the main house as well.

Athena was surprised at how much he ate. It took until Late Bailem before he was able to get on the road. He said goodbye to his beautiful wife and made sure Maldwin understood he was leaving. In parting, he had one last thing to say to the rat: "Everything is A-okay, man."

The Next Day
Just After Late Bailem

Double D had made his way into the city of Brandor just after the Peak of Bailem. The closer he came to the city, the larger presence the king's army commanded. It took quite a while to get to where he now stood. As he looked up at the massive torches being lit on the top of the arena, he could only assume the crowd was cheering for the final fight of the evening.

The assassin decided when the perfect moment would be to kill the General Absolute. He knew from previous trips to this city, the general fought the tournament's winner on the ninth day. He would take this opportunity to dispose of Justin. For now, he would use the next six days to scout the castle for the best place to slaughter the prince. He wanted to make a statement and the king's son deserved to die in front of as many people as possible.

This assassination would not be an ordinary killing. This murder needed to be horrific, disgusting enough that all the kingdoms of Grayham would talk about it forever. He wanted everyone to tell tales about how sadistic the slaying of the prince had been. This killing would be a statement of his artistry.

Double D couldn't find a place to stay, as all the inns were booked for the tournament. He wanted to speak to as few people as possible. He scouted the area until he found an old man who had left the tournament by himself. He watched from a distance, careful not to step into the light cast by the scattered torches throughout the city and followed the man to his home.

After ensuring the man was not going to be joined by other company, Double D pulled the hood of his cloak over his head. He vanished beneath the veil of magic. He walked to the front door, opened it, then slipped inside. He could hear the man in his bedroom, singing as he prepared to get into his bathing tub.

Ignoring the man's jovial sounds, Double D moved through the rest of the home, looking into bedrooms which had not been opened for nearly a season. Nothing was out of place, the beds were made, and a layer of dust was on the nightstands next to them. This was the home of an unmarried man. Even the bathing room, meant for the woman of the house, had nothing in it. This sad old man was perfect. From the look of things, no one would be coming to visit any moment soon. Double D's face turned dark.

The assassin waited for the old man to lie down and fall asleep before making his move. Without a sound, he put his pack on the floor and shut the heavy door. He walked toward the bed, stalking like a cat, keeping his breathing normal. He had done this so often it was second nature. He reached down and pulled the covers back to get a better look. He now had his target in sight and reached forward with both hands, but he had to pull back to stop himself from sneezing—a close call. Once again, he reached forward and concentrated on his target. There would be no interruptions and he would finish the job.

He snatched and squeezed. There would be no struggle. Double D relaxed his grip on the pillow from one of the spare beds in a guestroom. He fluffed it and crawled beneath the covers.

He had much to do tomorrow and wanted to be up and gone before the old man woke. He would hate to be a source of irritation.

Over the next six days, Double D scouted the castle and settled on the spot where he would assassinate the prince. He moved around the royal house keeping his hood up, remaining invisible to everyone. The plan was perfect and required just the right set of circumstances to carry it out. But first, the general needed to die.

Gessler Village

George arrived in Gessler, with Kepler not due for another 6 Peaks. There was still plenty of daylight. The mage asked around until he found the Bloody Trough Inn. He figured out which room's window would be best for Kepler to enter and paid the owner of the inn to reserve the room as he left to survey the area. The mage needed to find the perfect spot to teleport when returning to the village. After a while, he stumbled across the entrance to one of the village's mines.

About thirty feet to the left of this opening was a tree tucked against the hillside. He walked over, looked around its base, and realized there was enough room between the hillside and the branches to make his entrance. Just to be sure, he watched how many people came and went from inside the mine. There was little traffic.

Using his sword, George created a pocket within the limbs, clearing away the branches he felt would interfere. At the base, he smoothed the ground to make sure it was level. By the moment he finished, he was familiar enough with the area to avoid a mistake while teleporting. He stood inside his wooden cocoon and memorized every detail. Once he was confident everything was committed to memory, he walked to the other side of the village and took a practice run. Crossing his fingers and taking a deep breath, the mage closed his eyes. When he opened them, he was standing behind the tree, tucked in his branched alcove. A big smile crossed his face. Satisfied with his success, the next stop was his mother-in-law's guesthouse. George closed his eyes and disappeared.

The General Absolute Prepares for Battle

Double D arrived at the arena early and hid beneath the stadium where the fighters prepared for battle. He had been invisible, wearing his cloak since leaving the old man's home, and was now lying on the wooden rafters above the staircase which ascended to the fighting surface.

The moment was approaching for the trumpets to sound. The assassin reached inside his pouch and produced a tiny dart. He had laced its tip with his finest poison and put it into a skinny tube about twelve inches long. Double D lifted the weapon to his mouth and waited.

The trumpets sounded. As expected, the general ascended the dark staircase. There were torches on the walls, but the light cast was only enough to keep the men from falling. Watching as the general passed beneath, Double D blew hard into the tube as soon as he saw the base of the man's neck. The dart flew through the air and hit its target, delivering the wicked poison into the general's bloodstream. Justin reached back and slapped at his neck, knocking the dart into the shadows below.

Double D watched as the men around Justin questioned if everything was okay. Justin held his hand up to see if there was blood, but the darkness of the passageway prevented him from seeing any. The assassin was apprehensive, but the general shrugged it off as nothing more than a mild irritation. The murderer relaxed and watched as the big man continued to the sandy surface of the arena. He smiled as the crowd erupted at the sight of their champion.

Justin Graywind absorbed the screams of the adoring fans into his soul. He had been in this position on many occasions, and his nerves were chiseled from the hardest of stone. He walked into the sunlight and took his spot where no other fighter had been allowed to stand. After lifting his sword in the direction of his opponent, Justin pulled it back in front of his face and bowed to honor him.

The general watched as the king gave his signal for the battle to commence. He turned to face his new enemy. The man began his assault and darted toward him. Justin met this advance with equal measure. The warriors' blades clashed. They spun in unison, as if their actions had been choreographed, before their blades met again.

General Graywind backed away and nodded, acknowledging the skill his enemy displayed. He attacked again. A series of rapid metal clashes followed from many angles before the general's foot made contact with the man's chest and sent him rolling backward.

Justin motioned for the man to stand, and smiled as the fans screamed with pleasure from the exchange. He circled for a bit, feeling his excitement growing. He lived for this atmosphere. It was his heartbeat. He circled and held his arms high, absorbing the chanting of his name, waiting for his enemy to engage.

As Justin turned to face his foe, his eyes began to dim. He tried to rub the cloudiness from them, but this didn't have the effect he was after. *What's wrong?* he thought. *I feel fine. This doesn't make any sense.*

Through the fog, he caught a glimpse of his enemy's attack and his instincts took over. He stepped to the side of the advance and sent a crushing left hand to the side of the man's face. The impact was enough to send his enemy to the ground, unconscious. The general realized he didn't have the moments to waste before he wouldn't be able to see at all, and now, his chest was beginning to hurt. Toying with his opponent was not wise while in this condition. He followed up his strike with a downward stab of his sword to the back of the man's head. The point of the blade passed through his skull and exited the right eye. The mighty Graywind left his sword buried in his victim and grabbed his chest in pain.

The crowd, unaware of what was happening, erupted with sadistic joy. The general, despite his condition, raised his hand to acknowledge them. Stumbling toward the center of the arena, his sight was almost gone and now, his breathing was wrong. Justin dropped his arms and stood motionless. He was frightened, the way children are frightened when they are sure something is under their bed. The same man who had seen bloody wars was scared. The beast in his own chamber closet was emerging to take him.

The crowd continued to cheer, but he felt no comfort. Coldness consumed his body as his heart pounded against his ribs. He grabbed at his chest, lifting his voice to scream for the king's healers, then collapsed to his knees.

The crowd silenced as they watched. The king commanded his medics to hurry. Justin's breathing was becoming shorter. He was gasping for the air he could not find. His lungs began to fill with blood and the weight of his body was becoming too much to handle. Falling to his back, he could not see the sun's brightness. The only sound he could hear was the blood in his lungs bubbling with every short breath he managed.

Sam jumped from the king's box and ran to Justin. The healers were taking too long. Sam laid the leader of the army flat on his back and lowered his ear to the man's mouth. He heard the gurgling of blood and knew he had made a mistake by leaving the griffin's essence in his chamber. There was no other medicine on this world which could save him. He called for Shalee. She lowered to the sand and ran to his side. Pointing to Justin, Sam said, "Use Precious! Hurry!"

Shalee cried. "Sam, my power doesn't work this way. I can't do anythin' for him."

The horror in Sam's eyes served as his response. Shalee lowered to the sand and lifted Justin's head onto her lap. All anyone could do was watch as they surrounded the dying. The king moved in to take Shalee's place. Keldwin leaned over to whisper in Justin's ear. "You will always be my champion, my friend," he said with love.

The last gasp of blood-filled air escaped the warrior's body and his eyes closed. The king, full of rage, called for his guards to secure the arena, commanding no one be allowed to leave. The healers took the brunt of Keldwin's misplaced anger.

"What good are you if you can't stop this man from dying?" he screamed. The pain in his heart was agonizing.

Keldwin and Justin had been friends since they were boys. Justin's father also served under the late King of Brandor as a high-ranking officer. They had the same teacher when studying the arts of war, and during countless engagements, his friend had thrown him to his back when practicing. The boys had done everything together: hunting, fishing, riding, playing, and, when they were old enough to appreciate women, hunting of a different kind. The general had always been the stronger fighter and, when Keldwin ascended to the throne, he watched Justin fight his way to becoming the military's finest leader. When Justin slayed the previous General Absolute, Keldwin honored the army's new leader.

Their friendship had come full circle. The memories of their lives together were surfacing. Keldwin was shattered. The king made everyone wait until the general's body was cleared from the arena floor. One by one, as the spectators left the arena, each was searched for clues which might pertain to Justin's death.

There was no logical reason for this man to die. He had not been struck by his foe. His death tore at the king's mind and he could not let it rest. He marched around the arena, screaming orders. The people who watched were full of anticipation of what he might do, having never seen their king act this way. No one could predict what royal power he would invoke to appease his irrational mind.

The search for a killer lasted through the night while the king found solace with Sam in a small, secluded room off the arena. Keldwin collapsed in the future General Absolute's arms. Even the prince had never been this close to his father. Sam motioned to the prince that everything would be okay, and sat with Keldwin until he could pull himself together.

Sam propped the king up. "Keldwin, I need you to listen. I know your pain is great, but remember how Justin would have wanted his king, his friend, to remember him."

The king pulled away. "I don't know what to do, Sam. My heart is destroyed. No one knew how close we were. We've been friends since we were boys. I confided everything to this man. When my queen died, Aaron was devastated, and it was Justin who helped me be the father I needed to be to ease the boy's pain. What do I do?"

"I think you know what Justin would say. He would tell you to be strong and remember him with honor. He would tell you to live and enjoy the last few days of your life. He would say he looked forward to being reborn with you and he admired you. He spoke of his admiration when he was preparing me for my position."

The king's face softened. "He admired me, Sam?"

"He did. He admired you for your military mind. He admired you for your strength and honor. He told me of the things you did as children. I believe your friend knew he could have no finer friend than you. If he were the one in your place, he would be just as devastated. I would tell him the same thing I'm telling you. Be strong and honor the fallen. Don't be sad. Celebrate him. That's how you would want him to honor you if the roles were reversed."

"Sam, you're right. I'll honor Justin and hold my head high. Thank you for your counsel. When I die, my son could have no finer advisor."

"Thank you. It will be an honor to serve Aaron." Sam walked with Keldwin to the room where Justin's body rested. Until now, Sam had not realized the situation he was in. When the king died, he would be the second most powerful man in the kingdom. He swallowed hard.

They stood above the general's body, watching the healers as they tried to figure out what caused Justin's death. The king would not allow them to prod, knowing Justin would not have wanted to be torn apart to satisfy their need for answers.

After a while, Sam encouraged the king to leave. He reminded Keldwin there was one day left of his tournament. Even though the general had lost his life, he had won the battle. Sam could think of no better way to honor Justin than to have his Passing Ceremony in the same arena the general loved so much.

Keldwin liked the idea and called his slaves. He ordered them to spread word within the city that the ceremony to honor the general would be held in the arena after Late Bailem. The slaves scattered. Sam walked with the king to the royal carriage, then comforted him during the ride.

Sam was exhausted when he arrived in his room. Shalee was waiting. They avoided talking and went to bed.

When Late Bailem arrived the next night, the arena was filled with royalty, nobles, and every member of the senate. The adoring fans of the general filled what was left of the seats. Two hundred of the king's personal guards lined up in four formations around the platform at the center of the arena. The king entered, followed by Aaron and Sam. Shalee, Helga, BJ, Michael, and a few other officers who had made it back from their assignments, took seats in the king's box. Keldwin led Sam and Aaron to the top of the platform to stand next to the general's body. They took turns saying their final goodbyes, touching the blade of the warrior's sword before leaving Keldwin alone with Justin's corpse.

The king knew Justin would not want words to be said. He would honor his friend one last moment. He bent over to kiss Justin's forehead and lit the fire before descending the stairs. The arena sat in silence as the flames consumed the structure. No one was allowed to leave until the flame subsided. This was the Kingdom of Brandor's way of showing respect. The dying of the fire signified the ascension of the general's soul.

The next day, Sam was brought into the throne room and sworn into the General Absolute's position. Michael returned to the position of second in command and Sam sent word for all his officers to return home before the king died. Eighteen slaves delivered the royal message that all officers were to be given access to the hippogriffs so they could arrive before the king passed. Observing Keldwin's demeanor, Sam knew he did not have many days left to live.

The Grayham Inquirer

When Inquiring Minds Need to Know about their Favorite Characters

5 MORE PEAKS OF BAILEM have passed since Sam sent the slaves to retrieve his officers throughout the kingdom. They have returned. The senators, who remained in the city after learning of their king's failing health, have been directed to the king's throne room with the army's officers. The king is weak and wants to make an announcement before passing. What he will say to his men is of utmost importance. The king has spent much of the last two days working on the details of the passing of his crown with Aaron, Sam, and Michael.

DOUBLE D is hiding in the castle, waiting for the perfect moment to kill the prince. He was sitting in the corner of the throne room, with his hood pulled up to hide his presence, when he learned of the king's failing health. Keldwin told his subjects where he wanted his viewing to be held. The way the king described how his casket should be placed was the perfect set-up for Double D's plan.

GEORGE kissed Athena goodbye and teleported back to Gessler to meet with Kepler. He is napping in his room at The Bloody Trough, waiting for the jaguar and his brothers to enter through the window.

CELESTRIA is only 40 Peaks of Bailem from giving birth. She sat the elven witch family down to have a long conversation about how they are wearing on her nerves. They have promised to change their attitudes because of this stern talk.

MOSLEY is going to attend the King of Brandor's meeting and wants to ensure the transition of power was perceived to be supported by the gods. As it turns out, his team has decided to take an interest in this event and they are now en route. The gods know Double D is in the city and they are curious. Although they cannot intervene in this matter, they want to show their support of the king's decision to turn his crown over to the prince before he passes. Mosley, although pleased his team is coming, is having trouble imagining the reaction of those in attendance when the gods make their appearance.

LASIDIOUS is planning to entice the Serpent King, Seth, to make a trip to see George in the city of Bloodvain. He knows George is now only 7 Peaks from the Barbarian King's city. If everything goes right, and he has his doubts they will, the mage will be king before the reptile arrives. He hopes George will steal the crown and create an alliance with the Kingdom of Serpents for the upcoming war. So far, the Earthling has been impressive, but taking the Crown of Bloodvain will be difficult. The Barbarian King has a group of mages as counsel and, even though none of them are as strong as George, they could combine their power to defeat him.

Lasidious has given George the weapons necessary to gain power. He would have given George a solution to defeat the Barbarian King and his mages, but this was a different situation.

The Book of Immortality's rules forbid the gods from providing information which would change the balance of power on any world. It was okay to tell George that killing the king would bring power, but he could not give the mortal advice on how to do it. Until now, he had not crossed the line, but he had walked up to its edge. If George succeeds, this will be the largest shift of power Grayham had ever seen.

Lasidious has not been paying attention to the situation developing in the Kingdom of Brandor. He is not aware of Sam's new position.

SENCHAE BLOODVAIN is training harder than ever. His mind has not been able to find rest.

ONLY 4 PEAKS remain until the people harvest their crops across the Kingdom of Brandor. All of the oversized harvest wagons are finished and the massive barns are complete and ready to store the excess until it can be taken to the coastal cities. Sam has dispatched part of the king's fleet to wait for the wagons to arrive with their cargo.

Thank you for reading the Grayham Inquirer

Justice

Sam rose from Justin Graywind's old chair, wearing his new armor to symbolize his position as the leader of the king's army. This would be Sam's last series of moments as General Absolute. By meeting's end, he would be the advisor to the new king, Aaron Brandor, and Michael would move to take his spot as general.

Over the last couple of days, Sam got to know Keldwin's son. There were many things he admired about the royal offspring. They were about the same age with many of the same likes and dislikes. All in all, Sam figured his service to Aaron would be a pleasure.

Sam started the meeting. "Gentlemen, I've called you here to listen to the king's wishes. He's weak and any questions you may have will need to wait until after the king has left. I will be the one to address them. The king is on his way, and..."

Before Sam could finish his sentence, Mosley and the rest of the gods on his team appeared around the table. The men reacted defensively to the surprise visit. Sam had to do some quick thinking to calm everyone.

Mosley spoke. "General, we are here to show our support. We have no need to participate, but our presence will be good for the kingdom. We would like to acknowledge the new leader of Brandor's pack."

Mosley had learned of Double D's arrival in the city. This was the main reason why he wanted to come. He wanted to inform Sam of the assassin's presence, but he had to abide by the same law as Lasidious. Although his team had no idea what was about to happen in the Barbarian Kingdom, the law was clear: no god could provide the mortals with information or instruction on how to handle an event which could change the balance of power. This rule prevented the gods from gaining followers through such powerful manipulation. Mosley knew if the assassin killed Aaron, the laws of the land would make Sam the new king. Aaron did not have a son or a wife to survive him, and Keldwin's queen died many seasons ago.

Now...fellow soul...allow me to explain why Sam is in line to become the new king. It was once the law that the crown would go to the eldest relative, if the king did not have a direct descendant. But now, the Senate's law states: the crown will pass to the highest-ranking member of the military during periods of war.

The reason the law changed is for the security of the kingdom. 732 seasons ago, war engulfed Southern Grayham. Brandor's king perished during an invasion on barbarian soil.

When the nobles of Brandor heard the news, they fought amongst themselves for the crown since there was no surviving heir. This fight left the kingdom vulnerable to attack, with many losing their lives when the barbarians invaded. After the enemy was driven back to the north, the Senate was created and a new law, giving the highest ranking officer the crown, was passed.

The nobles of the fallen king would forever have a royal bloodline, but the crown would stay with the bloodline of the new monarch. If the new king fell in battle after assuming the crown, this law would also apply to his monarchy in times of war.

During times of peace, if a king passes without an heir, the law allows for an election. All nobles of the kingdom are allowed to campaign for the monarchy. The Senate recognizes the two nobles who secure the majority vote, then vote again for the one they believe will best fit the kingdom.

Sam took control of the meeting. "My Lords, we are honored to have you watch over these proceedings." Sam sent a messenger to inform Keldwin of the gods' attendance. He wanted the king to be prepared when he entered the meeting.

Moments later, the king entered, sitting in a wheelchair pushed by the prince. Everyone, except the gods, kneeled in reverence. Keldwin motioned for them to stand and take their seats. When the king saw the room was settled, he spoke in a weak voice. "Thank you for coming."

As he spoke, the coughing began, spewing blood into his hands as he covered his mouth. No one reacted. They dared not dishonor their king.

Keldwin regained his composure. "I'm giving my crown to my son.

From the moment I finish this address, Aaron will be your king. I expect you to serve him like you have served me. Sam will become his advisor and Michael will become the General Absolute. There have been many changes because of my health and General Graywind's passing, but I have confidence my son will lead this kingdom with honor. I hate to say farewell, but when you see me next, it will be to say your goodbyes."

The king said each man's name and bid them farewell before he motioned for a servant to take him to his chambers. Once Keldwin was gone, Sam led the group in bowing to their new king, Aaron Brandor.

Meanwhile, Mosley stared into the corner of the room, looking through the magic of the assassin's invisible cloak. He was careful not to allow Double D to notice, but the wolf wanted to see the killer's face.

Aaron addressed the leaders of his army and the Senate. "Much needs to be done to make this kingdom ready for the upcoming harvests. In addition to my father's Passing Ceremony, we need to ensure the crops are harvested efficiently. I would like to hear the status reports from those of you who carried out General Graywind's orders."

Aaron was speaking with the authority of a seasoned veteran. Sam was impressed with the young man's powerful presence. The meeting lasted until the middle of the night, with the king giving direct orders to Senate members to make preparations for his father's death. He laid out the plans for a proper viewing.

Aaron was pleased with how Justin Graywind had been honored when the fire was lit in the arena. He told the men his father would be honored in the same manner, knowing Justin and his father would approve of the idea. It would bring their friendship full circle.

After Aaron left the room, Sam called a close to the meeting. He waited for everyone to leave and motioned for Mosley to wait. When they were alone, Sam spoke to the wolf-god. But, Mosley's attention was elsewhere as he watched Double D leave the room. Sam watched the wolf's eyes and became curious, as he could not see anything but the walls.

"What were you looking at, My Lord?"

"Nothing, Sam. What can I do for you?"

"Everything is changing so fast. I'm feeling overwhelmed. I'm wondering if you could give me one of your blessings to help me sleep. I'd be grateful, My Lord."

"Sam, you and I do not need these formalities when others are not present. Let us continue as we were before I ascended. Let us treat each other as we used to."

Sam smiled. "You mean like the way you called me a fool when I started my training with BJ? Like the moments when Kael yelled at me for not respecting him as a sword of the gods? I can think of nothing better than to go back to our old ways and create more fond memories." Sam moved in and lowered to one knee, then hugged the wolf's neck. "Thanks for being there, old friend."

Mosley enjoyed this exchange, but could see Sam had something else on his mind. Sam took a deep breath. "I was wondering if you could see to it that Justin and Keldwin's souls are allowed to communicate with one another. You know, when they arrive inside the Book of Immortality. They were good friends, and it's irritating to know there's no Heaven. Can you do anything about this and ask the Book to allow two old friends to continue their relationship?"

"I may be able to," the wolf replied. "I can talk with the Book and see if he will allow them to speak with one another, but it is up to the Book to make the final decision. It seems like a simple request."

"Thanks. That's all a guy can ask."

Gessler Village

Kepler and his brothers squeezed through the window of George's room at The Bloody Trough. Standing around the bed, their massive bodies filled the large room. They watched what they thought to be a sleeping George and joked as they looked down at the mage.

"Ahhhhh, how cute," Kepler chuckled. "I didn't know something so ugly could look so adorable."

Keller responded, "Don't give him too much credit, he's still a human. They don't have the ability to be adorable. But, the furless freaks try."

Again they laughed as Koffler made an attempt to jump into the conversation, but the youngest of the triplet jaguars was not known for his wit. "Yeah, yeah, human, yeah, can't give him credit without being furry, you guys."

Kepler and Keller looked at each other and rolled their eyes. After a moment, Koffler realized his brothers were mocking him.

"What, what...hey, mother said you guys need to be nice to me."

"Mother was destroyed many seasons ago, imbecile," Keller replied. "Do we need to take you out back and bloody you up?" He turned to look at Kepler. "I hate to say this, but I think every family has a member that's not fit to be a territorial leader."

"What?" Koffler growled.

George sat up, catching the three cats off guard. "If you think I'm ugly, then I hate to tell you what I think of your looks. Every moment I see you, I feel I should put out a freakishly huge saucer of milk and say, 'Here kitty, kitty.'"

"That's not funny," Kepler snarled. "You know I hate those words, especially when you say them." He looked at his brothers. "That's the same thing he said as he stood over the Saber Lord and tortured him with the tip of his sword." The dark cats muttered amongst themselves about George's poor taste in jokes.

"Looks like we're even." George mocked.

"I suppose," Kepler responded. "Where's Amar?"

George shrugged. "I killed him."

"You did what? Why?" The room became tense.

"He was going to hurt our chances to take over the throne of the Barbarian Kingdom."

Kepler started to shift in place, the room being too crowded to pace. "And, exactly how would he hurt them?"

"Lasidious told me he'd create problems. Do you remember the woman I told you about...the one I came to this world with?"

"I do."

"She has become powerful. Lasidious revealed Amar had been to Luvelles to study the dark arts, and had plans to kill Shalee to take her power. If I allowed this to happen, Amar would've become powerful enough to destroy us all and take the throne for himself. I wasn't about to allow this. I led him into a smith's shed outside the city of Champions. I ripped out his heart and ate it."

"What?" Kepler snarled. "You ate his heart? Wasn't it enough that you killed him? What could you possibly gain from eating everything you kill? Would you have eaten Kroger if he wouldn't have been stone?"

George smiled. "Of course I wouldn't have eaten Kroger. I ate Amar's heart because it was the only way to steal his power before his soul left his body."

"What are you talking about?" Kepler's eyes flashed.

George figured he would show the beast instead of arguing. He lifted his hands into the air. Once they were level to the bed, he turned his palms up and lifted them further, causing all three jaguars to rise from the floor. Just over six tons of undead cat hung suspended. Kepler's brothers became angered and started to snarl, but George silenced them with a glance.

Kepler, on the other hand, remained calm. "I get your point, George. You have Amar's power. Are you saying you had to eat his heart to steal it and this was the only way to take it from his soul before it ascended?"

"Ding, ding, ding...we have a winner," George shouted as he lowered everyone to the floor. He turned to look at Keller and Koffler. "Relax. Everything will be alright."

"So what else can you do?" Kepler questioned.

The mage smiled. "I can do many, many things, but let's talk about them on our journey to Bloodvain."

The giant cat agreed. George stated they would leave in the morning. The rest of the mage's night was splendid. He told Kepler and his brothers he would be back at Early Bailem and would meet them on the far side of the village. Then George stood and closed his eyes. When he opened them, he was standing over his wife. He leaned over and ran his fingers through her hair. When she woke, she smiled, and made room for him to crawl in beside her.

The Next Day
The Castle of Brandor

Aaron stayed with his father throughout the night. Keldwin had intended to go to the throne room and pass the crown from his head to his son's, but found he was too weak to get out of bed. He tried to apologize to Aaron, but could not get the words out. Breathing his last breath, a father said to his son, "I am proud of you, boy."

These six words tore at Aaron's heart. Without control, he cried as he laid draped across his father's body. Sam found Aaron kneeling by the bed with his head lowered into one of his father's palms. He lifted the young king from the floor and led him out, signaling to the healers to prepare Keldwin's body for viewing while the servants were sent to tell the senators of the king's passing.

Now, the senators would need to do the jobs Aaron assigned while Sam comforted his royal friend. Keldwin's viewing was scheduled for the next day at the Peak of Bailem, with the celebration to honor his passing to follow after dark.

He took the young king out to the garden and sat him down to console him. "Aaron, talk to me. Let's get this off your chest so you can breathe."

"Sam, I'm fine. I think I've had more than enough moments to prepare for his death. It hit me hard, but I've shed many tears already. I'll continue to grieve, but not without performing my duties. My father would have wanted it that way. The last thing he said to me before he died was he was proud of me. Many men never get to hear their father say something so special."

Sam helped Aaron from his seat before speaking. "I thought I was going to have to console you, but you have everything under control. What do you say we go and get a mug of ale? I don't know about you, but I could really use one."

The king agreed the idea sounded pleasant. Both men headed for the kitchen with their arms draped across each other's shoulders.

City of Serpents

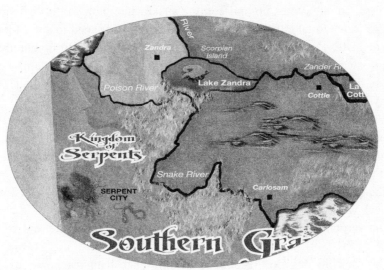

Seth was slithering through his underground kingdom toward his royal rock, the serpent's version of a throne. Far beneath this boulder, with a flat top, was an underground lava flow. The heat from the molten river produced enough energy to warm the rock. This was the giant snake's favorite place to rest. It was also the same rock his great-great-great-grandfather, King Sotter, had rested on many long seasons ago. His kingdom, for the most part, did not interfere in the matters of the two dominant human kingdoms of Southern Grayham. Every now and then, his snake army needed to chase neighboring soldiers away so they could continue to live in peace. His kingdom spread from south of the Poison River where it left Lake Zandra to west of the Snake River, which also exited the same lake.

His kind was known for their poison, and thus maintained a simple existence. They sold their poison, and various forms of plant life which grew in the marshy areas of his kingdom, to Merchant Island. The coin collected was kept in an overflowing underground cavern. His reptilian population did not have a need for wealth. The sale of these items kept the other kingdoms out of his borders and allowed them to live without worry of invasion. When he became the new king, he continued to do what worked and kept it simple.

There were four ways into Seth's cavern, all of which were guarded by two reptilian guards. These soldiers were not there to protect from outside invaders, but rather to protect the king from his own kind. Every now and then, an ambitious, up-and-coming snake champion would feel strong enough to try to take the king's rock. The guards managed to spoil this attack and life, as usual, moved forward. If a serpent was strong enough to fight his way to the king and kill him, he was given the throne and would remain the new monarch until he was either killed or died of old age. The rock would then be passed to another snake within his bloodline.

When Lasidious showed up in front of Seth's boulder, the snake was warming himself and taking a nap. The Serpent King's soldiers attacked, but Lasidious, careful not to hurt them, put up a wall of force and watched as the giant reptiles slammed into it.

The god made sure Seth was the only one who could hear. "Seth, I wish to speak with you."

The serpent hissed, "So I see. Who are you to stand in front of my rock?"

The Mischievous One responded to the Snake King's ignorance. "I'm Lasidious."

The reptile knew the name belonged to a god, though he had no knowledge of what Lasidious looked like. He knew his ancestors served Celestria, but in many of the stories about Sotter, his great-great-great-grandfather, there was mention of this particular god's name when referring to their goddess.

He ordered his guards to back away. "What is it that you need, Lord Lasidious?"

Lasidious knew the Serpent King's hissing would drive him mad. He decided to tell the snake everything he had to say, without interruption, and let the snake dwell on it.

"Seth, you've proven to be a good leader over your kind. You've continued the ways of the kings before you. This has kept outsiders from crossing your borders. I'm here to tell you a great threat has emerged which will destroy your way of life. The Kingdom of Brandor has decided to go to war with the barbarians."

"War?" Seth hissed. "Over what will they fight? Why bother me with this?"

"What, matters not. This war will consume your borders and will not stop until you are dead. The only way for you to protect your way of life is to ally your kind with the barbarians. They have a new king who is powerful, although he is not a barbarian. He has defeated King Bloodvain in a battle for the crown. If you align yourself with this man, your kingdoms can work together to defend the advances of Brandor. Once their bid for power has been stopped, you'll be able to continue life as normal. This is a friendly warning, Seth. What you do with this information is up to you. The man's name you'll need to seek, if you choose this path, is George Nailer. I wish you luck in whichever decision you make. I must take my leave."

Before Seth could respond, Lasidious disappeared. Agitated, the Serpent King looked at his soldiers. He called for the Council of Serpents to convene. He would announce his trip to Bloodvain.

City of Brandor

Sam woke early on the morning of Keldwin's viewing. After he left the room to get breakfast, Shalee opened her eyes. After stretching, she prepared her morning bath. Dropping her towel to step into a tub of warm water, the sorceress let out a shriek, then ran to the bed. She pulled the blanket over her and looked at the wolf. Mosley had materialized in front of her.

"What are ya doin' poppin' in on a girl like that? I was fixin' ta bathe. Can't a girl have some privacy? That really chaps my hide."

Mosley gave a wolfish grin. "Do not worry, Shalee, you do not appeal to my senses. You do not have enough fur, or a bushy tail for me to find satisfaction from seeing you without your clothes. Now, if you had a tail, I just might..."

"If ya finish that sentence, so help me, I'll turn ya into a god-frog," the sorceress said with a cold look.

The wolf laughed and turned away. Shalee wrapped her towel around her, then the wolf turned to face her. "Shalee, I have come to speak of things you should know as a sorceress. I want you to think about this and make sure it weighs on your mind at every moment. This will be the one thing which will keep you alive when other magic users find themselves facing death."

"Holy cow, Mosley, ya really know how ta ruin a girl's bath. Ya pop in unannounced, tell me I don't have a cute tail, ya have somethin' I need ta know, then scare me half ta death by sayin' if I don't think of this always, I could die. Nice work. I think I'm goin' ta change your name ta Mosley, The Wolf-god of Bad News." Shalee ruffled her hands through Mosley's fur.

Despite the fact the wolf came for a serious discussion, Mosley enjoyed the woman's affections. After a moment, he pulled away and asked Shalee to sit. When she did, she left a clear view. The towel had ridden up and Mosley was forced to turn his head. "Ummm, Shalee, could you please?"

Once Shalee realized what Mosley was referring to, she squealed and pulled the covers over her. "All boys are the same, no matter what species ya are. Human or wolf, you're all dogs, and every stinkin' one of ya puts your eyes where they don't belong."

Once Mosley stopped laughing, he continued. "Shalee, I need you to take me seriously. I cannot tell you why I have come to say these things, but I can tell you that it is for good reason."

"You're scarin' me, Mosley."

"You should be scared." The wolf's eyes grew dark. "You always need to be on the lookout for things which do not seem normal. You should have a plan prepared for when these things happen. If there is one lesson you can learn, it is you have the power to take control of most any situation. You need to heighten your senses.

"I must go, but remember, be ready, no matter what. I am sorry I cannot say more. Always be ready, Shalee...always be ready."

Mosley's voice echoed throughout the room even after his departure, leaving Shalee sitting on the bed, shaken and trying to process this new information. After taking a faster-than-normal bath to make up for lost moments, she headed out to be with Sam.

Aaron decided to change the venue where his father's body was to be viewed. The young king ordered Keldwin's corpse to be moved to the theatre in Brandor.

Invisible, Double D heard the order from where he stood behind the new king's throne. The tip of his blade was pressed against the chair's back and he was ready to shove it through and stab Aaron where he sat.

He pulled back the heavy knife. This change of venue would make the killing more public. Keldwin's body would be on display a short distance from the stage's curtain. And, better yet, this would make the assassin's job easier. The theatre would also provide a smoother getaway. He departed to familiarize himself with the structure's layout.

The assassin now stood on the stage where a few souls were preparing for the viewing. Within his veil of magic, he dodged between them, plotting his escape. It did not take long before he felt he was ready, prepared for anything unexpected which might happen.

The morticians entered the building carrying Keldwin's body. They entered from the back to avoid the masses of people who came from all over the city and lined up for miles to say goodbye. Double D watched as they placed Keldwin not more than five feet from the curtain. Seeing the placement and knowing his escape route would be perfect, he relaxed.

He listened as the morticians spoke of how they would usher the people on stage to say goodbye. Viewers would walk up one side, pay their respects in front of the casket, then exit on the other. To keep everyone from standing outside in the rain, they would bring in the nobles, followed by the senate, and then the high-ranking officers of the army. These first VIPs would sit in assigned seats and everyone else would be ushered in to fill the remaining seats.

The part of the plan discussed next caught the assassin's attention. Aaron had decided he would address the people. Ten guards, five on each side, would stand at either end of the casket. The casket would be placed parallel with the front of the stage. The back side of the casket would be wide open for his approach.

To the far side of the stage would be the king's throne. His advisor, the General Absolute, and their wives would be joining them. All Double D had to do was wait for Aaron to lean over his father's body.

The assassin was not concerned about the guards. He knew they wouldn't find him once he darted behind the curtain. Their reactions would be slow. The king wanted them to stand at attention and face the crowd. He could not have dreamed a more perfect scenario if he had tried.

Double D watched as the Peak of Bailem passed and the doors to the theater opened. Just as planned, the family was ushered to their seats, followed by the members of the senate and their families. These first two groups were placed, one behind the other, in front of the stage. Key members of the military and their families were next, numbering nine hundred souls. With the other 3,000 seats filled, it would be the biggest assassination ever witnessed. If not for his greed, Double D would have killed Aaron for free.

Many moments passed before the theatre settled. Double D watched as Sam stood from his seat next to his wife, gave her a kiss on the top of her hand, then walked to the center of the stage.

"Ladies and gentlemen," Sam shouted to make sure everyone heard. "Please, everyone, come to order." The crowd quieted.

"In a few moments, your king will arrive to make his way through the theatre. He has requested no one speak until he has made his address and said goodbye to his father. Once the king has left the building, you may talk amongst yourselves. You'll be told when it's your turn to pay your respects. I ask all of you to show respect for the dead, as well as for your king."

A young, well-dressed servant boy approached. He informed Sam the king had arrived and was waiting outside the doors to be introduced to the crowd. Sam signaled the trumpeters. He shouted, "Ladies and gentlemen, please rise. I give you King Aaron Brandor."

The trumpets sounded and filled the expansive room with wonderful music as Aaron entered through the double doors and made his way to the stage. Sam lowered to one knee and bowed his head, symbolizing the respect of the audience who could not kneel from their seats. Sam kissed the king's hand before being signaled to rise, whereupon Aaron embraced him and whispered in his ear, "I find much strength in you, Sam. Thank you."

Sam was touched by the compliment. He nodded, then returned to his seat. Aaron turned to face the audience and began his address.

Shalee listened from her seat. She was still bothered by Mosley's words, which had left her with a heightened sense of awareness. She scanned the theatre, looking for something out of the ordinary, but could not find anything. Despite this failure, the sorceress gripped Precious with white knuckles as she directed her attention to Aaron.

"You'll always be remembered, My Great King." These were the last words Aaron spoke as everyone watched him make his way to say goodbye to his father.

Double D waited on the other side of the casket and looked across as Aaron approached. His knife was ready and laced with poison to ensure he completed the job if an imperfect thrust was made. This was the same knife he used to kill the barbarian in Gessler. He waited for the right moment, then stepped toward the head of Keldwin's coffin. He moved his arm into position. Double D made sure the hood of his cloak was secure. He did not want his actions to cause the hood to fall. His invisibility was the key to escape.

As Aaron stood above his father, tears fell from his cheeks, but the assassin felt no compassion. The pain which filled the king's eyes could find no soft spot in Dawson Drake's killer heart. In fact, Double D smiled as the grieving man leaned over to kiss his father on the forehead.

He would allow Aaron to have this final kiss. As the young king began to straighten up, the assassin plunged his knife under Aaron's chin, shoving it so hard the tip of the blade pierced the top of his head. Double D licked his lips and savored the penetration.

⚓❖⚓

Shalee had watched the king move across the stage toward the coffin. Mosley's earlier comments had scared her to the point she had used Precious to heighten her senses. Something was not sitting right in her gut. Though she couldn't explain what it was, she was ready. As the sorceress watched the king bend over to kiss his father, she almost exhaled with relief, but the hole in the king's head opened and blood spurted.

⚓❖⚓

This would be the last series of moments the killer's blade would harm anyone. He would leave it buried in the king's skull to make a statement. *Let's go get my money*, Double D thought as he let go of the knife.

⚓❖⚓

Seeing the knife appear in Aaron's head, Shalee slammed Precious against the wood of the theatre stage and screamed, "Precious, *putta iluve*." Everyone and everything within the structure stopped moving, both seen and unseen. The sorceress stood from her chair and moved in to study the scene.

Blood was everywhere, with drops falling from the knife, suspended in midair. Shalee gathered her emotions, then took a closer look. *How could a knife just appear like this? Focus on every detail.* She saw that a drop of blood was out of place. It was falling toward the curtain on the far side of the coffin. *That's impossible. There's no way for it ta fall like that. Somethin' had ta be movin' away from Aaron's head.*

Shalee moved to get Sam and released him from her magic. She held her hand to his mouth and explained the situation. It took Sam only a moment to look at the scene and bring himself up to speed. He moved around the guards and to the backside of the coffin. As he did, his foot tripped on the extended leg of the assassin. "Something is here."

Shalee reached down to touch what felt like soft cloth. Upon further investigation, she realized it was a leg. She rubbed her hand along the bottom of it, toward what should be the rest of the body.

"Oh, my gosh, Sam, it's a man...and he's...yuck. Come and see. He must get his lil' rocks off this way. I can't touch this pig. You're goin' ta have ta do it."

Sam shook his head and moved in to take her spot. He took a deep breath and sure enough, the guy was excited to be there. He moved his hands up the rest of the killer's body until he came to the head and realized the killer had on a hood. Sam pulled it back, revealing the rest of the assassin's body.

They took a step back and caught their breath. "So, what should we do with him?" Shalee asked.

Sam did not answer right away. He circled the frozen figure instead, rifling through his pockets. "I want to know who we're dealing with."

"Be careful," the sorceress said, though she knew there was no chance the killer would move.

Sam reached in and pulled out a small wooden case with the initials "D D" burned into the top in a beautiful script. "Hmmm, D D. I wonder if these are his initials."

"Who cares what his name is?" Shalee snapped. "What're we gonna do with this creep? I can't keep these people frozen foreva', ya know."

Sam agreed. He lifted the assassin from the floor and carried him back to the coffin. He straightened Double D's legs to a balanced position and placed his hand back on the handle of the knife which protruded from the king's skewered head.

"Goodness-gracious, Sam, what're ya doin'?" Shalee asked in a frantic whisper.

"I'm making our killer look guilty. We don't want him getting away, now do we?"

"That's a good idea. Make him look guilty-like." She took the cape from the killer's back and held it up in front of her. She figured it might come in handy one of these days, but then she took a closer look at the garment. "This is downright nasty, Mr. D...D. There's blood all ova' this thing. Your motha' would be appalled if she had any idea you left your clothes so filthy." The sorceress draped the cape over her arm with two fingers as if it was diseased.

"Would you please focus?" Sam snapped. "Help me with him. You can criticize him on his lack of fashion sense later."

Once Double D was in the perfect position, Sam adjusted Aaron's weight to fall toward the coffin. They took their seats. Shalee slammed Precious into the floor and commanded everyone to be released from her magic.

The next thing Double D knew, he was standing with the knife still in his right hand and the weight of the king falling toward him. He released the blade and looked at the crowd. Everyone could see him. He heard Sam shout for the guards to seize him. He snatched at his hood, but was only able to grab air. He tried to run for the curtain, but one of the guards tackled him before he could take his second step. Nine different blades of the king's guard were pointing down. Double D was captured.

The theatre was frantic and everyone screamed as they saw their king fall across the top of his father. Sam took center stage and motioned for Shalee to use Precious to amplify his voice. "People of Brandor, sit and be quiet!"

Everyone stopped at and looked. Most of them didn't realize it, but Sam was their new king and he was about to make the chain of authority well known. He shouted again. "King Aaron has been murdered. I will not have this gathering make a mockery of this man's death. Sit down, now!"

Everyone took their seats. Sam turned and motioned for the guards to bring Double D to the front of the stage. The guards knew Sam was their new king and did not hesitate to comply. Sam ordered the morticians to take Keldwin and Aaron from the room. They were to return the kings in clean attire, inside two new coffins.

Sam faced the crowd. "People of Brandor, you will remain seated until our kings have been returned. Justice needs to be delivered, and I intend to give the fallen the respect they deserve. We won't leave until this has been accomplished. Do you understand?"

Michael, as if he had been prepared to say it all along, stood from his chair and shouted. "The king has spoken. Hail, King Goodrich."

The entire theatre was now aware of Sam's new role and responded appropriately, "Hail, King Goodrich!"

Many long moments passed before the morticians returned with the bodies of the late kings. During their absence, Sam forced Double D to kneel and face the crowd with his hands tied behind his back. After being beaten, Double D confessed his profession, and admitted to slaying the great, General Graywind.

Upon hearing the confession and seeing the crowds reaction, Sam shouted. "Double D has dishonored three great men with his actions! They will receive the justice they deserve! Two of our fallen were great warriors, but all three were leaders this kingdom cannot just replace! They will be missed! They will be avenged! They will be honored on this very night!"

Sam turned an event meant for a viewing of the dead into a pep rally of sorts. He did not want the people to leave without having closure, knowing full well all three of his fallen friends would approve.

When the bodies were in place, Sam commanded they be tilted to face the direction of the people. Michael ordered six of the ten guards to hold the caskets in position.

Motioning for the remaining four guards to lift Double D to his feet, Sam made another announcement. "People of Brandor, on this day, in front of our beloved kings, there will be justice! This man will tell us why he has killed our great leaders!"

Double D spit on the floor. "I will say nothing! Beat me if you must, but I will die before I speak another word."

Without acknowledging the murderer, Sam pulled Kael from his sheath and commanded the blade to bring forth its fire. The king lifted the weapon in front of his lips. "Are you ready for action?"

The blade's confirmation was sadistic. "Make the torture last, Sam. I want to savor his cries. He deserves to be punished. I want to feel the warmth of his blood as I slice him in two. Allow my blade to bathe in his life source."

Sam relished the thought as he lifted Kael above his head. The people within the theatre were awed by the blade's power as he addressed them. "People of Brandor, I hold in my hand a sword given to me by Bassorine himself. This is Kael, the one and only Sword of Truth and Might."

The entire theatre, especially the military leaders, watched with great admiration as their murmurs filled the room. They all knew how treasured such an item was and the fact their new king possessed a weapon of this magnitude was glorious.

"I will use this sword to strike down our enemies! I say we start with this traitor! What say you?" Sam pointed the tip of the sword in the killer's direction.

Everyone in the theatre exploded. Seeing their late king's murderer brought to justice would give them great pleasure. They screamed in unison, "Hail, King Goodrich! Hail, King Goodrich! Hail, King Goodrich!"

Sam brought his hand up to silence the crowd. He commanded the blade to invoke a new element. Kael brought forth the destructive force of water as Sam looked at Double D. "Why did you kill these men?"

Again, the assassin spit on the floor and cursed him. The crowd shouted profanities. Once again, their king held up his hand to command their silence.

Sam placed Kael's blade on Double D's shoulder. "Why did you kill these men?"

The assassin screamed as the watery flame ripped at his skin. He wanted to spit on the floor, but Kael's power was overwhelming. "I was hired! It was only a job! I did it for the coin!"

Again, the people cursed the assassin. Sam silenced them. "Who hired you?"

"I don't know," he cried. "I get my work through a man called Assistant Kane. He pays when I'm finished."

Sam held his hand high to quiet the people as he asked his next question, "When are you to meet this man to get your money?"

Again, the power of the sword ripped at the assassin's skin. "I don't know! I seek him out after the job is done!"

Sam only had one more question before bringing down judgment. "What's your name, murderer?"

Double D fought to avoid the question. It took many moments before Kael was able to break through the man's determination to stay silent. The killer had not said his name since he was a child and uttering it pained him to such a degree he wailed in agony as the memories of his dead father returned. "Dawson Drake. My name is Dawson Drake," he sobbed.

Sam motioned for his guards to lift Double D to his feet and spoke for all to hear. "Dawson Drake, I hold you responsible for your actions. The murders committed against King Aaron Brandor and General Justin Graywind will be brought to justice on this day, in front of the people of this mighty kingdom."

Sam was not about to make this man's death an easy one. He was enraged at how this piece of garesh caused so much pain to so many people in such a short period of moments. He took Kael and placed the point of the blade against the front of the assassin's right shoulder and commanded the fire to come forth. He pushed the blade at a slow, steady pace into the assassin's flesh. The killer cried out as the heat cauterized the wound.

The crowd cheered as they watched their king twist the weapon. The louder the man screamed, the happier the people became.

Sam withdrew the sword and used Kael in the same manner, except now, he dug the blade into the opposite shoulder. The screams of the killer were horrific as the crowd continued to savor his torture.

Sam abused Dawson Drake until he was satisfied the pain had degraded the man to his lowest point. After having the killer placed into the perfect position, Sam lifted Kael into the air, commanded the blade to quiet its power, and brought the sword down on top of Double D's head as hard as he could. The force split the assassin in two as if a warm knife had cut through a stick of soft butter. After a few short moments, the assassin's weight shifted and both halves opened like a fisherman's net while dropping its catch on the deck. The life spilled out of Double D as his guts spewed across the stage. His two halves fell in opposite directions.

The crowd glorified their new king's actions, screaming their praises and asking the gods to grant Sam a long life. Sam held up his hand to silence the mob, then commanded the guards and every member of the military present to leave and build a platform to celebrate Keldwin and Aaron's passing. "I command you all to go to the arena after Late Bailem. We will celebrate these men and light the fires to set their souls free."

He turned and looked at Double D's remains. "Cut him up. Throw him into pails and feed him to the birds."

The people of Brandor cheered as Sam took Shalee by the hand and exited through the back of the theatre.

Gods Who Bet
The Hidden God World of
Ancients Sovereign

Lasidious went to the home of Yaloom on Ancients Sovereign to deliver a message. When he arrived, he found that Mieonus was present. They were watching the assassination of Aaron take place as they glared into an indoor waterfall which fell into a large pool far below the level where they stood. This flowing sheet of water was a lot like watching a giant TV, except the images being portrayed were of an event in progress.

The God of Greed had exquisite taste. His home represented everything he considered to be the best. Though he was plain to look at, his fingers covered with priceless rings, he was self-centered and his home showed his vanity.

The pool at the bottom of the waterfall had many large gems which shimmered from the bottom of its depths. The water continued to cascade over many other smaller falls while moving through the structure.

The base of this mansion had been built into the center of a 1,100 foot fall. A hole had been created in the top of the structure. Every ounce from the fall funneled into this opening and moved throughout the home before it exited the bottom and fell the remaining 500 feet.

Despite the massive force which poured into the top of the structure, it was pleasant where they stood. Yaloom had engineered the mansion in such a way the deafening sound was not heard on this main level. He had smoothed the walls inside to direct the flow for good conversation.

Lasidious had come to the home to call a meeting about the pieces of the Crystal Moon, but instead, he watched the events unfold within the water, seeing everything as it happened in the theatre of Brandor. Realizing the images were of current events, it was too late to do anything to stop them. He watched as the assassin shoved his knife into Aaron's jaw and through the top of his head. He saw Shalee freeze the crowd and release Sam from the magic to help her figure out how to deal with the situation. He admired the way the mortals worked together.

To his delight, Lasidious could see Mosley sitting on the stage, but the people did not know the God of War was present. An orange glow surrounded the wolf within the water's projections, signifying his invisibility.

Lasidious screamed at Yaloom and Mieonus after watching the guard tackle Double D. "Why would you have wanted this assassination? What on Grayham would you expect to accomplish by manipulating this event?"

Yaloom was defensive. "The Kingdom of Brandor will be weakened by this. Brandor's army and their government will be disorganized for the upcoming war."

"Don't you realize what you've done? I'm surrounded by idiots."

"We aren't idiots," Mieonus snapped. "This event will benefit the plans of our team."

"Your team? Most of your team is doing nothing. There's so much more that could be done. You order one assassination and expect it will win your team the pieces of the Crystal Moon? This assassination will not accomplish what you want it to."

"It will," Yaloom shouted. "I..."

Lasidious trumped Yaloom's voice. "No! It will not help. The two of you may have ruined your chance to secure the first two pieces of the Crystal Moon. You have created stronger leadership in Brandor. How could you be this stupid?"

"Stop calling us stupid, or we'll..."

"You'll what, Yaloom? You'll do nothing. You're scared of the Book. You're scared of what it will do if you try. Spare me your idle threats. You don't even understand why I'm angry."

Yaloom rebutted, "Then explain."

Lasidious took a few deep breaths and spoke in a calmer tone. "Sam's mind and the power of his wife will not create a weakness. Have you forgotten how smart Sam is? Have you forgotten, Bassorine gave him the Sword of Truth and Might? Have you forgotten, Shalee is becoming a powerful sorceress? She's already a phenomenal power on Grayham. For you to make her a queen is ridiculous. Bassorine brought her here for a purpose. Don't you think there was a reason? He must've known something we don't. Whatever his secret was, I intend to find out."

"We didn't know the extent of Shalee's power," Mieonus barked. "We weren't watching her growth. When we instigated the assassinations, how could we have known Sam would end up as king, and Shalee, as queen? We couldn't control the changes Keldwin made to hold his tournament early. When we set these events in motion, we didn't know Sam would be given an invitation to fight. Somehow, he..."

Lasidious interrupted, throwing his hands in the air. "Yet, somehow he found a way to become king without lifting a finger in Brandor's arena. You would've known these things by paying attention. Come with me. I'll show you what the situation is like. Meet me at Brandor's theatre next to Mosley." With a grunt, the Mischievous One disappeared.

When Lasidious reappeared, he was standing next to Mosley on the stage, invisible to the people who filled the royal theatre. Soon, the four deities stood together. They said nothing as they watched Sam place the blade onto Double D's shoulder. This was going to be an event worth watching. Each took a seat on the stage's floor.

Sam commanded the blade to search for truth. They listened as Dawson Drake cried out his name. The agony of the assassin's screams, along with the smell of his burnt flesh, filled the air as Sam dug the blade of fire into his body. The people cursed Double D as he cried out. When Sam finished the torture, they watched as Kael sliced through the killer, spewing his guts across the stage.

Lasidious decided the moment was right to make conversation, a conversation which could only be heard by gods. "Mosley, you've managed to get Sam into the best position possible to use his full potential in the upcoming war. I must admit, I'm impressed, my four-legged friend. Not only have you made Sam a king, but you've convinced the mortal to make Shalee his queen. I should keep a better eye on you. It looks like you're a born manipulator, just like me."

The wolf turned and looked at his fellow gods. "Sam is impressive to watch. It did not take more than a few simple suggestions to turn him into a leader. I would not say I am a master of manipulation like you, Lasidious. I was not a god when I first began the journey to help Sam. I could tell him what to do rather than make suggestions like we do now. I had an unfair advantage. It is easier to make things happen when you do not need to obey the laws of free will within the Book."

Yaloom cut in. "Fair or unfair, I'm impressed." He began to polish one of his many rings. "I should have been watching to see what was going on in Brandor. I had no idea you had Sam in a position to become a king. I decided to watch the assassination and ignored everything else. Mieonus and I felt this would weaken the kingdom, but I fear we've made an error in judgment."

"Ya think?" Lasidious snapped. "You two managed to kill everyone who stood in Sam's way. You just handed him the crown within a matter of days. Nice work. Please remind me why you're gods."

"Okay, we get it already," Mieonus sneered. "It's clear this isn't what we intended to happen. Answer this question, Lasidious. What have *you* been up to?"

Lasidious rubbed his hands together in front of a sinister smile. "I just might show you."

Mosley ignored his response and took a few more of his moments to brag. "Sam has taken control of this situation. Look at how the people love him for his leadership. I am surprised at how Shalee's power is advancing. She has only failed to command her staff once."

"Shalee is quite impressive," Lasidious responded.

Mosley changed the subject. "I found your George."

"Really?" Lasidious said without showing his surprise, "I was wondering when someone would find him."

"I sensed his presence yesterday just before Early Bailem. He teleported to meet Kepler and his brothers on the north side of Gessler."

Mosley turned and looked into the God of Mischief's eyes and waited for his response. "And, what did you find? It seems our game is coming full circle. It will be harder to deceive one another now that we know what to look for."

Lasidious knew he could still speak with George in his dreams if he needed to. Whether Mosley was watching or not, this would not be an issue once he spoke with the mage. This was going to make things easier to keep an eye on the gods involved in the game.

"I found out they were headed north into the Barbarian Kingdom," Mosley answered. "If he is able to teleport, someone has given him information on how to find power of his own."

"Really?" Mieonus oozed. "I thought you were staying neutral and allowing the teams to manipulate the people."

Lasidious laughed. "No, I said I wouldn't cheat and tell either team anything in an unfair way. I said I wouldn't help the team I was on. I pulled myself off for a reason. I needed to be able to do what I wanted. As it turns out, it was a good thing I did. The two of you don't seem to have a good grasp on how to get things done."

"Stop with all the digs," Yaloom snapped. "We get it already. You're the master of manipulation. That was made clear when you found a way to kill Bassorine with the Book." Yaloom paused. "It was a clever manipulation."

"Thank you, Yaloom. There may be hope for you yet," Lasidious said with a verbal pat on his own back.

Mieonus rolled her eyes. "Could you possibly have a bigger opinion of yourself? For your sake, that over-inflated head of yours best not leak."

Mosley sniffed Mieonus' lifted heels. "Delightful."

The wolf looked at Lasidious. "I will be watching George from now on. I noticed he teleported without a spell or staff. He's controlling advanced magic for this world. We both know the only way he could accomplish this."

"You're perceptive, Mosley," Lasidious responded. "What else have your senses been telling you?"

Yaloom and Mieonus agreed with Lasidious the wolf's perceptions were accurate, although they did not know why they were agreeing and waited for the wolf to answer.

"Well," Mosley said in a calm voice, "we all know George had no natural magical abilities when you retrieved him from Earth. The others would have known if you tried to bring a magical being forward. The only way George could have gained his abilities is by eating the heart of someone before their soul left for the Book. How about we level with each other and you tell me how I am doing so far? You have given George the ability to command a grand pack of his own."

"All I did was tell the horse where the water was. George chose to go and drink it. I have been careful not to break the rules within the Book, as I'm sure you have. Just like you, I've done nothing more than make a few simple suggestions to motivate the mortal while starting on his road to glory."

"I would not call eating someone's heart a simple suggestion," Mosley responded. "I would like to know whose heart he ate. Who did he kill for his power?"

"Whether it is a simple suggestion or not is a matter of opinion. I'll answer your question as to whose heart he ate, but everything I say will fall under the rule of Fromalla."

Mosley thought a moment. He knew Fromalla was a rule, or rather a law, created by the gods and written in the pages of the Book of Immortality. It was created due to the overwhelming lack of trust the deities had for each other after the God Wars. Though they had fought together, once the wars were over, a battle of a new kind began. Each needed a group of worshippers to increase their power after the worlds were created. In the process, they shared each other's secrets to try to undermine each other's campaigns.

It was Bassorine who had called a meeting to suggest they vote to pass this law. The rule was long and covered all angles. It basically meant, if two or more of the Collective gathered to share something which was said to be under the rule of Fromalla, it could not be divulged to any of the others without penalty of being made mortal.

"I agree. Our conversation will be under Fromalla," the wolf responded. "Who is the person George killed?"

Lasidious looked at Yaloom and Mieonus. He watched as they nodded and verbally agreed to obey the law. The Mischievous One continued. "The mage, Amar, from Lethwitch."

Yaloom and Mieonus gasped. Mosley snorted, "Are you referring to the same Amar who studied under the Head Master on Luvelles?"

"Yes, I am referring to *that* Amar."

The wolf scratched the back of his ear. "How was he able to do this without Amar using his magic? Amar was easily the most powerful mage on Grayham."

"He was powerful, but he didn't have the drive to go after the kind of power George does. The power Amar commanded was wasted on his inhibitions. He was scared to do anything with it. Sure, he had his moments of courage, but when it came down to it, he was a sheep."

Mosley snorted again as a wolf would. "So, you're saying Amar was a follower and not a leader, but that does not tell me how George killed him."

"I was getting to that. It happened like this. He shook the mage's hand and turned the most critical parts of him to stone."

Again, Mosley was confused. "Okay, I will bite, how did he do this?"

Lasidious lied back on the stage before he responded. "I told him where the Staff of Petrafaction was in the Cave of Sorrow. He went in to get it and drank the liquid inside of its hollow center."

"Never mind the fact he got past Maldwin," Yaloom jumped in. "I'm sure that's a story of its own. How did he learn to control the ability to change things to stone once he drank the liquid?"

Lasidious smiled again. "Now that's the best part of this whole story. Amar taught his killer how to control the power which killed him. Quite the irony, don't you think?"

Mieonus shook her head and pushed her long brunette hair clear of her face as she allowed a sadistic smile to appear. Her brown eyes showed her pleasure. "I'm sure you enjoyed yourself when you watched him die. I know I would have. It seems you've been positioning George for great things. What do you feel he will be able to accomplish with his new power?"

Lasidious shrugged. "Now, now, now...you don't think I'm going to give you all the answers. You'll just have to tag along and see."

"Ha! You can't blame me for being anxious to know more," the goddess chided. "I think your manipulations are wonderful, Lasidious." Mieonus clapped. "I must hang out with you more often. You play in a much better sandbox of evil than I do."

Lasidious laughed, "What do you say we head over to Grayham's arena and watch them light the fire to celebrate these men? We can talk more there."

"That sounds like a good idea. I haven't been to an event like that for a while," Yaloom commented as they all disappeared.

The gods sat on top of the highest point of the arena as they watched the fire consume Keldwin and Aaron's bodies. Sam lit the wood with Kael's flame and sat on his new throne within the royal box to watch.

Four Days Later

The harvests for the Kingdom of Brandor were moving forward as planned, and the crops were replenishing themselves as promised by Alistar. Today was the last day for collecting the harvest and all of it would need to be stored in the barns.

770 wagons, built by the king's army, were making their way to the coastal cities. The harvest was so plentiful most every man with a wagon was helping in the effort. In total, there were over 38,000 wagons on the roads, each overflowing with crops.

To the north, the Kingdom of Bloodvain was also gathering their crops, but there was nothing special about this event. Life moved forward as usual for everyone—everyone, that is, except Senchae Bloodvain and his mages, who would be meeting George outside the city walls. The Barbarian King's scouts had located the man, along with his jaguar, and returned to inform Senchae George should arrive at the city gates around Late Bailem.

Senchae wanted to confront the human before he challenged him in front of his military. The warning of the talking bull had made him fearful he would lose his crown, and he was not about to let things go that far. He would meet the human with his mages and kill George before he had the chance to step foot inside the city.

Since the meeting was not until later, there was a meal to be eaten first. At that very moment, Kepler, Keller, Koffler and George were sitting down to have a nice breakfast. They were a half-day's walk from Bloodvain and figured they would arrive before dark. Keller caught a baby fawn, and the mage was sitting by the fire with his stick outstretched to cook his portion.

"Yuck," Keller growled. "How can you stand to eat it that way? You're cooking the flavor out of it, George."

"Yeah, the flavor out of it," Koffler added in his normal idiotic way, his mouth full of bloody flesh.

"Shut up," Kepler snapped. "I'm in no mood for your stupid antics today." The demon turned to George. "We're not far from the city. What's the plan?"

"As soon as the tigers you sent for arrive, we'll continue on to Bloodvain."

"I like the idea of back-up," Kepler responded between licks as he cleaned himself. "But, if you win the fight, do you really think the king's mages will let you just take over the kingdom? I don't think they'll want an outsider running their way of life. We both know their invitation to fight for the crown will be revoked if you manage to defeat their champion. I doubt they'll serve you."

"Kepler, my friend, my black, furry friend, you underestimate me still. Allow me to show you how I'm going to get the people to love us and stop the king's mages." George reached into his pack and pulled the sleeping Maldwin from it.

The demon looked at the rat and was up to speed. "Hmmm, nice, you teleported to Lethwitch to retrieve the rat."

Kepler said hello to Maldwin in the rat's language, then turned to George. "What do you want me to tell the little guy to do? I could tell him, you said to tell him, that I should tell him that you said telling him was a good idea, to tell me something that I could tell you, so you could tell me, to tell him it's a good idea, for him to tell me, to tell you that he understands."

George laughed, "You're never going to let me live that one down, are you?"

"Nope, never gonna, George," Koffler said with a stupid laugh as he started to choke on his food.

Kepler and Keller growled at their brother as if they were using the same mind. "Shut up, idiot!"

George continued. "Anyway, I want you to ask Maldwin, not tell him, to please give the barbarian people a vision of how great we are when I give him the signal. I want to walk around Bloodvain and not worry about our safety. I also want him to send his visions to the king's mages if we find ourselves in trouble. Just tell Maldwin to keep an eye out."

Kepler did as asked. Maldwin said he understood. Once the four tigers arrived, George waved his hand over them to hide their presence, then asked Koffler and Keller if they could see the beasts. Once the demons said they could not, George asked Kepler the same question. The jaguar confirmed he could see them just fine. Once again, George waved his hand to hide Kepler's brothers, then the group was on its way to take the crown of Bloodvain.

The four gods—Lasidious, Mosley, Mieonus, and Yaloom—now in their invisible state, watched the conversation between George and the cats.

"I guess I understand what George is up to," Mosley said as he watched the group head out. "It will be interesting to see how this turns out. He is smart and a decent tactician."

Lasidious smiled. "I was worried about how he was going to take the crown, but I must give him credit. He has a good plan. Seven giant cats and the rat can be a powerful force. When I told him about the staff, I never expected he'd turn Maldwin into an ally. He intends to use the rodent's talent as a tool to accomplish his goals. If he does everything right, he might pull this off. I wish I could tell him how to do it. I'd like more of a guarantee this is going to work."

Mosley nodded. "I know what you mean. I wanted to tell Sam Double D was about to kill Aaron, but I'm bound by the same law you are."

The deceiver chuckled. "Sometimes we make the damnedest rules."

"Agreed," Mieonus interjected. "But, I suppose the rules have their purpose or they wouldn't have been made."

"I think it makes the game more fun," Yaloom said as he turned his attention away from George's group. "Shall we follow them to see what happens?"

Lasidious responded, "Yes, let's follow. It will be interesting to see how this plays out."

Mosley sighed as they began to walk. "Being a god, and having the ability to summon anything you want, kills the idea of betting on whether George will become king. I enjoyed betting when I was mortal."

Lasidious nodded, "Instead of a reward for winning, we could require the loser to perform embarrassing acts as punishment for losing."

"I like that idea," Yaloom added as he pulled a ring from one hand to put it on the other. "We wouldn't be as bored and it would give us a few laughs. Let's swear on the Book of Immortality we have to do these things, providing it doesn't embarrass us in front of our followers, of course."

Lasidious smiled. "I'll agree to that. How about you, Mosley?"

"I can do that." The wolf grinned. "This is the most cub-like thing I have agreed to, but it should be fun. I must admit, I never thought that, as a god, I would be doing something so foolish."

Later that Evening, Outside of Bloodvain

The gods found a large rock and took places on top of it to watch the meeting. Yaloom was unable to sit. He had lost the first bet as to when George would dispatch his invisible cats to circle behind the barbarians. He had to stand with his robes draped over his right arm and a red bow placed over his privates until the next bet was lost.

Senchae and his mages were now within eyesight of George. They dismounted their specially-bred horses and tied them to a nearby tree. Everyone walked toward each other. Both sides were cautious as they drew closer, but George was relaxed.

❖⊱⊰•⊱⊰❖

"This isn't what I had in mind," Yaloom said, disgusted.

"Shut up and pay attention," the others responded as they watched the two groups converge.

❖⊱⊰•⊱⊰❖

George took a deep breath as the group stopped in front of the barbarians. The king was massive, a true force of nature, the likes of which George had never seen. Senchae's dark skin only added to this perception. He whispered to Kepler, "Holy garesh, this guy has muscles in places I never knew existed. Maybe you should tell Maldwin to be ready."

"Agreed," the demon whispered. "You should be careful." The jaguar spoke to the rat to make sure he was prepared to use his visions.

George smiled and addressed Kepler again. "Don't worry, I've got it all under control. I have a plan." George took note of the positions of Kepler's subjects. As instructed, they had crept up behind the king's five mages and were ready to attack.

The groups stood on a well-used road of packed dirt which led to the city. They had stopped by a rock, surrounded by trees, the same rock which held the invisible gods. They were alone and George loved the idea.

The human addressed the king. "I'm assuming you are Senchae Blood-vain."

The big man responded, "Who are you to call me by my name? You're a sorry excuse of a man. You haven't earned the right. I should kill you where you stand for such disrespect. I'm a king, and you'll address me as such."

Kepler watched as George began to laugh. Senchae didn't know how to respond. Kepler had seen George do this before. It made him nervous. The jaguar remembered how he felt when he was unsure what George was made of. He knew the human intended to pick a fight.

"Do you meet everyone outside your city's walls?" George asked. "I think someone told you I was coming. You obviously know I'm here to take your crown off that thick head of yours. It'll look much better on me than on top of that nightmare you call a face."

Without waiting for a response, George gave the signal for the cats to attack. He squeezed Maldwin's tail to send the king a vision of helplessness. The claws of all the tigers, along with Kepler's brothers, tore into the sides of the unsuspecting group of magic user's heads. The sheer force of the blows knocked all but one unconscious. This man, though he tried to speak his words of power, did not have the moments necessary to finish before Keller's jaws closed about his head and slung him from side to side. The barbarian's head separated from the rest of his body. Keller spit it to the ground and watched it roll before lowering his snout and smelling the barbarian's life source as it poured out. The cat slurped from the pool of red, still in his invisible cover.

Senchae had grabbed his head and was struggling to fight off Maldwin's vision. To everyone's surprise, he was able to overcome the emotion and attack George. The mage reacted by lifting his hand. George pinched his fingers together (just as his favorite villain had done in yet another one of his movies while on Earth) and lifted his arm into the air. The barbarian rose from the ground and grabbed his throat as he began to choke. George grinned as he thought, *May the force be with me.*

The gods were making bets. Lasidious was first to speak. "I bet he takes him prisoner," he said as he looked at the others.

Yaloom hoped to be able to put on his robe. "I say he kills him."

Mosley was next. "Taking him as a prisoner is the best move."

Mieonus laughed as she chimed in. "I agree with Yaloom. George will kill him. The mortal's emotions will get the best of him."

The mage spoke with a coldness Kepler had heard once before. The cat heard this wickedness on the day George's eyes had changed color. "Are you freaking kidding me, Senchae? Did you really think I'd come unprepared? I told you I was here to take your crown. Do you think you're so powerful you could get rid of me? I should snap you in half."

As George spoke his voice grew louder. "I should allow my friends to feast on you!" George waved his free hand and the cats appeared below the gasping man as he hung suspended. "Do you really want to die, King of Barbarians?"

Senchae searched for the breath to respond. "I'll die before I serve you. Kill me now."

George lowered the big man to the ground, but instead of choking him, he bound his arms and legs with unseen cords. With a calculated approach, he moved his face only inches from the large man's. "You'll die, don't worry about that, but not before I use you as my puppet. There are many things I can do to make you cooperate. We can do this the hard way, and I will choke you to the point of suffocation, then bring you back from a near death, or you can do as I say.

"When I'm done, I'll spare your family a painful death, and allow them to have a peaceful existence and enjoy their lives. The only one who has to die, once I have your crown, is you. I'm sure you don't want your family to suffer."

George paused, waiting for the king's response. But, when one never came, he added, "What's it going to be, Senchae?"

"My family would rather die than serve you," he refuted, spitting in George's face. "Even my son would not serve a swine like you."

George wiped the spittle from his cheek, not allowing his emotions to control the situation. He took a few deep breaths as he thought about how he would react if he were in the big man's shoes. He wouldn't have given any information about his own son if he were in Senchae's position, and now, he realized he had an opportunity to use the Barbarian's information against him, but he needed to know more.

"So, how is your son?" the mage asked as he led the barbarian into his set-up. "Is he still as proud as his father?"

The reaction was just as George expected. "Of course he's proud! He's a Barbarian King's son. We're not like the swine from the south. We are a people of strength."

"Hmmm, funny you should say that. From where I stand, looking down at you, there isn't much strength in front of me. I see a king who has been defeated, one who would rather kill his family before admitting to his weaknesses."

The barbarian showed his rage. "Take your magic away and you'd be nothing! You'd be just another weak excuse of a man from the south!"

George laughed. "Does your son have the same weaknesses as his father?"

"You don't know my son. All barbarians are strong. You'll die for your insults."

The king twisted and turned, struggling to break free of his magical bonds. Once again the mage laughed, then he returned the insult, spitting in the face of his enemy to amplify Senchae's rage.

"My daughter, who is only eight seasons, could beat your son in battle. Do you think we should see whose kid is stronger, and let them decide our disagreement?"

George hoped the king's son was close to the age he used for his fictitious daughter. If he wasn't, there was a back-up plan.

"The big man scoffed. "Your child commands magic, or you would not be wasting my moments with such nonsense."

"She doesn't command magic. She's a scrapper. I'd be willing to bet everything I have she would kill your son in the arena of Bloodvain."

"Your child is no match for a barbarian. You're wasting valuable moments. I'll never serve you, and my family will not serve you. They would rather die first, you piece of garesh."

Once again, the king spit in the mage's direction. George knew the reaction was a sign Senchae's son wasn't old enough, or he would have accepted the challenge. The moment had come for Plan B. He turned to Kepler and spoke to the demon as if the barbarian was not present.

"Kepler, I thought you told me the people from the north were strong. This man won't let our children fight for the crown. Don't you think this is a pathetic display of weakness? I think we should spread word of how weak their king is."

Kepler had an idea of where the mage was going with his questioning. He could already see the barbarian biting his tongue, his pride baiting him.

The undead cat responded, "I agree. I'm disgusted. I thought a man from the north would have enough pride to accept such a challenge. Maybe his son is a daughter."

George laughed. Out of the corner of his eye, he could see the king was about to blow. "How true that is. I think Senchae has no clue that his son should be wearing a dress."

George and all the cats were now laughing. Even Maldwin began to laugh, though he didn't know why. It just felt like the proper thing to do to fit the mood.

This was all it took to instigate a reaction. Senchae's pride now gripped his emotions. "My son is not a girl! If he were old enough to fight your daughter, I would allow it. I would get no greater satisfaction than watching your daughter die in my arena."

George turned the heat up a notch, screaming his next statement, taking a stab at a confession. "Are you telling me your son is weak? Can't he beat a girl of only eight seasons? You're lying to me, Senchae! You're scared to put him in the arena!"

Bloodvain cursed. "A boy of only three seasons cannot be expected to fight! Let it be. You and I can settle this."

The king sighed. He realized he had said too much and had given George the information he was fishing for. He softened his voice. "Please, there must be a way to settle this dispute. I can give you anything you want. What can I do?"

Once again, George started to laugh. He had retrieved the information he was after. He stopped, and after a moment of dead silence, looked into the eyes of the begging king, speaking in a tone which sent a chill running up the gods' spines. "I want your son to die," he hissed.

The king screamed as he watched George give orders to the demon-jaguar. "Kepler, when it gets dark, take one of your brothers into the city. Find Senchae's son and bring him to me. I'll need your other brother to stay behind so I can communicate with the tigers."

George leaned over and whispered in Kepler's ear, "I would prefer the smarter of the two, if you don't mind."

"Ha! I understand. I will take Koffler with me, but what of the noise the child will make when we carry him out of the city? We'll be discovered when he cries."

George took a piece of cloth from his pack, tore a long thin strip from it, and tied it on Kepler's neck. He waved his hand across it twice and the strip disappeared. "This will make everything you carry silent. As long as you have the boy hanging from your mouth or even your teeth, he won't be heard. I suggest you take the baby in the middle of the night and use the darkness of the city to make your escape."

The demon enjoyed the cries of the Barbarian King. "Hiding is what I do. You forget, I'm the Master of the Hunt." The two demons ran toward the city in the fading light.

Once they were gone, George faced the begging king. After a moment, he found the anticipating eyes of the tigers and asked Keller to give the order for the cats to drag Senchae's mages into the trees. "Tell them they can dine on their flesh."

Keller gave the order. "I'm sure they'll enjoy the meal, but I don't think they like you."

"I don't need them to like me. I just need them to obey."

"Agreed," Keller said. The jaguar moved into the trees to join his feline companions in severing limbs for their meal.

George listened to the deep growls of the feeding cats for a moment, awed at the viciousness of their snarls, then turned back to the king. "That could be you, Senchae."

He lifted his hand into the air and used his magic to carry Senchae's big frame into the brush, taking another piece of cloth from his bag to use as a gag. He wanted to keep the road clear until Kepler returned with his brother. He hoped they would arrive before dawn. In the back of his mind, he knew the king's guards would come looking if Senchae was gone too long. He could only assume the barbarian had left his city without the knowledge of the others, since he had intended to confront George before he made it to the city. He was glad Lasidious had warned him this may happen, but he had been frustrated the god could not tell him how to kill the Barbarian King and take his crown.

The Grayham Inquirer

When Inquiring Minds Need to Know about their Favorite Characters

NIGHT has fallen across Grayham. George built a fire he could put out if need be. Maldwin ate his cheese and fell asleep. The mage has commanded two tigers to stand guard over the Barbarian King and directed the others to watch for unwanted visitors from the edge of the tree line.

MOSLEY, Yaloom, Mieonus, and Lasidious are sitting by the fire, invisible to the mortals. Yaloom and Mieonus are in the betting penalty box since they were wrong about George taking Senchae as prisoner. They are wearing each others' clothes.

CELESTRIA is 32 Peaks of Bailem from having the baby. The elven witch family is more pleasant to be around since their last conversation. The goddess has cooked everyone dinner and, despite her obvious lack of talent for the culinary arts, the family is eating the dried-out platter of meat she set before them.

SAM is elated to hear the news: **Shalee is going to make him a father.** They have just returned from a dinner with the members of the Senate where they announced her pregnancy .

At dinner, some of the senators expressed concern. They have no idea when the war will take place, and wonder if the full mobilization of the military is necessary. Sam spoke of the gods' warning to be prepared, reminding them the kingdom would not have had three bountiful harvests if not for the blessing from Alistar.

This seemed to appease the members of his government. It was now just a matter of Peaks before Merchant Island would assign a value to the first shipment of the kingdom's harvests. Soon, they would be dispersed throughout the land and the kingdom's vaults would be full of coin. The funds to support the war would no longer be an issue.

Thank you for reading the Grayham Inquirer

A Babysitting Jaguar

"This is silly," Yaloom snapped as he walked around the fire in Mieonus' lifted heels. The dark blue of the shoe's surfaces clashed with the hair on his legs. "I don't like this game one bit. I never dreamt I'd be doing something this stupid. Lasidious, your cunning mind is dreadful."

"Quit moving that sniveling snout," Mieonus barked, with arms crossed and eyes gleaming with irritation. "I can't bear the thought of wearing those shoes ever again after you've touched them. You're disgusting. I have to sit here in your body odor-filled robe and I'm not whining."

Yaloom stumbled as one of his heels doubled over, sending the god face first into the flames.

"It appears we have our own personal jester," Lasidious said, slapping his knee. "Yaloom, you're a fool."

"Ha, ha, ha, very funny. Enjoy your little moment at my expense. You'll lose a bet soon enough, then it'll be my turn. I'm sure we'll see who's laughing then."

The wood shifted as the God of Greed pushed clear of the fire. They all watched as George looked in their direction. They knew the mage felt their presence.

<hr />

"That's odd," George said as he waved his hand in the direction of the fire. He was sure something was there, but his attempt to reveal the unseen did not work. "Why would the fire do that? The logs shouldn't shift like that," he muttered. He waved his hand again for good measure and still nothing. He shrugged and waited for Kepler's return.

Before dawn, the jaguars appeared with the child. As soon as the Barbarian King saw his boy suspended with his cloth diaper caught on the tip of Kepler's massive tooth, he cried, begging George to listen.

"I'll do anything you want! Please, don't do this! He isn't old enough to understand why you're killing him. If you want my crown, take it."

George ignored the plea and took the baby from Kepler's mouth. The child was screaming. The morning filled with the child's cries. This amplified Senchae's desire to stop the boy's execution. George grabbed the baby by his right leg and lifted him. The child's face showed his horror as the mage dangled him upside-down.

Senchae begged, "Please! Please! Spare his life! Do what you want with me. Just let him live. He hasn't seen enough seasons. What is it you want? I'll do as you command."

Finally, the king said the words George wanted to hear. His manipulation had come full circle. He now had a marionette whose strings he intended to pull. He lowered the baby back to Kepler's mouth to shut it up, hanging it once again from the tooth.

"Time to bet," Lasidious said, "I think George is going to leave the child behind with Keller and take the king into the city."

Mosley placed his bet next. "I say he does the same thing, except he leaves Kepler behind, since he has the cloth to keep the child quiet."

As soon as Lasidious heard the wolf's logic, he said, "Damn, I forgot about that. Good call, Mosley."

Yaloom and Mieonus saw an opportunity to get back into their clothes and jumped at the chance to agree with Mosley. Lasidious rolled his eyes. "You two are sheep."

The group laughed. Once again, George turned his head in their direction and waved his hand to reveal the presence he felt, but nothing happened.

"He knows we're here," Yaloom whispered. "Do you think he's powerful enough to reveal our location?"

Lasidious smacked Yaloom's forehead with the palm of his hand. "What? Are you serious? Come on, Yaloom. He may feel a presence, but he isn't powerful enough to reveal our location. You use your moments to say the damndest things."

George turned back to the task at hand. After collecting his thoughts, the mage faced the big barbarian. "Your child cries to live, Senchae. Why would

I let him breathe another day? I know you came out of your city to meet me. I also know it was without the knowledge of your army. You wanted to kill me before I had the chance to challenge you. Tell me why I should change my mind. Why wouldn't I kill this boy of yours?"

Senchae, all 550 pounds of him, cried like a baby as he answered. "I'll give you my crown. Just let him live. I'll do whatever you tell me. I give you my word as a king. I swear it on my father's soul. Just take him back to the city. I'll go with you in peace."

George stood and grabbed the baby from the demon's jaws and held him in front of his father's face. Again, the chilled morning air filled with the boy's cries. The child reached for his father, but George pulled him back. "Do you take me for a fool, Senchae? Do you think I'm stupid? Do you believe I'd go into the city without a plan?"

The mage hung the child by his diaper on the jaguar's tooth and moved within inches of the king's tear-filled eyes. He hissed as he examined the puffiness of Senchae's dark skin surrounding them. "You'll go with me, barbarian. I'll leave your baby behind with my demon. If you make so much as one wrong move...your son is dead.

"We will go into the city. I will release your son once I send word I have the crown. As to your fate, you'll die in the arena as payment for sparing your boy's life. You'll be given your burial at sea and I'll harvest your organs myself. If you try anything stupid, I'll turn your son to stone."

George reached into his pack and took out a small worm he had found under a rock. He lifted it in front of the big man's face and smiled with a darkness that sunk into the heart of the king. The worm's flesh turned solid gray. George crumbled it in his fist, then dropped the dust to the ground.

The barbarian cried at the hopelessness of the situation. "I'll do as you ask. Please, give your word you won't kill him once you have the crown."

"What's the boy's name, Senchae?"

The man sobbed, "Sadridz."

"I'll spare the child. I give you my word." The mage sat. "But, if you so much as think one wrong thought, I'll gut him like a fish."

"I understand. What must I do? My general will soon be wondering where I am. It would be a good idea to get going."

George agreed and began giving orders. "Kepler, stay with the boy and keep an eye on him. When he gets hungry, feed him some of the bread from my pack. If I'm not back by tomorrow night, or if anyone tries to rescue the child, kill him, then get out of here."

George made sure the king was paying close attention to everything he said. "Tell Maldwin the moment has come to implement our plan with the king's people. Inform the tigers I'll be taking them into the city with me. Make sure they know they'll be unseen like before. Ask them not to attack unless I give the signal." Kepler did as he was asked. "Keller, once we're in the city, give the order for the tigers to attack, if needed."

"I can do that. Just say the word," the demon sibling replied.

George looked at the king as he walked over to Kepler. He lifted the baby by his leg and smiled as the child cried. Again, he dangled the boy in front of the frustrated father, but during this series of moments, he allowed the child's hand to touch his father's face. "Are you sure you're ready for this, Senchae? I'm only going to give you one chance to get it right." He backed away and pointed at Kepler's teeth as the cat yawned. He held Sadridz close to Kepler's gaping mouth. "I'd hate to see your son torn apart by those jaws."

"You don't need to remind me. Please! Allow me to say goodbye before we go. I won't ever see him again. Please! Allow me this last request."

George waved his hand and the barbarian could feel his magical bonds release. "Don't overestimate my generosity."

Senchae shook his head. George tossed the boy to his father. The barbarian caught him by an arm and a leg, then turned the child right-side up to cradle him, quieting his cries.

George allowed the barbarian to hold his child for quite a while before he ordered Senchae to put him down. Senchae shook his head and took his heavy, sleeveless shirt off to make a spot for the boy to sit.

In the back of George's mind, he was thinking, *There just might be a better use for you, Senchae. Killing you and your family may not be necessary. I'll investigate this on our way into the city. Oh, crap! I've got to prepare for the Serpent King's arrival. My hell, Lasidious, you could have given me a few more days to prepare.*

George barked another order. "Let's go! We don't want to worry your men."

"Agreed," the barbarian replied. "How do you want to do this?" It was like the king was a new man since he had the chance to say goodbye to his son. He seemed at peace, resolved to the idea of his death.

George took a long deep breath. "I may have thought of an idea which will make us both happy, Senchae. I'll tell you about it along the way. You might not have to die after all."

"Mosley, you won the bet," Lasidious said. "He left Kepler and took the rest, just as you said he would. Looks like I lost. What would you have me do?"

"I have a few ideas," Yaloom interjected while removing Mieonus' dress and grabbing his robe.

"So do I. There are many things we could do to him," Mieonus giggled as she rubbed her hands together.

Mosley turned to follow George. As he passed Senchae's son, he reached out with his invisible paw and touched the boy's head to give him peace. Kepler was sitting near the child. The wolf decided he would appear to the giant cat. He informed the others he would catch up, saying he wanted to comfort the frightened youngster further. The others agreed and left him behind.

There were other reasons the wolf wanted to stay, but he did not want the others to know. He needed to look his wife's killer in the eyes. He knew the laws within the Book bound him from taking revenge, but hoped the confrontation would give him closure. Although he could not punish Kepler for her death, the wolf needed to let the demon know he knew the cat had killed her.

Once the others were out of sight, Mosley allowed himself to be seen. The jaguar took a defensive position. "Relax, Kepler, I have come to speak with you. Do you know who I am?"

"I do," the demon responded. "I know who you are. I know you took Bassorine's place. What do you want with me?"

"I know I am not the god you serve, Kepler, but I am the god who is watching over this baby. I have blessed this child. You will not be able to kill him. He will remain quiet until George gets back. Play with him. Keep him entertained." Mosley nudged the boy with his snout and the child chuckled. "I think you will find him wanting to play. He has soiled his backside."

The demon shook his head in disgust. "You want me to *play* with it? I don't play with weaker species. It's degrading that I should have to sit with this foul creature in the first place."

A stern look appeared on Mosley's face. "It would be upsetting if this child does not find his stay in the woods to be peaceful." The wolf growled. "Keeping the child-cub happy is the least you can do, Kepler, since you killed my wife when you attacked the Unicorn Prince. I have not healed from the events of that day."

"I never meant to harm your wife, Lord Mosley, I swear it. She was in the way. I didn't even know who she was. Her death wasn't intentional. The weight of my body knocked her into the Prince's horn. I meant her no ill will."

The intensity of Mosley's growls increased. "She ended up dead anyway! You do not need to speak of it. I'm not here to seek revenge. I am here to ask you to care for this child. *Do not* let harm come to him. Play with him. Make him smile. That's all I ask.

"Forget your pride. You will make a fine toy for this child. Kids love furry things. Let him pull your tail, bite your ears, poke you in the eyes, and grab your tongue. The boy will enjoy his moments. He can use your coat to wipe the snot from his nose. You can lick his backside clean. I am sure you are willing to do this. Consider this small task my way of forgiving you for killing my Luvera. It is your choice, Kepler. What do you say?" Mosley looked the cat square in the eyes.

"I give you my word I'll take care of the boy, Lord Mosley," Kepler said, bowing. "Thank you for your forgiveness."

With that, the wolf-god disappeared from the cat's sight. He took a few moments to watch Kepler to ensure the jaguar would hold true to his word. After the first lick of the child's bottom and seeing Kepler cringe, Mosley grinned, then ran to catch up with the others.

Meanwhile, George talked with the king as they traveled. "You know, Senchae, we could handle this a better way. It's obvious you're a man who's willing to give his life for his family. I respect that. It's also obvious the people you have surrounding you aren't powerful enough to protect you. The mages you had as your counsel were weak. You know this."

"It would appear this is true."

The mage hesitated. "I wonder...why do you find the people of the south to be so pathetic? Is it because you perceive them as weak?" The barbarian hesitated to answer. "Speak freely. Let's talk as friends, Senchae."

"What on Grayham is he doing?" Lasidious asked as he listened in on the conversation. "This is a twist I didn't see coming. If he does what I think he's going to, it will be brilliant. Yaloom, do you see the brilliance?"

The God of Greed had a deer-in-the-headlights stare. Mieonus wasn't much different. Lasidious snapped out a retort in frustration. "Where's Mosley when I need to speak with someone who understands strategy? How in all the worlds could either of you be gods?" He didn't wait for a response. Instead, he turned his attention back to the conversation between George and Senchae.

The mage could see Senchae's hesitation. "Look, I already know how you feel. So, give me a straight answer."

"Yes," the big man replied. "We feel the people of the south are weak, but I've never met anyone like you. I must say you've changed my mind in some ways."

"My name is George. I allow only my friends to call me this. You can call me George, if you wish."

The barbarian was now more confused than ever. "I don't understand."

"I imagine you wouldn't. Let me explain. The more I think about it, I feel you and I can help each other. Your goal is to defeat the people of the south, correct?"

"Yes. What does this campaign have to do with us?"

"Maybe, we can work together to kill everyone in Brandor who won't serve us."

"I'm listening," Senchae said without hesitation. "I like what I'm hearing. To dominate the south would bring honor to my kingdom."

"You need a consulate to protect you. I also want the power to defeat the Kingdom of Brandor. We could join forces to achieve our goals."

George stopped and looked up at the royal wall of a man. "I don't need to be a king to get what I want. The two of us can accomplish great things without sacrifice. Let's go back to get your son. We will bring him with us. You'll announce me as your counsel. I'll use the rat's visions to give your military leaders the idea everything is okay. All I want is for my family to be treated as you would treat your own...and we'll need to feed my animals."

George passed his hand through the air. All six invisible cats appeared next to Maldwin, who had been walking with them. The rodent jumped into

George's arms and began to nervously twitch his nose. He still felt like dinner being around the big cats. Maldwin looked up at the mage and with as brave of a face as he could muster, said, "Everything is A-okay, George!"

Senchae laughed at the rat's attempt at gallantry. "Then...you would like to form an alliance...and...I...still get to be king? You want to kill everyone in the south and take over their kingdom? What else do you want?"

"As I've said, my friend," George bowed to the ruler with his manipulative mind in full swing, "I want you to provide for my family and my pets. I want you to use me as your counsel and allow my power to protect you when I'm around. I never wanted to kill you, just get you to listen."

Senchae could not believe his ears. "I was convinced you were after my throne."

"Did you truly believe that? Think about it for a moment. Your city wouldn't listen to an outsider without your support. If I hadn't commanded your respect, you would have never taken me seriously. Besides, you intended to kill me first. I didn't have much choice. I had to force your hand. I couldn't allow you to rip me apart, now could I?"

Senchae gave a thoughtful grin. "You have demonstrated strength worthy of my respect." The king pondered these new ideas. "I like your mind. As allies, we could go after the lands of the south, but this will take a stronger army than I command. What other support can you draw to this campaign?"

Realizing his deception was unfolding without flaw, George reached up to pat Senchae on the shoulder. "Damn, you're a big S.O.B."

Senchae's brow furrowed, "S.O.B.?"

George chuckled. "It means nothing. Don't worry about it. Anyway...to answer your question...Kepler rules the giant cats on Grayham. You can see the alliance I have with him. Between his cats and his skeleton army, we will have a powerful force against Brandor. There is one other thing I'm working on, but you'll need to set aside your pride to make it work."

The Barbarian King was intrigued. "And, what would this be, George?"

The mage smiled when he heard the big man say his name, knowing for sure the barbarian was his puppet. "The Serpent King is on his way to meet me. He thinks you're dead and I'm the King of Bloodvain. I'm sure you can see we have a problem. I thought you would make me kill you, but as it turns out, we are going to be able to do great things together. How would you like to handle this situation?"

Senchae thought a moment. "My scouts could find him. We could meet him in his own territory. I don't think he has any idea what I look like."

George scratched the top of Maldwin's head as he pondered the situation. "I don't think we should go to his home without having an alliance first. Is there a place outside the city where your scouts could bring Seth? We could allow him to think I'm king until he leaves. Then, I'll follow him back to his kingdom once we have this alliance. I'll familiarize myself with his home, then teleport back and forth to deliver pertinent information. We should be able to coordinate our attacks this way."

The king enjoyed the mage's scheming. "Blood will flow in the rivers of Brandor. Your plan is strong. But, why would the serpent want to get involved in the affairs of war when his kingdom has lived in peace for so long?"

The mage held his free hand above the ground with his palm facing down. A pebble from the road floated upward. After capturing it in his hand, he responded while tossing it up and down. "That's an easy question to answer. Someone put it into his head Brandor is going to attack." George gave the barbarian the impression it was he who had done this.

"You are an ambitious soul. I would've never employed such tactics. I hate snakes. Perhaps, you can attend this meeting on your own. My scouts will tell the serpent you're their king. You can hold this meeting south of where we met. I have a home I often use to get away when I need moments to myself. With your hidden cats, my guards, and your rat, you should be safe."

"I agree," George replied. "Let's go back and get your son. Maybe you could have your cook prepare us a grand feast when we get to your castle."

"We will feast, but you cannot expect my military leaders to be eager to accept your presence. They are barbarian men. This change will challenge their pride."

Mosley lowered his head and began gnawing on his front paw. "I never saw that coming. I think George is smart to form this alliance. If he had killed Senchae, he would not gain the respect of the barbarian people. Senchae's support will be the key to his success."

"I agree," Lasidious replied. "I'm becoming more and more impressed as we go. George is brilliant. He can dispose of the king later. It will be interesting to see how he handles the barbarian's military leaders and the Serpent King."

Mieonus added, "George is, indeed, worthy of being a king." She adjusted her breasts to a sexier position within her gown. "I hope he succeeds." The goddess was becoming a fan of the mage. She was going to keep an eye on him. "I'm taking my leave. Mosley, I must say I have enjoyed your company." She vanished.

Mosley and Yaloom agreed and followed suit. Lasidious smiled as he vanished. The God of Mischief had avoided the consequences of the lost bet.

An Example Made

George, Senchae Bloodvain, the Barbarian King's son, Maldwin, and Kepler, along with the rest of their feline companions, arrived at the king's castle. As they had passed through the barbarian city, they turned many heads. Most men did not travel with seven man-eating cats and an oversized rat.

Bloodvain was a rugged city. Their surroundings reminded George of a national park with equally rugged people living in it. The expanse of the city was built within a heavy forest. It extended to the north until the tree line ended at the beach of the Blood Sea.

The Bloodvain River flowed from the Pool of Sorrow, through the Dark Forest, and through the center of Senchae's city. Heavy wooden bridges spanned its depths and the river was full of fish. In the short period it took to cross into the town, the group had seen two different men catching their dinner.

As they walked through the trees, George's frustration grew. Everywhere he looked, the place reminded him of log cabins—a lifestyle he loathed. He was careful to keep his feelings to himself, not wanting to strain his new relationship with the king. It was bad enough he had been sleeping on the ground, something he would never have done on Earth, but now he was faced with the likelihood of spending the rest of his life in a wooden shack. He hoped the king's castle was nicer. If it was, he would find a room there until he could build something better. He was not about to live like an animal. He missed his Gucci clothes.

As it turned out, Senchae's home was nothing more than a giant lodge. It was nicer than the rest of the city, but the mage felt it looked like the home of the Brawny paper towel man. It was not a place for George. He would have to figure out a way to renovate, but for now, this termite buffet would have to do.

Everywhere George looked, he saw trophies from the king's hunts. Heads of animals which resembled deer, boar, mountain goat, minotaur, mounted fish, and various birds hung all over the walls. Life-sized, stuffed animals in various poses were scattered throughout the structure. He saw bears, gorillas, buffalo-looking beasts, and after the third giant cat, he stopped Senchae.

Kepler and his posse were agitated. The idea of their feline family being used as trophies was not sitting well. George insisted this issue be resolved. The king apologized, then had his servants remove the trophies of every cat in the castle-lodge. This seemed to suffice. Kepler calmed his subjects.

Once in the throne room, the king's general entered with three high-ranking officers of the Barbarian Army. From the door they entered, they missed seeing their king's travel companions. Fergus expressed his concern about the company Senchae was said to have been keeping. "Sire, rumors are spreading through the city. They say you travel with undesirables."

George, being the wisecracker, had to comment. "I wouldn't call us *undesirable*. I'd call us, diversified."

The leader of the army spun around. Realizing he had spoken in front of the king's company, he faced his king and bowed. "Sire, forgive my intrusion."

Bloodvain frowned. "Get up, Fergus. If the moment of your intrusion had been less than perfect, I would have had you beaten. Introduce yourself to George Nailer. I met him south of the city. He shall act as my consulate."

"What?" Realizing his tone, the general added in a softer voice, "My King, your consulate, how could you possibly let this, this..."

"This what, General?" Senchae sat on his throne as he held Fergus' glare.

George interrupted. "Are you suggesting I'm not capable of doing the job? Or, are you bothered because I'm not barbarian?"

Fergus looked at Senchae, as if asking to confront the man from the south.

Senchae smiled, then looked at George. "Are you prepared for barbarian hospitality?"

"Definitely. That's what I'm here for."

Senchae slapped his hand on the arm of his throne. "Speak your mind, Fergus."

George decided to say something to stir things up before the general could speak. "I can handle this, My King."

The thought of George calling Senchae his king angered Fergus. His dark complexion portrayed his hostility as he pulled his braids clear of his eyes. "You're one of those pathetic souls from the south! Who are you to come into my home and act as if *my king* is your own?"

The manipulator held the general's chaotic gaze. "I'm the guy who is going to be protecting your king from now on. It seems you have a shortage of qualified people around these parts. Where were you when the king's mages failed him? Where were you when his son was taken from his bed in the middle of the night?"

"Bahhhh! I don't answer to you! I'd rather kill you. I despise ignorance."

"Ignorance? The last series of moments I checked, there was no ignorance in true statements. Let's face it, Fergus, you were nowhere to be found during either of those events. You didn't know where your king was. I'll bet no one knew his son was gone until this morning. Maybe you should have used the word *insolence*. This would better describe how I'm speaking. I'm pretty sure I'm being insolent."

The leader of the army removed his fur cloak, then pulled his war hammer from his hip and pointed it at George. Each one of the seven cats took defensive positions and snarled in a display of power. They spanned the width of the throne room and warned the overzealous barbarian he was making a stupid decision. Even Maldwin was ready to use his visions. His head was sticking out of George's pack. As he looked over the mage's shoulder, his nose twitched with excitement.

"It seems you do not fight your own battles," Fergus sneered as he studied the opposition. "If you didn't have your companions to protect you, you'd be dead."

George laughed, then looked at Senchae. "Maybe a demonstration is in order."

The king stood from his throne and spoke to the general. "I'll allow you to fight, but if you get blood on my trophies, you'll replace them with your own. I warn you, it's a mistake to fight this human. He's not weak."

"I know what I'm doing. I can protect you, Sire. You don't need this swine spreading his stench throughout our kingdom. I will govern your protection...not this piece of garesh!" The general spun his hammer in his hand.

The king gave George a glance. "What of your cats?"

The mage turned and motioned for them to move toward the walls. He lowered Maldwin to the floor and asked Kepler to call the rodent to him.

"Tell the tigers I don't need their help. Make sure they don't interfere." He turned to Maldwin and held up his thumb. "Everything is A-okay, man!"

"Everything is A-okay, George," the rat responded in a high pitched voice, twitching his nose.

Again, the general rolled his hammer in his hand. "Are you going to play with your mouse, or are you going to fight?"

George rolled his eyes. "Yeah, yeah, yeah, blah, blah, blah, whatever, Sergeant Slaughter! Maybe there are others we should invite to watch. I'd hate for the people of this great kingdom to miss this event."

Senchae understood what George was thinking. He knew George was going to make an example of Fergus. He would allow an audience. It was long past the moment for apologies.

The king clapped his hands, summoning his servants, then sent them to retrieve all those who were in the castle-lodge. It was not long before the room was packed with onlookers, tucked between the giant cats, with an area cleared for the men to fight.

Senchae commanded the room's attention. "This battle will be to the death. These men have points of view they need to express. May their blood stain the stones of my throne room. Glory is in victory!" Bloodvain was anxious to see the extent to which George would go to make his point.

Fergus nodded, then looked at George. "This is to the death, swine! Leave our kingdom and I'll let you live! Go back to your pig-of-a-mother and crawl back into the hole you came from!"

George yawned. "Blah, blah, blah, blah, blah! Are we fighting, or are you going to talk me to death?"

Kepler growled. "Kill him, George! You can eat him like you eat every-one else."

Maldwin was excited and screamed as loud as his tiny body would allow, "I like cheese, George!"

Everyone in the room turned, including General Fergus, to look at the rat. After a moment of awkwardness, the barbarian shrugged, then turned his attention back to his enemy.

"What can I say?" George said with a sinister grin. "He likes his cheese!"

Without another word, Fergus attacked, swinging his hammer toward George's head. The mage dodged the advance, rolled out of the way and stood up. "General, is that the best you got? You're killing me, man. You've got to be better than that. Please don't disappoint by missing again."

Fergus screamed as he made his next advance. He missed. George shook his head and ticked his tongue. "How could you be the leader of a powerful army? Your movements are slow. My King, you need a new leader."

Senchae nor Fergus knew the mage had used his magic to increase his speed. George would toy with Fergus a bit more before taking the offensive. "Maybe you could hit me, General, or is the hammer too heavy? If I'm not mistaken, that's what it's made for, right? I think I'm right."

"You talk too much for a dead man," Fergus snapped as he charged. Again, his hammer found only air as it smashed into the floor without hitting its target. During this series of moments, he wouldn't give George the chance to make another comment. He lifted his hammer and took another swing. Again, he hit nothing but air.

"I'm disappointed, General. Are you freaking serious? My King, is this the best our army commands? I guess they can't all be built for war as you are, Sire." George knew he made Senchae sound strong with his comment, and slammed the general's pride during the same moments. With his point made—the moment had come to demonstrate his power.

The mage waited for the next swing of the general's hammer. As expected, Fergus raised the weapon over his head. George lifted both hands. Just as the hammer began its descent, a wicked storm of lightning arched from the tips of his fingers and slammed hard into his enemy's chest, sending the barbarian flying across the room toward Senchae who sat on his throne.

Senchae, seeing he was in jeopardy, was quick to react. As his general flew toward him, the king pushed from his chair and jumped skyward to avoid the collision. Fergus passed just beneath Senchae's feet and slammed into the throne. The general's weight carried the throne with him as he slammed into the wall some ten feet behind. The chair crumbled under Fergus' momentum. The general slid unconscious to the floor as the pummeled pieces of wood landed around his massive form.

Kepler was shocked. The demon cat studied the peoples' faces as the spectators' murmurs filled the room. The jaguar knew his friend had stolen Amar's power, but he didn't realize just how powerful George had become. The undead cat had seen other mages throughout his seasons, but had feared none of them. He needed to have a serious conversation with his partner.

"Garesh," Senchae shouted as he released his grasp on the heavy iron, candle chandelier. With his feet planted on the stone floor, he turned to face George. "That was my favorite throne! You destroyed a family heirloom. It's been in my family for 1,300 seasons. Perhaps, you could kill him without breaking anything else, George."

George had to laugh. "Allow me to fix it, My King." He waved his hand and the shattered pieces of wood began to float around the room. The crowd cried out. The king gave them a look. The room silenced. Piece by piece, the wood came together, the magic uniting them until the chair rested in its original position.

"I trust that's better, Sire?" George said while watching the king shake his head in disbelief.

George moved to stand over his unconscious opponent. Looking around, he noticed the wooden rafters (maybe 30 feet high) which spanned the room. He removed his dagger from its sheath and stabbed one of Fergus' feet.

The pain woke the general as George twisted the blade. The general tried to fight, but with a simple wave of his hand, George sent the general's head into the stone wall hard enough to render him unconscious again.

George yanked the dagger free and allowed the blood to flow. He stood and lifted his hands. Fergus began to float toward the wooden beams.

Screams filtered from the crowd. Now, with Fergus' body pressed against the beam, the mage took his free hand and with a forced motion of his wrist, used his magic to drape the general's arms around it. George made sure the barbarian's arms overlapped as he walked to a position beneath him. Looking up, George began to levitate. He ascended toward the beam and touched the general's bloody foot as it drained down his boot. He listened to the frightened sounds of the crowd as the general's arms turned to stone, then lowered to the floor.

Once again, the king demanded silence, and motioned for George to continue. The mage walked over to Kepler and whispered in his ear. The cat lowered to the floor and allowed George to sit on his back. Kepler lifted, his burgundy eyes glowing as he moved to a position near the repaired throne.

The undead beast stood tall and let out a deafening roar to wake the general. Everyone in the room had to cover their ears, including Kepler's feline subjects who lowered to the floor and used their paws to cover their heads.

George knew the people were taking this in like a sponge. Once he left, gossip would spread throughout the city about the day's events. He wanted to leave an indelible impression.

Saying his final words, George lifted his hands, then shouted, "General Fergus, you aren't worthy to serve our king! You cannot command an army when your actions are filled with weakness! It is your moment to die!"

Lightning arched from the mage's fingertips. He allowed the magic to flow until the general's body was cooked. The smell of burnt flesh filled the room, a stench George would not stick around for. Kepler called the giant cats around them, and instructed his subjects to make sure they were all touching one another.

George looked at Senchae. "You might want to buy some air fresheners. I'm getting the hell out of here. This place stinks. I will return in the morning, My King." The mage touched Kepler's back and motioned for Maldwin to jump in his arms. They all disappeared.

The Grayham Inquirer

When Inquiring Minds Need to Know about their Favorite Characters

GEORGE and his companions appeared in Mary's barn. The mage took one of the corgans, a large cowlike beast, from its stall and turned its lungs and its spinal cord to stone, providing the rest of its flesh to feed his giant feline friends. The large piece of meat fell over and became one big rare steak. Before he left to be with Athena, he waved his hand across the bloody scene and made it invisible. Maldwin was still in his arms when he entered the house. He gave the little guy some cheese to satisfy his hunger.

Lying in bed with his beautiful wife, he talked to her pregnant belly. Athena was happy with her husband's affections and rubbed his head. He would go back to the barn and clean up the mess, then leave for the Barbarian King's throne room in the morning.

He knew the impression he made in Senchae's palace-lodge would be the talk of the barbarian's rugged populous when he got back. Despite his love for his pregnant wife, he was anxious to return and see the results of his handiwork.

SAM was sitting with Shalee at breakfast, feeding her grapes, when Mosley appeared. The wolf come to inform them that Lasidious would be holding a meeting to announce where the two pieces of the Crystal Moon have been hidden.

CELESTRIA was bored until she thought of a project. She would learn how to make an ospliton pie. An ospliton fruit tree grew near the elven witch family's home, and the two squirrels she had been feeding from her windowsill had offered to help her pick the best fruit. She now has a basketful and is carrying it back to the house.

SENCHAE BLOODVAIN left General Fergus's body hanging from the rafters. He called for the barbarian's family to come and collect him for his burial on the Blood Sea. From the looks of it, there would not be anything left of his organs to harvest, since his guts had been fried to a crisp.

The Barbarian King spent many, many moments after George's departure explaining to his military leaders that he intended to start a war. The moments have come to begin a new campaign to take control of the Kingdom of Brandor. He bragged about his new consulate's power, using the lifeless general as a visual aid to convince his men he was right in aligning the barbarian people with the mage. All in all, the meeting went well.

As Senchae sat to eat his breakfast, he realized his army could win a war against the south. With the Serpent King's army, Kepler's giant cats and the demon's skeletal warriors fighting alongside his barbarian army, he would soon be king of all Southern Grayham. He smiled as Sadridz ran into the dining hall, screaming for his daddy to play with him.

LASIDIOUS was with Yaloom and Mieonus when he informed them his meeting would be held before Late Bailem in the Hall of Judgment. He then left to go meet with George. There are a few matters which need to be discussed and he cannot wait for the mage to dream again.

Thank you for reading the Grayham Inquirer

Ao Loose Ends

When Lasidious appeared to George, Athena had just left her mother's guesthouse to fix something to eat. The mage was sitting in a hot bath he had conjured and wasn't fazed when the god appeared.

"Hello, my friend," Lasidious said as he looked down at the deceiver. "I felt speaking in person would be a pleasant change. How are you?"

George smirked. "Yeah, whatever, man. I'm sure you already know how I am. You were watching me outside of Bloodvain's city. I think the barbarian's castle is a joke. It reminds me of an oversized Elks lodge. It figures I'd end up trying to take charge of a bunch of rednecks. I'm going to have to renovate the place, maybe even rebuild it. I won't live like Grizzly Adams, Lasidious."

The god chuckled. "I'm sorry you don't like the king's style. The barbarians are a rough people."

"Really," George mocked. "Ya think? I would've never been able to tell. Damn those redneck idiots. The stuffed animals they have all over the place drive me nuts. I bet the king's wagon is on some cinder blocks in his barn. Once we take over Brandor, I intend to take full control and send that blockhead, Senchae, back to the north. I'll stay down here and run the south."

Lasidious laughed at his ranting. "I'm sorry you dislike the king's lifestyle. But, to change the subject, it's true, I was watching you the other day. But, I wasn't the only one."

"Really! Hmmm, I'm intrigued. And, who else was watching? Did you get the show you were after?"

"And, more, much more. We were impressed. You did things even I wasn't thinking about. I was worried how you would work your way into the hearts of the people of Bloodvain. I must admit, killing the king wasn't a smart idea. I applaud your decision to use him as a tool. When you dangled his son in front of his face to find his breaking point, that was an exceptional piece of work. So, how did it go inside the city? We weren't there. Do tell."

"You would have shared in my delight," the mage responded, lifting a cloth. "Do you mind if I finish while we talk?"

"By all means."

George began to wash and explained the events from the night before. "It's safe to say the general didn't like me much..." George finished the tale by saying, "...then, I sent lightning into his ass and kept at it until he was Kentucky-fried."

Lasidious' brow furrowed, "Kentucky-fried, George?"

"It means I cooked him until he was crispy. But, I didn't hang around to do a taste test."

"Well done, well done, my friend. This will give you quite the reputation in Bloodvain. With the king on your side, the people will be more apt to listen, despite you being an outsider."

"We shall see," George responded. "When I left Senchae's throne room last night, I left the general hanging from the ceiling."

Lasidious smiled. "I wish I had a hundred of you, George. You continue to impress. I look forward to the day I can retrieve your daughter's soul."

The mage smiled at the thought of his baby girl. "I've been thinking. What is the best way to handle the Serpent King when I meet with him?"

The god walked to one of the bathing room windows. "I'm not able to answer your question, George. It is against the gods' laws. You'll have to finish the events we've started in motion without my assistance. Besides, with the way you have done things thus far, you don't need anyone telling you how to win friends and influence people."

"Ha! That's the funniest thing I've heard all day. Winning friends and influencing people...an excellent resource book. I used that book as my bible to perfect my skills of manipulation. I wish I had it here so you could take a gander at it, Lasidious. The principles I learned to win people's friend-ships are also the same principles I use to undermine them, though the book wasn't meant for this."

"Sounds like a fine read. But, I have a reason for my visit. I want to warn you to be careful when you talk to others. The gods are watching and we can't afford for you to say something you shouldn't when they are present. I don't wish to have our plans divulged." Lasidious disappeared before Athena walked into the room.

"Who were you talking to, honey? I thought I heard voices."

"You know me, babe. All I do is babble." He stood from his bath and grabbed a towel.

City of Brandor

After breakfast, Shalee left Sam and went into the royal garden, wanting to add to her magical foundation. The gardeners were asked to leave. Over the last seven days, she had made significant advances in her abilities, and could command most of what she had learned without using Precious.

Walking through the foliage, she passed her hands over the flowers, causing them to grow and change color. But, today wasn't about flowers. Today was about making her first attempt at teleportation.

When Helga arrived, the ladies embraced as they always did. "Child, I've never been able to command magic this strong. All I know...for you to make it work without killing yourself is, you'll need to be familiar with your destination. There's only one other on Grayham who can use this power, and that's Amar."

Shalee's face displayed her curiosity. "Exactly how would I kill myself if I fail? What could possibly happen?"

Helga placed her hands, one on each cheek, on Shalee's face. "You could appear too high above the ground and fall to your death if you fail to teleport again out of the fall. You might appear under a large rock, inside a wall, under the ground, deep below the surface of a lake, in a lava flow...or, if you're really lucky, you could appear with your head stuck in a corgan's backside. No pressure, child, I'm rooting for you." She winked.

"Ha, ha, ha, very funny, smart aleck. Thanks for the confidence boost. I can't seem ta rememba' why I love ya so much. Will ya please remind me?"

"Because, child, you need your mother."

"Yeah, sure." Shalee laughed as she threw her hands in the air and moved to a spot she had picked out. "I've been studyin' this area for a while. I figured this would be the spot ta start. For some reason, I already knew I needed ta be familia' with the place I intended ta teleport to...don't ask me how. I was fixin' ta make a trial run."

"That's insightful, child. Where's Precious?"

"I want ta do this without the staff. I want ta work on commandin' my power without that kinda crutch."

Helga looked worried. "I understand your desire to master your power, but do you think it's wise to teleport without it? Maybe you can use Precious to get a feel for it. Once you know what you're doing, you can try without it later."

"No, that won't work. The staff uses words, and lately I've been controllin' my magic nonverbally."

Helga gasped. "Since when, child?"

"Oh, ya know, here and there...when you're not around. I didn't want ta worry ya."

"This is a blessing. This is incredible. Are you telling me you can control your power without words at all?"

"For the most part," Shalee replied.

"Goodness-gracious!" Helga giggled, stealing Shalee's phrase. "You're rubbing off on me, child. To command your power without words is almost unheard of on Grayham. I don't know of anyone who has this ability. Amar can command lesser skills without words, but even he cannot command this type of magic without his staff."

The queen smiled. "Well, I'm able ta control most everythin' without Precious. I don't know how, but it feels natural."

"The gods have blessed you. I think we both know this must be your decision."

"Shall we give it a trial run, then? I'll stand near the statue ova' there." Shalee looked at the stone figure as she moved to it. "Ya know what, Helga?" the sorceress said, becoming sidetracked.

"What, child?"

"Some things neva' change from one world to anotha'. Look at him. Back on Earth, we had statues of men which didn't have their privates covered. They called this art, but I think it's silly. What do you think?"

Helga thought a moment, then grinned with a suggestive twist. "Don't we all like them rock solid, child?" she responded, as she patted the statue's mid-section.

"Lordy, you're incorrigible." The ladies gave each other a high-five. They each kissed their hands and blew toward the statue's area of conversation for good luck.

"Oh, I forgot to tell you. I did what you said and had BJ touch me on that one spot you told me about and..."

"Stop!" Shalee cried as she covered her ears. "T.M.I...too much information." Again, the ladies laughed.

"If you aren't going to use words, you should try concentrating, child. Close your eyes and focus on what you want to happen. That's what I would do if I were in your shoes."

Without answering, Shalee closed her eyes and took a deep breath, then thought of the grassy area next to the blossoming bushes. She pictured herself standing there.

Helga screamed. "Ohhhh, child, child, child!"

Shalee did not want to open her eyes. She could not tell if her friend's tone was good or bad.

"You did it! Oh, my, you did it! I'm so proud of you!"

Shalee opened her eyes and gave a big grin, then enjoyed a long embrace as they bounced around.

Sam walked up. "Is there something you two need to tell me? What's going on?"

Shalee grabbed him, winked at Helga, then told Sam to close his eyes. The next thing the king knew, he was standing in their bedroom. He would have said something, but Shalee held her hands over his lips to stop him.

"We have something to celebrate. Just relax." She licked her lips. Sam smiled as he watched each button of his shirt be undone.

The City of Bloodvain

George teleported to an area near the wooden bridge outside the king's castle-lodge, arriving with all his cats cloaked in a veil of invisibility. He wanted to know how he would be received if the people thought he had arrived alone and, to his surprise, the people in the city bowed as he passed.

He left Maldwin visible and on this sunny day, the rat sat inside George's pack with his head sticking out, shouting at everyone as they passed, "Everything is A-okay, man!"

As the mage entered the throne room, seven barbarian men and six large women were collecting the general's body. One of them had climbed on top of the beam where Fergus hung. The goal was to break his stone arms and lower his corpse to the floor. George didn't know it, but the man who held the hammer was the general's son.

As the mage stood there, no one spoke. After the king showed up, George learned the man with the hammer was also the new champion of Senchae's arena. "His name is Churnach Fergus. He's the general's son. I wouldn't expect a warm reception if I were you. I had a long conversation with the family to calm them. They understand the general challenged you. But, still..."

George turned to the barbarian king and made sure Senchae was the only one to see his smile. "Well, this is a bit awkward."

The big man, despite the lack of sensitivity of George's reaction, had to smile. "Walk with me for a moment, my friend. I think it's best if we take our leave and allow this family their chance to grieve."

The king walked with George into the hallway leading south out of the throne room. The mage just shook his head. Everywhere he looked, more stupid trophies.

"I've been doing some thinking, George. It should take the Serpent King 20 Peaks to arrive once leaving his city. Do you know how long he's been traveling?"

"I do," the mage responded. George no sooner said this when screams echoed from behind them. They were coming from the king's throne room. The men glanced at one another, then ran to the doorway. As they entered, bodies were flying everywhere, falling lifeless to the floor. The king looked at the horrific sight. All he could hear was the angry roars of the invisible beasts. After a few moments, the only one left alive was the barbarian champion. He was swinging his hammer through the air, but it was not long before he, too, laid dead.

George waited for the commotion to stop. He waved his hand through the air. Seven blood-soaked cats appeared standing over the family's bodies, some with large mouthfuls of fresh barbarian. Between Kepler, his brothers' 4,000 pound frames, the thirteen dead barbarians, and the four 2500 pound tigers, the throne room felt like he had just stepped into an episode of The Twilight Zone.

The mage glanced at the king and shrugged. He walked into the room, careful to avoid the pools of blood. "Kepler, what's going on? Look at the stinking mess you guys made."

The demon's eyes flashed. "The son of the general said they were going to kill you. The men with him said they should do it now, while you were close and not heavily guarded. The women agreed, and said you were ripe for a killing. It wasn't wise to wait. I commanded my subjects to attack. So, me and the boys...well...let's just say, we took care of it. That's what a master of the hunt does."

"I can see that," Senchae responded before George could reply. "Your friends are creating quite the body count. Maybe we could save the killing for the people of the south from now on, if that's okay?"

Kepler walked over to the king, looked him in the eyes, and growled. "The big guy, Churnach Fergus, the one you said was your champion, stated his king wanted them to attack. He said they would be rewarded for killing you." The jaguar watched closely for Senchae's reaction.

Bloodvain turned to look at George. "I swear, my friend, I said nothing about a reward for killing you. I have sworn my alliance. I won't break this promise. I say this on my son's honor."

The demon stared at the king and made his judgment. He knew George would be angry and would believe the king to be untrustworthy. The demon spoke before George could use his magic. "George, may I speak with you a moment?" Kepler said in a tone which redirected the mage's attention. "This is important. You can kill him later, just as easily as you can now. Please, speak with me in private."

The king found he was unable to move. Senchae had been bound like this before and knew it was pointless to fight the magic. George followed the demon to the other side of the throne room, weaving their way through the shredded bodies and the snarling cats. The beasts feasted as if they had gone days without food.

"What is it, Kepler?" George snapped. "I should've killed him already."

"No, George. I lied. This family said nothing of attacking you."

"What? Why the deception? Explain your logic."

Kepler sighed. "The general's family was angry. I don't believe in leaving loose ends. Without them around, there's no one to seek revenge. The killing of these fools gave me the chance to see if the king was loyal. When I told Senchae his champion said he ordered the attack, I watched his eyes to see if there were signs of deception. If he had ill will toward you, I would have known it. The king considers himself to be aligned with you. I don't think he'll ever be a problem.

"Besides," the demon continued with a sarcastic tone, "It has given me and my followers something to eat. If you look behind you, I have some fresh skeleton warriors to command. Granted, after we pick what we want from their bones, it will take a while before their flesh rots. Soon, they will be a fine addition to my undead army."

George turned to look. One of the cats tore off a large chunk of a bloody thigh muscle as the future skeleton rose from the floor. One by one, they stood, then moved in front of the demon. The mage had to move out of the way to allow them to fall into formation. Clearly, Kepler was commanding them with his thoughts. Without a word, the dead left to sit among the trees with the cats in tow.

Kepler smiled. "I find it easier to leave them in an open area of the forest. The other animals and the bugs will clean their bones. Give it about 10 Peaks and I'll have some fresh, fighting skeletons who refuse to die. The only way to kill them is by using fire or..." Kepler stopped his sentence. "Well, that part doesn't matter."

"I already know, Kep. You die, they stop working. You know you're one sick cat." George said as he reached up to pat Kepler on the side of his head. "You're my big, furry ally. Your secret is safe with me."

Kepler cringed. "You don't need to be affectionate, George. It's degrading and wrong."

George walked across the room. With a smile, he waved his hand at the king. He did not offer an explanation of the events, but instead, spoke with Senchae as he released the power over him. "9 Peaks. The Serpent King has been traveling for approximately nine days now. Where does this leave us?"

The king stared into the throne room and marveled at the bloody scene. After a moment, George yelled from down the hallway, "Senchae, are you coming, or what?"

𝔚ater 𝔐ist 𝔐ares

It was almost Late Bailem before Lasidious showed up at the Hall of Judgment to announce where the crystals were. The god knew the others, including the Book of Immortality, had been waiting. They all sat around the large stone table where the Book's golden stand rested.

"Thank you for coming," Lasidious announced. "The moment has come to give the location of the first piece of the Crystal Moon which has been hidden on Grayham."

Mosley interrupted. "I was under the impression you were going to divulge the location of the first two."

"And, I'll do that, but not today. Shall I continue, or does anyone else have questions?" Lasidious looked around the table. "As I was about to say, the first piece has been placed on Scorpion Island at the center of Lake Zandra. I'll..."

Now, Alistar interrupted. After adjusting his robe and running his hands through his short brown hair, he looked at Lasidious through a pair of soft brown eyes which complemented his thin face. "That lake is haunted by the mares you created when we molded these worlds. You know they're deadly. The people of Grayham make it a point to stay away from its shores. The mares could destroy the armies of every kingdom if they weren't bound to the water.

"How do you expect the mortals to get to the island? The mares patrol the lake's surface. If they aren't there when the people try to cross, they'll be there before they get to the other side. We all know what will happen. It will be a quick death, not to mention what the Scorpion King will do if they manage to set foot on his island. I don't see any way for either side to get this piece of the crystal."

Lasidious chuckled. "Do you think I'd put the crystal where it stood no chance of recovery? There's no fun in failure. I told all of you, I don't want the worlds destroyed. This is just a game. The mist mares have a weakness."

Everyone in the room nodded, but none of them remembered what the mares' weakness was. Calla spoke with a soft voice. "I would like to know their weakness." She brushed her short auburn hair aside and made sure the sapphires of her headpiece, separated by two strands of pearls, were centered on her forehead. She sat with her dress tucked around her knees.

Lasidious shook his head and laughed at his own cleverness. "Ha! Calla, you can't be serious. Do you think I'm going to tell you the answer? That would ruin the game."

Mosley could not believe the ignorance of his team. They had known the God of Mischief for too many seasons. Yet, still they insisted on asking questions which would never be answered.

Walking around the table, the wolf decided to control the conversation. "Lasidious, correct me if I am wrong. There must be a twist. I believe you have a clue of some sort, or perhaps, a riddle we could reveal to the people. This way, they might stand a chance to fight the mist mares."

Lasidious admired the wolf as he watched him sniff the base of Yaloom's chair. "You know, Mosley, I'm proud to have you as one of us. There are moments when I get sick of how witless the others have become."

The room exploded. Mosley and Lasidious held each other's gaze, a mutual respect passing between them as the voices of the Collective echoed off the hall's marble walls. The fact they were pursuing different goals did not matter. Lasidious ignored the fuss for a bit longer before turning his attention back to the table.

"Shut up! I don't care if you dislike how I feel. If it were up to me, the only one in this room I'd keep around would be Mosley. If I had the power to do so, I'd destroy all of you."

The god glanced around the table at the angry faces. When he came to Mieonus and Calla, he offered some piece of mind. "Now that I think about it, I would also keep the two of you. You too, Jervaise...your beauty is without equal when you materialize. Your ghostly form is far too beautiful to destroy. But you, Lictina...you're about the most unsightly thing I've ever seen. Put your tongue back in your mouth and sit down." Those complimented smiled, while Lictina lowered to her chair and continued to express her hostility.

The Book of Immortality spoke. Its voice commanded everyone's attention. "It doesn't matter how Lasidious feels. As long as he doesn't act on his impulses, he's allowed to hate every last one of you. You came here for a reason. Get the information you came for, then leave until Lasidious is ready to give you the location of the next piece."

Lasidious reached into his robe's pocket. He produced two scripted scrolls and laid them on the table. "I have written a riddle on each. They read the same. I'll give one to each team. If any of you try to give the answer to the people on Grayham, or assist in any way, the scroll will disappear and return to me. If this happens, I'll destroy the Crystal Moon, and we all know what that means."

The god handed Mosley and Yaloom the parchments and waited for the wolf to walk to the head of the table and lower the parchment from his mouth to the surface.

Water mist mares of Zandra,
beautiful, but yet so deadly.
A sole reflection,
their nature is in war,
to govern the lake from shore to shore.

Mosley sat on his haunches and scratched his neck. "Sam will figure this out before he is finished reading. It is clear what you are trying to say."

Yaloom looked at Mosley. He played with the rings on his fingers. "You understand what has been written? What's so clear about it? Speak, wolf."

Mosley shook his head. "Yaloom, I would rather leave you in a state of confusion. You dominate no pack of your own and would divulge the answer to George."

"Who says I'm going to give the parchment to George?" Yaloom snapped. "Maybe I intend to take this information elsewhere."

Mosley shook his head and turned his attention to Lasidious. "You are right. The intelligence in this room is far from suffocating. I have never seen this much ignorance. You know I am right. Sam will figure out how to defeat the mares."

Lasidious smiled as he patted the wolf's back. "It's hard to get one over on Sam with his superior intellect, but I don't think it will be as simple as you think. There is a twist, I assure you."

"When can we meet again to discuss the second piece of crystal?" Mosley inquired.

"In 10 Peaks." Lasidious plopped into his chair. "Remember, you aren't to assist the people of Grayham while they seek the first piece." The God of Mischief disappeared.

Without a word, the wolf vanished. He had a destination of his own in mind. When Mosley appeared, he was standing in Brandor's royal dining hall. Sam, Shalee, BJ, Helga, and the General Absolute, Michael, were discussing who would be Sam's new advisor.

Prior to the wolf's arrival, Michael had asked to remain in the position of General Absolute. He did not want the burden, politics not being his strongest asset to the kingdom. He realized there was a level of politics in his current position, but he didn't want to be pulled out of the day-to-day dealings of the army. He knew being the king's advisor would require heavy involvement with the senate. This thought was not appealing.

Sam had agreed to Michael's request. This left the king with a decision to make. Who would be his advisor? Sam was pleased when Mosley showed up. Now, he could ask the god for his opinion. "Mosley, it's good to see you. What brings you here, My Lord?"

"I bring news of the first piece of the Crystal Moon. I have come from a meeting held by Lasidious. This piece is on Scorpion Island."

BJ and Michael began to speak at the same moment. Realizing he was not a proper part of the chain of command, BJ held his tongue.

"Thank you, BJ," Michael said. "Lord Mosley, the lake surrounding the island is a doomed body of water. It's haunted by the mist mares. No one has ever set foot on the island, except for one man. Barutomus has long since passed. From the writings about his exploits, the island is covered with giant scorpions. He wrote they have a king with a poisonous tail over eight feet long. You can't toy with beasts of this nature. If this island is covered with these creatures, it will be a nightmare to find the crystal."

Everyone at the table turned to BJ to hear his response. "I agree with the general. But, I am more concerned about the mist mares." He turned to Sam. "The army can fight the scorpions and win, but the mist mares are spirits. Neither sword nor any other weapon known to this kingdom will kill these beasts. They walk above the water and have killed everything which has tried to cross the lake's surface.

"For reasons we do not know, they don't come on land. No one has ever seen them anywhere other than the lake. They don't make their way up or down stream. They look like ghosts, and from what I've heard, they breathe a mist which kills anything it touches.

"Some stories call them demons, others shades, and still others, spirits. No one has dared study their nature. Everyone within Grayham stays clear of the lake's shores. To fight these beasts would be to doom us all."

Sam stood after hearing each man speak. He looked at Mosley. "Is this all we know about the situation?"

Mosley smiled. As expected, Sam was thinking beyond the obvious. "Lasidious has given me a scroll. I am not able to explain its meaning, but it is a riddle which will give you an idea of how to deal with the mares." Mosley nodded and the scroll appeared on the table. The king opened it and placed it flat to read aloud. He wanted to make sure everyone had a chance to give input on its meaning.

Water mist mares of Zandra,
beautiful, but yet so deadly.
A sole reflection,
their nature is in war,
to govern the lake from shore to shore.

Sam lifted his head after reading the scroll and scanned the room for clues. He had a good idea what the answer was, but wanted to see if anyone else had a guess. He smiled at the commotion and watched as everyone passed the scroll around. He knew Lasidious hoped they would look too deep for the meaning. By the blank stares around the table, they were doing exactly that. After a while, he took the scroll and asked for answers.

Michael spoke first. "My King, none of us have an understanding as to its meaning."

Shalee reached forward. Sam's mug, filled with water, slid across the table and into her hand. She took a drink. "Sam Goodrich, ya stop this right now and tell us the meanin'. I know ya know. Ya figured it out as soon as ya saw it. Stop toyin' and give us the answer or I'll…" The sorceress tapped the butt end of Precious on the floor and smiled at her lover. The message had been delivered, warning Sam of a future butt-zapping.

Other than Shalee, the only other people in the room who understood her actions were BJ and Helga. They laughed. BJ said, "You have to admire her tact, Sire. Only your queen would threaten her king in a meeting of this magnitude."

"Agreed," Sam replied as he winked at his radiant, pregnant wife. "You've got to love our queen. She's a handful."

Michael and Mosley looked at each other with blank stares, then shrugged.

Sam pulled Kael from his sheath and looked at the sword. "Do you know the answer?"

"Don't be foolish. Of course, I know the answer," the blade responded as it pulsated.

"Then tell us," Sam retorted.

"If I must! The power of the mist mares is in a reflection. The problem you need to solve, is which one holds the power. If you kill it, the others will most likely die or become harmless."

"What do you mean by a reflection?" Michael asked.

Kael sneered, "Who are you to speak, mortal? You are not my master. I have given you no permission to speak to me. Utter another word and it will be your last day."

"Whoa, whoa, whoa, Kael. Take it easy," Sam said while maneuvering the blade toward his hip. "Let's just put you away. We'll talk about this later. These people are our friends."

"No, Sam. They are your friends. They are beneath me." The blade grew hot before Sam could sheath it, forcing the king to release him. The blade lowered itself into Sam's sheath. "Figure out who you are so things can be the way they used to be."

Shalee gasped. "What in tarnation does he mean by that? Well, if that doesn't just chap my hide. Sam, go on and pull him right back outta that sheath and give him what for."

Sam shook his head. "It's best just to leave it be. Besides, we have a riddle to solve. What Kael is referring to is the sole reflection of the mare which is created by the water beneath its feet. I believe this is the source of the herd's power. The problem is, which mare within the herd is responsible for casting this reflection?"

Mosley looked up from sniffing the corners of the room and announced he could not help. He bid the group farewell, then disappeared. After he was gone, BJ looked at the group. "I swear, the gods meddle in our lives too much. I liked life better when I didn't have to worry about such things."

Sam walked around the table and put his hand on BJ's shoulder. "Just think of how interesting your life will be, now that I have decided to promote you to the position of advisor. You'll have to deal with the gods and the senate."

Helga screamed, jumped from her chair, ran around the table, and pulled BJ from his. She hugged him as Michael looked at Sam. It was easy to see the General Absolute had a question. Sam motioned for him to speak.

"Sire," Michael said, careful to choose his words. "I'd like to understand your decision. I mean no offense; exactly what qualifies a teacher of weaponry to perform the duties of running a kingdom?"

Sam pulled his chair out and took his seat. "No offense taken. Let's just say I feel he'll do a good job. I'm making my decision on a gut feeling. I'm sure you know what I mean. When you're in a battle and the fighting is chaotic, it's your instinct which helps you make decisions. You know and trust these feelings, despite what anyone else thinks. I want you to support my decision and understand my instinct tells me this is a good thing."

Michael stood from the table and bowed. "Shall I prepare our advance on Lake Zandra? The Scorpion King's island is small enough we should be able to take one of our legions to hunt for the crystal. I'll prepare the army and leave the problem of the mist mares to you."

Sam agreed.

Michael added, "I'll send word to Branson, the legion leader of Cottle, to be ready within 3 Peaks for our arrival. We can leave tomorrow, as it will take us 2 Peaks to get there by hippogriff. We can march on Zandra and prepare to cross to the island from its southern shores. It will take 5 Peaks to get there, maybe fewer, if everything goes well. We can use Cottle's new harvest wagons to carry the boats. Since the city is close to the shore, they should be finished taking their crops to the coast. By the moment we arrive, everyone should be ready. Does Your Majesty agree?"

Sam was impressed with Michael's quick decision-making. "It sounds like a fine plan, General. BJ will stay behind and run Brandor in my absence while Shalee and I go with you to retrieve the crystal. If there are no further questions, I say we adjourn."

Helga jumped from her seat. "What about me, Sam...I mean, Sire? I also have abilities which could be useful. I did train your wife to use her magic. I should come with you...in case there's a magical emergency."

Sam laughed. "A magical emergency, eh? Well..." He would have objected, but he watched as Shalee gave Helga a high-five and knew it would be a waste of his moments. "I guess it's settled. Let's get moving."

2 Peaks of Bailem Later
Ancients Sovereign

Lasidious appeared in Yaloom's home. The Mischievous One wanted to find out what the God of Greed was planning to do with the scroll he had been given.

"What do you want?" Yaloom snapped.

"I want to know when you're going to tell George about the scroll. I've watched you for the last 2 Peaks. All you've done is sit here and look at its words. What's the problem?"

Lasidious watched Yaloom move to look at his waterfall. He placed his hands on the railing as he looked down to the pool filled with shimmering gems. "I can't figure out the parchment's meaning. This bothers me," he said as he played with the ring on his pinky. "I'll give it to George as soon as I figure it out."

Lasidious became enraged. "Are you stupid? Only you would allow your ignorance of the scroll's meaning to stop you from giving George the extra moments to go after the crystal. Meanwhile, your chance to win this piece is fading. Sam is on his way to the city of Cottle to meet with his army and march on the lake."

Mieonus appeared. On this day, she wore a short yellow gown which was stunning and complemented her olive skin. She pushed her brunette hair from her face and agreed with Lasidious. "I've been telling him the same thing for a couple of Peaks. He won't listen to me. I agree with you. He doesn't need to know the scroll's meaning to allow George to see it, but he won't move from this spot."

Lasidious screamed, calling for the Book of Immortality to make an appearance. It was only a brief moment before the Book appeared. "I've called you here to let you know I've decided to take the team lead away from Yaloom and give it to Mieonus. It's obvious Yaloom doesn't have the intellect or the ambition to lead his team to victory."

Before another word could be said, Mieonus ran across the room, grabbed the scroll from the table, and disappeared to meet with George.

Yaloom's expression grew cold. "I have the mind to..."

"To what?" Lasidious hissed. "Even if we weren't governed by the Book's laws, you aren't powerful enough to challenge me. I'd destroy you. You're pathetic, and always will be."

Yaloom started to raise his hands to invoke his power, but the Book floated between them. "I suggest you think about your actions. If you do this, I'll retaliate, and you will be destroyed."

Lasidious laughed as he taunted the God of Greed. His eyes turned red and he flashed a mouthful of sharp teeth, daring Yaloom to use his power. "You're weak! You're spineless! You are a father's mistake and a mother's misery! Strike me down!"

After listening to this verbal assault, the Greedy One managed to calm himself. Disappointed, Lasidious vanished.

Bloodvain's Throne Room

Mieonus appeared in the Barbarian King's throne room. The only person present, besides the guards, was Senchae Bloodvain. The guards took defensive positions, preparing to attack, whereupon the goddess simply held up her hand and caused everyone in the throne room, except the king, to vanish and reappear outside the castle-lodge.

"Senchae, where's George?"

"Who are you?"

"I'm Mieonus," she sneered while looking over his person with a disgusted countenance.

Senchae held her gaze, despite his confusion. "Is this name supposed to mean something to me?" The woman in front of him was using magic like George and he was careful not to sound too bold. He had been aggressive before and it nearly cost him his life.

Mieonus was annoyed the king didn't recognize her name. "You're wasting my valuable moments, barbarian," she snapped. "Where's George?"

"I'm here," the mage replied, entering the room. "How can I help you on this fine day? To whom do I have the pleasure of speaking?" As always, George was charismatic toward a woman.

"Mieonus. I'm here to give you this scroll."

George was not familiar with the name, but he was sweet, careful not to ruin a chance to gain an advantage. "It's nice to meet you, Mieonus. May I say, you look lovely? Yellow is your color. Your heels slender your calves. Your beauty is rare in this kingdom. To what scroll do you refer?"

The goddess enjoyed his compliments and tossed him the parchment. "This should have been given to you days ago. Brandor has a headstart. It's the key to get past the water mist mares of Lake Zandra." She watched as George opened it and read the contents of the riddle.

Looking up, George said, "Should I know what this means?"

Mieonus stomped the heel of her shoe on the stone floor. "I can't answer your question. It's for you to figure out. All I can tell you is Lasidious has placed the first piece of the Crystal Moon on Scorpion Island."

George looked at the Barbarian King to see if the information rang a bell. "Do you know where this Scorpion Island is?"

"My people haven't spent many moments scouting the area. I can't tell you much about the island, but I do know it's at the center of Lake Zandra in the Kingdom of Brandor. The lake is said to be haunted by demon horses which live on the water."

Mieonus was taken aback by the king's lack of knowledge, let alone his total ignorance of the mist mares. She knew she couldn't say anything to assist. Her visit was a complete waste. She vanished.

Senchae grinned as he looked at George. "It appears burs have infiltrated her undergarments. Her mood was vexed. She spoke of the Crystal Moon. The moon is what keeps the worlds..."

"Yeah, yeah, yeah, I know, I know. It keeps the worlds separated. If the pieces aren't put back together soon, everything will end. Blah, blah, blah, blah, blah. So, it's missing. But...does this riddle mean anything to you?"

The barbarian looked at the scroll and shook his head as his guards re-entered the room. Seeing the king's response, George sent one of the confused men to retrieve his pack. When the big man returned, George studied his map to find the lake. He realized he could make it there within 6 Peaks of Bailem if he left now. This was a good excuse to do some reconnaissance. After thinking a while, he devised a plan.

Before George gave his orders, he motioned for the king's guards to clear the room. Though he was not the king, the men were under no illusion who was running the kingdom. As long as George kept Senchae's pride intact and gave his orders out of earshot of the king's subjects, he could do whatever he wanted.

Once they were gone, George commanded, "Senchae, I want you to gather the army and prepare for war. From the way it sounds, there won't be much the army can do to collect this piece of the crystal. The Serpent King isn't due to arrive for another 7 Peaks. I'll leave now and teleport to the city of Champions. From there, I'll circle the east side of the lake to its southern shores and see if I can gather information. If we're lucky, I'll learn more about these demon mares."

George paused, waiting to see if the king understood the plan. "I'll make it back before the moment comes to meet with the serpent, then teleport the slimy bastard back to his home, or at least as close to his home as I can. He can mobilize his army and wait for further orders."

The mage paused again, but during this series of moments it was for a different reason. He knew Kepler was watching from the shadows. The demon had crept in to listen to their conversation.

George had put a spell on the demon and his siblings to alert him when they were around. The mage didn't like the idea the demons could hide in the smallest of shadows without him knowing. The way Kepler's brothers had appeared outside the Cave of Sorrow the day Kroger died was eerie. He knew the beast was his ally, but he also knew the cat was a master manipulator like he was, and manipulators always had to be alert to other manipulators.

"Kepler...dude...if you wanted to listen to what I was saying, you only had to walk in and make yourself at home. I keep no secrets from you. We're partners, remember?"

The cat emerged from the shadows. "How did you know I was there? And, what does this 'dude' mean?"

"Relax! It means buddy, friend, or pal. Some hot chick appeared and threw me this scroll. I assume she was one of the gods, but I didn't confirm it. Her name was Mieonus. Does her name ring a bell?"

"Yes, she is a goddess, though I don't know what she stands for," Kepler responded. "What's the message on the parchment?"

George held it up. "It's about the mist mares of Lake Zandra, but Senchae doesn't know what it means. I was about to leave to gather information. Apparently, the first piece of the Crystal Moon is located on an island at the center of the lake."

Kepler growled, then lowered to the floor. He began to lick himself as if he didn't care. George rolled his eyes. "Damn it, Kep, what do you know?"

The demon yawned as he lifted his head. "Well, my dude, it's..."

George interrupted. "No, Kep. Just say, dude. 'My dude' sounds stupid."

Kepler cleared his throat. "Hmmm, hmmm. Dude, it's a good thing I showed up when I did. I know something of the mist mares, man."

George slapped his forehead. "Knock it off, Kep. You're starting to sound like me. You're not cool enough."

"I'm cool, George. I'm like ice." Kepler stood and moved to scratch his back on one of the wooden pillars. "Ahhhhhhh."

George rolled his eyes. "And, why is it a good thing you showed up when you did? You said you know something about the mist mares. Maybe you could tell me during one of your free moments."

Kepler licked the inside of his right front leg and rubbed it across the top of his right ear before responding. "I know about the mist mares. I also know the island at the lake's center is covered with scorpions. We will have no problem moving around the island if you can keep us from being seen by the Scorpion King's subjects.

"It's the mist mares we have to worry about. They can see everything unseen to the naked eye. I know this firsthand. I tried to take a drink from the lake one night while traveling to Carlosam. Somehow, they saw me. They charged, but I was able to get away from the shoreline. They stopped before coming on land. If they could have left the lake's surface, they would have. I've never seen such anger in a beast. They must be bound to the water. If we could get past them, we'll have a chance to get the crystal.

The shortest distance to the island is from the north side of the lake. This is where we should go. If we can get past the mares, it will only be a half-day swim. I hope you're in good shape."

"Swim? Who needs to swim?" George mocked. "I'll create a raft and we can sail across. The only problem I have is with this riddle. I don't know what it means. Apparently, it holds the key to getting past the My Little Demon Pony problem." George lowered the scroll to the floor and spread it out so they could read it.

"This seems straightforward," Kepler said as he explained the answer.

After listening to everything the jaguar had to say, George looked at his map. "This is good. We'll go to Athena's home tonight, and in the morning, teleport to the city of Champions. We will depart for Zandra's northern shore. We'll have two days to find the crystal before the Serpent King arrives. Senchae can have his scouts keep the snake busy until we get back."

George reached up to hug his demon friend around his huge neck. "You're turning out to be a regular book of knowledge, Kepler. What would I do without you?"

"I'm glad you're happy, George," the demon responded as he tried to back away. "But, do you think you could stop touching me? It's appalling to have a human be so caring. I've spent too many seasons eating your kind. My brothers have been jesting about our relationship. I want us to rule this world, not become your pet."

George took the opportunity to poke some fun of his own. With the same voice he used to speak to his dog back on Earth, he walked toward Kepler in a stalking manner. The cat backed up as his friend came closer. "Doesn't my furry little demon Kepler love his Georgy-worgy? He needs kisses...oh yes he does. Come here and give daddy kisses. Daddy George loves you so much...oh, yes he does."

The Barbarian King laughed as he watched George chase the massive pussy cat out of the room.

The Grayham Inquirer

When Inquiring Minds Need to Know about their Favorite Characters

GEORGE left the city of Bloodvain, teleporting with Kepler and one of his tiger subjects to Athena's home. His wife's pregnancy is causing her emotional distress. Rather than leave in the morning, George has decided to stay to pamper Athena, reinforcing his love for her. They will not teleport to the city of Champions until Early Bailem the following day.

SAM'S hippogriff has landed along with the others. As Michael ordered, the king's army was ready. They have begun their march toward Lake Zandra, which will take nearly 5 Peaks to get there.

While preparing for their journey, Shalee gave Helga the cape she took from Double D the day he died. Knowing the Island of the Scorpion King was going to be a nasty place, they figured they would need every advantage they could find and the cape was perfect for the occasion. The army will be busy fighting the giant scorpions. Shalee will help Sam while Helga plans to use the cape to search for the missing piece of the crystal.

The ladies have agreed not to tell Sam about their plan. They want to surprise him with the news once Helga returns with the crystal.

Shalee has given her friend the other half of a pendant necklace she created with her magic. The ladies have been giving each other high-fives while riding with the army.

LASIDIOUS is on his way to the world of Luvelles. He is not going there to meet with Celestria, but rather to talk with the Head Master, Brayson Id. He will appear to the Head Master in Amar's image, Brayson's good friend and old Mystic Learner.

There are many details which need to be discussed, and planning the future is in order to create diversions to keep the gods' attentions away from his soon-to-be, newborn son. Amar was the only man capable of pulling this off, but since Amar is dead, thanks to George's handiwork, Lasidious will have to make it appear as if Amar is alive.

BJ sat on Sam's new throne. He was pretending to be the king. He asked everyone to leave the room, then lowered into the chair to get an idea of how Sam must feel. As it turned out, he pushed his luck a bit too far by having the cook bring him his meal where he sat. When the large woman arrived, she scolded BJ and pulled him from the room by his ear. She dragged the advisor into the royal dining hall and sat him in a chair.

When BJ tried to object, the woman, almost 20 seasons his senior, instructed him to be silent and eat his dinner without causing further trouble. The advisor had to smile. He had always been taught to respect his elders and ate without question.

BJ will fall asleep this night and have wonderful dreams of Helga. In his visions, they will be standing near a brook which peacefully cascades down a small embankment into a shallow pool. Sam will be standing in front of them with Shalee standing to Helga's left as her maid of honor. To BJ's right, Michael, the General Absolute will hand BJ the ring he will use to promise his love to Helga for the rest of his life. The ceremony will be short, but lovely and the kiss between them to celebrate their new union will be full of promise. It will be the best dream BJ has ever had.

Thank you for reading the Grayham Inquirer

May the Best Man Win
5 Peaks of Bailem Later

Sam, Michael, Shalee, and Helga stood on the shores of Lake Zandra. It wasn't long after the lake's surface had been disturbed that the water mist mares appeared. As night approached, Sam gave the order to have the army set up camp.

Michael did as instructed, then established a post at a safe distance to watch the ghostly beings throughout the night. He ordered six men to throw rocks, allowing them to observe the mares' behavior. Despite the aggressive nature of these creatures, they were beautiful, like spirits, hovering above the lake's surface as they threatened the army. Their hooves never touched the water, nor did the mares come ashore. Their bodies moved with a graceful deadliness which complemented the glow of their white coats as the light faded.

The cries of the beasts sounded like any normal horse, but every now and then, a shriek penetrated the air from the one isolated a few hundred feet away. During the moments when this cry occurred, Sam noticed another member of the herd would move to take its place, as if relieving it from guard duty. By Early Bailem, Sam had the solution to their problem.

Lake Zandra's Northern Shore

George, Kepler, and the accompanying tiger arrived on the north shore, opposite Sam's army. Kepler disturbed the water waiting for the mist mares to appear, but nothing happened. "This doesn't make sense. They should be here by now. These creatures are fast and dominate the lake."

George sent a rock skipping. "I don't know where they are, or why they aren't here, but I know I can teleport us all to shore if they come. Let's get going and make a run for it."

Kepler growled. "Exactly how do you intend to run across the water?"

"Not literally, dumbass. Watch this."

Kepler grumbled as he watched the mage touch the water. An ice raft formed. Once they were aboard, George lowered his hand into the water and conjured a powerful wind with his fingertips. The big sheet of ice glided through the water toward the island.

Back on the Southern Shore

Michael ordered the army to prepare the boats for crossing. All that remained was for Sam and Shalee to figure out the problem with the mares.

"Shalee," Sam shouted, "Come here for a moment! Do you see the mare which keeps itself isolated from the rest of the herd?"

"I do."

"Use your magic to hold the beast in place. I'll use my bow to disturb the water beneath it and we'll see what happens."

Shalee tried. "Tarnation!"

"What's wrong?"

"I can't reach it. It's too far offshore. I need ta get closer."

Sam reacted, "General, have the men throw stones into the water down shore. I need them to keep the herd's attention while the queen moves closer to the waterline."

"Yes, Sire."

The herd took the bait and Shalee made it to the water's edge, waving her hands through the air. During this series of moments the mare was in range and it became stuck in place as a result of the queen's magic.

The ghostly horse cried for the others. They charged. Shalee teleported from the water's edge to avoid the herd's deadly mist. "Goodness-gracious," Shalee yelled after she reappeared. "That was too close! I felt the chill!"

Sam shook his head. "Maybe this isn't such a good idea. I don't want to get the men killed going after the crystal. Maybe, I should send the army home."

Shalee grabbed his arm and pulled him away from everyone. "Look, we both know we need this piece of crystal ta save the worlds from destruction. It was a close call, but this is our lives now. We're just gonna have ta buck up and get the job done."

"I know, but if you get hurt, I'll fall apart. You're the only thing keeping me together through all of this. It's one thing to sacrifice myself, but to sacrifice you and all these men, I can't do that."

"I understand how ya feel. But, you're strong, Sam...Bassorine saw ta that. I shouldn't be tellin' ya this, but the reason you're so gifted is because Bassorine made sure you were blessed. Haven't ya eva' wondered why ya have the abilities ta rememba' the things ya do? Don't ya eva' wonda' why ya learn so quickly? Haven't ya eva' wondered why ya were so athletically inclined? All this is because of Bassorine. He asked the gods of Earth ta give ya the abilities ya have. You and I were selected ta come ta Grayham before we were born. I need ya ta be strong. Without your strength, I would fall apart. I look up ta ya." She pointed at the men, "And, so does this army. Show 'em why the gods chose ya."

"How long have you known this?"

"That doesn't matta'. I can't tell ya anymore. What matta's is you and I have no Earth ta go home ta, and this isn't a dream where we can just wake up. Unless we figure this mess out, we won't have this home eitha'. Sam, I need ta feed from your strength." The sorceress lifted his chin with her fingertips. "There's some good news, though...news I think will make ya happy."

Sam took a deep breath. "What would that be?"

She winked. "The mare is still bound by my magic."

Sam smiled and took another breath before responding. "Since when did you become a leader?"

"How 'bout we finish this conversation later, maybe when we're alone?" Shalee pinched his butt. "Now get ta work."

Sam lifted his bow and aimed at the feet of the bound mare. As soon as the water beneath was disturbed, the others shimmered as if losing their form. He waited for the water to settle. Once again, the herd solidified.

"Did you see that, General?" Sam yelled. "Get over here! Watch this!" Again, Sam shot the bow and again, the herd shimmered. "General, the herd is affected when the water beneath that mare over there is disturbed. I want all the archers to aim for this spot."

"Yes, Sire!"

Soon, the herd of mist mares no longer had the power to maintain their form and faded into nothingness, leaving only the segregated mare. Sam looked at Shalee. "Okay, okay, now that we've got just the one mare to deal with, how long do you think your magic will hold her there?"

Shalee sighed. "Not long enough for the army ta cross the lake. And, we still have ta get back."

"That's not quite what I had in mind." The king scruitinized the situation. "Okay, okay, the mare is unable to come on land. What if we put it on the dirt? Maybe it will lose its power."

Sam pulled Kael from his sheath and commanded the blade to protect him from ice, and started to walk. Shalee grabbed his arm. "Ya don't need ta go out there. She still may be able ta use her icy breath, and you have no idea if Kael's protection is strong enough. Let me bring her here."

Sam lifted the blade in front of his face. "Is your power strong enough to protect me from the mare's breath?"

"Of course, but protecting you will not fix the problem. Shalee is right. Bring the mare on land."

Hearing the blade's response, the sorceress raised her hand and the mare floated toward them. The archers adjusted their aim to keep the water beneath her disturbed. Everyone cleared a large circle for Shalee to set the beast down, careful to stay far enough away so the mist could not reach them. As Shalee lowered the mare to the ground, the creature cried, filling the air with a horrid shriek. The men grabbed their ears. The cry was so loud, Shalee lost her concentration and the beast fell to the dirt. As soon as the first hoof touched the ground, a brilliant burst of light shot into the sky. Even though it was only the Peak of Bailem, the beam could be seen in all directions equivalent to a three day ride on horseback.

The army was thrown to their backsides as a burst of air smashed into them. The rest of the herd reappeared and hurried off the lake's surface, running through the army and out of sight. Their hooves touched the ground as they ran across the countryside with a trampling thunder. Grayham had its first pack of wild ghosts.

Sam made sure no one was hurt. "It seems they no longer have the ability to kill. They ran right through us. General, send two men to capture one. Have them take it to Brandor."

Shalee slapped his arm. "Hey, don't forget ta capture me one, too."

"Make that four men, and capture two, General."

"Yes, Sire." Michael picked himself up and rubbed his eyes. "You six men go after those horses! Capture three and take them to Brandor!"

Michael turned and saw that his king and queen were staring at him. He shrugged. "Don't look at me like that. I want one, too."

Michael changed the subject. "I've never seen anything so amazing. When that mare exploded, it had to be the brightest light ever created."

Sam walked forward and wrapped his arm around the general's shoulders. He pointed to the sun. "What about that light?"

"Very funny, Sire. Maybe you should try your hand at theatre."

"I've already tried theatre. Didn't you enjoy my performance with Double D?"

Michael rolled his eyes and shouted for the men to ready their boats. Sam smiled at his reaction and took Shalee by the hand. Leading her to one of the crafts, capable of holding thirty men, they jumped in. It wasn't long before the legion was rowing to Scorpion Island. As they crossed, Shalee winked at Helga and gave her the thumbs up. The elderly sorceress smiled and draped the cape over her shoulders.

George, Kepler and the Tiger
Approach the Island

George waved his free hand over the group as they drew closer to the island. Each of them vanished as they prepared for their secret invasion of the Scorpion King's kingdom. They all had seen the bright flash to the south, but could only guess its origin. They blew it off without much discussion.

As the raft ran onto the shore, the ice crunched as it slid across the rocks. The noise captured the attention of three giant scorpions who turned to investigate. Everyone exited the raft and moved away, observing the creatures' movements from within George's veil of magic.

George was awed by the anthropods' size, but he did not feel the need to get a better look. They were massive and, from where he stood, what he could see was enough. Their tails were at least six or seven feet long, with stingers sharpened to a fine point. Their mouths had two mandible-like scissors. Their big, beady eyes gave him chills, and he was sure they would zoom in on him at any moment. The top of their shell-like backs were waist-high and the pinchers at the end of their two front appendages could tear a man in half. He had never seen a scorpion up close and these three were more than he ever wanted to see again. The mage motioned for the group to move on.

The shores of the island were rocky, but as they traveled inland, the ground became more like a desert, attracting attention as the sand flipped up and into the air with each footstep. Their footprints were leaving a trail right to them.

They needed a diversion. George released the magic which kept the tiger hidden. Once the cat was visible, the beast became the scorpions' new target. The big cat took off running. The scorpions gave chase. Once they were far enough away, George spoke. "I think the tiger is quick enough to outrun them for a while, don't you?"

"That was mean, George. I love it," Kepler growled. "Let's pick up the pace."

"Yeah, let's go."

They ran within his spell of invisibility. After much searching, they found a cave leading into the ground. The sand gave way to a much harder surface where they no longer had to worry about leaving tracks. They began their descent into the hole. George used his magic to help him see through the darkness.

Sam's Army has Landed
The South Side of Scorpion Island

Sam jumped from the boat while the general ordered the army to form ranks. The king steadied the boat and motioned for Helga to come close. After securing his hands around her waist, he lifted her out of the boat. Turning to assist Shalee, he could only smile as the sorceress used her power. She floated over the side of the craft and lowered to the beach.

Irritated, Michael shouted, "No, no, no! I said seven ranks, not six! I want you 30 abreast and 12 deep!" Michael tapped the flat of his blade across the legion leader's breastplate. "Branson, you best get these men organized."

"Yes, sir, right away!"

Before the men could organize, the tiger crested the hill with over six hundred giant scorpions in tow.

"Prepare for battle," Sam cried. He grabbed Michael's arm. "You and Branson stay close. Fight by my side."

Sam grabbed Kael and pulled the blade free of its sheath. "*Val arrna, coia, ngw, vara poy.*" Kael burst into flames, extended his length an additional eight feet, and protected the king and those closest to him, within fifteen feet, from the scorpions' venom.

The legion's battlecries filled the air as they prepared for the massive collision. Shalee waved her hand in a half circle and toughened the army's skin against the scorpions' stingers. She lifted her staff and shouted, "*Val arrna, coia korons.*" The air filled with meteoric balls of fire which fell to the top of the hill, killing forty-seven of the giant anthropods in the blast. Scorpion body parts were sent flying in every direction as Sam's army cheered for their queen.

The tiger, seeing the group ahead, hoped to find a way to shake the scorpions. The beast was frightened, knowing full well a sting from one of their tails would end his life. As he drew closer to the army, the cat spun around to face the charging horde.

Sam yelled, "Shalee, protect the cat! Use your magic to capture it!"

The sorceress did as instructed. Lifting the cat into the air with just a wave of her hand, she placed the beast into one of the boats and sent him floating across the lake. The queen turned and moved to stand beside Helga. "Are ya ready?"

"Don't worry about me, child. Looks like we found ourselves a magical emergency."

Shalee chuckled as Helga put the hood of Double D's cape over her head and disappeared. The older sorceress began to walk around the oncoming horde as Shalee lifted her hands to send another wave of meteors crashing into the skittish invasion of poisoners. The body parts of another fifty-three scorpions were sent flying in countless directions. Again, the army cried out as the general ordered the soldiers to attack. An enormous eruption filled the air as Sam's legion of men, 2,520 strong, ran into battle. Kael called for blood as Sam charged into the horror to join his men.

Cave of the Scorpion King

The cries of Sam's army echoed off the cave's walls as George and Kepler descended into the cavernous underground lair of the Scorpion King. They found themselves pushed up against the cave's wall. Although still invisible, George had to use a protective barrier to keep them from being trampled. The scorpions were responding to the screams above. Over 1,100 passed their position as they hurried out of the cave. Whatever was happening up top was commanding a lot of attention. It left the cave empty and allowed the pairing to walk wherever they wanted.

The cave was dark, dismal, and smelled of waste. It was impossible to take a step without getting garesh all over Kepler's paws and George's boots. Many moments passed before they found an entrance to a branch of the cave which felt man made. The rough rock of the cave became polished, flat and formed. It was as if they were entering some sort of catacomb or dungeon.

Two torches sat on either side of a columned entrance. Both were spent. *Someone or something had been here before,* George thought. Beyond the entrance, no more than 100 paces away, sat a sole pedestal at the branch's end. *Only one way in and one way out. This feels bad.*

George whispered, "Kepler, hide while I investigate."

The demon snarled, "We should stay together. I don't like this."

"Relax. How does a demon as big as you get scared?"

"Bah. I'm not scared. I'm sensible. Splitting up isn't smart."

"I'm just going to be right down there. I'll be right back. I want to see if the crystal is here. Just stay put and keep an eye out. Come get me if you see anything."

"Okay, but hurry."

At a slow pace, George moved in to stand over the pedestal. To his surprise, a piece of the crystal, just like the one he had in his hand before falling through the floor of the temple, rested on top of it. He snatched it from its resting spot—keeping his magic at the ready.

Once the mage realized there would be no consequence, he motioned for Kepler to join him, then touched the cat's back. They closed their eyes and when they reopened them, they were still standing beside the pedestal.

"Garesh," George whispered.

"What is it?"

"I've used too much power. It'll be a while before I can get us out of here."

"This isn't good. They could come back at any moment."

"I know, I know, let me think a moment, will you?"

"What do you need to think about? You're out of power."

"Shut up already. I need to figure out a damn plan. Just be quiet." The mage scanned the area. He still had two unused snare scrolls from his trip to the Cave of Sorrow. He pulled them out. "Just stay away from the areas where I use the scrolls. Their magic should stop anything that wanders in. We can hide until I can get us out of here."

Kepler chuckled.

"What's so damn funny?"

"I can hide. You're screwed."

George rolled his eyes. "Thanks, pal."

Helga Begins Her Descent

Helga entered the cave having discovered its entrance by following the scorpions' trails from the southern shore. She had also used her magic on her eyes and was disgusted by the smell. She lifted her dress to keep it from touching the garesh-covered floor. Despite her revulsion, she moved at a steady pace. The way in was surprisingly easy. It appeared to be clear of the poisonous creatures. It wasn't long before she found the corridor leading to the pedestal. *This has to be it,* she thought. *Shalee is going to be so proud. I can't wait to see Sam's face.*

She tiptoed through the entrance and toward the pedestal, scanning her surroundings. It appeared she was alone. Without knowing, Helga gave her position away.

From his hiding place in the shadows, Kepler's ears snapped to attention as his eyes searched the area. He saw nothing, but the cat knew something was there. He lifted his nose and searched for a scent. *Woman,* he thought. *She's heading toward the pedestal.* The demon gave a wry smile. He didn't have to wait long.

Helga whispered curses as she found herself trapped in George's snare. "I can't believe this. How could I be so stupid?" She kept her voice low to avoid attention, unaware the humongous cat was listening, trying to determine the height and place from where the voice was coming.

Kepler crouched and was preparing to strike with a blow to her head, when a large scorpion entered the corridor. The monster was nearly a foot longer in its poison-filled tail than the others. This had to be their king.

Helga stared at the columned entrance and marveled at how the scorpion's form filled the gap between the pillars. She knew her whispers had attracted the beast, but she was still invisible. *It must have heard me,* she thought. *Stay still and don't make another noise, old girl.*

The Scorpion King scurried toward her. She stood as still as she could, but the sorceress knew, as the creature grew closer, it would run into her leg. She stayed quiet. *Maybe the beast will move on.*

Helga wanted to use her staff's magic. To do so, she would have to remove the hood of Double D's cape. The cape's power would not allow for offensive magic. The cloak was designed for stealth and to combine the different arts would destroy the one invoking the power.

If Helga lowered her hood and spoke the words of power necessary to kill the beast, others would come. She would be in a worse situation. She did not have the magic to fight them off. She decided to stay silent and hope for the best.

George watched from behind the pedestal as the scorpion approached. He could see the creature's size difference. It was unnerving. He was hiding behind the pedestal, and his power had not yet been restored. He could not see Helga, nor had he heard her when she became trapped. All he knew was he might have to use more of his power if the beast did not cross one of the snares' locations. He readied his sword to kill the creature, encouraged by the path the scorpion chose.

The mage became aware of Kepler's presence. Given the current situation, it was obvious why the cat had moved. Kepler whispered from the shadows. "There's a woman. She must be using a spell to hide herself. She's stuck in your snare. The scorpion is going to run into her."

George smiled, but did not respond. Sure enough, the giant killer made contact with the invisible woman. The mage listened as Helga made a fatal mistake.

"Aahhh," Helga squealed, then cupped her hand over her mouth. She watched in horror as the Scorpion King took a defensive position and began to use his massive pinchers to feel around.

Please move on. Please move on, she thought. *Just move on. There's nothing here for you to feed on.*

Helga watched as the first of three passes of the giant's powerful pinchers missed finding her location, but the fourth found her leg. The beast squeezed. The sorceress bit her lip, but the pain was too much. She ripped the cape's hood back and began to speak her words of power.

"Your Majesty, *na*..." Helga was stopped in the middle of her command. The scorpion's massive stinger had barreled its way through the air as she spoke and buried itself deep within her chest. She would have finished speaking her final word, but the force of the collision knocked the air out of her. The word was lost forever as the poison filled her body. The last thing the sorceress would ever see would not be the love of her life, BJ, or Sam, or Shalee, but would be the beady eyes of the royal killer as it moved in to take her face in its mandibles to rip it apart.

Now...fellow soul...I'm sure you are just as bothered by Helga's death as I was when I learned of this truth. I truly loved her. You see, the problem was, Helga's staff was given a name with too many syllables. This was a name her teacher hated when she was a young sorceress in training, "Your Majesty." It simply took too long to be spoken. As you can see, this was the day Helga realized the consequence of her mistake. She had named her staff in fun, never realizing what she might face one day. Once pronounced, the staff's name could never be changed. Unfortunately, as I continue this story, the fire for Helga's passing will need to be lit. I would cry if my soulful eyes would let me.

Back on the Southern Shore of the Island

Shalee's body count was growing as she sent magical arrows, covered with fire, into the masses of the Scorpion King's army. The skiddish horde was falling at a rapid pace. Body parts of both beast and man were everywhere, the ground saturated with blood of men and the oozing green slime of the scorpion's life source. By the end of the battle, the sorceress would kill over 356 of these giant anthropods, but not before many casualties plagued Sam's army.

Sam's men had slain another 980 as the king and the general continued to plow their way through the horde. The magic Shalee had used to toughen the army's skin helped to prevent the scorpions' stingers from penetrating their bodies, but in many cases this was not enough protection. In fact, it was Kael's power which spared Sam and Michael's lives. Despite Shalee's magic, both men suffered small venom-filled punctures which were ignored because of the blade's protection.

Sam's sword cut through the beasts like butter. Michael was careful to stay within the fifteen foot radius of Kael's protection and fought beside his king. They were tearing through the enemy like forces of nature.

Sam enjoyed the frenzy as Kael sliced through another of the giant beasts, causing it to squeal like an 800 pound lobster being dropped into a pot of boiling water. Back and forth, Sam swung Kael's extended blade through the air as the sword of the gods cut through their numbers. Now and again, the sword would pass, without ill effect, through Michael and Branson.

"This is what I call a fight," Sam screamed as they moved toward the top of the hill.

"Agreed, Sire," Michael shouted, catching one of the tails in his hand and severing it with his blade. He gave a downward thrust to the giant's back and listened to its nightmarish scream.

"Thirty-seven, Sire."

"That's it? Seventy-one here." A few moments later Sam screamed again. "Seventy-four!" The general shook his head and kept fighting.

A long while later, the fighting stopped as the last giant scorpion lay dead. In total, Brandor's army lost 502 men, with another 943 lying wounded. 643 of these men would not live through the night as the poison injected into their bodies was too toxic. The general ordered the healers to attend the wounded while the rest of the men stacked the dead on the boats.

Sam and Michael watched as the poison oozed out of the small holes scattered about their bodies. Kael's power also flushed the blood of the men who managed to stay near Sam during the battle and cleaned it of the poison's wickedness.

Meanwhile, Shalee was worried about Helga. She hoped the older woman would have returned by now. She searched the army to find Sam. "We have a problem."

"What's that?" Sam asked, tossing one of the giant's stingers to the ground.

"Helga was wearing the assassin's cape. She went ta find the crystal. I'm fixin' ta go look for her. I'm worried."

"What? Why would she do that? Where did she go?"

"Ta find the crystal."

"Damn it, Shalee!" Sam shouted, then assembled a hundred of his men and followed the scorpions' tracks. Shalee had to use her magic to keep up with the group. Her fear for Helga's safety increased as they ran.

They entered the cave. "This is where the tracks lead," Sam shouted. "This must be the place."

Shalee commanded the darkness to give way to the light. The king led the way and, after a while of searching, they found the corridor where Helga had been snared. The Scorpion King had severed Helga's legs and tried to back out while dragging her body. The giant had become caught in George's second snare and was fighting to free itself.

Sam tried to stop Shalee from rounding the pillar on the left side of the corridor's entrance once he saw the bloody mess. "You don't want to go in there. Why don't you let me handle this? Go back to the boat."

The queen could see the sorrow in his eyes. She needed to look for herself. She pushed past. As she rounded the corner, she lifted her hands to her mouth. "No! No! No! Helga, No!" She thrust her right hand forward. Thousands of iron needles flew from her fingertips and buried into the Scorpion King's body. The cave filled with the monster's piercing cries as it fell to the floor with a thud. It thrashed about, for a short period of moments, until its nerves perished.

George watched from behind the pillar as Shalee took the beast's life. He realized his power to teleport was once again his to command, but this scene was priceless. How could he leave? He wanted to watch its conclusion. This was going to be an Academy Award-winning performance from his favorite blonde ditz. If only he had a camera. George could see the pain as Shalee knelt beside what was left of her friend's mutilated body. The only thing identifiable was a pendant necklace which he watched Shalee pull free from the pulverized mass which once served as Helga's chest.

"I gave this ta her, Sam. I gave it ta her only eight days ago," Shalee cried. "This is my fault. She would've neva' been here if I hadn't agreed. I'm responsible for her death. I should've stopped her from usin' the cape." She buried her face in her bloodied hands and sobbed as the king gathered her into his arms.

"I'm sorry for your loss," George said, feigning his sincerity as he came out from behind the pedestal.

Shalee spun out of Sam's arms and sent her magic in his direction. George held up his hand and diverted the power. The needles penetrated the cave's wall. "Relax! It's me, George!"

Sam grabbed his wife's arms to keep her from doing anything else. "What're you doing here? Are you here for..." Sam chose not to continue.

George drummed his fingers on top of the pedestal. "If I was to take a guess, I'm here for the same thing you are. I was present when your friend died. I wish I could have saved her, but it wasn't in my best interest." The mage moved to stand next to the hidden demon.

Sam shook his head. "Why would you be after the crystal? What power are you talking about? And, why wouldn't it be in your best interest to save someone's life?"

"Look, man, you and I are on opposite sides. I am running the show in Bloodvain. It's my kingdom now. The power I'm referring to has been demonstrated. Shalee knows I should be dead, but she isn't strong enough."

"He's right, Sam. He should be dead. Where did ya get this kind of power, George? I would neva' try ta hurt ya. Ya startled me." Shalee paused. "What do ya mean, you're 'runnin' the show in Bloodvain?'"

"Like I said, we fight for different sides. From this point forward, it looks like we're going to be enemies. This kinda sucks when you think about it. But hey, it's all about getting my daughter back. This is the only way I know to make it happen."

Sam tried to reason. "George, your daughter? She's dead...like the rest of our families. You know this."

"No! She's not dead! I can save her. I can bring her back. I know how."

"Okay, okay, George, think this through. They all died when Earth was destroyed. I know it's hard to believe. It hurts to..."

George lifted his right hand. A single dart shot from the tip of his middle finger and stopped only inches in front of Sam's face. The energy of the dart caused it to hum as it remained suspended. "One more word and you're a dead man," he hissed.

George lifted the piece of the Crystal Moon into the air. "My baby girl can be saved and there's nothing you can do to help. May the best man win, Sam. May the best man win. No offense, but this is just business. This is the only way to get my Abbie back." With that, the mage closed his eyes and disappeared after touching the invisible demon. The dart fell to the floor.

Shalee turned to face Sam as he removed the dart from the floor to examine it. "For heaven's sake, what's goin' on? None of this makes sense. How could George be our enemy? What did we eva' do ta him? How did he get so powerful?"

"I don't know. Let's just get what's left of Helga's body and get out of here."

Shalee looked at Helga's pieces as she united her friend's half of the pendant to her own. She wished with everything in her it would fix the pain. As she placed the trinket close to her heart, she studied the bloody scene to determine how best to collect the parts. She felt queezy. The cave began to spin as she started to vomit.

The Grayham Inquirer

When Inquiring Minds Need to Know about their Favorite Characters

THAT NIGHT, after George collected the crystal from Scorpion Island, he appeared with Kepler in the Barbarian King's throne room. The mage opened his pack to place the crystal inside. To his surprise, the object began to glow as he let it go. He was not sure what to think. He showed Kepler what happened, but the demon did not know what to make of it.

SAM took his grieving wife out of the cave and ordered his men to collect what was left of Helga's body. They traveled to the southern shore of the island where Michael commanded Branson to take the men back to the city of Cottle to light the fires for the celebrations of their passing.

The king informed the general that Shalee would be teleporting the three of them, along with Helga's parts, back to Brandor. They would return to Cottle in 5 Peaks of Bailem to pay their respects once the army arrived.

Once this had been accomplished, Shalee instructed them to close their eyes and touch one another. When the group reopened them, they were standing in Sam and Shalee's bedroom chamber. Shalee asked Michael to have the morticians prepare the remains of Helga's body and have her friend brought back in a closed casket by Early Bailem. Shalee wanted to allow BJ one more restful night's sleep before giving him the bad news. She didn't want Sam's advisor to see his lost love in this condition.

LASIDIOUS has been sitting in his home far beneath the surface of the Peaks of Angels. After the images appeared within the green flames of his cube-shaped fireplace, he watched the events unfold on Scorpion Island. He was elated at George's luck, never guessing the mage would end up with this piece of the Crystal Moon. It certainly made things more interesting, but an adjustment in future plans will be necessary.

Lasidious knows the others are going to be furious when he informs them George has the second piece. The mage has had it since his arrival on Grayham. Even George does not know it.

He remembers Sam told Mosley that George fell through the floor with it, but the wolf never questioned its whereabouts. The Mischievous One never intended to take the crystal from George. Instead, he made sure it was invisible to the mage, and the others, until the moments were right to reveal the location of the second piece.

This piece is in George's pack. As the visions in the fireplace change, he watches George lower the crystal inside. He can see George has questions about why the crystal is glowing. An explanation will have to wait. He will avoid making an appearance in the mage's next dream until he has addressed the gods, tomorrow, at Late Bailem.

His visit to the world of Luvelles was productive and his conversation with the Head Master of that world was encouraging. His disguise as Amar provided the perfect deception. It is now a matter of manipulating a few more details before the next part of his plan can be implemented.

CELESTRIA is only 20 Peaks from having the baby. She can hardly wait to hold her son. She is looking forward to seeing Lasidious once the baby has been left in the care of the elven witches.

ATHENA'S morning sickness has been rough. Mary has been rubbing her back while talking her through it. Mary wishes George was here, but unfortunately, she thinks he will not be around until the baby is born. She has no idea George has been teleporting to see her daughter. The couple has managed to keep this secret.

BJ is approaching Sam's throne room. One of the castle servants was sent after breakfast to fetch him. For the last two days, the advisor has been preparing a home for Helga and him to share. He cannot wait to see his love.

While Helga was gone, BJ went into the city to purchase an extraordinary wedding ring. He is looking forward to being her husband.

Thank you for reading the Grayham Inquirer

What a Tangled Web George Weaves

The City of Brandor

BJ was as joyful as a man could be when he walked into the throne room. His head was held high as he searched for Helga, only to see Sam, Shalee, Michael, and the king's guards. It took only a moment for his eyes to focus on the coffin. A chill ran down his spine. Without a word, he knew Helga was inside. His happiness was stolen in less than a single breath and there was nothing he could do or say about it.

He turned to look at Shalee. A thousand questions filled his expression. The queen's legs crumbled as she collapsed under the pressure of his silent accusations.

Sam managed to catch his queen. He ordered the servants to take her to their bedroom chamber. Once gone, the king turned to look at BJ's hopeless face and watched as his friend walk across the room. Not a single word was spoken as BJ knelt next to the coffin. He lowered his forehead to rest against its cold surface. Despair filled his body. The pain tore at his soul as he fell into a fetal position.

Sam rushed to BJ's side. The king stopped as his advisor's scarred hand opened. The ring meant to symbolize his greatest happiness—a happiness which BJ had intended to cherish for the rest of his life—rolled from his palm and fell to the floor as nothing more than a useless symbol.

BJ wept.

Athena and George's Home in Lethwitch

George popped in for a few short moments to give his wife a kiss and a cuddle. He is scheduled to meet with the Serpent King at Late Bailem and knows what he is going to tell Seth.

He was sitting at the table when Athena walked in with her mother. George stood to greet them. "Hey, I happened to be in the neighborhood," he joked. "I wanted to tell you, our family should be together on a permanent basis not long from now. How are you, mom?" Athena ran across the room and threw herself into his arms.

Mary said, "I'm better, now that you're here. This young lady is doing nothing but throwing up. I can't wait until this phase of her pregnancy passes. Your wife is unbearable at the moment."

George tilted Athena's head back from his chest and looked her in the eyes. "Are you still being a priss?"

Mary did not give her daughter the chance to answer. She spoke for her. "Ha, you could say that again. You keep her for a while, I'm leaving. I'll see you tomorrow, little girl."

"Hi, honey. How long are you here?" Athena asked.

"I have a meeting tonight up north, but it won't be anything that will take all night. I'll come home once it's over. Other than that, I'm yours tonight and all day tomorrow."

Athena pried away from George's grasp. She ran toward a pail sitting near the front door and began to throw up. Her morning sickness was now a midday and night sickness as well.

The God World of Ancients Sovereign

The gods had traveled to the Hall of Judgment and are sitting at the table where the Book of Immortality's stand rests. It was just after Late Bailem when Lasidious appeared.

"I'm sure you watched the finding of the first piece of crystal with eagerness. I was impressed by how everything transpired," he said, gloating a little.

Mieonus jumped into the conversation. "So am I. I thought for sure, when I left that idiot barbarian's throne room, there was no chance George would capture the first piece."

Mosley snorted. "What do you expect? The leader of Brandor's pack was doing all the work. The door was left wide open for George to walk in and take it. I have to say, the fight between Brandor and the scorpions was most impressive. But, no matter how I feel, George won the crystal fair and square."

"It was also impressive to watch Shalee's power," Lasidious added. "I wish I knew what Bassorine did to her to make her grow so fast."

The wolf grinned and Lasidious caught a glimpse of it. "You know some-thing, don't you?" the God of Mischief questioned. "You know what Bas-sorine did, but you're not going to tell me, are you?"

"You give me too much credit, Lasidious," Mosley responded. "I do not know anything more than you, but it does make me happy to know I have a chess piece who can hold a candle to George."

"Agreed," Alistar chimed in. "It was sad to see Shalee's friend die. I'm sure this will set her back."

"Mosley," Lasidious said, ignoring Alistar's sentiment, "Do you remem-ber I said there would be two pieces of the crystal placed on Grayham?"

"I do."

"Do you also remember the day you and Bassorine appeared before Sam and Shalee in the temple?"

"I do."

"Do you remember when Sam and Shalee said three of them had appeared in the Temple of the Gods and George had fallen through the floor?"

"What are you getting at, Lasidious?"

"Give me a moment, I'm getting there...just relax. I was about to ask, do you also remember George was the one who picked up a piece of the crystal, causing the rest of the Crystal Moon to vanish?"

"I do. He was the one to touch the crystal. What does this have to do with where you put..." Mosley stopped mid-sentence. After a moment, he began to laugh in his wolfish way. "You cannot be serious." He looked at Lasidi-ous. It was clear to both of them the wolf had figured it out.

"What's so funny, Mosley?" Alistar inquired, acting as if he didn't al-ready know. He winked at Lasidious and smiled, careful not to allow the others to see the exchange.

Mosley responded, "I am laughing at the irony. I have known where the second piece of the crystal was during this entire series of moments, but I had not thought of it until now."

"So where is it?" Mieonus snapped.

Mosley turned and looked at the goddess. "Patience, Mieonus. Have pa-tience. Lasidious said the crystal would be on Grayham...and it is. It has been with George during his entire journey."

Mieonus' team exploded with laughter while the other four members of Mosley's team began swearing at the God of Mischief. All Lasidious could do was stand at the head of the table and grin. He had expected a mixed reac-tion and now that it was happening, he was enjoying every moment of it.

George Meets the Serpent King

George teleported to the home of the Barbarian King, south of Blood-vain. As planned, the king's scouts have brought the snakes to this secluded destination for their meeting. The Serpent King has been told George is the new monarch.

"So, you're the new King of Bloodvain," Seth said in his hissing voice as he watched the human enter the cabin.

It took the mage a moment to gather his thoughts. He had never spoken with a snake before, and this particular one had a body over seventy feet long. His fangs were large, sharp, and intimidating. Seth had an aura which made George quiver inside. However, the manipulator refused to show this weakness.

Seth saw George staring at him. He hissed again. "Is there something wrong with you, human? Something to cause you to stare at your guests so rudely?"

George apologized. He moved to the fireplace and took a seat on the hearth. This home of Senchae's was more of the same: mounted animal trophies everywhere in yet another stupid log cabin. The mage was thankful none of the barbarian's trophies involved a snake of any kind.

"I'm glad you were able to visit with me, Seth. You have a problem head-ing toward your kingdom. I wish to help."

The snake slithered into a better position to converse. "What makes you think I need a human's help?"

George shook his head in disgust. "The island of the Scorpion King was attacked by Brandor. They'll be headed your way soon. From what I know of your numbers, you can't defend yourselves against Brandor's legions. You know I'm right."

"Brandor's army couldn't get past the mares. I sense no serious threat to my serpent nation."

Because of the snake's hissed words, George found himself leaning forward, impatiently waiting for each syllable to be spit out. It was as if the slithering king had some sort of speech impediment.

"You're wrong," George retorted. "They destroyed the mares."

"You expect me to believe this? The mares are deadly. How did they perish?" The serpent adjusted his coils as he waited for the response.

George decided he would turn up the heat and spoke with a forceful conviction. "I don't give a rat's ass if you believe me, Seth. I know I speak the truth. If you don't want my help, leave and don't come back. You can die like the scorpions...and the mares. Do I need to show you before you'll listen?"

"That's a safe question to ask, since you know it's imposible to do."

"Not impossible, Serpent King. I can take you to the island, if you'd like." George stood from his seat and waited for the reply.

Seth studied the human's face prior to answering. "I have no desire to travel this evening."

George rolled his eyes. "I'll take us there. You don't need to move from the spot you're in. Close your eyes and we'll go."

Seth and his guard coiled their bodies tighter. "You expect me to close my eyes, human?" The Serpent King's tail rattled. "Do you take me for a fool? You're up to something, King of Barbarians."

George had heard enough. He waved his hand and put his magical bonds on Seth and his guard. "Look, you slimy bastard, if I wanted to hurt you, I could've done it already. There's nothing you could do to stop me. Do you want my help or not?" The mage waved his hand again and released just the snake's wicked tongue.

The snake tried with all his might to break George's magic, but could not move. After a while, Seth realized he could speak. "Release me, two legs, and I will accept your offer."

George clapped his hands. "Send your guard from the room and we'll get going."

Once Seth did as instructed, George waved his hand to release the guard. The snake slithered off as it collected the others to leave.

"Look. Stop being a pain in the ass. All you need to do is close your eyes. I'll take care of the rest. When you open them, we'll be on Scorpion Island."

Seth was astonished when he opened his eyes. "Magic has never been used on my coils. Are we truly on the island?"

"This is the place. I'll release you. But, you need to understand I can do far greater magic than what you've just experienced. I don't want to be put in a position which would cause me to use it."

"I understand."

George released his power and allowed the serpent to investigate the island's southern shore. The mage followed until the snake believed he was on the island. The scorpions' bodies lay everywhere.

George looked at his map while he waited and saw the snake's kingdom was south-southwest of their current position. He moved to the shore and once again created an ice raft. "When you're done slithering all over the damn place, let's get going."

Once on the other side of the lake, George spoke. "Look, Seth, I've shown you everything I said is true. I want to create an alliance."

"I trust your words, human."

"Then, we are allies?"

"Yes, we are allies."

"Splendid. The moment has arrived for you to go home. Prepare for war. The Kingdom of Brandor will attack soon. Make no mistake, the Barbarian Kingdom will help, but you will be at war before I can get my army here. Prepare a good battle plan. You know your lands. Take advantage of this. Make Brandor's army come to you. Fight them from inside your underground kingdom. Don't fight them on the surface. You will lose the war if you do. My army will attack as soon as we arrive."

"My kind will forever be in your debt. A victory over Brandor will mean freedom for my cousin, Farogwain."

George had no idea what Seth was talking about, but he didn't let his ignorance slow him down. "See what I mean, Seth? We need each other. You're going to get your cousin back. How awesome is that?"

"You speak strange, King of Barbarians. We shall meet again in battle."

George nodded, then closed his eyes. When he opened them, he was standing by his sleeping wife. He smiled as he looked at his peaceful beauty, then climbed in to take his place beside her.

Soon, the mage was asleep. Lasidious appeared in his dreams. George was glad to see the god, but angry since the dream of his baby girl was pleasant. Despite his annoyance, there were business matters which needed to be addressed. "Damn, Lasidious," George snapped. "You interrupted a dream about my Abbie."

"I'm sorry, George, but I have news to discuss. You possess both pieces of the Crystal Moon on Grayham."

"I was wondering why the crystal began to glow when I put it in my pack. Is the other one in there as well?"

"It is. You have had it since your arrival. I have kept it hidden. When you get up and open your pack, you will be able to see them both. Do you understand this will bring war to your doorstep?"

"I've already thought of this. When I got the first piece, Sam and Shalee were there. They know I have it. I figured this would force them to attack Bloodvain, but I've got other ideas. I'm going to bring the fight to the cavern of the Serpent King. I've already taken Seth to Scorpion Island to show him what Brandor is capable of. He's willing to align his kingdom with Bloodvain. He thinks Brandor is going to attack."

Lasidious was unsure about George's new plan. "How do you intend to get Brandor to attack Seth when you have both crystals? I don't see why Brandor would attack his underground city. There's no reason for this."

"It makes sense when you know what I know. I have a plan, Lasidious, but it requires a small amount of help from you."

"George, I've told you before...I can't help with any direct event which could change the balance of power."

"I know, I know, I know. Blah, blah, blah. I don't need you to do anything like that. All I need you to do is get the gods, who were with you when I threatened Senchae with his son's life, to show up tomorrow night in the Barbarian King's throne room. I have a few things to say the gods will find interesting. Could you make sure they are there?"

Lasidious smiled. "I sense a plan of genius. I'll grant your request. May I know what this plan is?"

"You can wait. Just be there by Late Bailem and I assure you won't be dissatisfied. Once I leave Bloodvain, I'll be heading to Gessler Village. Bring the gods to The Bloody Trough to hear the rest of my plan. I'll be at the bar drinking. Just keep them from following me to the shed when I take a leak. Maybe you could bump into a chair or something to let me know you're there."

Lasidious agreed and left George to enjoy the rest of his dream. In the morning, the mage woke up with his wife and attended to her as she once again began throwing up.

The God World of Ancients Sovereign

Lasidious called Mosley, Yaloom, and Mieonus to the Hall of Judgment. "How are you today?" Lasidious asked.

The gods and the Book of Immortality—who always rested in the hall—said they were fine, but demanded the God of Mischief get down to business.

"Did any of you hear what George said to the Serpent King last night?"

"I did," Mosley responded. "Why?"

"Did you get everything I got out of that meeting?" Lasidious sat at the table and played with the Book's golden stand, waiting for a response.

Mosley thought a moment. "Nothing more than George telling the snake that Brandor was going to attack his kingdom. I know he wants them to fight underground."

Lasidious had not known this information, but he did not let on about his ignorance. "So, I see a problem with his plan, don't you?"

The wolf moved to the head of the table and sat on his haunches on the floor. "I see many flaws in his plan. Brandor has no intention of attacking Seth. Why would they fight the Serpent King's army when George possesses the pieces of the crystal? Sam will attack Bloodvain, not Serpent City."

"I agree, but I overheard George telling the Barbarian King he needed to meet with him tonight. I thought we could listen in on this meeting. It will be intriguing to see what he's planning."

The Book of Immortality floated to a hovering position in front of Lasidious. The thin slit in his binding opened. "Do you want me to attend this gathering?"

"Why not?" Lasidious responded. "All you do is sit here and collect dust. Maybe you should get some fresh air in those pages of yours."

The Book took a few moments. "I don't see any reason why I can't. When shall I appear?"

Lasidious patted the Book's cover. "Be in the barbarian's throne room just before Late Bailem. Remain unseen to the mortals."

Late Bailem, Bloodvain's Throne Room

Lasidious, Mieonus, Mosley, and the Book arrived in their invisible form and stood behind Senchae's throne. Yaloom stayed home, stating he no longer cared what happened. Despite the god's anger toward Lasidious, his curiosity got the best of him. He is watching the meeting from his waterfall.

Senchae, the new general of his army, Corvin Hurthon, his guards, and a few of the army's military officers are in attendance. George appeared at the center of the room with Kepler and his brothers surrounding him.

"Thank you for coming," George announced, without wasting another moment. "I've called you here to let you know I intend to make sure the battle for the pieces of the crystal is fought on non-barbarian soil. I'll be traveling to the Serpent Kingdom to hide the Crystal Moon's pieces until we can defeat the Kingdom of Brandor."

Senchae interrupted, "How will you keep the crystals from being used by the snakes as a bargaining tool to create an alliance with Brandor?"

"I'll hide the crystals within the Serpent King's underground city. Seth will not know he has them." George paused for effect. "I have things I must do and won't be able to be contacted by anyone for the next 15 Peaks. I will be creating other alliances. We must gather enough of an army to crush Brandor."

"Where will you go?" Senchae asked.

"My King, this is a matter best left between you and me. These brave men around us do not need to worry about such things. They have much to do to prepare for war. With your permission, maybe we could speak of this during some other series of moments."

Senchae liked the diplomacy displayed by his consulate. "Agreed. We'll speak of this later." Senchae knew George had no intention of telling him anything, but the mage made everyone feel he respected his position, and this was good enough for the king.

George looked into the many eyes around the room, watching to make sure the men liked the idea of using the snakes to fight Brandor. After a brief question and answer session, he made his exit.

⋆⋇⋆⋇⋆

"Sounds like George is worried Brandor will defeat the barbarians," Mosley said after watching George disappear. He turned to face Lasidious. "Let's meet at the Hall of Judgment to discuss this." Everyone agreed, then vanished.

Soon, Lasidious lifted his feet onto the table in the hall. He leaned back, enjoying his position of power. The Book of Immortality took its place on the golden stand while Mieonus stood behind the God of Mischief, rubbing his shoulders.

Mosley spoke first as he lied on the table. "As I said before, it sounds like George is worried the barbarians will be defeated by Brandor. The human wants to ensure he does not lose the crystals. Hiding them in the Serpent King's city is a great idea. Sam will never know where they are. I wonder where George went after he left the meeting? Why does he need 15 Peaks before he can make another appearance in Bloodvain?" Mosley lifted his leg and scratched behind his ear.

"That's what I want to know," Lasidious responded. "I say we find out." The god waved his hand and a map of Grayham appeared. He told the map to search for George and it revealed the mage's location. "Hmmm, Gessler Village."

"I like your new toy," Mieonus said after seeing how it found the mage. "When did you create it?"

"You know me. I'm always tinkering with one creation or another. Shall we go?" They agreed and once again disappeared.

<hr />

When George appeared with the cats, they were underneath The Bloody Trough. It was good they had appeared in the spot they did, as there were two horses drinking underneath the inn on the opposite side of the troughs' wall. The presence of the three jaguars would have scared the life out of them. Instead, the demons hid within the shadows and waited for George.

The mage walked into the inn, found a seat at the bar, ordered an ale, and waited for Lasidious. After a bit, he was able to relax and enjoy his drink.

<hr />

Mosley was the first to appear outside the inn. Once the others arrived, they entered together, unseen as before. Finding a spot to sit, they watched to see what the mage was up to.

"Why would we want to watch him drink?" Mieonus whined. "All he's here for is some ale. This isn't worthy of a god's attention."

Lasidious shook his head. "We don't know why George is here. Leaving would be stupid. He must have a reason. Maybe he's meeting someone.

Let's see what happens. It's not like you have anything better to do. I'll summon us a drink."

Lasidious waved his hand across the table and soon everyone who could drink had frosty ale. The Book, feeling a bit left out, opened the thin slit within its binding to speak. "I wish you had created me with the ability to enjoy a stiff drink. I have always wondered what food and many of the liquids you pour down your throats taste like. I hear you talk about them, and find that I am curious."

After a brief debate, the gods agreed it wouldn't do any harm to give the Book a set of taste buds, eyes, rosy cheeks, arms, teeth, a tongue, nose, and a small stomach buried deep within its pages. They decided the waste, normally exiting the body, would be stored in the form of excess random letters toward the back of its heavy binding. The Book would open and dump the letters to the ground every so often when the page was full. The idea the Book would take a dump by dropping piles of letters all over the ground gave the gods a good laugh. They wondered if the piles of text would have an odor.

As they laughed, Lasidious used the distraction to make sure George knew they were there. He caused one of the chairs to make a noise, acting as if it was unintentional. Everyone in the room turned to look in the direction of what they thought to be an empty table.

"Do you think he knows we're here?" Mieonus asked as she watched George stare in their direction.

Mosley chided. "Between Yaloom falling in the fire and you bumping into chairs, we might as well put up a sign that says: 'Hey, George, we're watching you.'"

The gods laughed as they watched George turn back around to face the bar. Soon, a massive man walked in and sat down to order a drink. The gods watched as a conversation between the big man and George began. The mage ordered another drink and, after a while, excused himself in the middle of the conversation. He would leave more than once, and every moment this happened, Lasidious kept the gods busy. This was an easy task. They were keeping good company.

George walked to the back of the inn and entered the shed where Double D had killed the barbarian. He poured his glass of ale in the hole. He figured he would make a few more trips before putting his plan into action.

After a few more ales, George stepped up his drunken act, singing out the whereabouts of the Crystal Moon. "Hey, big man, did you know the Crystal Moon has been stolen from the Temple of the Gods?" He raised his voice so everyone could hear. "I know where two of the crystal's pieces are. I have them on me. See, look, I have them right here...yep...I do." Lifting them high into the air, he continued as he stumbled around. "I spoke with the Serpent King. Shhhh, don't tell anyone. He's going to let me hide the crystals in his underground city."

Lasidious acted surprised. "What's he doing? He's going to ruin his plan. Why would he do this?"

Mieonus responded, "I don't know, but he's your puppet, not mine."

"Be quiet," Mosley snapped. "Listen!"

George continued. "My buddy, Sam, is the King of Brandor. I'm sure you've all heard about this. I don't have to tell any of you he'd be pissed if he knew I had these."

The mage fell on his butt as he put both crystals back in his pack and continued speaking from his seat on the floor. "I bet Sam would pay a reward if he knew I was taking the crystals to the Serpent King's city. You know what? That bastard is too cheap to see this information is worth good coin. Maybe, I should explain it to him. I bet everyone here thinks this information is worth good coin."

George stumbled up to a big man and threw his arm around him. The mage noticed the bar was filling with many interested ears. All he had to do was play up the story a little longer and someone would confront him. He took some coin from his pocket and started throwing it around.

"If I were a king, I'd pay for this information, but Sam is too stupid." George moved away from the big guy, making sure he fell to the floor again. "Does anyone want to go to Serpent City with me? Oops, none of you can teleport. You're all pathetic. I don't know why I'm hanging out with any of you spineless idiots."

As he picked himself off the floor, a voice from across the room called out, "I'd be careful who you call names. A swine like yourself would be an easy target for a killing if he didn't watch his tongue."

George turned to find the source of the threat. Standing near the door of the inn was an intimidating barbarian. With his clothes made of furs and protruding muscles, George could not have picked a better person to finish his drunken demonstration if he had hand picked him.

The mage stumbled in his direction. "I bet you think you're the one to do it, don't you?" George slurred. "I have bigger fish to fry than you. You're just a stupid barbarian."

The gods watched in disbelief as George stumbled around, acting like a drunken fool. "He is being careless and stupid," Mosley said.

"I can't believe this," Lasidious added. "I think George has allowed the ale to effect his judgment. He's picking a fight with the biggest guy in the bar. George is going to kill him. He'll need to leave after this. Is anyone in a betting mood?"

All the gods wanted in on the action. "I say he kills the barbarian and heads for the Serpent's Kingdom to hide the crystal," Mosley said.

Mieonus rubbed her hands together. "I think he'll kill the barbarian, then go sleep off his intoxication before going to the snake's city."

The Book of Immortality decided to bet as well. "I think he'll kill the barbarian and teleport to Scorpion Island. He'll hide the crystals there. No one would ever think he'd do something like that. The island is empty. There's no chance anyone would go there to look for them. I think George is sober and this is just an act to draw Brandor to Seth's city of snakes. He's counting on someone to run and tell Sam about his secret hiding spot for the crystals."

Lasidious laughed. "I have to admit...that's pretty deep." The god thought a moment, then realized they had never given the Book a name. It was odd to be chatting with it and be unable to address it in any kind of formal manner. "I agree with Mieonus, but something's bugging me."

"What is that?" Mosley queried.

"It's silly, I suppose, but do you realize we've all been sitting here talking to the Book and it feels like it's one of us? Do you know what I mean? I feel like it's a part of our group. Maybe we should give it a name." Lasidious looked at the Book. "Would you like a man or woman's name?"

"That's a great idea," Mieonus clapped. "I agree we should name it. It is awkward, now that you mention it."

Everyone was in agreement as George turned the big barbarian to stone and left the bar. The gods were enjoying their conversation far too much to care. They dismissed the killing with little more than a glance. They would finish their conversation before tracking the mage.

After a good while, the Book spoke. "I think I like the name Thomas."

"Thomas?" Lasidious questioned. "How about something which suits the power you possess? Thomas is a weak name."

Mieonus jumped into the conversation. "How about using the name Dagan or Drake? Either of those sound more powerful."

The Book did not like their choices. Mosley added a comment to the mix. "Thomas does sound weak. You are far too powerful for a name like that. How about a name fit for the dragons on Dragonia?"

The Book declined. "The reason I chose Thomas is because, of all the souls within my pages, he's the one who stands out above the rest. This specific Thomas I'm referring to was from Dukas and died when it was destroyed. I've grown to know Thomas' soul quite well since I collected him. Granted, he was one of the billions I collected when I left to gather them all. He provided good company while I traveled. He was ten seasons old when he perished and..."

"So you liked the child," Lasidious interrupted, "but the name you choose will be with you for eternity. Make it a strong one. Don't settle for something feeble."

The Book tried to finish his story. "The child's one concern when he found out he died..."

Mieonus interrupted. "We aren't going to call you Thomas. You might as well pick something stronger. Give us another one."

Mosley stopped gnawing on his right front paw. "You need a strong name."

Exasperated, the Book thought a moment longer and spit out another one. "How does Gabriel sound?"

All the gods agreed and, since it was a man's name, the gods adjusted the Book's new facial features to something more masculine. Mosley tried it on for size. "So, Gabriel, it is nice to meet you." The wolf laughed at how silly it seemed to refer to the Book as a real person.

"It's a boy, everyone," Mieonus screamed. "But, the baby has a square head. Don't tell its mother...she'll want to put it back on the shelf."

The joke made for a good chuckle. Mosley changed the subject. "Gabriel, maybe we should look for George and see who won the bet."

Gabriel agreed. The gods checked Lasidious' map to see where the mage had gone. As he rolled it out onto the table, the Mischievous One thought back to his conversation with George the night he sat with him near the fire. He remembered what he said outside of Lethwitch within the trees of the Enchanted Forest. He told George his daughter was the only soul saved from the darkness of space around the destroyed Earth and was glad George had not heard that everyone's soul had been saved.

As it turned out, the Book was right. George was inside the cave on Scorpion Island. They decided they would join the mage, but on this occasion, they would not stay hidden. When they appeared, the gods stood behind the unsuspecting man.

Lasidious was the first to speak. "Nice act, George. I thought you were drunk."

George whirled around as Lasidious spoke, and sent his magic flying. The god caught the pulsating arrows in his hand like they were nothing more than minor inconveniences. The mage regrouped once he saw who it was and apologized. "What are you doing here, Lasidious? Why are they with you?"

Kepler and his brothers stayed in the shadows as they watched Mosley sniff around as he spoke. "Relax, George. I have to admit, you had me fooled in Gessler." Once Mosley realized the jaguars were present, he snorted his disapproval. He continued to speak without acknowledging their presence. "You are creative, George. You did all this without the assistance of your useless feline companions. Tell Kepler I look forward to our next meeting."

"Oh, shut up, wolf," Mieonus snapped. "You know the beast is hiding." She looked at George. "You play the game well. You'd make a fine god. Your deception will keep Brandor busy for quite a while. I hope you win the war."

Gabriel floated to a hovering position in front of George. "You're a far cry from the soul I have within my pages. Your daughter isn't deceitful like you. I find it hard to believe your daughter's gentle spirit was given to you to be her father. How could your gods of Earth expect a man with evil in his heart to raise a child? Abbie is nothing like you...nothing like you at all. Yet, she still loves you."

George dropped to his knees at the thought of his daughter. He was about to ask Gabriel a question, but Lasidious cut in. "George," he said in a louder-than-normal tone. The mage picked up on his subtle hint and dropped the subject. "What's next, my friend? What happens in this cave stays in the cave."

George rolled his eyes as he stood and used his magic to clean the scorpion garesh off his knees. "Sounds like Vegas."

The gods looked puzzled as he studied their faces. "Oh, forget it. Since when do you all watch me?" the mage asked as if he had no clue. "I guess I must be turning heads, eh?"

"You are," Gabriel responded. "What's next in your plan?"

The mage shifted his feet. "Seems strange to be talking to a book." He walked around Gabriel and studied him from all angles. "But, hey, who am I to say anything. You're just another freak this world has in it."

George tossed the two pieces of crystal on the ground. "I don't think I'm going to tell you what I'm up to. You can watch. Isn't that what you guys do best? Now, if you don't mind, I've got a hole to dig."

The gods agreed they were going to learn nothing more. They arranged to meet at the Hall of Judgment, then vanished. Before Lasidious left, he gave George a wink. "Keep up the good work."

A Ticket Out of Here

George buried the pieces of the Crystal Moon behind the pedestal, then patted the top of the podium's smooth surface. He looked at the blood-stained area of earth beyond and thought of how the Scorpion King had torn Shalee's friend apart. The memory kept replaying in his mind. The more he thought about it, the more it bothered him. He could have saved her. After a long series of moments, he sighed, *I'm sorry! I truly am sorry. But, my Abbie is more important than you were. I couldn't risk my life for someone I didn't know.*

He moved to stand over the spot where Helga's pieces had been scattered. *Perhaps, if I would have had more power. Maybe, I can pay you back in another life. No one should have to die like that.* He lifted his head, then, after a moment, his grief turned to scorn. *What the hell were you doing here anyway?* He looked down and kicked a blood-stained rock. The rock bounced across the cave floor and landed in a pile of scorpion garesh. *Stupid woman!*

George closed his eyes and teleported outside the city of Champions. He made his way to a hole-in-the-wall tavern. Once there, he saw the caliber of men who were drinking. Tonight was his lucky night. This would be his last stop. He couldn't believe his good fortune. A group of Brandor's soldiers were celebrating their buddy's last night as a single man.

George noticed the future groom happened to be an officer in Sam's army. Just like at The Bloody Trough, he delivered his message, but during this series of moments he had Kepler and his brothers pin everyone against a wall. Amongst the cats' snarls, he professed to his frightened audience he was going to hide the two pieces of the Crystal Moon in the Serpent King's underground city. His declaration was as good as gold.

Before George left the tavern, he turned the future husband into stone. He threatened the dead man's friends who were as highly ranked. Once the mage was sure his message about the crystal's pieces would get to Sam, he leaned over and whispered in Kepler's ear. "Kill everyone, but allow two of Sam's officers to escape. Meet me outside."

The jaguars did as instructed as George walked out of the tavern. As he sat on the heavy wooden railing of the porch, he listened to the sounds of death. Moments later, the two survivors burst out of the door and bounded down the steps with Keller close behind. After chasing them down the road a bit, the demon stopped, then returned. Once the blood-soaked cats finished feasting, George teleported the group south of Bloodvain.

"Keller, go into the city and deliver a message. Tell the king I want him to mobilize the army and head to the western shore of Southern Grayham. Tell Senchae, once they get to their destination, he needs to march the army south and stop north of the Serpent King's borders to set up camp. The army needs to mobilize before morning. I want Sam's scouts to think Senchae is after the crystals. Let's hope Sam takes the bait and takes his army to the serpent's doorstep.

"Take this note to Senchae. If you forget anything, it's all here." George rolled the parchment and tied it to the demon's neck. "Hurry! Once you return, we will go to Athena's. We'll sleep through the day and go to Angel's Village tomorrow night. We have a lot of work to do over the next 9 Peaks."

Once home in Lethwitch, he called to Athena as if it was any other night. "Honey, I'm home."

Athena ran into the room and jumped into his arms. "Oh, I missed you. How long are you here?"

"I have to leave tomorrow. I'll be gone for a while, but I should be able to put this family together real soon. You won't have to work if you don't want to. The family can come with us as well."

Athena hugged him, "Where will we be living?"

George took a deep breath. "In City View. I think you'll love it there. So will the family."

Athena gasped. "That city is full of barbarians. What about our safety?" She cupped her hand over her mouth. "What about our baby's safety? My family won't want to go."

"There's no reason to worry. I'm beloved within the barbarian kingdom for the work I do. No one will harm us. We will be safe and so will your family."

Athena shook her head. "I'll follow you anywhere, as promised, but I don't think my family will go. That will be hard."

"You're forgetting I can bring you home whenever you want. Besides, I'll talk to your family. I'm sure they'll want to come. Don't worry, okay? I have everything under control. Have I ever let you down? Do you trust me?"

"Of course I trust you." She led him into the bedroom. "Let me show you how much," she said with a grin of promise.

After a good while, George lay back on the bed, exhausted from their activities, and snuggled his wife. He had chosen to move the family to City View because it was the one place in the Barbarian Kingdom that would not see war.

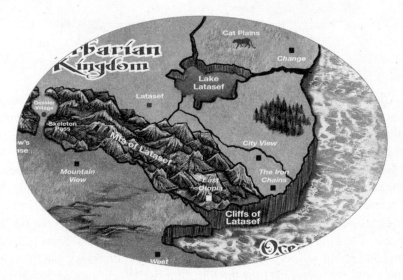

If Sam believed his deception about where the Crystal Moon's pieces were said to be hidden, war would not extend this far east. Although he did not plan for Lethwitch to see war either, he knew his face would draw attention. It would be impossible to live here. From here on out, when he visited Athena, he would not be able to leave the walls of their home until they moved.

It was just before the Peak of Bailem when his mind settled and he was able to fall asleep. His slumber would be shortlived. Kepler and his brothers were hidden in the Enchanted Forest. George was scheduled to meet them at dusk.

The City of Brandor

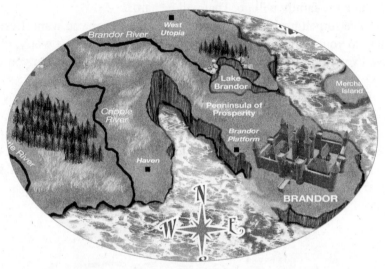

After saying goodbye, BJ left with Helga's body in the back of Sam's royal wagon. He wanted to find a spot on the western coast of the peninsula to light the fire to honor Helga's passing. BJ's heart was heavy. He had loved Helga more than any other.

Sam and Shalee had left for Cottle to attend the Passing Ceremonies of the men who died on Scorpion Island. Shalee had offered to stay behind, but BJ wanted to be alone. When the queen tried to object, Sam pulled her aside and suggested she let him go. It would be good for BJ to begin the healing process. The king needed his advisor's head to be clear as soon as possible. Sam had apologized, saying he was sorry for his callousness, but he had to think about what was best for the kingdom. BJ's face showed his disdain, despite understanding Sam's position.

The wagon held Helga's coffin on one side and the wood for her pyre on the other. This was the second series of moments in which BJ had to say goodbye to a woman in his life. The problem was, with Helga's death, his heart was destroyed. He was lost. His first relationship did not have the same passion he shared with Helga and his sorrow was unbearable. He traveled for as long as it took to find a spot which complemented his lost love's beauty.

When BJ found this perfect spot, he jumped from the wagon and made his final judgment. The sand of the beach was white and clean. The waves rolled onto the shore, adding a sense of peace BJ knew Helga would have enjoyed. The trees sat back from the shoreline and created an alcove of privacy. Within this alcove, there were two boulders which sat close to one another. They would serve as the perfect spot to light the fire.

As he lifted the wood from the wagon, BJ's heart became heavier with each step. Never had he felt so overcome with sadness. He longed for his love to return and claim an evil jest had been played. It consumed his thoughts as he stacked the wood the way Helga deserved. He would not settle for anything less than perfection with the placement of each plank. BJ was losing more of himself with each piece. His heart was falling into a pit, one from which he could not crawl out.

He read from a scroll Shalee had created. The magic gave him the strength to carry Helga's coffin from the wagon and lift it onto the pile. He made sure it was centered, adjusting it a hundred different ways before he felt its placement was perfect.

Dusk was approaching. BJ watched the sunset cast its beautiful array of colors into the darkening sky. This would be the last series of moments they could share. The urge to hold her as the sun descended behind the horizon pulled at him.

He hurried to grab an iron bar to break the lock which secured the coffin shut. He lifted the latch, not knowing his love lay torn apart inside.

Unsure if this was the right thing to do, BJ paused. How could he pass on this opportunity? How could he pass on showing his love? He convinced himself Helga would have enjoyed the idea of being held before lighting her fire. He lifted the lid and looked inside to find Helga's beautiful face. Seeing her mutilated pieces, his expression turned from one full of passion to one of horror and excruciating agony.

BJ took a step back from the coffin. Losing his balance, he fell to the beach and crawled away from the nightmare. He collapsed into the cascading water which flowed onto the shore. He lifted his head to the heavens and screamed, cursing the gods for stealing his happiness, cursing Sam for allowing Helga to go into the mouth of danger, and finally, he cursed Shalee for not being there when Helga needed her most.

A long series of moments passed before BJ stood and retrieved his dagger. He lit a torch and grabbed a container of oil. He poured the liquid over the wood beneath the coffin, but only on a single side. He cleared a place next to Helga and lied next to her pieces. With the torch in his left hand, he plunged the dagger into his stomach with his right. Dropping the torch onto the wood below, BJ laid back, closed his eyes and waited for the dagger's wound to end his life.

The flames spread much quicker than BJ anticipated. In his grief and confused state, he had used too much oil. His eyes had not closed forever before the intense heat consumed the coffin. His horrific screams filled the night before his soul left for the Book of Immortality's pages.

George Meets the Minotaur King

George spent the last four and a half days putting his plan in motion. Kepler had been instrumental in its execution. George realized the moments necessary to implement his plan were short—critical, in fact. He needed to hurry to ensure the war would happen in the Serpent King's kingdom.

George used his power to strengthen Kepler's body and has been riding the demon for the last 4 Peaks of Bailem. The jaguar's brothers tagged along, poking fun as Kepler complained about the saddle the mage created. Despite the taunting, Kepler was accepting of his demeaning task.

Now, they were approaching the rolling pastures where the Minotaur King grazed. George put a wall of force around the group as he rode Kepler into the area. The group's intrusion was not welcome. The part-bull, part-human subjects of the Minotaur King bellowed curses as the intruders passed.

George had never seen so many of these creatures. Their large bull heads, attached to human-looking torsos, and human-looking arms, were massive. The bottom half of the beasts' cow-like legs rippled as their weight shifted. They stood upright and walked like any normal man. It was odd to watch them reach down near their hooves, tear the grass from the earth with their hands, then place it near their mouths, only to scoop the plant in with their large tongues to consume it.

As they drew closer to the king, the beasts became aggressive and attacked. They bounced off George's magic like a child's ball would bounce off a wall. The mage laughed as the beasts picked themselves off the ground, dazed from their collision against the invisible shield. Kepler stopped in front of the Minotaur King. After watching his strongest subjects fail to break through George's magic, the king addressed the mage.

Kepler translated as the beast king spoke, asking if George was a god. George allowed Kepler to confirm he was, in fact, a god.

"Kepler, tell him my name and ask him his."

Kepler did as instructed. "He said his name is, if I'm translating it right, Horace."

"Horace?" George chuckled. "What the hell? Was his mother pissed when she named him?"

Kepler growled. "This might not be the proper series of moments to jest, George. A little more tact would work in this situation."

"Blah, blah, blah, I get it. Tell Horace it would be wise to send his scouts to watch for Brandor's army. Tell him Brandor is going to kill all beasts who live under a monarchy. Tell him the Scorpion King is already dead. It is only a matter of moments until he's next. Tell him Brandor's next target will be the Serpent King's underground city and tell him I can show him some of Brandor's handiwork."

Kepler rolled his eyes and thought, *Tell him, tell him, tell him, tell him. What an idiot.* The demon spoke with the Minotaur King. George smiled within as the beast bellowed.

Kepler turned to translate. "He's angry, George. He hates Brandor's new king. He feels their champion was cheated out of victory. He wants revenge."

George tilted his head. "He feels like he was cheated by Sam? I saw that fight. This is freaking perfect. You couldn't ask for a bigger silver platter."

Kepler's eyes flashed as he twisted his head to look at the mage. "Silver platter? What does a plate have to do with this negotiation? Have you become dense?"

"Bah! It's just an expression. Just tell the king I can take him to the Scorpion King's island and show him the carnage."

Kepler translated. "He said he's willing to go."

"Tell him to close his eyes."

Once done, the mage teleported the group to the location of the Scorpion King's body. When they appeared, they were next to the pedestal. George commanded the darkness to dissipate, then pointed to the giant anthropod's body. The minotaur bellowed, then walked up and out of the cave to take a look around the rest of the island. George was quick to direct him to the southern shore, watching the minotaur's anger grow as he witnessed the gruesome scene.

"Kep, ask Horace if he knows anything about the water mist mares."

Again, Kepler did as instructed. "He says they are powerful."

"Well then...tell the king the mares are dead, thanks to Brandor. Tell him I can prove it."

"George, are we starting this tell me, to tell him, to tell me, to tell you thing again? You're killing me."

"Shut up and tell him, will ya?"

Kepler obeyed. "He says, if Brandor can defeat the spirits, there is too much power in their army. He wants to know what can be done. He says his army is not strong enough to fight Brandor."

"His army doesn't need to be strong enough. I don't want him to attack Brandor right away. He'll need to wait until they attack the Serpent King. Make sure he understands I have a plan. If he attacks Brandor from behind, he'll have assistance. The Barbarian King's army will march from the north of the serpent's kingdom. The barbarians will be his allies for this war. Tell him Senchae's army is on the way."

"He wants to know why the barbarians would help."

"Tell him it's because Senchae does not want Brandor to gain too much power. Once the war is over, they'll go home. Senchae only wants to weaken Brandor's army. He wants to keep them from killing the beasts of Grayham. Senchae believes the beasts of this world are necessary for the survival of all kingdoms."

Kepler translated. "He agrees with your logic, George. He also doesn't want Brandor to have this kind of power. This would provide the chance for his kind to avenge the death of their champion."

"It's settled then. Make sure he knows the bears of the bear clan will be fighting as an ally as well. Tell him I will bring the Bear King to see him. They can devise a plan and work together."

Sam's Throne Room

Sam walked into his throne room with the general in tow. The nobles of the city and their families were placing gifts meant for the fallen men of the eleventh legion around the throne. They bowed as their king approached and moved to the base of the steps as Sam took his seat.

It was clear Sam was disturbed. "What do you mean, General. Are you telling me George is going to hide the pieces of the Crystal Moon in the Serpent King's underground city?"

"I am," Michael answered. "Forgive me, Sire, but I have only just received this information. There was an attack. One of our surviving officers has come from the city of Champions to deliver this message."

"Then, bring him in, damn it! Why is he in the hall? He can't talk to me from out there."

Sam's heart was heavy. His emotions were getting the best of him. No one had ever seen their king act this way. As a result, the nobles and the castle's servants were walking on eggshells.

Sam had just learned that BJ's hunting knife had been found at the center of a pile of ash. From the looks of it, his friend had committed suicide. The scouts had said the pile was found on the beach where BJ had lit the fire for Helga's passing.

The nobles gave way as Joshua entered from the hallway and moved to the base of the steps leading to the throne. Sweat rolled down his brow as he took a knee. For a long series of moments, Sam kept his head lowered into his palms, unaware of Joshua's presence.

Eventually, Sam cleared his mind of all thoughts concerning BJ and looked up to address his officer. "They tell me you heard a drunk bragging he had two pieces of the Crystal Moon. I was told you heard he was going to hide them. Is this right?"

"Yes, Sire," Joshua responded.

Sam took a deep breath. His face hardened. "Joshua, tell me why a group of my officers was not able to stop this man? Why didn't you bring him to me? Were you drunk? Why were you in the tavern in the first place?"

After hearing the king's tone, Joshua swallowed hard. "We were celebrating our friend's last night as a single man, Sire. The man who entered the tavern traveled with the demon cat, Kepler. There were two others who looked just like him. They were massive, My Lord. We tried to stop the man who spoke such traitorous words, but he wielded magic like I've never seen. He turned our friend to stone. We weren't strong enough to stop his beasts. They slaughtered everyone. I was lucky to have survived. I give praise to Mosley for my escape."

Sam leaned forward. "I'm sure Lord Mosley appreciated your prayers, but it is my forgiveness you should be praying for."

Joshua lowered his head. "Sire, forgive me. I serve this kingdom with honor. My family would die for your crown. There was no way to capture this man."

Joshua's testimony confirmed it was George, but why would George act this way? Once again, Sam's voice was cold. "Why would this man say such things, Joshua? Does it make sense for him to divulge critical information? What else do you know? Look at me."

Sweat dripped from Joshua's nose as he lifted his head. "My King, I swear to you, the man was drunk when he said these things. When he came into the tavern, he was happy, buying the lot of us drinks. Many moments went by before his cats entered. We tried to take him into custody, but the man's demons pinned us against the wall. He told us he knew you from a place called Earth. He called you words I've never heard before."

"And, what were these words?"

"Your Grace, I don't know I care to say them with so many ladies present."

Sam leaned forward and looked Joshua in the eye. "You've found me on a day when I don't have patience for things you care about. I'd tell me now if I were you." Sam pulled Kael from his sheath. "I would hate to place this blade on your shoulder. It doesn't feel good."

Again, Joshua swallowed hard. "Yes, Sire. The man said you had garesh for brains. He said you were spoiled. He called you weak. He said he was smarter than you and you could stick all the languages you speak up your... well...I think he meant your backside, Sire. Shall I continue? There were many other, much stronger sounding words."

Sam leaned back in his chair and laughed. "I bet he did, Joshua, I bet he did! That sounds like a drunk." Everyone in the throne room looked at each other. They would have been embarrassed by the things Joshua said, but their king just laughed.

After a bit, Sam stood and motioned for Michael to come forward. "What do we know of the barbarians? When we were in the cave, George said he was running things up there. Has there been any movement of their army?"

"Sire, we should be getting word from our scouts within days. I dispatched them after we left the island. They were told to report 4 Peaks from now. I have sent additional scouts, every 2 Peaks, to make sure we remain informed. If the first group of scouts doesn't know anything, the others are sure to discover something."

Sam formulated a plan. "I want the first five legions of the army to stay here and protect Brandor. I want the other five and what's left of the eleventh to assemble at the city of Champions. If the information the scouts deliver suggests George is hiding the crystals, we will attack Seth's kingdom. If it's not accurate, we will head north and attack Bloodvain. I'm not about to wait here for something to happen. You have only 8 Peaks of Bailem to do this, General. Do not fail, or I'll lead the army myself!"

"Sire, what of the blade Double D used to kill our king? It was barbarian. The assassin was fulfilling a contract created by barbarians. Should we not forego the crystals to avenge his death?"

Sam moved to stand in front of Michael. He leaned over. The general could smell the ale on his king's breath. "The pieces of the crystal are more important than one man's death, General. The quakes across the kingdom are becoming stronger. Would you have me sacrifice everyone for the sake of revenge?" The king did not wait to hear Michael's reaction and stormed out of the room.

Sam knew it was possible to make his orders work, but right now, his main concern was to make sure Shalee was okay. He knew his queen would be grieving. Since they had arrived on Grayham, they had seen far too much death. Grieving for someone else they cared so much about was hard. He would take his queen and go to where BJ died. He was sure their friends would want them to stand over their ashes to say goodbye.

2 Peaks of Bailem Later

George rode Kepler into the caves of the Bear King with the demon's brothers on either side. As before, they made a strong impression. The conversation was similar to the one with the Minotaur King and included a trip to Scorpion Island. When Groth saw the king's body, he became angered. The kodiak-looking bear exited the cave and walked along the southern shore, speechless as he studied the remnants of the massacre. George was quick to point out Brandor had killed the water mist mares. Groth's reaction was like Horace's. The beast felt Brandor's army was too strong. Something had to be done.

The mage teleported the bear to the Minotaur King's pasture. Kepler translated for both beasts. Horace and Groth formulated a plan to fight together. The minotaur would fight alongside Kepler's skeleton warriors while the demon's giant cats would join the fight with the barbarians. This pleased both kings. With nearly 11,000 barbarians, 1,500 bears, 1,900 minotaur, 600 giant cats, 2,100 snakes, and 500 skeleton warriors, the forces attacking Brandor's army would be over 17,000 strong.

The mage took the bear home after watching his plan fall into place. George asked Kepler to say goodbye and watched as the bear rose up to show his appreciation for George's help.

George teleported the cats to the north side of Lethwitch before heading into town to spend the evening with Athena. He wrote out a message and gave it to Koffler to deliver to the Barbarian King. He explained everything Senchae would need to know, writing this would be the Barbarian

Kingdom's greatest victory and the glory would be Senchae's. He would go down in history as the king who defeated Brandor.

The mage figured this would be enough of an ego boost to solidify the final part of his plan. He told Koffler to be swift on his journey, and for the cat's effort, he would give the demon something special once he returned. He teleported Koffler north of Angel's Village, then returned to Lethwitch to retire for the night.

George would have been proud of Senchae if he knew what the big barbarian had done—he sent his scouts to retrieve the unicorns to join them for battle. It was an unexpected gathering of force the mage had not counted on. With the fifty unicorns entering the battle, Sam would be facing a nightmare of an army comprised of many beings, each with a unique style of fighting.

Kepler went into the Enchanted Forest to send out his orders. He sent one of his tigers to gather the giant cats of the land. They were instructed to move at night and travel toward Zandra. They were to hide north of the lake until Brandor entered Seth's kingdom. Then, they were to circle west of the lake and join the barbarian army for the attack heading south.

Kepler also sent one of his grave raven friends with an order for 500 skeleton warriors to join the fight. This verbal message included code words which only the demon's skeleton commander understood. They were to travel day and night and stay away from populated areas. He wanted the commander to join his cats at Zandra. Once Brandor entered the Serpent Kingdom, the commander was to circle east of the lake and attack with the minotaur.

2 Peaks of Bailem Later

George collected Athena's family and teleported them in small groups to Gessler Village. He paid the innkeeper enough coin to clear everyone out. He intended to keep her family there until he was able to travel. The journey to move Athena's family to City View would take over 12 Peaks of Bailem. Before they could leave The Bloody Trough, George would need to recover. Teleporting the family to Gessler was a massive power drain. Rest was mandatory.

Since they would never set foot in Lethwitch again, George retrieved Maldwin from his mother-in-law's barn. Kepler told the rat the moment had come to get his family. George was keeping his promise and Maldwin twitched his nose in excitement.

The mage asked Keller to go to the Cave of Sorrow to retrieve the rodent's family and bring them to City View. There would be enough moments before their arrival for George to figure out a place for them to live. He figured there had to be a cave where they could stay until he finished building something special.

George slept next to his wife while Kepler and Maldwin kept watch over The Bloody Trough's doors to ensure the family's safety. They would leave in the morning for City View.

George had just fallen asleep when Lasidious appeared in his dream. "Hello, George, I'm impressed by what you have been able to accomplish. But, you're needed somewhere else. City View isn't where you need to go to get your daughter back."

"Kiss my ass, Lasidious! Look, man, I'm tired. I can hardly move. I need rest." There was a short period of silence. "Bah...what do I need to do to get Abbie back?"

Lasidious smiled as he looked at the images of George through the green flames of his fireplace on Ancients Sovereign. He waved his hand through the flames to refresh George's soul. "I have replenished your strength. You can sleep later, my friend," he said as he stared at the wild movements of the fire. "I need you to go to the world of Luvelles. There's work to do."

"What? Are you freaking kidding me? Why would I want to go there? I just got myself into a good position here. A little more manipulating and I'll own this world. What about my wife? What about her family? What the hell would I say to them?"

"George, you're forgetting with whom you speak. I have a solution to your problem. Your wife and her family will be able to go with you. I have made arrangements for Kepler to go as well."

"What about Kepler's brothers, and Maldwin? I can't leave them behind. Kepler won't go without his brothers." George thought a bit. "I promised Maldwin a home for his family, and Keller has gone to get them. Koffler is delivering a message to the Barbarian King. This is terrible planning, Lasidious, just terrible, man."

"Do I detect a soft spot in that cold heart of yours, George? You don't need to worry about Kepler. He's a demon. As far as Maldwin goes, I'll see to it his family has an amazing home inside the cliffs of Latasef. I'll make sure they are protected and ensure they are well fed.

"George, Southern Grayham will not be safe for you and your family. You'll be a hunted man. I'd rather see you use your skills elsewhere. You've proven to be an asset. You've masterfully manipulated this world and your daughter will be with you soon because of it. It won't be long before I have the power to do so."

"You better not be gareshing me, man. How do I get to Luvelles?"

"You need to teleport your family to Merchant Island. Find a man named Hesston Bangs. He will put you into a special container which will be carried by the Merchant Angels to Luvelles. Once there, I'd like you to travel to the village of Floren. You will need to find an elven witch family named Rolfe from the Clan of Ashdown. They'll have a new baby living with them. I want you to kill this family and raise the baby as your nephew. The baby will be born before you arrive. This may come as a shock, but this baby is my son. It is this boy who will give me the power to get your daughter back, but not until he's a season old."

"Holy garesh, Lasidious, that's crazy, man! You want me to raise your child as my nephew? How in the hell am I going to convince Athena's sister to go along with something this outlandish? That's heavy garesh to be springing on someone out of the blue. I mean, how would I break this kind of news anyway? I can just see it now. Hey...Susanne...by the way, you have a kid you forgot plopped out of you. That's just freaking nuts, man. Don't get me wrong, Lasidious, I'd love to take care of your kid. But, how do I make a woman believe something like that?"

"I'm sure you'll figure it out."

"Nice...just leave it up to me. Nice, man. I better get a sweet house out of this if I'm going to be babysitting. I want something that reminds me of Earth. You've been in my head enough to know what I like. I want the whole family to have houses of their own. Do we have a deal?"

"I can manage that, George."

"Right freaking on...then it's settled. So, how can I get everyone to Merchant Island? I've never seen the place before. And, what about the crystals I buried?"

"I want you to take the pieces of the Crystal Moon with you. I'll hide the third piece on Luvelles, but I'll save the revelation of its location until later. As far as Athena's family, have Maldwin prepare their minds to perceive the baby as one of their own before you leave the inn. Use the rat's visions to make them believe my son is Susanne's child. I'm sure you know how to make this happen. The Head Master of Luvelles is expecting you. He thinks his good friend, Amar, has referred you as his new Mystic Learner."

"Why would he think that? Amar is dead."

Lasidious gave an evil grin as he continued to wave his hand through the flames. "Let's just say someone who looked like Amar told him how powerful you are. The Head Master was happy to see his old student. He is making preparations based on Amar's recommendation. You'll have your nice houses, and yes, I'll make sure they're built to your style. Amar told the Head Master to give you plenty of coin when you arrive. It's waiting for you at an inn called Kebble's Kettle.

"You'll be rich. But, you will have to work to keep the gods busy. I need you to make a mess, just like the one you did here. Keep the gods' attention off my son. I think the safest place for the boy is under the gods' noses. They don't have any clue if Susanne has a child or not. It will seem normal for you to call my son your nephew. This will be my greatest deception and you'll be a part of it."

As he slept, George rolled to his other side. "You still haven't told me how to get to Merchant Island. Don't you think Amar visiting the Head Master after he was dead will raise a red flag regarding the moments in which his death occurred?"

Lasidious laughed. "Head Master Brayson thinks he saw Amar a while ago, before he died. He has no clue Amar is dead. He was easy to manipulate. I'll have to show you how I did it someday. Besides, the gods won't be thinking about Amar. Out of sight…out of mind. You just have to love that."

The Mischievous One reached into the flames and scooped the image of the sleeping George into the palms of his hands. He carried the burning vision to the stone table at the center of the room and took a seat after pulling the chair out with his foot. The fire remained hot and strong as the god set it on the table.

Lasidious leaned back in his chair, put his feet up, then stared into the flame as he continued their conversation. "George, there is something you need to know. You have the ability to look through Kepler's eyes and see into the demon's mind if he allows it. The demon has been to Merchant Island. You can find a place to teleport by using his memories. The cat's memories are trustworthy. You have grown close to the demon. Ask for permission and explain why you need to study his mind. Open your own and I'll show you how to do this."

George shook his head on his pillow. "How could you forget to tell me something this useful? Do you realize how much more I could've accomplished if you had told me this sooner? I could've teleported everywhere and not wasted all my damn moments walking."

Lasidious grinned. "Who said I forgot? I'm sure you could have made a bigger mess on Grayham, but I think the one you've made will do. I need you to hurry to Merchant Island. You'll be leaving for Luvelles in 2 Peaks of Bailem. You're scheduled to be transported by the Merchant Angels that night. The trip will take another 2 Peaks to get there. This should give you the moments necesary to rest."

George thought a while. "I think this will work. I'll get the crystals and stay here until Late Bailem tomorrow. Maldwin can make the family understand Susanne has a child and we can leave for Merchant Island after dark to find this Hesston Bangs. Luvelles, here we come. Wow, we have a ticket out of here. I'm relieved now that I think about it. Where will I find this Hesston?"

Lasidious smiled. "Tell Kepler Hesston works at the docks of the Merchant Angels during the day. Kepler will know where to go once he hears this information. The angels appear at night. They transport everything which needs to be traded to the other worlds. You will have most of the day to get into the container which has been prepared for your family. Amar took good care of you, don't you think?"

Lasidious laughed with George. "I'll speak with you once you're on Luvelles, but it may be a while before this happens. Be patient, my friend. Until then, have a good trip. It won't be long before your Abbie will be with you." Lasidious imparted beautiful visions of Abbie into George's mind as he left the mage to his dreams.

The Grayham Inquirer

When Inquiring Minds Need to Know about their Favorite Characters

GEORGE, his family, and Kepler are on the world of Luvelles. The ride provided by the Merchant Angels to this new world was dark and dismal. Their special container was a tight fit. Despite the fact everyone had to sit in their own waste, they remained in good spirits.

George has led the group to the village of Floren but has no idea how to find Head Master Brayson. The only thing he knows, for sure, is he has an elven witch family to kill and a nephew to take care of.

The family believes Susanne has had a son. Their minds were manipulated by Maldwin before leaving Gessler. Athena is talking about a baby she has never met.

Maldwin's visions were specific. After the baby was born, there were health issues which had to be dealt with. The family believes George rushed the child to Luvelles to receive the attention he needed. But, there is one detail about the baby's birth Maldwin's vision never delivered into the family's minds, a detail George never thought about, one which could cause a problem.

KEPLER left word for his brothers to govern Skeleton pass in his absence. As it turned out, Lasidious was right about the demon. The jaguar was more than happy to leave his brothers behind.

CELESTRIA has given birth. She cleaned up the child and after holding him, handed the baby to the elven witches. Once home on Ancients Sovereign, she waved her hand over her belly, removing all evidence she had been pregnant.

SAM asked Shalee to stay behind in Brandor. She is not handling the stress of losing BJ and Helga. She has been crying for days and the healers have warned Sam their baby could be in danger. As a doctor, he knows they are right. This kind of stress is not good. Her depression has made her a prime candidate for a miscarriage and the king is not about to risk his baby, or his queen, despite the asset Shalee would be in battle. When Shalee tried to object, Sam would not consider her position, saying, "No."

After arriving in the city of Champions, Sam received word from his scouts the barbarian army was headed south to the Serpent King's city. They are following the Latsky River in Neutral Territory. By the sound of the reports, the barbarians and Seth's serpents will be outmatched in this war. Days ago, Sam ordered Michael to turn the army in the direction of the serpents' underground city. The army has crossed the Snake River, and is now 2 Peaks of Bailem from the entrance to Seth's kingdom. This is where the pieces of the Crystal Moon are said to be hidden.

A HEAVY QUAKE has struck the city of Brandor. Many of the city's smaller buildings sustained damage.

The roof of the Senate's hall collapsed and 11 senators perished in the disaster. Word of the city's suffering will reach Sam's ears before the war begins.

Thank you for reading the final edition of The Grayham Inquirer

Surrounded

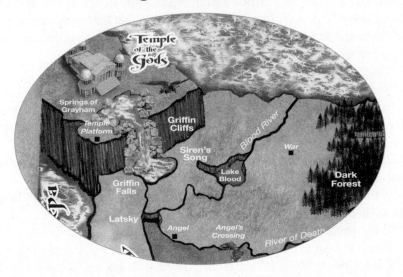

Mosley is sitting with Soresym inside the mouth of the griffin's cave below the Temple of the Gods. The wolf is agitated. "Sam is walking into a trap and there is nothing I can do. To have the power of the gods and be bound because of our laws is frustrating."

"Trap? What are you referring to?" Soresym questioned while looking across the beauty of the valley below. "I have heard nothing."

"Do you know Sam is the King of Brandor?"

The griffin fluffed the feathers on his head to allow the breeze to refresh his skin. "I possess this knowledge. Information of this nature travels fast."

The wolf scratched the back of his ear as he responded. "Sam is leading Brandor's pack toward the Serpent King's city. He has no idea he is about to be attacked from all sides. The bears are working with the minotaur. They plan to attack Brandor from behind once they cross into Seth's kingdom.

The barbarians are approaching from the north and the serpents will fight from the south. This is not the worst of it. The unicorns travel with the barbarians, along with Kepler's giant cats. The demon's skeletons travel with Horace. Sam has no idea what he is about to encounter."

Soresym looked confused. "Why would the minotaur or the bears break their alliance with Brandor? Brandor has done nothing but allow them to live in peace. They have been allowed to compete in the arenas. This does not make sense."

"Sam was the one who defeated their champions."

Soresym cringed as a griffin would. "I knew the minotaur fell by Sam's hand. I know Sam was close to losing his life in that battle. However, I did not realize it was Sam who defeated the bear's champion. This does not look good. I'm sure the pride of both kings is wounded."

"Did you know the Crystal Moon has been stolen?"

"Stolen?" the griffin questioned. "How?"

"How is unimportant. What is important...the moon is missing. Its pieces have been scattered throughout the worlds. Two of these pieces are on Grayham."

Soresym tapped his talons on the cave's floor. "What do the missing pieces of crystal have to do with the bear and minotaur kingdoms?"

"A trick has been played. They believe Brandor plans to attack all beasts on Grayham who rule with a monarchy."

"Why would they think this?"

"Brandor went to the Scorpion Island to retrieve one of the missing pieces of the Crystal Moon. When Sam arrived with his army, the scorpions attacked. There was no chance of negotiation. All scorpions were destroyed in battle, yet Brandor was still unable to retrieve this piece."

"Why would a piece of the Crystal Moon be there?"

"Lasidious put it there to start a war."

"Why would Lasidious do this?"

"Again, my friend, why is not important. Lasidious does things for his own reasons. What is important...a man named George has secured the first piece of the Crystal Moon. George also has the second piece. He has claimed to have hidden both pieces within Seth's underground city. Brandor is going to fight for them."

Soresym nodded. "This explains why the temple was sealed. I suppose this was to keep the faithful from knowing. Panic would have filled the land."

"Indeed. But, I am more concerned for my friend's life. It looks as if Sam will perish while trying to retrieve the crystal's pieces. I have been watching Grayham with a keen eye. I have seen the movements of the armies. Sam is in a hopeless situation."

Soresym shrieked. "Sam is a good human. It isn't his season to die. The gods must do something to stop this."

Mosley stood and moved to stand at the edge of the cliff. "The laws of the gods will not allow us to intervene. Soresym, you are mighty and the leader of your kind. Yet, even you are bound by your laws. I am sure you understand."

The griffin stood and stretched his splendid wings. After a moment, he shook his head in disgust. "What I understand is...Sam is the king Brandor has always needed. I've come to know this human as I have traveled with him. Something must be done."

"But, who is left to help? I must be going, my friend. There are matters to which I must attend. Let us hope Sam is strong enough to survive the battle."

The griffin sighed and looked out across the valley in deep thought. "I need to think." Soresym leapt from the edge of the cliff and fell over 2,000 feet before opening his wings and swooping over the landscape of Grayham.

As Mosley watched the griffin soar, he began to laugh. A moment later, the image of the wolf changed into a persona of someone more mischievous. The god's eyes glowed red and his teeth turned to sharp points. "Celestria, my love, here I come." Lasidious vanished.

The Home of Lasidious and Celestria

Lying in bed, Lasidious reached up and adjusted his pillow, then put his hands behind his head. "George masterfully manipulated this world. He was always two steps ahead and made the most unlikely allies."

Celestria rolled over and cupped his face with her hands. "I so missed your smile, my love, my sweet, my adorable little devil-god. I cannot tell you how often I thought of the fun you must be having. I would love to have watched your scheming mind carry out our plans, my pet." She licked the lobe of Lasidious' ear. "So, you sent George to Luvelles to take care of our baby."

"I did."

"Susanne will act as a good mother until we bring our son home. I hope George gives our baby a good name."

"If I know George, our child will be given a strong name."

"And, the war? Will it be enough to keep the Collective's attention?"

Lasidious kissed her forehead. "This war will be the biggest Grayham has ever seen. I have kept the gods busy. Mosley managed to get away now and again, but he doesn't know anything useful. I have a good idea how everyone is thinking. None of the gods have any knowledge George is on Luvelles. It will be a while before they figure it out."

"It gives me peace to hear your confidence, my sweet."

"I'm glad you're comforted."

Lasidious began to run his fingertips along the contour of Celestria's body. "The Head Master of Luvelles isn't scheduled to meet with George for many Peaks. After George kills the witches, there will be no reason to use his magic. There will be nothing to draw attention to his family. George will arrive in Floren soon. The gods will not divert their attention from the war because of the death of a few useless witches."

Celestria snuggled into her lover. "I knew you had everything under control, my pet. Please! Never make me have another child without using my power. It hurt. I do not think I could suffer the pain. The witches drove me crazy."

The goddess reached up and pressed the end of Lasidious' nose. "But, on a positive note, I did learn how to bake. I shall make you a pie." The gods enjoyed this simple thought as they embraced.

<hr />

The next morning, Lasidious woke and vanished, leaving his goddess lying in bed. When he reappeared, he was standing in front of a large group of rats. As instructed, Keller was guiding Maldwin's family to the cliffs of Latasef.

Seeing the man appear out of nowhere, Keller took a defensive stance and growled at Lasidious. The demon was about to pounce when Lasidious held up his hand and spoke in the ancient language of demons. *"Ered'nash ban galar."*

Keller snarled. The phrase Lasidious used was a command to invoke conversation. He was obligated to respond. "What do you want? This family is under my protection. I will not allow their journey to be hindered."

"You are a mighty escort. I am not seeking conflict." The Mischievous One looked at Maldwin. "We need to speak," the god said in the rat's language.

Maldwin replied, "Who are you?"

"A friend. George informed me of his promise to give you a home."

"Where is George? Kepler's brother is taking us to the cliffs of Latasef, but he has no knowledge of what we are to do once we get there."

Lasidious smiled. "George has seen to it you will be taken care of. He has asked me to give your family a home like no other. Follow the mountains east until you come to a small opening just before the edge of the cliffs. What you will find there is a glorious existence. Your new home is protected by the gods. Your family will always be safe."

Maldwin twitched his nose. "Thank you. I did not know George had such powerful friends. When you see him, tell him I am honored. I will be there for him if he ever needs me."

Lasidious squatted and waved his hand over the ground. A huge cheese wheel appeared. Moving out of the way, he smiled as he watched the rat's family swarm the meal. Again, he waved his hand and Maldwin floated into his arms. He positioned the rat so he could see the rodent's eyes. "You can tell George yourself. I'm sure you'll see him again." With that, Lasidious lowered Maldwin to the ground, then vanished.

Keller looked down and watched the rats eat. After a moment, he looked up, "Well, you could have left something for me."

The World of Luvelles

When George arrived in the village of Floren with Athena's family, it was past Late Bailem. The mage loved this new world. Everything he had seen since their arrival had some sort of magical influence used to create it. The magic here was much, much stronger than anything on Grayham and, in some places, the air smelled of it.

The people of Luvelles seemed to be pleasant, but George and Kepler noticed there was a dark side. Some of the people they met on their journey seemed two-faced, despite their outward appearance.

This journey had taken them through villages of similar size, but they did not appear on his map. Their general look and feel was more to George's liking, with smaller homes being constructed, or rather created, in such a way they exuded class. Magic was used for many things which did not exist on Grayham. It was nice to have a cold drink instead of a warm ale.

As the family entered the inn, Kepler did not need to hide. Along the way, they had seen others walking throughout the countryside with various types of animals. The inn was called Kebble's Kettle. George was amused at the quaint originality of its name.

The inn was comfortable, almost like an upscale hotel on Earth, but with many magical upgrades. The walls looked as if they were made of some sort of construction material, but upon closer inspection, they were flesh. The walls were alive. They felt strange as George passed his hand across them. Millions of tiny hairs grew on their surfaces and tickled the palm of his hand as it passed across. The walls possessed a natural warmth, just like the human body.

This is fascinating, George thought. *It's like this place lives, but with the appearance of a regular building. I wonder how this is done. The magic on this world must be powerful.*

Aside from a small check-in counter to the left of the entrance, the dining area and the tavern occupied the rest of the spacious room. George watched as one of the patrons ordered a drink. The man reached out and pulled the beverage from mid-air as the drink floated over to his table. *Now, that's pretty freaking cool. I'm going to like this joint.*

Athena tugged at George's sleeve. She whispered, "George, I'm scared. My family is nervous. What should I tell them?"

George pulled Athena close. "Tell them I've got everything under control. I won't let anything happen. Besides, just look at this place. It's amazing. Let's pass judgment once we've finished looking around."

There was a vaulted ceiling five stories high. The colors of the inn were earth tones and pleasing to the eye. There were no stairs leading to the remaining levels of the structure, nor were there elevators. They watched as a woman stepped up onto a small circular platform, then vanished only to reappear on the balcony of the next floor. *No way. This is like some kind of Star Trek garesh. The magic in this joint is nuts.*

As George stood there, a dustpan flew past his head and asked to be excused as it made its way to the far side of the room. A small broom followed and pushed the dirt from the floor onto its surface. The dustpan lifted, then disappeared through a large set of double doors. *You've got to be kidding me! Even the cleaning is done by magic.*

Again, Athena whispered as she tugged on his shirt. "Honey, wouldn't it be great if our new homes clean themselves."

"Yeah, this is cool, huh?"

"Hello, friend," the innkeeper said after watching them a while. "I see we need a number of beds for the night."

A short wobbly man, barely able to see over the counter, climbed up a set of booster steps. He had narrow, long, pointy ears and a pudgy nose, and a billowing pipe pinched between his teeth. The pipe smelled of a sweet cherry-flavored tobacco which had stained his graying mustache a yellow-ish-brown over the seasons. Somehow, the stains managed to complement his rosy cheeks. George found the smell of the tobacco to be pleasant. He could not help but notice how the innkeeper's ears poked through his gray-ing hair.

The mage smiled as he approached the counter. "Yes, we do need rooms. Thank you. My name is George and this is my family. And, your name?"

"Hee, hee, hee, if you saw the sign out front, then you know my name," he said with a jolly grin. "I'm Kebble. You can call me...well, Kebble works," he said with a chuckle. "Everyone in this village calls me Kebble, hee, hee, hee. Welcome to Kebble's Kettle. So, what can Kebble do for you today? He's in a delightful mood."

George turned to look at Kepler as if to say, *Is this guy for real?* He turned back around and reached out to shake the elf's hand.

Kebble stopped laughing and took the mage's forearm. He counted ev-eryone in George's group, needing to do it on three separate occasions since he kept losing count. After a while, he said, "I see you need enough beds for thirty-one and one giant kitty."

Kepler growled, "I'm not a kitty. I am jaguar. We need beds for thirty-four humans and one *jaguar*." The demon further thought, *What an idiot.*

"Whoa," Kebble responded as he looked at George. "Looks like you have a testy little pussycat on your hands. You can keep him in your room, but we have special places for goswigs to relieve themselves. If you'd like, you can take Kepler to the sandbox to the right of the inn."

"Goswigs," George repeated with a confused look as Kepler continued to growl. "What's a goswig?"

Kebble stopped a moment to look at the human. "You don't know what a goswig is?"

"Should I know what a goswig is?"

"Well, of course. If you travel with one, you should know something so trivial." Kebble pointed to Kepler. "He's larger than most and I'm sure one pile of his garesh will fill my sandbox, but...he looks goswig."

"Kepler isn't a goswig. He's a friend of mine. We're new to this world and have no clue what you're talking about. We have recently arrived by the Merchant Angels."

Kebble's fat cheeks wrinkled as his smile widened. "You are the one who has come by pass of the Head Master. I have been expecting you. It is an honor to meet you, George. Allow me to give you complimentary rooms for your first night. I have a substantial sum waiting for you as the Head Master requested."

George leaned over the counter. "Perhaps, you and I could speak of this during some other series of moments. I'd like to get my family settled."

"By all means. I also have a package for someone named Mary. Is she in your group?"

Mary heard her name and approached the counter. "I'm Mary. I doubt you have a package for me. I have only just arrived on this world a short while ago."

Kebble grinned. "I think we'll let the package decide if you're the correct Mary it seeks."

"I don't understand."

"You don't need to understand, young lady. There are many things a young woman of your seasons has not experienced. Give me your hand."

Mary looked at Athena. Her daughter's response was nothing more than a shrug. Susanne was the one who spoke up. "Mother, give him your hand. I want to know if the package is yours."

Mary held out her hand and Kebble took it. His hand was much smaller than hers as he pulled it close. He removed the note from the top of the package and placed her fingertips against it. Sure enough, the paper changed color from a bright yellow to a passionate red. The package was for her.

As George watched the note change color, he thought, *Holy freaking Harry Potter.*

Kebble puffed his pipe, then nodded. "Yep, yep, yep, this is your package, madam. The parchment's magic is never wrong. Someone has their eye on you." He leaned in and winked. "Someone important."

Mary was not sure if she should be happy or scared. She never had anything like this happen. "Thank you, Kebble...I think."

"You're welcome, my lady." The chubby elf turned his attention to George. "You must be a talented apprentice to be given such an honor. To be invited to this world by the Head Master is a rare thing. I'm sure you'll be assigned a goswig. You'll be able to learn about them for yourself."

"Ohhh, mother," Athena exclaimed, seeing what was in the package as Mary lifted its lid.

Mary gasped. "I know! Have you ever seen anything so beautiful?" Mary held up an elegant dinner gown. "Blue is my favorite color. And..." she gasped, "...it's my size. I wonder who it's from. How could this person know so much about me? Should I be happy? Mr. Kebble, do you know who sent this?"

"I do, but I cannot say. I will say, however, you have nothing to fear. Your admirer isn't a threat to you or your family."

Once again, Kebble turned to George. "As I was going to say earlier," the happy elf leaned in and whispered—although Kepler still managed to hear—"tell your kitty not to pee on the floor. I don't normally allow animals who are not goswig to enter my inn, but I'll make an exception since you're new to this world. I know it's hard to keep an unbonded animal in line. Filthy little critters, don't you agree?"

George could feel the jaguar's agitation. He thanked Kebble for his generosity and asked for their rooms. Each of them stepped onto the circular platform and appeared in front of their doors on the fourth level. Once in the room, George familiarized himself with every detail.

After Athena was settled, George gave Kepler the nod. "You ready to go?"

Kepler lifted from the floor and stretched. George shook his head. "Damn, you're a big S.O.B. It's a good thing this room is huge. I'll meet you out front. Let me tell Athena good-bye."

The demon left the room without responding. George grinned as he shut the door behind the cat. He walked into the washroom and put his arms around his beautiful wife. He rubbed her belly as he spoke. "I'll be back. I'm going to get Susanne's baby."

"Ahhh, that sounds wonderful, honey. Take me with you."

George had to think fast. He needed to kill some witches. Taking Athena was impossible. "You know, babe, I think I need some moments to myself. I'll make it up to you later. Can you feel me on this?"

Athena slapped his arm. "Sometimes, I can't get over how funny you talk, George Nailer. Our trip has been stressful. You go on ahead. But, hurry back with...with...ummm, I can't remember the baby's name, honey. I'm such a terrible aunt."

"Garrin. His name is Garrin," George replied as he kissed her. "Tell your sister I'll be back soon. I'm sure you're going to be the best aunt this world has ever seen, sweetheart. The whole family will be happy to see the little guy."

George hated lying to Athena, but he could not figure a way around this one. The lie was necessary to get Abbie back. If he had to raise Lasidious' child to get his daughter's soul released from the Book of Immortality, then so be it. But, he would be damned before he would allow lying to his wife to become a habit. He wanted to protect their relationship from deception.

Once downstairs, George asked Kebble if he knew of the elven witch family, Rolfe. "Sure, I do," the innkeeper responded. "Kebble knows everybody. They're from the Clan of Ashdown. It's not a far walk. When you leave the inn, just take the road south. You'll come across two bushes. You'll know they're the right ones because they fight a lot. The..."

George interrupted. "Kebble, you want me to look for bushes? Aren't there any signs or something better to navigate by?"

"Well, of course. But, this is far more fascinating. Trust me. The roses think the bushel berries have no right to be planted on the other side of the road. Just between you and me, I agree. The roses are pleasant. I've seen the bushel berry bush throw its rotten berries at the roses on many occasions. It's not neighborly. I..."

Again, George stopped him. "Kebble, maybe you could just tell me the signs I need to look for."

"Well, Kebble could do many things. Let me write it down for you."

After a while, Kebble handed George a parchment. Everything was written in the Elvish language. George looked up and smiled. "Thanks, Kebble. I'm sure this will help. I will have to visit them one of these days. I'll find you in the morning and get the package you have for me, if that's okay?"

"That's fine by Kebble. He has a safe place to store your things. The Head Master asked me to give you anything you needed. I wouldn't want to keep that much coin on my person if I were you, especially in this village. We have many shady characters who come through here. I'm sure you understand."

"Thanks again, Kebble. See you tomorrow."

Once outside, Kepler spoke. "Kebble is an irritating man. Can you believe the nerve of that elf? He called me kitty. Ever since you tortured the saber lord, I hate that word. I have half a mind to go in there and devour him. 'Tell your kitty not to pee on the floor.' 'It's hard to keep an unbonded animal in line.' The nerve of that guy! He makes me sick. If his soul didn't smell innocent, I would see to it I had my first skeleton on this world."

George reached up to pat Kepler's enormous back. "Once we kill these damn witches, you and I need to lay low for a while. We've got to chill out until we're contacted by the Head Master. Let's not do anything until we hear from Lasidious. Please...tell me you agree and will deal with the changes for a while."

Kepler snarled. "I agree, but I refuse to garesh in his stupid sandbox. I'll find some bushes like any self-respecting jaguar."

George smiled within as they continued their midnight walk toward the witches' home, his magic lighting the way.

George stood over the stone bodies of the elven witch family and studied their lifeless faces. The mage had used his power to keep them silent while Kepler feasted on parts of each of them, then turned what was left to stone. After a moment of staring at his handiwork, George looked for the baby. He found the god-child in one of the bedrooms and lifted Garrin into his arms.

On his way out of the room, he waved his free hand over the witches' statues. They crumbled to the floor into mounds of powder. George opened the front door and used his magic to command a small whirlwind to enter the home. After gathering the piles of dust, the funnel disappeared into the night sky. It was headed for the outskirts of the village to scatter the powder across an open field.

George looked at the baby. "Hey, little guy," he said, holding the child's hand in the palm of his own. "My name is Uncle George. I'm going to take care of you. Let's go find your mother."

The mage reached down and touched Kepler's back. After teleporting to his room at the inn, he handed the baby to Athena. He smiled at the joy the newborn brought to his wife's face. Soon the entire family was in their room, loving and googling over the god-child, Garrin.

War has Begun
The Serpent's Kingdom

2 Peaks ago, Sam's army crossed the Snake River into the Serpent King's kingdom. They passed through an enormous mire. It was cold, wet and mossy, waist-deep in spots, and slowed the pace of every legion. The army was not able to sleep that first night due to the conditions. The mire was a dreadful place, full of predators, which under normal circumstances, would have attacked any single man. However, due to the size of the army, these predators fled—all, that is, except the leeches. They attached to the men and

were unable to be removed until the army found dry land. When a tent could be pitched, they burned the blood suckers, tore them from their skin, then found sleep.

The underground city of the Serpent King rested underneath an enormous area of lava stone. Sam could not figure out how these massive serpents burrowed into this type of earth, but since his arrival on Grayham, he had seen many things he never thought were possible.

The General Absolute was nervous about the army making camp in such a vulnerable position. Michael feared a surprise attack, but one never came. It was as if the snakes wanted to stay below ground and wait for Brandor to enter—or better yet, perhaps they did not know the army was there. Either way, none of this bothered Sam—he had an idea and had come prepared.

Over the next 2 Peaks of Bailem, Brandor's army moved into position. As Sam looked up, the sun had reached its highest point. "General, I want a report."

"Sire, the four legions you ordered to meet the barbarian army should be in position by Early Bailem. I have sent Dreston and his legion into the serpents' city. We have 1,500 men waiting outside the cave's entrance once Dreston flushes them out."

Sam patted the side of his horse's neck as Michael maneuvered his to a position next to the king. They had hoped to find a tactical location in which to command the army, but the terrain was fairly flat. This small hill would have to do.

The heavy trunks of large trees had broken through the lava stone. There was no clear line of sight. Both men needed to rely on their scouts to deliver updated information. It was a miserable battleground.

Serpent City

Dreston and his legion descended into the opening of Seth's reptilian hideaway with torches held high. Their swords were drawn and every man's eyes searched for the enemy.

The air was putrid with the sound of shed skin crunching beneath their feet. Every so often, a rattle or hiss could be heard, but their origin could not be determined. It was as if the serpents were toying with them.

Many moments passed before they came to a path, no more than 20 feet across. To the left was a drop into darkness with no visible bottom and to the right, more of the same. The path of lava stone was too narrow, an impossible crossing for 2,500 men. The cavern's ceiling could not be seen, their torches not strong enough to penetrate the darkness.

By Dreston's estmate, the men had descended almost 500 feet. Something was not right. He held up his scar-covered hand. "This will have to do," he whispered. "We can go no further."

Dreston was a strong man, with nine previous battles to his name, some with barbarian scouting parties. His legion was Sam's finest and his men were known for their fearless acceptance of impossible tasks. Today's task was no exception.

"Lieutenant, bring the barrels forward and place them every twenty paces on either side of the ledge."

The lieutenant sheathed his sword and handed his torch to one of the sergeants. "How many?"

"All of them. I want them opened and their wicks set. We'll burn these slithering bastards out."

The lieutenant hesitated. "All of them? There are over 60. The cavern will become toxic. The men will not be able to breathe."

Dreston looked over the ledge. "By the moment the barrels hit the bottom, our men will be clear of this pit. We can outrun the smoke to the surface. The serpents will be left with no choice, but to come to us."

The lieutenant turned and looked at his sergeant. He nodded, "Make it happen. Spread word to prepare to run." The sergeant smiled and did as instructed.

With barrels in position, three men were assigned to each to ensure they were pushed into the pit. Once again, Dreston moved to the edge and held his torch over the side. Something moved toward the ledge, trying to escape the light. "Lieutenant, they're underneath us. They're under our damn feet. This is an ambush. We're exactly where they want us."

Dreston signaled to light the wicks. As the torches were lowered, he took hold of the lieutenant's hand and leaned over the ledge. His eyes widened as hundreds of holes covered the surface of the wall below and twice as many eyes were beginning to climb toward them.

Dreston shouted, "Get those damn barrels over the edge, now! Prepare for battle! They're coming! Retreat to the surface as we fight."

As the legion leader finished his orders, the first of the giant snakes crested the ledge and began using its powerful body in a whip-like fashion, knocking three of the men into the darkness. Their hopeless cries echoed throughout the cavern as they disappeared.

As the barrels were pushed over, some were caught in the serpents' coils as they fell. The liquid splashed onto their cold-blooded bodies and burst into flames. The heat caused a frenzied reaction which worked against Dreston's men and their own kind, knocking serpents and men alike to their deaths.

Dreston pulled his sword from the eye of his first kill, then turned to look for another as two fangs surrounded his lower body from behind. Agony filled his eyes as the serpent snatched him up and slung him from side to side. The legion leader's leg gave under the pressure and shredded at the hip as if it was nothing more than an overcooked piece of chicken being picked apart. The serpent swallowed the appendage, then turned to find the rest of his delicacy.

Dreston landed in an awkward position, his arm breaking beneath the weight of his body. His fall knocked two more of his men from the ledge. The coils of the giant snake encompassed his body as the snake's head lifted to a position above him.

The legion's leader maintained his wit and, with his last ounce of heart, thrust his blade into the serpent's mouth as it struck. The creature cried out in a bloodcurdling, hissing scream, then twisted into a tight ball of death as the smoke from the exploded barrels began to consume the ledge.

The serpents disappeared as the toxic fumes turned into a black fog. The men who could move retreated to the surface.

Back on the Surface

"Sire," a scout shouted as he stopped in front of Sam. "The barbarians have allied with the giant cats of the north, and this isn't the worst of it. The unicorns were hidden within their numbers. I saw them appear. Their magic is enough to destroy us!"

"How many cats and how many unicorns?"

"Hundreds of cats and at least forty, maybe fifty unicorns," the man answered. "We can't fight this kind of force. Our men will perish. Sire, we need to retreat and establish a new plan."

Sam thought for a moment. "General, sound the horns. Let's get out of here."

Michael had not given the order before the second scout rushed up from behind, screaming and nearly out of breath. "Sire," the scout blurted as he bent over to capture the air needed to continue, "The minotaur are behind us. They travel with the skeletons of the demon cat, Kepler. Their numbers are impossible to determine. The skeletons can't be killed. They killed four of us, but I was able to break away and remain unseen."

Sam turned his mount toward Michael. "Why would the minotaur fight against us? I was told they are our allies!"

Michael shook his head. "This doesn't make sense. Perhaps, their king seeks vengeance for the loss of their champion."

"Bah. I beat him fair and square. Retreat to the southern shore. We'll work our way home from there. Sound the horn."

Michael began to raise the horn to his mouth when another voice called out. "My King, the bears are coming!" The third scout approached on horseback.

"What the hell is going on here?" Sam snapped. "Are they also angry because I beat their champion?"

Michael steadied his mount. "No, Sire. They are allies. This is a blessing. We can use this to our advantage. We can ask for their assistance."

"No, My King," the scout cut in. "The bears have killed two of us. They approach as enemies. They're over a thousand strong. They are angry."

Sam looked at Michael. "Any bright ideas? We're surrounded."

"The majority of our army is too far north to stop this kind of force. Today appears to be a good day to die, Sire." The general ripped his sword from its sheath. "It has been a pleasure to know you, My King, but the moments for plans and useless words have passed. I say we fight like dogs and die like men. To die beside you will be my honor."

The king lifted Kael high into the air and commanded the sword of the gods to bring forth its fire. The blade screamed with joy at the thought of the pain they were about to inflict. "Michael, you're right. It is a good day to die."

Sam thought of Shalee and his unborn baby. He knew there would be many wonderful things he would miss: his child's first step, first smile, first word, and the joy they would bring to Shalee's face. He could only hope his queen would be strong enough to handle raising their baby on her own. He looked into the sky and was about to shout out his love for her, but as he did, he noticed a dark fluttering cloud approaching.

"General, look!" Sam shouted.

"My Lord, it is the griffins. They are powerful. It looks as if every creature on Grayham is coming for us."

"Don't be so quick to judge." Again, Sam lifted Kael into the air and commanded the blade to burn with a bright light. "Soresym," he screamed.

From high above, Soresym's eagle eyes spotted the King of Brandor's signal. Before altering his course, he ordered his family of over a hundred griffins and two hundred hippogriffs into battle.

◆═•═◆

The dark gray steeds, with pure white horns, had been ordered to act as the first wave of Senchae's attack. The unicorns moved ahead of Kepler's giant cats and the Barbarian King's army. Numbering fifty strong, the magical steeds galloped into battle as lightning shot from their horns and arched between the men of Brandor. The joints of their plate and links of their chain were welded solid as they fell to the ground, charred and lifeless.

The magic was overwhelming and Brandor's men retreated, dodging from side-to-side to avoid an electrical death. But, on this day, at this very spot, Nathan, a sergeant, and four of his men would hold their ground. They would not run. They had found an alcove within the lava rock to hide and were waiting for the unicorns to pass.

Nathan's father, Fordamus, had been a tactician of war for most of his life and had advised the late King of Brandor, Keldwin, for many seasons. Fordamus was essential when it came to planning different battle strategies to protect the kingdom. These strategies had been embedded into Nathan's nature as a small child and allowed him to recognize a helpless situation when he saw one. He knew their current location was without an exit strategy, but he would not go down without a fight. The sergeant and his men could at least narrow the odds before they perished.

The five men crept up behind the magical steeds after they passed, their armor removed to ensure a surprise attack. From a stealth-like run, their blades plunged deep into the sides of an equal number of unsuspecting unicorns and, as quickly as the men killed the beasts, they chopped off their horns and clenched them in their hands.

Realizing what was happening, the rest of the unicorns began an assault against Nathan's small group. Nathan shouted, "Hold the horns tight! They'll protect us from their magic! Stand ready! Ready your blades and fight together, no matter what! No surrender!"

"NO SURRENDER," the men yelled in the direction of the unicorns.

The steeds encircled the small group. Lightning, fireballs, and storms of ice were used against them, but the horns' magical resistances kept them safe. The eyes of the unicorns were full of rage, knowing their magic was useless against their own power. They began to scuff their hooves across the lava stone and tightened the circle around Nathan's group.

Nathan shouted, "Today, we die with honor! No surrender!"

Suddenly, Soresym's mighty family began to plow into the tops of the unicorn's backs. One after another, like meteors, the griffins fell with their wings folded against their bodies to increase speed. Before impact, razor-sharp talons and lion-like claws were extended as they drove the steeds into the ground. Blood sprayed in all directions as if bombs of red liquid had been dropped from a tremendous height. The force of the spray stung Nathan's face.

The screams of the unicorns filled the air, only to be matched by the griffins as they shrieked their battlecries. The smallest of the winged attackers—weighing over 3,900 pounds—buried its talons deep into the flesh of one of its enemies and severed the unicorn's spine. Thirty unicorns perished with no chance of defense. The others, though injured, responded by using their magic to teleport home to the Dark Forest. The strongest threat to Brandor's army had been disbanded in a matter of a few short moments.

Nathan's men lifted their swords and cheered for their winged allies. The moment had arrived to turn their attention to the next big threat. Kepler's feline subjects were the next wave they must face, which included the support of the Barbarian archers.

The rest of Brandor's army stopped their retreat and rejoined the battle. Nathan and his men climbed back into their alcove of stone to retrieve their armor. Once again, the mighty griffins and their family of hippogriffs torpedoed out of the sky. Ten of the giant cats perished—another thirty lay injured and unable to fight. But, during this series of moments, the winged army was not without casualty. Many of the giant cats were ready, their quick reflexes allowed them to avoid the crushing weight of the griffins. The cats responded by leaping onto their backs and tore into their flesh with their powerful claws.

Barbarian archers darkened the air, causing little damage to the griffins—their thick hides protected them as they descended for another attack—but, the hippogriffs were not so fortunate. Their hides were not as resistant to the projectiles. Thirty-eight hippogriffs fell in an uncontrolled spiral, their blood staining the ground as they splattered.

The largest of the griffins, nearly twice the size of the hippogriffs, snatched the giant cats, carried them high into the air and used their bodies as projectiles against the barbarian archers. The men of the north were in tight formation and could not avoid being crushed beneath their weight.

⁕⁕⁕

Soresym shrieked as he landed in front of Sam. "It looks as if I've come at a moment of need, King of Brandor."

Sam let out a sigh of relief. "I can't tell you how happy I am you're here. We're outnumbered and surrounded. I could use your help."

"I must have taken a liking to you, Sam. I find you intriguing and can see the value in protecting your position as king."

Soresym shrieked again, "The unicorns are no longer a concern for your army, but I fear the hippogriffs are no match for the barbarian's projectiles."

The griffin shifted and looked over his back as he scanned the area. "Order your army to the north to assist your other legions. We will deal with the serpents since they have no air-born weapons. I, on the other hand, will fly south and speak with Groth. I'll convince him to fight with us. The minotaur should stop their attack once they realize I'm fighting at your side."

Sam pulled back on his mount's reigns. "The minotaur are angry about their champion. They may not listen."

"Do as I say, King of Brandor. Let me handle Horace."

"I'll do that. It would be a good idea to separate the horns from the unicorns and fly with them into battle against the serpents. I have received word the snakes are coming to the surface. We are smoking them out. They are far more powerful than I estimated. The unicorns' horns will even the odds."

Soresym raised his massive eagle head and called out in a language Sam somewhat understood. Another griffin, flying overhead, responded and departed for the others to relay the orders to gather the horns and fly south.

Sam shouted, "General, take the troops north to join the attack." He turned his attention back to Soresym. "I'm in your debt. I don't know how you knew I was in trouble, but you're a sight for sore eyes."

"I suggest we speak of this later. There's a fight to be won." With that said, the griffin launched into the air and headed toward the bear king, Groth.

The serpents were making quick work of Dreston's men as they fled from Seth's underground city. The snakes' fifty foot long bodies out-slithered the running men and delivered their deadly poison. For every one serpent to fall, five men perished. The battle was hopeless for the 520 men left alive of just over 2,500 who entered, but relief soon came.

With swords held high and voices raised, they watched as the snakes burst into flames. The griffins and the hippogriffs descended on the serpents with unicorn horns grasped in their talons. With each swooping pass, their slithering bodies disintegrated into piles of ash. The serpents' retreat was inevitable as they hurried to the safety of their underground city, only to realize the toxic fumes would not allow it, but to stay topside was hopeless against such a power as well. Seth called for his army's surrender.

The Bear King stopped his army when Soresym landed in front of him. The griffin spoke in the bear's language. "Groth, stop your advance! You have been deceived. Brandor isn't your enemy. We must work together to stop the minotaur from attacking Brandor's army. You have no real enemy. Brandor does not plan to attack your kind."

Groth grunted, "You're wrong, griffin! I saw the body of the Scorpion King! Brandor attacked his island!"

Soresym thought back to the conversation he had with Mosley. "Yes, Brandor was there, but with good reason. This war isn't necessary."

"What reason would justify Brandor's attack against a group of beasts who live separate from all others?" The bear shifted posture as he pointed a claw at the griffin. "If this wasn't an act of war against all beasts, then what was it?"

"Brandor's actions were necessary to save our world. A piece of the Crystal Moon was hidden in the Scorpion King's home. Brandor went there to save us all. They would not have attacked if the scorpion had peacefully greeted them. On my honor, I assure you this is true. You know I live in the service of the gods. I would not lie. We don't have the moments necessary to debate. Join me in talking with Horace. Don't fight this war against Brandor."

Groth growled as he pondered Soresym's words. "I trust your service. Carry me with you. I'll stand at your side. If what you say is true, then a lie has been told to us all and we need to stop the skeletons' advance."

Groth turned to face his army. "Head north to join the minotaur! Go now! I'll be back soon!" Facing Soresym, he roared. "Shall we go, griffin?"

Soresym took the bear into his massive talons and carried him to find the Minotaur King.

Horace and his army were following the southern edge of Lake Zandra when Soresym landed in front of the beast-man. The minotaur lifted his hand to stop his army, then shouted in his language. "What is the meaning of this, griffin? Why do you carry Groth? There's blood to be spilled. He should be with his army."

Soresym took note. The leader of the skeleton army was at the minotaur's side. This gave the griffin pause as he spoke in the minotaur's tongue. Soon, Horace raised his head and bellowed.

Though anxious, the skeleton commander waited. He had been instructed to attack Brandor's army at the minotaurs' sides. The bony commander would not move until the bull-king ordered the army to continue.

After a moment, the Minotaur King shouted for his scouts. "Spread word throughout the army. The skeletons are traitors. Wait for my order to attack. We will..."

Soresym interrupted, "The skeletons will not die. A plan is necessary before dispatching your men."

Meanwhile, Sam shouted, "General, sound the horn and pull the troops back. Night is coming. We will regroup and attack the barbarians as a single unit in the morning. The barbarians will most likely follow our lead and also regroup. We'll attack at first light. Signal the griffins to land and rest among us."

"Yes, Sire!"

Once Sam's orders had been carried out, Michael approached. "The barbarians are regrouping and setting up camp. They won't attack in the dark. We have an opportunity to use this to our advantage."

"It will be pitch black. What advantage are you referring to?"

"I have spoken with Goss. He is the brother of Soresym and a respected leader amongst the griffins. I have asked him to come to a meeting."

"Okay, okay, but how will this give us an advantage?"

Goss landed. "Because, King of Brandor, my kind can see through the darkness. We shall have an advantage from this alone, but also, one of the fastest of our kind will arrive in a matter of short moments with your queen. I can't imagine why you would have left her in Brandor."

Sam's face tightened. "I left her because she's pregnant! Damn it, I don't want her here! Whose bright idea was this? I swear, it better not be yours, Michael!"

"No, Sire. Blame your queen."

"What do you mean, blame the queen? I don't want the future of our kingdom on the battlefield."

Goss lowered next to the king and folded his wings. "If you fail to obtain victory, there will be no future for Brandor. Your queen is strong. Soresym has informed me of her sorcery."

"How could Soresym know the full extent of her sorcery? He has never witnessed it."

The griffin reached out and with a single flip of one of his talons, thumped Sam's breastplate. "Let's agree he has been informed. How, matters not. Your queen will be helpful in this battle. Besides, she was already on her way to join you. She was just south of Angel's Village when we found her. Your queen has ignored your order. Soresym was the one to convince her to wait until we had a chance to fly her in unharmed."

"How could she possibly..."

A screech from above filled the air as the gusts from a large set of wings stirred the earth. Sam watched as the griffin settled a short distance away. He hurried to help Shalee down. "I asked you to stay home. We can't risk our baby like this."

"Goodness-gracious, Sam, take a pill. I missed *you*, too." Shalee put her hands on her hips. "Don't ya think I know I'm pregnant? Do ya think I've gone bonkers? I was fixin' ta go nuts in Brandor."

Sam sighed. "Stop. You know I'm happy to see you. I don't want you to get hurt."

"Me? Get hurt? Who do ya think you're kiddin'. From what I've heard, *you* could've died today. Without the griffins, I wouldn't have a husband. Don't ya tell *me* about the danger! You walked right into a trap...a trap George set, I might add. You're lucky a lil' birdie decided ta make sure ya had some extra help. I'm here and I don't care what ya say. I'm not leavin'. So, ya might as well let me use my magic. That's why I teleported ta Angel's Village and hitched a ride. I can't keep cryin', Sam. I need ta be here with ya."

"I'm the king, Shalee. I want you to go home. I won't let you stay and risk our baby's life."

Shalee's right brow lifted as she leaned in to whisper in Sam's ear. She was careful not to allow the others to hear. "If ya think I'm leavin', you're nuts. Who do ya think ya are, tellin' me what ta do? I'll teleport your sorry backside home and return without ya. You just try and play the king card on me, stud. I'll give ya what for. I'm here ta help, whetha' ya like it or not. All I've done since ya left is cry. I need ta help, Sam. I need ya ta believe in me. I can't go home. I can use my magic ta fight from a distance."

Sam pulled Shalee close and hugged her. "Promise me you'll teleport someplace safe if you get into trouble. I couldn't bear the thought of losing you. We've lost too much already."

"I promise," she responded, then kissed him.

"Sire," Michael said, clearing his throat. "We need to plan."

Goss interjected, "Yes, this is a tender moment, but we should be planning. Have your army gather as many heavy pieces of lava stone as you can. We will fly through the night and drop them from above. I'll take your queen on my back and head north of the barbarian's camp. She can rain down her magic. This should keep Senchae's army from resting through the night and give Brandor an advantage. We should be able to kill a fair number before dawn."

"Sire, this is a good plan," Michael confirmed as he mounted his horse. "The queen will be safe while on the griffin's back. She'll be hidden within the darkness. Her magic will kill many and she'll never need to set foot on the ground. If we're lucky, the barbarians will retreat before morning."

Sam thought a moment. "General, you will fly with the queen. If you feel she's in danger, I want you to have Goss fly to safety. She carries the future of Brandor in her womb. I'll not risk her life."

"Yes, Sire!"

Shalee kissed Sam, again. "Thank you!"

As the griffin ascended into the night, Shalee lifted Precious high into the air. Her voice was strong as she commanded fire to rain from the sky. The camp of the barbarians began to burn as the griffins and hippogriffs released the lava rocks.

Panic filled the camp as the men of the north scattered for their lives. Bodies fell lifeless, burned, and crushed.

Senchae looked toward the darkness. Realizing the hopelessness of the situation, he shouted for his new general. "Order the army to attack Brandor's camp. We need to merge the armies so the griffins will have no choice but to stop dropping their rocks. Set the trees on fire to light the battlefield."

High above, Goss observed the barbarians' movements. He turned his eagle head to look over his back to inform the queen. Shalee teleported, then appeared next to Sam. "The barbarians are headed this way. They didn't retreat like we thought they would. They'll be here soon. Ya need ta prepare."

Sam shouted. "General, prepare the army! We attack now!"

"Yes, Sire!"

"Shalee, use your magic on the men's eyes so they can see. This should give us an advantage."

"Charge," Sam shouted as he ordered the army into battle. Kael screamed with glee, his sharp edges begging for action. Kael quieted once he realized Sam would be keeping watch from the top of a small mound of lava stone, away from the battle.

Shalee had hitched a ride on Goss' back, sending her fireballs into the advancing barbarian army, wanting to inflict as much damage as she could before they collided with Brandor.

Swords, maces, war hammers, shields, and bodies slammed into one another as the full force of Brandor's army met the large men of Bloodvain. Bodies fell, blood saturated the earth and the griffins, along with the hippogriffs, once again descended from the rear of the barbarian horde, smashing them like grapes.

Soon the fight was too tight. They had to pull back. Goss landed next to Sam. "We can no longer assist. It is up to you from here. My kind is large and fighting in close combat would hurt your men, not just barbarians. We will keep watch and attack when we can."

"Thank you, my friend," Sam replied. "Brandor owes you a debt. Shalee, stay with me, I need your help."

"Any friend of Soresym is a friend to all griffins. Consider it my pleasure. I will be watching from above." With that, Goss took to the sky.

Sam turned to look at Shalee and tossed his torch to the ground. "I need you to use your power on my eyes. I need to be able to see through the darkness."

"Why?"

"Just do it...please!" Once Shalee's magic took effect, Sam lifted his bow and began firing his arrows into the night.

By the next morning, the bears and minotaur had torn apart Kepler's undead army. Hundreds of skeleton heads had been tossed into three large piles. Each skull was furious, cursing and calling out orders for their arms to work their way back to their torsos. The shifting of the piles caused a frightful clattering as the bones bumped against one another. Despite the noise, the beasts enjoyed the spectacle as they picked the arms off the ground as they inched their way across it and tossed them to the top of the pile. Every moment this happened, a much stronger curse filled the air from the skeleton's head who owned the arm.

The Peak of Bailem had come and gone. The moments had come for the General Absolute to create his legacy—or solidify his death. Michael lifted his sword horizontal to the ground and pointed it at the Barbarian King, despite his exhaustion. "I challenge you! We can settle the outcome of this war!"

Michael's plate armor was battered, and in some places, offered no protection to his body due to the abuse of the countless confrontations he had survived throughout the night. His blue eyes were bloodshot and it took every last ounce of strength to stand in front of the Barbarian King and call him onto the battlefield.

Senchae lowered from his mount and moved to take his position in front of Michael. The barbarian stood two feet taller than the General Absolute and outweighed him by more than 300 pounds. His armor was covered with blood. Michael, though a large man, appeared diminutive compared to the Barbarian King.

The horn of the Barbarian General sounded. Both armies stopped fighting and turned their attention toward the two men. Senchae spoke, "I admire your courage, swine. I'd like to know the name of the man I'm going to kill."

It took everything within Michael to claim his bravery. "Knowing my name seems insignificant. When you are dead, a memory is unnecessary. But, if it appeases Your Highness, I am Michael, the General Absolute of the Kingdom of Brandor. It isn't I who will be dying today, Senchae."

The men of Brandor who had gathered and managed to hear the General's response, cheered. Senchae waited for the noise to die. "You seek a fool's death. After today, you will no longer be able to address a king by his first name. Tonight, my officers will feast on the meat of my best bull once it has been cooked over the flames of your body."

Senchae lifted his heavy blade. His army began to stomp their feet as the men from both sides watched. With shield in one hand and sword in the other, Michael engaged, rolling forward, and slicing at one of Senchae's legs. The king lifted his leg and smiled as the blade passed beneath his foot.

"You have a quickness about you, but it won't do you any good. Nothing will spare your life."

Michael thumped his sword against his shield. "I will not miss again."

"Who said there will be an again?" The barbarian lunged forward and smashed his two-handed sword into Michael's shield. The force sent the general backward and to the ground. Senchae followed his assault by kicking Michael on the right side of his chest as he tried to recover. The force of the impact lifted the general from the ground. The leader of Brandor's army cried out as he heard two of his ribs crack.

Senchae backed off. "To think...once you die, I'll command your army. Your men will serve me."

Michael gathered his last bit of strength and lunged toward Senchae with his blade extended. The barbarian stepped to the side, grabbed Michael's wrist, and lifted him into the air. The king squeezed until the leader of Brandor's army was forced to drop his blade. Michael tried to hit Senchae with his shield, but the Barbarian King simply dropped his sword and caught the shield's edge with his hand. After pulling it free from Michael's arm, Senchae threw it to the ground.

After securing the General Absolute by his throat, Bloodvain pulled Michael close. Spittle from the barbarian's speech landed on Michael's face as the big man spoke. "You are weak. You have failed your army. You have brought shame to Brandor. You're pathetic."

Senchae threw the leader of Brandor's army against what was left of a tree which had burned throughout the night. The general fell to the ground, spitting blood into the ash. Senchae spoke as he moved to stand above Michael. "I never thought a pile of garesh from the south would have this much heart. It's a shame you must die. All garesh needs to be disposed of."

The Barbarian King retrieved his blade. The heavy metal began its decent, but the tip of an arrow exited the front of Senchae's throat. The king's eyes glossed over as he began to gasp for air. He stumbled before falling to his knees. Michael pulled himself to his feet and lifted his blade. Plunging it deep into the Barbarian King's heart, he screamed, "Attack!"

Brandor's army reacted, fueled with renewed vigor. Their blades moved with swift conviction as the battle commenced. From across the battlefield, Sam lowered his bow to his side. He grasped Kael and summoned the blade's extended fire, then charged down the mound of lava stone into the chaos.

It was not until Early Bailem the next day when Sam found Soresym. The last thing Sam imagined he would ever see would be the hundreds of skeletons' arms inching along the ground as they tried to reunite with their torsos. To his delight, he saw nine piles being watched by both minotaur and bears—three for their heads, another three for their torsos, and the remaining three for their arms and legs.

The separated limbs were being tossed back onto their respective pile, again and again, as they tirelessly tried to reunite with their torsos. The bony heads were becoming more frustrated and screamed yet another curse with each failed attempt.

The Bear and Minotaur Kings met with Sam, along with Soresym. Sam was the first to speak as Soresym translated his words. "My Lords, it appears there has been a grievous misunderstanding. It's good to know we've been able to solve this problem without more bloodshed."

Groth responded, "Why did you attack the Scorpion King's island?"

Sam took a deep breath and explained everything. After a few moments, the shock of the Crystal Moon's disappearance settled.

Horace spoke. "If we can help in any way, we are at your service."

"We are as well," Groth added.

Sam thought a bit. "We must go into the serpents' underground city to find the missing pieces of the Crystal Moon. We can use the unicorns' horns to hold the serpents at bay, if need be, but for now, we have bones to deal with. Any idea on what we should do to kill these things? We can't leave them here."

Soresym agreed. "We need to separate their parts and make sure they'll never be able to rejoin. I know of no other way to stop them. If they're allowed to unite, they'll attack Brandor as ordered by Kepler. They won't stop until this has been accomplished."

Sam sighed, then unsheathed his blade. "Kael, do you know of a way to kill these things?"

Kael responded, "I do. Fire."

"That's it? It's that simple?"

"Simple if you know the answer. Put my blade into the piles and command my flame. I'll do the rest."

Sam looked at Soresym, shrugged, then moved to the first pile. He commanded Kael to produce his flame. Soon, all nine piles were ablaze. The sounds of the skulls' screams were hellish as the temperature rose. One by one each skull cracked, releasing the soul which had been trapped by Kepler into the air. The soul ascended into the atmosphere until it was out of sight. It was not long before every spirit found its way to the pages of the Book of Immortality.

Sam turned to Soresym. "We need to find Kepler. He's responsible for creating these creatures and needs to be stopped. Will you ask the griffins to take to the air and search for him? I want to make sure we put an end to his life and stop this kind of evil from running free on Grayham."

The griffin thought a moment. "I suggest you finish what you started. Go north into the Barbarian Kingdom and bring all of Southern Grayham under one monarchy."

"I will. But, first we have some snakes to deal with."

"The snakes are of no concern. They have surrendered. You will be able to search for the crystal's pieces without interference."

The Home of Lasidious and Celestria

Celestria backed away from the green flames within their fireplace, the visions of war fading as she turned to cup her lover's face in the palms of her hands. "So, my love, I can't wait to see Sam and Shalee's faces when they realize Seth doesn't have the crystals."

Lasidious sat down and put his feet on the stone table. "Yes, their expressions will be entertaining. I must admit, I didn't think the griffins would offer assistance. I wasn't sure if my ruse worked. I thought I was going to have to save Sam myself."

Lasidious lowered his legs to the floor and motioned for Celestria to sit in his lap. "I think there's enough confusion on Grayham to keep the gods watching."

Celestria reached down and rubbed her favorite part of her devil-god as she spoke. "I agree, my love. You are conniving, my pet."

The Mischievous One smiled as he brushed her hair clear of her neck. "Our baby is safe and in Susanne's care. The moments have come to turn our attention to Luvelles. Everything is going better than we could have hoped. The next stage of our plan is ready to be implemented. But first, let's offer George a well-deserved rest. When the moment is right, he'll make us proud once again."

Lasidious lifted his goddess and carried her into their bedroom. "Allow me to show you how much I have missed you." Celestria giggled as the door shut.

The End

Keep reading for a SNEAK PEEK
inside the pages of Book 2.

Sneak Peek
Book 2

Magic of Luvelles

Black skies threatened the land below as the clouds continued to rumble their raged-filled curses. The morning had been unkind to Western Luvelles, punishing the terrain with pebble-sized hail and earth-scarring strikes of electrical fury. The forest had taken the brunt of the storm, the high winds had abused many of the tall evergreen trees, causing their branches to fall to the ground.

Countless mud-filled puddles were hard to avoid and stained the white dress of an injured woman. Shalee Goodrich, powerful sorceress and queen to the Kingdom of Brandor, grit her teeth in agony. Her moans could be heard as she crawled along the muddy road leading away from the swamp. The open wound across her abdomen marked an easy trail for the dark figure stalking her. Her flight had slowed and now, the once sporadic drops of blood were turning into smaller coin-shaped areas of saturated earth.

The hunter knew his prey was beginning to tire. He smiled as he bent down, rubbing his hand across the stained dirt. "You can't run forever," he whispered. "Your blood gives you away. It didn't have to end. I'm going to miss you." He rubbed the essence of her life between his finger tips and tasted it.

Shalee crawled off the road and into the forest. Her forearms were torn from the gravel embedded in her skin. Her teeth chattered as her body continued to lose its heat. She managed to force herself into an upright position against a large stone. The blade of her assailant had made a clean cut.

She tried using her magic to cauterize the wound, but failed. *Why can't I use my magic?* she thought. Her mind screamed for an answer, but one could not be found. She closed her eyes and tried to teleport. Nothing. There was no escape. *I've gotta get outta here. He's gonna kill me.*

It wasn't long before her attacker stood above her, looking down with eyes full of evil intent.

Please enjoy the following concept art
inside the pages of book 2.

Cindy Fletcher
Cinfl37@yahoo.com

Kathleen Stone
www.kastone-illustrations.com

Angela Woods
www.angelawoodsfineart.com

Sam Goodrich

Athena

Mary

Susanne

Gage

Ultorian King

Lord Dowd

Hepplesif

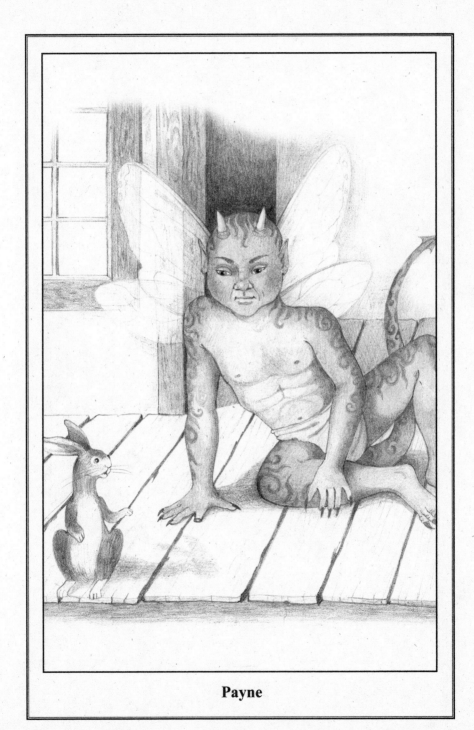

Payne

Shaban

Joss

Kiayasis

Head Master Brayson and Bryanna

Boyafed

Books, apparel and other Crystal Moon products:
www.worldsofthecrystalmoon.com

Facebook:
www.facebook.com/worldsofthecrystalmoon

You can email Big Dog at:
phillip.jones@hotmail.com